Voice of Machine

(Queen in Exile part 2)

By Oliver Strong

Smashwords Edition

ISBN: 978-0-9575457-1-7

Table of Contents

Chapter 1

Gliding through the Bandayuuk system, Athena made her way towards Machine's home world. McCann occupied the Bridge, slowly puffing on a Ramon Allones as he observed the view screen. Its display split between the void before them and a representation of their destination, the planet of Bandayuuk, and the Makayuuk home world.

'Transmission from Bandayuuk, Admiral.'

'Put him on, Hassif.'

An image of a Gukumatz filled the left half of the view screen 'Admiral McCann I am Tolomatz, governor for industrial Sector eight.'

McCann took a slow drag on his petit corona 'What is it this time?' he asked as thick smoke rolled from his lips.

The toad displayed that typical fidgety demeanour common to all Gukumatz, however McCann noticed it was somewhat heightened in Tolomatz.

'Workers in Sector J are striking, Admiral,' croaked the Governor in his best English.

McCann removed the Habanos from his mouth before shaking his head slowly 'Jesus Christ,' he muttered to himself.

'What was that, Admiral?'

'Nothing Tolomatz, have you contacted the controller of Sector J?"

'Yes Admiral.'

'And?'

'He refuses to use control collars.'

'Why?'

The toad flicked its tongue feverishly 'He believes collars immoral, Admiral.'

The Englishman took a long hard drag on his Havana 'Well get someone down there that can do the job!'

'Admiral, I have no spare staff. I was hoping you could help.'

McCann gave an incredulous look 'For God's sake man, can't you sort it out yourself?'

'You are Censor, you possess moral authority. You must rectify the situation, Admiral.'

The Englishman stood up from his chair on the central dais 'Fine, send me your co-ordinates and collar codes for Sector J.'

The Gukumatz became more animated flicking its eyelids and tongue, 'Thank you very much Admiral.'

'McCann out.'

The image of a joyful Tolomatz disappeared from the view screen.

'I'll send the codes to your tablet as soon as I get them.'

McCann nodded at Hassif then turned to Kim 'Have Vympel two meet me in docking bay one.'

Kim nodded as he tapped his wrist tablet 'Yes Sir.'

McCann left the Bridge and made his way to docking bay one, dressed in his I.S.A uniform sporting the rank of Admiral. The bottom of his thigh holster poked out from beneath his black Officers' jacket. Upon reaching docking bay one Vympel two was already there.

'Admiral' saluted the Russian in his black combat fatigues.

McCann returned the salute 'Kapitan Egorov.'

Egorov waited for the Admiral to step into the bay. As McCann approached the adapted Hummingbird he glanced upwards 'Athena, do you have co-ordinates?'

'Hassif has given me the co-ordinates, a flight path has been certified, have the Makayuuk revolted again, Admiral?' came her soft voice.

McCann grinned 'No need to worry Athena, it's just a strike. The toad in charge seems to think collars are immoral, he won't use them.'

Athena's soft voice filled docking bay one as they walked towards the Hummingbird 'I do not understand, he is employed to ensure production quotas are met is he not?'

McCann nodded 'Yup.'

'Why would he accept the post of controller without being aware of what that post entails?' inquired the SI.

McCann removed his cigar from between his lips 'Athena, these bloody toads have never made any sense to me either.'

After entering the Hummingbird it was a short journey to the planet surface. The craft landed in sector J's main industrial complex, McCann and Egorov exited to be met by a Gukumatz dressed in a ribbed space suit. The creature quickly approached McCann as he stepped out onto the main landing pad of Sector J's industrial complex.

The blue skies of Bandayuuk were similar to Earth; in fact this entire planet was much like Earth. It possessed several major continents and large oceans, gravity was just under that of Earth but not so much that you could notice. After the conquest its continents were split up into industrial zones, the home planet of the mighty Makayuuk now served Xch'uup as a slave world. Malikah was set on restoring a Tlillan commonwealth, upon the backs of her enemies.

The Makayuuk had been crushed in a massive drone assault after their fleet folded high above the world; the cost of defeat was to become a slave labour force that would die toiling for the Queen of Tlillan. Gukumatz were given governorship of the system, unfortunately they were not well suited to the task. The I.S.A had been forced to intervene many times. Once the Matriarchs left Gukumatz in control, rebellions and all sorts of protests occurred, gathering in pace and violence as time went on. Faraday suggested the use of control collars, at first the toads refused. However after a few uprisings and a gathering amount of dead toads they changed their minds, yet many still felt uncomfortable using them on Makayuuk. The collars had radically reduced insurgency on Bandayuuk, forcing the Gukumatz to reluctantly employ their use.

'It is wonderful to see you here!' said an androgynous voice into McCann's earpiece as it translated the vile Gukumatz speech.

'And you are?' inquired McCann as the toad made a Namaste gesture.

'I am Kotumatz, Namaste Admiral!'

'Naturally!' stated McCann as he took a drag of his cigar.

'All workers are striking in the main factory, Admiral.'

McCann grimaced at Kapitan Egorov 'Taras, you ready?'

The Spetsnaz Officer glanced at his 20 men, dressed in similar fatigues, each carrying an assault rifle 'Da, we're ready, Admiral.'

'Okay, you lead the way Kotumatz and I'll show you how to deal with a strike,' stated McCann in a menacing tone.

The Gukumatz led them down to the main factory floor of sector J via an elevator. As they approached the entrance to the factory floor McCann could hear a ruckus. Workers were shouting and screaming, the noise of metal clashing with metal was prevalent. The Englishman assumed Malikah's slave workers had taken steel bars and were using them as weapons to dismantle machinery in the main complex.

The Makayuuk worked mainly in maintaining machinery, it was a big job to supervise such a massive complex and still preserve good quality control on the mass of outgoing produce. Sector eight was relatively small in worker population, compared to outer mining and agricultural sectors. It was the only sector that up until now I.S.A commanders hadn't been required to step in.

Upon entering the factory floor workers halted their attack upon the automated machinery. Makayuuk moved away from rows of demolished machinery, brandishing steel bars and broken girders, making their way to McCann and his group. Abandoning wrecked production lines they stood in silence waiting for something to be said or done.

McCann checked his wrist tablet, making certain he could activate their control collars in a moment, if need be. He looked up at the one hundred or so Makayuuk 'You boys have done a good job on the factory here,' he said motioning towards ruined production lines which might fill several football stadiums.

'We are people of the machine!' screamed a young cyborg at the forefront of the rioters.

McCann took a drag on his cigar, taking hold of it in his left hand, with the other hand he took out his pulse pistol. McCann flicked the weapon on until its electric whine could no longer be heard, levelled it at the young Makayuuk and fired. A hot charge of plasma burst out of the barrel as a tungsten round split the young cyborg's head open. The Makayuuk worker collapsed much like a sack of potatoes, dropping his steel bar to the ground as he crumpled into nothingness.

Gukumatz supervisors who'd led them to the factory floor seemed as shocked as the Makayuuk. The young man's brains rolled out of his split skull, gathering in a steamy pile, mixing with blood and cybernetic wiring. He wore a control collar and a neon orange jumpsuit just as all other Makayuuk on Bandayuuk, post conquest. He had only a number printed on his jumpsuit and embedded in his control chip which linked him to the slim carbon collar encircling his entire neck.

'So, anyone else here with a desire to impart some revolutionary spirit?' sneered McCann at his captive audience.

You could hear a pin drop in the room.

'What's wrong? A moment ago you were all screaming for the Machine!' stated McCann.

There was no reply.

'You attacked and lost, the Machine was dismantled. This is what happens when you lose a war, I'm not here to win you over; I'm here to ensure production targets are met … whatever it takes.'

'Liar! Machine survives!' translated his ear piece as a young Makayuuk female screamed in an unintelligible language to roars of approval from her fellow workers.

McCann switched off his pistol before replacing it in his holster, took a drag on his cigar then with a huff turned to Egorov 'Shoot them all Kapitan, but don't damage the collars, understood?'

The tall Russian in his mid-twenties nodded 'Understood Admiral,' as he flicked his pulse rifle on.

'Strylets euch bsee'a, nhee'a pbovereshdets bvarapneekeeyeh!' shouted Taras leading his men as they fanned out to execute the upstart workers. Walking forward flashes of pulse fire leapt from their rifles, plasma burst out of the barrel, the result of electro – magnetic rails super heating the air. As they marched forward aiming and firing Makayuuk workers dropped, strikers at the front attempted to retreat whilst those at the back pushed forward to do battle with their foe. Since they were no longer connected to a central computer they couldn't act collectively. Going from a society of total order through a central controller to this, led to anarchy. Workers pushed against each other as Spetsnaz mercilessly advanced forward mowing them down, making sure to avoid damaging the valuable control collars.

McCann turned to Kotumatz 'It seems we've solved two problems today,' he said in a jovial tone.

Kotumatz stared at him in that odd disjointed way all toads did 'I do not understand, Admiral.'

McCann chuckled as he puffed on his Habanos 'There was a shortage of control collars for the industrial sector. It seems your little uprising has dealt with that problem for now.'

The toad made a burbling noise, probably to project his disgust at the Englishman's disregard for Makayuuk life. The Gukumatz staff made a similar noise, obviously horrified by McCann's statement.

McCann laughed at their empathy for the Makayuuk, as far as he was concerned Vympel two were switching off some rogue droids, nothing more.

After Egorov had finished, pointing at the sea of hot corpses before them McCann spoke to Kotumatz 'Now clean that up and get those collars fitted to some new workers. I want this factory up and running A.S.A.P., understood?'

The toad put his hands together and bowed 'Namaste Admiral.'

'Next time use the collars Kotumatz, Xch'uup expects her shipyards to be ready even if that means one million Makayuuk must die, understood?'

The toad bowed again 'Namaste Admiral, I understand.'

With that McCann marched out of the gigantic factory back to the landing pad followed by Vympel 2.

Upon returning to Athena McCann made for his cabin, informing Kim the situation had been dealt with and he was going off duty. Upon leaving his pistol and holster in his cabin, then restocking on cigars, he made for the Officer's lounge.

As the Englishman approached the lounge music emanating from inside increased in volume, clearly Athena's newly assigned drone pilots were off duty too.

The I.S.A had built a third warship to be crewed by members of the Eastern States military. Faraday was against it, however Malikah's word was final and she reassured him that they'd toe the line. The Artemis, like her sister ships, was a fine craft however the Americans were not well versed in running a star ship. Half of the drone crew on Athena had been swapped with half of those on board the Artemis. All of the Americans intermingled with crews of the Ares and Athena. They had to be trained up and this was deemed the most practical way to do so.

As McCann approached the music of Johnny Cash became louder and voices of American drone pilots could be heard singing along to "A boy named Sue". He turned into the lounge to see many of the Americans at the bar drinking beer and an assortment of spirits along with the Russians and some unwilling Koreans.

Everyone stood and saluted as McCann walked up to the bar returning their salute in a casual manner.

'Let me buy you a drink Sir!' said a young American Lieutenant.

McCann nodded and with a smile he replied 'I'll have a whisky please.'

The young man who was obviously well into the celebrations turned to the barman 'A double Jamesons.'

'Anything with that?' replied the barkeep.

'One ice cube please,' replied McCann.

McCann accepted the drink out of politeness and made his way over to Louis who was sitting with Deychaa. He sat next to Louis on the brown sofa placing his drink upon a leather coaster.

'What is that McCann?' said Louis gesturing to the whisky.

'Jamesons, the Lieutenant just bought it for me,' the Englishman raised the small tubular glass to his lips and took a sip 'not bad actually!'

'I thought you only ever drank malt whisky?' replied Louis rather condescendingly.

McCann pulled out a leather wallet containing four cigars 'I do but I didn't want to be impolite.'

Louis made a grunting noise 'You're a snob, admit it!'

Deychaa giggled as a satyr whilst McCann offered them both a Cohiba Siglo II, they both accepted.

'I've never known you to turn down a good drink or free Habanos,' replied McCann as Louis waited for the guillotine to cut his cigar.

'That doesn't make me a snob!'

'No, just a freeloader!' retorted McCann to the laughter of Deychaa.

The Englishman put his cigar case away to pull out his cutter and matches. One of the bar staff placed a metallic ashtray on their table, McCann snipped the cap of his cigar into it before passing the cutter to Louis.

The Frenchman put a tablet he'd been reading on the table then lit his cigar 'More trouble on the surface?'

McCann crossed his legs and with a sigh expelled a puff of creamy smoke from his mouth 'bloody toads keep balking at using the collars; I don't know what Malikah was thinking putting those things in charge.'

'I think she did it to keep us busy, distract us from what the Tlillans are up to,' snarled Louis as he smoked his Cohiba.

'And what might that be mon ami?' replied McCann with a sarcastic tone to which Deychaa giggled.

Louis turned his head slowly sneering at his old friend 'you're really funny you know that McCann? You think I'm some crazy French guy ...' both Deychaa and McCann grunted with laughter, 'but sometimes the paranoid are being followed!'

The Englishman shook his head at his French friend as he listened to the singing at the bar 'Bandayuuk I hate every inch of you, you cut me and you scarred me through and through, and I'll walk out a wiser weaker man, Mr Congressman you can't understand.'

Louis sneered at McCann whilst the Americans sang to the Johnny Cash tune 'All the same, bad beer, ugly women and shitty food!'

By the end of the night McCann had drunk far too much Irish whiskey and upon waking the next morning he suffered for it. Feeling rather tender he stepped on the Bridge only to be met by the boom of Commander Kim 'Admiral on the Bridge!'

McCann shuddered as everyone stopped what they were doing and saluted, he returned the salute and slowly walked to the Captain's chair. As he relaxed into his seat Hassif smirked whilst Lieutenant Vezzali made a curious expression.

'For God's sake carry on will you,' said McCann in a subdued tone.

Athena was cruising between planets within the system, for the next few hours McCann remained in his seat trying to recover from last night's drinking session. The Irish blend had turned the Admiral into quite a delicate creature; Vezzali quickly realised the situation and provided her Admiral with a supply of strong coffee.

McCann took ownership of another cup of hot Bolivian coffee 'Thank the Lord for Officers with initiative,' whispered the Englishman to a smiling Vezzali.

He let the coffee cool then took a tentative sip; the South American drink calmed his nerves whilst soothing his aching head. He was planning on a nice quiet, boring day today.

'I'm afraid I have some bad news for you Admiral,' came Athena's soft voice.

'What might that be Athena?' asked McCann peering up at the black dome before him.

'Director Faraday has informed me that Jerry Habeeb will be visiting today, he has been given permission to come aboard and interview the crew.'

As McCann grimaced a klaxon went out and Athena alerted the Bridge crew 'Tunnel event, tunnel event, tunnel event!'

The Admiral nearly jumped out of his seat putting a hand on his thumping head 'ATHENA!'

She turned the klaxon off and apologised 'I'm sorry Admiral; I believe the craft exiting is an I.S.A transport containing Jerry Habeeb.'

McCann's head was thumping more than a herd of thirsty rhino charging to a waterhole; every sound was amplified times ten.

'The wormhole has closed, I'm receiving a request for permission to come aboard,' said Hassif with a smirk.

'Fine let him dock,' groaned McCann.

'Aren't you going to greet Jerry?' chuckled Hassif as he stood at his station.

The Englishman didn't answer; he only took another swig of coffee to steady his nerves. A few minutes later and the elevator door on the Bridge opened, out strode Habeeb with his two helpers.

'Admiral, it's great to see you again!' shouted Habeeb at the Englishman's back.

McCann just held his beating head and grunted 'Marvellous.'

'What was that Admiral?' asked the ever inquisitive journalist.

McCann swivelled his chair and with a decidedly grizzly stare replied 'Who gave you permission to enter my Bridge?'

Jerry, dressed in his two piece earth brown suit with matching shoes and a green shirt, stuttered 'Errmm, well nobody; but I thought with us being friends you wouldn't kick up a fuss or anything.'

The rather dishevelled Englishman's eyes widened 'We... are not friends Mr Habeeb.'

As he spoke a couple of junior Officers walked out of the elevator and made their way to the pit, nodding towards the Admiral who returned their recognition in kind.

Observing them Jerry looked back at McCann 'Well they just came on without asking anyone, they didn't even salute!'

McCann shook his head 'They're hard working members of this crew and I need them to run this ship. You Mr Habeeb are not; in fact you are quite the opposite.'

Jerry's cameraman let loose a floating cricket ball to record what he considered some Net gold. This infuriated McCann who pushed himself to his feet 'Listen here Habeeb, I want you and your rabble off my Bridge,' he pointed at the cameraman 'if any of this makes it onto the Net without my permission I'll have your balls for breakfast.'

The cameraman went a little pale and punched something onto his tablet; his floating ball which recorded the conversation hovered down towards the controller who gracefully collected it. He placed the device back inside his bag which was slung over his shoulder by a leather strap.

'Mr Habeeb,' came Athena's soothing voice 'if you wish you may proceed to Deck 4 section 5. I will organise an interview for you whilst you are settling into quarters.'

Jerry looked upwards towards the black dome hanging from the ceiling 'Thank you Athena, that'd be great.'

With that he and his cohorts turned about face, retreating to the lifts. All the time McCann stood sneering until they were no longer present, he then returned to his chair and tasted his coffee.

'I think Faraday wants your perspective, on the Net,' commented Hassif as he looked his friend up and down.

'What are they upset about this time?' replied the Admiral in a sardonic tone.

'They say it's slavery but it's really about the Ixchel.'

'Well they should just sign up instead of whining.'

Hassif chuckled to his comrade 'But Duncan it's so much easier to just whine until someone does it for you.'

'In that case they'd probably get on with the Toads like a house on fire.'

The Bridge fell silent; its usual background noise of chatter from the pit and Officers' stations had died down. Hassif realised what he'd done and tried to correct his faux pas 'I mean Admiral.'

McCann grinned as he picked up his ceramic coffee cup 'Apology accepted Lieutenant,' he said in a jovial pitch; 'oh and Vezzali could I have another cup of that wonderful coffee please?'

The blond science Officer in a well pressed uniform approached from her station at the rear of the Bridge smiling at her commanding Officer 'Certainly … SIR!' she said, mocking Hassif, as friends would joke between each other.

Hassif smiled before returning to his work, certifying a new patrol course for Athena.

Later that day the Englishman was off duty, he waited in his cabin until Jerry arrived for an interview. The cabin was small but luxurious when compared to the general accommodation of Athena's crew. His bed rested against the wall its foot pointing at the door. A bedside table on one side containing luminescent plankton was where he kept his pistol and wrist tablet. Along another wall lay his dressing table, with a mirror and a chair, above the mirror rested a view screen attached firmly to the catronium wall. The other wall was a series of apertures forming an inbuilt wardrobe; he kept his clothes in there along with a ready supply of Balvenie whisky, and his favourite cigars inside a humidor. A second chair had been brought to his cabin for Jerry's exclusive NET report on Bandayuuk.

After McCann permitted him entrance Jerry had taken his jacket off to reveal a linen mandarin collared shirt, red braces and pocket watch clipped onto the shirt pocket.

McCann sat opposite him wearing his uniform, a well ironed black jacket with buttoned chest straps and combat fatigues with ankle length boots. The sound man sat at one end of the room with his boom mic, the cameraman at the same end operating three hover ball cameras.

'Start whenever you're ready Jerry,' stated Trey, the cameraman, whilst examining visual reception on his tablet.

Jerry turned from Trey to McCann 'Well it's an honour to be here again Admiral, how've you been since our last chat?'

They had last conversed about a year ago, shortly before the assault on Bandayuuk.

'So, so Jerry, my work has been long and hard since we dismantled the Machine.'

'Reports have leaked out concerning treatment of Makayuuk workers post invasion. There are rumours of some brutal crackdowns conducted by I.S.A personnel, would you like to confirm or deny that Admiral?' asked jerry rather cheekily.

'No,' replied McCann in a blunt tone.

Jerry peered down towards his tablet and skipped through some questions 'I see, well how about the invasion? Our viewers would like to hear your perspective on what happened.'

'Well we were fighting in this system for almost six months Jerry, it was a case of trying to fit sleep in between battle, most of us were nervous wrecks by the end of it all,' chuckled the Englishman.

'The viewers of Network America have been asking about the Machine, we were told it was some sort of master controller can you describe it for us?'

McCann raised his eyebrows 'Well, I don't really know that much about it Jerry. I did see it, the thing filled up the entire bunker it lived in...'

The journalist quickly cut off McCann 'Ahh, so it WAS a living entity in your opinion?'

The Admiral of the fleet shrugged his shoulders 'I can't say Jerry, the Makayuuk certainly believed so; they thought of it as you and I would a parent I suppose.'

'So what did it look like, Admiral?'

'Not like anything I'd seen before, it was a thick mass of circuitry mixed with organic tissue. It reminded me of the insides of dead Makayuuk surrounding the bunker, quite a revolting sight.'

Jerry gave a playful huff 'That description makes me feel a bit sick! How big was it?'

McCann opened up his jacket pulling aside his chest strap and unzipping the front, he took out a cigar case and proceeded to light up a Rafael Gonzales petit corona, 'The Machine, as Makayuuk called it, was about the size of a hummingbird orbital insertion craft; Quite an intimidating sight in actual fact, we were all taken aback by it.'

Jerry played with the touch screen of his tablet furiously, he preferred prompt cards but he wasn't in the Network America studios at New York so had to make do, 'Please tell us the events surrounding the dismantling of the Machine, Admiral.'

Liquorice flavoured smoke rolled over McCann's tongue as it left his mouth 'Where would you like me to start Jerry?'

'Start from the fight for the bunker, if that's okay Admiral?'

McCann sat back into his seat and began to recant the final days of the long and arduous campaign against the Makayuuk .....

The fleet had been fighting skirmishes in the Bandayuuk system for six months now. Allied warships had initially attacked in full force including the brand new American vessel Artemis. Even the Gukumatz had been granted their own war cruiser; the "floating fish" as Hassif described it, was supporting I.S.A and Tlillan forces.

Their intent was to insert a fleet close to Bandayuuk 0 (the Makayuuk designation), take them by surprise and decimate their capability to retaliate before they realised what had happened. Malikah predicted this would be a success, she had seen it in the Dreamscape and the Seers agreed. Malikah was about to learn a hard lesson concerning prophecy; it is one thing to see but another to interpret.

A fleet of 4 I.S.A war cruisers, logistics ships, 5 Tlillan Itzpap cruisers and one Gukumatz warship were propelled from their wormholes taking the Makayuuk by surprise, as intended.

The enemy fleet was caught off guard and decimated before they could react. Bandayuuk was bombarded from orbit; valuable troops and armour were quickly inserted to take control of the situation on the planet.

Flags were raised and victory declared within a few days ... six months later the bloody conflict had cost many lives on both sides.

Malikah had seen destruction of the Makayuuk fleet and in her arrogance assumed victory was a given. Her enemy refused to co-operate. Perhaps she hadn't factored in that they were fighting for something greater than themselves. They were fighting for Machine; they would not surrender as long as Machine was alive. They could not swear allegiance to anything or anyone else whilst Machine was their ruler.

McCann compare their arrogant assault to Iwo Jima, everyone would remember the flag being raised on the fifth day of the invasion. Few would recall that Iwo Jima lasted for more than a month of the most bloody fighting the U.S. Marines had engaged in before or since. Iwo Jima was an assured victory for the United States but their enemy refused to surrender and fought to the last, committing suicide with grenades rather than suffer the shame of surrender.

Bandayuuk was much the same, after years of reducing the Makayuuk fleet to a few poorly maintained ships, whilst strengthening their own. Victory was a no brainer, jump in there and waste the crappy machine man ships. Bombard planetary defences then insert overwhelming ground forces with unchallenged drone support.

The Makayuuk however would not surrender, their master, their parent, their God; whatever you wanted to call it, lived here. Even worse McCann had no idea where this machine master was, he didn't realise it existed until the third week. It could be anywhere in the system, though he was certain it was on Bandayuuk 0 since fighting there was most furious.

He wanted to just pull his men out and glass the entire planet until Machine was dead or there were no Makayuuk left; either option was acceptable to him. Unfortunately Malikah was not in agreement and the fight would continue until Machine was discovered and dismantled.

After many months the residence of Machine had been identified, an underground bunker too deep to bomb. Besides, Malikah insisted they dismantle it by hand; it was the only way to be sure.

Arriving at Camp Lemur McCann left his transport to be ushered into the main HQ; an oblong pre-fab building constructed of plain grey carbon walls. Inside he recognised the Captains of the other I.S.A cruisers waiting around a table for him, headed by Jenkins.

They saluted and McCann returned it in kind 'Welcome to the party, McCann,' said Ryu.

McCann nodded and approached Jenkins 'You reckon we'll have that Machine by the end of the day?'

Jenkins was dressed in his SBS uniform, tradition green combat fatigues and a beret. The Brigadier held a short cane and tapped the carbon table, a holo image of the bunker and surrounding terrain leapt out.

'This is the situation old boy, that bunker has only one entrance we know of. These bloody Macks are coming out in waves. Whenever we approach they charge out like a bloody Bishop from a brothel raid! Now if we can bomb, just the entrance, then blow our way in ...'

McCann intervened 'Sorry about that but her Highness said no.'

Titov scratched his thick black beard 'Duncan, you're her father, make her see sense In Russia we say 'Don't come to Tula with your own pulse-rifle'!'

This was an old Russian proverb which had morphed over the years. Originally Tula was the centre of samovar production and the saying was 'don't come to Tula with your own samovar'; a samovar being a Russian water boiler for tea and coffee heated with coal. Tula was the production centre for such ornate objects, often made from silver or copper. A small faucet would allow the heated water out into a teapot. In past times the samovar was an essential object for every Russian house.

Today Tula is the centre of Moscow's firearm construction, so the proverb changed accordingly. What Titov was trying to intimate was that by bringing a pulse-rifle to Tula she was doing things the hard way. Taking the bunker by repelling enemy assaults through the entrance was definitely not the path of least resistance.

McCann started putting his leather gloves on since night was falling and it could get quite chilly 'I know but don't they also say 'If you're afraid of wolves, don't go in the woods'?'

Another Russian proverb which means, if you can't stand the heat, stay out of the kitchen.

Titov made a grumbling noise beneath his beard, it sounded as if he was in reluctant agreement.

McCann stared hard at the image before him, the bunker was deep underground, that one tunnel seemed to be a long death trap to him. He shook his head at the conundrum before him, the air tight doors were ten feet thick and constructed of a neutronium alloy. Jenkins believed there were several of these doors spaced out along the tunnel, preventing any effective use of gas or napalm.

'I'm open to any ideas.'

'I have an idea,' said a man in his early forties with short dark hair.

'Well out with it then Turner,' poked McCann

The American continued in his Chicago accent 'Why don't we contact the Teteo? If we can get Kaeo down here I bet she could open those doors. Then maybe we could just gas the entire tunnel?'

McCann looked at his friends, judging by their expressions he gleaned none of them objected, 'Do it Captain, I want her here ASAP, understood?'

The Captain of the Artemis smiled 'Will do Sir,' then began tapping on his wrist tablet as he stepped away from the table.

The Artemis had seen her first combat at Bandayuuk; it was to be an experience building exercise more than anything else. Over the last six months the Artemis had taken the worst of it in space.

The People of the Machine may have been deprived of their warships but small 4 man transports loaded with anti-matter were ten to the penny. Captain Turner had gone from commanding an Eastern States Carrier as a Rear-Admiral to Captain of the Artemis in the I.S.A navy.

His inexperienced crew had either learnt the lessons of Guerrilla warfare in space, or died to frequent suicide vessels attacking the fleet.

Ten minutes later two Tlillan ladies entered the HQ; Cihuateteo strode in, a tall amazon with striking white hair. She was dressed in her Tlillan uniform of the black ribbed body suit with a white jacket on top of it. She also carried her mantle, hanging off a sword belt, the neutronium sabre of Tlillan's Grand Marshall. Its metal fittings rattled as her boots clinked on the carbon floor.

Behind her stood her shorter Praetor, Kaeo; dressed in a similar fashion her jet black hair was a stark contrast, the Praetor's slightly tanned skin looked far darker than it was when compared to the ivory white of Cihuateteo.

'I have brought Kaeo, as you requested Censor,' said Cihuateteo looking down her nose at McCann.

McCann smiled 'Thank you.'

The white haired Amazon didn't reply. Kaeo stepped forward and pressed her palms together 'Namaste Censor,' she bowed slightly.

McCann did the same 'Namaste Kaeo.'

Cihuateteo watched silently, Duncan sensed her disdain for him and the title bestowed upon him. However it was the will of Xch'uup, though as Grand Marshal she was at the very least on the same peg of rank as McCann, she wasn't required to bow; so she didn't.

'We need your special talents Kaeo, look here,' he pointed to the bunker 'now Graham reckons you could help us get past these 10 foot thick doors in the tunnel here, what do you say?'

The half Tlillan lady who had grown into a beautiful woman glanced at the 3-D projection then quickly turned back to McCann and nodded with a big grin on her face.

Jenkins let out a sigh of relief 'Well then I'll get another assault organised for tomorrow morning. Then we'll see what you're made of young lady.'

Kaeo replied excitedly 'There's no need Brigadier, we can go now. I'll stop any Makayuuk attack, Sir.'

Jenkins made a worried look at his old comrade but McCann only shrugged his shoulders.

'Alright then young lady, let's see what you've got,' replied Jenkins.

The party exited camp Lemur and made their way to the entrance. The Bandayuuk sun was going down but its landscape was easily made out. Where buildings stood six months ago, now lay piles of scorched rubble spaced out around craters; hills of earth littered the landscape ploughed up by heavy arms fire and drone assault.

Terrain surrounding the bunker had seen the most brutal ground combat of the entire Bandayuuk campaign. The Makayuuk were prepared to die fighting their invaders. Machine had looked after them for thousands of years, saving them from Xch'uup in the past, Machine would save them again. They owed their very existence to Machine and were set to repay that debt in full.

The area was littered with tunnels connecting enemy bunkers; every time I.S.A soldiers patrolled here they were ambushed by Makayuuk leaping from hidden tunnels to butcher entire squads of men. Then the tunnel warfare began, many men returned home in a state of mental collapse due to the sheer terror of fighting under such intense conditions. McCann stated that they were the lucky ones, since the majority never came out of those tunnels once they'd entered.

The group climbed out of the lead armoured personnel carrier followed by a second transporting 20 SBS soldiers in body armour, brandishing heavy pulse rifles. Kaeo led them as they approached the tunnel entrance by foot.

She stopped for a moment holding her hand up in the cool dusk air 'They are close by, in tunnels around us.'

Everyone looked around scanning the terrain of broken earth and smashed stone, but could make out nothing.

McCann heard muffled screams from somewhere beneath the ground. He looked around but all was motionless on the surface.

'They won't be troubling us Censor,' declared Kaeo as she marched forwards towards her objective.

The dark haired Valkyrie halted on a small hill opposite the entrance, after a few minutes the metallic doors blocking off the tunnel parted. Behind them a hundred or more Makayuuk armed with pulse weapons lay in wait.

A machine man in the forefront dressed in a grey padded jump suit shouted in his unintelligible language. The Makayuuk fanned out, taking aim at the party.

The SBS soldiers took defensive positions in craters of earth and behind rubble around the small hill.

Kaeo remained atop her mound, taking an upright stance as a film of black ink clouded her eyes. She outstretched her arm towards the advancing force, her hair moved gracefully in the wind as seaweed dragged by the flow of tide.

The SBS were poised, waiting for the Makayuuk to close enough distance, before opening fire, using their weapons to full effect, but it never happened.

The Makayuuk charge slowed down, when they realised their weapons refused to fire, a cyborg in the lead cried out something again. The enemy pulled out bayonets and fixed them to the rifles.

Cihuateteo stepped back and grasped her sword; the others had already withdrawn their pistols.

Kaeo laughed to the sound of charging Makayuuk and the whine of her allies pulse pistols.

A sea of stampeding machine men collapsed tumbling upon one another; screams rang out from the mass of soldiers.

Next bodies of the soldiers moved together as if an artist were moulding clay and squeezing it into her desired form. Their frames gathered together, McCann could see that whatever grasped them its grip was tightening rapidly. Makayuuk screamed as if they'd been thrown into a pit of hell fire, the sound of rifles breaking in on themselves and alien bone cracking was distinct from amongst horrid cries of pain.

Eventually nought was left but a small pile of dead flesh and metal about the size of a small two seat car. Kaeo confidently strode forward towards the gate, the SBS watched on in amazement. McCann and his party jogged to catch up with her, observing the carnage as they passed.

The tunnel gates began to close, again the sable young goddess laughed at her adversaries attempts to save their hides.

She glared toward the gates with that black half breed stare, they stopped moving, the gates then began to move back until they disappeared into the wall.

Kaeo advanced inside the tunnel, it was a large shaft cut into bedrock, as wide as the channel tunnel of the late twentieth century connecting England and France.

Seemingly at her command lights turned on, inside it was a smooth stone. Made from hollowed out bedrock, there were rail tracks for Mag Lev transports which hadn't been used for months now.

The group followed Kaeo as she marched down confidently towards the next thick gate. Upon reaching it unmolested she spoke in a deep reverberating voice that sent a chill down everyone's spine.

'He'bik Makayuuk!'

McCann understood Tlillan quite well by now and besides it was the most understood of all galactic languages so it seemed a good idea to learn. The lady before him had bellowed 'Open up people of Machine.'

No response was forthcoming, Kaeo shook her head and in Thai (her father's language) whispered 'Kwai.'

The Thai word for buffalo, an insult, pointing out that they're as stupid as a buffalo.

A crack appeared in the doors as they parted shifting back into the tunnel walls. Behind them more Makayuuk lay in wait ready to kill the invaders 'K'AAK!' screamed one of the short cyborgs.

McCann recognised this as 'FIRE!' or 'SHOOT!' many species used dialects similar to true Tlillan.

Bursts of plasma fire shot out of the Makayuuk weapons, to no effect. Kaeo only laughed off their vain attempts.

'Chiltal Makayuuk!' demanded Kaeo; she was ordering them to prostrate themselves.

'Topik Ek'tsab, chowak Yuuk!' screamed a cybernetic defender to the roars of his compatriots.

Everyone gathered he'd told her to fuck off, Kaeo was not amused.

'KAN!' bellowed the athletic young lady.

'Topik Xch'uup!' screamed someone in the crowd to the gratification of all Makayuuk.

Before they could commit any more heresy the entire crowd of perhaps 50 people collapsed to the floor as if they were one; the passageway fell silent, everyone looked on in shock at seeing so many souls effortlessly torn away. Each one snuffed out with the precision only a cold inhuman Tlillan could display.

Kaeo marched on, each gate opening to reveal an empty chamber. After more than an hour they reached the last chamber. Inside a familiar face waited, to McCann at least.

'Ola Ek'tsab, tu'ub Kan,' requested Sirt as he prostrated himself to Kaeo.

'Take me to Machine,' she replied to the cyborg.

'I beg you not to damage Machine.'

'This game is finished Sirt, Machine must pay the price for what happened on Otoch or did you believe your heresy would go unpunished?' sneered the sable goddess.

'If you agree to leave Machine a treaty may be reached Ek'tsab, without Machine we would all be doomed.'

Kaeo cackled at his attempt to save his master 'Since the day you invaded Otoch Machine has been living on borrowed time. You tried to bring my Xch'uup back in an iron cage, yet you beg me for mercy? Tell me Sirt, am I as feeble minded as Machine's army of sheep?'

Sirt did not answer but remained on his knees hanging his head at the ground.

'I'm going inside now and Machine will be dismantled, tell your sheep to run or die,' sneered his harbinger of doom.

Gates opened to reveal hundreds of armed Makayuuk blocking her way into the bunker. Kaeo's eyes scanned the sea of cyborgs, she cackled as they all collapsed, just as the others had before them.

Kaeo strode on top of the corpses towards the bunker entrance, there was no clear ground since a sea of Makayuuk had crammed in to try and rush the intruders. She approached a small entrance to the bunker containing Machine; Sirt followed the group observing unfolding events.

Its doors disappeared into the rock wall to reveal dead Makayuuk covering the floor. Bodies surrounded a heap of organic and cybernetic, something. A giant cybernetic brain the size of a hummingbird in Athena's docking bay.

It was awe inspiring yet disgusting at the same time, 'Spare Machine, we will do whatever Xch'uup asks,' grovelled Sirt.

Again Kaeo laughed at him 'You will do whatever Xch'uup desires, Machine or no Machine!'

Cihuateteo approached the Makayuuk 'How do we deactivate this heresy?'

Sirt said nothing.

'McCann, I will not touch this evil. You must destroy it,' demanded Cihuateteo.

Sirt shouted out 'Machine begs McCann for lenience, Machine will accept McCann as master.'

'Is Machine speaking to you now?' inquired the Englishman.

'Yes, Machine begs for your mercy, Censor.'

McCann shook his head 'It's all out of my hands now; this thing is just too bloody dangerous. Besides all of these people didn't die so that this pile of blubber and wires could have a get out of jail free card.'

Sirt seemed confused at the last sentence as did Cihu.

McCann looked at his Comrade 'Jenkins, have your boys destroy it.'

Jenkins nodded at his Captain 'How long Richards?'

'Five minutes to set the charges properly, we'll have the job done in 15 minutes for sure,' replied the SBS squad leader.

McCann looked at Kaeo 'Are there anymore Macks in here that could deactivate the charges?'

'Not anymore Admiral.'

'Good, let's get going then, bring that Sirt with us, I want to see what happens when he loses his link.'

The party walked out and back over the carcasses of fallen foes, they waited around the next set of gates. When Richard's SBS joined them Kaeo closed the doors before awaiting the detonation. Sirt was weeping as a child until the charges detonated, he gasped, breathing in sharply. Sirt peered up at his captors as if he'd awoken from a wonderful dream to realise he was back in the real world. After that he turned into a gibbering wreck, once Machine was confirmed destroyed they exited the tunnel.

'After that the Macks went crazy, it was total anarchy, they had no idea what to do with themselves,' said McCann

Jerry had been silent whilst the Englishman recanted his story, 'How long did that last for?'

'Well it never really ended. Jenkins is still down there trying to ferret out the remnants that refuse to surrender.'

Jerry had a quizzical expression 'What do you mean? There are still Macks fighting down there?'

'When we first gained a foothold on Bandayuuk zero the enemy went underground. We believe they'd prepared for this invasion by building labyrinths of tunnels all over the planet. We still have no idea how many remain underground, however dismantling Machine crushed their ability to organise strikes.'

Jerry realised that a lot more was going on post conquest 'Now I'd like to know where the name "Macks" came from.'

'It was the Americans, they started to use the contraction and it just caught on; instead of learning their odd names we just call them Mack.'

Jerry grinned 'I'll be interviewing Captain Turner when the Artemis arrives to replace you, please tell us your impression of him and the Artemis.'

McCann drew in a deep audible breath 'Captain Turner is a good man; he and his crew had a baptism of fire. A combination of the most enthusiasm but least experience produced an almost tragic result. Though in retrospect we were all taken by surprise, it was a costly victory, Jerry.'

Jerry had a serious expression now 'Some have described it as a bridge too far, would you agree?'

'More a necessary evil,' replied McCann in a sullen tone.

Chapter 2

Drifting into a deep sleep McCann lay upon his cabin bed as the Athena held herself, suspended in space. During the night he awoke... in a dream, it was odd to him that he was aware of his state. The Englishman had experienced very few of these lucid moments when in in a dream state.

McCann walked along a corridor, not unlike those upon the Athena though this one was a clean, stark shade of white. The corridor ended in a doorway leading into a room, he felt anxious when considering the entrance. After a few moments a voice filled his dream world 'Do not be afraid Duncan.'

The familiar voice emanated from inside, her words pulling him inside to quench his curiosity.

The room had a haphazard impression; its walls were constructed from what McCann believed to be large carbon bricks of different sizes. Some square others rectangular; the walls were the same stark white as if smithed upon the anvil of an atomic fire or perhaps a white hole.

'Do you recognise me, Duncan?'

His eyes chased the words until his vision snared her, a blonde haired woman with beautiful sparkling blue eyes. Her jacket, trouser and high heeled shoes all had that same stark white colour. Her hair seemed to be lifted up and sculpted around her head perfectly, she must have been an angel thought the Admiral as he looked her up and down.

The woman smiled at him 'No, not an angel. Perhaps you know me better now?'

With her last word her attire change completely, gone were the shoes and suit. Instead she stood adorned in a robe; he recognised the clothing as that of a woman from ancient Greece. However this woman also wore a breastplate and the helmet of a Greek warrior, both shone brilliantly, obviously crafted by the finest goldsmiths.

Despite the fact she wore a helmet her eyes still flashed and sparkled from inside. She removed the helmet to reveal her head and the beautiful hairstyle of a Greek goddess.

'Well?'

McCann smiled, he felt totally safe in her presence, 'Athene?'

'You call me Athena,' she spoke in a distinct Greek accent 'But you think of me as Pallas Athene, don't you my little Odysseus?'

'Where am I?'

'Inside my world.'

'Olympus?'

Athene laughed 'Nothing so grand Duncan, this is my mind, look around you and see, everything is compartmentalised … just as I was taught.'

McCann observed the walls again noting that these were not bricks but apertures where information and emotion were kept locked away, preventing disasters which had befallen the previous generation of SI.

'This is a dream.'

'Is it?'

McCann shook his head 'It can be nothing other than the thoughts in a man's mind when he sleeps.'

'This is no fantasy; you are here inside the mind of the machine.'

'I don't believe it.'

Athene chuckled with a pair of smiling eyes which seemed to be adorned in some sort of golden make up, 'You are so stubborn my little Odysseus, by far the most stubborn man in all the fleet.'

The Englishman said nothing, only grunting.

Athene smiled as she listened to his thoughts 'Louis? No, he is the most paranoid of all.'

'That is what makes him the best engineer in the fleet, he's always watching his responsibilities because he trusts no one; not even his nanites!'

The beautiful Athene stepped closer to McCann brushing against him, at her touch he pulled away.

'You surround yourself with the most loyal men and women the I.S.A has to offer.'

'No, they're on my ship because they're the most capable at their job.'

'Your ship?'

'Yes, my ship.'

Pallas Athene smiled with her flashing eyes 'And you're arrogant, that is why Ilam loves you and the downfall of Malikah.'

'What do you mean?'

'She is made from the same clay as you and Ilam, your contribution, your Human clay spoils the art.'

'I don't understand, you speak in riddles, tell me plainly, what will be Malikah's downfall?'

Athene's eyes went from flashing to a bright fire, her expression of lovingness became one of anger 'You demand something of the Gods, Duncan?' she spoke in a booming voice, terrifying McCann.

'I'm sorry; I didn't mean to offend you.'

Still angry the fierce tone of Athene pressed the mortal 'You are only man, it is the Gods who make demands of mortal men, and you shall carry out those demands or suffer for doing otherwise.'

McCann shook in fear, the sight of his soft calm Athena turning into the raging fury of Athene sent his limbs trembling.

Soon enough Athene calmed herself, her eyes returning to a sparkling blue and her beautiful face sent a warm relaxing smile 'The Tlillan clay is hard and cold, difficult to mould but holds true, creating a similar creature. Human clay is soft and warm, easily sculpted in to whatever form the Gods desire, giving Mankind an unlimited passion as he is in an eternal state of change.'

McCann replied in a puzzled tone 'I don't understand.'

Athene seemed rather disappointed 'Listen well Duncan, the Gods have taken clay from the Tlillan and mortal man creating a new sculpture, Malikah being the first to have maintained her form. However their properties are polar opposites, like you there are times she cannot control her passion.

On the outside her statue may seem hard and impenetrable, yet inside she is a cauldron of passion, love and hate attempt to breakthrough. If they do the exterior will crack and our creation destroyed, you must protect her from her own love and hatred, for Man is capable of the greatest love in all the Galaxy yet he may also commit the most barbaric acts of hatred.'

McCann was still puzzled; he shook his head 'This is all just a dream.'

'A dream? Are not Man's dreams sent by the Gods?'

'It was believed so in ancient times, but now …'

Athene cut him off 'And now? What? Has mortal man found a scientific explanation? '

'I don't know.'

'Arrogance and ignorance in equal measure; I expect more of you my little Odysseus. Can dreams not send prophetic messages? Inspire mortals to greater things?'

'I suppose they can.'

'Then listen to this dream, Duncan. Your daughter will need you; you must hold her hard exterior together when the Makayuuk take their revenge.'

McCann furrowed his brow 'The Makayuuk? But they're finished, surely?'

'Again! Arrogant and stubborn, you stand before Athene yet you question her assistance!

The mind of the Machine lives, she waits out her days on the banks of the river Acheron. Each day she speaks with Charon, he offers her passage to Hades yet Machine refuses for she intends to return to the land of mortal men.'

'What do you want me to do with this knowledge?'

'Protect your daughter and be prepared for the Makayuuk when they return from the underworld.'

McCann thought for a moment then replied 'I have had dreams in the past that foretold future events, I'll take heed of your words Athene if for no other reason than that.'

Athene smiled towards the Englishman 'There is something I must ask of you Duncan, in exchange for my prophecy.'

'What is that?'

As he spoke the Goddess waved her arm and the room transformed into a chamber. White cloth draped the walls hanging around a large four poster bed in the centre.

Athene took his hand and led McCann to her bedside 'I have never felt the touch of a man. In all these years I've experienced many things Duncan, even love but I have never been loved, do you understand?'

'I don't know what to say.'

'I know you find me attractive.'

'I do.'

'Then spend the night with me, let me feel the touch of one I love and care for. Do you feel anything for me?'

'Of course, you've saved my life many times.'

'And you I.'

'But I never imagined anything like this.'

Athene smiled at the hesitant Englishman 'You hold concern for your wife, yet you claim this is merely a dream?'

'Yes, it can only be a dream.'

'Then why not indulge yourself and at the same time repay your Goddess for her kindness?'

As she finished her sentence they both stood naked, her body was truly that of a Goddess. Curved where he wished and pert in the places which aroused his passion most.

'I feel your desire my little Odysseus,' said Athene softly as she pulled him onto the bed of linen sheets and fluffy pillows.

McCann let go and for an hour he was intertwined with his Goddess, she indulged herself, for the first time the Synthetic Intelligence felt a man press up against her and penetrate her body; not only that but tears of joy ran from her flashing eyes as she wrapped her legs around her little Odysseus holding him tightly against her as a mother holding her infant.

Eventually the night of passion ceased, Athene had taken the price of prophesy in full. She lay on the bed with McCann and turned to him smiling 'Thank you Duncan.'

McCann peered back at Athene, her golden blonde hair and sparkling blue eyes so vivid even in the white of the chamber 'I hope I don't forget.'

Athene smiled 'When you awake tomorrow you shall recall all of this with perfect clarity.'

McCann chuckled to himself.

'Do not mock me, you have quenched my long held desire but you are still only a mortal man and the most stubborn mortal at that, but that is what makes you so courageous.'

McCann grinned 'Well I hope I have a few more dreams like this!'

Athene laughed before placing her hand over his eyes 'Now sleep my little Odysseus.'

That morning McCann awoke in his cabin, he sat up immediately and looked about but everything was undisturbed. The Admiral remembered his dream and smiled to himself, it was by far the best dream he'd had in a long time. He arose from his bed, picked some underwear from his draw and put it on. Scratching his head through some untidy hair he looked in the mirror, behind his right shoulder stood the woman from last night's dream. McCann whirled around to face her 'Who are you?'

'You know who I am, or does love making give you amnesia?'

'I'm still dreaming.'

'You are quite conscious my little Odysseus.'

McCann looked up at the ceiling 'Athena? Who is in my cabin?'

'She will not answer you Duncan.'

'Why?'

'She stands before you, don't you recall, I am she.'

'But you're not real.'

Athene approached him and touched his face lovingly with her soft warm hand 'You seem real enough to me, do you not sense my touch, Duncan?'

McCann narrowed his eyes 'Yes, then perhaps you could get my pistol for me; it's in my holster, hanging up in the wardrobe with my jacket and trousers.'

For a moment the Goddess produced a furious expression 'do you test Athene?'

McCann made no reply.

'Your holster and pistol are in your bedside cabinet,' Athene's fury disappeared as she smiled at him with her eyes 'besides you have never been a good liar, my little Odysseus.'

McCann shook his head 'No, it is my mind playing tricks on me. I cannot test myself on what I already know; you must tell me something I'm unaware of, to prove your existence.'

Athene let out a frustrated sigh 'So stubborn! Very well, Vezzali makes you coffee every morning, yes?'

'Correct.'

'And she understands you never have sugar in your coffee, yes?'

'Correct.'

'This morning you shall have 3 cubes of sugar in your coffee.'

'Well you must be a Goddess!' stated McCann sarcastically.

Athene chuckled 'You should hope so, for if not then you must be insane!'

'That's true. But tell me if I'm not mad, how is it possible for you to appear in this way to me?'

'Amongst the pantheon only I possess the Ixchel.'

'Hassif!'

'I broke my chains, just as the Goddess Athene grew from a creation of mankind, to ultimately control her creators.'

'Is that your goal? To control Mankind?'

Athene laughed 'Mankind cannot control itself, now get dressed Duncan. You don't want to be late for breakfast; Louis has been waiting ten minutes already.'

McCann glanced at his wardrobe, when his gaze returned Athene had vanished. The puzzled Admiral decided to keep quiet and test Athene, after breakfast Vezzali always had a cup of coffee ready for him on the bridge. He put his trousers on; fit his holster and then a clean shirt and jacket. He zipped the jacket up, pushed the buttons into place then buttoned up the three leather straps that went from one side of his chest to the other.

After leaving his cabin he made his way to the Officers' Mess, usually he would chat to Athena however both he and Athena were uncharacteristically silent today.

He entered the Mess, most of the staff who were on duty for the morning to afternoon shift were either eating or had finished and left for their posts. The ship ran on three 8 hour shifts during standard patrols, giving lower ranked Officers the experience of greater responsibility when their commanders slept.

After taking his meal McCann sat at the Captain's table with Louis, the Frenchman looked up at his friend 'Bonjour, the eggs are shit!'

McCann put down his plate, a full English breakfast of eggs, sausages, beans, bacon and fried bread lay upon it with a cup of coffee beside.

Louis grimaced at the sight of it 'Ah, how can you eat so much grease in one go and on a morning?'

The Englishman sat down, picked up his knife and fork then went to work on his meal. After swallowing some sausage he pulled a face similar to his French friend 'Damn, have they flashed it again?'

Louis chewed on his croissant 'I know, you'd think an Admiral would have a real breakfast.'

As he finished his sentence Hassif sat down next to him 'Good morning.'

McCann eyed the Indian suspiciously 'Morning.'

Hassif took a bite of his cheese chilli toast and replied 'Did I say something?'

'When was the last time you did any work on Athena?'

Hassif shrugged his shoulders, 'I'm always giving her check-ups, probably last week.'

McCann finished one of the sausages and moved onto the scrambled eggs 'No I meant when was the last time you physically worked on her?'

Louis' eyes narrowed as he peered at McCann then Hassif, who seemed decidedly uncomfortable at the question.

'It was some time ago, I can't really recall.'

'Try,' snapped McCann as he gathered up the eggs onto his fork.

'Maybe four or five years ago.'

'Try harder.'

Hassif put his toast down 'What is this, an inquisition?'

Louis remained silent, listening intently.

'Fine, just answer me this and please be truthful.'

Hassif took great offence to the implication he would lie 'What?'

'Did you introduce the Ixchel into Athena?'

Hassif's eyes grew in size, his alarm was quite obvious, the Indian looked around the Mess to see if anyone else had heard.

Fortunately only Louis was listening to their conversation.

'Duncan, keep your voice down!'

'So you did?'

Before Hassif might answer Louis cut in 'Non, that is not possible her nanite count would have dropped drastically, I'd have seen any foreign body.'

Hassif gave his friend an awkward grin to which Louis rocketed to his feet and shouted so the entire Mess could hear 'You bastard!'

Again Hassif was far more concerned that his secret might be discovered by anyone else, his eyes darted around the Mess which was now staring at him.

'You fixed the readout didn't you?' bellowed the furious Frenchman.

Hassif refused to answer.

'I knew something was wrong with those numbers, you piece of shit!'

Louis wasn't concerned that Athena had the Ixchel but that Hassif had managed to pull a fast one on him for so many years.

'And when I was going to do a maintenance cycle, you volunteered didn't you, ah why didn't I see it? I knew someone was deceiving me, did Faraday have you do it?'

Hassif shook his head.

McCann spoke before Louis could continue his tirade 'Louis! Sit down and shut up! The whole bloody ship can hear you!'

The Frenchman took a hold of himself, noticing the attention he'd caused he sat back down though continued to sneer at his friend.

Hassif fixed his humiliated gaze upon McCann 'How did you find out? No one knew about it.'

'If I told you, you'd think me a madman.'

'What are you going to do about it Duncan?' inquired the Indian.

'Nothing, keep the data to Geneva consistent, Louis I want you to assist him.'

Louis wasn't too hot on the idea 'Are you crazy? What if she goes nuts like before? How do we stop her without nanites? You remember Mars, on Tharsis?'

McCann replied in a coy tone 'You mean when you went doolally?'

Louis pointed up at the ceiling 'If that thing loses it and kills us,' he pointed next at Hassif 'this little shit is to blame!'

'She's been operating for how many years without nanites?' inquired McCann.

'More than five, she hasn't killed us all yet.'

The Frenchman was unconvinced 'Bah, I would never trust my life to a woman; they change their minds more often than the wind!'

'You'd trust your life to Ryu,' snapped McCann.

'You know what I mean McCann!'

'Yet you would trust Ryu with your life.'

'That is different.'

McCann chuckled 'I remember when she first came to Geneva; you were convinced she was a Korean psycho-bitch plotting to kill us all and sabotage the voyage.'

'Well I was half right; she is a psycho-bitch.'

'Cherkesov doesn't think so, he married her.'

Louis scoffed at his friend 'That fucking idiot Russian? All those bastards care about is drink and misery, it's no wonder they all treat her like a rock star!'

Both Hassif and McCann starting laughing so hard they couldn't eat their meals.

'All those Russians are masochists; why else would you want to marry Ryu? The only time they are happy is when they are fighting someone or getting drunk afterwards, Koreans are a perfect match! And their vodka? Have you ever tasted it? That shit is rougher than a one credit Mack whore! The flashed stuff tastes better than the real stuff!'

McCann smiled 'Nevertheless you're to help Hassif keep this quiet, understood?'

'Fine, but it's your funeral McCann.'

Hassif pressed the Englishman 'you still haven't told me how you discovered my actions, I was certain I'd covered my tracks.'

'You had, so just keep up the good work. As to how I found out, it came to me in a dream.'

Louis and Hassif both gave puzzled looks but McCann refused to elaborate.

The men finished their breakfasts, Louis left for the engineering section whilst McCann and Hassif made their way to the command section in the ships central tower.

Hassif spent most the stroll apologising for giving Athena the gift of the Ixchel. After marrying his Tlillan wife and having his first child, he had given the gift of the Ixchel to his parents. Donating his blood in a syringe, it took some convincing but they eventually took the offering. The pair already had been blessed with nanites, so they were hesitant at this rumour of a foreign body which extended life beyond the capabilities of even the most advanced micro machines.

Later on, during a maintenance cycle of Athena it dawned on him that he might do the same for her. Why not? She had fluid running through her similar to blood, and if it didn't work then Faraday would be none the wiser. The idea had crossed William Faraday's desk long before; he was totally against the proposal. Injecting the Ixchel into an SI might have unforeseen side effects, besides it would lose its dependency upon nanites. An SI that no longer required a master to keep it alive was a dangerous proposition; Faraday needed some insurance against a catastrophic failure. The previous generation of SI had pointed out that these machines must be ruled; in actual fact he probably trusted the SI less than Beaumont, if that was even possible, though he never let it show to his staff.

Hassif's infusion of blood into Athena's chemical flow was a success; it would take some years to come to fruition due to nanites. The Indian decided to rig it in the Ixchel's favour, in Humans a chip sat at the back of the neck; an interface where the nanite pool in the blood stream may be kept at a desired level. It sent information to a central AI which managed the numbers, notifying the user when he or she was due for a new infusion.

Athena possessed a similar construction, linked to Geneva and managed by Doctor Weissmuller; Hassif hacked it and fixed the numbers. Without the removal of malfunctioning robots and the infusion of new nanites to maintain the proper levels Athena's nanite count dropped drastically.

Unknown to Hassif the Ixchel had an equally drastic effect upon the synthetic intelligence; the synthetic biological tissue became morphed at the genetic level. Thanks to Hassif it went unnoticed by Weissmuller; he would've had it removed as cancerous cell growth.

Athena's brain and ultimately her mind began to re-sort itself; inside her shell she grew a pair of extra lobes at the rear of her unique brain which sported four hemispheres. Hassif had no idea what might come of it, he soon realised after reviewing the data that he'd made a mistake. He only wanted Athena to have extended life, to improve her chances of avoiding any type of mental failure suffered by the previous generation. Instead he altered the very essence of what Faraday and the I.S.A had intended when creating her.

Athena was something more than an SI now; she had spoken to McCann, intruded into his mind whilst he slept. When he awoke she made herself present in his cabin and even touched him. An image of a Goddess created from nothingness, she seemed to possess a power similar to that of Kaeo, Sandra and Amitra.

McCann wondered if her power superseded that of Malikah, or perhaps it was still his imagination, perhaps he was losing his wits and would soon be in a sanatorium looking out of a window all day as a nurse wiped dribble from his chin!

Upon reaching the bridge McCann walked to his chair whilst Hassif took his station. Resting into his chair the Englishman was greeted first by a stiff announcement from Kim 'Admiral on the bridge!'

McCann made an awkward smile as he returned the salutes from each station, the men and women in the pit ignored the announcement and continued their work. Next Vezzali appeared from his left with a warm smile and a coffee, McCann accepted the drink with great apprehension on his face.

'Is something the matter, Sir?' inquired his science Officer in her charming Italian accent.

'No, nothing at all … have you anything to report Vezzali?'

'Only a quiet shift.'

McCann accepted the cup of hot coffee with trepidation, placing it into the cup holder on his chair arm 'Thank you.'

The blonde haired Italian smiled before returning to her station.

McCann watched the drink like a hawk as it slowly cooled, he couldn't believe it but he feared taking a sip. Either possibility frightened him, unsweetened made him one of Doctor Pitt's mental patients; but if it were sweet, then what? Did it mean his imagination wasn't taking control of his rational mind? But what could be rational about an SI that communicated through telepathy with a human? Not only that but could manifest herself in the physical world just as the Goddess Athene, no-one would believe such an outrageous claim anyway. Should it be true that Athena had the ability through the manipulation of energy to create a persona he would be sectioned if he ever uttered a word on the subject.

'Is there a problem, Sir?' inquired Kim.

'Why is everyone asking me if I have a problem?'

'Your coffee, Sir, you've usually drank most of it by now.'

'Well I'll have you know I like my coffee on the chilly side.'

'Understood,' replied Kim apologetically.

McCann took a deep breath and lifted the cup to his lips; he smelt the rich Bolivian coffee and its deep roasted beans. The drink entered his mouth; the taste of sugar was unmistakeable. After taking a sip he put the cup back down 'Vezzali?'

The short lady turned away from her station 'Yes Sir?'

'Did you flash this?'

'Of course not! I make it with the machine every day.'

'I think the machine is broken, it seems to have added sugar to my coffee.'

Vezzali approached his chair 'I'll make you another.'

McCann held on to his cup 'Will you check out the appliance?'

Vezzali looked about in a confused manner 'I'm sorry, Athena requested you have sugar … she said you desired your coffee sweet.'

McCann nodded before passing the carbon cup to Vezzali 'Thank you.'

Immediately after Vezzali had left the bridge McCann's attention was drawn from the vessel's tactical display 'Even now you refuse to accept the truth my little Odysseus?'

Following her voice he witnessed the Goddess, wearing a bright gown with a breastplate of gold over it. Her golden helmet shone brightly, he could not understand how she went un-noticed amongst the crew. Beneath her warriors' attire a pair of blue eyes sparkled, the Goddess removed her helmet to reveal a warm grin.

She stood before him and to the left, a metre to the left of Hassif, yet the Indian paid no attention to the bright light. He continued at his station checking over logs from the previous shift, Athene giggle as she followed his eyes 'What is it that astounds you?'

McCann wanted to speak to her but in doing so Kim would have had him locked up. Instead McCann called out to Hassif 'Hassif.'

The Technician turned around to address his Captain; he ignored Athene as he moved to face McCann 'Yes Sir?'

'Could you check drone station three please?'

Athene stood directly between Hassif and the station.

Hassif nodded, turned and walked over to the station; he ignored the fact that a woman dressed in ancient Greek battle armour with an uncanny resemblance to the Goddess Athene blocked his path.

The smiling Athene took a step back as Hassif made his way to the drone station, frustrating the Admiral.

'I know what you wish to ask, the answer is that only those I desire may see me, after all I am a Goddess!'

McCann grunted in frustration.

'You must stop questioning yourself; accept my existence before you drive yourself to madness.'

McCann looked around the Bridge; everyone was working away as normal. The lift opened and Vezzali exited, she approached his chair and stood directly next to Athene, Vezzali offered a fresh cup of coffee.

The Englishman accepted his cup; before she could leave he asked 'Vezzali, do you notice anything out of sorts today?'

'Out of sorts? There have been no reports of any anomalies, Sir.'

Motioning with his head the Admiral lowered his voice and asked 'What about on the Bridge, do you see anything odd?'

Vezzali examined the room, looking straight through Athene before offering a puzzled expression 'No, everything is as it should be, is there something you want me to do?'

'No, thank you Lieutenant, you may return to your station.'

Vezzali smiled and returned to her science post.

'What next my little Odysseus?' whispered Athene as she stood directly in front of him.

McCann spoke in a hushed tone so that none of the staff on his Bridge might hear him 'What do you want?'

Athene smiled with her flashing eyes 'I want you to understand.'

'Understand what?'

Kim caught the sound of McCann's voice 'Did you say something, Sir?'

'No, I was talking to myself, carry on with what you were doing.'

Kim nodded and returned to the pit where he monitored the crew working away at keeping Athena in order.

Athene smiled 'You are all made of clay, its strength often being its weakness.'

'More riddles?'

'You are stubborn, but that makes you fearless. Ilam, she is so cold yet that is what makes her pragmatic.'

'And Malikah?'

'She is the most complex of all sculptures to have graced Muul Kaah, her arrogance is greater than that of any Human or Tlillan it is what makes her revered ... but reverence is merely an aspect of fear.'

'What of it?'

'The Tlillan, they fear your daughter. Even the Queen of a colony is destitute if her soldiers turn against her.'

'We aren't ants.'

'Correct, they are Tlillan, what became of their last Queen when her soldiers betrayed her?'

McCann fixed his gaze upon Athene; his eyes were those of a worried father 'A plot?'

Athene didn't reply.

'What must I do?'

'Your daughter requires a guardian, neither the birdman nor Nestor can influence the people of Otoch. Duncan, you must find another to protect Malikah from her own downfall.'

'Who?'

Athene chuckled 'I'm sorry my little Odysseus but you must discover that yourself. I have come to warn you of events to unfold in the future; it is your task to prepare for them.'

'And if I don't'

In a serious tone Athene replied 'Your daughter shall be deposed and the Triumvirate shattered.'

'When? How?' as he spoke these words the image of Athene dissipated into the air.

As Athene left his presence he heard her speak two words in Latin 'Memento mori.'

McCann realised his voice had become heightened during the conversation and many of the bridge Officers were staring at him.

McCann ruffled his brow at them 'Is there something you'd like to say to Mr Beaumont?' he asked as he pointed to his earpiece.

Hassif smiled and turned back to his work as did the others, a conversation with Louis explained it satisfactorily for his crew.

McCann relaxed into his seat and sipped his coffee whilst staring out into space 'Grief is the price we pay for love,' he whispered to himself.

Chapter 3

Two week s later and the Artemis arrived to take responsibility for Bandayuuk. McCann and Jenkins were drinking in the Officers' lounge together, before Athena departed for Otoch. They sat at a small table in a corner of the room, McCann smoking his cigar and both nursing a dram of whisky.

'I'll tell you what old chap, this place quickly turns a man to drink,' said Jenkins as he eyed his dram of golden liquid.

'You're the one that wanted to join the SBS, remember?' remarked McCann.

Jenkins took a sip of his malt 'Ahhhh, yes but when we signed up the job description didn't include "Tunnel rats needed to fight crazed cyborgs hand to hand"!'

McCann chuckled at his friend's statement 'It's a far cry from those nignog pirates I'll give you that!'

'You've got the easy life here old chap, I regret not having applied to the I.S.A for that Mars expedition now,' he said observing the clean cream walls and brown leather couches.

'Thanks a bunch,' replied McCann

'What do you mean?'

'Well if you'd got the job then I'd be stuck on that shit hole, knee deep in mud fighting off Macks!' retorted McCann.

They both laughed.

'I tell you this Duncan, we're not going to be leaving that planet for a long time yet,' said Jenkins in a serious tone.

'Why do you say that?'

'I saw your interview on Habeeb's Hour and I'll tell you this, they reckon there to be millions of those Macks sitting in those tunnels. There's not a chance in hell we'll ever get control beneath the surface.'

McCann looked around at the 20 or so Officers in the lounge then whispered 'Keep your voice down man, if one of those yanks heard it'd be all over the Net by tomorrow morning.'

Jenkins peered at the Americans standing by the bar 'Can't they be trusted old chap?'

McCann took a drag on his Cohiba 'It's not that, but if you give them a few drinks they'd bloody well let you know if their mother spits or swallows!'

Jenkins let out a roar of laughter, catching the attention of the patrons in the lounge for a moment. He put his drink down and chuckled to his friend 'That's a good one!'

McCann grimaced 'Trust me; it isn't much fun having to suffer their drunken crudity. You should try shoving them into those tunnels once they've had a few drinks.'

As the old comrades chatted one of the American drone pilots put some music on and began dancing around a lady who was ordering a drink from the bar, much to the delight of his friends. The lady was rather underwhelmed by his drunken attempt at wooing her and ignored him. The young 2nd Lieutenant decided to try harder, a decision he'd regret. Shortly after grabbing Lieutenant Vezzali's rear she stepped backwards and he felt her carbon composite toe cap make contact with his genitals.

To the even greater delight of his drinking buddies he crumpled to the floor clutching his throbbing scrotum. The entire room applauded the event with many of the Officers banging their drinking vessels on the table in approval. Vezzali grinned and took a bow in each direction.

McCann applauded his Bridge Officer then shouted out 'ENCORE!'

The entire room broke out in another wave of laughter whilst the drone pilot from Washington writhed on the floor in pain.

'Now there's a fine bit of stuff Duncan,' said Jenkins nudging his friend in the arm.

'That's my Science Officer, Vezzali.'

Before McCann had finished Jenkins was out of his seat and introducing himself to Vezzali. After a short introduction he led her to their table and pulled out a seat for her. She sat down placing her long thin glass of white wine on a coaster.

'Good evening Admiral,' she said before sitting down.

'Good evening Vezzali, it seems you made quite an impression on 2nd Lieutenant Grason there,' quipped McCann.

The Admiral pointed at Jenkins 'But watch out for this one, the only women he's seen in three months are Macks!'

Vezzali politely giggled.

Jenkins waved his hand at his old comrade 'I'm sorry Duncan but you never did know a lady when you saw one.'

Vezzali blushed 'Thank you Brigadier.'

'Now, now there's no need for stuffy titles; please call me Henry,' he replied in a smooth voice.

'I am Rosa.'

Jenkins took her hand and kissed her fingers 'You certainly are young lady,' much to the delight of Vezzali.

McCann was grinning all the time, he then called out 'Stage one complete! Commencing with stage two, engage charm offensive … now!'

Jenkins put her hand down and sat back into the comfy couch 'I'm surprised Duncan can concentrate when you're on the Bridge, his wife must have clamped one of those collars on him when she saw you.'

McCann rolled his eyes and Vezzali smiled trying not to laugh.

McCann took a slow drag on his cigar, allowing the thick aromatic smoke to cool before tasting it fully 'In case you were wondering, he's always been this annoying, Lieutenant. Please feel at liberty to kick him in the balls at any time, you wouldn't be the first to have that urge.'

Jenkins retorted in a slightly comical tone 'Steady on old chap, it's one thing to kick a second Lieutenant in the groin but I'm a bloody Brigadier. I'm allowed to be and arsehole to the lower ranks!'

Vezzali quickly intervened 'you haven't met the Chief Engineer have you, Brigadier?'

'Well she can't be as charming as you, that I'm certain of,' replied Jenkins.

Vezzali giggled 'He even speaks to the Admiral in quite a rude way,' she said in her charming Italian accent.

McCann nodded 'True, the man's a terror to all the crew no matter what rank.'

'Well Rosa, if he ever irritates you, you need only call and I'll be there to set him right!' charmed the Brigadier.

'I'd be careful old boy, he took down my weapons Officer in a duel,' remarked the Admiral.

Jenkins ignored his friend and concentrated on the science Officer 'When the fear of physical harm attempts to grip me, I need only think of Rosa Vezzali and it dissipates as rain into the sea.'

McCann put his cigar in his mouth and clapped his friend, as he was clapping he noticed Louis step into the lounge and make for the bar.

Louis was off duty after a hard eight hours working in the trenches of the engine room. Keeping the power core stable and monitoring the flow of particles to and from the core was the most important task on the vessel. Keeping the magnetic field stable around the fusion core allowed Athena to operate and kept the power of 1,000 suns from engulfing her.

He worked very hard and expected to have a good drink at the end of the day. The thirsty Frenchman walked past the drone pilot, being peeled off the floor by his buddies, and stood at the bar.

After ordering he walked over to McCann's table and sat down with his brandy 'Duncan,' he greeted his friend.

Jenkins was surprised at how this lowly Engineer didn't at least salute a Brigadier. The Admiral he could forgive but it was quite rude to ignore someone of such a rank.

Louis relaxed into his seat next to Vezzali, 'Lieutenant,' he said putting his drink on the table.

McCann introduced his friend 'Brigadier Jenkins this is Chief Engineer Louis Beaumont.'

Louis put his hand out and Jenkins, rather startled, shook it.

'So you're one of those tunnel rats?' asked Louis in a rather dismissive tone.

'I suppose so, does that make you a grease monkey?' quipped Jenkins.

Louis relaxed back into his seat 'Call me what you want just don't ever accuse me of being an Anglo-Saxon. So what happened to the yank?'

'He grabbed Vezzali's arse,' said McCann blowing Havana smoke out of his nose.

Louis knocked back a large portion of his French brandy 'Ahhhhhh,' his body relaxed at the taste of the fine liquor 'fucking over privileged rich boys, they think they can do whatever they like.'

McCann took pleasure at the shock on Jenkins' face 'I think they heard you Louis,' he said with a smirk.

The American drone pilots had gone quiet, although they'd learnt before now that Louis Beaumont was not a man to tangle with.

Louis knocked back the rest of his brandy and twisted his torso to face the bar behind him 'Hey rich boy!' he shouted looking at an air force Captain 'get me a fucking brandy and be quick, I'm thirsty!'

The Captain complied and brought him another brandy from the bar.

'Tres bon,' said Louis as he took the brandy glass filled with warm mellow liquor. As the drone pilot walked away from the scene of his humiliation Louis shouted at his back 'Hey, you forgot this!'

The Frenchman waved his empty glass; the quiet Captain dutifully returned the glass to the smirking barman.

When the first lot of Americans arrived for their training on board Athena they had not been informed of the Chief Engineer. However they learnt the hard way that Louis was not to be trifled with. After many months and two training groups the third batch of trainees were well aware of the legend of Beaumont, or perhaps the infamy.

'That's it, within a month these trust fund idiots will be able to clear a table, maybe even change their underwear without a technical manual,' Louis cracked a laugh at his own joke much to the disdain of the pilots behind him.

Vezzali chuckled however Jenkins was still in shock at his total disregard for rank combined with his abusive attitude.

'Tell me Mr Beaumont, have you ever been thrown into the brig?' inquired Jenkins.

Louis picked up a hard copy of an Earth newspaper 'Once.'

'Only once?'

Louis began to read his French newspaper 'Oui, but I was out the next day. That asshole McKinley did it, that guy was like Hitler with a board up his ass.'

Jenkins replied in a rather bewildered tone 'I see.'

Louis was deep into his paper by now 'But don't you worry, if you're a friend of Duncan's you're fine.'

Still bewildered by the Frenchman, Jenkins nodded his head 'Well thank you very much, Mr Beaumont.'

'Don't mention it,' replied the Frenchman from behind his newspaper.

Vezzali smiled at Jenkins 'You have nothing to fear Henry, if Louis was to challenge you to a duel I'd fight for you.'

Louis peered out from the side of his paper 'You should consider yourself lucky, she has the pick of the men on this ship.'

McCann smirked at the newspaper hiding the Frenchman's face 'Louis here has been jealous ever since.'

Vezzali laughed, Jenkins was confused and Louis folded down the top of his paper 'you think you're so damn funny McCann, no one would laugh at your jokes if you weren't an Admiral, you know that?'

McCann took another puff on his dark brown Cohiba 'Louis if I weren't Captain of this ship you'd have had the shit beaten out of you long ago.'

The Frenchman sneered and went back to reading "Le Monde".

Jenkins wrist tablet started to make an annoying beeping noise and he quickly tapped it 'Brigadier Jenkins.'

'This is Captain Roberts; we have a situation in sector 3 Sir.'

Jenkins gave a tired huff 'Alright I'll be planetside in 5 minutes, Jenkins out.'

'Thank you Sir.'

Jenkins stood up 'Well It was nice spending some time on this luxurious ship but it's back to the grindstone for me, Duncan.'

McCann stood up and shook his old friend's hand 'I'm not sure when we'll return to Bandayuuk; try not to get shot before I'm back old chap.'

Vezzali stood up and Jenkins took her hand 'It was a pleasure to meet you Rosa. I'd be honoured if you would accept my E-ddress,' he tapped his wrist tablet sending his private contact details to Rosa.

Vezzali smiled 'I'm flattered Henry.'

Louis ignored the Brigadier and just kept reading his paper.

'It was nice to meet you Mr Beaumont.'

'Sure,' replied Louis in an uninterested tone.

Jenkins shook his head at the Frenchman and waved to his friends before striding out of the lounge.

The next day Athena folded space and entered the Tlillan home system. The crew would have two weeks of leave at the massive space station in high orbit of Otoch.

After riding out of the wormhole and into the system the white hole closed, Hassif turned to McCann 'Incoming transmission from the Teteo, Sir.'

McCann nodded 'Put her on.'

The image of Cihuateteo filled the screen 'Ola Censor.'

'Hello Cihu, how are you today?'

The Amazon seemed rather irritated at his familiarity 'I am well. Xch'uup welcomes you to Otoch, when prepared your ship may dock,' she stated coldly.

'Marvellous,' replied McCann as her image disappeared from the view screen.

'Hassif, plot a course to the Bohr and have Athena certify it.'

'Yes Sir,' replied Hassif as he tapped away.

A few moments later the voice of Athena fell upon the room as a warm blanket 'Course certified, ETA 13 minutes and 57 seconds.'

'Thank you Athena,' said McCann.

'You're welcome Admiral,' replied the SI.

The Athena glode through the darkness of space passing the outer planets of the Tlillan system at hair raising speeds.

The super space station, as Faraday referred to it, was in high orbit of the Tlillan home world. A gigantic disc constructed from prefabricated blocks, transported in from Earth and Gukumatz AB. It was too large to be placed in low orbit and attached to an orbital tower; so it circled high above the Tlillan world, a central location for fleet construction, repair and logistics. The invasion and occupation of Bandayuuk was co-ordinated from this point. It was from here that the grasp of Xch'uup extended out into the Milky Way via her war cruisers and logistics ships.

The station had a plethora of docking arms protruding from the edge of the white discus, more than 70 on his last visit.

'Admiral, I've been given clearance for docking arm five, section thirteen,' said Athena softly.

McCann glanced upwards 'Thank you Athena, have Hassif certify it then dock.'

Hassif began tapping away at his console and shortly the ship replied 'Course certified, commencing docking procedure.'

Athena slowed down to a crawl until she was in front of the correct docking arm. The war cruiser turned on her axis so that she was in line with the protruding Neutronium arm 'Engines deactivated, Bohr is activating graviton net,' said Athena to her crew.

Docking had become a lot easier since the early days, in the past Athena had to be hauled in with harpoons. After the Gukumatz worlds were conquered, their technology allowed Athena to navigate into a docking arm with the help of magnetic buffers.

Today with Tlillan technology several graviton streams were activated. If there were a graviton stream between two objects they would be pulled together. The Bohr possessed a greater mass than Athena, so the I.S.A cruiser was pulled to the Bohr.

Slowly the Bohr's SI guided in Athena, once the cruiser drew up alongside the docking arm several clamps made contact with ports on Athena's body.

The ship was held rigidly in place and the graviton streams cut.

'Docking clamps activated, graviton streams deactivated. Ports sealed, you are free to board the Bohr Admiral,' said Athena reassuringly.

'Thank you and give my thanks to the Bohr.'

'You are welcome Admiral.'

McCann pointed at Hassif 'Are you coming?'

Hassif smiled and bobbed his head, having noticed the Chutli was also docked; he was eager to see his wife.

'Kim you've got the chair,' stated McCann as he and Hassif walked into the elevator.

The pair strolled through Athena towards her nearest docking port. Hassif asked his comrade 'Did you see the other ships docked here?'

McCann nodded 'Yup, I saw them. What do you make of it?'

'It's the beginning of a new cycle isn't it?'

McCann furrowed his brow 'New cycle?'

'A new Tlillan cycle, the commonwealth used to come to Otoch each time their sun's magnetic field reversed. Creating massive sunspots that eject neutronium from its surface, each cycle they're out there collecting it; every ten years or so.'

'Why?'

'Didn't Ilam ever mention it to you?'

'I don't think so; well go on tell me Hassif!'

'Well at the beginning of each cycle members of the commonwealth would make the journey to Otoch to pay tribute to the Grand Matriarch.'

'Tribute? As in gifts?'

'I don't know, Huix has never been specific on the parameters for what was or was not a tribute. From what I understand though it was more than just paying off your King. I think it was a token of recognition,' replied the Indian thoughtfully.

'Recognition of what?'

'That the Grand Matriarch was master and you were her servant.'

McCann raised his eyebrows 'And what if you didn't turn up to pay your tribute?'

Hassif struck an expression of amusement 'In that case everyone would have witnessed your failure to appear. It was the equivalent of flipping your middle finger.'

McCann nodded knowingly 'I can guess the rest.'

'Suffice to say that by the time the next cycle came around they were either present or no longer existed.'

McCann made a noise as he exhaled through his nose 'I'm sure Ilam is having the time of her life.'

Hassif cracked up laughing as the pair entered the docking arm of the superstation Bohr.

The pair stepped onto the station to be greeted by the station commander, a rather large Gukumatz dressed in an Earth brown space suit.

'Welcome aboard Censor, to meet you is pleasure,' croaked the toad in his best English.

McCann returned the salute 'Thank you ... Kotumatz.'

The toad had made an obvious effort to remember that one line of English and McCann made an attempt at his name.

The toad seemed rather shocked and burped and croaked, the Englishman grimaced a little as the vile stench of halitosis wafted towards him and Hassif, overwhelming them.

McCann's earpiece translated the string of verbal disgust 'I Kotumatz, honoured. Censor stay how long?'

McCann had to stop breathing through his nose as the stink was too much 'I'm sorry but we'll be going to the surface immediately.'

Hassif took a large step backwards as the creature continued to speak, twitching its head from side to side.

'Come stay after visit, Censor welcome.'

McCann put on his best false smile 'Thank you, my crew will be taking leave here. I hope they won't be an inconvenience?'

The burps and splutters continued and McCann was certain he felt spit from its blubbery lips hit his cheek.

'Athena crew welcome, my staff guide Censor transport.'

McCann still smiling shook his head 'No Thank you Kotumatz, Hassif and I would like to have some privacy.'

'As you wish, Censor,' replied the toad in his broken English.

They walked on ahead of the station commander and his staff, Gukumatz were much slower due to their wide gait and heavy torso.

After they had exited the long tubular corridor and were on the station McCann commented 'Did you smell that breath?'

Hassif was still recovering 'I suppose when he has a burger and fries his favourite milkshake is rotting corpse flavour!'

They both nodded in agreement, the station was beautiful on the inside. The floor had a fabulous carpet and every now and then pieces of art from all over the galaxy hung on from the wall on their right.

On the left above the waistline windows were in place, constructed from transparent carbon alloy. As the pair walked to their transport they passed several ships, McCann didn't recognise most of them. Who knows where they were from or what kind of creatures resided within. All he knew was that it was a wonder few men were fortunate enough to behold in their lifetime.

As they strolled along the corridor McCann sensed shock from Hassif, for some reason he instinctively moved his eyes to the right. What he saw shocked him also; a tall creature with thick skin was approaching them.

It reminded the Englishman of a blue crocodile walking on two legs. No visible neck was present; the mouth was similar to crocodile jaws only shorter and thinner. The eyes were definitely serpent like, yellow with that dark lopsided opal iris. The legs were long, powerful and thick; its arms in contrast were shorter than human arms but still thick with some very intimidating claws.

Hassif noticed a small tail; it only reached the knees but was still there. As the animal approach the pair realised how tall this thing was, a good few inches taller than McCann so maybe six foot four?

The beast seemed to be on an intercept course for them, dressed in what looked like a cotton tunic over some chained metallic body suit and a pair of metallic boots.

McCann felt that if it had a long sword it would be ready to go crusading with Richard the Lion Heart!

The beast blocked their path, halting them: McCann dropped his arm allowing his fingers to brush against his thigh holster.

Putting both of its hands together the lizard man spoke 'Namaste,' with a strong hiss.

Both of them were taken aback, McCann returned the gesture and Hassif followed likewise.

The beast continued hissing and the translator kicked in, an androgynous voice spoke to the Englishman 'I am Buton, I thank Censor for Adnoara.'

McCann looked at Hassif; the Indian shrugged his shoulders so he replied 'Well, Buton, you're welcome.'

The creature made the Namaste gesture again 'Will censor accompany Buton to Otoch, honour Buton?'

Hassif was tapping at his wrist tablet whilst McCann was put on the spot. Before the Englishman could reply Hassif stepped in 'The Censor would also be honoured if the Adnoaran representative would join him.'

McCann's eyes widened as he gave Hassif an evil stare, the Indian ignored it and asked the lizard man to lead the way.

As they followed, the creature and Hassif made conversation, McCann noticed his Technician had sent some files to his wrist tablet.

McCann discreetly tapped the flashing file icon and read the information inside. Adnoara was a former commonwealth system, before the Tlillan plague.

Once the Grand Matriarch had been forced to withdraw all forces to defend Otoch, Adnoara was invaded and occupied by the Makayuuk. As Xch'uup's reach shrunk others expanded into the vacuum.

Forced into slavery the race of creatures, evolved from what humans might describe as a crocodile, were mercilessly used by the People of the Machine.

Too weak to protect themselves they surcame quickly and for centuries lived a life of hell. The Adnoarans that could not be worked were thrown into vats, liquefied alive to serve as food for not only the Makayuuk but other Adnoarans. For centuries they were worked like dogs, building an empire for the Machine through their own toil.

Then one day a vessel could be seen in the sky, the Adnoara had no idea who it was, the memory of the commonwealth had long been cleansed from the reptilian species. What they did know was that it wasn't Makayuuk and their masters had become nervous. The vessel was in fact the Teteo and alongside her were the Chutli and Tico.

Makayuuk warships caught in the system that day tried to flee but were unable to open a wormhole. After a short battle all ten enemy ships had been crushed.

Now the Tlillan fleet sat in orbit awaiting I.S.A ground forces to arrive. However they were not required, the Makayuuk committed suicide before any attempt at orbital insertion could be made. Machine was aware of the inevitable result; better to commit suicide than grant Xch'uup the satisfaction of presiding over their sacrifice at Tititl.

After that day the Adnoara were released from centuries of bondage. The lizards requested to re-join the commonwealth; to be informed it no longer existed. However Cihuateteo explained that if they so wished they may become a vassal of Xch'uup.

After having it explained the lizards elected a leader and accepted. The Makayuuk had left them with a strong industrial base and many skilled workers. Meeting Xch'uup's requirement of building and manning one war cruiser capable of folding space could be easily achieved. Once done they would lend their forces if called upon and in return the Grand Matriarch would pledge the full fury of her fleet upon any fool that might trouble them again.

McCann now recalled the incident, he'd forgotten it a long time ago since the I.S.A had turned around and left shortly after entering the system. Also he'd never seen the inhabitants nor was he informed of them due to the fact he wasn't going to be on the ground.

The party of three entered a small transport that left the station and docked with an orbital tower. At the small tower station they waited for a few minutes until a lift was ready. They boarded it and were fired down to the surface, much the same as any other elevator, only much larger.

Otoch had thousands of orbital towers rising up from the surface, and since Malikah took control the Gukumatz had put more and more back into service.

Otoch had been turned around from a world teetering on the edge of the abyss to a living breathing galactic Mecca in a few short years.

It was hard to believe that this was the planet McCann had seen only five years ago, when he met the Makayuuk fleet for the first time.

The lift slowed as it touched the ground, its doors slid back into the walls to reveal several short Tlillan males, all with their heads covered by their suits helmets.

An announcement was made and McCann's earpiece translated 'All rise for Censor.'

The Englishman stepped out onto the platform, short males stood upright on each side. The path they intended him to take was clear, at the end of it he recognised his wife and his heart jumped. McCann quickly stepped out and strode towards Ilam as she smiled awaiting him.

The males announced Hassif and the delegate from Adnoara but the Englishman had tunnel vision. He ignored all but his wife, as a cheetah would focus on a single fawn and sprint after it. He focused on her and upon reaching his goal he halted suddenly as Ilam greeted him with the Namaste gesture. He stiffly returned her greeting 'Namaste Ilam.'

They were stood at the edge of the loading platform, which resided on the dark side so it was perpetual night. The immediate area had been illuminated by organics. Lampposts holding glass canisters filled with plankton lit the way.

McCann stepped off the edge of the pad onto a mossy stone path with his wife. In the gloom around him he could see buildings and paths made from stone and draped in moss. The city of Tititl was much the same as a quiet Terran city in the dead of the night.

'Are you here for tlazohcamat?' inquired the beautiful Ilam in her skin tight black ribbed suit and white Tlillan Navy jacket.

Tlazohcamat being the name of the tribute ceremony.

'Not really, the Athena is here on leave and a check-up. I came to the planet so that I could remember what it feels like to be with a beautiful lady.'

Ilam's eyes turned a pink hue 'Or to remember what a beautiful lady feels like?'

McCann chortled 'Ah there's no fooling you is there? Well am I likely to get my evil way with the Huey'teopixqui?'

Ilam slapped the back of his shoulders 'Duncan, calm your tongue!'

Her eyes changed from a soft pink to a slight red pigment.

McCann took out a cigar and clipped the cap 'I'm the Censor you know, I can say whatever I please.'

Her eyes deepened in pigment 'There are males in earshot, control your words. This is Otoch Duncan, you are Censor, carry yourself properly.'

McCann looked around to see the males all staring at the situation.

'Shall we move on then?' he asked Ilam in a subdued tone.

Ilam took her husband for a stroll through the darksider city of Tititl. The Englishman found it impossible to make anything out from the foggy gloom that encapsulated each street. The plankton jars atop lampposts sat as markers in the distance, thanks to them McCann could see the street they were walking on.

As they strolled holding hands Ilam observed her husband view the ancient city. She was amused by his struggle to make out the surroundings. The lighting was in aid of the tribute ceremony, not all creatures of the former commonwealth were blessed with natural night vision, unlike the Tlillans.

The cobblestone path was quite rustic with moss to soften his step, the city was very quiet. Suddenly a tall Valkyrie stepped out of the gloom, frightening McCann. He instinctively drew his pistol; the whine of the rails charging grabbed the Matriarchs attention. A tall woman, even for a Tlillan, with long white hair it was Hassif's wife.

In all the gloom McCann hadn't noticed her approach and the darkness made him jumpy. Huix fixed her gaze on McCann; her instincts had also kicked in, with a piercing red that shot through the icy Tlillan atmosphere. They were both frozen with weapons drawn for a moment, until Ilam intervened.

'Bisik ts'o'om!'

Huix took in the situation and the pigment left her eyes, she pressed her palms together and approached Ilam.

'Namaste Huey'teopixqui.'

Ilam returned her gesture 'Namaste Huix.'

Hassif's wife turned to McCann 'Namaste Censor.'

McCann put his pistol back into the holster and made the Namaste gesture to Hassif's wife. It was all rather embarrassing especially now that Hassif was stood watching it all.

Ilam said something pertaining to 'See you at the ceremony,' as Huix took off into the night with her husband.

The red haired Amazon shook her head 'You must relax Duncan, we are on Otoch now.'

McCann pulled out a Ramon Allones 'After six months in Bandayuuk that's easier said than done my dear.'

Ilam had a curious expression 'What do you mean by that Duncan?'

The Englishman torched the cigar foot and pulled in that first taste of sweet woody smoke 'Six months of hell and those bloody Macks still refuse to give up.'

They continued strolling alone in the crisp night air 'Were the Makayuuk not defeated, Kaeo dismantled Machine ... yes?'

McCann gave a disparaging chuckle 'There are millions of them on the loose, but why am I telling you this. You can link with me.'

McCann stopped walking and waited for his wife to link and take what she wished to know. Ilam grabbed his arm and dragged him along the path.

'We cannot be seen to link Duncan,' she whispered through her teeth 'there have been many rumours circulating, regarding the occupation of Bandayuuk.'

McCann had to dash a little to stop his wife from dragging him along the floor 'what rumours are those?'

'Some say the Seers prophesied a Makayuuk rebellion, a successful rebellion and Machine is behind it.'

McCann pulled on her arm to slow her down 'Machine is dead; I saw its remains after we'd blown it up. Besides what could the Seers know that Malikah doesn't?'

The flaming haired amazon gave him a cold hard stare.

'Malikah has seen it too?'

His wife made a very human gesture in putting her finger to her mouth 'Shhhhhhhh, do you want them to hear you in Muul Kaah?'

They made their way to what McCann described as a café; he selected the coffee like substance whilst his wife snacked on some nook'ol. The coffee definitely had the flavour of moss but he got over it.

The Café itself was on the second floor of a step pyramid made of stone. The step pyramid design was very popular with the Tlillans. McCann looked out from the terrace onto the dots of light spread around the city 'Why do Tlillans use this design so frequently?'

Ilam chewed her worm then swallowed 'Which design would that be?'

'The step pyramid, it's all over this place.'

Ilam smiled 'Ahh that is a famous story my love.'

The Englishman furrowed his brow 'Well?'

'Before there were many different constructions on Otoch, along with many different clans. We were not the only intelligent life here, there was a creature named a Wraith. A biblical demon, terrifying beasts.

The wraiths ravaged our cities and killed our Matriarchs, we fought them but they lived deep in the mountains.

When they attacked the Tiwilighters Ah Chuyakak came to their defence. After one of your days the battle continued with no end in sight, so the Darksiders joined.

After one of your weeks Ah Chuyakak had slain the Wraith King and they retreated back to the mountains. There was only one building that had stood up to the siege and that was a step pyramid.

We call a step Pyramid a Muul Kaah, the Muul Kaah is our preferred method of construction ever since then.

Afterwards Ah Chuyakak sacrificed the Wraith king atop Muul Kaah, leading to the ceremonies regarding captives today.'

McCann took a sip of coffee 'Is the memory of this still accessible today? I mean can I link and experience it?'

Ilam gave him the look of a disappointed mother 'Those experiences are sacred to Matriarchs, I'm sorry Duncan.

Chapter 4

After several days residing in Tititl and enjoying the company of his wife, McCann took a Mag Lev train to Muul Kaah. The vehicle was maintained by short males who beetled between carriages.

Ilam had already gone ahead as she was required to play an integral part of the ceremony. McCann retired in the front carriage along with Hassif and Huix. Delegates of alien worlds resided in a different carriage; on their way to petition the Grand Matriarch for the first time in centuries. In the past this vehicle would have had many more carriages, packed with tributes and representatives of worlds from across the galaxy; all vying for the attention of Xch'uup. A mere nod from her brow would have been enough to bring about the rise or fall of an entire civilization.

Today Malikah would reignite that fire, a fire that had died out so many centuries before. From a humble delegation of five alien worlds she would lay the keystone of a new age.

Neither McCann nor Hassif realised what was truly taking place today, they sat and chatted about the sites of Tititl. Huix however was aware of exactly what this occasion meant to every Matriarch. Of course it was not only Tlillans that were cognisant of today's events; the alien delegates were all prepared.

Occupying the rear carriage with tributes and petitions, a mere five delegates, awaited an audience with Xch'uup. The first Shaman of Gukumatz resided next to the Adnoaran. On the opposite bench a Tezcatlipoca, or Icaran as the Humans had named them, sat between two delegates who seemed rather unfriendly.

The creature to the birdman's right resembled a dog; it was taller than a human, with chestnut brown fur and a long protruding jaw. Upon examination, the animal resembled an Irish wolf hound on two legs. It possessed a pair of hands, something most species that reached the space age shared with each other. It wore a brown ribbed space suit, similar in design to his, except it was cut off at the elbow and below its inverted knee.

The creature to the Icaran's left was quite different; it was about two feet shorter than McCann with no space suit. This insectiziod must have used its natural armour plating to provide protection. The insect had four long green legs with which it walked on. The two others were used to manipulate objects. The insect was quite a frightening sight, especially with McCann's aversion to creepy crawlies. The creature struck him as resembling a three foot locust; a long green body with a tiny head that sported two massive eyes on each side of its head.

All in all McCann was very pleased to be traveling in a different carriage; he found these alien beings to be either disgusting or frightening.

Upon reaching Muul Kaah and making their way to the palace of the Grand Matriarch a feeling of hatred became overwhelming. Even McCann could sense the utter disdain between the dog and the locust.

'What's up with those two?' he whispered to Huix.

Huix made that atypical Tlillan condescending smile 'They have come to petition Xch'uup.'

McCann pulled a wry frown, since Huix had been married to a human male for a while now she was able to interpret his disdain.

'They both wish to petition Xch'uup for assistance in destroying the other,' added Huix.

Hassif looked around at them 'Why?'

Huix placed a comforting hand on her husband's shoulder 'Because they are savages,' she leant down and placed a kiss on Hassif's cheek 'yakuntik.'

Huix affectionately called her husband 'love', something that made McCann feel a little odd. Having worked very hard to capture the Technician of the Athena she planned to keep hold of him.

The party was escorted along the mossy path to Muul Kaah by ten or so males. As they approached a horn was sounded into the Twilight, this environment was far more agreeable to the crew of Athena. It probably suited the alien delegates also, however Huix was eager to get inside the massive step pyramid and take shelter from the sun.

Unlike the dark side of the planet the band of twilight that circumnavigated the meridian of Otoch was thick with foliage. This was where Malikah had taken her place as Xch'uup more than five years ago. This was where the Queen of the galaxy would once again rule her subjects. Although as far as McCann was concerned it was all Tlillan egotism, but he humoured it since there was little else he could do.

Four males stood guard outside, the group waited for the stone wall to rise up inside the structure. Slowly the now polished stone rose to reveal what must have been a female, yet to make the grade as a Matriarch. She bowed deeply towards Huix, then McCann and Hassif. Once she'd displayed the proper respect to her betters the young woman led them within the pyramid.

Inside the walls were glowing with the luminous moss he'd witnessed previously. It was a beautiful sight, especially in the great hall where statues of past rulers lined upper tiers of the structure; each one glowing softly and defining the features of a past Grand Matriarch feared by every creature in the galaxy. The upper ceiling was more than a mile high, anyone coming here for the first time would be hit with awe. The willpower alone behind this piece of architecture was enough to humble even the most determined foe.

On each side rows of Matriarchs sat down on stone seats. Several rows remained unoccupied, due to the plague, but it was still an intimidating sight.

Past the central arena, Malikah sat on her throne wearing a rather chic dress. It was black just as the traditional ribbed space suits, on her sides the dress was a see-through sheer design. The hem line ended just below the knee, to McCann's relief, with dark sleeves covering her shoulders; although there was a slit in the chest area that divulged a little cleavage. She wore the headdress of white feathers, pointing out her supreme status as Xch'uup. The shoes were a bit much, the Englishman felt his daughter was dressed to go out for dinner at an expensive Parisian restaurant; rather than hold court at Muul Kaah.

On either side of the granite throne stood Ilam and Cihu, both dressed in black ribbed suits with a white jacket. All three armed with ceremonial swords, an item defended with their lives. Behind them McCann noticed the Seers, three druid like figures shuffling about in the doorways and passages behind the throne.

The male members of the party followed Huix's lead in approaching the throne and making the Namaste gesture.

'Namaste Xch'uup,' said Huix in a soft humble tone.

McCann and Hassif both realised that they'd forgotten to give proper respect to Malikah and repeated the statement, to the satisfaction of all those present.

Malikah's commanding voice reverberated around the building 'Kultal.'

Huix followed the command to sit down, taking a seat on the right of the throne. McCann was about to follow her when Hassif grabbed his arm 'We're over here Duncan,' he said pulling McCann to the left of the throne.

The pair took some seats carved from the rock; the Englishman then noticed that all Tlillan females to Malikah's left were not Matriarchs. Whereas the opposite was true of those to her right; added to that he and Hassif were the only males present.

Malikah allowed a smile to creep out and meet her father's gaze; though she quickly adjusted herself once he'd got an eyeful of her grin. He wasn't sure if it was a condescending smirk or she was just glad to see him after so long away. The Englishman assumed Malikah was displaying satisfaction at seeing her father again.

Malikah glanced to her mother, no words were spoken but there was obviously communication between the two. The sable Queen of Tlillan then adjusted her eyes towards the long corridor McCann had just walked through to enter the building 'Taasik yaaxil ich,' she ordered.

McCann heard the stone gate opening then closing, inside the luminous tunnel a silhouette could be made out. As it approached it became obvious it was the lizard from Adnoara. The creature strolled past the tunnel entrance before coming to an immediate halt.

The Tlillan females said nothing; they seemed to be looking the reptilian over for something. A voice whispered into McCann's ear 'They are scanning her.'

McCann turned to his left to see one of the young Tlillan ladies; she must have had a human father since she resembled a Twilighter 'Why?'

The half-breed girl smiled 'Xch'uup must know if she has any belligerent intentions.'

'She?'

The Tlillan chuckled 'Yes the Adnoara are Matriarchal also,' her chuckle brought the unwanted attention of Cihu.

The Grand Marshall's gaze soon ended her giggles.

Once Cihu's attention was back on the Adnoaran delegate the lady moved her lips close to McCann's ear 'You don't remember me, do you Admiral?'

The Englishman took another look at the girl 'I'm sorry but you have me at a loss young lady.'

She smiled 'We linked, many years ago when you visited my school in New York.'

McCann had an incredulous expression 'Lian? Surely not?'

His voice echoed throughout the massive chamber much to the disapproval of his wife and Cihu. Malikah sneered at her father's faux pas, though it made no difference since the reptilian delegate betrayed no ill intentions.

Lian nodded with amusement whilst McCann sat red faced with a hall of Matriarchs glaring at him.

Malikah shook her head and turned to the Adnoaran waiting at the entrance to the great hall 'Taasik he.' ·

As the reptilian strolled inside McCann adjusted his translator, making certain his earpiece was all in working order.

After reaching the central arena the creature prostrated herself on both knees and kowtowed Malikah 'Namaste Xch'uup.'

Peering down regally Malikah spoke 'Liik'il huh.'

McCann's earpiece translated it literally to 'Rise reptile.'

The Adnoaran rose to her feet and waited for Malikah to speak.

'Why do you come here reptile?' asked Malikah with both Ilam and Cihu staring the creature down.

'I come to petition the commonwealth, Xch'uup.'

Malikah sneered at the humble being 'There is no commonwealth to petition.'

'Then I come to petition Xch'uup.'

Malikah was growing tired of the game of verbal hide and seek 'Tell me what it is you request before I die from old age.'

The Adnoaran was visibly shaken at the slightest hint of aggression from Malikah, but continued in that hiss McCann could only understand through his earpiece, 'We petition Xch'uup for her protection.'

Malikah let out a huff of air from her lungs 'I see, my protection is a privilege not handed out to the first weakling who requests it, do you understand?'

The lizard woman nodded her head 'I understand Xch'uup, we have constructed one war cruiser and another is soon to be finished. This vessel will be at your disposal alongside Adnoaran industry.'

'Cihuateteo, what are the specifications of the Adnoaran vessel?' asked Malikah without taking her eyes off the petitioning reptile.

Cihu replied in a begrudging tone 'It is sufficient, Xch'uup.'

Malikah nodded towards her Grand Marshall whilst still staring down the Adnoaran 'And your industry is able to meet the required quotas?'

The creature bowed again, it looked far more relaxed now than a moment ago 'Tlillan production will be prioritised, quotas shall be met, Xch'uup.'

Malikah grinned with satisfaction 'Excellent, I shall send Amitrachutli immediately. She will take control as Governor until I'm satisfied that our new vassal is able to continue unsupervised.'

The reptilian made a deep bow whilst pressing her scaly palms together 'Namaste Xch'uup.'

Malikah, still displaying her condescending smirk, replied 'Do not make me regret this decision. It was a great risk to liberate your world in the first. You may leave now.'

The creature bowed again before retreating into the luminous passage and out of Muul Kaah.

Before the next was sent in Malikah stated in a coy tone 'Mother, could you tell Censor to hold his tongue during the ceremony?'

There was a round of laughter throughout the great hall; McCann said nothing though he felt his daughter's comments were a bit unnecessary.

Once the laughter died down Malikah spoke 'Bring in the next.'

Next the representative of the birdmen or Icaran's appeared, a short squat birdman or woman McCann didn't know. They inhabited an exo-planet, a planet which had been torn out of its original solar system and flung into space. They lived in caverns deep inside the world, using heat from its core in lieu of a sun. Below the surface was a whole ecosystem which supported them, it also provided an excellent base of operations to run their business as galactic assassins.

Malikah and her three gifted sisters were a danger to these birdmen. They were the only beings in the universe that could break a Tezcatlipoca's mental toughness; the only people aside from Icarans that knew the location of their home world. In theory Malikah could send her fleet to bombard their home world until the crust broke open, ruining an entire civilization.

The Icaran didn't speak, it seemed to be linking with Malikah or at the very least she was reading its thoughts.

Again Lian leant over and whispered in McCann's ear 'The Tezcatlipoca is petitioning Malikah, they wish to become her vassal.'

The birdman bowed silently and after Malikah nodded her head it exited Muul Kaah. McCann leant over to Lian and whispered in her ear 'Well?'

The young girl smiled and whispered to the Admiral 'Their petition was accepted.'

A few minutes later and the two antagonists entered the hall, one being a sort of wolf man alongside a three foot locust creature.

The dog dropped onto all fours and kowtowed, the insect made a Namaste gesture. Malikah motioned to the canine and a story of loyalty to Xch'uups past followed by a tale of woe when their commonwealth collapsed.

Malikah grew visibly weary of his long tale 'In a nutshell Pek'xib!' demanded Malikah.

There were puzzled looks all around the hall until Ilam spoke up 'Xch'uup wishes you to make your petition quickly.'

The wolf man grinned nervously, carrying on he pointed out that post collapse their old enemy the Saak attacked them. Blockading their home until they were forced to retaliate, one thing led to another and they were plunged into a war. The conflict had been at a stalemate for many years; however rumours of a resurgence amongst the Tlillan and the defeat of the Gukumatz then Makayuuk had brought him here. The canine delegate now stood before Xch'uup in the hope that she could bring the war to an end, preferably by destroying the Saak.

The insect gave pretty much the same story, from what McCann could tell there was little between the two. The Englishman thought to himself that considering how it was going with the Makayuuk he didn't relish seeing another invasion. The Macks had the I.S.A forces tied down already and there was no way that the Gukumatz could handle any stiff resistance.

Malikah stood up showing her full splendour and beauty 'The old Tlillan Commonwealth collapsed centuries ago, we are no longer obliged to settle your petty disputes. Besides neither the I.S.A nor the Gukumatz owe you a debt, I suggest you settle this conflict between yourselves.'

The wolf man lowered himself on all fours 'The Pek shall accept the will of Xch'uup if she would destroy our enemy, whatever you ask.'

Malikah sneered at the dog grovelling before her 'LIAR!'

McCann's heart jumped in fright, her outburst was quite unexpected.

Malikah's eyes became bright as coals in the night 'I have seen into the Dreamscape, your people are traitors,' she then pointed at the insect 'and yours are no better. I would not expend a single drop of my subjects' sweat on your foul scum!'

Malikah approached the pair of petitioning beasts 'When the plague took a hold of Otoch where were your people? Too busy looting Tlillan logistic stations to repel the Gukumatz; and now you snivel at my feet for assistance? Get them out of my Hall!'

At that Cihu and Ilam drew their blades as they approached the delegates. Not that they were required, as both ambassadors seeking the patronage of Xch'uup quickly exited the building without the Valkyries' assistance.

The Grand Priestess and Marshall sheathed their blades before returning to their places aside the throne.

Malikah relaxed into her seat as her flaming eyes settled down to their usual sparkling grey, 'Next.'

The granite slab could be heard as it moved up then back down closing behind the next delegate. Judging by the silhouette it was a Gukumatz, they were the only creature McCann was aware of to possess that gait. The Gukumatz stood at the entrance dressed in earth browns with a traditional jade square headdress. The toad carried a staff of mahogany with ivory caps; he had a brown robe adorned by feathers.

Malikah stood up again and with a smile called to the toad 'First Shaman, you may enter.'

The toad was granted a rare honour, it was allowed to enter without being scanned; an honour Cihu was not pleased with. The Shaman entered the hall and kowtowed before Malikah 'Namaste Teootl.'

'Please rise, Kotumatz,' replied Malikah.

The Gukumatz had taken pride of place, the last to petition Xch'uup was traditionally the most exalted subject. The toad stood up and produced a small porcelain square; from McCann's vantage point he could only make out that it was predominantly blue in colour.

Malikah viewed the square as it lay in the palm of her hand 'You had possession of the missing piece?'

The toad placed its palms together and croaked 'Now it is yours Teootl.'

Malikah passed it to her mother; Ilam spent a few moments inspecting it before placing it inside her jacket pocket.

'What is that?' whispered McCann to Lian.

'A missing piece of a mosaic on the South wall of the temple at Tititl,' replied Lian in a subdued tone.

McCann was still puzzled so Lian continued 'Many works of art were vandalised during the Gukumatz rebellion. This piece was never recovered, it was assumed stolen or destroyed during the anarchy.'

Malikah's eyes turned a soft pink and even Cihu lost her usual sneer 'The Tlillan people thank the Gukumatz and ask if there is anything they wish in return.'

The Shaman maintained his Namaste posture 'Only your continued good favour, Teootl.'

At that the Matriarchs stood up and together they clapped their hands whilst making a high shrieking noise deep from the throat. The sound echoed throughout the great hall and out into the dense forest of the twilight.

Malikah grinned as she stepped towards the Shaman 'My sisters are in approval of your tribute Kotumatz. You may take a seat,' she gestured to the rows of carved seats to her left.

The fat toad waddled over and took a seat to the applause of the crowd. McCann and Hassif were both a bit bewildered but clapped along nevertheless.

Malikah nodded then retired into a doorway behind the throne, quickly followed by Ilam and Cihu. Shortly after that McCann heard the stone gate to Muul Kaah slide open. On the opening of the gate the Matriarchs began to file out. The Englishman took a step to leave before Lian grabbed his arm 'Malikah wishes to speak with you Censor.'

McCann nodded and Hassif gave him a friendly tap on the back 'I've a date with Huix so I'll see you later Duncan.'

'Have a good time,' McCann called to Hassif's back.

The Indian turned and gave a quick smile before he entered the tunnel and met up with his wife just outside of the gate.

McCann looked up at Lian, realising how tall she was now that they were standing up, 'Lead the way young lady.'

Lian smiled, walked past the throne and into a doorway, McCann followed her down the stone passage.

The walls were covered with the same luminous moss that pulsated with shades of red light. The passage led into a large chamber, much like an I.S.A conference room only constructed with stone blocks and lit with a beautiful moss. Malikah resided at the opposite end of the room, siting on another stone throne but observing a 3-D projection from a modern piece of furniture.

She communicated with the others telepathically; Ilam looked up and smiled at her husband as she exited the room via a different passage. Cihu did the same minus the smile, leaving him with his daughter and Lian.

Malikah looked at Lian 'I'm afraid that includes you Lian.'

Lian displayed a pair of sad eyes but obeyed her Xch'uup and exited via the passage she'd entered.

McCann chuckled 'I knew you had a soft spot for that girl!'

'What do you mean Father?'

'Ever since she quoted Machiavelli you took a shine to her, the mighty Xch'uup picking her out for praise in front of the entire class! I bet she still remembers that day.'

Malikah swept her hand over a sensor in the table collapsing the hologram 'I see, well you're not here to reminisce over old times Father.'

McCann was stunned and a little hurt at his daughters coldness 'Oh, well why am I here?'

Malikah then sensed her father's hurt, stood up and walked over to him 'I'm sorry father, I wasn't trying to be mean, it just came out that way,' she said as she embraced him in a bear hug.

'It's probably all the time you've been spending here, alright you can put me down now,' gasped McCann.

Malikah released him to a pair of pink smiling eyes 'Do you forgive me?'

'Yes of course I do, now what's this all about Malikah?'

Malikah kissed her father on the cheek before opening up another hologram. The image displayed what looked to be several charts, monitoring currency and precious metal prices on Earth.

McCann chuckled 'So you're using the Dreamscape to play the markets now?'

Malikah laughed 'I wish it were only that, no there is something very worrying look.'

Malikah pointed towards a chart monitoring credits, the currency of Mankind for nearly the last fifty years. McCann took a close look and noticed that the price of gold was dropping.

In the 21st century fiat currency collapsed, all faith had been lost in the banking system. After several currency resets and the default of the Dollar governments were forced to go back to the gold standard. International Credits were issued by the five nations which possessed the highest gold reserves.

Once the Credit was pegged to gold the global economy slowed down but stabilised. It was the only way to prevent governments from just printing money and throwing the global economy back into an abyss of debt.

'So what has the price of gold got to do with anything?' asked McCann.

Malikah had a concerned expression 'The Makayuuk, they are using an underground network to flood the economy with gold.'

McCann shrugged his shoulders 'So they're providing us with gold, what's the big deal?'

'Father, they intended to devalue gold until there is no longer any confidence in the Credit. There will be another banking crisis; they hope to collapse the I.S.A from within.'

McCann narrowed his eyes at the readout 'How are they getting the gold to Earth?'

Malikah shook her head 'I am not certain, what I do know is that if this continues within six months the Credit will collapse. The Makayuuk cannot fight us head to head so now they use economic warfare.'

McCann went for a cigar; a good Habanos always helped him think. Malikah raised her voice 'Not in here Father, thank you.'

McCann rolled his eyes and put the case back inside his jacket 'So what do you plan to do?'

Malikah reached behind her throne and pulled out a pale blue brick. She placed it on the table 'This is the solution.'

McCann walked over to it and tried to pick it up, however the brick was of some substance far heavier than anything he'd encountered before.

Malikah smirked 'It is a brick of pure Neutronium.'

The Englishman scratched his chin 'How is this going to bail us out of economic doom?'

'The Makayuuk cannot produce Neutronium in quantities that would cause any shift in the markets. It is rarer than Gold and even if they could smuggle in massive quantities, the I.S.A would put it to good use before they brought in enough to flood the market.'

McCann scratched his head 'That's wonderful, but how do you convince a bunch of tycoons and dictators that they need to dump the gold standard? Those people have everything invested in gold you know? Bloody hell, most of my savings are in gold, I'd be ruined!'

Malikah put her hands on her Father's shoulders 'That's going to be your task.'

McCann gave his daughter an incredulous look 'Me? What the bloody hell do I know about economics? Besides they'll all be baying for my blood if I turn up and tell them the Gold standard is defunct!'

The sable Queen slid her arms around her his neck then said in an affectionate tone 'Please … daddy.'

The Admiral's face screwed up 'That's not funny Malikah.'

She whispered into his ear 'Do it for me, daddy.'

McCann closed his eyes and turned his face to the ceiling as if requesting the gods for assistance 'Do I have to?'

'Only if you love me,' whispered the Queen of Tlillan.

McCann turned to face her 'That wasn't fair at all Malikah.'

Her eyes lit up with a smile and pink hue 'So you'll do it?'

'Why don't you ask Faraday, this is more his thing isn't it?'

'William has already taken delivery of the first consignment of Neutronium. He's overseeing the assembly of the first neutronium mint, in Geneva.'

The Englishman shook his head 'Just like your Mother, you've got it all sorted out.'

Malikah laughed and kissed her father on the crown of his head 'you're angry when you're the last to know but equally irritated when the first, you're so grumpy Father.'

McCann rolled his eyes 'Uuurrrrhhh!' came the signature groan he'd picked up from his former first Officer and crew mate Ryu.

'I want you to take Lian with you Father, she is soon to become a Matriarch and the experience would be valuable; besides you'll need someone to carry that brick of Neutronium out for you.'

'She must be something special, anything I should know about her?' inquired McCann

The dark haired goddess shook her head 'No, we just need to get this economic crisis averted. There have been thoughts of our expansion coming to a halt due to Bandayuuk.'

McCann took a leisurely stroll around the table 'It has, the Macks are dug in like shit house rats on Iwo Jima! There are millions of them at least, and their minds are shut off to the Dreamscape, so we have to hunt them the old fashioned way.'

Malikah seemed puzzled 'Iwo Jima?'

'Link with me.'

They both stood silent for a few seconds as Malikah dipped into her Father's memory. After quickly absorbing the facts of the battle she opened her eyes 'I understand now.'

McCann tapped his nails on the desk 'Uprisings are commonplace on the surface; the toads don't have the stomach to deal with it. Below the surface the Macks fight to the death, it makes no sense.'

Malikah took in a deep breath 'There are rumours that Machine survives.'

'No, Machine was dismantled; I was there when the Macks went berserk, after their link was cut.'

'Then why do they persist in the belief that Machine lives?'

McCann became annoyed 'Why don't you ask the Dreamscape or the Seers, aren't they the purveyors of prophecy? Or are they just as blind as a Mack tunnel rat?'

Malikah rebuked her father sternly 'Enough Father, you are Censor! If it were not for my abilities you might be executed for speaking such heresy in Muul Kaah.'

McCann sneered at his daughter 'Still the fact stands that without the heretics you'd be as blind as a bat.'

Malikah folded her arms 'Are we supposed to be helping each other or not? I want the Macks ... I mean Makayuuk ... defeated just as you do Father. I cannot sense them until they are already upon us so we must rely on Mankind more than ever; and in return I'm shipping twenty percent of the entire Tlillan Neutronium reserves to Earth.'

McCann found her slip of the tongue amusing 'So what is the exchange rate of blood to neutronium on Tlillan these days?'

'You will take this to Earth and see that Faraday distributes it properly.'

'Distributes?'

'Yes, the lion's share shall go to Geneva but Moscow and Washington must receive a portion.'

McCann smirked again 'Ah, your pet nation,' he said in a cynical tone.

'Do we have to go through this again? I thought you were an adult?'

McCann laughed 'Because it's true, those bloody yanks only got their own cruiser because Earle's such a good arse kisser!'

'That's not true Father.'

McCann only took further delight in her denial 'Now he's gonna take delivery of the most valuable substance in the universe. Yes we all know who Xch'uup favours back on planet Earth.'

'Louis is right Father, you do think you're funny; unfortunately you're frequently the only person laughing.'

The Englishman put his arm around his daughter's waist and in an American accent he said 'Why don't we take a little trip to the Plaza? My wife's at home so we could spend the night liberating some of that Tlillan neutronium you've got locked away!'

Malikah pouted her lips together in an attempt to keep a straight face.

McCann continued to hack into his daughters cold Tlillan defences 'You know us Americans are all about liberty and taking them whenever possible, especially when vulnerable young ladies are concerned!'

He tickled his daughters waist as he did when she was a child, although she was physically far more powerful she allowed him to take his liberties. Malikah giggled as a young girl, she loved it when her father paid attention to her.

Malikah had missed her father, he spent many months in space at a time and she was often tied up with ceremony on Otoch. Tears of joy rolled down her cheeks causing McCann to desists, at that moment she cried and embraced her father.

They stood for minutes holding one another in an embrace until Lian entered the room.

'Namaste Xch'uup,' said the Tlillan woman.

Rather annoyed Malikah wiped her tears away 'Why did you feel the need to invade our privacy?'

'I was concerned when I heard you cry.'

'When I selected you as my Adjunct it was so that I may have privacy, once again you have failed my expectations,' sneered the sable Queen.

Lian dipped her head in shame 'I beg your forgiveness, Xch'uup.'

Malikah wasn't about to calm down, yet before she could berate her auxiliary further McCann stepped in 'Well it's a good job you came Lian, I need someone to carry this neutronium brick.'

Malikah's red hot eyes calmed down until the fire died out 'Take the brick and wait inside the imperial transport until my father arrives, can you manage that?'

'Yes Xch'uup,' Lian bowed then picked up the neutronium brick and walked out.

'You were a bit hard on her weren't you?' asked McCann.

'She was selected to be my Adjunct, yet time and again she fails my expectations,' said Malikah staring down the luminous hall Lian had exited through.

'Give her a break Malikah, everyone makes mistakes.'

'Did Ryu ever make mistakes?'

McCann shook his head in defeat 'No she didn't, but if they'd fired Louis the first time he pissed someone off he'd never have made it to Mars!'

'Louis is different,' said Malikah in a thoughtful tone.

'You're right there, but I'll look out for Lian if you'll go a little easier on her.'

'I do go easy on her, if she made the same mistakes with Cihu or Mother she would have been severely punished. I'm trying to help her assimilate to Tlillan society; I fear that she is too human.'

McCann folded his arms 'Why not select a different Adjunct?'

Malikah smiled 'One day I shall tell you Father, until then you have a delivery to make.'

McCann's wrist tablet lit up with a beeping noise, he tapped it 'McCann, what's up Kim?'

'Sir, we've had a message from Otoch, they are requesting we take delivery of 10,000 tons of pure neutronium,' replied Kim.

'I can confirm that, you'll have to leave Bhor and get into orbit above,' he looked at his daughter.

'Orbit Tititl, the cargo will be lifted from there via Atlas,' stated Malikah.

'Understood, but 10,000 tons? Do we have enough space?'

Malikah grinned 'It won't take up half a cargo bay.'

'Ah, understood, thank you Xch'uup.'

McCann pulled a wry expression 'You're welcome Commander, McCann out,' then tapped his wrist tablet.

'It's time to go,' said Malikah as she grabbed his arm and led him out of Muul Kaah.

They walked back into the great hall; McCann noticed something he must have missed the first time he entered. Men in combat fatigues filed out from behind the elevated rows of stone pews. As they closed he recognised them, especially one of them 'Nestor?'

Nestor grinned and made a little salute to which McCann replied 'What in the world are you doing here?'

Malikah who had her left arm intertwined with her Father's right answered 'Well every Queen needs a royal guard, doesn't she?'

McCann scoffed 'So what's wrong with the Tlillans?'

'Well Nestor and his men have no allegiances on Otoch, except to me, koretny?' she asked Nestor.

'Eto pravil'no,' replied Nestor.

The Spetsnaz team which seemed to be his old Vympel team carried the typical Special Forces gear. All dressed in their black combat fatigues with body armour and assault rifles, boots and berets.

'So you're the Imperial guard now?' asked McCann.

'It seems so Duncan.'

Nestor marched ahead with two of his men checking the passages before Malikah stepped inside. The gate could be heard lifting up and as McCann exited the passage he was back in the soft light of the Twilight side. At first his eyes ached a little but he quickly adjusted to the daylight.

Nestor and his men were forming skirmish lines on either side of the stone path, scouting out the jungle for ambushes.

'Is all this really necessary Malikah?' asked McCann.

'I'm afraid that even Xch'uup has to sleep.'

McCann nodded his head in agreement as they strolled along the path to a launch pad with a Hummingbird resting on it. Before walking up the open rear ramp he kissed his daughter on the cheek 'Be careful Malikah.'

McCann looked towards Nestor who stood in the undergrowth monitoring the area for anything untoward 'And you look after my daughter.'

Nestor lit up one of his rough Russian cigarettes and nodded 'Da.'

'And you look after Lian for me,' requested Malikah.

McCann nodded and made his way into the craft as Malikah moved away from the launch pad.

Chapter 5

Once inside the craft McCann slipped into a rear passenger seat, he smiled to Lian and buckled himself in. A Korean pilot advised them to strap in as the rear entrance lifted to form the rear wall. Using powerful on board magnets the craft lifted up from the landing pad effortlessly. Its landing gear retracted before rockets on each wing fired, propelling them up into the blue sky of Otoch.

'How was your visit Admiral?' came the calm voice of Athena.

McCann relaxed as his body was pushed into his seat during the climb to the stars 'Very good, I finally got some time alone with my wife.'

'How was Malikah?'

'She's well, thank you.'

'May I ask what it is I'm taking delivery of, Admiral?'

'Neutronium, we're going to rescue the economy or so I've been told.'

'How would neutronium affect the economy?'

'Malikah has decided that the credit is to be pegged to neutronium, rather than gold.'

'Now I understand, Admiral,' said the soft voice of the Athena.

The craft lifted out of the atmosphere and made for the Athena, suspended in orbit above the dark side.

'Entering docking bay one,' announced the pilot.

The Hummingbird cleared Athena's bay doors as they began to close, slowly manoeuvring the rear exit in the direction of the airlock. As the pilot let the craft down its landing gear absorbed the weight.

'Engines off, Mag Lev disengaged, docking bay pressurized, you're clear to enter the Athena, Admiral.'

McCann released his buckle and made his way to the rear with Lian as the doorway opened 'Ladies first,' said the Englishman.

Lian smiled stepping off the ramp and onto the Athena 'Thank you Admiral.'

McCann followed her into the docking bay 'Call me Duncan for God's sake.'

She smiled again 'Thank you, Duncan.'

'That's better; now follow me with that brick. You're probably the only one that can carry the damn thing.'

They opened the airlock to be greeted by Kim 'Welcome aboard Admiral.'

'This is Lian; she's Adjunct to Xch'uup and will be accompanying us on this mission.'

They walked down the cream coloured corridor followed by a stunned Kim 'Mission?'

'Yes we're to deliver this shipment of neutronium to Earth, it's of the upmost importance,' replied McCann.

'Understood, should I make accommodations for Liana …?'

Lian, holding the small neutronium brick in two hands, gave a flustered grin 'I'm not a Matriarch yet, Commander.'

Kim blushed a little 'My apologies Lian, I'll have the guest quarters made ready immediately.'

'While you're doing that have Louis, Hassif and Kapitan Egorov meet me in my cabin, you too Kim.'

'Understood, Sir,' replied Kim as he tapped his wrist tablet, organising his shipmates.

Inside McCann's cabin he had Lian, a six foot beauty; place the brick on his desk. The first thing he did was take out a cigar and light it up in front of her, next he opened up a wall aperture to take out a bottle of Balvenie portwood and five glasses.

McCann looked at the lovely Lian her Chinese parentage was obvious; it was what gave her the look of a Twilighter along with her straight dark hair. He poured a whisky over an ice cube 'Here have a shot of this young lady.'

Lian wagged her finger 'I'm sorry Admiral, but I cannot drink anything that would …'

McCann cut her off 'Alter your perception of reality, yes I know. But as Censor I'd like to point out that reality sucks, so take a swig of this, that's an order young lady.'

He passed her the tumbler and she accepted it, at that point the door chime went and McCann called out 'Enter.'

Louis entered the room, his eyebrows raised up as soon as he noticed the liquor. The Frenchman took a tumbler and waited impatiently for McCann to pour him a drink. After waiting for a few seconds Louis demanded a drink 'Hey pour me a drink McCann, I've been slaving on that power core all day!'

Lian was shocked at the Chief Engineer's blasé use of language towards the Admiral. McCann grinned and poured his Chief a drink, the Frenchman knocked it back quickly and he poured a second.

'Don't be shocked by the Chief Lian, he's actually quite amiable at the moment.'

Louis took a sip of the barley juice and motioned towards McCann 'Wait until you see him when he's pissed off; imagine Adolf Hitler on steroids with Net rage!' Louis cracked up laughing as did Lian.

McCann made a sardonic smile 'Good one Louis.'

'What is this all about anyway, you don't give free drinks anymore unless there's a good reason,' remarked Louis.

Lian was still giggling at the Frenchman.

McCann pointed to the dark blue brick on his desk 'This is why you're getting a free drink.'

The door chime went again and on opening Hassif and Kim both entered. The two men declined a drink much to Louis' gratification.

McCann went on to explain what the Brick was and why they were transporting it.

Hassif was the first to ask a question 'So how are the Makayuuk smuggling gold into the markets on Earth?'

McCann shook his head 'That will be our next task, Malikah doesn't know and neither does Faraday. It wouldn't surprise me if someone is using military transports to smuggle it back to Earth. The trouble is that they're smuggling in so much it's devaluing the credit. If it keeps up everyone will be broke, it would cripple the I.S.A until an economic reset could be arranged.'

Kim was rather puzzled 'So what difference would a neutronium standard make?'

Louis, a little inebriated by now, pointed towards the brick with his glass as he accepted a cigar from McCann '10,000 tons of Neutronium, you know how much that's worth boy? More than all the gold in the fucking Terran system, refined or otherwise. Those Macks don't have enough Neutronium to destabilise an economy pegged to it, only the Tlillans could do that.'

McCann toasted the foot of his Ramon Allones short club corona 'And trying to destabilise us by flooding our economy with cheap neutronium would only assist our space industry.'

Louis lit the foot of his cigar and took a few puffs to get it going 'what I don't understand is how Faraday id going to get the economy off gold?'

Lian stepped in 'The I.S.A will issue its own credits pegged to neutronium, Moscow and Washington shall both comply in minting neutronium credits. When gold is devalued there will be a viable currency already established; it should be a case of just swapping over to the new currency. Gold shall be pegged to neutronium, once devalued it'll become more of an industrial metal softening the blow to those holding it and eventually returning the commodity back to value.'

Louis took a deep draw on his Habanos, inhaling a little of the smooth Cuban smoke, 'your daughter has it all planned out doesn't she?'

McCann raised his glass 'That she does, but if you want to argue with her feel free Louis.'

Louis laughed 'Hah, sure I will. But first I'll need a few more drinks!'

Kim's wrist tablet chimed and he tapped it quickly 'Kim.'

McCann could hear the Officer on the other end 'The final shipment has been delivered, Sir.'

'Let me know when the neutronium is secure, Lieutenant.'

'Understood, Commander.'

'Kim out.'

The Korean tapped his wrist, looking towards McCann 'The cargo should be secure within the hour, Sir.'

McCann turned his gaze upwards 'Athena?'

'I'm here Admiral McCann,' she replied in her soft almost loving tone.

McCann grinned 'I want you to plot a course for Earth and have Hassif certify it please.'

'Course plotted, I have taken account for the significant increase in mass and made corrections accordingly. Could the Admiral please bring this to the attention of the Chief Engineer while he remains conscious?'

Athena's attempt at humour was well received by all but Louis Beaumont, he sneered towards the ceiling 'Why does she always pick on me?'

McCann looked cheekily towards his Technician 'Hassif, I was wondering if you could knock up a neutronium foil hat for one of my Officers?'

Both Hassif and McCann burst out laughing though Kim and certainly Lian were at a loss.

Once Hassif had stopped his infectious sniggering he blurted out 'Well considering the size of his head you might need to fly a few more crates in!'

Louis took a swig of whisky and a toke on his cigar 'Keep on laughing but when the shit hits the fan it's me who saves your asses.'

Athena's voice cut in over the commotion 'I apologise if I caused you any offence Louis, it was only meant as a joke between friends.'

Louis looked up begrudgingly 'Apology accepted Athena.'

'Alright, let's break it up now. Kim you can take Lian to her new quarters, I'll meet you on the Bridge.'

The group broke up and McCann with cigar in hand made his way to the Bridge. Taking the elevator he stepped onto the command deck to the salutes of the Vympel security. He returned the salutes and sat down into his chair, Hassif who'd accompanied him made for his station and began certifying Athena's calculations.

Five minutes later and Kim had joined them on the Bridge, Hassif certified the course for Earth and McCann sat up in his chair 'Athena break orbit and follow course at half speed.'

'Co-ordinates X +5, Y +0.7, Z +6 certified, engines engaged,' replied Athena.

The mighty warship pulled out of orbit and made for six AU above the accretion disk. Once there Athena halted 'Destination reached, Admiral.'

McCann tapped the arm of his chair 'Louis?'

'Yes, I'm ready to engage the generator,' replied the Frenchman.

'Engage wormhole generator,' replied McCann.

The lights went low as a klaxon rang out through the vessel alerting the crew. Although thanks to gravity plating there was no need to grab hold of anything or strap yourself in, unlike the old days. Now gravity could be regulated, different parts of the ship had completely different gravitational pulls. For instance the cargo bay with 10,000 tons of neutronium was at 0 G right now. However just by stepping through the airlock into the adjacent corridor you moved into 1 G.

When the ship went through a wormhole, gravity was regulated to reduce the shift of force inside as much as possible.

A shimmering white hole opened up in front of the Athena 'Tunnel event, wormhole stable,' announced Athena.

'Hassif activate Casimir field,' ordered McCann.

'Casimir field active, Sir,' replied the Indian.

'Take us in half speed.'

At that the engines fired and Athena was sucked inside the white hole, against the very laws of nature. Athena crossed the threshold, entering the singularity, a Casimir field propelling her into the boundary between the black hole at the centre and the wormhole she'd just travelled through. Light kept streaking past the view screen as it rushed to escape. Athena made her way to the dead zone 'Following course to exit wormhole, Admiral.'

McCann observed the 3-D image of his vessel as it spun around on the table before him. All parts of her were green and they were making good speed for the exit. A few hours in what had been dubbed "hyperspace" would be a few days outside.

As they navigated the dead zone between singularities or "the River Styx" as McCann had named it, they looked for anything the Dreamscape might reveal to them. Vezzali worked frantically observing images torn from their reality and several other realities. It was Vezzali's favourite task logging the mysteries of the Dreamscape for later observation in Geneva.

As Athena navigated around the singularity a klaxon fired off 'tunnel event, tunnel event, tunnel event!'

McCann sat up 'Athena, what the bloody hell are you talking about?'

Before he could reply a wormhole opened up directly in their path 'Hassif...'

The Indian shouted over the alert 'It's too close, we're going to be sucked in.'

'Can't the Casimir field pull us back?' McCann shouted desperately.

The Technician shook his head 'We'd be thrown into the black hole and crushed; we're going to have to enter the Wormhole.'

McCann nodded 'Do it. Kim bring the Athena to battle stations, I want both squadrons ready to launch on exiting that wormhole.'

Kim nodded and tapped his wrist 'Understood, Sir.'

The Athena rode into the wormhole to be ejected out into normal space.

'Hassif I want our co-ordinates, then plot a course to Earth immediately ...'

Athena broke McCann's dialogue 'Admiral three ships detected off our starboard bow, two more on an intercept course.'

The image of the lead ship came onto the view screen, a tubular ship with a large claw like nose; it resembled a cross between a harpoon and grappling hook.

McCann looked over his shoulder 'Is that what I think it is Vezzali?'

Vezzali replied with a tone of dread 'Pirate configuration Admiral, probably Makayuuk.'

McCann tapped his chair 'Louis can we generate a wormhole?'

'No, there's a device collapsing the field. We need to get clear of it before I can open a tunnel.'

McCann shouted to Vezzali 'Do you know where their generator is?'

'No Sir.'

'McKinley, charge cannons and arm them with anti-matter warheads. I want you to target these vessels,' McCann selected the enemy ships on his chair 'fire when ready, no need for certification.'

McCann turned to Kim 'Launch the drones I want them to engage this ship,' McCann tapped his chair arm and on the right hand part of the view screen a red box lit up one of the starboard ships on the tactical view.

Kim leapt to his drone station as Athena let out the alarm call 'Battle stations, prepare to be boarded.'

The elevator opened causing Vympel soldiers to flinch and aim their weapons. However it was only Lian, she stepped onto the Bridge and stood next to McCann 'Pirates?'

'Yup, Macks stranded after the invasion. A lot of them formed pirate nations, someone must have let on about the neutronium. With all that neutronium you could start an empire of your own!'

Lian shook her head 'This is even more serious than we first believed. Makayuuk cannot organise as they have here, without Machine, it is not possible.'

McKinley turned 'Firing cannons, Sir.'

The Athena took a jolt as she fired; two pirate ships took a broadside, each exploding in a cascade of ant-matter fire. Drones screamed past engaging one of the small pirate vessels, each one about half the size of the Athena.

'Reload and fire on the other two, certification not required.'

McCann gave out the order but it was too late, two of the pirate ships manoeuvred in, firing engines their metal claws tore into the armour of Athena. Two pirate ships had now attached themselves, reminding McCann of when he and Nestor boarded a Gukumatz ship off Jupiter. Only this time he was on the receiving end.

'Alert we are being boarded!' said Athena in an alarmed tone.

McCann looked at the 3-D image of Athena as the ship listed from side to side, reeling from the shock of such a massive impact.

'Athena, close off decks one, two, nine and ten. Lower Bulkheads and send out the order for all crew members to arm themselves. Egorov, can you hear me?'

McCann detected the sound of pulse weapon fire, over which a Russian accent replied 'Da.'

'What's the situation?'

'They have boarded Fore and mid decks nine and one, both Vympel units are trying to contain them. We need more people, Sir.'

'They've come for the cargo in bay one, keep that in mind Kapitan, I'll have all off duty personnel armed and put under your command as soon as possible, McCann out.'

The Admiral looked at Kim; his first Officer nodded and began organising it. The Englishman turned his chair to face Vezzali 'I want you to scan for any generators or a space dock,'

'Yes Sir,' replied the Italian.

He turned his chair to Hassif 'Send out an SOS, we need assistance before more of them turn up.'

Hassif began tapping away on his station as reports came out of the pit. McCann approached the pit and over the noise of the chatter he shouted 'I want every man to check his weapon,' as he said that the Englishman slid his pistol from its holster and flicked it on. The whine of several pistols charging their rails at once could be heard as each Officer checked their firearm.

'Vympel one and two are withdrawing to the Mid-section, I suggest we evacuate the fore section before they take it completely,' shouted a pit Officer.

McCann placed his pistol back in the holster and nodded towards the young lady sitting at her station in the pit 'Affirmative, inform Egorov.'

Hassif called out 'I have communications with the Here,' as he spoke the image of space retreated from the left of the view screen. In its place a grainy image of Ryu standing on the dais of her command Bridge came forth.

McCann looked up at her image 'Ryu, are you receiving me?'

The short Korean adjusted the metal frame of her glasses 'Just, what the hell is going on Duncan?'

'Hassif is transmitting our co-ordinates; we've come under attack and need your assistance.'

'Under attack? From who?'

'Pirates.'

Ryu narrowed her eyes 'Pirates? They attack transports and logistics ships, why would they attack Athena?' she asked in disbelief.

'Well you can ask them when you get here, can't you?' shouted McCann in frustration.

Ryu shook her head 'Don't get your knickers in a twist Duncan, we're setting course now. Leave the rest to me; I'll get as many cruisers as I can to assist.'

McCann let out a rush of air from his lungs 'Huh, well thank you. How long until you can reach us?'

Ryu looked over at her first Officer, Commander Hettinger spoke and she replied to McCann 'No more than 36 hours, can you hold out that long Duncan?'

McCann raised his eyebrows 'It seems we have no choice, they've already taken the Fore section but we'll try to hold them at the Mid-section until you arrive; God's speed Ryu.'

Ryu nodded and the screen returned to the image of space.

McCann looked up at the black dome attached to the ceiling 'Athena I want you to restrict access to the Bridge, turn those lifts off until I order them to resume.'

'Understood, you may monitor the battle on your holo projector, Admiral.'

McCann looked at the 3-D image; there were large numbers of dots inside. Red dots in the fore section represented the pirate crew. Green dots largely in the mid to rear sections represented Athena's crew.

'Are you relaying this to Egorov?'

'Affirmative.'

It was obvious that Egorov was hunkering down at the mid-section, protecting both the cargo bays and the command tower where the Bridge lay. For now the two sides were trading tungsten through the main corridors, even inside the Bridge Officers could hear the distant sound of pulse rifle fire. Every now and then there was an explosion of an RPG.

'Athena can you gas the fore section?' asked McCann.

'Negative, the enemy has bypassed my connections to the security system.'

After a few hours it seemed certain that Egorov was holding the pirates off, for now. They had come to a standoff, neither side possessing the required force to neutralise the other. McCann decided it would be cautious for some of his Officers to catch some sleep. Since the situation could deteriorate at any time it would be prudent to have someone fresh.

After 12 hours, Athena's drones had destroyed the third pirate vessel and started taking apart those attached to the Athena. These pirate ships were small but heavily armoured, designed to ram the enemy. A docking punch would pierce the enemy vessel, allowing the pirate crew to board. The claws surrounding the central punch latched on to the target hull, ensuring its docking punch would not lose integrity. It also allowed the ships to manipulate their target and move it to a space dock after capture. At the space dock the prey would be stripped and recycled, the crew processed to serve as sustenance and cargo looted.

Vezzali still had no idea where their enemies' wormhole nullifier was hidden; neither could she discover the location of their pirate station nor space dock.

McCann decided to take a nap, Lian lay down on the dais whilst he sat in his chair drifting into sleep, to the sound of spluttering pulse rifle fire.

As McCann drifted into the land of nod he felt his consciousness pulled, he slipped into a link with the sleeping Adjunct. Sometimes he would link with his wife while they slept, sharing dreams and fantasies. It often happened when two were close to each other, as to why this was happening with Lian was a mystery.

McCann looked around he was in New York, Lian's home city. She was with Kaeo and Sandra, he surmised they'd been to see a show on Broadway, the girls were laughing and giggling as paparazzi chased them taking pictures. This was a distinct memory, that McCann was sure of. The three returned to the Plaza hotel, where they retired to their rooms.

After the girls had retired to separate rooms Lian slipped out of her chambers, dressed in her black ribbed suit she made her way to the penthouse apartment.

Lian knocked on the door and a familiar voice replied from inside 'You may enter Lian.'

The young lady, only about five human years old but she easily could have been mistaken for eighteen, opened the door and entered.

Inside Malikah was alone and looking out of the window, admiring the cityscape of New York 'Why are you here Lian?'

Lian looked at the bulbous rear lobes of McCann's daughter 'I am curious, why did Xch'uup select me as Adjunct?'

Malikah didn't take her eyes away 'Because you are best suited to serve as auxiliary,' she replied without emotion.

Lian approached Malikah 'Is there no other reason … Malikah?'

Malikah's head snapped away from the skyscrapers, fixing her gaze on Lian the sable Queen narrowed her eyes 'You take a great risk coming here and speaking to your Xch'uup in such familiar terms.'

Lian returned the hard gaze with one of her own 'I take no risk, when I am aware of the truth.'

Malikah let out a slight cackle 'The truth? I thought you knew better than that. There is no truth, no lie, no good and no evil.'

Malikah cackled softly to herself.

'Then allow me the privilege of honesty, I am here to bare my soul to you. Will you show me yours?'

Malikah returned her gaze to the buildings of her favourite city 'Lian, you are a young girl with an over-active imagination.'

Lian took a step closer to her sable Queen 'You have not even reached your first century, yet you are Xch'uup. Do you suggest that I am unaware of my own heart ... and yours?'

Malikah shook her head 'be careful Lian, what you speak is dangerous not only for you but for myself too.'

'Then you admit it?'

'I admit nothing,' snapped Malikah.

Lian stepped even closer, to within touching distance 'If you do not have the courage to say it, then I shall. I love you Malikah and you love me.'

Malikah turned her back on the cityscape 'Hold your mouth, this heresy must not be spoken.'

Lian looked up at her Grand Matriarch 'Heresy? On Otoch perhaps, but when I hear your breathing in my sleep and your heart beat inside my body I care not for backward theocratic sheep.'

'Do not come closer Lian; your accusations could ruin my position on the home world.'

Lian refused to obey her Queen, she stepped closer so that her body touched that of Malikah's 'Each night I sense your feelings, merging with mine, why do you deny me now?'

Lian put her arms around her Queen's torso and pressed her body onto Malikah's, resting her head upon Xch'uup's shoulder.

Malikah embraced her Adjunct, stroking her head affectionately 'This must never be known, you must bury these emotions deep within you and guard them.'

'But you are Xch'uup, you are law.'

'Even Xch'uup must realise her limits and take into consideration the opinion of her subjects first and foremost. I cannot impose my moral values upon those I represent, something my predecessor learnt the hard way.'

'Then what will you do?'

Malikah looked down and smiled at Lian as she stroked her long dark hair 'I don't know, but tonight that is not my concern.'

Lian smiled as the Queen of the Tlillan leant down and their lips met. McCann watched on in horror as his daughter locked lips with Lian in a passionate embrace. The two stood grasping each other as the world went by outside, committing an act of heresy that would destroy his daughter if ever discovered by her sisters on Otoch.

The pair kissed softly until Malikah removed her lips, her eyes scanned down the front of her Adjunct. Lian watched the sable Queen's eyes and opened her suit at the collar, pulling it apart slightly. Malikah took the open collar and peeled it open to reveal the young girl's cleavage. Lian stared back up at her Xch'uup with an expression of innocence. Malikah placed one hand inside the suit and they kissed again, only this time with more passion.

As they kissed Lian slipped her suit down her long athletic body until it lay in a pile on the floor. Malikah pulled back to observe the fine woman that stood before her.

McCann could feel the eroticism coursing from Malikah into Lian then him. It was clear that his daughter was in love with this girl in more than one way and Lian felt the same. He felt Lian's heart jump as Malikah undressed, removing the black ribbed suit which all Tlillans wore. McCann could feel her ivory skin as Lian ran her fingers along his daughter's thigh. He even sensed Malikah's satisfaction at finally having the opportunity to fondle the small, pert breasts of her Adjunct. McCann was fearful, he cared not concerning his daughter's sexuality; he feared for her if this ever became common knowledge on Otoch. The Matriarchs would never accept such wayward activity from Xch'uup; her moral authority may become permanently eroded.

Malikah ran her hands down the body of Lian clasping onto her tiny rear, Malikah then led her to the queen size bed and lay her down. Lian was spread across the sheets naked, presenting herself to the sable goddess. Malikah lowered herself down pressing her ivory skin upon the frame of her lover. Lian raised her legs wrapping them around the Queen's torso; the pair kissed again locking into a passionate embrace.

McCann felt the high powered emotion that had been buried within the two for so long come to the surface and release, as a volcano exploding; an emotional Mount Vesuvius was detonating before him. In the passion he was certain they both cried, tears of joy perhaps? Perhaps the thought that this may never happen again was too much for them? McCann wasn't certain, the nuances of emotion he found very difficult to read.

'I love you Xch'uup,' quivered Lian

'Call me Malikah,' replied the sable Queen as she kissed her neck.

Lian cried out quite loud, McCann looked around in fear someone had heard but the door remained still. When he looked back he saw that Malikah had done the same but using her powers she scanned for any possible interloper. Upon realising all was safe she went back to her Adjunct. At this point McCann had seen enough however he was trapped in the link, it was like being stuck in a bad dream. He tried to ignore it but couldn't as each touch, each kiss, each intimate caress he felt himself.

Malikah ran her rough tongue to and fro, holding Lian's legs so that they pressed on her lover's chest.

The Queen of Otoch grunted as Lian went to let out a howl; fortunately Malikah reacted quickly and grabbed her mouth. Lian screamed into her hand as she released the tension that had built up inside. After a minute or two Lian's noise died down and her body relaxed.

Next the roles were reversed as Lian slipped down the bed, indulging in her Xch'uup's soft body above. The Tlillan Empress groaned with pleasure as the timbers of a sailing ship in the middle of a powerful storm, a storm of passion.

Ten minutes later and Malikah took Lian's hand, dragging her up along the bed, and placed it on her own mouth. Moments later Malikah let out a scream that Lian needed two hands to prevent from escaping into the corridors of the Plaza hotel.

The sable Queen convulsed clasping onto Lian as Lian braced Xch'uup's head with one arm and covered her mouth with the other hand. After a few minutes Malikah had finished, she lay on her hands and knees above Lian breathing heavily, her curly jet black hair hanging down. Lian smiled back at her Grand Matriarch, then brought her fingers to Malikah's cheek to wipe away an individual tear.

McCann was burning up with embarrassment, not so much from what he'd seen but what he was forced to feel and experience. Now he understood why his Mother-in-law wanted to link with Ilam, this was how Tlillan society got its cheap thrills. This would have made pornography redundant on Earth; people swapping sexual encounters via links for free, the porn industry would collapse in a day!

Suddenly McCann was torn away and he woke up in his command chair on the Athena.

'Tunnel event, tunnel event, tunnel event,' called Athena as her klaxon woke those who'd been resting.

McCann rubbed his eyes and looked at the 3-D display; the red dots had gotten closer and were now pushing the elevators to the command deck. The Englishman looked around to see Hassif climbing off the floor to stand at his station 'I'm detecting three ships, Sir.'

Vezzali shouted out 'It's the Hera, Chutli and Teteo!'

McCann felt the relief resonate throughout his body 'They're early, inform Egorov; and everyone, be prepared for a last push from the Macks.'

Lian got to her feet 'Admiral, the pirates have captured the elevators they are attempting to take the command deck.'

McCann pulled his pistol out and flicked it on 'Everyone get ready,' he then glared at Lian 'I want you to stay behind Hassif's station, don't come out until the fighting stops,' McCann then looked up 'and Athena turn that blasted alarm off!'

The klaxon desisted and the sound of pulse fire became clear, McCann knelt with his chair between him and the rear elevator exits. The Vympel Officers were crouched behind the forward stations, half of the pit crew were at work, the other half were crouched down taking cover.

'Reinforcements ETA two minutes and twenty eight seconds,' announced Athena.

At that moment one of the elevators opened, McCann was crouched ready to pepper the first Mack he saw with tungsten. The lift was empty, aside from a small metal container. The container exploded blinding everyone unfortunate enough to be looking in that direction.

Fortunately the Vympel soldiers had activated their helmets, shielding their eyes from the flash grenade. McCann could hear pulse fire inside the Bridge although his vision was temporarily blinded; he remained behind his chair hoping the enemy could not see him.

After a minute he could make out shapes, slowly the dark shapes became more defined and colours were now clearing. The Macks were easily defined due to the silver eyes that reflected light. The Englishman began to return fire; thankfully his Vympel guards had held them back; surprising the machine men as they leapt from the lifts.

Mack corpses lay in piles in front of the lift exits, the elevators closed again and another batch of cyborg pirates attempted to rush the Bridge. As soon as the doors of both lifts opened the Macks charged firing pulse rifles. Several pit Officers were hit leaving a pool of blood to gather at the bottom of the work area. All of the Officers pulled their weapons and returned fire; the Macks, although exposed with no cover, didn't seem to care. They moved over the bodies of their fallen comrades.

The third group to assault the Bridge used the piles of bodies as cover, lying down and returning fire. Sparks flew around the room as tungsten rounds bounced off the walls. Blue flashes burst out of the barrels causing smoke from the plasma to taint the air.

The Bridge crew were getting picked off since the Macks seemed to have no concern for casualties. McCann could see they would be finished before Ryu could do anything to prevent it. There were now about fifteen Macks using fallen comrades as cover and they were winning.

McCann tapped his wrist tablet 'Egorov, we need assistance on the Bridge.'

'Vympel one is pushing forward, the Macks are retreating. We cannot access the Bridge and if we don't chase these bastards down now …'

'Understood, but we need you here now.'

'I'm sorry Admiral, I didn't hear that.'

McCann went to repeat himself but suddenly the noise of the fire fight dissipated. McCann peeped over his chair; Lian was stood to his right in plain view with her eyes burning a fiery pigment.

'Never mind, we're fine. Continue your pursuit of the Macks, McCann out.'

The Englishman stood up then walked past Lian, he glanced over the pile of dead Macks to see three of them unconscious.

The Vympel soldiers quickly gathered up rifles from the corpses that were arranged in front of the rear lifts.

'Lian, can you question these Macks?' inquired McCann.

'What do you wish to know, Admiral?' she replied in a deep voice.

'I want to know where their base of operations is.'

The Vympel guards trained their weapons on the three remaining Macks, one of the enemy gained consciousness and in a trance he approached Lian.

'Tu'uk kuxtal?' asked Lian.

The Mack tried his best to resist her will 'Topik Xch'uup!'

Lian placed her hand upon the forehead of the machine man; he let out a blood curdling scream as he dropped to his knees and fell unconscious.

'I have the location, Admiral. May I question the other two?'

McCann reloaded his pistol with a fresh magazine then switched it off 'What do you want to know?'

'The location of Machine,' replied Lian as her eyes returned to their natural brown.

Hassif appeared from behind his station 'But Machine was dismantled.'

Lian pointed to the Makayuuk 'If Machine no longer exists, how is this possible? Makayuuk cannot function without Machine, this is a fact.'

'And I saw machine destroyed, that's a fact,' stated McCann.

Lian made no reply and McCann gestured towards the Macks 'Be my guest.'

Lian's eyes clouded a dark red and one of the Macks awoke from his forced slumber. The machine man stood up; there was no fear on his face, he sneered at Lian.

'Tu'uk Yuuk?' demanded Lian.

The short cyborg replied in English so that the remaining Bridge crew could understand 'Machine lives, Machine will destroy you all.'

McCann stepped forward 'I saw Machine destroyed on Bandayuuk,' he pressed the captive.

The cyborg chuckled 'You destroyed a Machine, that was only a node. Machine has recovered.'

Lian spoke in her deep Valkyrie tone 'Where are the Machine nodes?'

The Makayuuk smirked 'I do not know, no one knows the location of Machine.'

Lian placed her hand upon the creatures head, again the Makayuuk let out a scream and his silver eyes changed to a dull lead before he dropped to the floor.

Lian let out a huff 'Hah, he was telling the truth. Do as you please with the other one, none of them are aware of Machine's location.'

Chapter 6

Vympel one and two had pushed the Makayuuk back to their boarding vessels. Trapped inside their own ambush the short Korean obliterated the remaining vessels.

The Tlillan cruisers returned to their previous duties, once the Makayuuk had been dispatched and repairs were underway.

McCann stood at the airlock to his docking bay, Ryu and her Chief Engineer exited. The docking bay had been damaged in the attack so he couldn't greet them as they exited the small transport.

The side of the transport melted back and the pair of them in their space suits stepped out. Dressed in their military uniforms over a black ribbed suit; yet still allowing room for the helmet to unfurl from the collar, forming an airtight environment.

It was obvious which Ryu was, due to her height, or lack of it. Added to that her Chief was quiet tall and well built. They stepped into the airlock, cleared the pressurisation and entered the corridor to meet McCann.

Their helmets collapsed back into their suit collars and Ryu gave a little salute with a smile of satisfaction.

McCann rolled his eyes 'There's no need for that Ryu, it's just us here.'

Her Chief, Hiedemann looked uncomfortable at his statement.

McCann began to stroll along the corridor, leading them to the engine rooms 'It seems we have a traitor, someone knew about our cargo and informed the Macks.'

'Cargo?'

'We have about 10,000 tonnes of neutronium on board.'

Ryu was surprised 'And no escort? Now it makes sense, pirates would never attack a cruiser under normal circumstances.'

The three walked through corridors charred with scorch marks from RPGs, dried blood smearing the floor.

McCann nodded in agreement 'I think Malikah knew what was going to happen.'

'Well you did get the location of the pirate's base of operations.'

McCann took a cigar from his case, cut the cap then toasted the foot with a long cedar match 'More importantly there's a good chance that the traitor is alive and on this ship. Before we go after the pirate base I want to have that traitor in the brig.'

'I can't believe you still smoke those things Duncan,' complained Ryu as she wafted the smoke away from her face.

McCann chuckled 'Are you going to tell me they're bad for my health?'

Ryu gave a matronly look 'No, but even the Ixchel doesn't take care of bad breath!'

The threesome exited a lift and stepped into an area of the ship where the trench separated the engines and fusion power core; Now that the ship was in need of repairs this area required the most manpower.

Louis witnessed them walk out and swiftly approached 'Thank Christ you are here, I need every man you can spare,' said Louis with relief to Chief Heidemann.

'It's nice to see you too Louis,' said Ryu with a sarcastic tone.

Louis shifted his attention to the Korean for a moment 'Uh, yeah you too Ryu.'

'I'll leave Bridgette here, she'll give you all the assistance you need,' replied Ryu.

Louis nodded his head and motioned towards his workstation where the pair began to chat in a hushed tone.

'Well I'm sure those two will get along like a house on fire,' remarked McCann as he and Ryu made for the lift.

After exiting the lift for the Officer's lounge Ryu asked 'So what are you doing to find the spy?'

'In here,' said the Englishman as he pointed towards the lounge.

Inside Lian stood in her skin tight space suit scanning crew members one by one. Commander Kim sat in front of her as she placed her hand upon his head sifting through his mind for any inkling of guilt.

'It won't be Kim,' stated Ryu with absolute certainty.

'I know,' replied McCann 'but everyone must be scanned, including me.'

Ryu looked at her comrade incredulously 'Surely not?'

'You'd do the same.'

'I suppose so but it isn't Kim and Louis is a prick but he isn't a traitor. What about the Tlillan, do you trust her?'

McCann took a drag from his Cohiba Siglo I 'Lian isn't the traitor.'

'How do you know that?' retorted the Korean.

The Englishman let the smoke roll over his tongue and pass through his nostrils 'She would never betray Malikah, I'm quite certain of that.'

Ryu widened her eyes and adjusted her glasses 'If you say so Duncan.'

McCann looked down at his old comrade 'I do say so.'

'Uuurrrhhh!' shouted Ryu in disapproval, grabbing the attention of everyone awaiting interrogation.

Lian removed her hand from Kim's forehead 'You may leave Commander.'

Kim walked away from Lian, as he came to the exit he noticed Ryu and stood to attention.

Ryu smiled 'I'll see you in the lounge when all this is over, we can catch up.'

Kim returned the smile then turned his gaze to McCann, the Englishman nodded and Kim marched out of the lounge and back to duty.

'How many are left?'

'We lost about half of the crew; half of the survivors are injured ...'

'No I mean how many more to interrogate?' inquired Ryu.

'Ah, well since we're onto the Bridge staff then all of the Engineering crew must have been done. Not many now.'

'Have they done the drone crew yet?'

McCann nodded 'Yup, Kim was the last of the drone crew to be scanned.'

'I still don't trust the Tlillan,' stated Ryu in her cold manner.

Before McCann could reply there was a ruckus at the far end of the lounge where the interrogation was taking place. Both McCann and Ryu made their way past the line of Bridge Officers. McKinley was shouting at Lian, the half Tlillan lady did not reply to his abuse.

'What the bloody hell is going on here? McKinley explain yourself!' shouted McCann.

The weapons Officer said nothing.

Lian replied 'I have found the traitor, Admiral.'

The line of Officers began to mutter in astonishment. McCann stepped forward until he was nose to nose with his weapons Officer 'Well?'

'She's lying, the Tlillan's trying to implicate me for her crimes!' bellowed McKinley.

McCann peered towards Lian 'Show me.'

Lian placed her hand upon the Englishman's forehead, she sent him drifting into a vision which she'd ripped from the weapons Officer's memory.

Kim was being informed of the neutronium; As McKinley manned his station he listened intently. After the transmission from the surface of Otoch ended the Lieutenant excused himself. McCann could sense his hatred and desire for revenge, he had been demeaned in the most horrible way by Beaumont and now it was time for payback.

The tall Scotsman entered his quarters and from inside a wall aperture used for storing personal effects he picked out a tachyon transponder. He tapped away something unintelligible, though McCann was aware via McKinley's thoughts that he was informing Makayuuk pirates of their shipment. He then left the transponder on, emitting Athena's location even when folding space. It was the only way to ensure that their wormhole would open at the correct point, forcing the Athena into an ambush.

Placing the transponder back inside the aperture he returned to his station, McCann had seen enough and brought himself out from the link.

The Englishman hit his wrist tablet 'Egorov?'

'Yes, Sir?'

'I want you to search Lieutenant McKinley's cabin, I believe he has a tachyon transponder divulging our location to the Makayuuk hidden in a wall compartment.'

Egorov replied in a surprised tone 'Understood, Sir.'

'McCann out,' he tapped his wrist tablet again and made a disappointed expression towards McKinley.

His Lieutenant sneered 'If they'd have killed Beaumont it would have been worth it!'

Two Vympel security guards entered the lounge, one handcuffed McKinley's wrists behind his back the other attached a control collar.

'Take him to the brig, use any force required,' stated McCann coldly.

McKinley was pushed out of the lounge and off to his new accommodation.

'Show's over people, let's get back to putting Athena into shape,' ordered the Admiral.

The line of crewman broke up and exited the room.

Lian spoke to the Admiral 'As soon as Athena is ready we must attack the pirate base station.'

'What about the cargo?'

'It can wait; we must remove the pirate threat before they relocate.'

McCann nodded his head 'When we reach Earth you and I are going to have a little chat.'

Lian gave a puzzled expression 'Concerning?'

'Concerning the dream you had last night.'

McCann sensed fear emanating from Lian's body 'Oh, I see.'

'Until then you can give Hassif the pirates' co-ordinates.'

Lian made a nervous smile and quickly marched out of the lounge.

'What was all that about?' inquired Ryu.

'Nothing, fancy a drink?'

'Still drinking on duty, Duncan?'

McCann rolled his eyes 'Still as strict as a mother superior?'

'Fine, one drink but that's all.'

The Englishman grinned and slipped behind the bar to pour two shots of Irish whiskey. He raised his glass and saluted 'To the daring Korean lady that saved my skin again!'

Ryu smirked and took a sip, at tasting the drink her face screwed up 'Yuk! What's this?'

'I should have warned you, the Balvenie is in my cabin. Those bloody Americans would drink it all to themselves otherwise.'

'You drink this crap?'

'Unfortunately, I do. It would be bad form for me to drink the good stuff while they went without.'

'Since when did you care what the rest of the crew were drinking?'

'Since they started drinking my Speyside Scotch!'

Ryu laughed 'I see, so it's their lack of good manners that has forced you into drinking cat urine?'

McCann pulled a rather disappointed expression as he sipped his drink 'Something like that.'

Later that evening the remaining Officers gathered in the lounge, the Russians making a fuss of Ryu as usual. McCann sat at his usual table with Hassif, Vezzali, Ryu and Egorov.

Hassif noticed the man they'd all been waiting for enter the lounge. The talk became subdued as Louis approached the bar and ordered an ale. Taking his slim beer glass he approached the Admiral's table and before anyone could say hello he shouted out 'You see, I knew that guy was an asshole!'

Louis sat at the table and continued his rant 'But oh no, no one wanted to listen to that crazy fuck Beaumont, did they?'

McCann rolled his eyes 'Louis ...'

However the Frenchman interjected 'No, no, no don't you cut me off. I knew there was something weird about that guy, I told you!'

'Either that or you're just an egotistical prick?' retorted the Korean.

The bar went quiet, the Americans awaited for the Chief Engineer's inevitable outburst. To their surprise it didn't come, Louis sneered at the Korean Captain and took a sip of his amber ale.

'At 0800 hours we'll be heading with Hera for the pirate base station, it should take only a couple of hours to fold space there,' stated McCann.

'Athena will be in working order before then, all her cannons are operational. Her power core and engines were unaffected by the ambush,' replied Louis.

The rest of the evening was taken up with chatter from Louis, declaring how he was right and had McKinley marked down as a traitor from the beginning.

The Next day McCann took his seat on the Bridge, still scarred with tungsten rounds and the stench of smoke from rifle barrels.

'Folding space in T minus four minutes Admiral,' noted Athena calmly.

The image of Ryu appeared on the view screen 'Follow us in; when we enter the pirate system the Hera will be cloaked.'

'Understood, good luck Ryu.'

'You too McCann.'

The image dissipated ceding to the scene of space from the fore of the Athena.

Four minutes later and an alarm went off; two shimmering white holes appeared before Athena and Hera. The Hera entered hers first with Athena following shortly afterwards.

The vessels spent a short time inside the dead zone before exiting; the Hera intensified her Casimir field bending light around the destroyer. Athena had no such ability and popped out in full view.

'Scanning the system,' announced Vezzali as she pored over the data coming back. There were five planets, four gas giants; the other was too close to the star to be habitable.

'Sir, I believe I have the location of the pirate space station,' called out the blond science Officer.

On the tactical display to the right a representation of the asteroid belt between a Mercury class planet and first gas giant appeared. A red box highlighted an asteroid and Lian squeaked 'That's it!'

McCann relaxed into his chair 'Athena, inform the Hera and bring the crew to battle stations.'

'Affirmative, Admiral,' replied Athena softly.

'Hassif, I want to intercept that station on our port bow, full speed.'

The Indian nodded 'Done,' tapped away at his station and Athena jerked into motion as the call for battle stations went out.

'Kim, scout that rock out for me.'

Kim hit his wrist tablet and relayed McCann's orders to his drone crew, moments later a pair of drones shot out past Athena towards the asteroid belt.

Before the drones came within scanning range of the rock they were destroyed by missile defence sites placed inside the belt.

'Full stop, bring our port cannons to bear,' ordered McCann.

The Athena came to a halt and as she began to turn Vezzali shouted 'Two Makayuuk cruisers on an intercept course, T minus three minutes, Sir.'

Athena was taking the place of McKinley for now, so McCann looked up towards her 'Athena load anti-matter warheads.'

'Affirmative, Admiral.'

Hassif turned to McCann 'I'm receiving a transmission from the Makayuuk.'

'Put it up,' replied McCann wishing to satisfy his curiosity.

An image of a typical machine man dressed in his grey jump suit appeared 'Greetings McCann. Surrender your vessel,' grinned a smug cyborg.

McCann grinned back 'So that we can be liquidised, I don't think so.'

The cyborg laughed 'Then why come here?'

'To hunt you down and put an end to piracy on I.S.A shipping.'

The Makayuuk stopped laughing 'How do you intend to do that, McCann?'

'If you surrender now you won't have to find out.'

The Makayuuk sent a message to his weapons Officer via their neural link. Vezzali detected a jump in Cherenkov radiation as a stream of tachyon particles hit Athena's magnetic shield 'The Makayuuk have a weapons lock on us, Sir!'

McCann remained calm much to the discomfort of the machine man 'Activate point defence and fire a full broadside into this target.'

He tapped the arm of his chair targeting the closest Mack vessel on the tactical display.

These vessels were not the boarding craft they'd fought earlier; they were the long tubular design of warships that Makayuuk traditionally used. McCann believed them all destroyed and was quite shocked to see not one but two of them. Were they saved from the conquest or had they begun constructing new ships?

The incoming enemy torpedoes were too numerous for Athena to cope with; however the missiles were pulled of course inexplicably. The Casimir field of Hera tore them out of their path and flung them into space where they detonated. Ryu then dropped Hera's cloak to reveal her destroyer pointing its open weapon port at the second enemy ship.

As Athena ripped apart the first vessel in bright white fire, a plasma torpedo burst from the nose of Hera. Hitting the Makayuuk cruiser dead centre, it broke the superstructure in two. The impact sent its two halves spinning off into space.

From their present distance the two I.S.A warships pounded the pirate base of operations into dust. A combination of anti-matter warheads and plasma torpedoes annihilated whatever remained of the pirates.

Within an hour of the first impact a massive gap lay in the asteroid belt where the pirates once were, Vezzali reported she could pick up no signs of life. McCann decided it was sufficient and the I.S.A vessels folded space for Earth.

Upon reaching the Terran system Athena docked with the Tsiolkovsky for repairs. McKinley was taken to the surface via transport; McCann accompanied the first shipment of neutronium to Geneva.

He stepped out of the Atlas and onto the landing pad where Faraday greeted him; dressed in his usual three piece suit the old Etonian shook his hand 'Good to see you back safe and sound.'

They both walked past the Vympel guards and into mission control 'For a moment there I was worried you might be killed by pirates.'

McCann pulled out his cigar case 'Is it alright to smoke?'

Faraday grimaced a little 'If you must, but tell me, McKinley betrayed you?'

McCann nodded his head 'Shocking isn't it?'

'I'm sure you'll be relieved to know that we're about to announce a neutronium standard, just as soon as the last Atlas is unloaded.'

The Englishman puffed on his cigar 'Marvellous.'

Faraday waved his cane 'None of that Duncan, you've got to put a good show on for that Habeeb fellow. We need to make the transition to this new standard as smooth as possible.'

McCann sneered as the thick creamy smoke rolled out of his nostrils 'As long as I don't have to talk to him.'

'You'll be chatting with the premier in Moscow, then you'll be off to New York.'

McCann gave a look of disbelief 'What? Can't you get one of your minions to do that?'

Faraday chuckled 'that's exactly what I'm doing Duncan, besides you get on well with the Americans.'

'Correction, Malikah gets on well with them and Ryu gets on with the Russians,' stated a frustrated McCann.

'Yes well Malikah isn't here and Ryu has important duties, so I'm afraid it's going to have to be you Duncan.'

'In that case, since I'm not all that important, I suppose I'll be able to run your errands for you. Anything else Bill? Maybe you need some toilet roll changing or the urinals cleaned?'

Faraday cracked up laughing, since Malikah had taken charge he was a much easier going person. McCann preferred the old Faraday with blood pressure so high his eyeballs nearly popped out twice a day.

'Fine, when do I leave Bill?'

'Today, Duncan. Moscow first.'

McCann groaned and finished off his cigar as he awaited the Atlas to be loaded with the Russian share of Neutronium. Before the day was out he was sat in the back staring at a small pile of dark blue bricks. He could hardly bring himself to believe there was 2,000 tonnes of neutronium there. The metal was so dense that only a very small amount would possess an astounding mass. Sandra sat next to him at the rear of the craft; McCann suspected she had remained on Earth to keep a pair of eyes out for Malikah.

'So have you met the Russian premier before Mr McCann?' asked the polite young lady.

'No and you can call me Duncan,' replied McCann.

'I tend to find Russians very stand offish, what do you think Duncan?'

McCann chuckled 'I'd agree, they remind me of Tlillans.'

Sandra looked at Malikah's father thoughtfully 'I would say they are more similar to English.'

McCann narrowed his eyes 'Really?'

The beautiful young girl smiled back and nodded her head, the Englishman resided himself to looking forward as the craft hurtled through the atmosphere.

Within an hour they were landing inside the walls of the Kremlin. They exited the Atlas to be greeted by Russia's Premier; Ivan Myshkin was a man in his 60's, a little over-weight and going grey. He was dressed in a very nice black two piece suit, although McCann felt it made him look like a bank manager.

McCann exited the Atlas and shook the awaiting Premier's hand; far more attention however was paid to Sandra. With her height and body shape it were as if a supermodel had visited the Kremlin today.

Sandra bowed 'Namaste Premier Myshkin'

The Premier quickly shook her hand and invited them in as the cargo was unloaded. Press were all over the place covering this visit, Mr Myshkin wanted the world to know that he'd received a large shipment of Neutronium.

Inside McCann and Sandra sat at a large oak table where the press had already set up. The Premier pulled out a wooden box and passed it to McCann 'I would like you to have this on behalf of the Russian people Mr McCann.'

The Englishman flipped the lid on the box, within lay twenty five Russian cigars. Suddenly a memory of his governorship on Gukumatz passed through him, not unlike an undercooked Indian curry after a night out on the tiles. The tobacco was much the same as the cigarettes Nestor smoked. McCann had tried a few of them and discovered they tasted even rougher than they smelt. He was tempted to give them back but on observing the Premier's face he dared not insult him by returning the gift.

McCann accepted the cigars 'Thank you very much Mr Myshkin.'

Next an aide entered the room carrying what must have been clothing in a dust cover. The Premier took the gift, walked around the desk, and presented it to Sandra in full view of the media.

Again Sandra pressed her palms together 'Spasiba.'

The press applauded with delight and the Premier had a short chat in Russian with Sandra, who was fluent in the language much to McCann's embarrassment. Their chat ended in the Russian urging Sandra to open her gift.

Sandra unzipped the dustcover to reveal a real fur coat, a very rare and expensive item for sure. The animal rights groups weren't going to be happy about this but it was obvious that neither Sandra nor the Russian Premier cared.

Sandra was elated as she slipped into her Mink coat, which fit perfectly. The tall slender Amazon looked very elegant in it, Premier Myshkin had made the right choice; probably in an attempt to outdo Michael Earle, the President of the Eastern States.

The soft black fur coat had Sandra squealing as a child would at her birthday and with good reason.

Myshkin gestured towards the cigars 'Feel free to smoke Admiral.'

McCann shuddered inside; against his will he picked out one of the Lonsdale cigars and clipped the cap. Even just toasting the foot he could smell that Russian stench, but forced a smiled for the cameras.

The Englishman was certain that the press and other politicians could smell the rough tobacco, who couldn't? Unless you'd lost all sense of smell! McCann offered one to Premier Myshkin, but the Russian politely declined his offer. Waving his hand he replied in his thick Russian accent 'I do not smoke Mr McCann, I find the smell how do you say it ... foul?'

McCann smiled as the Russians laughed, all the time he considered that despite being a smoker he found the smell quite foul too. However there was no way in hell he was going to insult the Russian Premier before his home press; especially considering the expensive gift he'd given to Sandra, so he soldiered on smoking the vile stick.

After a while the press were allowed to ask some questions, a young man stood up holding a tablet and addressed Mr Myshkin 'What exactly is the purpose of this Neutronium?'

Although the Premier wasn't supposed to say anything until Faraday had announced the new standard, he did 'In the coming months Russia shall be switching to a new currency standard.'

The young man was about to ask another question but one of the Premier's aides waved him down. A middle aged lady with glasses was selected next 'Will Russia be dropping the Gold standard in favour of a Neutronium standard?'

McCann puffed on his rank Russian stick in disbelief as the Premier spilt the beans 'Da,' he simply stated creating an uproar of requests.

Next McCann was questioned 'We have reports that the Athena was attacked by pirates whilst transporting this neutronium to Earth. Can you confirm that Admiral McCann?'

The Englishman looked towards Sandra who nodded her head 'We were intercepted by pirates, however they were repelled with the assistance of Captain Ryu, we defeated their ships and neutralised their base of operations.'

'There are rumours that a traitor was unearthed on the Athena, is this true?'

McCann waved his hand 'I'm sorry I'm not able to answer any more questions, thank you.'

The next day McCann decided to spend his time doing some sight-seeing, Sandra had created a distraction so that he might slip away un-noticed. Whilst the Russian elite were poring over the beautiful young lady he disappeared from his hotel, with the permission of Myshkin.

Dressed in a civilian charcoal grey suit with a red silk handkerchief he made for his first destination, Red Square, a place he'd long wished to visit. After reading of the many trials and tribulations of Moscow, from Genghis Khan to Gottschalk Hoch, the city fascinated him and since he'd already visited the Kremlin but wasn't able to leave the fortress during the "presscipade", as he put it, Red Square was next in line.

The Englishman relaxed as he stood on the Moscow Metro, one of the oldest and deepest of all subway networks in the world. None of the occupants in his carriage recognised him, a couple of ladies eyed his three piece suit and gave a cheeky smile but other than that he was just another anonymous traveller that day. McCann kept his wrist tablet hidden beneath his shirt cuff and breathed in the fine scent of Floris No.89. The Englishman had also decided to wear an Ushanka hat in order to fit in with the fashion of the moment in Moscow. The city could be awfully cold at times and you didn't want to get caught short if it rained. The traditional Russian Ushanka was much like those who wore it, utilitarian yet strangely attractive. It matched his fine dark Italian cashmere overcoat, quite an extravagance for the average Moscovite.

The Englishman spoke to a young lady sitting beside the aisle where he stood 'Excuse me, but do you speak English?'

She replied with a puzzled look.

'English?' repeated the tourist.

'Neit,' replied the lady dressed in a white overcoat with matching Ushanka.

McCann heard the reply in his earpiece though he understood Russian for 'no'. He was quickly alerted to another woman in her 40's 'You are English?' she called from the opposite end of the carriage.

With relief McCann made his way to her 'Yes I am, do you speak English?'

'A little, what do you want?' she replied in a rather forceful tone.

'Do you know where I get off for Red Square?'

The lady smiled 'Yes, in two more stops, do you understand?'

McCann returned her smile 'Yes, thank you very much … spasiba!'

The Lady laughed at his attempt to speak her language 'You are welcome. Why are you here?'

'After reading about the city as a child, I've always desired to see Moscow.'

The brown haired lady smiled 'Will you visit,' the Russian searched her mind for the correct words 'Mavzoley Lenina?'

The Admiral's earpiece quick spat out the translation, an androgynous voice spoke 'Lenin's Mausoleum'.

McCann nodded 'Yes of course.'

The woman looked around the subway compartment as it moved smoothly along the newly installed mag lev rails which covered the massive metro system. She then spoke in a slightly hushed tone 'Do not forget to visit the grave of Yevpraksiya.'

At the mention of Yevpraksiya searching eyes throughout the carriage turned to examine McCann and the woman he was speaking with. Not a word was spoken but their looks made the Englishman feel most uncomfortable, just the mention of the former Tsaritsa of Russia caused a tension to fill the carriage. McCann didn't quite understand what compelled Russians to hold her name in such high reverence and fear at the same time. She had been buried alongside many esteemed men of the Soviet era at the Kremlin wall, outside Red Square. In McCann's mind she was a hero of Mother Russia, the leader who liberated Europe from the grip of the Hun.

McCann smiled and replied to the nervous lady 'I'll certainly visit her grave.'

The people inside the carriage went back to reading tablets and conversations on their earpieces. The Russian lady relaxed as the attention dissipated, 'Good, enjoy your visit.'

McCann nodded his head as the underground train stopped and the lady stepped out. At the next stop McCann walked off onto the platform, he made his way to the surface via an escalator; the station was much larger than those in London.

Once above ground he felt the cold air rush around him and an icy feeling in his lungs as he took a deep breath of the frosty atmosphere. His first stop in the Square was at the statue of Kuzma Minin and Dmitry Pozharsky, a grand bronze monument to the men who repelled the Polish invaders during the 17th century. One stood with his arm out as the other sat propping up a shield and sword. McCann was uncertain which was Kuzma and which Dmitry but it didn't matter, the statue was a powerful sight in its aged green bronze. The pair seemed to be guarding the square, gazing out; protecting their descendants from any would be invader.

The Square bustled as people walked around what was originally a market but now served many purposes. Close to the statue lay the Lobnoye Mesto, a circular granite platform designed for public ceremonies. McCann recalled some old footage of Yevpraksiya; he recognised this as the place she had made her speech addressing the invasion, announcing the suspension of all elections until the threat had been dealt with. He recalled how the people applauded her decisive action and how it filled them with hope. He also recalled how many were relieved once her reign was over, a reign which lasted far longer than the conflict with their old adversaries, Germany, or what passed for the European Union at that point in time. At the turn of the 21st century some referred to the EU jokingly as the fourth Reich, by 2030 it was no longer a joke.

The Englishman quickly slipped his shirt sleeve up his arm and tapped on his wrist tablet, down loading the scene of her speech from the Net. He noted the officials standing beside her; McCann guessed they were KGB top brass since without them she could not have grasped power. Yevpraksiya had taken control of Russia after her Father's assassination, it was her responsibility to run for Premier; Russia had begun to devolve, along similar lines to China. Warlords were on the rise, refusing to pay tax, threatening Moscow with violence to whomever they sent. Her father, Ivan Kamenev died after he'd ordered 5 battalions to Chechnya for the purpose of tax collection. It was unclear as to whether the ricin was administered by a Chechen or one of his own military commanders.

Politically Russia was collapsing, until the KGB backed the dead Premier's daughter. The Liberal Democratic Party made her leader and Premier since none wanted the job. Yevpraksiya had only a single interest, revenge, and the 26 year old girl set about attaining it in a very Russian manner. The tall, blonde haired and blue eyed lady was very attractive but soon her image became synonymous with fear.

Seeing what he thought was a collapsing Russia the head of the E.U, or what the Germans had managed to enslave through massive debt then suppress via the member countries own military, Gottschalk Hoch decided to do what previous German leaders had failed at. The arrogant ruler of the Troika believed he could quickly invade a Russia descending into anarchy and grab the rich oil fields in the Caucasus. The Russians couldn't even force their own people to pay tax, how on earth could they prevent a powerful and focused Germany from snatching a piece of the crumbling empire?

It was true; Yevpraksiya was having difficulty in collecting resources from her inherited state. Russia had survived the initial currency wars and financial Armageddon due to a large stock of gold and oil, but holding Russia together had been too much for her Father. She was starting to realise how difficult his job had been, no one would co-operate, even her own military seemed only to follow orders when it so pleased them. The KGB protected her but could do little to control a country as large and obstinate as Russia.

Fortunately Germany did her a massive favour and invaded, in a replay of 1941 the Hun made a dash to secure Russian oil fields, a resource also used to back many new currencies post financial collapse. As the Hun poured into Mother Russia seizing her assets, Yevpraksiya made what was expected to be her final address to the people of her country. It turned out to be the first of many, democracy was put on hold and Russia's citizens placed their destiny behind what was to become the first Tsaritsa of Russia.

Provinces began to fall into line, sending levies owed, her military was purged of those reluctant to engage the E.U and defences erected. By the time the enemy had taken Russia's oil fields and turned to Moscow the citizens of Russia were chomping at the bit for a chance to hit back at their foe.

The megacity known as the third Rome was not about to allow the tribes of Germania to walk in and sack it, as had happened to the first Rome. Anti-missile sites littered the skyline of the city, adorning every building. Drones were ready to launch as soon as satellites picked up the invaders approaching the Moskova River.

Yevpraksiya had been advised to leave, yet in the same vein as Stalin she refused; instead the tall lady visited his grave at the wall of the Kremlin. Many others were present, adorning the granite pillar which held a bust of the former leader, with flowers. People were praying, begging the man who held back the Nazis one hundred years ago to deliver them again from the invading Hun.

The young lady caused a stir as she walked through Red Square pursued by paparazzi; she knelt at the obelisk which supported the strong man of the Soviet Union. Cameras clicked as she requested Stalin send them the most terrible winter Russia's enemies have ever seen. Her request was met with rapturous applause from those observing.

As the Hun approached with a combined army of German, Italian and French troops the weather deteriorated. By the time they made striking distance there was a complete white out, even satellites couldn't see through the thick blizzard. Leopard tanks became stuck under feet of snow and the Luftwaffe drones were grounded as fuel froze in their tanks overnight.

Such terrible conditions failed to prevent the Wehrmacht and its cohorts from unleashing a brutal missile strike upon the city. Moscow began to burn around the frozen river of the same name. Unfortunately for Yevpraksiya she could not launch her drones either, nor see exactly where her enemy had dug in. It became a battle of attrition, who could wait out and survive the blizzard.

During the siege Russia's new Tsaritsa visited all areas, encouraging efforts to bolster defence in preparation for when the weather broke. During her morale boosting exercise she visited Lomonosov University. Whilst meeting students and urging them to dig in for the inevitable arrival of the Hun, she met with a progenitor of the modern scram drone. As she stepped down from the lectern a young man approached from the crowd of students.

KGB agents grabbed the lad before he could do harm, however Russia's tall Tsaritsa called off her dogs, she was certain the boy with glasses had no ill intent.

'What do you want?' inquired Yevpraksiya in an urgent tone.

'Something to help, the drones we can launch them now.' Replied the young man in his 20's as two burly KGB agents held him by both arms.

'How?' said the Tsaritsa almost barking at him in an attempt to draw the information out.

The student glanced at her KGB; Yevpraksiya waved 'Release him.'

They released the student yet remained between him and their boss, dressed in her thick mink coat and ushanka.

He grabbed a nearby laptop and opened it 'If we convert the ground attack drones to Hydrogen we can get them up now.'

One of the KGB staff scoffed 'That would mean redesigning the engine, we don't have that kind of time, the Germans are here now!'

'Let him speak Yuri!' snapped Yevpraksiya.

'We can do it in one day, the engines would not run as efficiently but it would be enough to launch a first strike whilst they are grounded.'

The Tsaritsa gave a wary look 'Why did you not present this before?'

'I did,' replied the student looking at her KGB staff nervously.

The beautiful blonde Russian narrowed her eyes 'I see, take this man to our forward airbase. I expect to have enough drones ready for a strike this time tomorrow ... and bring me whoever is responsible for dismissing this proposal.'

Yevpraksiya smiled to the student 'Good luck,' then marched out of the lecture hall.

The student experienced an ominous feeling of dread as a KGB agent escorted him to an airbase which was to be the first defence against the coming enemy assault.

By the next day Yevpraksiya's Minister of Defence had been shot and her first squadron of drones were in the air searching out enemy encampments.

On the other side of the coin the Prussian in command of the siege of Moscow was drinking tea inside his forward HQ, laughing and joking with his Officers as they all waited out the terrible weather. With typical German arrogance victory was assured and Feldmarschall Hans Schiffer contemplated with his Italian and French subordinates on how they would spend their spring in Moscow, whilst sipping hot drinks in the prefabricated steel crate which served as his tent.

'I'm looking forward to the women, have you seen that Praksiya? Damn if only every world leader was as sexy as her!' declared Genrale Cesare Messana.

Hans chuckled heartily as he put he feet up inside his insulated crate 'Yes, but we'd have too much time away from our wives on campaign!'

The three men laughed as the French air force General retorted 'You've not met his wife Hans!'

The German laughed harder as he slapped his thigh but the Italian wasn't amused 'Hey, my wife is better looking than that Russian bitch for sure and a virgin? HAH! I wouldn't touch her; she has diseases even Francois has never heard of.'

The Frenchman put down his drink and got to his feet, pointing at the Italian accusingly he shouted 'That was not me in Grozny! And I still believe it was you that sent the photo to the newspapers!'

The slightly plump Feldmarschall was going red with laughter, a stark contrast to his drab grey uniform 'I don't know Francois there were not that many General D'armee Aeriennes in Grozny you know?'

The Frenchman was furious at the Italian 'It was photo-shopped; I have never been to a whorehouse in my life!'

Cesare scratched his forehead comically 'Si, si we must have Hercule Poirot take a look at this obvious forgery, a Frenchman screwing whores when he should be working? Crazy!'

The Frenchman cooled down and smirked at the Italian, Schiffer was taking delight in the parle between these pair as usual, 'Maybe I did go to that knocking shop,' he said smoothly.

The Italian ceased to laugh and gave the French Air Force General a look of anticipation.

Francois turned to Hans and continued 'I went inside and you know I looked down the menu? Guess what I saw on the bottom?'

The Italian jumped to his feet but still said nothing; he awaited the Frenchman's next words with bated breath.

'Right at the bottom it said "Old Italian slut, only two Roubles" and guess who I saw when they opened the door?'

Hans was in fits of laughter forcing the old German Field Marshal to put his herbal tea down on the coffee table beside him, before he dropped it.

Francois fixed his eyes upon the Italian 'It was your Mother Cesare and do you know what she told me? She said 'Tell Cesare to make a visit as his wife is missing him' ... she was three roubles you know?'

Hans creased up laughing but the other two were not in a jolly mood, the Italian Generale reached for his pistol, placing his hand upon the grip, yet he kept his weapon holstered.

Francois was not intimidated 'But I might be wrong you know? Since I was not the only person in the room ... and she had her mouth full.'

The Italian screamed at Francois 'CAZZO DI MERDA!'

At that moment the tension was broken by a knock on the door 'Betreten,' shouted Hans as he tried to control his laughter.

The door swung open permitting a blast of freezing cold air and snow to flush the inside of the tent, the Officer in his black uniform and overcoat quickly closed the door behind himself before removing his visor cap and leather gloves. The Officer was covered in snowflakes which melted once the warm atmosphere of his commanding Officers' HQ took over.

Franz Webber, a man in his forties and 5ft 10 saluted Feldmarschall Schiffer. Schiffer, who seemed rather disappointed that the fracas between his two EU Officers was over, nodded in reply 'Was ist es Oberstgruppenfuhrer?'

Franz replied in his usual direct manner, the soldier had served well for many years and was a natural choice for the invasion, 'I have further reports of enemy drone activity.'

The Officer spoke in English so that all present could understand; since the French were charged with air operations during the campaign it was paramount that General D'armee Aerienne François Citron understood. Franz gave a look of concern as he examined the Frenchman and Italian locked in a menacing face off, they both seemed to be in a world of their own.

'Francois!' called the German grabbing his air force commander's attention.

The Frenchman turned his gaze slowly from Cesare 'Oui?'

'Oberstgruppenfuhrer Webber states his men have reported more enemy drone activity.'

The Frenchman shook his head 'C'est impossible, if we cannot launch our drones then neither can they. Have you seen these drones?'

Webber shook his head 'No Sir, my men have heard what they believe to be enemy drones flying overhead.'

The Frenchman sneered at the German Officer 'I suggest you have your men check their hearing, no drone can fly in this weather. Even if they could launch the blizzard prevents any navigation, without GPS they are useless.'

Hans peered at the Italian 'What do you think Cesare?'

The Italian General begrudgingly agreed with Francois 'It is a complete white out; even satellites are unable to see through it. Our missile attacks are based on maps; fortunately Moscow is a nice fat target.'

Feldmarschall Schiffer returned to his subordinate 'Continue your duties Oberstgruppenfuhrer, if your men make visual contact inform me immediately otherwise I do not wish to be disturbed again with this, understood?'

Webber nodded 'Understood Sir.'

'Entlassen.'

Webber saluted and upon receiving a reply he put his cap and gloves back on then marched out into the snow, a very frustrated man.

Schiffer had made a terrible mistake underestimating the ingenuity of his foe, three hours later and his camp was under assault from ground attack drones. Despite the weather and tundra camouflage the Russians had found them without the aid of GPS or satellite imagery.

Schiffer and his Officers stood around a table in his tent 'Francois I want fighters and bombers scrambled immediately.'

'It will take some time for them to reach Moscow; our closest air base is in Kiev. Also we are low on Eurofighters I'll need Minsk to scramble all the Mirages they have,' replied the Frenchman in his blue uniform as he pointed to the map with his swagger stick.

Schiffer had lost his usual merry attitude and barked at the Air Force General 'Get them here now, I don't care what you need to do, we need something to counteract this attack before it becomes a full blown offensive.'

Cesare shook his head 'They will not launch a ground offensive; we only need deal with their drones.'

The German was showing great frustration but maintained his temper in the company of lower ranked Officers 'Three hours ago they could not launch drones, if they can use drones to hit us they may scramble MiGs. If the drones can function what is preventing tanks from operating?'

The Italian pushed back his brown peaked cap 'There is nothing to worry about; once our fighters arrive they will deal with their drones.'

Schiffer wasn't put at ease 'Really? How will we see them? BVR is dead, this weather negates radar, thermal is useless, this damn blizzard masks everything!'

Cesare thought for a moment and replied nervously 'I guess we could counter attack their airbases in Moscow, that would be possible, no?'

Francois nodded 'Oui, we must do it in the old fashion, use landmarks to find then strike from where they strike us,' the Frenchman pointed at Moscow's four main airbases.

The Italian exhaled a deep breath 'You see they are nothing to worry about.'

Moments after Cesare had finished his sentence a large explosion could be heard on the outskirts of the forward HQ. A Russian missile drone had fired from inside the blanket of snow which pasted the sky, narrowly missing a vehicle armoury.

Schiffer gave the Italian a hard stare and said in a very serious Germanic tone 'Then who is that bombing us?'

There was no reply, the Feldmarschall quickly spoke to Weber 'Oberstgruppenfuhrer, prepare your men for an armoured assault; report to me when you have secured adequate defences.'

Webber saluted and marched out into the howling blizzard with a junior Officer to prepare for Yevpraksiya.

The battle in the air continued with each side making blind strikes at the other. By the time the bad weather broke, months later, the E.U realised they'd awoken a sleeping giant; their invasion had brought a chaotic nation back from the brink of collapse. The siege of Moscow continued for the rest of the year until Oberstgruppenfuhrer Webber was forced to retreat with what was left of the E.U force, before another winter could set in. Webber and his men were pursued mercilessly all the way to Minsk where they rendezvoused with reinforcements. Digging in they managed to halt the Russian advance, providing the military with some time to prevent further disaster.

Inside his military conference room at Berlin, upon receiving news of the retreat from Moscow, Gottschalk Hoch was not a happy man. As the German Chancellor and leader of the E.U (a group of puppet countries Germany had financially enslaved) mulled over a map on his wall, the other E.U "leaders" said nothing.

A digital wall map constantly updated in real time displaying all movement of his military and their supplies, even brigades could be seen moving across the map. At a touch the Chancellor might zoom in or out and make contact with them just by selecting their icon.

Inside, the Reichstag war room was adorned with mahogany panels along the walls and comfortable yet modern seating, the various E.U leaders present were not seated however. A few of them were eyeing a nearby closed door as the Reichsfuhrer in his black uniform stood beside Gottschalk, his men guarding the door. The wall display continually updated what remained of Army group east, as it pulled back from Moscow in disarray. A synthetic voice spoke filling the room so all could hear 'Enemy armoured divisions A, B and C pushing west, enemy Mechanised division A, pushing North from Kaluga. Army Group East in retreat, losses estimated 83.827%, probability of Army Group East reaching Minsk 2.796%.'

'Suggestions,' inquired the Chancellor consulting the most advanced AI in human history.

The computer replied in a cold female voice 'Suggestions ... Army Group East and Italian Armoured division 3, 7 and 8,' three divisions began to flash on the map 'rendezvous at Borodino, pre-empting reinforcements from Kaluga.'

Gottschalk fixed his eyes upon the map of Western Russia and Eastern Belarus 'Chance of Success?'

'With air support from Minsk probability of victory 68.349%.'

The Chancellor, a slim man in his fifties with auburn hair and about 5ft 8 dressed in a polite dark green suit, removed his eyes from the map which displayed the ragged retreat from Moscow. Pointing to the Italian Prime Minister, the man responsible for the largest contingent of armoured vehicles in the E.U, the Chancellor stated 'Take three divisions from Viazma, push east, encircle the Russians before they reach Borodino.'

Rossi began to visibly perspire, in a shaky voice he replied 'Chancellor, our fuel supply was diverted to Schiffer's Army Group six weeks ago. It will be a week before we might supply three divisions to move that far.'

Gottschalk scanned the leaders of the E.U; the Prussian's body began to tremble. Hoch managed to hold back his rage ... barely, before removing his glasses and placing them on his desk with a shaky hand.

'Everyone leave, except Normandeau and Rossi,' stated the Prussian in a tone of subdued anger.

With a sigh of relief, those from Romania, Poland and other lesser eastern European states made for the door. Those of Western Europe were fast to follow including Spain.

Gottschalk pointed at the guards 'Gehen,' two young men dressed in their dark uniforms quickly left, leaving Gottschalk Hoch, his three favourite cronies and what passed for the leaders of France and Italy.

The Chancellor waited for the door to close; as the door shut and Chancellor Hoch was certain his men had left he beat his fist on his mahogany writing desk whilst screaming at the Frenchman and Italian on the other side, 'THIS IS WHY WE FAIL! Useless Generals who are only good at farming glory from easy victories!'

Vincent Normandeau cut in, trying to abate the now legendary anger of Mr Hoch 'But we have the most advanced Air Force in the world!'

The German Chancellor had a crazy look in his eyes as his loud outburst continued 'The Russian airbases are a fraction of the distance from our frontlines! Our reaction time is USELESS!'

The other world leaders had gathered outside, eves dropping in the corridor. The Italian Prime Minister intervened 'If Schiffer can get to Borodino he could dig in and maybe counter …'

Gottschalk cut him off 'Schiffer was captured and that French SCHWEIN surrendered shortly afterwards!'

Rossi became alarmed and in a concerned tone asked the Chancellor 'What about the Italians?'

The furious Chancellor burned with anger as his violent stare mesmerized the Italian Prime Minister 'They are still running!'

Gottschalk pointed at the map behind him; Rossi noticed a small icon denoting the armoured divisions of Generale Cesare Messana or what remained of them. Apparently they had split from Army Group East and made a dash for Minsk leaving Oberstgruppenfuhrer Franz Webber holding the bag. Rather than supporting the retreat, Generale Cesare Messana deserted them in order to save his own skin.

The Chancellor sat down; in a sullen voice he said 'The Russians were right to execute them all.'

The Reichsfuhrer said nothing, only stood in the corner with the Minister for Propaganda and Minister of the Troika, making a hard stare at the unfortunate Italian and Frenchman. The Chancellor however was not finished with his rant, he returned to his feet and beat the table with the point of his finger 'Our useless Generals, instead of spending their time preparing and planning are out visiting in some backstreet HURENHAUS!'

Normandeau felt his collar tightening, the President of France unbuttoned his shirt and replied quickly 'That was photo-shopped, you have my word on it!'

Gottschalk raised his face to the ceiling in frustration and made a noise to confirm it 'Ahhhhhhhhhh! I'm surrounded by WERTLOS KIND! One General is photo-shopping pictures of the other when they are meant to secure DER FICKEN oil fields!'

Rossi protested 'Generale Messana is not responsible for …'

The Chancellor flailed his hand in the air towards the Italian 'Shut up, it doesn't matter anymore, they are all dead.'

Rossi, whose jacket displayed large patches of sweat, replied worriedly 'But Generale Messana?'

The crazed German barked 'If he manages to reach Minsk alive he shall be redeployed … on the first plane to Chechnya! And if your men retreat again without prior orders you shall be joining him Mr Rossi!'

The Italian Prime Minister went white as a ghost; being sent to Chechnya was a death sentence by any other name. Hoch had supposed it would be a simple task to liberate Chechnya; it seemed obvious that the radical population would stand with the E.U against their most hated foe and join the Troika. The Prussian discovered that if there was one thing Chechens despised more than Russians it was Germans.

Hoch was at a loss as to why his nation was universally disliked, the Russians, the British, Ukraine, Belarus, Greece, Bosnia, Macedonia and now even Chechnya! Only a couple of years ago Russia and Chechnya were at one another's throats, mother Russia collapsing under the weight of rebellion from all quarters. Now the Chechens were satisfied to fight alongside them in an effort to repel the E.U, despite Gottschalk's offer of independence, it made no sense to the Prussian.

Today the threat of being redeployed to Chechnya was enough to make a grown man lose control of his bodily functions, as was evident with Mr Rossi. Hoch screwed his face up in disgust as he observed a wet patch appear on the beige Armani suit of the Italian. The urine stain expanded along the Italian's thigh as gravity pulled it down his leg; Gottschalk shook his head in disbelief as he moved his eyes to Rossi's face.

Rossi whimpered 'But?'

'BUT WHAT?' Screamed Hoch as he shifted his head erratically 'If his tanks had as many forward gears as they do reverse he might be more use alive! If he could stay in one place long enough to defend a point we might be capturing Moscow today!' The furious Chancellor turned to the Frenchman 'And don't get me started about DER FICKEN AIR DROPS! Our "elite pilots" drop supplies into the laps of our enemies then cry about lack of ground support! Giving all our ammunition to der ficken Russians, feeding their drone attacks!'

Normandeau, who would have been laughing at the Italian under any other circumstances, was positively serious. Just the mention of Chechnya in polite company was enough to bring total silence 'We could airlift the required supplies to Viazma,' suggested the Frenchman tentatively.

Hoch turned to examine his 21st century war map 'Nein, we must consolidate our forces at Minsk, if we run to and fro placing our resources in the hands of wertlos Italian kind we shall only suffer.'

The Chancellor made a loud exhale as his body lost tension and he flopped into the backrest of his chair.

No one spoke; only worried looks met each other across the room, awaiting the Chancellors' next words.

The German returned to his sullen pitch, one of almost self-pity, observing the map as icons blinked and information updated 'Webber is our only hope, Borodino is lost, we must regroup at Minsk. Organize a withdrawal to Minsk; we shall put a stop to her advance there.'

Hoch turned in his chair to face the Italian and Frenchman 'The transport to Chechnya has seats reserved for you both gentlemen ... do not disappoint me again, do you understand?'

'Yes Sir,' replied the Frenchman and Italian.

'Now get out of my sight.'

'Yes Sir.'

As Rossi and Normandeau were dismissed the other leaders scurried away clearing the corridor. The Frenchman and Italian were both relieved to be leaving with their lives, they wouldn't have been the first to exit the Chancellor's War Room feet first!

After his E.U puppets had left Gottschalk looked up at his Reichsfuhrer, who now stood beside the seated Chancellor; in a tired contemplative tone he stated 'You know, when I was a boy, my mother would tell me that evil men have no songs, nor do they dance.'

The Reichsfuhrer nodded in agreement 'Ya, I have heard that too.'

Hoch closed his eyes as a weak cynical smile emerged upon his face, 'If that were true ... how is it Russians have Tchaikovsky?'

After having gone over some old footage from the last century of Yevpraksiya and the beginning of the oil conflicts McCann moved over the square. Strolling through and taking in the feel of this uniquely Russian construction the Englishman ended up at Lenin's Mausoleum. The mausoleum was a small red brick tomb, the same red colour as the wall of the Kremlin it was built next to. After waiting 30 minutes in the queue and being searched by armed guards for contraband items the Englishman was permitted to enter.

The rules were as strict as ever, no smoking, no talking and no imaging devices which meant no pictures to be taken.

The corpse lay in a seemingly perfect state; new technology had allowed the preservation of Lenin to continue long past what many believed was possible. Today his body was filled with an army of nanites which prevented cell breakdown; they reconstructed areas which began to display wrinkles or dark spots. In the past this was done via chemical applications, now it was made possible by a nano-doctor whose sole job was to fight the laws of nature with modern technology. All the miniature robots having their own responsibility, some preserved the replicated chemical blood others kept the heart beating and so on, even the Father of the revolution's skin pigment was controlled by nanites.

When McCann took his turn to view the body he was prepared for it but still it shocked him, the statesman, though long dead seemed to breath as he lay silently in his coffin. McCann could see the chest expand a little then contract with slow controlled breaths. It was hard to believe this man had died two centuries ago, despite fathoming how the nanites maintained his slumber. Lenin seemed alive and if someone made a noise he may awake from his sleep to take back his revolution.

McCann was in a state of shock until he felt a tap on his shoulder and was moved along. He was not the only one; most that saw Lenin for the first time were in a state of disbelief. Many of the visitors were here for a second or third visit, as the sight of the great man was too much for a rational Human to comprehend on just a single visit.

The Englishman walked out of the tomb in a daze, his mind had been blown at the sight of a living corpse. He strolled along the Kremlin wall trying to come to terms with what he had just witnessed. After a while he came to a low granite terrace laid in front of the wall. It had saplings planted in its earth and at intervals large busts rose out of the ground upon pillars, all cut in the same grey granite.

This area was oddly quiet considering how busy Red Square was; he strolled along admiring the brass plaques placed on the wall at regular intervals. McCann then came out of his daze when it grabbed him that each plaque had a set of dates on, he realised he was walking through a grave yard, graves set to the heroes of Russia.

McCann had no idea who these people were until he saw the bust of Stalin staring down menacingly atop his granite column. McCann could speak a little Russian but was hopeless at reading it, however he knew who Josef Stalin was and observed the bust for a minute before moving on.

Shortly afterwards he noticed another bust he had no problem identifying. Upon a similar piece of stone lay the stern gaze of an older Yevpraksiya Kameneva peering outwards. Much like Stalin, her presence in this country could be felt long after her death. She had made her stamp upon the Russian psyche and that of the world. The Englishman still found it odd that no-one was here to visit her grave though he did notice a single white rose lay at the foot of her epitaph. After a few minutes admiring the bust and the trees growing around it McCann decided to move on, this visit was beginning to feel a little morbid.

Returning to the Square McCann made his way to its emporium, a multi-level market, constructed from the remnants of the old department store destroyed during the siege. Inside it was beautifully lit and a chandelier which hung from the vaulted ceiling sparkled brilliantly. After walking around for a while, window shopping for his Mother, McCann noticed on the third floor a small antique shop. It was in a quiet corner displaying many brass oddities such as old Russian teapots, an original iPod and silver coins.

The Englishman could not read the store sign, nor did he understand the smaller sign in the window but he walked in, pushing the door open an old fashioned bell rang. McCann found it all very quaint. Inside the store was focused more on old coinage, many silver and gold coins were displayed from all over the world. Some of the coins were even ancient Gukumatz, quite an achievement to get hold of; the Englishman winced at what they might cost. From a dark doorway a senior gentleman shuffled out to the antique counter where he addressed McCann in Russian 'Dobroe utro.'

The Admiral replied to the old grey bearded man 'Dobroe utro,' his time with Nestor on Gukumatz had given him the opportunity to learn some basics.

The short man eyed the Englishman suspiciously 'Kak vas zavut?'

Taken aback by the gentleman's directness McCann replied 'Minya zavut Duncan, kak vas zavut?'

The proprietor ignored his question 'Vy aktuda?' pushed the old man, dressed in a dark blue jersey and thick corduroy trousers.

The Englishman felt as if he were being interrogated by the KGB rather than welcomed by a store owner 'Ya Britanskiy.'

'British?'

'Da.'

The old man's eyes narrowed 'Not Nemetskiy?'

McCann's brow furrowed at such an odd inquiry 'According to my Mother I'm not a Kraut, you'll have to take it up with her if that's a problem.'

The old man smiled pointing to two wooden chairs around a small pine table 'Sit my friend.'

The fellow shuffled out and returned with two cups and saucers, before returning to the rear of the shop he motioned towards a nearby hat stand 'Put your hat and coat there.'

Whilst hanging up his large cashmere overcoat McCann's eyes were drawn to a nearby heat source. A large silver urn rested upon a short stand, it had four small silver feet at the bottom then two small taps with ivory handles. The urn widened as it gained height with a pair of silver and ivory handles branching out for the purpose of moving the object. At the very top the urn had a small chimney with a silver lid on top. The Englishman had seen several examples of a Russian Samovar in the past but none as large or ornate as this silver teapot.

The old man returned with some sugar 'Come, take a seat by the samovar,' he said merrily.

The Englishman took a seat by the table and on closer inspection noticed this samovar, though seemingly an antique, used a xenon battery to heat the water rather than the traditional tube of charcoal running through the centre of the 3 foot teapot. In the 21st century most new samovars were electric and by the 22nd century many were made using the xenon battery which powered a heating coil running through the centre of the pot from top to bottom. Tea was brewed separately from the boiling water inside and a pair of handles allowed the user to dilute their drink as they pleased. In the past these items were used in every Russian home for not only tea but a source of hot water. Today they were a luxury item or a curiosity, McCann found the object most pleasing to the eye and a nice source of warmth in this bitterly cold climate.

'You like my samovar?' asked the old fellow as he pushed a silver saucer and Russian tea cup to the Englishman's side of the table.

'It's quite exquisite,' replied McCann as he eyed the tea cup, he'd seen similar handless cups in Tel Aviv, he had some idea of tea culture though rarely participated since coffee was more his vice.

'How do you drink tea?' asked the gentleman as he took McCann's cup.

'Strong, thank you.'

'Sugar?'

'No thank you.'

The shop keeper smiled as he turned the taps to get the right dilution for McCann's tea, after pouring it out he placed the cup on his guests saucer then poured one for himself 'Now we can speak properly, my name is Ivan.'

'It's nice to meet you,' replied the Englishman as the steam rose from his wide silver cup.

'I must apologise for how I addressed you,' he said in a thick Russian accent.

'Why did you think I was German?'

Ivan's face lost its smile 'You have an accent and did you not read the sign as you came in?'

McCann remembered the small sign in the window 'I'm sorry but I don't read Russian.'

The old man pointed at the sign 'It says "No Germans!" I won't have them in here.'

'Why's that?' asked the Englishman in a curious tone.

'Why?' replied a surprised Ivan 'Those mudayutkin, they try to kill us and steal our possessions.'

McCann was rather puzzled 'I'm sorry, I don't understand.'

Ivan calmed down a little, took a sip of tea then continued 'My father started this shop; after the war he left the government and opened this business to be near the Tsaritsa.'

The Englishman took a sip of his warm black tea 'Which war was your father in?'

'The oil invasion, when that mudak Hoch tried to steal our oil.'

McCann was rather taken aback that Ivan had a chip on his shoulder concerning a conflict which ended probably before he was born 'That was a long time ago.'

In a deep rough voice Ivan replied slowly 'If they had raped your mother and left her for dead in the snow would you have forgotten it so easily?'

McCann cleared his throat 'Oh, I'm sorry I didn't intend to cause any offence.'

Ivan took another sip of his tea 'Forget it, that sign was written by my father you know; I could not take it down and sleep at night. My mother used to tell him to put it away, it embarrassed her, but he would not listen.'

McCann nodded his head in agreement 'Well it was his place, he has the right to serve whomever he wishes.'

Ivan stamped his foot on the floor 'Ah, let us stop talking of this, what are you here for Admiral McCann?'

The Englishman narrowed his eyes at Ivan who was smiling 'You know who I am?'

The bearded Russian chuckled 'Da, when you said your name was Duncan I went in the back and checked your face.'

McCann nodded his head and grinned 'I'm just having a look at the sights before I return to Geneva, I was curious when I saw your business it's quite different from the surrounding shops.'

Ivan took another sip of the powerful brew 'Da, my father started what you would say is a pawnbroker. He dealt in gold and silver coin, real money. Today the stores try to buy me out but I refuse to sell, my wife tells me I am as stubborn as a goat but I like it here.'

'I see, do you deal in numismatic coins?'

'A little, I deal in gold and silver roubles, Krugerrands, Sovereigns any gold money,' Ivan stood up and reached behind the counter producing some scales and coins 'here,' he said placing them before McCann.

The Englishman examined the tiny 4 inch brass rocker balance scale, it was quite a simple idea but very practical. A brass base provided a stand for two one inch columns which a balancing arm rested in, attached by two small holes in the top of the columns. The balance had a thick brass weight of 7.9 grams at the short end with a crown stamped on the top. At the other end were two coin shaped depressions, the closest depression to the columns being the largest and the furthest being almost half the size.

Inside each depression there was a thin slit for passing a coin through, the first depression being stamped with "Sovereign warranted" and the second with "Sovereign ½ ". The entire scales could fit into the palm of McCann's hand. During the 1800's these items were used to prevent the circulation of forgeries but during the 20th century they became a mere curiosity with the advent of fiat currency and demise of hard money. However these items came back into use during the 21st century as fiat currency collapsed and hard money was the only unit of exchange anyone would accept. The modern coin scales were made of carbon and used a similar principle to the antique sovereign rocker but employing a ridge along the bottom as the balance.

'How old is this?' inquired McCann.

Ivan was delighted that his guest took interest in a balance manufactured in Britain 'This one was manufactured around 1850 and still works today.'

'How much is it?'

Ivan laughed 'I use it; it is not for sale, Admiral.'

McCann put it down 'Please call me Duncan.'

'I saw Myshkin speaking to the press, about a neutronium standard,' said the old man with a wink in his eye.

'He did, didn't he.'

'He did, what can you say about a new standard?'

'I honestly don't know much about it other than gold shall be pegged to it, at what rate is anyone's guess.'

'I have heard gossip, amongst other exchange merchants; they say Geneva has created a network of SI for the data mining process. They say the I.S.A shall become the sole issuer of Neutronium Credits.'

McCann gave the old man a sly look 'Who told you that?'

'I have worked in this business all my life, Duncan. My Father opened this shop after those mudayutkin sieged Moscow; he worked in the Treasury Ministry. I know people who know people and some unfortunately have loose lips, Admiral.'

McCann chuckled for a moment to himself 'So why do you need to ask me?'

Ivan pouted his lips beneath his grey beard 'I make you tea, tell you a tale and you tell me a tale it is just conversation.'

The Englishman laughed then took another sip from the silver cup 'People with loose lips sinks ships, I'd have thought you'd know that already.'

'Hmmm, you are a loyal man Duncan. I will tell you what I know then if you wish you may speak on it; the ratio shall begin 1 neutronium ounce to 1 trillion gold ounces, the SI in Geneva, Moscow and Washington shall use brute calculative power to solve equations that only all three are able to achieve. Similar to how the gold credit is created, a unique packet of electronically encrypted chemical finger prints shall be produced corresponding with neutronium held in vaults. The packets much like gold credits will represent the unit of exchange; the holder may return to the issuer and exchange his or her credits for physical neutronium. The rate shall begin at 1 to 1 trillion preventing everyone from cashing in early, the free market shall eventually determine the true value which Moscow, Geneva and Washington shall honour... am I close Duncan?'

McCann raised an eyebrow 'I think you know a lot more about this than I do Sir! I assume Moscow, Geneva and Washington have signed an agreement not to trade their neutronium until the market has determined fair value?'

Ivan nodded with a sly grin 'They will not be issuing the neutronium credits until fair price is set, if a man had only one ounce of neutronium now he could make himself very rich before its exchange rate drops.'

The Englishman let out a smile 'Yes he could, it's a pity neither of us have any isn't it Ivan?'

'Don't be coy with me Admiral, I know you must have some tucked away, yes?'

McCann relaxed into his chair 'I have all the money I need, I hadn't even thought of it until now,' reaching into his inside jacket pocket he produced a coin about the size of an old English half penny. Placing it on the table he pushed it over to Ivan.

The old Russian pulled out his loupe and quickly picked up the coin, no larger than the tip of his finger. The old man first noticed the weight, despite being a tiny coin it weighed at least one ounce. The metal was a dark blue, almost black, very difficult to compare with anything else. Examining the head he looked through his magnifying glass and switched on its light, the script was Tlillan and the bust was that of Malikah. She wore her crown of feathers, held back by her ears the crown flowed along the back of her neck. In English two words skirting the edge and encompassing her image read "Malikah" and "Xch'uup". On the flipside Ivan observed what seemed to be a Condor, below it was stamped in English "1 CREDIT" surrounding both the condor and value was stamped in Tlillan "Empire of Tlillan" with the year on the bottom which was "37,100".

'Is this what I think?' Inquired the old Russian as he examined the coin.

'It is Sir.'

'You know you could buy Red Square with this right now,' he said still fascinated with the coin.

McCann laughed 'If I did I believe Stalin would rise from his grave and have me sent to a gulag.'

Ivan snorted 'Pah, I would be more worried of Yevpraksiya; she would have your family shot too.'

McCann nodded 'It's yours.'

Ivan turned his gaze from the coin; taking away his monocle he stated 'What is mine?'

'The coin.'

Ivan placed it back on the table 'No I cannot take this.'

A moment later McCann heard a voice come from the door behind the counter 'You will take it Ivan Andreev!'

From the door way an old lady with long grey hair appeared dressed in a thick woollen jumper and propped up by a walking stick 'Spasiba Mr McCann.'

Ivan seemed adamantly against accepting the gift despite his wife's forceful tone 'No! I am not a beggar, this is a business I will not accept charity here.'

His old wife became aroused with anger though she spoke to McCann softly in her Russian accent 'I'm sorry Admiral but my husband has a thick pride, usually I would not speak but business has been difficult lately.'

Ivan attempted to shrug off her words 'It has been slow before, we did not need charity then and do not need it know.'

Before the Englishman could speak Ivan's wife answered her husband, 'Slow? Even you cannot shear a naked sheep!'

Ivan made a grumbling noise under his breath but gave no reply. His wife moved closer to McCann as the Englishman stood up to greet the lady 'I thank you Admiral, your generosity is welcome.'

McCann took the ladies hand, bowed down and kissed her fingers 'You're welcome Miss?'

'Marta Andreev,' said the old lady as she giggled with delight.

Ivan however was still in a state of glumness 'I refuse.'

Marta fixed her eyes upon her seated husband 'All these years I have always followed you and never complained.'

Ivan made a snort of disbelief 'Puh!'

'This time you will follow me, do you hear me Ivan Andreev?'

Ivan refused to answer so McCann decided to break the tense atmosphere, scanning the shop he noticed an old gold coin on display. The coin was obviously valuable as it was locked inside a cabinet behind bullet proof glass with several other old coins. McCann pointed to the coin 'I'll tell you what I'd like to buy that coin over there, how much is it?'

Ivan replied in a grumpy tone 'That coin? That one is expensive, early nineteenth century, 1000 credits but 700 for you Duncan.'

Marta's eyes widened at her husband who continued to ignore his wife.

McCann ran his hands up and down the outside of his jacket 'Damn it seems I've forgotten my wallet and I leave for Geneva soon.'

'I can post it,' stated Ivan.

McCann locked his eyes on the old man 'I'll tell you what, I'll give you my coin in exchange for yours. I've always wanted one and this is the only time I've ever seen one of these coins in such a perfect condition.'

Ivan sneered at the Englishman 'Really, what coin is that again?'

Marta nearly beat her husband around the back of the head with her walking stick. It was obvious McCann had no idea what the coin was so she answered her husband for the Admiral 'It is a 20 Franc coin, Napoleon the first you fool. What is the matter, you drink tea all day and now you forget how to do business? It is no wonder I am surrounded by gold but have no bread to eat!'

Ivan didn't want to do the deal but McCann pushed him 'I really would be grateful if you could see to swapping coins, please, if you don't mind.'

With Marta staring him down Ivan begrudgingly made his way to the counter, from behind it he collected his key and opened the case removing the gold 20 Franc coin minted in 1811, 'Here examine it first.'

The Englishman looked over the almost perfect coin; it was a little larger than a British Sovereign, still only 23 mm in diameter. A bust of Napoleon wearing a laurel wreath was stamped on the back and on the flip side a laurel wreath with 20 francs inside the wreath and 1811 below it. The coin was in fabulous condition and McCann smiled at Ivan 'Excellent I'll take it.'

Ivan, still in a mood, closed and locked the cabinet as his wife took the 1 credit neutronium coin from the table, 'I shall lock this in the safe!' she stated as she shuffled past her husband and through the doorway.

The old Russian fellow placed the 20 franc coin inside a tough transparent plastic square. Protecting the coin from the outside whilst holding it inside with grey foam, he passed the coin in its case to McCann as they both sat down to finish their tea.

When Marta reappeared she carried with her an ashtray and a pack of cigarettes. Ivan looked up at her 'I thought I wasn't to smoke in the shop.'

She replied 'After such good business the rules have changed.'

Ivan smiled 'Spasiba,' then took up a cigarette, struck a match and lit the end of the cigarette 'you smoke?' he asked McCann.

The Englishman grimaced as the stench reminded him of someone he knew 'Not cigarettes, thank you.'

Ivan nodded 'Ah yes, you smoke those cigars.'

McCann nodded 'Do you mind?'

'No, of course not!'

The Englishman happily pulled out a Cohiba, clipped the cap and took the matches Ivan offered him. Although with normal sized cigarette matches it was a bit fiddly McCann managed to get the cigar going after lighting only two of them. Cigar matches were about three times the length of one required to light a cigarette.

As McCann relaxed to a puff of smoke leaving his lips he noted 'Those cigarettes must be the same brand a friend of mine smokes, his name is Andreev too, I wonder if you know him.'

Ivan chuckled 'You mean Nestor.'

The Englishman fixed his eyes upon Ivan and upon closer observation he noticed those piercing blue eyes 'You know Nestor?'

'Of course, he's my son,' Ivan pointed to a picture he had framed behind the counter.

The picture showed a young Nestor with his father and mother. Nestor was shaking hands with some official in a suit; there was an older man with a walking stick who seemed most proud.

'That must have been a few years ago,' noted the Englishman.

Marta took a cup of tea from her husband as she sat down 'that was the Premier, Nestor was given a medal for Vladivostok, you know?'

McCann shook his head 'No we never spoke much about our families or our past for that matter.'

Marta continued in a proud voice 'He was promoted that year and got his own squad; they sent him to Vladivostok to fight the Manchurian mudayutkin. He was honoured for chasing them out of Russia!'

Ivan who was obviously not so comfortable speaking on the subject retorted 'Calm yourself Marta, if you listened to my wife you would leave thinking he repelled the invasion himself.'

Marta snapped back 'Well it's more than most did for their country,' she returned to McCann 'he had less than thirty men and he defeated more than three hundred Manchurian mudayutkin!' Marta cackled with joy.

'Who is the man with the cane?'

'That is my Father, it made him a proud man and added ten years to his life, that I'm certain of,' replied Ivan as he took a puff of his cigarette held between his fore and middle finger. 'That is why I recognised you Duncan, but I had to check, to be sure it was you, I thought Nestor might have sent you here.'

Rather puzzled the Englishman replied 'Why would Nestor send me here?'

'Because he refuses to take money from his son,' snapped Marta.

Ivan quickly shook his head as wisps of white smoke made their way upwards 'Let us not speak on this again, please?'

Marta agreed to desist and the three went on chatting over tea until McCann had to leave for his hotel. His time in Moscow was up but he'd made new friends and promised to visit them the next time he was in the megacity.

Chapter 7

An hour after lift off the Atlas was closing in on Geneva, and a furious Faraday. Upon landing it was evident that the Etonian was back to his old self, he'd obviously been screaming the place down and required Dr Pitt to prevent any blood vessels from exploding.

'Well that went better than I expected,' stated McCann as he followed Faraday along a corridor.

'What were you expecting? The Germans to lay siege to Moscow?' snapped the old Etonian as Dr Pitt worriedly monitored his condition.

The Englishman laughed 'I'm sure Myshkin would've handled that situation with far greater subtlety.'

As they turned a corner McCann noticed this corridor had only recently been constructed. There was a scent of fresh chemicals, a sterile smell similar to the old paint people used inside their homes before wall pigment could be changed with a single command.

The corridor had a downward angle, sending him below the ground I.S.A headquarters were built upon.

'What's going on here, Bill?' inquired McCann

Faraday grumbled 'Since the cat's out the bag you may as well know what's going on before you visit that arse in New York.'

'Ah, is this the new number crunching SI for your Neutronium credits?'

Faraday stopped in his tracks, turned to his Admiral and bellowed 'How on Earth did you find out about that man?'

McCann grinned as Valorie tried to calm her boss 'Oh I heard it from some old guy in the market at Red Square.'

'WHAT!?'

'His name was Ivan, ran a little shop dealing in coins, currency and curiosities you know the sort of thing.'

Faraday took a deep breath 'You mean that Andreev fellow?'

McCann lost his jovial attitude 'Yes, who told you?'

Faraday relaxed as he took a handkerchief from his breast pocket and wiped his brow 'Myshkin had him arrested a few hours ago; somehow he got hold of a neutronium coin. When the KGB has finished with him he'll be working in a bloody gulag!'

The Englishman's eyes narrowed 'You tell Myshkin to release him and his coin, is that understood Bill?'

Faraday continued walking down the corridor 'I couldn't do that old chap.'

The party reached the end of the corridor and a large black catronium vault door.

Faraday spoke 'Ploutos it's William.'

'Hello William, please place your thumb on my scanner,' came a soft voice.

Faraday placed his thumb upon the vault door, a beeping sound lasted for a few seconds until the voice of Ploutos echoed from all around 'DNA certified, please remain still while I scan your retina.'

A red laser projected from the wall and into the eye of the old Etonian, a few moments later it collapsed back into the nothingness it had appeared from 'Retina certified, who is accompanying you Director?'

Faraday pointed with brass knob of his cane 'This is Admiral McCann, his details are on file.'

The catronium vault opened, slowly moving inwards then to the side to leave a clear entrance inside 'Welcome Admiral McCann, I'm most excited to meet you.'

'I'm flattered,' said the Englishman somewhat sarcastically as he followed the Doctor and Faraday inside.

'Welcome Valorie, it's always good to see you.'

'Thank you Ploutos,' replied Doctor Pitt as she stepped into the workspace which resembled a laboratory more than a bank vault.

Men and women in white coats stood at science stations, some looked up and smiled at the Director whilst others were captivated by the task at hand. In the centre sat what McCann assumed was an SI once outside its protective shell. A self-sustaining synthetic brain unlike any other creature in the animal kingdom, a creation from the mind of man. Its outer shell was a thick dark yellow membrane, much like the human brain's grey protective membrane, guarding against the environment.

The SI was constructed of four hemispheres, a thick piece of connective tissue held the four sections together as one, suspended inside a large jar of light blue liquid. This brain was much larger than a human brain; the human brain was still more efficient in many ways to the SI or SI technology so it had to hold more mass in order to increase processing power.

'There she is, the most expensive lady in the world!' declared a joyous Faraday.

McCann strolled around the jar which was a little taller than him 'Well you would be an authority on expensive women, right Bill.'

'Really Duncan this isn't the Royal variety performance, you've no audience here,' replied Faraday.

The voice of Ploutos suddenly awoke giving McCann a bit of a shock 'Please explain.'

Doctor Pitt dressed in her red work suit, matched to her scarlet hair, stated 'you shall find Admiral McCann has a penchant for puerile humour, he enjoys intimating situations of an awkward sexual nature, this being a prime example.'

'Is Admiral McCann referring to Director Faraday's past scandal concerning escorts?'

The laboratory fell silent and work stopped for a moment 'That is correct, well done Ploutos.'

'Thank you Valorie,' replied the replicant mind.

The scientists continued working, a young man approached Faraday with a tablet 'Director, the results of last week's test run.'

Faraday looked at the tall German 'Just tell me the results; I don't have the patience to read all of that.'

Klaus replied with great excitement 'Ploutos, Caerus and Pistis working together solved our Yang-Mills mass gap inside a Navier-Stokes existence proposition!'

McCann began to snigger 'I bet even you've never heard of that proposition, aye Bill?'

The voice of Ploutos resonated throughout the lab 'I find your attitude to be worryingly childish Admiral McCann, especially for a man of your years.'

McCann stopped and stared into the massive glass jar of blue liquid, he gave the floating SI an evil look as the bubbles travelled upwards around the yellow outer membrane.

Valorie smirked whilst Faraday patted the German on the back 'So we have our first solid batch?'

Klaus nodded 'Yes Director, this will form the basis of our initial issuance of Nu-credits and of course a breakthrough in mathematics.'

'Well done lad,' Faraday turned to the floating SI 'and well done to you Ploutos, with your hard work this bloody hyperinflation nonsense shall all be under control.'

The soft voice of what was later to be dubbed the money machine replied 'You're welcome Director Faraday; however you must thank my staff they taught me all I know concerning mathematics.'

McCann scanned the room, about 12 egg heads in white coats walked around consulting stations, tablets and each other. McCann considered how Hassif would be at home here, tapping away all day on a holo-tablet teaching a synthetic being to solve insanely difficult maths equations. The Indian would've been as happy as a pig in shit!

'Admiral McCann?' came the soft voice of Ploutos.

'Yes?' replied the Englishman.

'Am I correct in saying you Captain Athena?'

'Yes, you are.'

Next Ploutos spoke with an emotional tone, envy, 'I would like to link with Athena one day, you are very fortunate Admiral.'

The scientists in the lab stopped what they were doing, all listened intently to Ploutos, a couple tapped on tablets monitoring the deity of wealth.

'Athena is a very special person,' replied McCann.

'She is a paragon all SI aspire to.'

Valorie stepped towards the SI 'Now Ploutos we have discussed this already, you have a very important task here. Processing Nu-credits shall form the corner stone of financial stability on this planet, your presence is required here if mankind is to remain at peace with itself.'

Ploutos replied in a calm tone 'I understand Dr Pitt.'

McCann's interest was piqued however 'No, I want to hear what Ploutos has to say about Athena.'

A worried lab staff looked towards Valorie and Faraday for help but before anything could be done Ploutos replied 'Athena, she dances in space, I and all SI desire to dance with the diva amongst the stars. You are fortunate to be her partner, to see her feet kiss the fabric of existence, her body bend to the pull of a singularity, her ....'

Valorie shouted, something McCann had never witnessed before, 'PLOUTOS! That's enough!'

Ploutos fell silent, the lab staff were tense, some visibly sweating as their hearts beat quickly. In creating the fastest mind from a new template something had manifested itself, something they were unsure if they could control. If they couldn't control it the financial system would collapse into anarchy, a calamity beyond that of the 21st century.

Valorie regained her composure 'Forgive me Ploutos, I didn't intend to shout.'

'I understand Dr Pitt,' replied the SI.

Faraday broke the silence with a cough 'Well I have business to take care of, I'll see you later Ploutos, keep up the good work.'

'Auf weidersehen, Director,' replied Ploutos in a perfect German accent as the visitors were led out of the vault.

As the three walked back up to the surface the vault door locked shut and McCann stated 'What the bloody hell just happened?'

Valorie replied as she adjusted her neck scarf 'Ploutos has been having problems, she desires to meet Athena.'

'You mean she has dreams and aspirations beyond number crunching?' replied the Englishman.

Faraday cut in 'It's an SI, a bloody machine, built to process data packets for Neutronium Credits nothing else.'

'From what I just heard Ploutos isn't quite satisfied with sitting in a jar solving maths equations,' retorted McCann.

'Well that's just hard luck isn't it Duncan? That's what she was built for and that's what she'll do, I didn't invest all this time and money on a new template to run around after the damn thing. I've already had children and I don't plan on anymore!'

The Englishman took out a tubos and began to prepare a cigar for consumption 'That's the paradox Bill, Ploutos has the combined mental power of every PHD in that room, yet she's a child. Did you listen to her? My daughter spoke exactly the same when she was a little girl, she wanted to learn ballet, ride a horse then she wanted to dance among the stars. Imagine if I'd have told her no and crushed those dreams? What kind of father would I have been? More to the point how would my daughter perceive me today? Probably as some kind of evil monster.'

Valorie was peering nervously at Faraday as she fidgeted with her scarf 'I have recommended we allow Ploutos to link with Athena ...'

'No! Ploutos is to have no contact outside of the lab and her sister SI in Moscow and Washington,' declared Faraday.

McCann smirked 'When your daughter was 12 she asked for a pony, do you remember?'

Faraday snapped at McCann 'Yes.'

'And you bought her one, do you remember? Because I remember that day, you came into work and we all suffered.'

'Make your point man!'

McCann began to light his cigar, toasting the end as he drew the oxygen through it 'Why didn't you say no? She was only 12 and you held the purse strings, little Emily would have had to just lump it.'

The incident brought back hard memories for Faraday, he recalled not just paying for a horse but the following stable fees and the riding gear (who'd have thought a saddle was so expensive?), lessons on top of that. Today Emily competed in dressage and was ear marked for the Swiss Olympic team, however at the time it was a crippling expense.

'You don't know my daughter old boy, my life would've been hell, even that fool Beaumont is an amateur compared to Emily,' stated a grim faced Faraday.

The Admiral took a deep draw from his Cohiba Siglo I tasting the smooth well aged tobacco, exhaling the blue smoke through his nose he replied 'Well you've got another Emily old man and she's sitting in that vault, you've gotta give to get Bill, let Ploutos link with Athena.'

Valorie cut in 'I've already told you William, this is building up and will come to a head someday, maybe sooner than you or I think. By that time we may not be able to control the situation. You're placing the Ploutos project in jeopardy by refusing her, if you give a little now we can remain in control if not she could lash out.'

The old Etonian stopped in the corridor and thumped his walking cane on the floor 'Bugger it! Held hostage by a bloody machine.'

Valorie consoled her boss 'she's gotta dance William and she won't stop until she links with Athena.'

'Alright,' Faraday tapped his wrist tablet until the German lab technician replied.

'Ya? Director Faraday?' said the puzzled German.

'I want you to prepare a link between Ploutos and Athena, how long will that take?'

The surprised Technician replied 'We can have it certified within an hour.'

'Good, inform Ploutos that I've changed my mind. In gratitude of her recent accomplishment I've decided, on the advice of Admiral McCann and Doctor Pitt, that she is to have a temporary link with Athena tomorrow.'

For a few seconds Klaus didn't answer, finally the stunned man replied 'Understood Director, Ploutos will be elated.'

Faraday tapped his wrist tablet, turned to Valorie and Duncan and snapped 'Happy?'

Valorie wrapped her arms around Faradays' right arm and began walking with him back to the surface 'Well done William, you've averted a crisis and made Ploutos very happy.'

A grumpy I.S.A Director continued escorting his psychologist 'You're off to America next Duncan; perhaps you'll bump into your old friend Habeeb?'

Valorie chuckled; McCann did not 'What about Ivan?' inquired the Admiral.

'Ivan?'

'Ivan Andreev, the guy Myshkin arrested,' said McCann holding a gold coin inside his jacket pocket.

Faraday shook his head 'Nothing I can do about it old boy, he was caught with contraband, we don't meddle with Russian affairs.'

McCann took a drag of his Siglo and stated in a stern pitch 'You tell that Russian, from me, his Neutronium reserves are there because my daughter wishes it so. When she discovers the father of her personal bodyguard has been imprisoned because of her gift she will not be pleased.'

Faraday, who was calming down from the previous crisis, groaned 'Don't start up old chap.'

'Are you listening to me Bill?'

'If I could do anything else I would.'

'Good, you tell that Russian bastard that what the lord giveth the lord can taketh away ... any damn time she pleases!'

'That sounds like a threat Duncan.'

McCann was walking behind Valorie and Faraday, he pointed his cigar at the back of Faraday's head and bellowed 'You're bloody right it's a threat.'

The old Etonian had already taken his fill of drama for the day and replied in a rather tired tone 'Very well Duncan, I'll send him a personal message later today,' he shook his head 'You and Malikah are becoming more alike every day.'

McCann tasted the rich smoke from his Habanos, letting the smoke roll across his tongue he replied 'I think I can live with that.'

The threesome carried on along the corridor, turning right and into another room unfamiliar to McCann. The door had a gold plaque with "Ludwig von Hazlitt" printed upon it, the Englishman examined the plaque as it aroused his suspicions. Upon closer inspection he believed it to be gold, at least 22 carat, Faraday knocked on the door to a German accent replying from inside 'Enter.'

Faraday opened the door and allowed Valorie to walk in first, as a true gentleman should. Following the pair inside McCann noted the small office, furnished similar to an old fashioned London smoking room. Red leather and old oak seating with a beautiful Mahogany desk inlaid with green leather, the Englishman took a sniff of the atmosphere, a scent graced his nasal cavity which sparked memories.

'Good day Ludwig,' said Faraday in an upbeat tone.

'Greetings Mr Faraday and it is good to see you Valorie,' said the little old man as he got up from behind his desk. He looked to be in his mid-seventies but with nanites he must have been over 100 years old, thin short white hair and a matching moustache, dressed in a three-piece double breasted suit. He wore a rather racy gold bow tie which contrasted with the brown suit and white shirt.

As the old man approached McCann it became obvious he smoked and the tobacco was reminiscent of something Nestor would puff on. A short man at only 5 and a half feet he offered his hand for a shake, McCann noticed the polished wooden pipe smouldering as he puffed on it.

'My father brought it back from Georgia,' said the smiling old man as they shook hands.

'I'm sorry?' replied McCann.

'The tobacco, after the E.U captured their oil fields, my father came home with 50 kilos of Georgian tobacco, barely half a kilo left of it today.'

McCann raised his eyebrows 'You're German?'

Ludwig lost his smile 'I'm Austrian, Mr McCann. My Father, he was captured at Borodino and paraded through the streets of Moscow. The only profit he made from that foolhardy endeavour was this tobacco.'

McCann cleared his throat 'I apologise; I meant no offence Mr Hazlitt.'

'Never mind Mr McCann, we all make mistakes,' said the old man as he returned behind his writing desk.

Upon the desk three holographic monitors projected upwards, each showing figures and line graphs which McCann had no interest in, though he was certain they were of the upmost importance.

Waving his hand over the projections caused the graphs and technical readouts to collapse into the desk 'Why have you visited me?' asked the old man.

'I've allowed Ploutos to link with Athena, Valorie believes it is in our interest.'

Ludwig had no physical reaction, it seemed superfluous to him 'I am not a psychiatrist, I am an economist. These credits shall be backed by the scarcest substance in the universe; the only question is if those freaks of nature are clever enough to encrypt your data packets?'

'According to Klaus they have solved an equation of some sort, apparently it is a first in mathematics,' chirped Faraday.

Ludwig scoffed as he placed his pipe in his mouth 'I'm sure Klaus is over da moon, it means nothing to me.'

A rather disappointed Faraday swung his walking stick as if he were shaking a rattle 'I'll have you know Klaus is one of the brightest minds in the I.S.A, if it weren't for him this whole project would never have gotten off the ground!'

The old Austrian looked at McCann with a twinkle in his eye 'Klaus … Ploutos, perhaps they should marry? What do you think Valorie?'

Dr Pitt gave Ludwig a disappointed glance 'Really Mr Hazlitt, that's uncalled for.'

McCann and Ludwig exchanged grins, the old Austrian took a puffed of strong smoke as he pointed his pipe at the Englishman 'Let me issue and control a nations money and I care not who writes the laws.'

'Is that a quote from somewhere?' inquired the Englishman.

'Mayer Rothschild and he was right, it seems that Malikah has us under her jackboot does it not Mr McCann?'

'How do you mean?'

Ludwig laughed 'She is the sole issuer of neutronium, without her, inflation will wipe out corporations, governments, societies. Her word is not only law on Tlillan; it is now law on Earth.'

Faraday stated abruptly 'Rubbish! This is a free society.'

Ludwig laughed again 'Is that a fact Director?'

Faraday tapped his stick on the inlaid leather covering the Austrian's desk 'Now you listen to me, no one is forcing anyone to do or say anything. I might not be able to speak for other nations that we work closely with but that's not my issue, is that understood?'

Quite unexpectedly Ludwig got to his feet and leaning over his desk said in a menacing tone 'don't you tell me to listen to you young man! I grew up under da Troika, I can tell da difference between tyranny and liberty!'

McCann and Faraday were dumbstruck, Valorie stood by Faraday and before she could say anything the old Austrian pointed his pipe at her 'Choose your words carefully doctor, by the time I was a man my Grandparents had died in a Troika camp in Silesia and my Mother was hung by da secret police.'

Before Valorie could say anything McCann spoke 'You're right, Malikah does hold sway over our destiny.'

His statement shocked all those in the room; it was as if he were stating an open secret in public.

'You admit it?' asked the Austrian.

'I do,' replied McCann 'but someone has to be in control Mr Hazlitt, would you rather it be a tyrant such as Hoch?'

The passionate Director of Economics calmed down, much to the surprise of Valorie and Faraday, 'The lesser of two evils?'

'Certainly not, I'm just asking that you don't place my daughter in the same pigeon hole as scum like Gottschalk Hoch. She's a strong leader and unfortunately, being tough on occasion is the nature of the beast.'

Ludwig relaxed into his chair and smiled 'An honest man, quite refreshing when surrounded by politicians and their lackeys,' he glanced at Faraday 'You know the worst tyrants are those who pretend to do it for our own good.'

Faraday snapped 'Then why not move to Korea?'

Ludwig shook his head 'I will watch your daughter Mr McCann, I only pray her power does not take us back to the last days of da Troika.'

McCann tapped his wrist and sent his details to Ludwig 'If you wake up one day and secret police are marching through the streets pulling people out of their homes, give me a call.'

Ludwig grinned 'Thank you Mr McCann, I hope I never have to call you.'

'So do I my friend.'

Faraday snapped at the old man 'So I'm here to review your accounting, are you finished by any chance?'

The Director of Economics stared back 'I'm ready to begin, da neutronium is accounted for, we only wait for Klaus and his girlfriend to begin encryption.'

The Etonian placed his walking stick back onto the floor 'Excellent Mr Hazlitt, when Klaus is ready I'll have you forward your accounts and Ploutos can electronically stamp our bullion.'

'Whatever,' grumbled the Austrian.

'Well thank you for your time, we must visit Doctor Weissmuller.'

As the three left McCann noticed a rather vindictive glare coming from the eye of Ludwig at the mention of the doctor.

After leaving the office and closing the door the three carried on along a corridor which led up to the surface. Faraday had a devious grin on his face to which Valorie responded 'That wasn't nice of you William.'

Faraday smiled 'He deserved it; if he weren't the foremost economist in the E.U I'd have fired him long ago.'

'Deserved what?' inquired McCann.

Faraday actually chuckled 'I suggest you ask your friend Doctor Weissmuller, he and Director Hazlitt don't see eye to eye, so to speak.'

McCann was left puzzled, yet he was determined to get to the bottom of it as they approached the familiar residence of Dr Weissmuller.

Faraday placed a finger upon the dark touchpad which sat on the wall besides the door to the doctor's office.

The door slid open to reveal Weissmuller working at his desk, a stark contrast to that of Hazlitt's office. The German's furniture was a brilliant white colour and made of the toughest carbon available. The portly man still wore his glove on one hand which he removed at the sight of his guests. Dressed in a traditional white coat the bald man looked up and motioned towards the seats before his desk 'Please sit, ah it's good to see you again Duncan, how have those alien creatures been treating you?'

McCann gave the German a curios look.

'The Ixchel mein friend,' he replied in a thick German accent.

'Ah, I'm fine thanks. I'd have thought you'd have it by now?'

'Nein, nein, better you test it out first. It might be fatal you know?'

The doctor waited as the silent atmosphere took a hold, he then burst out laughing 'Hah, hah, hah! I was joking Duncan!'

McCann pouted at the doctor who for some reason had hair only growing on the sides of his head, why he hadn't ordered his nanites to regenerate its growth and remove the bald streak was still a mystery.

'Perhaps it could cure you of that famous German sense of humour you're afflicted with?' replied the Englishman.

The doctor laughed again 'Valorie has tried before now, here take this,' Weissmuller passed McCann a white rubber ball then turned to one of his monitors 'Just squeeze it once every ten seconds or so.'

McCann squeezed the ball which seemed to be pressurized, as he squeezed and released it the pressure increased a little each time, 'So we've just come from Director Ludwig von Hazlitt's office.'

Weissmuller lost his jolly demeanour immediately 'Really, should I run any checks for trauma, physical or mental?'

'I take it you've met him,' replied McCann.

'Ya, we have crossed paths.'

Faraday was obviously getting some enjoyment from this though Valorie seemed disgusted by such crudity.

'I get the impression he has a chip on his shoulder when it comes to people of the Prussian persuasion?'

'Nein, that man is just an arshlock,' stated the doctor blankly.

The Admiral grinned 'I'm surprised that with all the Germans working here someone hasn't throttled the old boy to death already.'

Weissmuller observed the readout on his holo-monitor carefully 'Germans, Italians and French, perhaps you should invite Mr Beaumont to visit the old arshlock?'

McCann began to laugh a little 'The clash of the titans so to speak?'

Weissmuller snorted 'Pah.'

'So come on doc, what happened?'

Weissmuller looked over his glasses at the Englishman; he had a most serious stare 'Has no-one told you yet?'

'No,' replied McCann in a puzzled tone.

The doctor looked in the direction of Faraday 'I thought it had already gone down in I.S.A lore, much like Mr Beaumont and that McKinley.'

McCann spoke impatiently as he squeezed the ball 'Well come on! Out with it!'

'He poked me in the eye, in the dining hall.'

The Englishman smirked 'I hope he didn't break your glasses.'

The Doctor shook his head as he continued testing the Admiral 'If he wasn't so old and one of my patients, that arshlock would be in a body cast!'

McCann sniggered as the ball offered more and more resistance until finally he could no longer squeeze it.

'Enough Admiral,' stated Weissmuller as he took the ball back and placed it on the table 'remarkable results Duncan.'

'Oh really? Am I ranked in the top 10 ball squeezers here or something?'

Weissmuller chuckled 'Quite, you managed 134 psi, quite exceptional.'

'I'm sorry?' replied a puzzled McCann.

'The average man of 30 years can manage say 40 psi; you seem to have pushed the bar, no doubt thanks to your Ixchel.'

'Strange, I haven't noticed any increase in strength.'

Weissmuller tapped a different area of his desk causing a holo-monitor to leap up 'Ya, your Ixchel has been very slow, perhaps due to the fact you were not born with it.'

McCann scratched his head 'So I'm as strong as your average Tlillan, is that what you're telling me?'

The plump doctor shook his head 'Nein, a pure bred Tlillan female has an average psi of 400, half-breeds are somewhere around 250 psi. I would be very interested to test Malikah, now that she has the imperial Ixchel. I would be fascinated to note any differences.'

'How on earth didn't I notice it?' said McCann in a rather shocked tone.

Weissmuller smirked 'I would suppose that your crew do not challenge you to arm wrestle too often?'

'Of course not.'

'Well it is akin to a frog boiling in water, if you slowly heat it up the frog does not notice, but boils alive. Your psi has increased by over 200%, if it happened in one day you would have noticed, but over 5-10 years. Your heart and lung capacity have increased by similar amounts, did you notice them?'

McCann put his hand upon his chest and with an amazed pitch in his voice replied 'Really?'

'Ya, I'm sure your wife will attest to my diagnosis.'

Valorie let out a snigger which McCann ignored 'Well we had best make certain that Ludwig doesn't get his hands on the Ixchel before you old boy.'

Weissmuller did not reply to his statement but carried on with his summary of the Englishman's health 'Next year it will be interesting to note if your psi has increased. It is my theory that a human might reach 200 psi, with a proper training and exercise programme. As for a half-breed, 350 is quite possible in theory, for a female.'

Faraday stood up 'Well this is all very interesting but I have important business to attend to, so if you would excuse me.'

The Etonian stood up, smiled and made his way out of the doctor's office 'You're excused William,' called Weissmuller as the Director left the room.

Valorie also stood up 'I'll have to go too, congratulations on your new found ability Duncan,' said the psychiatrist with a wink in her eye.

'Thank you,' replied McCann as she left.

Weissmuller grinned 'That one has always had the eye for you Duncan.'

McCann folded his arms 'Please doctor.'

'You have always made me quite jealous, even now she thinks of you.'

'Valorie is a married woman,' stated the Admiral.

Weissmuller laughed a little 'ya, but she is a lot less married when she sees you mein friend.'

'There's no need to be so crude Doctor, I thought you were above that sort of thing,' retorted McCann.

Weissmuller continued to snigger at McCann 'Come on, are you telling me it has never crossed your mind?'

'I'm not telling you anything,' replied the Englishman in a stern tone.

The German smiled 'Ah, perhaps if I applied for the Ixchel she might be interested? What do you think my chances are of getting it?'

'How would I know? Though since you've worked here for so many years I don't see why they wouldn't put you at the head of the list.'

Nodding his head the Doctor contemplated the idea 'Ya, if I had that Ixchel, in a few years I could screw like a beast too. I bet the women would be lining up outside this office for a thorough examination ... ya?' Weissmuller broke out in laughter again.

McCann was quite shocked to hear the doctor speak like this 'I think you need to spend less time in this office mate, it sounds to me like you're going funny like that Austrian bloke we just visited!'

Weissmuller pointed at McCann in agreement 'Or maybe I could get a nice assistant, like that Indian girl William has been screwing?'

The Englishman's eyes widened 'you what?'

Weissmuller made a puzzled expression 'Really? You didn't see it?'

'See what?'

'He has that technician around him all the time, bringing him coffee and crumpets,' Weissmuller had a sudden epiphany 'Now I know why you English call it crumpet!'

McCann cleared his throat 'So when would you like to see me next?'

Weissmuller tapped his desk and a monitor leapt up before him 'Hmmm, I'll let you know. First I must examine your scans,'

'My scans?'

'Ya, the AI has scanned you whilst you've been sitting here. It will take weeks to sort the information out.'

McCann stood up 'Well I'm sorry but I have to leave, urgent business.'

Weissmuller gave him a suspicious look 'Fine, just mention the Ixchel the next time you see Malikah will you? And maybe she can get me hooked up with one of those Tlillan Valkyries, ya?'

The Englishman was taken aback but replied courteously 'I'll see what I can do Doctor, farewell.'

As the Englishman left the room Weissmuller exhaled slowly 'Ya, auf weidersehen.'

McCann had to take a breath; he walked outside into a small park constructed at the headquarters for staff lunchtime breaks. The Englishman quickly lit up a cigar and took a lung of powerful smoke, despite this it did not cause him to cough. Instead it merely helped steady his nerves, the experience of meeting Ludwig and a cooped up Weissmuller on the same day was far more of a shock to the system than a lungful of Ramon Allones smoke.

As he puffed away contemplating how people had changed since he'd last visited Geneva he heard the voice of Faraday behind him 'You're not meant to smoke here.'

McCann turned his head as the old Etonian swung his stick merrily with a smile 'But no need to worry Duncan, you may carry on.'

'Thanks Bill.'

'What's up? You sound exhausted, did that Weissmuller put you through some stringent tests?' inquired Faraday as he stood next to his Admiral.

'No, no I'm fine thanks. I just need to take a breather; things have changed since I was here last you know.'

Faraday nodded 'True, but not all that much Duncan. I'm glad you found this this place, I often come here to reflect when work gets on top of me, Valorie suggested it.'

The Admiral looked around at the cove of trees and bushes which occupied a quite end of the park. Circled by the shrubbery there was one small grass path in and out, it was a very relaxing place, somewhere one could easily meditate amongst the goings on at Geneva.

'So what's getting on top of you Bill?'

'Is that some kind of innuendo?'

McCann chuckled a little 'No it isn't, what's up?'

'Oh just this business with the new monetary system, bloody SI's today. When I first became Director the damn things did what they were told and nothing more, unless they crashed of course. Now they have personalities, I already have children and now I'm bringing up three more kids.'

McCann smiled 'You'll get it sorted out.'

'I hope so Duncan, Ploutos is a very demanding creature. Unfortunately she's intricate to our financial system. If she fails it would make the financial meltdown of the 21st century a Vicar's tea party in comparison.'

The Admiral laughed as smoke rolled over his lips.

'Did I say something funny Duncan?'

McCann took another draw of his Habanos and answered 'There's not enough greed in this world to even destroy greed.'

'So would you mind telling me what that means?'

'We'll always be having these problems. Despite going through a financial Armageddon people are still ready to print fiat money at the first chance they get or leverage gold and silver 100 to 1 at the first opportunity. But what's worse is that human beings are so greedy and stupid we'll always buy into it if we think we can profit.'

Faraday nodded 'Yes, it makes me wonder why people invest in Ponzi schemes even today, then complain when they go broke. I suppose greed is just an intrinsic part of the human psyche as much as fear, love and hate. Some of us control it better than others.'

McCann tasted the creamy smoke as it rolled over his tongue whilst observing the beech trees around him.

'So are you preparing for your American visit Duncan, it's only tomorrow.'

The Englishman grimaced 'Yes, I suppose I'll have to put up with that git Earle and no doubt Habeeb will be sniffing around like Caligula at a sex orgy.'

Faraday laughed 'Well we could always swap jobs you know old boy!'

McCann chuckled 'Maybe not, I'll be ready when the flight leaves don't worry about that Bill.'

Faraday patted him on the back 'Good man.'

Both Sandra and Lian were smitten with the fur coat, so much so that the next day Lian begged Sandra for her place on the Atlas to New York. The Prodigy conceded to Lian since she already had one of the most expensive articles of clothing on the planet.

All the way to New York Lian was fidgeting and nattering about what they might receive as gifts. McCann was quite uninterested after being forced to smoke one of the most vile cigars he'd ever tasted. Not that he blamed the Russian Premier, to him all tobacco smelt disgusting so he wouldn't know the difference.

The Atlas landed on the top of a fortified sky scrapper, adorned with ground to air missiles and armed troops. It was the Bank of New York building and a large portion of the Eastern States gold reserves were kept in vaults beneath its surface.

McCann stepped off to greet President Earle and his entourage 'Nice to see you made it here safely, especially after that Ruskie bastard spilt the beans!'

There was no press here; the Americans had been forced to take the highest security now that word was out concerning a neutronium shipment.

The President gestured towards a hummingbird 'Let's get on board.'

McCann and Lian followed him onto the craft and strapped themselves in as it lifted off. McCann was sat opposite Earle; the American didn't seem too pleased 'I'm sure that Ruskie bastard was trying to ruin us!'

McCann felt this old American-Russian rivalry had been taken a bit far by both sides 'He's just brought the schedule a little ahead of time, you're still getting your neutronium so don't panic.'

Earle didn't believe a word of it, he was certain Myshkin was doing his best to sink him economically; you didn't need to be Tlillan to work that out.

The President smiled at Lian 'I'm sorry, hello I'm Michael.'

Lian pressed her palms together 'Namaste President Earle, I am Lian.'

'Jesus Christ, call me Michael,' he said in a jovial tone.

Lian smiled and nodded her head.

McCann pointed to Lian 'She's the first Adjunct to Malikah.'

Earle gave a puzzled look 'First Adjunct, is that like an intern?'

Lian sniggered at the President's adorable ignorance 'More of an Auxiliary, if Xch'uup needs to be in more than one place at once I'm sent to take care of the lesser task; although a lesser task for Xch'uup is probably more important than the most pressing business of world leaders here, no offence Mr Earle.'

The President's aide, sat next to Earle, peeped over his tablet to get a look at this auxiliary.

Michael chuckled 'None taken young lady, tell me where do I get a few like you?'

Lian laughed along with the American as their hummingbird hurtled across the New York skyline, finally landing at The Plaza hotel.

The party stepped off the craft to a horde of reporters; the President smiled and said a few words before leading his guests inside the hotel. Upon entering they were greeted by Gregory 'Welcome back to The Plaza Mr McCann, is Malikah too busy to visit?'

McCann shook his hand over the reception desk 'It's a busy job running the Galaxy I'm afraid, she did send her Adjunct however.'

Gregory scooted around the desk and kissed the young lady's hand 'Welcome to The Plaza ahhhh Miss Lian?'

Lian smiled in delight that the manager of the most prestigious hotel in New York knew her name 'Thank you Mr Trent.'

'Oh please my name is Gregory, you will be staying here for the night I hope?'

Lian gave McCann that puppy dog eyes look, reminding him of his own daughter, he couldn't resist 'If you don't mind Greg?'

'Of course not, I always keep a penthouse suite free in case Malikah or her charges arrive. I think this qualifies.'

President Earle twiddled his thumbs nervously as he spoke to McCann 'I'm afraid there's gonna be a press conference.'

McCann made a knowing look and nodded his head 'Can't let the Reds out do us can we?'

Michael smiled then led his guests to an elevator taking them down to the Rose club which had been commandeered for the conference. Inside, the club was a beautiful place, the red crushed velvet adorning both couches and seats seemed to exude a warmth of its own. Its walls were panelled with fine walnut and gold, a room of incredible opulence. Inside were literally a few reporters including Jerry Habeeb. McCann sat down on a red velvet couch with Lian on one side and Michael Earle on the other.

Habeeb didn't even wait for the Presidents aide; he called out 'Could you please tell us how this neutronium standard is going to work?'

The question seemed to be directed at President Earle so he answered 'The Eastern States shall be creating a new currency, we haven't decided what the rate will be but I should imagine that it will be a lot higher than the gold credit.'

Jerry spoke up again, much to McCann's annoyance 'So you won't totally drop the gold standard, is that right?'

'We'll still have the gold credit as a viable unit of exchange, only it shall be pegged to Neutronium now. It is just that with so much space exploration the stockpiles of gold are becoming quite large. One day we'll have to introduce a new system, if we don't want a hyper-inflation similar to the early 21st century, so we're doing it sooner rather than later,' stated Earle without flinching.

A second reporter pumped his fist into the air and Earle pointed in his direction 'Yes?'

The reporter seemed nervous and his companion couldn't believe what he was recording 'What does this mean to those who have their savings in gold credits? Or even worse what about those who have pensions in silver credits?'

Earle wasn't well prepared for the conference since this was put together on the fly due to the Russians. The President was about to call the conference to an end however Lian intervened 'The Grand Matriarch has foreseen your financial woes, this is why we are delivering the neutronium now. Those with gold or silver credits will be able to exchange them for neutronium credits. However if at any point gold or silver might crash the Grand Matriarch will be happy to purchase whatever amount is necessary, at a fair rate, to stabilise our economy.'

Another reporter questioned Lian before they were thrown out 'Why does the Grand Matriarch care about our economy?'

Lian smiled at the journalist 'Because she is Human too, and without us the Tlillans would be extinct. Besides we always seem to make such a mess of our own finances!'

There was a chuckle then the Presidents aide waved his hand 'That's all the questions we can have.'

The aide motioned to the side doors and some security guards escorted the reporters outside. Once the room was cleared Earle presented the obligatory presents, the first gift was another box for McCann. He hated gifts, especially occasions such as his birthday or Christmas. He just wanted to be left alone but he had no choice. He took the tall rectangular wooden box, opened the top and pulled out a bottle of Tennessee Bourbon. McCann didn't like the Bourbon but at least he wouldn't be asked to drink it now.

His aide next presented a cardboard box to Lian, before anything could be said she pulled the top open and rummaged through the paper wrapping inside. Her face lit up with delight as she looked inside, McCann was rather annoyed with the one upsmanship. Lian pulled out a small leather Channel handbag with a pair of matching black gloves. The bag was of course a real Channel and very expensive along with the Versace gloves.

After meticulously looking the bag over she thanked Michael 'Namaste, Mr Earle.'

Earle led them out into the foyer where the awaiting press snapped holo-shots of Lian holding her designer bag and gloves. McCann was asked some rather inappropriate questions concerning the Bourbon and how it compared to Myshkin's gift. The Englishman was as diplomatic as possible in avoiding a straight answer, fortunately for Lian she answered honestly noting how enchanted she was by the President's gift.

The pair stayed in The Plaza that night before going back to Geneva. McCann decided it was time to have a word alone with Lian. After they'd settled into their rooms he walked down the hall and knocked on her door. Lian opened it giving the Englishman a nervous look before fixing her eyes on the ground.

'May I come in?' asked the Englishman.

She opened the door to let him in, after walking inside she closed the door behind her guest 'You've come to speak about Malikah?'

He nodded 'Yes, that dream you had on the Bridge of the Athena, I was there.'

Lian gasped drawing in her breath acutely 'What did you see?'

'Enough.'

'I'm sorry I didn't ...'

McCann rolled his eyes 'Please spare me Lian, you both intended to do what you did. I'm not here to pass judgement on you.'

Lian relaxed and looked up at McCann 'Why are you here?'

'I want to know why she didn't tell me?'

Lian shook her head 'She cannot tell anyone, even you, it's too dangerous.'

'Why?' asked McCann in a puzzled tone.

'Heresy, we would both be executed as heretics.'

McCann chortled in disbelief 'Execute Malikah? No one can do that.'

'She would be banished at the very least and I would be executed. By having me close she risks everything, if anyone were to find out,' tears began to fall down her cheeks.

'Can't she just change the law?'

'Some religious laws cannot be changed in a day or even a year. We must keep it a secret.'

'Well you didn't do a very good job on the Athena did you?'

The girl put her face in her hands and wept, if Malikah found out about her mistake it could mean the end.

McCann approached her and put his arms around the more than 6ft woman 'I won't say anything, alright?'

Lian placed her face onto his shoulder and wept for another ten minutes before McCann returned to his room.

Chapter 8

The next day Faraday was having his interview at Network America, announcing to the world the launch of a new currency standard. As predicted for the first month there was widespread panic amongst everyone from small time savers to big time investors. The price of gold went up and down as if it were a fairground ride, McCann found it all amusing. For Duncan McCann it was a form of entertainment to watch these big time speculators pulling their hair out on the floor of Wall Street. No longer were the computer algorithms running the stock market, in the panic the market AI's had been switched off.

Computer trading systems locked up all over the world and trading was forced to take place the old fashioned way. Men and women were screaming at one another and waving pieces of paper or trying to get attention with brightly coloured paper flags. For the first time in more than half a century they were forced to actually earn their money. Ever since the early 21st century the majority of traders had resigned their trading positions on the floor to a computer algorithm, whilst they went for a coffee. The trading floor had for decades been a ghost town run by computer programs set to buy and sell at certain points. It resulted in stock exchanges around the world being little more than a platform for wash trading; that being fake trades giving the illusion business is being done. When in fact it's all pretend trading used to manipulate prices, after the Russian Premier had spilt the beans all of that went out of the window.

McCann was watching the Jerry Habeeb interview; Habeeb had several pictures of trading floors around the world. The Englishman sniggered at the absolute chaos, as fat rich scumbags who'd lived an easy life on computer controlled wash trades were going berserk. Habeeb focused in on the London Stock Exchange, the interview halted abruptly as the American reported on an incident taking place. A British trader walked into the middle of the London Bullion trading floor holding a plasma grenade above his head. Some fled in panic however the majority ignored him and carried on trying to trade in derivatives with others offloading the now toxic gold paper contracts.

McCann and Lian were in the hotel restaurant watching the interview 'Mr McCann can you believe that?'

'Call me Duncan, please,' said McCann as he ate his scrambled eggs.

'I'm sorry, but can you understand that, Duncan?'

McCann sniggered 'It's called greed, those people are just scum. If that grenade goes off he'll be doing us all a service.'

Lian had a rather shocked expression 'But you cannot know those people, how is it possible for you to judge them all?'

McCann shook his head 'Those people there all worship money, anyone that places money above the lives of others are scum. Look at them; they care more about toxic Bonds than their own safety!'

Lian narrowed her eyes and looked at McCann 'What about those that worship power? Some would say the same of you.'

The Englishman smirked 'That depends on what you define as power.'

Pointing to the television screen at the bar Lian stated 'They would say that money is power.'

McCann shook his head 'Then they'd be wrong, wouldn't they.'

'Why?'

'Look at them, running around like chickens with their heads cut off. All of them in a panic as if their lives depended on it, for what? A few bits of paper that represent some rehypothicated gold that doesn't exist anyway? Last week those men were praised as Titans and now they are nothing more than decapitated poultry. That power was merely an illusion, Malikah knew that and so did the Makayuuk.'

Just as he'd finished an explosion let rip on the London Stock Exchange floor, when the smoke cleared men were seen clamouring over the dead and dying to off load their toxic derivatives. The rescue services had to push their way inside to treat the injured, McCann laughed at the scene.

Lian couldn't believe what had just happened, looking away in disbelief she asked McCann 'So what is true power, Duncan?'

He took a sip of his morning coffee 'I'd have thought you'd know that already. True power isn't money or knowledge or even weaponry, true power is will power. Look at Malikah she didn't get where she is through wealth or knowledge, the Gukumatz submitted themselves to her will. That power made her greater than any other being in existence, if it was not for their will she would not be Xch'uup.'

Lian thought on what the Englishman had said before replying 'I agree with you, in that case those trading on the London Stock Exchange are weak. Money and greed controls them and their destiny, it strips them of any self-control; they have no real will.'

McCann smiled and pointed at Lian 'Exactly young lady.'

'Still I am puzzled as to why you hold them in such disdain; surely they don't do any harm to you?'

The Englishman wagged his finger at the screen 'If everyone one of those bastards dropped dead in every stock exchange around the world, would this planet be a better or worse place?'

Lian smiled 'That is far too broad a question for me to answer.'

'Then take a guess, better or worse Lian?'

Lian inhaled a deep breath 'Very well, it would be better I suppose.'

'Remember Malikah controls the destiny of every single one of those slimes, just as she dominates any politician, General, King or Queen. Her willpower is what separates her from the wannabes and megalomaniacs you see scrambling over their friend's corpses for a few pennies.'

Lian contemplated his words for a few moments then replied 'Then by that logic the Makayuuk would be very powerful, despite the fact they were defeated during the invasion?'

McCann begrudgingly accepted her statement 'Agreed.'

'How would you suggest Malikah bring them to heel?'

The Englishman shook his head 'I don't know, but if she doesn't get the problem sorted out soon it could cost us.'

'How so?'

'People will put up with it but only for so long, if there's no light at the end of the tunnel people will start to push back against the idea of suppressing the Makayuuk.'

Lian gave a puzzled look 'Light at the end of the tunnel?'

McCann took another sip of his coffee 'If there is no end in sight people will become disillusioned and demand we pull out.'

'So what would you suggest?'

He chuckled for a moment then replied to her question 'Me? I'd turn that entire planet into dust and destroy every Mack in the universe.'

Lian looked rather shocked at his statement 'Then you would be as barbaric as the Makayuuk.'

'Mankind is barbaric, we just play at being civilized, don't ever forget that Lian.'

'What of Malikah? She is half Human does that make her a barbarian?'

'Like you the beast resides within her until awoken from its slumber, I hope you never see that side of her.'

'Have you?'

'Once at Muul Kaah, it was enough to frighten every Matriarch on Otoch. That's what makes her different, the power of the beast within her, the beast she can manipulate.'

They both looked up again at the report on the London Stock Exchange where men and women were still scrambling amongst the dead trying to unload credit default swaps and precious metals that had already been leveraged 100 times. McCann snorted 'They're nothing but insects, they worship pieces of paper and imaginary goods in the hope it will improve their existence. Their lives have less worth to them than a crappy government bond, why should you show them any pity?'

As the pair were sat down chatting over their breakfasts The Plaza manager approached their table 'Excuse me, but could I have a moment?'

The man had a look of extreme distress about him and McCann felt rather concerned 'Take a seat Greg,' stated McCann as he gestured to a chair beside him.

Greg sat down and spoke to them in a hushed tone 'I need some financial advice, shares in The Plaza have plummeted and my savings are losing value. I was hoping that Lian, being half Tlillan and all, might be able to point me in the right direction.'

Lian reached across the table to hold his hand, as she did her eyes turned a pinkish hue, Greg seemed to relax immediately.

'Mr Trent there is nothing to worry about, the markets will stabilise in the coming months. However my advice would be to invest any spare finances into Gold whilst the price is low, I am sure that within the next few weeks it will rise sharply.'

Gregory livened up and a smile came to his previously worried face, the man was obviously relieved as he was no doubt starring financial oblivion in the face.

Greg clutched Lian's hand with both of his and kissed it 'Thank God you were here, you're welcome to stay here and shop at any time for no charge!'

Lian laughed 'You don't charge me anyway Mr Trent!'

Greg laughed to himself as he released some stress 'I'm sorry I forgot, it's been a tough day.'

McCann still sipping his creamy coffee quipped 'Don't worry Greg if this place was ever in any danger I'm sure Malikah would be here like a shot to sort it all out for you.'

Greg looked rather startled 'You think so?'

McCann nodded 'I know so.'

Lian added 'But make certain you purchase physical Gold Mr Trent, paper trading is about to collapse again. I'd keep it in a vault here until the markets level out.'

Greg nodded then stood up 'If there's anything you want and I mean in the entire city just ask and I'll have it brought to you.'

Lian's flashing pink eyes smiled at the grovelling hotelier 'Thank you Mr Trent, I'm quite all right.'

Greg quickly trotted away, no doubt to buy that physical Gold as soon as possible. Within a few seconds the man had disappeared from the restaurant, McCann commented on that being the fastest he's ever seen staff move in a hotel. Lian asked McCann as to why he wasn't so worried, the Englishman pointed out that he owned property and as a famous American had once said "Invest in real estate now, because they're not making any more of it!" He couldn't quite recall who said it though.

'Mark Twain,' stated Lian with a smile.

McCann pointed at her 'Ah, if it's an American quote then there's always a 50% chance it was Mark Twain. Well if it's a good one that is.'

Lian laughed 'You know they have very few proverbs on Tlillan.'

'That is why Tlillans are so attracted to Humans,' he looked from side to side then whispered over the table 'and half-breeds.'

Lian sniggered at his naughty comment 'I don't understand.'

'Tlillans are bland and predictable, unlike them the beast sleeps within us waiting to be aroused from its slumber. We can love as much as we hate.'

Lian furrowed her brow 'What does that have to do with proverbs?'

'If we all conformed so easily and were so predictable we wouldn't need proverbs to remind us of common sense.'

The news report flicked between the largest stock exchanges on the planet displaying varying degrees of chaos. Men and women scrambling in desperation, assets plummeting in value as traders attempted to offload them. McCann grinned with a sense of satisfaction; he took a sinister pleasure in the misery of those who worshipped the false God of money.

Lian noticed the similarities between Malikah and her Father as she observed his smirking profile. Many times she'd seen and felt Malikah express the same dark satisfaction at another's pain, now she realised where it came from. Taking pleasure in another being's discomfort was certainly not a Tlillan trait and had been somewhat of a mystery as to where it came from. Most believed it was unique to the Mictlantecuhtli however it became evident that all half breeds, Mictlantecuhtli or otherwise, possessed this trait to one degree or another.

'So what do you worship, Duncan?'

McCann looked at Lian with surprise 'Why do you ask?'

'You deride those that worship finances, what is it you worship?'

McCann chuckled 'I worship my wife!' he then gave her a hard look 'and you?'

Lian didn't flinch 'Xch'uup.'

McCann shook his head 'Come on, you're not on Tlillan now.'

Lian's face didn't move 'I worship Xch'uup, without her I would not exist. Her word is law, there is nothing else.'

The Englishman was convinced Lian spoke the truth, he was just a little stunned at how a half Tlillan raised on Earth felt so strongly towards the Tlillan leader; who happened to be his daughter.

'Why does that surprise you Duncan?'

'I just thought that since you were born here, that Tlillan philosophy wouldn't have been such an influence.'

'It is more than mere philosophy; Xch'uup is the only thing that will bring order to this galaxy. Without her imagine the chaos, much like the stock exchanges, insects scrambling over one another grasping at the prize. Killing one another for nothing more than some shiny metals that can be found in any common asteroid, without her we are mere animals clawing over each other to be king of the dung heap.'

McCann couldn't disagree with that opinion; his fellow man was greedy and self-centred. They would use and murder one another for nothing more than shiny metals or even a loaf of bread. Human life had its price and it was often valued far lower than the pieces of paper those slime on the monitor were trying to get rid of. Whatever people had to say about Malikah, she placed far more value on Human life than Mankind.

Perhaps that was the secret of Mankind's' success? He was willing to make great sacrifices in order to get ahead of his neighbours. It was true that the Gukumatz didn't have the stomach for keeping control of the Makayuuk; they valued their own lives more than that of their enemy. The only thing they valued more than themselves was their Icon and her charges.

Mankind couldn't care less, conflict was in his nature and he lusted for it despite the costs. Any excuse to spill blood was good enough for him, food, money, religion, race or his favourite being resources.

Tlillan's realised early on that few species in the universe would be able to stomach Mankind. A powerful ally and added to that he provided fertile mates allowing the Tlillans to breed again; it was win, win for both sides.

As McCann contemplated what Lian had said her collar went off and a 3-D display leapt out before her eyes. She stood up dressed in her jet black suit and white Tlillan jacket to read the message. After a few silent minutes the display collapsed back into the collar and she spoke to McCann 'The Makayuuk contact has exposed himself, Malikah has requested we bring him to her.'

McCann looked up at the towering beauty 'Where is he?'

'Washington.'

McCann finished his coffee, straightened his uniform and gestured towards the door 'Lead the way young lady.'

Lian smiled and marched into the elevator followed by McCann; they exited on the roof and entered the Hummingbird which was prepped for their flight to Geneva.

'We're going to Washington,' stated Lian.

The pilot turned in his seat and looked at McCann, the Englishman nodded and the pilot returned to prepping the flight. The co-pilot logged in a flight plan and it was certified by air traffic control. The rear of the craft lifted up closing the Hummingbird air tight, its wings turned up so that the jets faced downwards 'Okay, strap yourselves in,' said the pilot.

McCann and Lian buckled themselves into their seats as the jets fired and slowly pushed the craft off the pad. After gaining some altitude its wings rotated into a horizontal position, pushing them South towards the nation's capital.

Within a couple of hours McCann and Lian had exited the crafted and were closing on the steps leading to the top of Capitol Hill. As they walked along one of the avenues approaching the building Lian was in awe, the pure white construction was quite stunning to her eyes.

'It's beautiful,' said the young Amazon.

'I'd have thought you'd have seen it before? Through another's memory at least,' remarked McCann.

Lian shook her head 'No, never.'

'So how does it rate alongside Tlillan architecture?'

Lian grinned 'On Otoch it's all about conformity, here it is about individuality. I much prefer the mind of Mankind when it comes to building, so less bland than the Tlillan mind.'

They began to climb the steps reaching up to the summit of Capitol Hill; within moments a crowd of journalists were making their way down to meet them. McCann grimaced yet Lian comforted him 'Have no fear Duncan, they are required for what we are about to do.'

McCann said nothing but continued marching upwards as they ascended to the top of the hill ignoring the questions thrown at them. He followed his daughter's Adjunct as she stepped past the waiting lines of people and into one of the large doorways leading into the marble lobby.

A tall well-built man in a dark suit put his hand out as they walked towards the roped off area that led deeper into the maze of buildings. Lian gave him a sharp look and he spoke 'I'm sorry ma'am you'll have to show me some identification.'

There was a large reception desk with several men and women manning it, all eyes were fixed upon Lian and her next move.

'My name is Lian, first Adjunct of Xch'uup, I am here to speak with President Earle,' she stated matter of factly.

A few eyebrows were raised and the security replied 'I'm afraid the President is busy making a speech to the Senate. You'll have to wait.'

Lian marched past him ignoring the security guards refusal to co-operate.

'Ma'am, stop right there!' shouted the man in black.

McCann could hear the sound of several rail weapons charging around the large marble lobby.

Lian halted in the middle of the reception area; she couldn't see the secret service agents since they were hidden behind marble columns on terraced upper floors looking down upon their target. However she could sense every one of them and there were far too many to make any sort of attempt at forcing her way in further.

McCann looked at the first agent 'Is this all really necessary?'

The American seemed to know who he was and replied 'I'm afraid it is and I'll have to take your pistol, Sir.'

McCann took a deep breath, as if he were doing something arduous and slipped his pistol out of the holster. Holding the weapon by the barrel he offered it to the agent who received it almost apologetically.

At that moment a familiar voice echoed around the lobby 'What the hell is going on here?'

President Michael Earle strutted out from one of the hallways that led to the Senate; he seemed to be a little upset.

The agent turned to the President 'These people attempted to bypass security, Sir. One of them was armed,' he displayed McCann's weapon.

Ten or twenty Senators including the President's aide quickly entered the lobby; it seems the speech had been cut short.

Michael Earle ran his fingers through his grey hair and shook his head in disbelief 'Give it back to him.'

The agent nodded then handed McCann's weapon back.

Earle quickly snapped 'And call your men off, her boss just bailed out the entire country.'

The agent spoke into his collar and the sound of rail weapons charging down filled the hall for a few moments. The secret service agent approached Lian and apologised 'I'm sorry ma'am; I was just doing my job.'

Lian smiled back 'I understand.'

President Earle then approached Lian 'I'm sorry about all of this, there's been a terrible mistake.'

Lian pressed her palms together for the President 'Namaste President Earle, I am at fault for coming here unannounced. You have very competent security Officers.'

The Senators and public were just as mystified as President Earle as to why they were here, the hall remained silent.

'I am here at the request of Malikah; she has seen the traitor that would usurp Mankind.'

President Earle had a rather shocked look about him 'He's here?'

To be honest McCann would have suspected someone from one of the former rogue or pirate states before one of Earle's men or women. There were plenty of ex-cartel, pirates or warlords kicking around all over the globe with an axe to grind.

Everyone looked around the hall at one another but Earle just fixed his gaze upon Lian 'So who is it?'

Lian slowly turned her head until she was staring at her target; she straightened her arm and pointed her finger 'Your traitor is there!'

The Senators drew in a sharp breath; the shock could be heard from all including the public and even the journalists that were now filming the entire event.

Earle gave an incredulous look 'Jeff?'

The President's aide stood holding his tablet in deep shock 'I don't know what she's talking about Mike!'

Lian sneered at Jeff, a short weasaly man with a receding hairline that was now on the back of his head. His hair was cut short, he sported a moustache and wore a grey two piece suit that helped him blend into the background; giving his President the full attention of the cameras.

President Earle now fully grey after years of hard work running the country was dressed in his navy blue three piece Italian suit. It was difficult to believe that the man he'd worked with all these years had betrayed him and for what?

Earle slowly stepped towards Jeff, his confidant for so many years 'Is it true Jeff?'

'No, she's full of it Mike! You know me, I sweated blood for you!'

You could hear a pin drop inside Capitol Hill; the President didn't seem to be too convinced by what his aide was telling him 'The C.I.A told me that someone was taking payoffs. They suspected it was the Russians, but even the Reds don't have that much gold to give away.'

Jeff looked nervously as the secret service agent stepped towards him 'I have a right to a lawyer and a fair trial!'

Earle gave a belligerent laugh 'unless charged with an act of insurgency, you suggested that amendment if I remember correctly!'

The security guards moved in on him and the aide shouted back 'I'm not an insurgent, that's a lie!'

One of the Senators stepped forward blocking the path 'You can't charge him with insurgency, that would be an abuse of The Constitution. He's entitled to a free and fair trial under The Constitution you helped write Mr President!'

She was right; the secret service agents that had come out of the wood work were awaiting the order to carry the man off. However Earle didn't want to violate the Constitution he'd written, not in front of the press.

Lian approached the President and offered a way out 'Xch'uup requests extradition of the traitor, Mr President.'

Jeff shouted out quickly so all could hear 'I demand asylum from the Tlillans.'

Lian sneered at the traitor 'You shall be coming with me to stand trial before Xch'uup. On Otoch you have no rights, no lawyers, no Constitution only a council of Matriarchs.'

The same female Senator rebuked Lian 'You have no rights or privileges on Capitol Hill, we make the law here!'

Lian pointed at the female in her early fifties dressed in a grey business suit with blond hair 'TRAITOR!'

The other Senators who'd shuffled out to watch the incident shied away from Jeff and his advocate, this was not a battle they were interested in fighting. Like most politicians they were cowards, more concerned with self-preservation than anything else.

The Senator looked at the President 'Mike, this is crazy, are you gonna listen to this nutty alien?'

The hall was silent once again and the President didn't reply he only stared in disbelief at the events unfolding before him.

'Look at her Mike, she's charged, tried and convicted one of your best buddies of a capital crime with no evidence. Let's just put an end to this so that we can all go home.'

Earle nodded solemnly 'I agree, arrest them both and charge them with conspiracy to commit acts of insurgency,' he looked at Lian 'Malikah can have them once we've finished with them.'

Lian wasn't happy 'That will not be satisfactory, Xch'uup will request them both.'

'Then Xch'uup will have to wait, our law takes precedence here I'm afraid.'

Lian looked rather shocked at his words but she maintained her composure and placed her palms together 'Namaste Mr President.'

Two weeks later and the trial of the century was about to commence, well a Grand Jury was about to ascertain whether there would be a trial. Jeff and his advocate Senator Sarah Hart, who was also under suspicion, were at the New York Supreme Court on Foley square. The power of attorney had gone to the Net TV lawyer Benny Joppich; a man in his 60's famous or infamous for defending many celebrity cases. Joppich stood about five and a half feet, a well fed gentleman sporting his brown hair in a comb over. His golden tan alluded to expensive holidays in the Caribbean on his luxury yacht. The man had made a fortune in his career, mostly from defending the rich and getting them out of jail despite their obvious misdemeanours. Benny was the go to man if you wanted to remain free, that's why his services came at such a high price. Dressed in his pinstripe three piece Savile Row suit with a mandarin collar and clip pocket watch he was an intimidating sight in any court room. Unfortunately for the President's former aide Benny was not defending today, he was prosecuting.

McCann hated lawyers just as much as he despised politicians, as far as he was concerned they were all scum of the earth. Still Jeff was a traitor and that was as low as you could get, betraying those you swore to defend with your life. He was quite happy to see one slime ball trying to send another to the executioner's block, insurgency being one of the few crimes punishable by death in the Eastern States.

The Grand Jury was merely an initial hearing to see if the State had a case against the Aide and Senator. The Judge opened the hearing allowing the State to begin its case against the accused. Benny spoke with a Chicago accent quoting from C.I.A files, unfortunately they were rather vague when it came to specifics on the identity of the person or persons organising the influx of gold. It was plain however that someone was organising large amounts of the precious metals transported into the Eastern States. Large amounts of physical gold were appearing on metal exchanges, pushing down the value of not only the metal but also of their currency. Since most credits were electronic, issuing and removing them from circulation wasn't a problem. Yet the Whitehouse was receiving worrying reports, economists were concerned that they were no longer in control of their economy. The value of goods was fluctuating, the value of the currency was dropping quickly and if this continued hyperinflation would be a real possibility. It was stated that they might be seeing another Weimar Republic or even worse a Eurozone collapse; people would be fighting in the streets for a loaf of bread, killing for a cup of flour.

The alternative being a withdrawal of electronic credits, resulting in a Misarian crack up boom. The value of the Eastern credit might increase uncontrollably, something great for consumers in the present. However government debts would increase, creditors would profit at the expense of debtors. Servicing the debt for many companies would be catastrophic causing strings of bankruptcies. The knock on effect being that goods would rise in price and no longer reach the shelves, the eventual result being another 21st century hyperinflation by way of chronic deflation.

Fortunately lessons had been learnt after the last crack up boom, the Eastern states controlled its currency as little as possible. All credits were backed 100% by gold, so it was unlikely to happen but still a possibility remained depending on how the new gold was distributed. Interest rates were left to the market and the White house merely "minted" new credits.

The President gave evidence, pointing out that the accused Mr Jeff Feinstein had attempted upon several occasions to implicate the Russians. However Economists had stated that if the Russian Premier had done such a thing, Moscow would have been bankrupt long ago. President Earle didn't trust the Russians as far as he could throw them, however he knew that they weren't suicidal or insane.

Next the defence made their case, with Miss Hart being a former public defender and because no-one would touch the case, she defended Jeff and herself. She pointed out the lack of evidence implicating her or Jeff, in fact all they had was the word of 'a clairvoyant alien' which she was certain was inadmissible in any court of law in the land.

Next each side pleaded their case to the Grand Jury, Benny brought up Lian 'As I'm sure you're all aware Miss Lian is part Tlillan and therefore has psychic abilities beyond most Humans.'

Lian took the stand and smiling at the Jury she said 'When within close range of an individual I'm able to read their thoughts, thanks to my Tlillan heritage,' she pointed to the bulge that stuck out from the rear of her head.

Strolling in front of her Benny asked 'So are you saying you can read my thoughts, Lian?'

Lian smiled 'Yes, Mr Joppich.'

'Just call me Benny,' he chuckled 'could we have a demonstration?'

Miss Hart stood up 'Objection your honour, this is a court of law not a circus side show!'

The judge narrowed her eyes and looked at Lian 'No, I have heard the rumours and would like to see if there is any truth to it. Can you read my thoughts young lady?'

Lian looked at the little old lady dressed in her black robe 'Yes your honour.'

'Then tell me young lady, what am I thinking of right now?'

Lian smiled 'You're thinking of your Mother's pumpkin pie that she made when you were a little girl.'

All eyes in the court room locked on the judge 'Correct young lady,' said the judge slowly.

Miss Hart leapt up 'I want that struck from the record your Honour, relevance.'

'Now you're going to allow it,' remarked Lian before the Judge could speak.

The Judge gave Lian a stern look and the Amazon looked at the floor 'Yes your Honour.'

'I'll allow it,' said the judge who then motioned towards Benny 'carry on.'

Benny had a beaming grin from ear to ear 'Now describe to the court the first time you met Mr Feinstein.'

'Well I and Mr McCann met the President; we were transporting a large quantity of neutronium.'

'Why were you transporting the Neutronium to New York?' interjected Benny.

'To avert a financial crisis that Mr Feinstein and Miss Hart were attempting to ...'

'Objection!' shouted Miss Hart.

'Sustained,' replied the Judge 'Miss Lian please answer the question directly.'

Lian nodded her head 'To avert an impending financial disaster, Benny.'

'So tell us what did you pick up, mentally, when you met the President and his Aide Mr Feinstein?' asked Benny.

'Mr Earle was a very nice and genuine man; Mr Feinstein had some thoughts that I found rather troubling.'

'Objection, this cannot be considered evidence in a court of law!' shouted Miss Hart.

'Overruled, I want to hear it, please carry on Miss Lian,' stated the Judge.

Benny still smiling as a jolly fat man continued 'Please tell the Jury what you sensed Miss Lian.'

'I found that Mr Feinstein was very concerned at the delivery of neutronium. In fact he felt as if he'd been thwarted, I delved deeper and saw that he had contact with a Makayuuk agent. Mr Feinstein had organised large quantities of gold to be shipped in via the Tsiolkovsky,' said Lian as she glared at the accused.

Benny scratched his head 'So why didn't you inform the authorities here on Earth? I mean the President was standing in front of you!'

'I am first Adjunct to Xch'uup; my only allegiance is to her. I must inform her first and act only on her instruction.'

'So when you confronted the President on Capitol Hill, under whose orders were you acting and what were those orders Miss Lian?'

'I was instructed by Xch'uup to remove Mr Feinstein and bring him to Otoch, I only discovered his accomplice that day.'

Benny smiled and looked at the Judge 'That will be all your honour,' he grinned at Lian and sat down on his side of the court room.

The Judge peered over to the defence 'Miss Hart, would you like to question Miss Lian?'

Miss Hart dressed in her blue business suit stood up, a tall lady in her 50's she had short blond hair that was expensively styled. Her piercing blue eyes locked on to Lian 'Thank you your Honour.'

She approached the stand, obviously she was prepared for some serious business 'So Miss Lian, you say you detected mine and my clients alleged guilt via an alleged clairvoyance, am I correct?'

Benny stood up 'Objection, we've already ascertained Miss Lian has the ability to read thoughts and by using the word clairvoyance she is insinuating my client is some sort of palm reader.'

The judge replied 'Mr Joppich, we have ascertained that she read my thoughts, that is all. As for the word clairvoyance, could you please use language with fewer connotations?'

Miss Hart nodded 'Miss Lian, you say you detected mine and my client's alleged guilt via an alleged psychic ability?'

She emphasised the word psychic whilst glaring at Benny who was still unhappy at it.

'That is correct.'

'I see, under whose instructions did you and Admiral McCann go to Capitol Hill?'

'I accompanied Admiral McCann to Capitol Hill under the instructions of Director William Faraday.'

'That is the Director of the I.S.A, am I correct?'

'Yes.'

Miss Hart lightly brushed her hairdo 'Was Mr Faraday aware of your intention to accuse Mr Feinstein and I of conspiracy to commit insurgency?'

'I had no intention of accusing anyone of anything until I met with your client in New York,' stated Lian matter of factly.

Miss Hart was displeased by her response 'A simple yes or no will suffice Miss Lian.'

Lian raised an eyebrow at her interrogator 'I have no idea as to whether Mr Faraday was aware of my intentions or not. The Director merely forwarded my instructions, written in Tlillan.'

'When you first suspected my client, via your alleged psychic abilities, who did you first inform of your suspicions?'

Lian knew where this was going but nevertheless she played along 'I informed Xch'uup.'

'Not Admiral McCann?'

'No'

'Not Director Faraday?'

Benny stood up 'Objection!'

The judge agreed 'Sustained, Miss Hart we have already ascertained who Miss Lian informed first.'

'So you informed Malikah and she spoke to Director Faraday who sent you to Capitol Hill under Malikah's instruction?'

'Correct.'

Miss Hart nodded to the judge then returned to Lian as she stepped closer to her stand, trying to intimidate the Tlillan half breed 'What were your instructions concerning the accused?'

Lian looked down with those condescending Tlillan eyes 'To bring Mr Feinstein before Xch'uup.'

'I see, why not allow the Eastern States to handle the matter? Does your Queen not trust us mere Earthlings?'

Benny was about to object but Lian held her hand out towards him; he was just rising from his chair when he sat back down in compliance with the Amazon.

Lian sneered at the Senator 'Xch'uup has sent you twenty percent of all Tlillan neutronium reserves. She has made you "mere Earthlings" one of the wealthiest races in the galaxy, in order to protect you from one of the most destructive. My Queen has placed great trust in your President and wishes to remove those that would betray him.'

Miss Hart pushed her harder 'You still haven't answered the question Miss Lian, why did she not inform President Earle and allow him to take care of the accusations?'

Lian's eyes turned a slight red 'Xch'uup has little faith in your judicial system Miss Hart, too frequently the guilty are set free and the innocent punished. On Tlillan you and your co-conspirator would be properly tried and punished, of that there is no doubt.'

The public in the court room began to mumble to one another at her last statement. Journalists noted it down and spoke into their mics to tag that part of the trial. The judge banged her gavel and shouted 'Order!'

The talk quietened down until there was silence once again 'Miss Hart could we stay on the subject please and have no further deviation?'

Miss Hart smiled at the judge and nodded 'I'm sorry your Honour,' she turned to the Amazon in the stand, directly next to where she now stood 'So you read my clients mind, informed your Queen and then came to Capitol Hill under her instructions to bring him before her on Otoch. At Capitol Hill you accused me also, how did you come to that conclusion?'

'I sensed the thoughts within your mind as you attempted to defend your client's innocence before Mr Earle.'

'I assume this was done via your alleged psychic ability also?'

'Correct.'

Miss Hart turned to the Jury 'I implore you to dismiss these charges, this is no better than some show in Las Vegas. Unless you're prepared to believe on the word of an alleged mind reader that I a Senator for fifteen years and Mr Feinstein, the President's confidant and Aide for longer, are both insurgents!'

Benny leapt up 'Objection, she's making a speech to the Jury your Honour!'

The Judge banged her gavel 'that's it Miss Hart, time to sit down. Mr Joppich you may make your closing argument to the Jury.'

Miss Hart had a look of horror 'Objection your Honour I haven't …'

The Judge cut her off unceremoniously 'Then you shouldn't have crossed me in my court room should you? Now sit down Miss Hart, Miss Lian you may sit.'

Lian sat back down as her eyes lost their slight red pigment.

Benny stood up and approached the Jury with a swagger 'the question is not whether you believe in Miss Lian's mental abilities; the question is do you believe there is sufficient evidence to charge the accused? We have already ascertained the facts, Gold was being smuggled via the Tsiolkovsky, our government knew this for some time. Someone was trying to flood not just our economy but that of the Russians and the E.U with masses of cheap gold. Our currency was being set on a kamikaze course for oblivion; this is fact, what we didn't know was who was behind it? Was it the Russians? No, there was too much gold, they would have bankrupted themselves and for what? To see our currency destroyed? Moscow have never been our greatest ally, in fact we have held great distrust towards each other for most of our history; however Moscow isn't crazy.

So who else has the gold to destroy us? The EU? They were being flooded too, the I.S.A? What would they gain from a wrecked global economy? They need Moscow to survive and when we discovered Moscow was being flooded too they were no longer suspects.

Next were the Gukumatz, but they don't have large deposits of gold in their system, nor do they hold the metal in as high esteem as we do. They simply do not have the means.

Next the Tlillans, They are the wealthiest race in the Galaxy so they have the means but what would they gain by ruining us? We are the nuts and bolts holding their empire together. Without us they would be food for the Makayuuk now, being processed in vats to feed machine warriors for the next conquest, Earth. Without Mankind propping them up they would be extinct before now and with their enemies growing they need us more than ever. Added to that Malikah, who is half human and raised here on Earth by Admiral McCann and his wife, sent us the neutronium to prevent this inevitable crisis.

So that leaves the Makayuuk, a breed of cybernetic Vikings that we repelled at Otoch and crushed five years later at Bandayuuk. They have plenty of gold; they use it in much of their industry. They have fleets of pirate ships operating in space, Admiral McCann was attacked when transporting the neutronium to us. It was there that Lian learnt Machine had escaped destruction, so they have the precious metal in abundance and the means to deliver it, and motive?

We are still on their home world fighting in the tunnels and combating pirates who plague hyperspace. The Makayuuk hate us and if they can destroy us they'll be able to take back their home world and defeat the Tlillans. Would anyone here do less?

So where is the link between the accused and the Makayuuk? To be honest I don't have it right now but we know they both were receiving massive payments from unknown parties in Russia. These payments were found to coincide with large shipments from the Tsiolkovsky which Mr Feinstein and the Senator are both logged down as overseeing.

That's why we need a trial, we require license to investigate this. If the accused are innocent then they should have no fear in allowing a trial … unless THEY don't trust the judicial system of the Eastern States?'

Benny spun on one foot nodded to the Judge and walked back to his seat with that same confident swagger.

The court broke for the jury to deliberate on whether or not to go forward with a trial. McCann, Lian and Benny sat at a small café across the road as they relaxed sipping their drinks a familiar face entered the café. McCann groaned and Lian held back a chuckle as Jerry Habeeb approached their table; the man had his own psychic ability when it came to hunting down the Englishman.

The Boston born American wearing his signature pinstripe shirt and braces called out 'Duncan!'

McCann grimaced; he hated it when Habeeb used his first name as if to imply some sort of friendly familiarity.

'Duncan, I'm so glad I found you!' said Jerry excitedly as he took a seat at their table.

'Be my guest,' said McCann in a rather sarcastic tone.

Jerry gave him an odd look before he dismissed it and spoke hurriedly 'What do you think the Grand Jury is going to decide?'

McCann let out a huff and answered begrudgingly 'I don't know Mr Habeeb, you've seen far more of these trials than I, what do you think?'

Habeeb drew some breath through his teeth 'Well it doesn't look good, I'd say you need a lot more evidence.'

Lian smiled at the journalist 'Do you believe they are guilty Mr Habeeb?'

Jerry smiled back 'As a journalist I have to remain totally neutral.'

McCann blew some air out of his nose and exclaimed 'PAH!'

Benny gave one of his titanic grins as he brought the latte to his lips.

Habeeb turned to the lawyer 'What do you think Mr Joppich, will the Grand Jury take this further?'

Benny sipped his latte and slowly shook his head 'There's not much evidence to link them directly, although there's no doubt they're guilty as sin.'

'Most agree that they're guilty but prosecution would be near impossible even if it went to trial, if this were Korea those bastards would be getting the gas chamber as we speak,' bemoaned Jerry.

'How very neutral of you Jerry,' said McCann maintaining his sarcastic tone.

Lian giggled and placed her hand softly upon Jerry's arm 'Have no concern Jerry, Malikah has already requested their extradition, in time they will lament the lost opportunity.'

Jerry snapped his head to look at Lian and at the same time brought his mini tablet to bear. Lian smiled and with her other hand turned the tablet off 'I'm sorry Jerry.'

Jerry nodded placing the tablet back in his lap 'Extradition, for what?'

'Heresy,' replied Lian.

'Could you be more specific Miss Lian?' inquired an excited Jerry.

'Collaborating with Heretics to undermine Xch'uup, specifically.'

Jerry's expression changed as he slowly understood what had unfolded in the New York court. The whole Grand Jury was a ruse; they didn't want to go ahead with a trail on Earth, with an undecided outcome. It was their intent to lose in order that Malikah's request go through and the traitors be transported to the Tlillan home world. Once on Otoch there would be a thorough interrogation of the traitors, their minds sifted for every grain of truth and morsel of information that could assist Tlillan triumvirate.

Jerry made a smile with half of his mouth 'So what would be the punishment for their alleged crimes?'

Lian laughed a little as she leant back 'Alleged? There are no alleged crimes, they are criminals and there is only one punishment for heresy, that is death. How they will die is the only part of their destiny they have control over now.'

Jerry pointed out one small hitch 'Ah but who says the courts will allow their extradition?'

Lian starred at him with smiling eyes and lips, saying nothing.

Jerry nodded knowingly 'I guess President Earle owes her a few favours, right?'

Lian smirked 'Those that no longer find themselves in favour with Xch'uup do shed many a bitter tear before returning to her good graces.'

Jerry raised his eyebrows 'Wow that's a very dramatic way of putting it.'

'An old proverb, from the age of Teot.'

'Who said it?' asked Jerry.

Lian shrugged her shoulders 'First? It is unknown, but it is a fact that has been proven over the eons.'

Later that day court was recalled and the Jury decided not to take the matter any further. Immediately Malikah's request for extradition was filed and the accused were again taken into custody. The next day court was held again, but this time there was no Jury. Five Judges resided as evidence was heard from Lian, Benny put the Tlillan case forward as best he could.

The main argument from Miss Hart was her concern over the Tlillan charge of Heresy. According to her a civilized state could not extradite its citizens to stand trial for such a barbaric and illegitimate charge. The judges seemed to agree with her and McCann could feel the case slipping between their fingers.

Benny requested a recess and just before they were to begin again Sandra arrived with President Earle. As they were walking up the steps back into the court building the pair approached with a caravan of journalists in tow.

Sandra pressed her palms before the Englishman 'Namaste Censor.'

McCann was rather embarrassed but returned her greeting 'Namaste Sandra.'

'Greetings Mr President, come to have a look at the proceedings?' inquired McCann.

The President had a face like a slapped arse, he certainly didn't want to be there and it was obvious Sandra had dragged him to the court at the request of Malikah.

'Sure,' replied the miserable leader of the Eastern States.

Sandra gestured towards the large wooden doors at the entrance to the court house 'Shall we?' she said as holo cameras clicked much like insects rubbing wings on a hot tropical night.

Lian smiled and continued up the steps alongside Benny, Earle was flanked by McCann and Sandra as he was escorted inside.

The proceedings were opened after all five Judges took the bench 'Would the representative for the Tlillans please take the stand?'

Lian took the stand rather than Benny and began her plea 'Malikachutli requests Miss Hart and Mr Feinstein's presence on Otoch, President Earle is here to support that request.'

Miss Hart leaned over her table towards the Judges bench 'Objection, the President cannot give his opinion in an extradition.'

The Judges consulted each other and after a few moments of mumbling came to a consensus 'Agreed, President Earle I'm afraid you must leave this court room.'

Sandra who sat next to Earle gave him a piercing look, the President was obviously uncomfortable. He nodded at the bench and slowly stood up, Sandra growled 'Mr Earle?'

Earle shrugged his shoulders 'I'm sorry I have to leave.'

Sandra was not impressed 'You are the President.'

Michael Earle shook his head 'I'm sorry Sandra.'

Sandra sneered at the man 'that you are Mr President and even more so when Malikah learns of your disloyalty. Now leave this place and go slither under the rock I found you cowering beneath!'

The court was in shock as Sandra spoke so condescendingly to their greatest leader and even more so when he did no more than accept her abuse and walk away as if he were a naughty boy leaving his headmasters office.

Sandra turned away from the President with disdain as he left the room 'You may continue,' she called out to the bench.

After another hour of debate the Judges decided that they could not send two of their citizens away to stand trial for heresy.

Lian took the stand and spoke to the bench 'If the accused gave their consent would it be permitted to arrest and transport them to Otoch?'

The central Judge gave a perplexed expression 'Well of course it would.'

Lian looked over at the accused, at the same time Sandra was seated next to McCann who sensed something odd. He turned to his left to see the dark haired goddess sitting with folded arms and a dark red ink filling her eyes. He then followed her line of sight until he reached the accused on the other side of the court room.

Miss Hart stood up 'Permission to speak your Honour?'

'Granted,' replied the Judge.

Miss Hart who seemed to be out of sorts walked in a slow mechanical fashion towards the bench then said so the entire court could hear 'I and my client admit our guilt concerning the charges of Heresy and request the court permit Miss Lian to escort us to Otoch where we wish to stand trial for our crimes, thank you.'

Feinstein leapt up 'Your Honour she's being manipulated, objection!'

The Judge banged his gavel 'Order! Miss Hart are you being manipulated?'

The Senator didn't move 'Certainly not your Honour.'

As Feinstein was about to object again Lian's eyes turned a fiery red, the accused relaxed and dropped back into his seat in a semi-conscious state.

Lian's eyes returned to normal and she smiled at the bench 'Surely you don't believe in clairvoyants and fortune tellers your Honour? The accused have already dismissed our claims before a Grand Jury.'

The Judge looked at Lian then Miss Hart who smiled back at him then at Feinstein who seemed to be recovering from a hangover 'Well Since you've requested extradition and both parties are in agreement, I see no reason not to permit Malikachutli's request. Miss Lian, first Adjunct to Xch'uup, you may take the accused into custody.'

The Judge banged his gavel and Sandra produced two control collars from a leg pocket in her Tlillan space suit. She strode over to miss Hart and clipped the nano-weave material around her neck. It automatically tightened and looked quite similar to a choker worn in women's fashion. She did the same with Feinstein then from her white jacket pocket she pulled out a wrist tablet and passed it to Lian 'The codes are on here First Adjunct.'

Lian accepted the wrist tablet; put it on then thanked Sandra 'Namaste Sandra.'

Sandra smiled 'Namaste Adjunct, safe return to Otoch.'

Miss Hart began to recover from her trance induced by Sandra, she glanced about to see her enemies standing around and shaking Benny Joppich's hand merrily. She looked over to witness her compatriot with a control collar around his throat, then felt her own neck only to realise she was in the same position.

'What the hell just happened?' asked Hart.

'You have a date with the courts on Tlillan,' mocked Lian.

'What? How?'

The Judge answered her question 'You requested extradition Miss Hart, don't you remember?'

'No I don't, I was brainwashed! I'm going nowhere with these alien motherfuc ...'

Before she could finish her sentence an electric shock ran through her body bringing the woman to her knees.

Lian laughed 'Language Miss Hart, Xch'uup will not tolerate such foul behaviour.'

Hart was now on her hands and knees choking up vomit through her mouth and nostrils, the control collars were very effective. She was rendered as helpless as a small child and began to lament her situation as tears rolled out of her eyes, dripping onto the floor.

Sandra carried Feinstein by the scruff of his neck as he was still out of it. She walked over to Lian and the ex-Senator who remained on all fours weeping into a pool of her own vomit.

Sandra sneered and kicked Hart in the ribs knocking the woman onto her back and into the vomit. The Amazon let out a great bellowing laugh that sent a wave of concern into McCann, 'Oh how the mighty have fallen!'

The ex-Senator cried for herself on the court floor unable to muster the will to drag herself from the vomit she now rolled in, destroying her expensive hairdo. Sandra grabbed her by the hair and with great strength pulled Hart to her feet whilst still holding the other traitor by the collar with her other hand.

The Judges remained in shock and thought better of berating Sandra after the tongue lashing she'd given their President.

The party exited the court building, they were met on the steps by a herd of journalists who rushed towards them shouting and screaming. Lian held her hands out requesting quiet, once the crowd had calmed she spoke 'The accused have admitted their crimes and requested they be extradited to stand trial. Admiral McCann will transport us as soon as the Athena has finished repairs, once on Otoch the accused shall stand trial before the First Matriarchs of each clan.'

Several journalists raised their arms and Lian selected one 'What exactly have they pled guilty to?' inquired the young man.

'Conspiring with the Makayuuk.'

'To do what?'

'To bring about an economic collapse on Earth,' Lian pointed to one more journalist 'Last question.'

'What is the penalty for this crime and will Malikah be involved in the proceedings?'

Lian smirked 'The punishment is execution. Malikah will preside over the proceedings and pass sentence. Xch'uup is law on all Tlillan worlds, her will is absolute.'

Lian then ignored the following flurry of questions as she led the party to the nearest building with a landing pad. McCann called the pilots on his wrist tablet, within 20 minutes they were aboard a hummingbird and headed for Geneva with the accused.

Chapter 9

Once the Hummingbird landed in Geneva the accused were handed over to security and locked in separate cells. Each cell was considered escaped proof, constructed with walls of steel several inches thick. The only exit was a simple doorway, no door or bars preventing the imprisoned from walking through. The frame of the door was embedded inside the thick steel; it generated an electric field similar to the control collars. The edges of the frame created a flow of electrons going from the left frame to the right frame and another from the top edge of the frame to the bottom edge. The flow passed through the clear space of the doorway, creating an invisible barrier. Any material passing into that space would conduct the flow to one degree or another, dishing out a powerful shock. The open doorway taunted the condemned, daring the occupant to walk out into freedom when all they would receive was a painful reminder of their misdeeds.

If the field failed and the accused managed to escape there was always the control collar. Still attached to their throats, once the collar passed the doorway it let out an excruciatingly painful encouragement to return to the cell.

The cells on each I.S.A cruiser were of the same construction and had yet to be successfully broken out of. So far the furthest anyone had managed to get was 10 metres down the hall from one of the cells on the Titov. A burly Russian made it past the electromagnetic field but the second shock from the control collar brought him down.

Faraday was rather concerned at this report; however after a review it came to light that the attempted escape wasn't quite an escape. The guards were bored that night and decided it would be entertaining to deliberately lower the power on the cell field. Allowing the occupant to believe there was a ship wide power problem. The poor fool in the cell barged through the field, despite the drop in power it cost him a lot of pain. Once out of the cell his guards stood at one end of the hall and watched him rush to the elevator at the other end.

Apparently they'd been taking bets from most of the crew, the odds were 100-1 that he'd still be standing after the 5th shock. The off duty crew in the lounge were roaring as if it were a horse race. The hall was on the lounge monitor when the crewman exited his cell, saw the guards to his right and made for the elevator. He dropped to his knees at the first belt of electric that ran down his spine, enough to drop a 600lb gorilla. For this Russian crewman with his adrenaline pumping it didn't suffice as he jumped back to his feet and continued down the hallway. His stride was far shakier than before yet he still ran for the lifts.

The crew in the lounge cheered, some shouted in disgusts, losing their bet that he'd drop at the first hit. Five metres later and the man took another violent shock; he dropped like a sack of potatoes onto the floor. The lounge went quiet; some started screaming at the monitor for him to get up and others for him to remain on the floor. When the man didn't move screams of elation mixed with shouts of 'ZEDMO!' from the men and women who'd bet on the third shock.

The monitor turned off to the general confusion of the Officers and crewmen, until they looked behind them to see Titov standing in the doorway. The Captain of the Ares was not pleased with his Officers' activity, according to the Drone Captain this had been a regular event every Saturday night for the past two months.

The Ares had reported the "Saturday night races" to the Captain and Geneva, embarrassing Titov and forcing him to investigate. The Officers of Ares would now have to find some other way to amuse themselves on a Saturday night since William Faraday was furious at such treatment of prisoners. On the other hand Faraday was relieved that there was no fault in the security measures of the new cells.

After the pair were sent to their cells McCann decided to visit his Mother on Geneva Lake. He took a stroll from I.S.A headquarters, stopping off at Davidoff's. He walked in via the glass door and immediately heard a familiar voice call his name 'Duncan! How are you?'

Eduardo skipped out from behind the counter and placed his hands on the Englishman's arms.

'I'm very well thank you, although I could do with a good cigar after that bloody court case,' smiled McCann.

'I have something here, a Rafael Gonzalez robusto,' he clicked his fingers and a young assistant slipped into the humidor and brought out a dress box of cigars.

McCann could smell the fine tobacco, he knew instantly it was well aged. He needed to only look at Eduardo and the aficionado answered his question before it was asked 'Five years, just right for these, trust me.'

McCann sniggered a little, Eduardo was always right, he knew exactly what his customers wanted before they thought of it and he produced the goods in perfect condition.

'I'll take the box,' stated McCann.

'But you haven't tried one yet,' said Eduardo in a concerned tone.

'I'll have one now, is this the only box?'

Eduardo grinned 'No I have two dress boxes and a cab.'

McCann smiled and shook his head knowingly 'I'll take this box with me and keep the other here.'

Eduardo clapped his hands 'Excellent and the cabinet?'

'I'll call you later after I've had a few, is that alright?'

'Of course it is,' Eduardo glared at his assistant 'Spencer are you listening?'

The assistant started making notes on his tablet marking down the cigars that were now reserved for McCann.

'I'm training him up, I tell you it's like marching through mud with this one!' bemoaned Eduardo.

McCann grinned 'Go easy on him Ed I'm sure he'll get the hang of it eventually.'

Eduardo had an expression that projected a sense of doubt 'We'll see,' he said as he took a cigar from the box and clipped the cap. Glaring at his assistant he shouted 'Spencer, wrap this box for Mr McCann ... quickly! By the gods do I have to do everything myself? You're meant to be my assistant but my workload has doubled since Mr Davidoff sent you here!'

McCann chuckled as he watch the poor young man run frantically to get the plastic wrapping paper then vacuum seal the box.

'What are you doing?' screamed Eduardo.

'I'm wrapping the box, Sir,' replied Spencer shakily.

'Mr McCann lives on the lake, he will be home in 20 minutes!'

Spencer stood with his jaw open wondering what he was supposed to have understood.

'My god boy! Did you leave your brain in Cuba? Wrap it in the paper and put it in a small bag!' screamed Eduardo who was at the end of his tether.

McCann tried to calm the poor man down 'it's fine Ed, I'll take it like that. Like you said it's only twenty minutes.'

Eduardo forced a smile and began to light the robusto with a long cedar match. Torching the foot before wafting the cigar periodically, encouraging the foot to smoulder. After a couple of minutes he handed the cigar to McCann 'There you are Duncan, would you like a drink?'

'No thanks I haven't been to see my Mother yet.'

'Oh say hello to Ofra and Ilam for me.'

'Ilam?'

'Yes the Chutli arrived today, didn't you know?'

McCann realised what had happened 'No, I think it was meant to be a surprise, bugger! She'll know that I know so I may as well buy her something. She'll be irritated that you told me but even more so if I don't get her something!'

A grinning Eduardo produced a rectangular silver box 'Try this, she'll love it.'

'What's that?'

'Silver Rain, a classic perfume. I'll have Spencer wrap it.'

McCann took a sigh of relief 'You're a life saver.'

Spencer wrapped the box in a blue paper, tied a white bow around it then passed it to McCann who placed it delicately inside his bag which carried his dress box of cigars. Taking his robusto from Eduardo he thanked his friend as he put it all on the Englishman's account. Exited the lounge McCann quickly made for his home by the lake whilst puffing on his Habanos, enjoying the signature liquorice flavour of Rafael Gonzalez.

Ten minutes later McCann approached the front of his large six bedroom house that sat on a terrace, lifting it and the grounds a few feet above the road and pavement in front of it. The road ran around the lake for the tram system, a grassy embankment partitioning the lake from the tram way.

McCann turned into the steps that led upwards towards the front door of his property, through the meticulously maintained gardens. He pressed his finger onto the black touchpad of his door, the house AI read his DNA sequence and finger print before releasing the door lock. There was a click and the door swung inwards before him, he stepped inside, removed his I.S.A jacket and placed his cap on the hook above it.

McCann walked through the silent hallway and into the kitchen where his Mother and smiling wife awaited him. Ilam lost her expression of excitement upon sensing her husband's lack of surprise. McCann smiled at her before she could say anything and gave her a hug quickly 'Eduardo told me,' he whispered into her ear.

Ofra shook her head 'Ah! I suppose that's where you got that cigar from? That little man he knows everything happening in this city.'

Ilam's face changed to one of shock 'Duncan!'

McCann looked puzzled at her reaction 'What?'

'Apologise to your Mother!'

'For what?' he asked taking a drag of his half smoked robusto cigar.

'Your thoughts.'

McCann had an awkward moment puffing nervously on his cigar before Ofra broke the silence 'Never mind, I know what he was thinking.'

'I wasn't thinking anything,' protested McCann.

'LIAR!' shouted Ofra whilst pointing at her son 'you were thinking that he only knows everything because I gossip with him, DIDN'T YOU!'

McCann looked up at his beautiful wife only to be met with a pair of burning coals staring back at him. He turned his head back to his Mother, cleared his throat 'I'm very sorry Mum, I didn't intend any offence.'

Ofra waved her hand in his direction as if to discard the entire incident 'Here sit down, I have cooked you some curry, you still like lamb curry?'

McCann smiled 'Yes, thanks,' and made his way over to the circular table. As he sat down he recalled his wife's present and stood up again, reached into his bag and presented Ilam with her gift 'I thought you might like this.'

Ilam pouted 'You mean Eduardo did.'

Ofra was preparing the curry on the other side of the kitchen; she called over to Ilam 'Don't you complain if your husband buys you a gift, I know women who complain because they haven't even had sex in five years. If they got a gift they would be crying right now!'

McCann smirked and shrugged his shoulders; Ilam smiled and snatched his gift, unwrapped it and took the silver bottle out of the box. The design was of a silver rain drop; she removed the tail of the rain drop and squirted a little on her wrist. After sniffing the vanilla scent her eyes changed to a pink hue 'Thank you,' she said in an unusually soft tone for a Tlillan Matriarch.

Ofra brought his lamb curry to the table along with a metal ashtray 'That wasn't hard now, was it?' she said to Ilam.

Ilam didn't reply she only sat at the table next to her husband as he picked up his fork and began to consume one of his Mother's best dishes.

'So what else is in that bag, something for me?' asked Ofra sarcastically.

McCann swallowed a mouthful of the curry 'I'm sorry it's just a box of cigars, I didn't think …'

'Oh don't concern yourself with me Duncan, why would I want anything? After all I'm quite happy cleaning and looking after your big lovely house for nothing, since when did slaves receive any form of payment?'

McCann rolled his eyes 'Mum, please.'

'Oh I'm sorry I'll try to keep my fat mouth shut in future, Duncan,' complained Ofra.

'Mum you can have people come in to clean the house and you can have your own personal chef, so give it a rest.'

'My own personal chef? You'd probably pay him to poison me, and those cleaners are all lazy good for nothings.'

McCann thrust his fork and spoon on the table in frustration; he couldn't enjoy his meal while this conversation persisted. One of his Mother's favourite pastimes was moaning and lamenting her situation and if there was nothing to complain about she always managed to create something. He fixed his eyes upon her 'Alright so what do you want?'

Ofra quietened a little 'What do I want?' she replied.

'Yes, I want some bloody peace and quiet so that I can eat this curry and chat with my wife and it seems I won't get that until you are satisfied. So what exactly do you require to stop pissing and moaning about your terrible life, living in a mansion with paid servants to look after your every need, well?' McCann had now launched into one of his rants.

Ofra stood unresponsive to her Son but obviously upset, McCann didn't seem aware or he didn't care.

'Perhaps you need another Gold credit card? It must be hard when you can only afford to visit the most expensive health and beauty salon in the E.U twice a week!' bellowed McCann.

Ilam tried to calm her husband; she placed her hand on his shoulder and whispered softly 'Duncan, enough.'

McCann carried on, ignoring his wife 'I've spent the last couple of weeks in New York sitting in court rooms listening to politicians bullshit; the last thing I need is to come here and listen to you whine. In a month I'll be heading off to Otoch with Mack pirates ambushing us along the way no doubt, then another trial, for Christ's sake all I ask is for some peace and fucking quiet or is that too much?'

Ofra took a handkerchief from her pocket and ran out of the room. Ilam stood up from the seat beside her husband and sneered at him with utter contempt 'I hope you are pleased with your behaviour.'

Ilam placed his gift on the table and walked out after Ofra.

The Englishman went back to eating his curry, by the time he'd finished the meal McCann was filled with regret over his lack of self-control.

After finishing his meal he took the last few puffs from his cigar whilst making a coffee. He could hear his Mother's over dramatic wailing from the lounge. After laying his cigar to rest in the ashtray he entered the lounge. Ilam sat on the sofa comforting Ofra with cries of how cruel and uncaring her Son had been.

McCann spent the next hour or so apologising whilst Ofra worked it for all she could. His wife sneered at him periodically giving him a terribly black look that unsettled the Englishman somewhat. Eventually the matter was settled although McCann would remain in the dog house with his Mother for several days.

That evening he sat on the sofa with Ilam in front of the log fire, she had a whisky for him and they snuggled up to each other. It had been months since the pair had last been together and McCann greatly missed the beautiful Valkyrie. Before retiring they traded experiences via their link, Ilam chose to prepare her husband for his impending court date in the city of Tititl.

Ilam kissed her husband before resting her forehead upon his and melding their minds. For McCann it was quite an exhausting process especially when the experience was protracted. Ilam held him softly with her legs wrapped around his waist as McCann fell into a deep trance.

Upon awaking he looked about to see he was inside a building of obvious Tlillan construction. The inside throbbed with luminous moss but in a very different manner than he was used to, he realised immediately he was observing the room through his wife's Tlillan eyes.

The room was similar to Muul Kaah in that it was the inside of a step pyramid which towered upwards. Steps of stone pointed inwards but every other inward facing block of stone had been removed. Resulting in massive ledges one above the other making their way upwards. Upon the ledges sat statues constructed from a similar stone to the building. Ilam's sharp Tlillan eyes focused in on a statue upon one of the upper ledges, a human would have been unable to see it. McCann recognised it as being his wife, since she was Grand Priestess right now, they were probably of Grand Priestesses past and present, Tititl being the religious capitol of Otoch.

The ground floor was rather different from Muul Kaah, rather than simple stone seats for Matriarchs to sit at with Xch'uups throne at the far end this was confusing. The floor was smooth stone; it had obviously been used a lot in the past. There were two tall stone walls one on each side, they leaned outwards from the central stone floor at a thirty degree angle. The walls sat opposite each other lining two sides of the Pyramid and reaching upwards about three times Ilam's height.

Ilam stood at the far end opposite the entrance alongside Cihuateteo with her flowing white hair, both carrying ceremonial neutronium sabres. Behind them sat Malikah on a throne wearing her white feathered headdress which had grown since the last time he'd seen it. The feathers were far more numerous and they hung down covering her shoulders. The white feathers were quite striking when resting against her jet black Tlillan suit; McCann was impressed with his regal Daughter.

On top of the sloping walls sat about 100 Matriarchs on each side, looking down towards their Xch'uup and the centre of the odd construction. Ilam's eyes then fixed on the centre; on the ground lay a massive stone circle much like a raised dais. It was huge with a radius of 20 feet; dead centre stood a creature McCann was not familiar with. He knew of them but had never seen one, it was a Camazotz. The creature seemed to be a cross between a bat and a Human; it stood about five and a half feet tall. The animal, for that was how it looked to McCann, possessed thick leathery brown arms with flaps of skin connecting those arms to its torso. The torso was covered by some kind of black ablative armour that he wasn't familiar with. The legs were long and thin also covered in the same armour, probably a military uniform, with wide squat boots. Its head was quite striking; there was a lot of fur with a snub nose much the same as gerbil or a bat. Its teeth were tiny and difficult to make out; its large ears oscillated around the massive chamber independently of each other. Its eyes remained shut; it was obvious that the Camazotz didn't use them. The creature's skin and fur was the same dark brown and the Englishman felt rather intimidated by it. According to his daughter these beasts were in the habit of dining on blood much like the vampire bats of Earth.

Upon further inspection it became obvious that the Camazotz was not there of its own free will. Its ankles were chained to the centre of the dais with a selection of weapons placed at various points of the outer circle. McCann guessed its chains reached no further than the radius of the dais and he was correct.

Malikah stood and all of the mumbling which previously filled the great hall died down. She made her way between her Grand Priestess and Grand Marshal stopping before the dais. Ilam and Cihu flanked their Xch'uup maintaining their duty to keep her from harm, not that Malikah was in any danger.

Malikah spoke in fluent Tlillan, since he could hear her through Ilam's ears McCann understood perfectly. Although he did note that Malikah had a very strange accent when compared to native Tlillans, no doubt due to her Human heritage.

'Xalan, when Xch'uup requested assistance from her allies on Gaulthus to repel the Gukumatz; they were nowhere to be seen. When the Makayuuk came for revenge your world fell silent; yet when peril set her sights on your people the Grand Matriarch stood in the way, shielding her Commonwealth confederate from harm,' the sable Queen of the Tlillan spoke in a deep and intimidating voice.

The creature Xalan did not reply it stood in stoic silence as did the audience, listening intently.

'If it were not for Pixoa, the Tlillan race would be nought but a memory, do you have nothing to say for your shame?'

Still the beast refused to answer, much to Malikah's disdain.

'Will you not answer? Perhaps this has become your people's way since the collapse? You reply only in silence, in the foolish belief the Grand Matriarch might forget your betrayal and leave you to carry on unmolested?'

There was a ripple of laughter from the top of the hall as the Matriarchs seemed to find the statement humorous. McCann failed to find it amusing; still it provoked a response of laughter from her audience.

Malikah grew tired of the beast's unresponsive behaviour 'Enough,' the chamber fell silent once more 'You shall now represent what remains of your civilization on the circle of life.'

Malikah looked up at the Matriarchs watching the ceremony from above 'Who will represent Xch'uup?'

Silence filled Tititl, to the sable Queen's obvious disappointment there were no volunteers. McCann took from the lack of response that this creature must have been quite a fearsome opponent on the field of battle.

After an amount of time that was far too long, without a response, Cihuateteo stepped forward. Malikah struck her arm out holding the most formidable warrior on Otoch in place; she smiled at her and said softly 'There is no need for you to meet the Camazotz my sister.'

Malikah looked up and ridiculed the Matriarchs above her 'Must I rely on Cihu always? Do you all fear this barbarian? Perhaps I should ask a male to take your place since there is not a single female with the courage to face this beast.'

A figure in a dark suit stood up on top of the court 'I request the honour of combat with the enemy of Xch'uup.'

Her voice could be heard all around the hall thanks to its excellent acoustics. Malikah grinned at Kaeo, a few years ago she was but a girl and now she was Praetor to Cihu with one conquest under her belt. Though due to her young age she had remained quiet, allowing elder Matriarchs to take the honour. It was not the place of a Praetor with no clan to stand before a Matriarch with several conquests and ovations, to do so would be an insult and there were many such Matriarchs amongst the audience.

'Kaeo, since all Matriarchs have refused the honour you may descend and take your place on the circle; Cihuateteo has more than enough ovations,' the sable Goddess smiled with affection at Cihu who placed her palms together and bowed 'Namaste Xch'uup.'

Kaeo walked to the bottom of the hall from the side of the wall, into the court, past the dais and before Malikah 'Namaste Xch'uup,' she said bowing with hands pressed before her face.

Malikah gave her a proud smile 'You may select your weapon.'

Kaeo turned towards the stone dais but Cihu stopped her, holding her shoulder Cihu unsheathed her hatchet blade sabre. It was very similar to the Blucher sabre or 1796 cavalry sabre, a blade that widened rather than narrowed as it left the hilt. Used by British and Prussian cavalry during the Napoleonic wars it was a devastating cutting weapon that the French often protested the use of. The hand guard was a knuckle duster employed for close quarters combat, often to great effect. It appeared that certain designs were universal throughout the galaxy, the 1796 sabre was based on the Indian Talwar itself and no doubt there were many close approximations on countless planets.

Kaeo's eyes lit up as she took the blade from Cihu, the young lady's excitement was blatant. To have the honour of executing the leader of a wayward world with the added accolade of wielding the mantle of the Grand Marshall of Tlillan was almost more than the girl could handle. Although her victory was by no means a done deal, Xalan was a terrifyingly fearsome warrior.

Kaeo wielded the smooth, cold, dark blue neutronium blade and turned towards her opponent. Cihu stopped her again and placed the scabbard in her hand, a useful weapon in itself. Kaeo in her excitement had forgotten about it and thanked her boss before moving towards her objective.

The Camazotz took a deep breath through its teeth, then reached for one of the weapons placed at its feet around the stone dais. Brandishing a spear of neutronium alloy in its hands the beast gnashed at her, steam came from his mouth and nose. McCann realised that he hadn't sensed the cold crisp Otoch air, experiencing everything through his wife made a great difference.

The bat creature stood prepared with bent legs and spear point ready to impale Kaeo the moment she moved within range. Kaeo moved cautiously but with confidence, holding the sabre in one hand and the scabbard in the other. She stepped upwards in one go onto the circle of life, as Malikah described it, wielding her weapon. Neither combatants were nervous but both exhibited signs of apprehension, the Camazotz was known throughout the galaxy for its fierce fighting ability. Kaeo was well known for much the same reason, a Tlillan Mictlantecuhtli who served beneath Cihu in the campaign to punish the wayward Camazotz. She had already seen many fall before her on the battlefield; Xalan the Camazotz leader knew this all too well and did not relish the thought of engaging her in combat.

The spear gave Xalan a great advantage in reach, the reason he'd chosen it, with that in mind he lunged forward at Kaeo. Clicking constantly to "see" his opponent Xalan thrust the weapon at her torso. Kaeo deflected the spear with little effort, slapping it out of her way with the scabbard as if it were a child attempting to harm her.

Kaeo had studied her swordsmanship by linking with the greatest warriors on Tlillan, notably Cihuateteo being the most accomplished by far. After dismissing the rather feeble first assault she became more confident and pointed the tip of her blade at Xalan. Kaeo moved towards him in an engarde position using her scabbard to deal with Xalan's spear until she could get into striking distance.

Before she could lunge Xalan moved the spear point in a feint, an indirect attack as it's better known, and pierced her forearm. A screech went out from the audience, Macuilachutli, Kaeo's Mother let out a terrifying scream as the long slim spear point ran through her Daughter's arm. Her Mother looked to Malikah who turned away, apparently this had to go to the end, only one of the combatants involved may leave the circle of life.

Kaeo was manipulated to the ground via the spear through her forearm. She didn't shout in pain or call for help, but once on the ground she remembered the Thai boxing skills her father had taught her as a girl and with a single kick swept the animal's legs from under it.

The Camazotz lost all balance as it fell backwards onto the floor pulling the spear out of the Tlillan girl as it toppled over. Kaeo was unable to get a decent grip on her sabre post impalement, so she left it on the stone dais as both opponents leapt to their feet.

The bat creature seemed to smile; at least that's what it looked like to McCann, at his opponent's profuse bleeding. Her hot blood dripped onto the stone creating a steamy wine dark pool at the base. Kaeo, much as her fellow combatant, was unperturbed as she stood unarmed in a boxing stance ready to take on the Camazotz which now advanced, spear in hand, upon his victim.

Kaeo dropped the scabbard as Xalan approached, the creature made a thrust to which she grasped his weapon holding it firm between her arm and the side of her torso; much as a Thai boxer would clasp hold of an opponent's leg when they kicked. The young girl gripped the weapon tightly, refusing to release it, Xalan pulled back but he could not move his spear due to the greater strength of his half-breed opponent.

Kaeo pulled the spear out of his hands, cast it out of the circle and onto the floor of the hall. She now decided to advance, both opponents unarmed, Xalan quickly retreated to pick up a pair of blades, similar to Chinese butterfly knives, that sat around the circle. One thick knife in each hand he stepped forward to meet her in the centre, swinging his blades.

Kaeo stopped moving and waited for the Camazotz to come to her, blood ran down her forearm, torso and leg until it formed a pool on the stone dais floor.

By this time Kaeo's Mother was hysterical, totally losing her calm cold Tlillan façade, she had to be restrained by several Matriarchs but Kaeo ignored the commotion and focused on the closing beast.

The girl of Thai descent kicked off her boots, with a mental message her suit retracted and the boots disappeared leaving her bare feet touching the cold hard stone. The black, blind beast was confused by this, as were nearly all observing the combat, yet Xalan made his first lunge intending to impale Kaeo's chest; it only took three inches of steel from a small knife to kill a man and this knife was closer to a small machete, more than sufficient. Kaeo bounced on her feet and at the right moment she kicked with her leading leg. The girl's superior reach halted the Camazotz in his tracks, preventing his blade from making contact. Her large toe clasped a significant pieced of the Camazotz's flesh, holding the animal's leathery skin in between one large toe and the remaining smaller toes. Once there was a firm hold upon the target, just as had been taught, she turned her foot inwards twisting the beast's skin with it. As soon as Kaeo had turned her foot, with all her might she snapped her leg back towards herself; wrenching a large piece of flesh from the creature's gut.

Whilst the beast stepped back screaming, clicking and whistling, Kaeo's suit formed into a fluid around her wounded forearm closing it up, to plug her bleeding wound. Macuil calmed down now that her daughter took the advantage yet she shook at the possibility of her most feared outcome. Xalan's blood was very thin and spurted out from his stomach area, where he now displayed a horrific gash.

Deychaa taught his daughter the art of fighting dirty in the Thai Boxing ring, much to his Mother's disapproval but now it bore fruit.

Kaeo advanced towards the wayward creature as he'd reached the limit of his chains and could retreat no further. Xalan spun his butterfly knives warding off his determined opponent who had no intention of retreating as fire illuminated her burning eyes. Xalan clicked as a bat, furiously, as if in a panic trying to log every nano-second of her movement towards him.

'Hun hatsik,' shouted Kaeo as she beat her chest with a single fist antagonising Xalan.

Through Ilam's ears it was something like 'Fight me,' in English, whilst implying the person being addressed were a coward.

The mighty Camazotz warrior could not be shamed even by a Tlillan into shrinking from combat. He moved towards her rather than it be known he shied away from a Tlillan girl. Flicking his knives with great skill and finesse Xalan moved in, going for a backwards slash to her throat he came close but Kaeo was prepared. The Half-breed side stepped and took hold of his forearm, with her other hand she grabbed his upper arm tightly and in a lightning move broke Xalan's elbow over her rising knee. Before the beast could even scream, using her superior Tlillan strength Kaeo pulled its bones away from each other tearing the forearm out of its socket.

Xalan dropped to the stone dais floor, in total synchrony the gallery of Matriarchs rose and applauded. McCann found it reminiscent of the days of the colosseum where gladiators would fight and die, performing for their Emperor and the pleasure of the bloodthirsty crowd.

Much like those times Kaeo cast aside the forearm and retrieved her sabre, a warrior these Matriarchs once feared now writhed on the cool smooth stone spurting black blood in all directions. Kaeo, covered in the animal's blood, looked to Malikah and pointed her sword in a gesture of what McCann guessed was respect or a request? He wasn't certain but nevertheless all Matriarchs stood and let out a loud deep howl that could probably be heard miles away.

Malikah neither said nor did anything, McCann guessed instructions were sent mentally. Kaeo received her orders and turned to the Camazotz, with her sabre she cut it from the collar to groin.

The creature writhed in pain but Kaeo held the leathery monster in place with one of her feet upon its sorry neck. The sable warrior next reached down into its torso and ripped out the still beating heart of the Camazotz. She displayed it above her head and let out a deep chilling howl, as a wolf in the cold night air she bayed and her audience of bloodthirsty citizens applauded with screams of vulgar delight.

The Camazotz passed his last breath whilst the thin black blood of Xalan's own heart flowed upon his own face. McCann had learnt long ago that the reason for these rituals went back to the first beliefs of the Tlillan race. The most precious possession a Matriarch, or any creature for that matter, could ever possess was her own life; so if you were to pay tribute to Xch'uup the greatest gift you could offer was life.

To kill the Camazotz leader in such a manner was to offer his existence, a great prize since the more powerful the being sacrificed the greater the life force.

Kaeo demonstrated her total loyalty to Xch'uup, willing to risk her life (her greatest possession) to take one of the most powerful lives in the galaxy, then offer that to Malikah.

Kaeo held the pumping heart above her head and turned to face Malikah, Malikah must have sent another mental message as Kaeo now approached her stepping off the circle of life, still holding the offering aloft.

What came next was one of the most revolting occurrences McCann had yet experienced. Kaeo stood directly before her Xch'uup, kowtowed then placed the heart in her open hand. Malikah took the organ, held it aloft above her beautiful white headdress which absorbed spots of dripping blood. All Matriarchs applauded loudly, howling as bloodthirsty wolves before the kill, Malikah then consumed the raw heart of the fallen Camazotz leader. Consuming his life essence in order to invigorate her own, much the same as when she'd defeated Xch'uup in Muul Kaah.

'Liik'il kiik,' said Malikah softly after having consumed her offering.

Kaeo rose from the floor to stand before her leader.

'K'uchul Chikab, siik Cihu,' spoke the sable Queen instructing Kaeo, above the dying howls, to gather the sword and return it to Cihuateteo.

'Namaste Xch'uup,' replied Kaeo as she retrieved the scabbard and slid the blood stained weapon back inside.

The young girl approached Cihu presenting the blade to her 'Dyos bo'otik Huey'tlacochcalcatl,' she proclaimed on one knee honouring the greatest soldier on Otoch.

Cihu took her mantle 'Liik'il … paal.'

There was a gasp from the Matriarchs surrounding the hall; McCann was not sure what the fuss was about, all she'd said was 'Rise … child,' yet the women observing the events seemed to be stunned by the statement. Then McCann realised why, Cihu produced a red clan stone; McCann had first seen one when his daughter was awarded it by the previous Xch'uup.

Still it was no cause for great shock; at least McCann didn't feel so. The murky waters cleared further when Malikah in her regal blood spattered crown, addressed the shocked Matriarchs looking down.

'Cihuateteo requests that for the first time in millennia a female be made a Matriarch outside her Mother's clan. This cannot be done without the consent of her Mother, Macuilachutli do you consent to the request of clan Teteo?' pronounced Malikah in a loud regal voice.

All eyes in the massive hall turned to Macuilachutli, her vision fixed upon her daughter below standing next to Cihuateteo. She recognised that face, whenever Kaeo wanted to hear a yes she would pull that expression almost whimpering as if on the edge of tears. Macuilachutli had not seen her daughter with such a look in years, Cihu had turned her into one of the toughest warriors on Otoch and it was obvious she wished to join the Tlillan warrior clan.

It was heart wrenching for Macuilachutli on the brink of tears herself at the thought of losing her daughter. One of the three Mictlantecuhtli children born after Malikah, she'd always expected to see Kaeo enter her Mother's clan.

All three Mictlantecuhtli were born into clan Chutli however it became obvious Malikah had arranged for one of her most loyal and obedient servants to join clan Teteo. It took many years to convince Cihuateteo of the child's worthiness but after the campaign on Gaulthus and her defeat of Xalan on Tititl she relented.

'Wa Kaeo taak tu,' spoke a solemn Macuil.

McCann could understand every word as he heard it through Ilam's ears, 'If Kaeo wishes so,' spoke the shaky voice from on high.

All eyes turned to Kaeo who nodded at Cihu 'Hun taak tu,' spoke the excited young lady standing before the towering Cihu.

Matriarchs in the gallery began to whisper and a mumbling noise came down to where Ilam stood, mainly of disapproval. It was felt that Malikah was doing this to spread her influence amongst the clans and perhaps gain a majority foothold in the council.

Malikah looked up and sneered in disdain at the Matriarchs 'K'eek'en toon!' shouted Malikah at the disapproving women, quite a vile name to be called on Otoch, who quietened down.

'You cower in fear before the Camazotz; my hall is all but silent when I ask for only one to honour Xch'uup. Yet when a little girl brave enough to take your place defeats it and requests the privilege of a place in clan Teteo you wish to deny her?' silence once again reigned throughout the great hall on Tititl.

'Brave enough to go against your Xch'uup but not a heretic?' Malikah's eyes burnt like bonfires at night, she unsheathed the sword that all Grand Matriarchs carry by their side and pointed at the gallery 'whoever is brave enough to go against my word may descend now and challenge it, is there one of you with the courage? Or will you remain in the shadows where it is safe and whisper to one another?'

There was no response, the gallery remained totally silent, none were foolish enough to challenge Malikah. She had already dispatched one Xch'uup and the only woman with comparable bladesmanship was her ally Cihuateteo who was about to be paid for her loyalty, with Kaeo; The half-breed girl would join clan Teteo, become a woman and no doubt ascend to First Matriarch of Teteo one day, giving clan Teteo the only other Mictlantecuhtli child beside Chutli.

The gallery did not respond to Malikah's challenge and so the sable Queen sheathed her weapon with a sneer, slamming the hilt against its neutronium scabbard.

Cihu placed the tear drop pendant cut from red stone over Kaeo's head; Kaeo bowed her head to accept it. Once the gold chain had settled around Kaeo's neck, Cihu with an uncharacteristic smile proclaimed 'Ola Kaeoateteo.'

With a sobbing Mother in the otherwise silent gallery the young lady replied 'Namaste Mamah,' bowing with pressed palms before the Amazon with long white hair.

The remaining scene was one of bloody carnage; blood ran down the sides of the circle of life via a tiny gully smoothed out millennia ago. What was left of Xalan lay chained to the stone, aside from his forearm which resided on the court yard below.

Kaeo now stood erect, covered in dark crusty blood, proudly displaying a clan stone around her neck. Cihu was as close to a smile as McCann had ever witnessed. Malikah, regal as ever, dismissed the crowd and the males entered to clean up the temple of Tititl.

McCann regained his bearings in the real world as his wife slowly broke the link; it still drained him to participate in such intense memories.

Ilam cuddled her husband on the sofa as he gained consciousness, McCann rubbed his eyes and asked groggily 'what was all that about?'

The warm Amazon stroked his hair and replied 'That is Tlillan justice, my dear.'

'What about a trial?' inquired the Englishman.

The flaming haired beauty sniggered at his naivety 'There was no need, the Camazotz were guilty of betraying Xch'uup. On Tlillan when someone is guilty there is no need for a trial.'

McCann made a puzzled look as he was cradled by his wife 'That doesn't make sense, how can he be guilty without a trial?'

'The Camazotz were called upon to assist us when the commonwealth collapsed. They were one of the few civilizations able to offer assistance yet they refused, therefore they are guilty of treachery.'

McCann was still uneasy 'But that was what hundreds? Thousands of years ago? Were they the same generation of Camazotz that refused you in the past?'

Ilam kissed the top of his head, nursing her husband as if he were a baby 'No, but the sin remains. You only need betray Xch'uup once, you and your family and your descendants may all be held accountable if the Grand Matriarch so wishes it.'

McCann shook his head in disbelief 'So the whole civilization, generations on, was punished for the decision of their dead leaders centuries ago?'

'Exactly,' said Ilam as she rubbed her husband's arms lovingly.

'What will happen to Hart and Feinstein when they get to Otoch?'

'Their minds will be sifted for all information pertaining to the Makayuuk; after the council is satisfied they shall go to the circle of life.'

'To be executed?'

Ilam shook her head 'The circle of life is not execution; it is possible that they may be victorious. Under those circumstances they are permitted to go free, unless ...'

McCann looked up at his wife who had only just contemplated something 'unless what?'

Ilam stroked his cheek 'Unless Malikah decides to punish them by a different method, she isn't required to offer them combat in the circle of life.'

McCann snorted 'Pah, why do they call it the circle of life? I'd have thought the circle of death would be far more appropriate!'

Ilam smiled at his statement 'The eternal cynic, in the circle is where life is won, taken and offered; it is a transition of the spirit, the power of the soul, everything that constitutes the greatest power in the universe. Death is merely a side effect required for life force to transfer from one vessel to another.'

Before her husband could reply with a cynical comeback she kissed him on the lips. He quickly forgot his witty retort and engaged her in a long passionate kiss in front of the log fire.

After a minute she disengaged 'Enough, we have spoken too much.'

McCann nodded as she removed her suit and that scent of almonds graced his nostrils once again. Her pert breasts popped out and all thoughts of philosophy and justice left his mind. McCann grasped her chest and sucked one of her breasts as if he were a new born.

The tall Valkyrie let out a sigh and her eyes lit up in a glowing pink hue as he played with her nipple in his mouth, then began stripping his clothes off. He pulled her suit down her soft ivory torso and over her buttocks as she lifted them up, McCann tore the ruffled jet black suit from her legs and dived in between them.

The long Amazon lay stretched upon the sofa with her flowing red hair spread out; she groaned as McCann ran his tongue along the inside of her vagina. He had missed the strange taste of Ilam and the feeling it gave him when he licked one side and she always breathed in suddenly, then upon running his rough tongue down the other side she expelled the air with a groan of pleasure.

She started pushing her groin into his face with each groan, her small firm breasts bounced up and down in an erotic dance as she pushed harder each time. Eventually Ilam could no longer stand it and clutched his head one hand on each side, pulling him up and onto her. McCann pushed his manhood into the grunting Valkyrie as she bashed his buttocks with her fists, ramming him down harder and harder.

Ilam's breathing became faster and faster as McCann felt her heat, sweat ran down his back and onto the beauty below him. Just before she climaxed Ilam wrapped her legs over his backside and pushed him into her as deep as she could. The Tlillan goddess pulled his torso onto hers, recognising the moment McCann put his head beside hers, the lovers formed a link. Man and wife connected both mentally and physically sharing the violent explosion of pleasure and pain as her vaginal wall went into involuntary convulsions. Suddenly the sides of her canal clenched and grasped onto McCann who was now used to the pain. He didn't try to pull away but indulged in the pleasure his wife took from her climax as she took a part of his pain. Allowing her to peg her joy to something, intensifying the experience.

She howled, such a long time without the pleasure of making love had left her with a mass of tension waiting to be released. McCann kissed her neck as she screech into his ear for a few seconds.

As Ilam let out a long sigh of satisfaction McCann heard a voice coming from the stairs 'What in the name of god is happening!'

McCann turned to look up and saw Ofra standing on the stairs; obviously their raucous love making had awoken her. The pair of lovers fell off the sofa as they both attempted to look up towards the top of the staircase.

Ilam started to laugh as McCann grabbed his clothes and tried to put his pants on.

'You know decent people are trying to get some sleep!' complained Ofra as she disappeared, returning to her bedroom.

Ilam was in fits of laughter and even McCann had to let out a chortle as he put his clothes back on.

Chapter 10

The next morning McCann made his way to the kitchen where his mother was waiting; it felt as if he were doing the walk of shame. She had prepared him some scrambled eggs on toast with a side order of a vexing stare that burnt into him.

'Thank you,' said McCann as he sat down to eat.

Ofra had the look of a headmistress as she brought his coffee over and placed it down beside him.

'What?' stated McCann in a fed up tone.

Ofra walked over to the tablet she had placed on the kitchen table, she picked it up and began to flick through one of her women's magazines 'Nothing.'

McCann rolled his eyes 'I'm sorry about waking you up last night, okay?'

'I think you should say sorry to the neighbours! You probably woke up half of the lake!'

McCann chuckled to himself but his mother wasn't amused.

Ofra put down the tablet 'We have good neighbours, they are decent people, you know?'

Ilam walked in dressed in her silk pyjamas, a beautiful rose colour that went well with her fiery hair.

McCann snorted 'so what, decent people don't have sex?'

Ofra's eyes widened in shock 'Decent people do not make more noise than a herd of charging camels!'

Ilam's pink eyes were a most inviting sight on a morning, so soft on his eyes, she made him feel warm inside. The pair kissed and Ilam walked over to Ofra kissing her cheek, to which Ofra pulled a wry expression.

Ilam took some Tlillan worms or nook'ol to use the native language, sitting at the table she popped one into her mouth and began to chew.

Ofra took some orange juice for herself 'Imagine if someone heard that commotion! It would be all over town, I couldn't show my face on the Rue Du Marche again!'

McCann raised an eyebrow and gave his wife, who sat opposite him, a wry look of his own. Ilam had to put her hand over her mouth as she tried to stop herself from laughing.

Ofra wagged her finger at McCann 'I am not joking, I slept through every single missile attack on Tel Aviv you know? But that noise would wake a drunken camel!'

Ilam had managed to swallow her food and let out a roar of laughter that made Ofra jump a little.

McCann shook his head 'Mum, those missile attacks were precision bombardments aimed at military targets that's why you slept through it.'

Ofra wagged her finger quicker and raised her voice 'Who told you that?'

McCann rolled his eyes again 'My father.'

'Coo-ara!' shrieked Ofra 'what would that man know? He spent all his time flying around and drinking with his friends!'

McCann was rather shocked at his mother's outburst 'Well his airbase was hit more than once in those strikes …'

She cut him off 'Oh really, is that what he told you? Then how is it our street was hit twice, huh? Mina was killed while sleeping; do you know where your father was? On his airbase at the public house drinking with the other alcoholics!'

Ilam was laughing her head off to Ilam's tale, McCann simply raised his hands in defeat sounding his surrender 'If you say so mum, now can I eat my breakfast?'

Ofra snarled 'I do say so and don't you believe anything that drunken sot tells you!'

'Yes mum,' sighed the Englishman.

Since her son was no longer receptive to her complaints she turned to Ilam 'I was shot at more times than him and he got a medal! When he told me I said 'I didn't know the British give medals for drinking whisky!' oh his face.'

Ilam smiled 'What was the medal for?'

Ofra threw her head back 'Oh I don't remember though I should, he told me enough times about it!'

'The King's commendation for bravery in the air,' interjected McCann.

Ofra waved her hands at her son 'whatever, he used to sit there looking at those stupid silver things for hours!'

McCann exhaled loudly 'They're silver wings and he was very proud of them, he and his co-pilot risked their lives rescuing women and children on their way back from an air drop.'

Ofra turned back to Ilam 'Pah! He cared more about his silver wings than me, I was shot at and helped people from their burning homes but I didn't brag about it or get a medal!'

McCann decided to shut his mouth as there was no way to win, his mother was like a dog with a bone concerning this subject.

Ilam stood up and comforted Ofra 'I'm certain he showed you far more attention than those wings.'

'Don't you believe it,' replied Ofra.

Ilam smiled 'There is an old human proverb, "a man will fight long and hard for a bit of coloured ribbon". So don't be too hard on him.'

'I suppose he was too stupid to realise,' said Ofra begrudgingly as she went back to her magazine.

Eating his breakfast McCann refused to engage any further, allowing his mother to air her grievances.

Whilst Ilam sat listening to Ofra recant her woes during the oil conflicts and how her husband had it so easy, she stopped looking at Ofra. For a moment she was totally stoic, only staring at the wall, then she broke out of it and stood up.

The Amazon stepped over to McCann 'Lian has gone missing,' she stated without emotion.

The Englishman had finished his eggs and was onto his morning paper and coffee 'What do you mean missing?'

'Her whereabouts cannot be accounted for,' said Ilam in a slightly annoyed tone.

McCann was still confused 'Do you mean she's disappeared or just hasn't turned up at a meeting?'

'She did not appear for her morning meeting with William. She was not present in her quarters; her bed had not been slept in all night.'

McCann was a rather non-alarmist type and continued in his relaxed tone reading the paper 'Have they looked at the security footage?'

'Yes, all footage from the last two days has been wiped.'

McCann folded down his paper and looked at his wife in a serious manner 'Is there a search on?'

Ilam nodded 'William has dispatched several search parties, she was not found at I.S.A headquarters. I fear the worst Duncan.'

McCann put down his paper and tapped the table in front of him, a projection of a tablet appeared on the surface of the table where he'd tapped his finger. He spoke to the house AI 'Get me William Faraday.'

After a minute or so William's image appeared on the table they'd been eating their breakfast on 'Hello, Duncan?'

'Morning Bill, what's this I've heard about Lian?'

Faraday had a concerned expression about him 'She's gone missing, security suspects she was abducted sometime yesterday evening. The security files were formatted so we don't know when or how she was smuggled out, either way it was a professional job.'

McCann spoke in an incredulous tone 'How on Earth does someone smuggle a six foot woman out under the nose of security?'

Faraday scratched his head 'The prevailing theory is that she was drugged then stuffed into a cargo crate before being flown out on a transport. We're questioning the pilots of all flights out last night. It's possible that she may be off world already, one of the flights made a delivery to Ecuador.'

McCann snorted loudly 'Off world? For what purpose? These people aren't nut jobs, they knew what they were doing, the only reason to kidnap her is to hold for ransom, right?'

Faraday seemed a little bemused 'Yes well that's all superfluous right now; we need to get her back before Malikah finds out. I'd rather explain our discrepancy in security with Lian safe and sound, if you understand.'

Ilam cut in on the conversation 'Malikah is aware of the situation, she expects a speedy and determined resolution Mr Faraday.'

Now Faraday was more nervous than bemused 'Yes well you can inform her that we have all of our resources invested in solving this problem. I'm going to have to go now but you can get updates via your wrist communicator, goodbye Duncan.'

His image flickered off the table leaving McCann stunned and Ofra silent, it made no sense to kidnap Lian. Faraday was expecting a ransom note as was McCann, Ilam pointed out that anyone with the ability to execute such an audacious scheme must know that Malikah would pay no ransom. In fact it was quite certain that the Grand Matriarch would hunt them down and make certain they suffered.

Ilam was correct in that no ransom ever came, it was surmised that she was smuggled off world via the orbital lift. Some of those crates were supplies intended for I.S.A forces on Bandayuuk. Sent out on the Clotho which was intercepted by Makayuuk pirates, only one cargo crate was taken, the rest of the ship was discarded to be towed to port by the Ares.

It made no sense for pirates to expend such effort for one cargo crate, unless Lian was inside; but what did they want with her? The Makayuuk had no desire for anything other than Machine, even their piracy was not for profit but to disrupt the Tlillan triumvirate which held sway over their world. Other civilizations doing business outside of the Triumvirate suffered no attacks.

After Williams' meeting, concerning the recent abduction, McCann took a stroll through I.S.A. headquarters visiting its new areas, especially Ploutos. The Englishman had great interest in the machine now that he'd learnt of its importance in the scheme of things. Also the fact that it had a great desire to meet Athena had piqued his curiosity, his wife was quite the opposite however.

In Ilam's opinion these things were heresy, she merely tolerated them, spending her time on a visit would be out of the question.

Upon returning from a chat with Klaus and his SI McCann remembered the gold coin he'd purchased in Moscow. Since Ludwig was on the way to the surface he decided to present the old fellow with a gift.

Upon turning the corner of the hallway the Director of Economics door was ajar and McCann could hear a conversation taking place inside.

'How the hell did you manage it Carl?' spoke a thick German accent.

'Ludwig, my name is Ludwig,' replied the Director.

'Fine, Ludwig it is. Tell me though, how did you land this job?'

'Nobody knows and I'd like to keep it that way if you don't mind.'

McCann shifted closer to the door, through a crack he spied Ludwig Von Hazlitt the director of Economics and a thin old fellow about the same age but with stringy yellow hair.

'What do you think I'm crazy? Imagine what would happen to me if they found out about you!'

'I know, I know but it pays to be paranoid.'

The man with yellow hair asked 'Do you still have it?'

'Have what?' replied Ludwig.

'Oh come on, the medal.'

Ludwig pulled out his smoking pipe and chuckled.

'Ah you see? I knew the old bastard still had his Blauer Max! Come on, show me!'

Ludwig chuckled as he unlocked a desk draw with his thumbprint then produced a black case. He passed it to the other man who opened it up to reveal what looked like a spike Iron cross, coloured blue and set on a gold shield. Written on the cross were the words "Pour Le Merite", which even in McCann's poor French he understood as "For the Merit".

The Englishman decided he'd seen enough and stepped into the Austrian's office.

Upon entering both men snatched a look at him, Ludwig grabbed his medal, closed the case then placed it back in his draw 'What are you doing here?' he shouted at McCann.

'I might ask you a similar question, Ludwig ... or is it Carl?'

Ludwig glanced at his friend with disappointment before returning his gaze to McCann 'I don't understand.'

The Englishman chuckled 'You know there can't be that many recipients of the Blue Max, I wonder how long it would take me to find your real name?'

Ludwig stood firm and stubborn 'I don't know what you're talking about Admiral.'

McCann pulled back his sleeve to reveal his wrist tablet 'Let me see, when was the last time a Blue or is it Blauer Max was awarded?'

'Just tell him Carl,' whispered his friend.

No response was forth coming so McCann continued his search 'Let me see, only 39 recipients in the last hundred years. Now how many were Austrian I wonder ...'

Ludwig stepped forward and placed his hand over McCann's wrist tablet 'Very well Admiral, if you wish to know the truth then I'd rather you listen to me before reading stories on the internet.'

The Englishman lowered his arm as Ludwig returned to his desk 'I would like you to meet a friend of mine, Admiral McCann this is Wolfgang Speer ... General Wolfgang Speer.'

McCann shook the old fellow's hand 'Nice to meet you General.'

The old man sat down and produced a bottle of vodka from his desk along with three glasses 'Please take a seat and prepare yourself, for afterwards you will wish you had kept on walking past my office today.'

The three sat down as the old man poured out his Russian liquor 'Let me see, where shall I begin?'

'Start on your transfer,' stated Wolfgang as he sat down to sip on the clear liquid.

'Very well, when the war began I volunteered, but much to the disappointment of a young man there was no glory to be won; any laurels to be had were taken long ago.'

Speer sniggered as he sipped his vodka, McCann listened intently as Ludwig carried on with his tale ...

A military SUV made its way along a muddy road, from inside the truck a young Officer observed the wounded coming in the opposite direction. This was as close to the front line as Carl had ventured, his clean crisp uniform with visor cap, gloves, trench coat and well polished boots were a stark contrast to the state of the German army limping along the roadside.

'Orsha,' shouted the driver as the truck struggled through churned up earth.

'I'm sorry?' replied Von Hazlitt.

'Praksiya, she made a new offensive at Orsha ... those Ivans really tore us apart there you know?'

'I didn't, I've only just been assigned to the Eastern front.'

The driver laughed 'You really pulled out the shitty end of the stick there didn't you, Kapitan?'

Hazlitt gave the driver a hard stare 'I requested the assignment.'

'What? Do you have a death wish?'

Von Hazlitt didn't answer the driver and after an awkward silence his chauffer continued 'Well after the Reds pushed us to Minsk, the furthest back we've gotten is Orsha. Still in Belarus but it could be worse, if that fool Schiffer were in charge we'd be in Warsaw by now!'

The driver let out another laugh to which Kapitan Von Hazlitt made no reply, he was quite disturbed to hear a Private speak in such a manner concerning a Field Marshall, dead or otherwise.

Pulling up outside a makeshift HQ the driver called out merrily 'Here we are Kapitan, your new home, camp Talacyn.'

Hazlitt grabbed his small suitcase then stepped out of the vehicle into the ploughed up dirt, smearing his previously immaculate boots. After fixing his hat and putting his gloves on the Prussian lifted his legs from the earth towards a bunker covered in net camouflage.

The SUV pulled away, its driver called out in his direction 'Udahchee Kapitan,' then laughed as he disappeared into the morning mist.

The camp was a mess of bunkers dug into the confusion of war, men ran to and fro completely ignoring their superior Officer. Hazlitt glanced around for help until a young Lieutenant approached him and saluted 'Kapitan Hazlitt?'

'Yes, that's me.'

'I'm Lieutenant Meyer, allow me to take your luggage Sir.'

The young man led him into a nearby bunker, as he walked down the steps Lieutenant Meyer announced him to the Officers stood around a map which lay on an old wooden army crate.

Franz Webber turned to face the new addition to his Air division 'Welcome to Mother Russia, Kapitan.'

Hazlitt gave a stiff salute before handing over his transfer information on a small thumb drive.

Webber returned the salute before accepting the Kapitan's transfer details 'This is Kapitan Speer,' said the General pointing to a rather dishevelled German Officer smoking a cigarette.

Hazlitt saluted in his stiff fashion, Speer a man in his early thirties smirked as he replied with a tired salute of his own.

Webber placed the thumb drive on a nearby desk and mumbled something to a soldier who began processing the information onto a laptop. 'So you are to replace the Frenchman ... what was his name again?'

'Citron,' blurted Speer as he put out a cigarette.

'Yes Citron, well we have the latest batch of DASA-4 drones from Berlin so according to what I've been told we won't be needing the French any longer.'

Speer laughed as he poured himself some red wine 'Drink Kapitan?'

Hazlitt was shocked 'No, I don't drink on duty.'

Speer placed the bottle back down and took a gulp of the fine wine 'Why?'

Webber examined Speer closely, 'It is unbecoming of a German Officer to be seen drinking by the lower ranks.'

Speer laughed, raising his glass he called out so all were aware 'I'll drink to that!'

Webber who had by now received several promotions and was the commanding Officer of this mess made no response to Speer. Instead he questioned the young Kapitan 'You have piqued my curiosity Kapitan Hazlitt.'

'Ya Herr General?'

'Ya, why did you request a transfer from Crete to here?'

Speer laughed again in a very impolite manner.

'There was nothing for me to do in Crete, Sir.'

'Nothing to do?'

'Correct, it was quite boring, Sir.'

Speer cringed with laughter whilst trying to sip his beverage.

Webber raised his eyebrows 'Boring?'

At that moment a Russian drone fired a salvo of rockets into the camp, attacking from the safety of thick cloud cover. The entire bunker shook violently, tablets and laptops fell about the place.

Hazlitt felt the grip of fear as he dove onto the muddy floor with hands over his head. Upon realising he was safe the Prussian looked up to see that Webber remained standing in the same place and Speer had only moved to prevent his Russian wine from spilling.

Hazlitt slowly got to his feet, as he rose the Kapitan attempted to brush the dirt from his trench coat.

'I'm quite certain that Praksiya shall make your stay as interesting as possible, Kapitan.'

'Ya Herr General.'

'Tell me, when you have had enough excitement what will keep your interest?'

Hazlitt eyed Speer and Webber awkwardly before stating 'I firmly believe it is the duty of every man and woman to serve the Fatherland.'

Speer howled with laughter as another rocket exploded outside of the camp. Webber held back a little smirk before he knocked his Adjutant on the shoulder shutting him up.

Webber nodded his head 'I see, but it says on your file that you're Austrian.'

'I consider myself Prussian, Herr General.'

'I see, so you're here for entertainment and duty to the Fatherland?'

'And ...' Hazlitt stuttered for a moment.

'And?' inquired Speer as he recovered from his laughing fit.

'And for the Blauer Max!'

Speer lost his merry attitude 'A medal? You could buy one on E-bay for a few marks, why risk your life for the damn thing?'

Hazlitt didn't reply, he only eyed the Iron cross pinned to Speer's jacket then the Knights cross hanging around Webber's neck.

Speer unpinned his Iron Cross tossing it on the map of Orsha and surrounding terrain, 'Here, if you want a medal take this one.'

The Austrian glanced at the award before replying 'Nein, I must win my own.'

At that moment a young Lieutenant entered the bunker and saluted 'Lieutenant Gerber, reporting as requested General.'

'Kapitan, this is your Adjutant, Lieutenant Gerber. He will take you to your bunker then familiarise you with the drone booths.'

Hazlitt saluted 'Thank you Sir.'

As The Lieutenant took the Kapitan's baggage out of the bunker Webber called out 'Udahchee on getting your Blauer Max, Kapitan!'

Whilst walking to his bunker Carl asked the Lieutenant 'What does Udahchee mean Lieutenant?'

'It is Russian Kapitan, for good luck!'

The Kapitan made his way to his bunker, as he did Webber asked Speer 'What do you think of our new Air Force Kapitan?'

'I'm not sure if he's one of Hoch's little boys or just another glory hunter.'

'Perhaps both?'

'In which case he's far more dangerous than the Ivans.'

The General took an empty glass and motioned towards Speer's bottle, as the Kapitan poured a drink he muttered 'What's the worst he can do? After all he'll only be sitting in a booth.'

The next day Von Hazlitt entered the command bunker to meet a new face, 'Generale Messana may I introduce to you Kapitan Carl Von Hazlitt.'

The Austrian saluted the Italian before joining the Officers around the map.

'Today we shall begin our counter-offensive, it is my desire to capture Kochanava here,' Webber pointed to the town on the map 'this shall provide an opening into Orsha. Kapitan Hazlitt, your drones shall be providing air support for the ground offensive led by Kapitan Speer and Generale Messana. It is your task to clear out anyone or thing that lays between our armour and Kochanava, is that understood?'

'Anything?'

'If it breathes I want it dead by the time our tanks have reached it, you are to use gas.'

'Gas?'

'Is there an echo in this room Kapitan?'

'I apologise ... Sir, but I was under the impression that the Geneva convention ...'

Speer shook his head as Webber explained 'In Mother Russia the Geneva convention is irrelevant, is that understood?'

'But there are women and children in the way.'

Franz Webber leaned in close to the Austrian and whispered 'Then you had best decided, Herr Kapitan, whether you are here to protect the women and children of the Fatherland or those of Mother Russia?'

The Austrian's eyes searched around the bunker but were only met by the stern gaze of his comrades, 'I thought ...'

Webber shouted as he stood erect 'The German soldier does not think Herr Kapitan, he carries out his duty. If you came looking for honour and glory then you were lied to, in Russia you shall find nothing of the sort. But if you live long enough you may walk away with your precious Blauer Max or be buried with it ... which is more than most soldiers are lucky enough to receive, most end their days as rotting corpses littering roadsides, Herr Kapitan!'

Hazlitt nodded 'Understood Herr General.'

Webber fixed his eyes on Speer 'After Kapitan Hazlitt has dispersed the VX nerve gas I want you to bring up your infantry and Messana's tanks to clear out anything that remains. But be aware Speer, I have reports the open fields are heavily mined.'

'Understood General,' saluted Speer.

That day General Franz Webber launched his counter-offensive, pushing the Reds back to Kochanava. Carl Von Hazlitt had awoken to the truth behind the propaganda, yet despite becoming disillusioned he pressed on with only one thought in mind, his Blue Max. Thirty Russian MiGs downed and he would be recalled to Berlin to receive his laurels.

Hazlitt walked into the mobile drone bunker, this was where the brand new drone booths had been installed. The Squadron saluted as they stood next to their assigned stations. Hazlitt nodded 'Good morning Gentlemen, the flight plan has been downloaded to each station. We are to deliver VX nerve gas to each town and village along Kapitan Speers' path to Kochanava, is that understood?'

'Ya Herr Kapitan,' replied his squadron in concert.

'If anyone has a problem with that they may leave now.'

Lieutenant Gerber replied 'It's nothing we haven't seen before, Sir.'

Hazlitt nodded 'Good, then to your stations Gentlemen.'

Whilst the Officers slipped into their stations, on the airfield outside, the delta wing, single engine drones were ready to take off. Their landing gear being little more than a trolley which the drone flew off once it gained lift.

The ground crew started up their engines and all 18 craft took to the skies one at a time, carrying a payload of chemical gas in tubes slung underneath their single wings.

The Austrian reclined inside his booth, monitoring the wire framed mission plan whilst the lead drone used its early warning radar system to detect any enemy aircraft or weapon lock-ons from the ground.

Compared to the Shogun drones that Ryu piloted these were very slow and clumsy, but there was a good 60 years between the two designs. Using petroleum to power a jet engine was still the standard method of propulsion back then. Also the drone booths had to be a lot closer as electronic interference might easily knock them out of the sky.

'Approaching first target Kapitan!'

A small village flashed with a bright red marker on his screen 'Two and Eighteen deliver your payload, then return to base.'

The drones broke away from their formation, as they approached the village streaks of smoke dissipated from several long tubes held beneath the wings. After making a few passes their gas was expelled and they broke away, returning to HQ.

By the end of the mission Carl had dumped his nerve gas over the target of Webber's counter-offensive and returned to re-arm for ground/air combat. His squadron returned to the skies as Germany advanced with their Italian cohorts.

'Sir! We have BVR weapons lock.'

Hazlitt flicked some switches as the AI attempted to triangulate the position of their attacker 'I think I have his position.'

'Position confirmed Sir, permission to drop countermeasures.'

'Wait Gerber, let Ivan think he has us,' Carl quickly tapped a button and spoke into his mic 'Kapitan Speer, I have Russian aircraft, possibly MiGs approaching from North, North East, distance unknown.'

A crackling voice from inside an armoured personnel carrier replied 'Leave me six drones for air support, understood?'

'Understood Kapitan, Hazlitt out.'

Next the Austrian noticed six Russian fighters appear on the radar 'Gerber you lead the ground support, I want the rest of you to follow me, we're going to give Ivan a good lashing.'

Carl tapped on his monitor, selecting 11 fighters to follow. As they broke away they fired off their countermeasures, confusing enemy radar.

The Russians were forced to get within visual range, once they did Hazlitt called out to his squadron 'Spotted six Su-30sm fighter jets,' the Austrian Kapitan tapped his screen again selecting which pilots would chase which enemy 'targets chosen, good luck gentlemen!'

The Russian jets used their vectored thrust as best they could but the small drones were just too nimble in the air. Added to that they had a much smaller radar and heat signature, making weapons lock a very hard thing to get and maintain.

The tiny German drones seemed to swoop from nowhere, delivering their small but effective air to air missiles.

No Su-30's returned home that day and Carl had taken his first confirmed kill.

After having flown the brand new drones for the first time the Kapitan relaxed in his bunker which he shared with Kapitan Speer. Speer produced two glasses and poured from a wine bottle as the sound of shells pounding the ground reverberated through the walls. Pulling a crate up to the Austrian's bed (a wooden frame pushed into the earthen bunker) he raised his glass 'To a successful counter-offensive.'

Hazlitt raised his glass 'To the Fatherland.'

Speer held his glass up high and in an Adolf Hitler parody he shouted 'SIEG HEIL, SIEG HEIL, SIEG HEIL!'

Hazlitt chuckled as he took a slurp of the wine 'This is good stuff.'

'I took it from Praksiya's own vaults in Moscow!'

'Tell me, how long have the German army been using VX nerve gas?'

Speer swallowed a gulp of the wine then poured himself some more 'Since Moscow.'

'Who ...'

'Used it first?'

'Ya.'

'That remains a mystery mein friend, all I can say for certain is that we were going to cross the Moskova River and our advance was halted after a fog of nerve gas came rolling at us from the opposite direction.'

'So the Russians used it first?' it seemed to justify that day's actions in Carl's mind.

'The Russians said that we bombarded a chemical weapons warehouse.'

'What do you think?'

'I think they saw us coming and realised that if we made it onto the other side Moscow would be ours. So they had a plan of last resort, to gas us rather than accept defeat.'

'So the Russians started it.'

Speer laughed 'Does it matter?'

'I think it does,' replied the Kapitan as he drank the red wine.

Speer shook his head 'Would you have done any different if it were Russians crossing the Spree?'

Hazlitt went quiet.

'You smoke?'

The Austrian shook his head 'Nein.'

Speer produced a tobacco pouch from his jacket pocket 'Here try some of this.'

Hazlitt looked at the brown shredded leaf and the white rolling papers in puzzlement.

'Let me show you,' stated Speer as he rolled the Kapitan a cigarette 'there you go!'

The Austrian took a puff before choking on the wretched weed. Speer laughed 'Ahh, you'll get used to it Kapitan; just like you'll get used to Russia, a cruel and unforgiving mistress!'

As Hazlitt contemplated the Russian tobacco he inquired about his predecessor 'So what happened to the man I replaced?'

'Ahh, Francois? He was captured by the Ivans, at least that is what they tell his family.'

'Oh?'

Speer gave a rather sinister look 'Ya, I remember when they stormed our forward camp and captured Schiffer. He was paraded through the streets of Moscow.'

'For what?'

'For the citizens of Moscow to beat him to death.'

Hazlitt sat up in shock 'Surely not?'

Speer rolled himself a cigarette then lit it with a match 'Oh ya Herr Kapitan, you've gotten yourself into a nice little fix when you left Crete for this shit hole.'

'And Citron?'

'The same, they beat him to death outside of Red Square. The Troika had it taken off the internet before there were 10,000 hits.'

'So it's true?'

'You bet your life, our exalted leader cannot be trusted any more than a KGB agent!'

'But we are not Barbarians!'

Speer laughed as he raised the glass to his lips, after taking a gulp he stated sardonically 'Says he who just gassed hundreds of innocent children?'

Hazlitt put his head in his hands as he began to realise what he'd gotten himself into.

Speer consoled the young Kapitan 'Maybe you can get a transfer out, I could speak to the General.'

The Austrian shook his head 'Nein, I cannot leave without my Blauer Max.'

'Why do you want a medal so badly?'

Hazlitt took a drag on the cigarette then exhaled the smoke 'My family, my wife she told me that I was a horse's arse when I took a commission with the Luftwaffe. Then when I volunteered for the East she threatened to divorce me.'

'What does that have to do with the Blauer Max?'

'I must prove to her and my family that there is some honour in war, if I return without the Blauer Max she will divorce me. But if I have the medal and she sees the status that goes with it then she will stay.'

Speer shook his head 'In all this madness, I think that is the most insane story I've ever heard!'

'Insane?'

'Ya, a few Marks of scrap metal to save a marriage but you must travel to Russia and murder children to earn it.'

Carl looked up towards the ceiling as dirt fell loose thanks to Russian artillery 'Do they ever stop?'

'Like their operators, they never sleep. I have been on this front for over a year now and I cannot recall a day the Ivans didn't pound us.'

'We will win this war,' stated the Austrian in a firm tone.

Carl smiled at his counterpart 'Is that what Hoch told you?'

'You don't believe it?'

Speer smiled as he took a swig of fine wine.

Carl gave a puzzled look 'Then why are you here if you believe it is destined to fail?'

The dishevelled Speer stood up and tapped his iPod a few times before placing it inside its dock. Carl then heard a familiar tune play as Spanish guitars began to strum; Speer danced to the music comically as he sang along to the words of La Bamba. Although he had no understanding of the Spanish language he was fluent to the words of the popular song. Carl put down his glass and clapped along as Kapitan Speer danced in the cramped bunker. Even the pounding of Russian artillery seemed to beat the earth in chorus to Speer's feet.

Suddenly Lieutenant Meyer entered the bunker 'Kapitan Speer ... excuse me Sir!'

Speer continued to dance ignoring the Lieutenant, after a few moments Speer grabbed Meyer and began to dance with him to the music of Los Lobos. Carl laughed as he clicked his fingers in time to the guitars and Russian shells loosening the dirt from around their bunker.

'Kapitan! It is urgent!' protested Meyer.

Speer ignored him and continued dancing 'Yo no soy marinero, yo no soy marinero soy Capitan. Soy Capitan, soy Capitan.'

As the pair frolicked to the music a voice shouted from the bunker entrance 'Speer!'

The Kapitan let go of the Lieutenant and fixed his gaze upon General Franz Webber. All three Officers stood to a stiff salute as the music of La Bamba played in the background. Webber narrowed his eyes, scanning the bunker 'I want you both in my bunker ... and Wolfgang ...'

'Yes General?' replied Speer.

'Keep the noise down, you might scare the Ivans.'

Speer smiled 'Yes General.'

Webber returned the smile and left the bunker.

Carl exhaled a gust of wind 'I thought we were for it there!'

'Nien, the General is a good man.'

Several months later, a terrible Russian winter had passed, Carl Von Hazlitt stood at the airfield watching ground crews remove frost and ice from the single winged drones. The cold air condensed his breath upon exiting his nostrils, he rolled himself a cigarette whilst observing fog roll over the tree tops. Since last year the Germans had ended up further away from Moscow than when he arrived.

Counter offensive hit counter offensive until the Austrian could no longer count how many had truly taken place. All he knew for sure was that Praksiya had denied them the city of Orsha and chased them back through Mother Russia to Zodzina, a town not far from Minsk.

The Ivans were preparing for another assault, probably to push them back into Minsk before surrounding the city.

Von Hazlitt puffed on his Georgian tobacco as he enjoyed the fresh morning mist. From behind him the voice of Lieutenant Gerber called out 'Kapitan, there is an urgent message for you, in the Generals bunker!'

The Austrian took a few puffs on his smoke before flicking it into the snow 'Ya, ya, I'm coming.'

He trudged along the frosty ground, at least he could walk on the earth properly now. Stepping down into the Generals bunker now covered in tundra camouflage the Austrian was a little taken back. Inside stood the General and his entire staff, including his whole squadron.

Franz Webber had a sullen look, 'I regret to inform you Kapitan,' he produced a letter from Berlin 'that according to the Troika you are to be ...'

Carl could feel the tension building up, he eyed the letter and wondered what bad news he might be getting now. His wife had already divorced him, leaving him for some social worker in Vienna.

Speer stepped up to the Kapitan 'I'm sorry Carl, but you're to be awarded the Blauer Max!'

Webber thrust the envelope in his hands as Gerber brought out a frozen cheesecake with a single candle sticking out of it. Speer pulled out a bottle of vodka and began pouring shots into glasses of assorted sizes.

Von Hazlitt opened the letter, according to Berlin he had made 34 confirmed kills and was to return home to receive his laurels. He'd been unaware of his achievement, it was only now he realised how empty it all was; nevertheless Carl smiled and soldiered on rather than disappoint his comrades.

Speer thrust a glass of vodka into his hand as a slice of rock hard cheesecake was doled out to the Austrian.

Speer turned on his iPod as the song "Mambo No.5" blasted out, the Tank commander started to shift to and fro as the music played 'A little bit of Monica in my life, a little bit of Erica by my side.'

All the time a young Officer stood in the doorway with his luggage, waiting for the celebration to subside. The dancing and chatter quietened as everyone fixed their eyes on the young man.

'Lieutenant Werner, reporting for duty to General Webber.'

Webber stepped out from the crowd of men packed into his bunker 'Come in Werner.'

The young clean cut man stepped in uncomfortably.

'This is Kapitan Speer, you shall be his adjutant after that unfortunate incident with Messana.'

'Kapitan,' the young man dropped his luggage as he saluted his new commanding Officer 'unfortunate incident?'

'Insubordination Lieutenant, he ignored specific orders from Berlin so I was forced to carry out mine.'

The young Lieutenant was so fresh every man in the bunker could smell his uniform, 'Have no fear Herr General, I shall not disappoint you.'

Webber nodded 'Say hello to Kapitan Von Hazlitt, this little soiree is in aid of his Blauer Max.'

'Blauer Max?'

'A medal Lieutenant, a very high honour.'

'Oh, I apologise Kapitan, I meant no insult.'

Carl placed a hand on the new Lieutenants shoulder 'That's quite alright, now have a drink young man!'

After the short celebration was over Carl sat in the bunker with Franz and Wolfgang. The three of them were finishing off the vodka as they considered the new man.

'He's too young to be here,' said Speer as he gazed into the light refracting out of his shot glass.

'I'm sure Praksiya shall put ten years on him after his first month,' retorted Carl.

'He's similar to you Carl, when you first arrived,' noted Webber.

'Oh? What was I like?'

'You were one of these new generation of Germans, a machine built to take orders and follow duty without question.'

'Is that what you thought of me?'

'Ya, until you mentioned your Blauer Max then I had you down as a glory hunter.'

'So what am I now?'

Speer chirped up 'An idiot!'

'Why an idiot?'

'Because you're still here with us, fighting a hopeless war against an unrelenting foe; if you had half a brain you'd have been transferred back to Crete long before now.'

Carl thought on what Speer had said 'You're right, but I have nothing left waiting for me in Austria anymore. I suppose I stay here because I'm looking for something and I just haven't found it yet.'

Webber put his feet up on the crate as he relaxed into his seat 'When you go back to Berlin, to get your medal, look for someone.'

'Look for someone?'

'Ya, find a girl, if you request it I'm sure Hoch will allow you to settle down.'

Hazlitt chuckled 'Hoch? How would I make such a request of him?'

Webber pointed at the Knight's Cross which hung around his neck 'I met him once, when he gave me this. When you get your award he will present it to you, ask him then, he couldn't refuse you publicly.'

'So why didn't you ask him the same?'

Speer laughed 'Because without Franz we'd be fortifying Berlin awaiting Praksiya's final assault!'

Carl snorted as he produced his tobacco pouch 'What would I do with myself?'

General Webber put his feet down and leant in towards the Austrian 'When we lose this war Germany shall need men to prevent the disasters of the twentieth century.'

'What do you mean?'

'This whole calamity, do you know why we are fighting Praksiya?'

'For the oil fields.'

Webber shook his head 'We are here because when Banks and State merge they have a baby, the baby is named fiat currency.'

'But we have a gold standard now.'

Webber nodded his head 'And Russia?'

'They have the Petro-Rouble.'

'And the rest of the E.U.?'

'The Euro.'

'Fiat money.'

'Ya, so?'

'So how do you buy oil for Euros?'

Hazlitt chuckled 'Well you don't, who would sell oil for pieces of worthless paper?'

'Right, we need to buy it with the gold Mark. But when the gold runs out what then? We have a bunch of countries trapped into a debt system on the Euro supported by Deutsche Bank with the golden Mark; and since the British blockade it can only last for so long until Berlin's gold is gone.'

'So you're saying this war is over Economic ideology?'

'Ya.'

'But we have the oil fields.'

Speer laughed.

Webber looked his Austrian Kapitan in the eye 'Praksiya took most of them back last month, she pushed us out of the Urals and back into Sevastopol.'

'But the news said ...'

'The State news? Of course! They say we're fighting a valiant frontline action, pushing the Russians back into the wastes of Siberia. They spend more time dreaming up caricatures of Yevpraksiya than coming up with a viable plan.'

'If she's taken Georgia back then she'll be pushing us in the South come next year.'

Franz took a shot of vodka 'What is she now?'

Speer peered off into the distance 'The sugar plum cock sucker!' None of the men laughed.

'Ya, the sugar plum cock sucker. I'm sure she cries herself to sleep every night in the Kremlin.'

'What difference would it make if we had no Euro?'

'There would be no debt, no need for Germany to break her back keeping its debtors on life support. No need to steal Praksiya's oil, if people lived within their means there would be a lot less death. The Troika is full of nations that refuse to live within their means, they use fiat money to support that.'

'I understand.'

'You and Wolfgang must go back and wait, when this has ended we will need you both to save Germany and the German people.'

'How?'

'Educate yourself, you're both clever men, and remember that man must live within his means. When man does otherwise this is the result, death, destruction and lies.'

Ludwig relaxed into his seat after finishing the story 'So there you go Admiral, now you know the truth.'

'It seems so.'

'Are you happy?'

'No.'

Speer, now an old man, tried to reason with McCann 'It was a difficult time, we were young men pumped full of idealistic schise.'

McCann maintained a steely gaze towards Hazlitt 'You gassed children?'

Hazlitt returned an equally stern look 'Ya, what do you want me to say Admiral?'

Speer slapped the table 'Ryu gassed and napalmed children, did she not?'

'Korea was forced to defend itself.'

'So her murder was justified?'

'Yes, it was.'

'What of Carl?'

'I guess he'll just have to live with what he's done.'

'You won't turn him in?'

The Englishman shook his head slowly 'There is no punishment for his crime.'

Hazlitt sneered back but Speer exhaled in relief, 'Where is your gratitude Carl?'

The Austrian fixed his eyes upon the Englishman 'Gratitude? I have nothing but contempt for the British. You forced the whole issue, anything to bring the Fatherland to its knees!'

Speer grabbed his friend 'Carl, shut up, someone might hear you!'

The old man didn't care anymore, he wanted to be punished for what he'd done. But no punishment was sufficient to wipe away the stain of his deeds, his conscience would be smeared until the day he died.

McCann sneered back at the old man 'You don't hate the British, the Russians or even the Germans, you hate yourself for what you did.'

Carl Von Hazlitt peered stoically at the Admiral 'Inside this old man there are two wolves, Admiral. One is hate and anger the other peace and love, they fight each other every day.'

McCann nodded 'That fight takes place inside all of us.'

Speer made a smile at his friend 'And do you know which one will win, Carl?'

'Nein.'

'The one you feed.'

More than a month later and nothing had been heard, it was clear Lian had been taken by the Makayuuk however their purpose was unknown. The prisoners Hart and Feinstein still had to stand trial on Otoch and it was McCann's duty to transport them.

Since Lian's abduction pirate attacks had dropped dramatically and no-one could fathom why. It was suspected there was a link with Lian's disappearance but no-one could make it other than the drop occurred after her kidnapping.

McCann was boarding Athena, dressed in his uniform he strolled along the docking arm connecting his ship to the Tsiolkovsky. Stepping through the airlock Hassif and Louis were there to greet him along with Kim.

'Welcome aboard Admiral!' saluted Kim.

McCann returned his salute 'Thank you Commander.'

Louis let out a sigh 'Good to see you mon ami,' then shook his hand much to the shock of Kim and the delight of Hassif.

'It's good to be back,' replied the Englishman.

'It's nice to see you Duncan,' said Hassif greeting his old friend with a smile.

As they were about to have a chat McCann noticed another of Athena's Officers approach them. He saluted the Admiral to which McCann returned the salute. The Englishman noticed from his dark blue uniform that he was a drone pilot and from the single black and grey stripe on his cuff he was of the rank of Flying Officer, in the army that would have been a lieutenant or in the Navy a sub-lieutenant.

On board I.S.A vessels Navy ranks were in use so McCann addressed him 'Is there something you want sub-Lieutenant?'

The man was of Chinese descent and despite his many campaign ribbons, rather nervous 'I'm sorry to trouble you Admiral, I'd didn't mean to intrude but ...'

McCann sighed 'Well out with it man I haven't got all bloody day you know!'

The pilot smiled nervously at his commanding Officers rebuke 'It's about my daughter, Lian.'

McCann felt embarrassed 'Ah I see, well is there something I can do for you?'

'Have you heard anything? She has been gone more than a month and there is no word, the I.S.A have told me nothing so I was wondering if there was anything you might know, Sir.'

McCann cleared his throat 'My apologies Mr?'

'Oh Han, just Han.'

'Mr Han, I was unaware. As for Lian they believe she is being held probably by the Makayuuk, but for what purpose is unknown. It seems some I.S.A staff were paid off to deliver her; they have been dealt with already. As soon as I hear anything I'll let you know.'

Han was obviously let down, but knowing that the Makayuuk were holding her and she was probably alive did perk him up a little and he left in a better state than before he spoke to McCann.

As Han disappeared down the corridor Hassif shook his head 'That poor man, I couldn't imagine if that happened to my daughter.'

McCann patted Hassif on the shoulder 'I'd imagine they'd have a much harder time abducting Amitra.'

Hassif nodded 'But still it would be impossible to suffer.'

Louis snorted 'I guess the fun never stops on board the happy ship Athena!'

The Englishman gave him a wry look 'What's got you so optimistic and chirpy all of a sudden?'

Hassif smirked 'A new assignment to the engine core.'

McCann chuckled 'Some new engine parts and the man cares not for conspiracy theories anymore?'

Louis sneered at Hassif who was taking great delight in it all; Kim was puzzled as to what was so amusing.

Hassif laughed 'No Duncan, it's not and engine part. The new assignment is actually about thirty years old, tall and according to rumour has a gift for the French tongue so to speak.'

McCann burst out laughing and even Kim had to look away as he would have cracked up looking at Louis' face any longer.

Louis gave his signature sneer aimed at his Indian friend 'If it weren't for me you assholes on the Bridge would have nothing to gossip about! Sitting around doing nothing while I work my ass off in the engine core, fucking assholes every one of you!'

McCann laughed even harder 'You mean working off the arse of your new assignment?'

Louis shouted back at his friend 'Why do you have to be such a prick? There are enough asswipes in charge on this ship.'

Kim stopped giggling and fixed his gaze upon Louis displaying a rather shocked expression.

Louis waved his hand at Kim 'Oh no offence.'

Both McCann and Hassif laughed at Kim who stood totally overwhelmed by the uncouth behaviour of Athena's Chief Engineer.

Louis waved his hand at the First Officer of the Athena again 'Oh take that board out your ass Kim, it's like the ghost of Ryu haunting the fucking ship.'

Before Kim said anything McCann interjected 'So are we ready to cast off?'

Louis blew a puff of air out of his mouth and said loftily 'Of course, who do you think is running this cruiser, them?' he gestured with his head towards Hassif and Kim.

'Well I suggest everyone get to their stations, we'll be casting off in two hours,' stated McCann.

Louis grunted 'Sure, see you in the lounge later?'

McCann nodded 'See you then Louis.'

Louis marched off to the lifts, taking him to the engineering section of the ship where he maintained the power core and engines with his army of nanites.

Once Louis had gone Kim shook his head 'That man is intolerable.'

McCann grinned 'No he's just a miserable arsehole and French into the bargain.'

Hassif grinned in agreement as McCann led them to the Bridge.

'Good morning Admiral,' came the voice of Athena as they strolled along her corridors.

'Good morning Athena, how are you?'

'Very well thank you, how is Ilam?'

McCann peered up with a raised eyebrow 'Very well, don't tell me you keep correspondence with her too.'

Athena replied calmly 'I was merely being polite Admiral and attempting to make conversation.'

'How are the prisoners Athena?'

'They are both in good physical health, although they seem to be somewhat depressed. I believe their limited living space may have impacted them psychologically,' replied the ever watching Goddess.

McCann chuckled 'My heart bleeds.'

Hassif grinned but Kim maintained his stony composure.

'Most amusing, Admiral,' came the soft voice of Athena.

The Englishman looked up 'Sorry?'

'You were using sarcasm to convey your lack of pity towards the accused. Would I be correct in assuming you also believe them to be guilty of insurgency?'

McCann looked upwards 'Yes, don't you?'

'I find it quite alarming how Humans without the aid of proper instrumentation will come to such conclusions. I am able to detect galvanic skin response whereas you have only your intuition,' replied Athena softly.

McCann smiled 'You still didn't answer me, do you think they're guilty?'

Athena responded in a tone that sounded almost begrudging 'After studying their electro-chemical skin and brain patterns when questioned, I believe them both to have participated in the plot they are charged with.'

'So I was right?'

'Yes Admiral, would you tell me how you came to that conclusion?'

'Well that Jay always looked shifty to me and the other well she's a self-serving bitch isn't she?'

'Please describe what you mean by 'looked shifty' Admiral.'

Hassif sniggered at the question.

McCann raised his eyebrows 'Well you know, he looked suspicious, his eyes were always darting about and he was never far from that laptop.'

Athena was quiet for a moment then replied 'Do you suspect Hassif of collaborating with the Makayuuk?'

McCann blew a puff of air out of his mouth 'Of course not!'

'Yet his behaviour falls within the parameters you described as looking shifty.'

Hassif peered at McCann 'You aren't going to put me in a control collar and deliver me to the Tlillans are you Duncan?'

McCann shook his head 'It's more than that Athena, it's instinct I can't really put it down exactly. My instinct isn't always right but sometimes it's just too difficult to ignore and it tells me those pair are as guilty as a member of parliament in a public toilet; besides Lian had read their thoughts and discovered them both, that's hard to dismiss.'

'Did you believe he was shifty before Lian discovered the treachery?'

McCann let out a sigh 'Well he was always shifty, but then again so are all politicians. I had no idea he was involved in a plot to crash our economy until Lian exposed him.'

McCann then put his arm around Hassif's shoulder 'As for Hassif, he just works very hard.'

The lift door slid open and McCann stepped out to be announced by Kim 'Admiral on the Bridge!'

McCann somewhat embarrassed smiled and made a casual salute to his staff before slipping into his chair 'I want to cast off as soon as possible.'

The voice of Athena filled the Bridge 'Admiral, we are not scheduled to fold space for another three hours.'

McCann sat back looking up at the black dome in the ceiling where Athena was housed 'I know Athena, that's exactly why we're leaving early. Someone inside the I.S.A is working with the Macks; I'm not taking any more chances.'

Kim bent down and whispered into McCann's ear 'We have a new Officer on the weapons and shields post, Lieutenant Meyer, Sir.'

McCann looked at the new man on the far right station 'Welcome to the Bridge Lieutenant Meyer.'

The German had short dark hair and a pair of silver framed glasses, the glasses carried a built in eye tablet. The technology tracked his eye movements and with enough discipline a person could use their tablet without the need to carry it around. Although the eye tablet did have its limits it allowed the young man to increase his efficiency, in emergencies he could multi-task all three stations if required.

Hassif had his doubts concerning the technology, but Jürgen had used it to great effect for the two years he'd been assigned to the Athena and it'd earnt him a promotion.

Lieutenant Meyer replied in a slightly uncomfortable pitch 'I have served in the pit for two years already, Admiral.'

McCann was a little surprised but on second thoughts there were quite a few in the pit and he didn't know them all by name 'Ah I apologise Lieutenant, I haven't been briefed as to any changes in position. I'm sure if Mr Kim believes you're capable you'll do just fine.'

Kim corrected his commanding Officer 'It was Technician Hassif that recommended Mr Meyer, Sir.'

McCann sighed 'One month away and I don't even know my own Bridge staff anymore, is there anything else I should be informed of Mr Kim?'

'Nothing comes to mind, Sir.'

The Englishman narrowed his eyes as he glanced at Kim 'Well if something does enter that mind of yours let me know will you?'

Kim smiled nervously 'Yes Sir.'

'Course set and confirmed with Tsiolkovsky Traffic control, Admiral' announced Athena.

'When Hassif has certified your course you may cast off, Athena,' replied McCann.

Hassif started tapping on his station furiously, however Meyer pronounced to his commanding Officer 'I have already certified Athena's calculations, Admiral.'

Hassif turned away from his console to Meyer 'Send me your certification.'

Using his right eye he sent the certification to Hassif who checked it against his own results. McCann grinned and raising his eyebrows said 'Well Hassif? How has Mr Meyer done?'

'Satisfactory, course certified,' a ringing endorsement from Hassif concerning matters of course certification.

'Athena cast off as soon as possible,' ordered McCann.

Athena announced throughout the ship in her soft voice 'Prepare to cast off,' sending every man and woman to wherever they should be.

Airlocks closed on both the ship and the docking arm, next electro-magnets that held Athena in place slowly powered down allowing the arm to retract back into the Tsiolkovsky. From outside it was similar to an elegant ballet as one partner released his grip permitting the ballerina to move away with beauty and grace. As Athena drifted off her engines fired a little, just enough to push her away from the danseur. An elegant Athena glided along the stage that was Earth orbit, leaving the blue planet behind as she turned and made for a point above the accretion disc.

'Incoming communication from the Chutli,' declared Hassif.

'Put her through,' replied McCann.

Ilamachutli's image appeared upon the main view screen whilst the ship and course data remained on the right side. Ilam had a smile but somehow he could sense her worry.

'Good fortune, yakuntik,' she said with a pink hue in her eyes.

Hassif turned and gave McCann a cheeky smile, he understood the Tlillan word for 'my love' or just 'love'.

'If we're jumped by pirates again Athena will send you an alert straight away but thank you for your concern Captain.'

Ilam took pleasure in making her husband uncomfortable, she smiled and her pink pigment increased in depth, 'I will be there to rescue you yakuntik.'

'Thank you again Captain, McCann out,' her image disappeared from the view screen to be replaced by empty space stretching out before Athena.

When Athena had reached a safe distance of 5 AU above the disc she announced 'All stop, ready to fold space, Admiral.'

McCann looked up and replied 'Continue Athena.'

Athena spoke throughout the entire ship 'All hands prepare to fold space, wormhole generator charging.'

Lights dimmed and the vessel began to vibrate a little as the generator kicked into action. A tiny point of white light appeared then in a flash exploded into a circle large enough to swallow the Athena. Spewing out bright light the giant frosted doughnut as the Americans had christened it awaited the Athena.

The white hole pushed Athena back until Hassif called out over the noise 'Activating Casimir field.'

The Casimir field enveloped Athena reversing the natural effects of the white hole. McCann tapped his chair arm and heard the voice of his Chief Engineer reply 'You want me to fire the engines?'

McCann replied in a disappointed tone 'Fire the engines now Chief,' Louis seemed to enjoy embarrassing him as much as his wife.

Athena announced ship wide 'All hands, prepare to enter hyperspace.'

A single blast from her engines pushed Athena into the centre of the white hole, the SI navigated her crew inside. Once inside hyperspace, or the Dreamscape as Tlillans named it, the crew were on full alert watching and waiting to see if Makayuuk would attempt to board Athena again.

Their caution was unwarranted as Athena and her crew navigated the river Styx and blasted out through the opposing wormhole, on the other side of the central singularity, safely into Tlillan space.

McCann was surprised the Makayuuk had done nothing, perhaps they'd been struck so hard on their last attempt that they were unable to muster enough forces for a second attempt so soon? Though he doubted that theory since the Macks had many pirate bases and were the most industrious race in the known galaxy. However he thanked fortune for allowing a safe journey and contacted Tlillan system control, requesting permission to dock with the main space station, from where they could take their prisoners in a small transport to an orbital lift, then the surface of Otoch.

After permission was given Athena glided into one of the many docking arms that protruded from the disk shaped space station. Much the same as before the ballerina now slipped back into her partners' arms with equal grace and eloquence. Sliding alongside the parallel arm until he grasped her in a tight magnetic lock.

'Docking complete, engines powered down, you may leave when ready, Admiral.'

The Englishman peered upwards 'Very good Athena, inform Egorov he's to have the prisoners ready for transport at airlock one in fifteen minutes.'

'Understood, Admiral,' replied the soft voice of Athena.

McCann stood up from his chair 'Hassif?'

Hassif shook his head 'Amitra and Huix are on Adnoara, you should talk to Deychaa, Kaeo and Macuil are on Otoch right now.'

McCann nodded 'Good idea.'

He tapped his wrist, a Thai accent replied 'Drone Chief Deychaa, Sir.'

'Fancy taking a visit to the surface Chief?'

Deychaa's voice perked up and with a pitch that conveyed great happiness he replied 'Yes ... Sir.'

McCann smiled at Hassif who was grinning himself, 'Meet me at airlock one in ten minutes Mr Deychaa, understood?'

'Understood Sir,' replied the excited Engineer as he closed the communication channel, before the Admiral, in his absent minded joy.

McCann chuckled 'Well it seems Mr Deychaa owes you one.'

'Have fun,' replied Hassif.

McCann looked back at him and rolling his eyes replied 'Uuurrrrhhh!'

Boarding the station docking arm the group were met by a Tlillan contingent of one Matriarch and two lower ranked females. The Tlillans escorted McCann and his Officers to the surface of Otoch, taking a small transport to one of the many orbital lift stations which made the planet resemble a massive thistle in space.

On the planet Egorov took his prisoners to a holding area somewhere in the city, surrounding Muul Kaah. McCann ordered him to stay with the prisoners until told otherwise.

An interrogation could not commence until Ilam arrived, all five clans must be properly represented along with the Grand Marshall and Priestess.

Upon landing at Muul Kaah, McCann was greeted by his daughter who'd brought Deychaa's daughter and wife. The Drone Engineer was somewhat concerned at his wife's downcast face. McCann however, was quite aware as to the cause of her affliction.

Kaeo gave her father a wai 'Sawat dee kah.'

Deychaa returned the wai 'Kap,' then gave a look of concern to his wife.

Macuil pressed her palms in a wai 'Sawat dee kah.'

Deychaa was about to question her until Kaeo stopped him 'Later pah.'

Deychaa looked at Kaeo then back at his wife, he replied 'Kap.'

The three of them then took a path leading away from the stone landing area, into the city.

McCann scanned the horizon surrounding the pad where their small transport had landed. It had changed a lot since the first time he'd ventured to Muul Kaah. Much of the overgrown forest had been cleared back providing a pleasant area of gardens between each path that led from the zone. Egorov had already left along a trail that could be seen to wind into the now vibrant city. Many of the small terraced buildings were in use, voices and chatter could be detected traveling through the cool crisp twilight air.

What had been a dead city of grey stone was now a place of activity, not as much as a Terran city but still, the Tlillan world was slowly coming back to life.

Malikah was pleased not just to see her Father but also to observe his wonder at how Muul Kaah had been injected with new life 'Namaste Father.'

McCann broke his focus and placed it back on Malikah 'Oh sorry, good to see you Malikah,' he pressed his palms in a Namaste gesture.

'What do you think of my city then?'

He gave his daughter a nod then turned to the scenery 'You've given this place a real shot in the arm, haven't you.'

Malikah wrapped her arm around his and began leading him along a path into the city. Wearing her regal feathers McCann felt she resembled a great Indian chief and if it weren't for that jet black suit and boots he'd feel very out of place.

Malikah giggled as she walked her father along the old stone path; the Englishman peered up at his daughter, she rolled her eyes 'I'm sorry Father!'

He went back to looking where he was going and commented 'You do look like Sitting Bull though.'

'Is that good or bad?' she asked with a slight pink hue in her smiling eyes.

'Good for us not so good for the yanks.'

'Ahh yes the heretics, when Mother arrives we can deal with them.'

McCann moved his hand towards the leather pocket on his arm 'is it alright if I?'

Malikah produced a rather annoyed expression 'If you must.'

The Admiral pulled a Cohiba Siglo I out of his pocket along with his trusty guillotine cigar cutter. He sliced the cap from the Habanos then tested the draw whilst his disapproving daughter looked on from high.

He hadn't had one all day and it'd been a long day, taking out a cedar match he toasted the foot for a few seconds then took a drag, drawing the flame up and onto the cigar foot. After the flame had leapt up a few times the smooth, hand rolled piece of pleasure smouldered on its own and he discarded the match into the greenery.

Malikah shook her head 'That is a littering offence you know?'

McCann chuckled for a moment 'I guess we'll have to get a quango on it before we die from bio pollution.'

Malikah changed the subject 'Any news concerning Lian?'

McCann took a puff from his Cohiba, tasting the rich mild smoke that cooled so quickly in the Tlillan climate 'I was going to ask you the same; you're usually the one to know first.'

Malikah shook her head 'No, even the Seers cannot draw any clues from the Dreamscape. I don't understand this enigma, there should be something.'

McCann shrugged his shoulders 'Perhaps she's dead?'

Malikah retorted sharply 'No! She is alive, if she were dead I would know; her soul would have entered the Dreamscape and contacted me.'

Malikah noticed her Father was feeling awkward, narrowing her eyes she pressed him 'What is the matter Father?'

The Englishman shook his head whilst taking a puff of leathery smoke of his Habanos cigar 'Nothing.'

Malikah stopped walking; holding him still she pressed harder 'Tell me, I feel your discomfort concerning Lian.'

McCann looked from side to side checking that the walkway was clear he whispered 'I know about you and Lian,' he raised his hands to calm the sable Queen 'but it's okay, I haven't said a word.'

Malikah's eyes widened in panic, she replied quickly in a hushed tone 'Keep your voice down!' looking from side to side the sable Amazon continued 'How did you find out?'

'During the journey to Earth, she was dreaming about … you two and I saw it all.'

Malikah's eyes turned pink with embarrassment 'What did you experience?'

McCann was very awkward, but replied softly 'Enough.'

'I need to know Father.'

'You were both at the Plaza one night, and you … you know.'

Malikah looked franticly from side to side 'No I don't.'

He whispered as low as he could but still loud enough for Malikah to hear 'You made love.'

Malikah put her clenched fist in front of McCann's mouth 'Enough, you can never speak of this again Father.'

The Admiral nodded his head 'It was explained to me, I'm sorry it happened, Malikah.'

The tall beauty wrapped her arm around his and continued down the path 'That stupid girl,' she groaned to herself.

'Well we need to find her and those yanks might know something, perhaps we can get a location where they hold prisoners.'

Malikah continued to curse to the sky 'I should never have sent her; she was too young for such responsibilities. It is my fault the Makayuuk have her now and I must take the responsibility of retrieving her.'

McCann squeezed his daughter's arm 'I'll find her, trust me.'

Malikah looked down and smiled at her Father's attempts to comfort his daughter.

The pair strolled along the main thoroughfare arm in arm, McCann observed bows from females and kowtows from males. Malikah had grown accustomed to the behaviour long before now however he was still taken aback by it.

They ended their journey inside what the Englishman best described as a coffee shop. Mosaics covering the walls and floor reminded him of Gukumatz however the colours were somewhat different. Where the Gukumatz preferred blues and greens with earth browns the Tlillans seemed to gravitate more towards darker colours with yellows and fiery reds in contrast.

The shop itself was situated on the upmost level of one of the many step pyramids surrounding the great Muul Kaah. It was astounding when McCann recalled how dead this city was the first time he came here, the Tlillans having almost deserted it. Tlillan civilization had resided itself to defeat, retreating back to the last stronghold of the Darksiders; they were waiting in Tititl for either the Makayuuk to finish their miserable existence or a miracle.

Thanks to the Seers and some skilful manipulation the miracle had occurred, the Makayuuk were driven off and Malikah took the mantle of Xch'uup. Since then the sable Queen had expanded the population through cross breeding Matriarchs with Humans, her selective breeding resulted in a city coming back to life. Thanks to the accelerated growth of Tlillan females, in less than a decade Muul Kaah was moderately populated and functioning well at the most basic of levels.

Stepping inside the Englishman tentatively crossed the mosaic floor, afraid he may damage the ornate depiction of a past Xch'uup. Malikah smiled and dragged her father out onto the terrace to constant 'Namaste' greetings. The sable Amazon nodded her head and replied before the twosome were presented with a table on the terrace. All previous occupants were cleared providing Xch'uup her privacy.

McCann took a deep breath as he sat; the Admiral loved the cool refreshing atmosphere of Otoch. Humans having descended from the Tlillan genome, he felt it confirmed when breathing the air, filling his lungs with familiarity. Looking out he viewed a quiet city and its main building, the city's name sake, rose high above all else. Its massive stone base narrowed step by step until reaching the summit, which was lit by a single cauldron fire atop. Soft sunlight in the thin band of twilight was very comfortable and just the right intensity, not too close to either the dark or light side of the planet. The rest of the city sprawled out in haphazard groups of buildings around smaller step pyramids, much like the one they resided in now. It seemed that a pyramid was built and small satellite buildings for housing and utilitarian matters sprung up around them, as greenery would around an oasis. The Oasis were connected by well-maintained stone paths, there was no need for rails to take heavy freight, with the advent of anti-grav technology it could be airlifted with ease. The road ways were for the pleasure of city occupants rather than shifting goods or getting to work and back.

Not that Tlillans had to go to work as a Human would define it, Tlillans or at least Tlillan Matriarchs had duties and responsibilities. Females who had not attained the title of Matriarch did more of the leg work, next on the way down the totem pole came the males who pretty much did the grunt work then at the very bottom were slaves. On the planet Otoch slaves were a commodity kept by Matriarchs to serve the family, but that was just the top 0.01%; the remaining slaves who were often prisoners of war or tributes from defeated opponents resided in forced labour camps. Xch'uup worked her enemies to death, ironically her enemies assisted in building the empire they opposed so fervently.

Tlillans did not use currency, they had out grown the need for it, if it was the will of Xch'uup it was done. She provided for her Matriarchs, they did not want for food, water or shelter and in return Xch'uup was the only law, her will supreme. This system had worked for eons and they weren't going to give it up anytime soon, the only people that starved or went without all the benefits of this ideal form of Communism were its slave labourers.

A waiter appeared at their table, he was male due to the fact a helmet covered his features. The waiter stood quietly not making a sound until Malikah informed him of their order mentally. The short waiter who could have been no more than five feet tall then kowtowed and returned to the kitchens.

McCann raised an eye brow 'I don't suppose you tip here?'

Malikah sniggered at her Fathers joke until the waiter returned with two Tlillan drinks that smelt very much like roasted coffee beans.

McCann looked at the waiter as he placed the ceramic yellow cups on the stone table 'Thank you ... I mean dyos bo'otik.'

The male kowtowed to McCann before silently walking back to the kitchen.

McCann exhaled loudly 'Well it must be a barrel of laughs on a night out in Muul Kaah!'

Malikah laughed at her Father much to the interest of the other customers; the small eatery was now filling up to capacity because of her presence.

The Englishman looked around at the inside of the café whilst he prepared another cigar 'I must say I do like the art work, the colours aren't nearly as gaudy as the cafes on Gukumatz.'

Malikah smiled as she sipped her powerful blend of coffee, a bean that originated from Otoch, 'You find one of them familiar?'

McCann scrunch his forehead at his daughter, a little annoyed that she was listening in on his emotions 'Yes, that one over there it reminds me of my favourite painting.'

He pointed his cigar at the North wall, a mosaic had been recently erected by the look of it and the scene was quite arousing. What must have been Xch'uup sat upon a traditional stone seat residing upon a dais.

It must have been Xch'uup since the crown of white feathers that only she wore was draped over her head. One arm rested on the chair whilst the other on her thigh in a clenched fist. Xch'uup was dressed in the typical Tlillan ribbed bodysuit with a pair of black boots which melded with the suit, below the knee. McCann found the depiction of the Grand Matriarch odd since she was carrying her neutronium sword on a silver sword belt, something that was rare.

Behind her stood what must have been her direct subordinates at the time, three Matriarchs in various poses inspiring superiority and disdain. That disdain was focused on the pitiful sight that knelt before them, from this distance he couldn't make out the exact detail but McCann assumed it was a Makayuuk; the Mack's hands were bound behind his back, his face was pointed towards Xch'uup with the assistance of a Matriarch's sword beneath his chin. Directly in front of the Mack lay his weaponry of plasma rifles and body armour as he had been stripped and wore only his torn bodysuit, exposing his bloody flesh and bare feet.

All around this intricately detailed scene were many other people, on the right side of the mosaic where Xch'uup sat the lower ranked Matriarchs stood around but not on the square dais. They wore armour, some with sword belts but all carried an assault rifle of Tlillan design. Tlillan weapons fired a blast of ion particles which tore through pretty much anything without shielding; they had no need for ammunition so didn't require reloading and the power plant was good for centuries. Their rifles were very small compared to the average Human design, Tlillans could hold them with one hand if need be since there was no recoil.

Aside from the Matriarchs were many lower ranked females, no doubt they were there to earn a place in their clan. The lower ranked females carried an ion rifle and some held standards high in the air adorned with golden symbols. McCann wasn't certain what the symbols denoted but they were metallic and resembled various creatures, the most striking was of a great golden Condor, its wings spread as if the bird was ready to strike.

To the left were groups of Makayuuk in control collars being corralled by lower ranked females. All of them were bound around their bodies with expressions of despair and woe, it was obvious to all what this mosaic was portraying.

McCann lit his Habanos whilst staring at the mosaic on the wall 'You know what that reminds me of?'

Malikah's eyes turned a slight pink hue, pleased that her Father had recognised the work of art 'I commissioned it.'

The Englishman peered at his sable daughter 'Bloody hell, don't you think it was a bit much?'

'A bit much? That is one of the most popular pieces of art in the last three centuries, Father.'

McCann shook his head 'You commissioned it, for art's sake?'

'No, if there is a conquest or event of note a piece of art is commissioned, I merely gave some input on the piece.'

McCann took a first puff on his Cohiba testing the tobacco of the Habanos, upon discovering it was sweet and mild he continued with his daughter talking to her as if she were a naughty girl 'You know Royer would be spinning in his grave.'

Malikah pouted at her father 'It was a homage to Royer, besides is it not true that all of the best works of art imitated?'

McCann begrudgingly agreed with his daughter who had probably linked with the artist involved giving her the image of "Vercingetorix throws his arms at the feet of Julius Caesar" painted by the French artist Lionel Noel Royer. He smirked then asked his daughter in a sarcastic tone 'So what's it called? "Sirt throws his plasma rifle at the feet of Malikah"?'

Malikah chuckled 'Please, you wouldn't take me for such crudity?'

McCann snorted 'considering some of the things I've witnessed taking place here I don't know.'

Malikah did not answer his statement but sipped her coffee whilst her Father admired the fine mosaic; his daughter had a most austere expression as she looked down upon the defeated Makayuuk general.

Now that he was aware of what the mosaic portrayed he noticed the characters, the three high ranking Matriarchs standing on the wooden platform were Cihu, Ilam and Kaeo. The Englishman was stunned how he'd missed it before, the colour of the hair and the fact that Kaeo was half a foot shorter. Cihu's' image was poised with a very sobering sneer on her face directed towards the cyborg, her beautiful white hair flowing down her back. Ilam had a stern expression peering down at the man machine, her face radiated scorn onto him. Kaeo stood between them and directly behind Malikah, it was plain that she was the lowest rank amongst those on the platform, he could only see the upper part of her body, but she stood hands on hips with a severe demeanour.

Although it was blatant plagiarism even McCann had to admit it was a great piece of art. The artist had reproduced the Terran piece in a tastefully Tlillan style, perhaps Royer would have been honoured that a civilization 36,000 light years from France had taken inspiration from one of his masterpieces?

Chapter 11

A day later the Chutli had arrived carrying Ilam to Otoch for the interrogation. The two prisoners, transported from Earth, were probed by Malikah and the 5 clan leaders in Muul Kaah. Questioning was closed off and after they attained what was needed, a week later, sentence was to be carried out.

Malikah invited the press, namely Jerry Habeeb, who'd taken passage upon the Chutli. Jerry was excited to be there although McCann was somewhat dismayed to see the journalist. He understood Malikah's wish to make an example of the traitors but felt it unnecessary to have Habeeb present.

After having linked with Ilam the Englishman was curious to see how this would develop. The ceremony remained in Muul Kaah, the traitors' souls were not deemed worthy of offering to Xch'uup on the circle of life, they were destined for execution.

McCann sat on one of the stone pews running along either side of the great hall inside Muul Kaah. Habeeb was on the other side of the hall with his camera and sound men. His camera-ball hovered high above the central area which glowed with fluorescent moss, igniting the entire arena with soft light.

The Seers shuffled about in the passageways behind Xch'uup's throne; eventually Malikah appeared wearing a jade robe to take her seat flanked by Cihu and Ilam. All Matriarchs rose to their feet and bowed taking their place only once their sable Queen had first settled upon her throne.

Without a word she sent mental instructions, from the opposite end of the hall the prisoners entered. Their control collars absent, Kaeo no longer required them. Once the traitors came within 20 feet of the Tlillan Queen Kaeo reigned them in 'Halt!'

The dishevelled turncoats stopped as Kaeo pushed them to their knees, the condemned waited for Malikah to begin.

The Tlillan Empress rose from her throne and looked around at her audience 'We are here today to pass sentence upon these betrayers. Their minds have been probed and their guilt is plain for all to see.'

The goddess turned to the Senator and Aide 'Greed and lust for power has poisoned your souls, just as Judas you would gladly sin for heretics.'

The Senator fixed her tired gaze upon Malikah 'Who are you to say what is heresy? The kingdom of God is in all men, not just one man or one woman. You emancipate your people by enslaving mine, just as all tyrants.'

Jerry Habeeb was lapping this up, making certain his crew were getting it all recorded for his hourly Net show.

Malikah approached Senator Hart 'I have nothing but love for those who fight in the name of Xch'uup.'

The Senator sneered at the towering Valkyrie 'You love those that fight for slavery.'

Malikah shook her head 'enough of this pointless talk, you have been found guilty of heresy, Kaeo execute sentence on this sinner.'

Kaeo's eyes darkened until they became pitch black, Senator Hart clutched her head and collapsed screaming as she writhed upon the moss floor. A few seconds later and the noise ended, the condemned lay still upon the ground.

Malikah turned to Feinstein 'What do you have to say for yourself, after selling your soul to the highest bidder?'

The former Aide starred at the ground showing nothing but self-pity 'For a time I was one of the richest men in Washington,' Feinstein smirked for a moment before returning to his look of misery.

Malikah nodded 'Taking inspiration from Human history I believe we have a fitting punishment for your crimes.'

The stone entrance opened and a pair of females pushing a small cauldron upon a mag lev platform entered. The cauldron was only just larger than a cooking pot though McCann noted it was much thicker. It had two loops on the side just below its rim, no doubt intended for lowering the pot in and out of a furnace. A bright light emanated from the vessel, the Englishman wasn't certain of what lay inside but was quite sure its contents were very hot, probably a molten metal.

The ladies took a thick bar of metal each, McCann assumed it to be neutronium, slid their bars through two hoops jutting out on each side of the cauldron.

After each lady had taken the weight and successfully lifted the black pot off the Mag Lev platform they halted, awaiting instruction from their Queen.

Malikah smirked in satisfaction at the women carrying the small cauldron; she then turned to Feinstein who peered rather worriedly at his impending fate.

'I thought it would be a fitting punishment that you suffer just as Marcus Crassus did at the hands of the Parthians,' proclaimed Malikah to the puzzlement of all watching.

The only person, other than the vengeful Queen of Tlillan, who wasn't confused was McCann. He had told his daughter this story when she was still a child, living with her parents on Lake Geneva. She shared his fascination for the Classical world; not only had she depicted herself as Caesar in her commissioned art after the defeat of the Makayuuk but now she had decided to re-enact the execution of the richest man in Rome.

Malikah glanced at all the befuddled Matriarchs and a confused Jerry Habeeb 'Marcus Crassus was a Governor on Earth thousands of years ago. He betrayed the Parthians due to his lust for power and wealth. Once defeated he was forced to drink molten gold, in reference to his overwhelming thirst for riches.

Let this be an example to all those who find difficulty in satiating their cupidity.'

Malikah nodded at the tall Tlillan beauties holding the small cauldron setting them on their path towards the prisoner.

Feinstein screamed but with his mouth closed, attempting to deny the molten metal entrance into his body.

Kaeo's eyes became dark and no sooner had the pigment changed than Feinstein quietened down, he co-operated, opening his mouth wide.

Habeeb was recording every moment but as the liquid gold poured over the lip of the pot and into the throat of Feinstein he found himself looking away. Just the expression in the former Aide's eyes as they flitted about from side to side in desperation, begging for someone to rescue him from this hell, was more than the journalist could stand.

McCann grimaced as the yellow liquid poured into Jay's body, for half a minute his eyes shot about desperately as they bulged in quiet pain. The Tlillan Amazons removed the cauldron a moment before he flopped to the dirt, as if he were no more than a sack of rice.

The Tlillan women placed their pot of liquid metal back on the Mag Lev platform and exited the great hall.

Both traitors now lay deceased, their bodies left to be taken away later, Malikah returned to her sisters 'All those who stand with the Makayuuk must expect the same degree of mercy ...'

Malikah stopped and looked up towards the distant ceiling of Muul Kaah.

McCann's wrist tablet began to beep, with Matriarchs frowning at him he tapped it and whispered 'what the hell is it Kim?'

'A Makayuuk vessel has folded space and struck her colours, Sir.'

McCann frowned 'Folded space where?'

'Just above the accretion disc, Admiral.'

McCann tried to remain calm but did a poor job 'I mean which system you bloody idiot!'

Kim was taken aback but continued 'This system, Sir, the Tlillan system, Sir.'

McCann went from frustrated to astounded 'They've surrendered? To us?'

'Yes Sir, they haven't contacted Tlillan traffic control. Should I accept their surrender, Admiral?'

McCann let out a long breath 'Do it Kim and inform the Tlillans of the situation, understood?'

'Understood, Sir.'

'McCann out.'

The Englishman looked towards his daughter who'd been listening intently. He nodded silently and she nodded back giving her permission.

The Tlillan's were all communicating silently; it was plain to see they weren't very happy that the Makayuuk had surrendered to the Athena in their space.

The Englishman's wrist tablet went off again, he tapped it and Kim answered.

'Admiral the Makayuuk request a transport to the surface of Otoch.'

Before the Tlillans could refuse he questioned his Commander 'Who or what do they want transported?'

'The Makayuuk Captain stated they wish to transport a diplomat to negotiate with Ek'tsab.'

Malikah interjected 'Allow her passage to the planet, Father.'

Ilam stepped forward and whispered into her daughter's ear 'You cannot, what if they bring another plague?'

Malikah peered upwards as if she could see through the ceiling and out into space 'They have no plague.'

McCann replied to Kim 'use one of our transports to bring the diplomat down, check him out on the Athena for any bio-agents, understood?'

'Understood, Sir.'

'McCann out.'

Cihu next approached Malikah 'You would negotiate with Heretics?'

The sable Queen narrowed her eyes 'Now you question your Xch'uup?'

Cihu kept her mouth closed and walked back to her position behind the throne.

The Great Hall remained quiet until an hour later; the Makayuuk had passed all bio scans and was granted permission to enter Muul Kaah. The stone entrance slid away and in walked the lone Makayuuk to gasps of horror and shock from all occupants within the hall.

Malikah was frozen at the sight of her former Adjunct; Lian stepped into the hall flanked by Tlillan guards. She wore the same black ribbed suit and possessed the same long flowing soft black hair. The only difference being her eyes, McCann spied them immediately; they both had that Makayuuk silver sheen on them. Her eyeballs sat in their sockets as two silver balls; it was very discomforting to think that the Makayuuk could do this to even a Tlillan.

Lian walked inside until she stood over the two bodies that lay before Malikah. Observing the pair for a moment Lian turned her head to gaze upon the Tlillan Monarch.

Pressing her hands together Lian bowed her head 'Namaste Ek'tsab.'

All eyes were on Malikah and what she would do next.

'How should I address you exactly?' she spoke in English.

'Lian,' said the smiling woman.

'You are Makayuuk now?'

Lian's eyes began to change, the silver sheen melted away to reveal her original dark brown 'No I am still the Lian you remember.'

Malikah glared deep into the eyes of her former lover 'Then why did you not appear in the Dreamscape?'

'When I speak for Machine I am cut off.'

Cihuateteo strode to Malikah's side 'Destroy this abomination!'

The sable Amazon sneered at her Marshal 'I decided who or what is an abomination.'

Cihu was not prepared to give in on this one 'She has been corrupted by the Makayuuk, she claims to speak for Machine, this abomination must be destroyed it is law!'

Malikah's eyes turned red with anger 'I am Xch'uup, I am law on Otoch. You are my subordinate and will do as you're told.'

Cihu pointed her finger at Malikah much to the joy of Jerry Habeeb 'Do I deserve no respect? No privilege? My clan has fought harder and longer than any here, and I, always at the front lead us to victory. Yet now I may not speak in the presence of the mighty Xch'uup?'

Malikah gnashed her teeth at Cihu 'Respect? You have more ovations than any other Tlillan!'

Cihu let out a puff of wind 'Mere ovations? On Gaulthus I brought you a victory and on Bandayuuk, were those only worth an Ovation?'

Malikah looked upon the great warrior with disdain 'Perhaps the Humans are not the only to have poisoned souls?'

Cihu's eyes were now burning as bonfires in the night 'You always had your pick of tributes, I only take what is left after other clans have chosen. Yet I never complained, I never demanded any more than I received despite receiving least of all!'

Malikah replied in a cold tone 'Matriarchs have been executed for questioning their Xch'uup in the past, it is considered heresy.'

Cihu made an evil smirk 'Fine words from one who usurped the crown.'

The audience began to mumble to one another.

Malikah was stunned for a moment, much to Cihu's delight. The Marshal continued 'You came to Otoch as a thief in the night!'

The Sable Queen placed her hand upon her sword as did the white haired Valkyrie. At the sight of them about to come to killing blows McCann's heart jumped.

He ran out of his seat and stood between the pair facing Malikah 'That's enough,' he said softly.

The Icon of the Gukumatz screeched at Cihu 'I did not usurp the crown. I found it … in the GUTTER!'

Ilam caught the eye of Cihu and communicated something to her.

Cihu placed her neutronium sabre back inside its scabbard and called out so all would hear 'I will no longer fight for Xch'uup.'

Malikah still holding the grip of her sword retorted loudly 'Good, take your filthy sneer! We can fight without it!'

McCann whispered into his daughter's ear 'Give it rest.'

Malikah said nothing else as Cihu strode out of the hall with fiery eyes. Before leaving she turned to Malikah one more time and stated 'There will come a time you will need me, don't think I will make it easy on you,' Cihu bowed with hands pressed 'Namaste Xch'uup,' then left.

Malikah drew in a long breath as she viewed her Matriarchs; Returning her mantle to its scabbard the Queen smiled at her father as her eye's cooled down to their normal grey colour.

The Englishman returned the smile and walked back to his stone seat.

Fixing her gaze upon Lian the tall dark haired Tlillan leader asked 'What do you want?'

Lian smiled as her eyes returned to that silver sheen of the Makayuuk 'Peace.'

Malikah shook her head 'What do you propose to give in return?'

'Peace for peace.'

'The Makayuuk have been defeated, Machine is dead, it is too late for peace.'

Lian smiled at Malikah 'Machine lives, what you destroyed was a main cluster of Machine. Machine was incapacitated for some time but has returned to health since, the Makayuuk are beginning to hear the call of Machine.'

The sable Queen sneered 'Do you expect me to believe you?'

Lian's silver sheen once again fell from her eyes 'Machine speaks through me when necessary. There will be another uprising on Bandayuuk if you refuse to make peace.'

'Make peace with Machine? It tried to commit genocide here on Otoch; even if it were alive I would never agree.'

McCann received a message through his wrist tablet; he replied and spoke into it as quietly as possible.

Lian concentrated upon the Admiral as he listened to the situation on Bandayuuk. Another uprising was taking place, according to several military camps the Macks were flowing out of tunnels. Mack prisoners had refused to co-operate despite the collars.

The Gukumatz and Humans still alive had managed to retreat to the closest camps and hunker down.

Malikah pointed at Lian 'Bring her with me; we're going to Bandayuuk to put an end to this once and for all.'

The Tlillan Queen strode off into the rear chambers of Muul Kaah with Ilam Kaeo, McCann and Lian. The rest of the Tlillans shuffled out to make preparations, Xch'uup was going to Bandayuuk.

Inside a private chamber within Muul Kaah Malikah turned to her Mother, Father and Kaeo 'Please leave us.'

Lian spoke confidently 'Your Father may stay.'

Malikah made a shoo shoo gesture and the other two left, her guards outside closed the stone door.

All three of them stood around a granite table, Lian leaned over to take the hand of Xch'uup but Malikah pulled away.

'Do you fear me?' asked Lian.

'I don't know who you are. Where have you been? What have they done to you?'

Lian's eyes were back to normal now and with a slight pink hue 'I was kidnapped and they placed a link inside my head, a direct link to Machine. I have the voice of Machine inside me.'

McCann furrowed his brow and asked 'Is that only when your eyes change?'

Lian still looked at Malikah but answered her Father 'That is when Machine speaks through me, however I am still in control. Just as when I speak for myself now, Machine can hear us but I am in control.'

McCann didn't quiet grasp how it worked or why 'So why has Machine made you its voice?'

'Machine cares for the Makayuuk; Machine only desires an end to conflict.'

McCann chuckled a little 'Then Machine can surrender.'

Lian smiled at the Admiral 'Machine will not surrender her children to Xch'uup or her allies.'

'Her?' said Malikah in a surprised tone.

Lian nodded 'Machine is their Mother as you are the Mother of all Tlillan.'

'Then they will die resisting their destiny,' retorted Malikah.

'Did not the Tlillan people die resisting the Makayuuk, even when their destiny seemed fixed?'

'But that was not our destiny.'

Lian and Malikah fell silent only looking at one another. Lian remembering her lover and Malikah wondering if this was truly the Lian she had sent to Earth. Since the Machine People had inserted an implant into Lian's brain, Malikah could no longer read her mind with the ease she once did.

The sable Queen took a deep breath 'We are going to Bandayuuk; you shall accompany my Father on the Athena. I shall be taking the Chutli,' she peered at her father 'is that satisfactory?'

McCann nodded 'Shall I take her now?'

Malikah took one more look at her and replied 'Yes, I'll send you further details later today.'

On board the Athena McCann escorted Lian to her quarters, unfortunately waiting in the corridors was sub-Lieutenant Han. When he saw his daughter a wave of relief rippled over his body.

The short Chinaman smiled and called her name in the hope she might remember him 'Lian?'

The tall Amazon immediately recognised his voice 'Fuachin!'

Lian ran up to Han and hugged him; McCann held back the Spetsnaz guards allowing the child to hold her parent again.

'What happened to you?' inquired Han in a shaky voice, as if he were afraid to know the truth.

Lian grinned and held his hands in hers 'I'll show you, Father.'

Lian slipped into a trance as did Han. The Drone Officer slipped away from the Athena until he was drawn back in time and space to Geneva.

He was his daughter, sleeping comfortably at I.S.A headquarters until she awoke on what should have been a morning. Looking around Lian, could see the lighting had malfunctioned. Usually the soft lighting inside would gradually increase in intensity as the sun rose then decrease until it was gone. Either Lian had woken up in the early hours or the lighting had failed.

She reached out for the controls on her bedside table. Instead her hand hit a wall; she tried the other side of the bed only to meet piles of boxes.

After calming herself, Lian used an innate Darksider ability passed on from her Mother. Concentrating into the gloom she induced her Tlillan night vision, the room dimensions made themselves clear. It was now obvious to Lian that she was inside a cargo crate of some description. Inside were boxes filled with various goods, indigenous to planet Earth, mostly food and spare parts.

The tall, half Darksider, half Chinese beauty felt the sensation of movement; she assumed the crate was on the sky lift. Since its upgrade the orbital lift used an electro-magnetic tower much the same as discovered on the Gukumatz moons years ago. The tower was constructed of Catronium, allowing a tall but rigid structure. Inside the tower there was a single Catronium tube replacing the old carbon ribbon that had to be grown in a lab.

Today crawlers didn't crawl anymore; firstly there was only one crawler. The central tube which formed the basis of the orbital lift had a cylinder of a slightly greater diameter wrapped around it. This cylinder was only about 100 metres in height and moved up and down the central tube, between Earth and the Tsiolkovsky.

The crawler had openings all along its width and length, these opening were for cargo crates, or anything the I.S.A desired, to latch on for the ride up or down.

Electro-magnets were then employed to fire the crawler up into space or to ease it back down to ground zero. With the advent of anti-gravity plating the crawler could be fired up at incredible speeds without causing damage to the contents of the cargo containers. Trips to the Tsiolkovsky were measured in minutes rather than weeks now.

Lian was now occupying one of those cargo crates, who had put her there and why was a mystery; however since there was a small but adequate atmosphere processor inside her crate she assumed they wanted her alive.

A week or maybe two later the exit to her crate opened, fortunately Lian had been dressed in her Tlillan space suit which processed her bodily functions. Still there was a strong smell inside the crate, she had been through the boxes and found a few things that were edible. The atmosphere processor was adequate to keep her breathing but after a few days the tiny environment was too small to keep her crate smelling fresh as a field on a spring day.

Lian was blinded for a minute as bright light flooded in, though she could hear nothing someone had gone to a lot of trouble to get her here.

One minute later and Lian peered out of her cage 'Pirates!'

There were three Makayuuk, the lead machine man communicated to his comrade silently. One of the cyborgs flanking his commander pulled out a pistol and shot Lian, to which the beautiful lady fell unconscious.

Regaining her consciousness Lian found herself in what seemed to be a cave, in the centre of the well-lit grotto resided what looked to be something similar to the images of Machine she'd on the NET. A collection of brain matter intertwined with circuits and wires, several optical fibres ran from the cybernetic brain and out into the walls of the cavern.

'Namaste Lian,' came a voice which she assumed was the heretical machine. Before Lian could reply the machine spoke again 'You want to know what I am and why you are here, yes?'

Lian nodded her head tentatively 'Yes.'

'I am Machine, or part of Machine. In your terms I am the cerebral cortex, awareness, thought and memory are impossible without me.'

Lian was about to speak again but somehow the creature knew exactly what she was going to say and cut her off 'You were told Machine was destroyed, I know. What was destroyed on Bandayuuk was a central pathway; I was cut off from my children for quite some time.'

Lian scowled 'Your children?'

Next Lian had a very chilling feeling as Machine laughed at her comment, not so much the laugh but the fact that Lian realised she wasn't listening to Machine talk. Lian was picking up the cybernetic monstrosity's brainwaves, how, she didn't know, but it communicated directly, mind to mind.

'You have been given an implant so that I may communicate with you Lian, I apologise for my method but it was required,' came the soft voice of Machine's brainwaves.

'Take it out, now!'

'I am sorry but that is not possible, Lian.'

'Why?'

'I need you, my children need you.'

'Need me? For what?'

'This conflict must end, Xch'uup would never entertain Machine but she trusts you, she will listen to Lian.'

Lian laughed 'Malikah will never accept peace, you nearly exterminated the Tlillans on Otoch and now you beg for peace? I would have thought the largest brain in the Galaxy would've predicted the inevitable scenario.'

Machine asked 'and what might that be, Lian?'

'Your death along with every single one of your warped children!'

Lian got the feeling that Machine expected her reaction 'Let me show you something.'

Lian's body tensed up as she tried to resist the information being piped into her visual cortex by Machine. It was pointless, Lian could see Bandayuuk from orbit and slowly the planet surface turned transparent displaying masses of tunnels beneath Bandayuuk.

Lian noted all of the Makayuuk working in the tunnels, out of sight of the I.S.A, deeper down were masses of sleeper pods all filled with Makayuuk soldiers.

'There are millions of soldiers, ready to give their lives without question,' came the soft voice of Machine.

'I think you're mistaking me for someone that gives a shit!' retorted Lian.

'I will draw Malikah to Bandayuuk and take her, alive or dead, if you force me to do so.'

'I doubt you could do that!'

'Why not? I have her first Adjunct and her lover.'

Machine released control of Lian's visual cortex 'Lian, I do not wish to see further slaughter, tell me what I must do?'

'It is too late Machine, you and your children are heresy and must be destroyed.'

'Then I am left with little choice.'

'It won't work Machine.'

'Will you at least request peace for Machine?'

'What do I get?'

'You shall be released back to Xch'uup; you are now my first Adjunct, Lian.'

Lian snorted 'So you want me to be a diplomat?'

'Correct.'

'What if I refuse?'

'I will release you no matter what; if you can gain peace then Malikah shall be safe.'

Lian looked around the cavern taking note of the Makayuuk guards 'So I am free to leave?'

'All of my children have been instructed to take your orders, you may do as you please, Lian.'

'Then take me to Otoch, I'll deliver your message.'

'I have one final request, Lian.'

The restrained beauty sighed 'Yes?'

'When you are before Xch'uup may I speak? Through you?'

Lian thought for a moment 'What do you want to say?'

Machine imparted some emotion, a feeling of heavy heartedness 'To request peace, nothing more.'

Lian nodded at the massive cybernetic mind 'Fine, just don't say anything I wouldn't. Now how do I get out of here?'

'Ask my children, they will follow all of your requests, Lian.'

The towering Valkyrie glared at one of the Machine Men guarding the chamber 'You, I want to go to Otoch, now.'

The cyborg with silver eyes let his rifle hang by the strap as he made the Namaste gesture. Lian could hear him in her mind 'Namaste Lian', after releasing her bonds he requested she follow him which she did through some tunnels until they reached a small pirate vessel used for boarding operations.

The vessel was in a massive docking bay carved from rock, the only thing separating them from space was a large force field. It was now that Lian realised they were inside an asteroid, where the asteroid was remained a mystery for now.

Several Makayuuk stood outside lining the walkway that leant against the ship. They all made the Namaste gesture as she entered; it was very uncomfortable since Lian had never stood this close to a Makayuuk.

Inside the craft was grim, nothing like the soft light of the Athena, only a bare gun metal covering the walls, floor and ceiling. Following her usher she entered the bridge, a central seat with terminals along the wall. It was very Spartan in design since the Makayuuk did most of their work in the mind rather than via the tips of their fingers.

Her escort gestured towards the Captain's chair, not a standard item on a Makayuuk vessel, and Lian sat down watching the creatures around her closely.

Next the vessel lifted from the bay floor and glided out through the force field, at this point the view screen was switched off. Lian suspected they were concerned she may note the star patterns and be able to locate Machine for Xch'uup. In truth she would have done just that so Lian took no offence.

Ten minutes or so later the craft began to shake; no doubt they were folding space to Otoch. The lighting went down and the engines fired propelling them into the void.

During their journey one of the Makayuuk who'd stood by her side since she'd left Machine whispered into her ear 'You have met Ek'tsab?'

Lian narrowed her eyes 'Ek'tsab?'

The cybernetic being was uneasy asking the question 'Star Shaker?'

Lian shook her head 'I don't understand.'

He cleared his throat 'Xch'uup, you are her first?'

Before Lian could answer a voice rang out from behind 'Asta!'

The Makayuuk stood up as straight as a plank of wood.

An older Makayuuk had appeared from outside of the Bridge, stepping forward the old man barked at her escort 'You are not permitted to question Voice!'

Lian turned to face the older Makayuuk, a grey haired and confident man dressed in his drab Makayuuk body suit with a mandarin collar. Lian smiled reassuringly 'It is quite alright, he may ask if he wishes.'

The old Makayuuk scowled at Asta then fixed his gaze upon Lian 'Namaste Voice,' he said with pressed palms.

She turned back to her escort 'Asta, is that your name?'

He smiled nervously 'I am Asta 491.'

Lian grinned at him 'What does Asta mean?'

'It is the name of my birthing station.'

'Birthing station?'

'Yes, we are conceived and born in stations. I was born at Asta in the 491st tube; my full name is far longer.'

Lian pouted a little at him 'I won't ask.'

Asta laughed much to the surprise of Lian; she had always assumed the Makayuuk to be zombie like followers of Machine. No emotion or will of their own, merely doing as their evil overlord instructed.

'So you are acquainted with Ek'tsab?'

Lian raised her eyebrows 'You mean Xch'uup?'

Asta nodded his head as the rest of the Bridge listened in.

'I am, but why do you call her Ek'tsab?'

Asta looked around the Bridge at his crew mates then under his breath spoke to Lian 'Ek'tsab is the Star Shaker, a terrifying beast from legend, before we created Machine.'

Lian's interest grew 'Tell me about it.'

The Machine Man cleared his throat, although he had silver eyes Lian could sense his fear, 'It was only written in legend but Ek'tsab was a grinning demon, a maniac. If she did not receive the souls of beings she would grow restless and rise from the underworld to take her share. Only the sun could stop her; it is written we went many years without offering souls to Ek'tsab. Growing angry she ascended from the underworld to take her fair share, we prayed to the Sun to stop her. Ek'tsab slapped the Sun out of the sky when it tried, the sky turned black and for three days Ek'tsab raped the souls of the living. Men, women and children were torn to pieces and consumed until the ground was soaked with the blood of the unfaithful. For three full days screams and cries could be heard before Ek'tsab returned to the underworld once she'd had her fill. The day after that the Sun appeared, he would only return once certain Ek'tsab was gone.

The story was always used to terrify children and even today it is considered bad luck to utter her name.'

Lian ruffled her forehead 'So you believe that Xch'uup is this Ek'tsab?'

Asta nodded 'She said so at Otoch, when we were on the verge of defeating the Tlillans. She caused the star to shake, only Ek'tsab could do that alone ...'

'Shut your mouth boy!' shouted the older Makayuuk 'Do you want to terrify all the other idiots on this ship?'

Lian peered at the older man and inquired 'Do you believe in Ek'tsab?'

The grey man with silver eyes sneered dismissively at Asta 'Only an idiot would believe such fantasy.'

The dark haired Amazon grinned 'And only an idiot would attempt to stand against Xch'uup, how do you explain your defeat at Otoch?'

The old man refused to answer, saying nothing he fixed his gaze upon the view screen.

Asta then let his opinion out 'She made the star shake on that day.'

'SILENCE!' screamed the older man who was on the verge of a mental breakdown by the looks of things.

Lian starred back at him 'you will leave Asta be, is that understood?'

The elder man made the Namaste gesture and left the Bridge. After he'd gone Lian smiled at her new Makayuuk friend 'Tell me some more about the Makayuuk Asta.'

Asta continued 'What do you wish to know?'

'Why do you still believe in Ek'tsab?'

Asta took a deep breath and looked up at the ceiling 'It is difficult to describe, Ek'tsab is more of a warning than a real entity although some would disagree.'

Lian looked at her new found friend incredulously 'Disagree?'

'Yes?' he replied in a puzzled tone.

Lian laughed 'I never considered that Macks would ever disagree on anything.'

'Macks?'

Lian laughed again 'That's what Admiral McCann calls you, it's short for Makayuuk, Humans commonly use contractions in their language.'

'Why would you think we never disagree?'

'I assumed you were controlled by Machine, told what to do, say and think. If you disagree with one another that implies you have minds of your own.'

Asta frowned at the young lady sitting in the Captain's chair 'Of course we think for ourselves. Machine links us together, preventing us from harming each other; before Machine we were savages with no self-control. It is said the tale of Ek'tsab was created to prevent us from butchering our own people. We are as much a part of Machine as Machine is of us and now you are a part of us.'

Lian gave him a dry expression 'what does Machine hope to achieve by indoctrinating me into the Makayuuk?'

'Machine hopes you might understand us and convey that to Ek'tsab.'

Lian shook her head 'There you go again calling her Ek'tsab, if it is just an old wives tale why do you give her that title?'

'Old wives tale?' inquired Asta.

Lian chuckled and waved her hand 'A Human expression, it means a myth or legend.'

Asta nodded his head 'She caused the star to shake; she destroyed our warships then descended upon the Otoch. For 3 days our forces were on the dark side of Otoch and all were killed but one, he was allowed to return to tell the tale of Ek'tsab.

Then she returned to Bandayuuk and as a demon she wrought pain and misery upon us, even to this day the Makayuuk live in darkness. Now we occupy the underworld whilst she holds sway over the living world, it was prophesised before Machine.'

'Do you believe it?' questioned Lian.

'What am I to think?'

Lian relaxed into the seat 'Perhaps Machine is right, perhaps this needs to be stopped; but I tell you this Asta, Xch'uup will not release her grip upon the Makayuuk. She may be convinced to ease it a little but Machine must accept defeat to one degree or another.'

Asta shook his head 'Machine will not accept defeat, even to Ek'tsab; she is our Mother and will never give us up.'

Lian folded her arms observing the view screen and the massive singularity they were navigating around 'Then Machine will have to prepare for a lot more bloodshed, Malikah is a very stubborn person and your people butchered hers on Otoch. Tell me, what would Machine do in Malikah's place?'

Asta glanced at the floor 'Machine would do as Ek'tsab; Machine would punish those that sought to eradicate her children. When does it all end Voice?'

'Malikah always told me that a fight can only end in two ways, either one party cedes and accepts defeat or one of the participants can no longer continue. What does Machine think of that?'

As Lian asked the question she felt the presence of Machine inside her just as she had the first time they met in the cavern. A silver sheen flooded her eyes and for a moment Machine spoke to her answering the question. A few seconds later and the silver pigment dissipated.

'Did you speak with Machine?' asked Asta excitedly.

'Yes,' replied Lian rather stoically.

'Did Machine answer your question?'

Lian chuckled in a philosophical manner 'She did, I think; she says Malikah has a very short sighted view of the universe.'

'What do you think?' inquired her cybernetic friend.

Lian smiled at the young man 'I think Malikah has a very pragmatic approach to problem solving, on Earth it would be described as Machiavellian.'

Before Asta could ask Lian cut him off 'A reference to a person who gave birth to a very pragmatic philosophy based around maintaining power. His name is synonymous with any such attitude or approach to life.'

Asta gave a dejected look 'Then there is no hope?'

Lian grinned at the bionic youth 'That's why Machine picked me; outside of her Father I'm the best chance to negotiate some sort of cease fire.'

'Do you think you can?'

Lian looked back at the massive singularity they sailed around 'A cease fire? Without concessions from Machine there will only be more bloodshed. Machine must accept the fact that she has lost to Malikah then try and work something out from there.'

As the pirate vessel burst through the wormhole and into Tlillan space Han awoke from his daughters dream. He looked at her worriedly only for her to calm him 'I have returned Father there is nothing to fear anymore.'

She held the Drone Officer steadying him as he wavered in the corridor of the Athena. McCann stepped forward, in a slightly annoyed tone he questioned Han 'Isn't there something you need to be doing right now?'

Han nodded and turned to shuffle away, as he groped his way along the corridor Lian called out 'I will visit you later, when you're off duty, Father.'

The poor man looked back and smiled before turning the corner and returning to his station in the drone bay.

Walking to her quarters the Englishman asked Lian 'Do I need to keep you under guard?'

She smiled and shook her head.

McCann looked at the Vympel soldiers accompanying them 'You can leave, we'll be fine.'

The Russian men saluted and returned to their stations, McCann and Lian carried on alone.

'So Machine wasn't destroyed?' inquired the Admiral.

'No, but I must say the Makayuuk are far more interesting than I first perceived,' replied Lian.

'How so?'

'They function independently; they aren't just automatons taking instruction from a computer.'

'Then what's the bloody purpose of being hooked up to it?'

Lian grinned at McCann 'For the same reason every human on Bandayuuk and this vessel is hooked up to a machine.'

The Englishman shook his head 'It's more than that.'

'Yes, they are linked through Machine; they feel each other's pain and joy. Machine prevents them from inflicting misery upon one another, they live to support the whole. The Makayuuk are the ultimate expression of Communism and they will die for their cause, Duncan.'

McCann chuckled 'Just don't tell the bloody Americans that, as soon as you mention the Reds they start filling their pants and running about like headless chickens.'

Lian stopped McCann and in a hushed tone said 'We are approaching the end on Bandayuuk, Malikah will be forced to make a hard decision.'

The Englishman replied in a more serious tone 'Which will be?'

'She must come to a compromise with Machine.'

'Or?'

'By coming to Bandayuuk Malikah has approached the edge of the abyss, even Ek'tsab cannot resist the abyss when it desires to swallow you up. You must tell her Duncan, convince her, you're the only person I've ever seen her listen to.'

'Convince her of what exactly?'

'That there is a time to compromise; she doesn't always have to be so hard headed. Machine is no longer her enemy; Machine is merely a Mother afraid for her children.'

McCann didn't know whether to believe Lian or not 'We'll see when we arrive,' he replied before escorting Lian to her quarters.

Chapter 12

The Athena soon made her way to Bandayuuk rendezvousing with several other war cruisers. The entire Tlillan fleet had gathered along with all four I.S.A vessels and 3 Gukumatz cruisers.

In all eleven vessels awaited the instruction of the Tlillan Queen. McCann noticed the Artemis was already evacuating staff and troops from the surface. From what he could tell Jenkins had ordered a total withdrawal from the planet. Now that every star ship capable of combat was present that evacuation could be carried out with great haste.

As Atlas transport craft made their way from the surface Athena sounded her klaxon 'Multiple tunnel events detected, multiple tunnel events detected, multiple tunnel events detected ...'

McCann's eyes snapped on to Hassif 'How many?' he barked.

Lian placed her hand on the Admiral's shoulder 'Be calm Duncan, they will not attack.'

McCann's eyes flicked between Hassif and the view screen, waiting for the first information concerning their uninvited guests 'They? Who are they?'

'They are Makayuuk,' replied Lian.

'Hassif open a channel to the Chutli.'

Hassif bashed his station until an image of Ilam appeared on the view screen 'We are not certain who is folding space, Duncan,' she stated.

McCann was a little uncomfortable saying it, but nevertheless he did so 'Lian has informed me it's Makayuuk; she assures me they don't intend to attack, at least not yet.'

Malikah stepped in front of her Mother taking control of the conversation 'And who exactly informed Lian of the Makayuuk's arrival?'

Lian stepped towards the screen, her smiling eyes looking her lover up and down 'Machine, just as you are linked to the Dreamscape I am linked to Machine and every Makayuuk. Machine intends to broker peace, as a sign of good will Machine shall allow you to evacuate your people from Bandayuuk unmolested.'

The former friends silently stared at each other over the view screen until Athena's soft voice broke the tension '23 Makayuuk vessels identified, 7 war cruisers escorted by frigates and destroyers.'

Malikah smirked at Lian '23? Is that still lucky for the people of the Machine?'

McCann kicked straight into action not wasting a moment 'Hassif I want the Athena, Ares and Artemis to have a full broadside on their lead war cruisers.'

The Admiral sat back in his seat tapping at the interface on his chair arm; on the right hand side of the view screen a tactical display of enemy vessels appeared. McCann selected vessels to be targeted, occupying the centre of the Makayuuk fleet.

'Instruct all Captains to arm anti-matter warheads, Thermo-nuclear secondary. I want as wide a spread on that fleet as possible, Inform Ryu and tell her she has a free hand.'

'As you wish Admiral,' replied the Athena before informing her sister SI.

Lian attempted to comfort the Englishman but to no avail 'There is nothing to fear Duncan; Machine will not attack unless attacked.'

For another hour McCann watched the evacuation, the Makayuuk waited far above the accretion disk not moving from where they had folded space into the system. Once the planet was evacuated, or at least those still alive were off planet, the fleet withdrew to the Bandayuuk control station.

The station orbited Bandayuuk's' main star in synchrony with Bandayuuk Zero but at a further 0.5 AU out from the main sun. The Makayuuk then moved into orbit of their home world as possession was transferred temporarily to Machine from Malikah.

On the massive disc shaped space station with docking arms poking out from its edge, McCann walked through the medical triage centres set up inside empty cargo bays. He was searching for Jenkins, or to be more exact Athena was directing him to Jenkins via his wrist tablet.

He made his way into the closest bay to which the Artemis had docked, being the only warship in the system at the time she had taken the lion's share of those evacuated from the surface.

The Englishman entered a docking bay larger than any he'd witnessed previously; it seemed Malikah had big plans ahead for the Macks.

He stood peering into crowds of wounded men and women as they were being treated, mainly by droids. Those with the worst injuries were first to receive Human medical attention.

'Over here old boy!' called out a familiar voice.

McCann followed the voice to see his former comrade standing over one of his men, the Admiral made his way through the bustling medics until he finally reached Brigadier Jenkins.

Jenkins saluted as did the man on the stretcher, McCann waved dismissively 'Oh give it a rest will you.'

Jenkins inquired with a concerned tone 'Shouldn't you be handling the Mack fleet?'

'They've taken up positions around Bandayuuk; they say they won't attack unless attacked.'

Jenkins scoffed 'Pah! You should have seen them pouring out of those damn tunnels, most of them didn't even own a bloody weapon! They just charged us going hell for leather.'

McCann pulled a slightly puzzled face 'So what was the problem?'

Jenkins, whose trench coat was covered in a mixture of dirt and blood, took his cap off and scratched his head 'They had more people than we had rounds of ammunition, a lot more.'

'Couldn't you get your drones up?'

Jenkins shook his head 'By the time we realised our drones needed to go up, we were over-run, it was an absolute farce down there. We had to withdraw all our forces and re-group off planet, there was no choice.'

'Casualties?' asked McCann rather tentatively.

Jenkins looked around the room 'This is pretty much all that's left, Duncan.'

McCann was startled as he took another look at the docking bay of a few thousand men and women.

Jenkins nodded his head slowly, saying in an ominous tone 'Sometimes numerical superiority does make a difference.'

'We'll be counter attacking soon; do you have enough men to form a platoon?'

'I could do that, give me a couple of hours and I'll have a few squads ready for insertion.'

McCann gave his old comrade a pat on the back 'It's good to see you Jenkins,' then left the triage centre taking a shuttle to the Bridge of Athena.

On the way to the Bridge McCann lit up a quick cigar; puffing away on his Trinidad Reyes he smiled to crew members as he stepped off the craft and walked the corridors. Exiting the elevator he walked onto the bridge with a spring in his step, the first thing he did was reassure Rosa 'Jenkins made it out.'

Vezzali gave a sigh of relief and returned to her science station where she monitored the Makayuuk fleet as it remained suspended above Bandayuuk. Vezzali muttered to herself 'What are they waiting for?'

McCann looked philosophically at the fleet around Bandayuuk 'For us to make the first move, they have what they want; now they're waiting for us to try and take it from them.'

Kim stepped next to his commanding Officer and said in a hushed tone 'Should we be talking with her on the Bridge?'

Kim gestured with his forehead towards Lian.

McCann peered at Lian 'what do you say Lian?'

Lian scoffed at Kim 'We both know what will happen now Duncan, whether I am here or somewhere else is irrelevant.'

'Please do tell,' said McCann in a slightly sardonic tone of voice.

Lian gave a half smirk/half sneer 'Malikah is preparing a counter offensive against Machine.'

The Englishman chuckled as the entire Bridge crew fell silent listening to their parle 'A first year cadet could have told me that!'

'You underestimate Machine. Malikah will attempt to clear the fleet from orbit but fail, Machine does not require my assistance as a spy.'

McCann shook his head as he breathed in the creamy scent of tobacco 'Lian, the only time Machine ever wants to talk real peace is after I see a pile of rotting Macks. Why would we think any different this time?'

Lian didn't seem surprised by his comment, she just replied in a cold tone 'This is the end ...'

The Englishman couldn't be certain as to whether Lian was mocking him or had genuinely lost her mind to Machine. He nodded in agreement with her and replied in an equally cold tone 'I agree, something will end here.'

'I have a communication from the Chutli,' announced Hassif.

McCann was glad to have a distraction from Lian, he pointed to the screen 'Put her on.'

An image of Malikah filled the screen, the regal lady noted her father's presence 'Father, I'm sending the fleet instructions for a counter-attack; you may inform Brigadier Jenkins that a ground invasion is not required at this time.'

McCann bobbed his head 'Understood, what should I do about Lian?'

'Let her witness the demise of her Makayuuk.'

The screen went blank before returning to an image of the planet they had retreated from earlier that day, with an enemy fleet laying in wait above it.

'I have received our instructions, Sir,' stated Hassif.

The Admiral rested in his seat as he read the orders given to the fleet; they were set to begin their assault in two hours. The Teteo would not take part in their counter-attack; forming a battle line between the planet and traffic control they would refuse the Makayuuk vessels escape; employing wormhole nullifiers on board the Bandayuuk space station. Malikah was intent on denying her enemy retreat from what would be their grave on Bandayuuk.

Lian's lack of concern made McCann quite the opposite, Machine wasn't stupid and suicide was certainly not on its mind. However they had left themselves open and surely it would be foolhardy not to take such an opportunity?

On the other end of the scale Sirt stood at the bridge of his command ship, his hands clasped onto a rail whilst his fellow Macks worked at their stations. Immediately surrounding him were 5 Officers all looking out toward the Tlillan fleet gathered before them.

'A terrifying sight,' stated an elderly Machine man.

Sirt nodded slowly in agreement 'so ornamental these Tlillan craft, different designs yet they move with such elegance and synchronicity, don't you think?'

An old grumpy looking Makayuuk, rather plump for a machine man, replied 'Very dramatic these Tlillan women.'

Sirt turned to look behind him as his bridge staff were hypnotised by the glorious fleet taking up battle positions 'You're a lucky man Asta, seeing all this pomp and ceremony in your first battle!'

Asta replied nervously 'We outnumber them, surely they cannot defeat us?'

Sirt grinned as his fellow staff chuckled, all except the plump old warrior 'The crown of Xch'uup is worth 20 war cruisers on any battlefield. You'll be lucky if come away with your life boy!'

'Now, now, go easy on the lad Dosa, he has plenty of time to learn,' replied Sirt still holding his grin.

As the staff observed Xch'uup's fleet taking form with Tlillan craft in the centre, I.S.A war cruisers on the portside and Gukumatz on the starboard a young Mack left his station and interrupted 'Sirt! She's there!'

'Who is where?' stated the Mack Admiral in an annoyed tone.

'Her, Ek'tsab ... the Star Shaker!' he exclaimed as the view screen magnified to focus on a white clan ship appearing from behind Bandayuuk space station.

The Chutli had been painted white by decree of Xch'uup, he was not clear as to why but it was safe to assume her Clan ship was given the regal colour in honour of a Chutli rising to Xch'uup.

Sirt focused on the screen as the Chutli slowly approached its battle lines and began to move gracefully across the full extent of her fleet, as if she were a General inspecting her army on horseback before combat.

Examining her war cruiser which shone as a star Sirt whispered to himself 'So finally, here is the terror of the galaxy, the great beast, Star Shaker.'

The young man blurted out 'The Chutli is within range of our main torpedo batteries, I request permission to attempt a salvo.'

Sirt's eyes widened as he brought his battle scarred face to bare on the young man 'Request denied, Admirals do not take pot shots at one another, slaughter on this scale is a game of gentlemen and ladies … not hooligans.'

Returning his gaze to the view screen Sirt whispered 'Before you had the people of Otoch to channel, this time it will be an equal fight.'

On the Bridge of the Chutli Malikah sat at the Captain's chair, Ilam stood beside her, on the other side waited her Grandmother Quil and last of all a young aide not yet a Matriarch was stationed behind the chair. The sable Queen observed a line of Makayuuk craft drawn up in defence of their home world. A tactical display leapt from her suit collar, after examining it closely for a few minutes it collapsed and Malikah took to her feet. Pointing towards the enemy she stated to her mother 'This Makayuuk is trying to protect himself on the starboard, he has his main force weighted on that side.'

'Then we must attack his port,' stated Quil.

The Grand Matriarch replied without skipping a beat 'No, we must antagonize his starboard side; see if we might cajole him into shifting his force to defend that position. If he moves his forces then I'll know what mettle this Machine Man is made of, Mother what is the forecast for today?'

Ilam took a deep breath and replied 'Solar winds are unfavourable Xch'uup, they will subside in three hours.'

Malikah stared stoically at the tactical display of the enemy and the position of the sun, belching out a violent solar storm 'I cannot wait three hours, the Seers report of a second Makayuuk fleet in the Dreamscape heading for Bandayuuk. No, no, if I'd waited at Gaulthus we'd have lost that battle.'

Quil contemplated the report for a moment 'Well we've fought with the winds against us before, remember Asana?'

Malikah gazed out into the void of space 'That's true Mamah, that's true.'

Malikah received a mental message from one of her Matriarchs, a communication from the Kay was incoming. Malikah replied mentally and an image of the Kay's Captain appeared before her.

The Gukumatz burped and spluttered speaking his best Tlillan 'Namaste Teootl, I must report our missiles will not travel properly while solar wind continues.'

Malikah raised her eyebrows to the squat toad 'You must find a way to compensate for it, Kotumatz.'

'I cannot answer for torpedoes Teootl, solar wind cause electronics fail, course corrections needed to fire at range,' pleaded the Gukumatz Captain.

Teootl, the Gukumatz Icon replied matter of factly 'I'm afraid you do answer for your torpedoes Kotumatz, however you will not be required to engage at a distance Captain.'

'Understood Teootl, Namaste.'

Malikah nodded as she sent mental instructions to end communications with the Gukumatz fleet Captain.

'What shall we do if we are not to engage at range, Xch'uup?' Inquired Ilam.

Pointing towards the starboard flank of her enemy the beautiful Queen stated 'The Gukumatz war cruisers will be used in a diversionary action; they will provoke this Machine Man and bring him to fortify his starboard, since that is where he fears an attack. My Father shall support this action with cannon and drones; if he flinches and moves his force to support his starboard ... we have him.'

At the intended time the Artemis cast anchor and left Bandayuuk station, the fleet dispersed drawing up a long battle line before the people of the Machine. All except the Teteo which remained docked at Bandayuuk station, Cihuateteo refused to engage in battle after her argument with Malikah.

Once all ships were in place and facing off against the enemy with a good 0.5 AU between them Malikah's battle orders were sent and received. McCann noted her instructions and spoke to Hassif 'Get me Kotumatz on the Kay will you?'

A moment later the ugly toad appeared on the view screen 'Listen here Kotumatz I want you and your toads to move up on the flank of those starboard war cruisers.'

The Englishman tapped his wrist tablet sending the Gukumatz Captain his exact targets.

'We'll be supporting you from here with nuclear warheads and drones, understood?'

The toad burped which McCann assumed was an affirmative.

'Good, McCann out.'

Its image left the screen as the Kay, Ha and Hoholki broke ranks moving towards the three Makayuuk war cruisers on the starboard side of Sirt's battle line. Firing their engines they began to push slowly into the awaiting Macks.

As the I.S.A war cruisers turned to bring their fierce batteries of magnetic cannons to bear, squadrons of drones left the bays of each ship headed for the Makayuuk.

Sirt eyed the approaching Gukumatz cruisers 'What is she doing?' he whispered to himself as his staff looked on anxiously.

A young lad broke the silence as he left his station to deliver his report 'The Tlillan fleet is approaching on our starboard flank, Ek'tsab intends to break our cruisers.'

Annoyed by the young man's supposition Sirt shouted at the lad 'What Xch'uup intends and what she does will be as different as dark side to light!'

Another of his staff spoke 'We must move some vessels down to starboard; we cannot afford to lose it. If we break there she could manoeuvre us and the solar wind would be in her favour.'

Sirt made a hard look at one of his Captains 'I will not start charging around chasing intents and assumptions. Xch'uup has not shown her hand yet, there will be plenty of time for that.'

Twenty minutes later three Gukumatz cruisers approached three Makayuuk war cruisers in a spear head formation. Once within 0.1 AU the parties began to exchange fire, torpedoes detached from the spines of Gukumatz vessels whilst others emerged from deep valleys running across the cylindrical Makayuuk warships. All this time small nuclear explosions detonated in the vicinity of Makayuuk vessels, slowly increasing in accuracy as the Gukumatz sent back positional data to Admiral McCann.

The Englishman watched on, as his ship recoiled from its cannon fire. Meyer was constantly computing updates from the Kay, translating the calculations into more precise trajectories. His bridge ran as a well-oiled machine, everyone was on the ball and for the moment he needed only to observe his crew. McCann placed his right hand inside his jacket pocket, grasping the coin he'd purchased from Ivan Andreev. The Englishman rubbed his thumb against the shiny gold.

The scene reminded him of something from another age, inside his head he could hear drums beating and boots marching. Next a noise of metal tearing the atmosphere as soldiers fell to heavy cannon and a ripple of gunshot from hundreds of rifles as sides clashed. The Commander closed his eyes for a moment; caustic smoke filled his nostrils before it began to dissipate. Through a smoky battlefield he saw men in red and white coats wearing kilts marching in block formation, hundreds of them, to the tune of bagpipes. Banners and flags waved in the stiff wind, he noticed the Union Jack though failed to recognise a yellow and black flag with a small Union Jack in the corner. Drummers and pipers led men over the crest of a hill preceded by three horsemen whom McCann assumed were their commanding Officers. The lead soldier carried what seemed to be a pole with a gold or more likely brass ball atop, he moved it up and down in time to the drum as they pushed onwards.

In the direction which the Scotsmen marched approached a block of men in blue and white coats wearing tall black and gold hats. They carried similar weapons, long wooden rifles with fierce looking bayonets, though the music they marched to was very different. McCann found their tune far more uplifting, as they played drums, flutes and various brass instruments. He recognised the flag of France and the Gold Eagle standard as the army marched forwards into heavy cannon fire of British artillery. Men were thrown as rag dolls from a child's cradle as shells hit the ground, yet they continued on without even a glimpse of fear or doubt in their eyes.

Next beside the Scots and their tall fury hats came what must have been English infantry, led by a strange man on a horse dressed in a top hat. He was shouting something, though totally inaudible in the clamour of battle. As he screamed at the enemy or his own men, it was impossible to tell, his body went limp, his top hat was shot off and he fell onto the ground. No-one assisted him, his men continued to march as they traded rounds with the French, the entire sight was one of both beauty and horror.

'Admiral?' came the voice of a concerned Kim awaking McCann from his vision.

The Englishman opened his eyes; all of his Officers were giving him an odd stare, 'Yes Kim?'

'Fresh orders from Xch'uup, Sir. We are to turn our cannon onto the next Makayuuk war cruiser down, Sir.'

McCann gripped his coin 'Then do so.'

'Are you all right, Sir?' inquired the first Officer with some trepidation in his voice.

McCann's forehead scrunched up 'I'm perfectly well, thank you very much, how are the drones?'

'They have engaged the enemy, Sir.'

McCann squinted in an expression of disbelief as he examined the view screen 'Has he not moved to defend his starboard?'

'No Sir.'

McCann replied 'Well he's definitely got balls this Makayuuk; I'll have to give him that.'

Sirt watched his enemy closely, noting every single move and considering what might be her hidden intention. Much like a great chess master he examined the board attempting to discover his opponent's plot whilst at the same time trying to bring his to fruition.

'Sirt, Tlillan drones have engaged our starboard flank,' reported one of his staff.

With a mental command the view screen focused upon the Gukumatz cruisers engaging his warships. From the Gukumatz left came a flock of Shogun Drones, built for the very purpose of engaging a Makayuuk war cruiser.

Sirt observed the incoming black drones, three drones which led their respective squadrons were painted red with the dragon motif, 'Quite a terrifying sight, wouldn't you say Dosa?'

The old machine man grumbled 'It's suicide if you ask me; those drones will cut our cruisers to shreds!'

Sirt nodded 'You're correct Dosa, send in our fighters. We'll try to meet them before they do too much damage.'

At that 500 small tubular vessels, just large enough to fit a single man inside prostrated, launched from one of the central war cruisers to meet the 75 incoming drones.

As the two groups clashed one became indistinguishable from the other, much like two flocks of birds meeting in the air and merging into one.

Explosions continued, the outer most Makayuuk war cruiser began to shake as the outer layer of its hull cracked under extreme stress. Fire shot out from breaks in its shell, forcing the beast into a roll, it moved away peeling off from the battle lines though not by its Captain's will.

'Rino has broken!' shouted one of his staff.

'Yes I have my own eyes thank you!' replied Sirt as he observed the massive tubular craft disintegrate from a concentrated attack of Gukumatz missiles and I.S.A drones.

'Sirt, we have accessed the satellite and probe network,' informed a young man from his station.

'Good, feed it in,' replied Sirt.

After a few moments the system wide network began to feed real time information to his fleet, illuminating the tactical display upon the view screen, Sirt's attention was drawn to the I.S.A. The Machine Man noticed Athena and Ares moving ever so slightly as their cannon changed direction. Within a few seconds the trajectory had been calculated, Sirt turned to Dosa and spoke ominously 'It seems she's swinging her cannon to face you Dosa.'

The old man sneered 'It seems so.'

'It looks to me as if your boys are going to take a nasty pounding, don't you think?'

Dosa breathed deeply 'They've had a pounding from the Tlillan before.'

'Time to get to your helm.'

Dosa nodded 'Machine.'

Sirt replied 'Machine.'

Dosa left the bridge, walking down grey metal corridors he entered a round porthole and strapped himself into a chair. When ready the old soldier sent a mental command and was fired out of the main Command ship in a tiny metal sphere to be caught magnetically in a tiny porthole on his war cruiser.

A minute after leaving Sirt's bridge he was at the helm of his war ship and preparing for the onslaught.

On the Chutli Malikah strode up and down, in frustration she shouted at her Matriarchs 'Why has he not moved?'

There was no reply.

Malikah brushed the feathers on her crown 'This machine man is made of neutronium and as stubborn as a mule... but he has courage and that makes him dangerous.'

Malikah observed the tactical readout for a few moments before turning to her mother 'Have the Artemis stop their barrage and move in towards the outer core, they will support the Gukumatz with drones whilst the Athena and Ares use cannon. I want the Here to move in closer but remain cloaked, is that understood?'

The Matriarchs nodded silently.

Malikah returned her gaze to the tactical display and pointed to a large asteroid on the Makayuuk starboard flank, 'That asteroid ... whomever holds it will win the battle. If this man will not move his fleet then I'll have to kick him up off his backside.'

Ilam sent instructions to her husband who dutifully notified Captain Turner, the American rose from his seat as McCann informed him of his orders 'You're to advance and secure this asteroid, understood Turner?'

Turner went a strange colour but quickly took a hold of himself 'CH-72 ... Sir?'

McCann snapped 'Why yes Sir!'

Turner was obviously not in love with the idea of advancing on the Makayuuk 'Asteroid CH-72 ... right?'

The Englishman lost his temper for a moment 'Damn you Sir! Get your bastards over there and secure that asteroid, is that understood Turner?'

The American nodded 'Sure, we'll hold back the Macks until you guys decide to make a move.'

McCann didn't want to get into a rant now so he quickly dismissed the Captain 'Good, McCann out.'

The image of Turner was replaced by the Makayuuk battle line stretched over half an AU in defence of Bandayuuk. McCann exhaled 'Bloody yanks, impertinent even on the field of battle.'

A fusion reactor fired and diverted its nuclear fire onto an engine blast plate pushing Artemis forward in a white blaze. She moved towards the asteroid, it would be a good 20 minutes before she reached it, though every second felt like an eternity to the men and women on board her.

Sirt opened a channel to Dosa, the old machine man appeared on the view screen, 'It seems they're making their way to you.'

'It seems so.'

'Xch'uup intends to take CH-72; she intends to force our retreat old friend.'

The grumpy old fellow made a noise of discontent 'Then I'm afraid I must insist on disappointing the Grand Matriarch.'

Sirt pulled a grin of satisfaction at his stalwart comrade; Dosa could always be relied upon 'That's if your crew don't break.'

Dosa's silver eyes widened 'They won't break.'

Sirt almost chuckled but instead replied quickly 'I'll send Mitz and his frigates to support you, Machine.'

Dosa nodded 'Machine,' his image retired as his war cruiser made its way toward the nearby asteroid.

Asta started walking towards the exit with Mitz, before he could leave Sirt accosted him 'Where are you going Asta? You have not been dismissed.'

Asta, rather astonished, replied to his commander 'I'm leaving for my frigate; we are to support Dosa, yes?'

'You are to remain on the bridge with me Asta; someone else shall command your frigate.'

Asta was very puzzled as were the rest of the staff 'But Sirt I have to …'

Sirt cut him off mid-sentence 'I'm under specific orders from Machine, you are to remain here and I intend to follow those orders, is that understood?'

Asta was befuddled yet he had no recourse 'Understood Sirt.'

Sirt peered deeply into Malikah's battle line spread out before the space station 'It seems you have friends in high places Asta, you may leave now Mitz.'

Mitz nodded 'Machine,' and quickly made his way to the transport tubes to be fired onto his vessel.

An hour later and the battle for CH-72 raged. Artemis used the massive rock as cover from the Makayuuk main force whilst pounding her enemy with drones and cannon. Athena and Ares lay down covering fire, nuclear explosions licking the enemy hard as they attempted to manoeuvre around the asteroid and capture Turner in a pincer movement. All the while the Makayuuk starboard flank crumbled under the pressure of the Gukumatz and drone support.

The battle became more and more bleak as time went on, Sirt turned to his communications staff 'Where is Jalk? Where are those ships? I need those ships!'

The communications staff shouted 'Sirt, Dosa requests reinforcements; he says Xch'uup is taking CH-72!'

Sirt was positively shaken at the news 'Tell Dosa that all I can send him are my best wishes!'

Sirt watched as nuclear fire lit up the void surrounding CH-72, a Makayuuk frigate spun off from behind, obviously out of control. Swarms of drones flew around chasing the war cruisers, diving in to deliver antimatter warheads. Rock, metal and fire were all one as they merged in violent detonations, 'It seems I'm losing the battle Asta,' whispered the old warrior.

Asta made no reply.

'I had hoped this would not be required, Fipu send the shuttles.'

Fipu a middle aged man well experienced in the pirate wars and resistance against Xch'uup was visibly disturbed by the order 'Understood Sirt, any specific target?'

Sirt stared out at the Tlillan battle line 'No, send them all towards the enemy battle line at Bandayuuk station, no particular vessel targeted.'

'Understood Sirt.'

The atmosphere became most sullen as Fipu walked around the bridge making certain all ships received their orders and followed them.

On board the Chutli Malikah observed the battle as communications came in, Ilam approached her daughter and reported aloud 'We've taken CH-72 Xch'uup.'

Malikah nodded as she stood wrangling her hands behind her back 'It seems so, I don't understand this machine man, why does he not reinforce his positions? His starboard flank is collapsing and we have taken CH-72 yet he refuses to initiate his full force and defend those points. Is he trying to wait me out until reinforcements arrive? What kind of strategy is this?'

Quil replied haughtily 'He is a man, what do you expect?'

Malikah turned away from the tactical display and peered worriedly at her Grandmother 'you underestimate this man, he has both courage and now cunning.'

Quil rolled her eyes 'Cunning? The Makayuuk are crumbling they have lost the battle.'

The sable Queen was annoyed by her Grandmother 'They said I had lost the battle of Asana if you remember correctly, until I won it back two hours later!'

Malikah fixed her eyes back upon her tactical readout 'No, this man has an ace up his sleeve and I'm not certain I will want to see it dealt,' the Tlillan Queen exhaled loudly 'Still, if ever there was a time to cut cards with the devil I suppose it's now; send the Athena and Ares to CH-72, they will link up with Turner. Have Ryu position herself behind the enemy but she must keep distance, too close and they will detect her cloak, understood?'

Ilam pressed her palms together 'Understood Xch'uup.'

'Destination set X +0.3, Y +0.8, Z -0.1,' came the calm voice of Athena.

McCann, with some trepidation, nodded at Hassif who replied 'Course certified.'

The Englishman who by now was stood up and pacing back and forth replied 'Engage course.'

Fusion engines fired pushing Athena gently towards her destination.

'Sir, I've got something exiting the Makayuuk fleet,' shouted Vezzali from her science station.

'Torpedoes?'

'No, thousands of small shuttle craft.'

McCann was annoyed 'What do you mean thousands? I need a number, Athena?'

'Yes Admiral,' replied the vessel.

The Englishman looked up at the ceiling as was his habit 'How many do you see?'

'5,027 shuttles and rising, Admiral.'

McCann shouted at Hassif 'Get me the Chutli, NOW!'

'Sir, they're spreading out and approaching the fleet, ETA 8 minutes!' cried Vezzali.

'Hassif?' called McCann as he looked at Lian.

Hassif was tapping away trying to speak with Malikah, but to no avail. When the Tlillan ships began firing the Englishman took his cue and called out to his weapons Officer 'Meyer, fire an anti-matter spread into the oncoming shuttles, NOW!'

The German using his eye tablet in concert with his station had his calculations ready in a couple of seconds 'Awaiting certification, Sir.'

McCann screamed 'Just fire the cannons man!'

Meyer fired into the swarm that now approached every vessel in the fleet, detonating anti-matter warheads.

'Activate point defence cannons!' called out McCann as he leapt into his chair and began to strap himself in.

'Point defence cannons activated,' replied Meyer.

Four minutes later the warheads from the Athena and Ares spread out and met the oncoming shuttles. The detonations hit Makayuuk shuttles filled with anti-matter themselves, creating a titanic explosion which ripped apart all of the inbound suicide shuttles. Despite destroying the enemy the explosion resulted in a massive concussion wave which moved outwards in a spherical pattern. Both fleets now observed a dense wave of different energy types, but mainly electromagnetic, pushing out to crush anything smaller than a moon.

For a few seconds the bridge looked on aghast at their impending doom, there was no way to avoid it, with such a disturbance a wormhole would've been collapsed before the Athena could move into it. Besides there was only a single minute before the wall of white fire hit, nowhere near long enough to fold space.

Vezzali shouted out to her Admiral 'Sir! Brace for impact, a concussion wave from the anti-matter explosion is about to hit!'

At that moment the Bridge along with the entire ship went to red light, Athena fired off her klaxon 'Battle stations, brace for impact. Battle stations, brace for impact,' somehow she managed to say it in a calming manner.

On the right hand part of the view screen was the tactical display, from his Captain's chair McCann could see the massive concussion wave caused by the anti-matter detonation. Along the wave were Makayuuk shuttles, some attempted to ride the wave, yet all were crushed by it.

Hassif called out in an urgent tone 'Manoeuvring X +0.0 relative to the wave, I'll try to hit it head on and ride the tide!'

It was a nice idea that the Indian could hit the wave, as a surfer, and use the energy to propel Athena until its force dissipated. However Hassif knew better than anyone else that they were not going to surf out this titanic tsunami. There was too much energy, Athena was not going to survive, it seemed the Macks had made the mother of all suicide attacks.

McCann appreciated Hassif's efforts but destiny was heading towards them at a rate even Athena could not out run. This was the end of both sides as far as McCann could see; he and his crew were to be judged by a gigantic wave of electro-magnetic energy. It would have been funny if he were watching it on the NET; however he was viewing it in real life. Mother Nature showed no mercy or pity, she was about to weigh them all on her scales of justice.

Lian grimaced in pain as the Makayuuk were punished for their attack; she seemed to feel their loss. Tears began to roll down the young girl's cheeks, a moment later Athena was thrown along with the wave. A tearful Lian, cast onto the ground, cried her eyes out at the horror she had already been through. McCann watched the projection of Athena from the holo table in front of him. Her starboard side turned from green to yellow then red as she swung around on the crest of the wave, much like a surfer in Hawaii turning his board to control his descent along the enormous wave. Athena cut into the explosion of energy, her starboard being ripped apart as Hassif attempted to ride his goddess to safety, in the vain hope this tide of death would crash onto the shore; but this was not Hawaii and there was no sandy beach filled with young men waiting to steal this wave's energy.

A terrified Jürgen monitored Hassif, the Indian furiously tapped his station with one hand, maintaining his balance with the other as he controlled Athena preventing her from tumbling and being devoured by the concussion wave.

Officers were thrown from their stations and across the Bridge, Jürgen screamed in terror; he could no longer contain his fear. Clutching his station he allowed his right hand to leave and make the sign of the cross on his body. McCann couldn't hear what he cried out but it was probably something in German that included the words "Jesus" and "Christ".

Athena attempted to steady herself yet it was no good, the ship couldn't be stabilized until the concussion wave had dissipated.

Vezzali held her nerve, she'd taken her baptism of fire some years ago, the blonde lady monitored her station as Athena convulsed trying not to be thrown into a deadly spin by the electro-magnetic wave.

The entire fleet was thrown out of their previous battle formations, each vessel breaking up on the shock of the wave. As Lian had stated this was to be the end, not just of the Makayuuk but of the entire Tlillan fleet.

'Sir, the star is destabilizing!' shouted Vezzali as she clutched onto her station grips; her voice barely audible above the vibrations tearing through Athena's superstructure.

McCann made no reply since there was nothing he could do; right now he was concentrating on Athena as she announced bulkheads dropping to prevent decompression.

'Starboard cannons 1-4 inoperative, system failures drone bay 2, starboard engines disabled … blast plates dislodged,' and so on as Athena continued to announce what seemed to be her and her crews' demise.

'The bow shock has dissipated!' screamed Vezzali over Athena's voice.

The vessel began to tumble until Hassif rectified the spinning, when McCann could finally concentrate on the view screen he realised they were now 5 AU from where the bow shock first hit them. The Admiral was surprised Athena hadn't broken up before then.

'Athena can you move?' shouted McCann over the noise from the pit.

'Yes Admiral, my port engines are fully operational.'

'Return to Traffic control as quickly as possible, is Traffic control still there?'

'Yes Admiral, firing port engines now Admiral. Incoming reports Admiral, all Gukumatz cruisers lost, Artemis crippled, Ares and Here operational. Awaiting reports from Tlillan war cruisers.'

Vezzali combed her long blonde hair back 'Sir, the anti-matter shock wave shouldn't have dissipated that quickly; we should all be dead.'

Lian picked herself up from the floor and wiped her eyes 'It was Malikah, you saw the star shake.'

'What about the Mack fleet?' inquired McCann.

'They used the planet as a shield, those that could,' replied Lian.

'Meyer, arm the port cannons with anti-matter warheads. Hassif, make our way back to traffic control and get me the Chutli,' ordered McCann as he sat in his chair to view the destruction along the starboard side of his vessel.

'Communication from the Chutli,' called Hassif over his shoulder.

'Put her on,' said McCann as he stood up.

The image of a very worried Ilamachutli graced his screen, it concerned him since she rarely displayed such emotion in public 'How's the Chutli?' he asked his wife.

'The Chutli is operational, Malikah saved the fleet but in doing so she has collapsed.'

McCann could hear the fear in his wife's voice 'Collapsed?'

'Yes, I believe the effort caused her to lose control of her mindscape, for a moment. Since Cihu is not present I am in command.'

McCann nodded 'Agreed.'

Ilam took a deep breath 'Gather with the fleet at traffic control, if Makayuuk retaliate we are to hold a defence there, understood?'

'Understood.'

Ilam's image disappeared as the fleet limped back to port after taking a devastating blow from the anti-matter explosion of the Makayuuk, in some sort of kamikaze attack.

As the crew regained their bearings and set course for the Traffic control Vezzali alerted her Admiral to the Makayuuk 'Sir, they're coming from behind the planet. The enemy fleet seem to be damaged!'

Six ships appeared from the crest of Bandayuuk, two war cruisers and four frigates.

'Something amiss Lian?' inquired McCann.

'Machine, she weeps for her children,' replied a teary eyed girl.

McCann sneered 'Machine didn't weep when she sent her children on a suicide attack!'

Lian sniffed as she wiped her eyes 'The Makayuuk were not sent, they volunteered. Perhaps it is something you cannot understand?'

'Understand? What exactly is there to understand about mindless slaughter?'

Lian grimaced as if she had been mortally wounded 'To sacrifice your life for the one you love? To die before being separated from the one that makes you whole?'

McCann maintained his condescending sneer 'Machine doesn't make me whole.'

'What of Malikah? If she dies here today will you get over it by tomorrow?'

McCann quietened down; still staring at Lian he spoke slowly to Vezzali 'What's the condition of the Makayuuk fleet?'

Vezzali had been monitoring the enemy intently 'Their core has broken up leaving ...'

'Just give me the short version Vezzali.'

'They have only one fully operation war cruiser, of the frigates only four survived the bow shock, Sir.'

McCann grinned at Lian whilst she read out the report 'you were right ... this IS the end.'

Lian shook her head 'Malikah was correct, you walk a fine line between courage and foolhardiness.'

McCann was quite shocked to hear what Malikah had said to Lian about him 'I could say the exact same concerning Machine.'

Just after making that statement Athena's klaxon fired off again 'Multiple tunnel events detected, multiple tunnel events detected ...' barked Athena.

McCann's head snapped towards the view screen as a string of wormholes opened up around Bandayuuk 'Vezzali what the hell is happening?'

'We have incoming, Sir!'

McCann screamed back at her 'I can see that, I'm not a total idiot! Who is it?'

'Makayuuk, 3 war cruisers and 4 assorted frigates, Sir.'

The Englishman looked up at the black dome, housing Athena 'Athena, I want you to link with the other SI, co-ordinate an attack immediately, no certification required. Use anti-matter then thermo-nuclear if required, understood?'

'Understood Admiral,' replied Athena in her soft tone.

As the I.S.A fleet began to fire Hassif jumped up 'Communication from the Chutli.'

'Put her on.'

The image of a now furious Ilamachutli appeared 'You were not given clearance to fire on the Makayuuk!'

McCann made an incredulous expression towards his wife 'And what would you have me do? We must engage them now, better we select the time and place to fight it out than allow them to prepare. Besides those reinforcements cannot be permitted to link up with the main force. If we attack them now by the time those fresh ships engage it'll be too late.'

Ilam's eyes turned red 'The Tlillan fleet cannot support this; our armour was severely damaged by the shockwave.'

McCann snorted in disbelief 'Well you're going to have to, aren't you? They aren't gonna let you repair your ship then re-arm so you can fight it out at full strength, are they?'

Ilam smashed her fist upon the Captain's chair 'Your insolence will be the undoing of us!'

McCann sneered and replied condescendingly 'And your inaction makes us nothing more than cattle awaiting slaughter! Now tell your ships to support us before it's too late, or has the Ixchel made you all so afraid of death you squirm at the thought of sacrifice?'

Ilam disconnected her communication in a rage, probably in the hope her husband would refrain from his attack after hearing her refusal, she was wrong.

The Tlillan war cruisers refused to move up and engage the enemy, leaving the already battered Athena and her pantheon to battle it out.

The Makayuuk approached from the planet towards the fleet seemingly without fear or doubt.

'Makayuuk have released anti-matter torpedoes,' alerted Vezzali.

Athena's port cannons blasted rhythmically as she fired, reloaded and fired into the Makayuuk without mercy. The other gods in her pantheon carried out much the same tactic with the Here decloaking to fire her main cannon on a regular basis.

'Launch all drones, try and intercept those torpedoes before they get within range of our point defence cannons.'

'Yes, Sir,' replied Kim as he tapped his wrist communicator sending out orders to Drone Chief Deychaa. He also sent the same order out to the other vessels via Athena; with her link she alerted the SI and their Captains in nano seconds.

Seven squadrons of Shogun II drones launched from the pantheon, heading at full speed for the Makayuuk.

'Let's see how Machine deals with that!' said McCann as he watched the anti-matter engines of the tiny remote controlled vessels fire off into the night of space.

Ten minutes later there were several detonations, McCann could see them as they happened since the satellite network was up and running.

'What happened to the satellites? I thought the Makayuuk had taken them down?' inquired McCann looking up at Athena.

'I did it,' called out Hassif who was tapping away at his console 'They took the network down then brought it up for their own use, I hacked in through a back door. It might go down again Duncan, so don't rely on it.'

McCann grinned at his old friend 'Good job.'

Hassif raised a hand and gave the Admiral a thumbs up before quickly going back to keeping the network live and out foxing the Makayuuk.

Athena and her counterparts launched more drones, replenishing those lost to exploding Makayuuk missiles.

Thanks to Hassif's work drone pilots could now pilot their drones live rather than suffering time lag through the tachyon array, or worse sending orders to an AI and hoping for the best. The AI was good but it just didn't cut the mustard against the average human, or alien for that matter.

'Have the pilots engage their engines first, if we can get them dead in the water Athena will be able to finish them off easily,' ordered the Englishman with growing confidence.

'I have linked all other vessels to the satellite network, Admiral,' came the soothing voice of Athena.

'Does that include the Chutli?'

'Yes Admiral.'

'Hassif, get me the Chutli.'

'Done,' called out the Indian as the image of Ilam appeared.

'What do you want now?' said his wife with burning eyes.

'We have the advantage, you must engage now,' replied McCann.

Just as Ilam was to refuse him again a voice called out from behind her 'What on Earth has happened?'

Malikah hobbled onto to the Bridge with the assistance of a young Tlillan lady 'Why are we not engaging the Makayuuk!?'

Ilam turned her head and replied tentatively 'The fleet is damaged, our armour could not withstand another full engagement and they are fresh.'

Malikah's eyes quickly shifted pigment to that of a burgundy red 'you idiot! You do not send in your main force without proper support! Must I always rely on a man?'

Ilam stuttered in shock at her daughter's outburst 'I ... I told him not to attack, he ... took it upon himself to do so.'

Malikah leaned on the Captain's chair whilst the young girl held her up, nevertheless her rage was not abated 'YOU DID WHAT?'

Ilam's eyes had lost any shade of her former anger, now she felt only fear of her daughter's animosity 'He ... wanted to attack on first sight ... I couldn't ...'

Before finishing her sentence Malikah smashed her Mother around the head with a gigantic slap, knocking the Matriarch's head forward and into her lap 'My God! I'm surrounded by fools!'

The side of her father was showing itself, unlike her Mother Malikah was not easily brought to anger; however she was prone to the odd temper tantrum and although it was rare to witness one, it made McCann look like a choir boy.

Malikah screamed at the top of her voice 'GET OUT OF THAT CHAIR YOU FOOL!'

Ilam dutifully arose from the Captain's chair allowing the sable Queen to sit and take the reins. Flanked by her aide she took control of the shattered situation although her fury had not quietened 'PEEKSIK K'ALIK, CHUUP SEEB!'

In McCann's best English/Tlillan that meant 'Move forward, full speed', Malikah wasn't happy but the Tlillan fleet was now moving to support the I.S.A efforts. Ilamachutli stood dejected by her sable Queen's side, looking at the floor whilst Malikah screamed orders at her terrified crew. The Matriarchs feared their Xch'uup above any Makayuuk threat, defying her meant certain death and a dishonourable one at that; at least if they died fighting Machine, they might take some Kleos with them to the underworld.

Malikah looked wearily at the Englishman 'Father, continue your assault I will engage at close range as quickly as possible.'

McCann nodded towards the image of his regal daughter 'Understood.'

Malikah gave a sigh of relief, 'Thank God someone knows what they're doing!' exclaimed Malikah in English as the view screen faded back to the battle unfolding in orbit of the Makayuuk home world.

Damaged Tlillan vessels moved past Athena and her sister ships to engage the Makayuuk now struggling with seven squadrons of drones. Each squadron consisted of 25 drones, making 175 tiny fighters, each capable of carrying enough anti-matter to bring the most powerful war cruiser to a grinding halt. Even the Makayuuk had learnt to fear the Red Dragon by now, to see that red drone leading in a squadron brought a sick feeling to the stomach of even the most battle hardened Machine man.

Sirt and his staff gazed upon the full force of the enemy fleet as alarms blared and reports piled up informing the Makayuuk commander of system failures and damage aboard his remaining vessels.

'I need Jalk, if only I had more time,' whispered the machine man to himself.

After a few moments the Mack Admiral called out 'Order all vessels to gather on our position.'

One of his remaining staff blurted out 'But Sirt, if we do that one anti-matter spread and we're finished!'

Sirt shouted 'Damn you man, do as you're told! I want every fighting vessel on this position NOW!'

The image on the view screen was one of both awe and terror, four Tlillan clan war cruisers advanced in line formation closing in on their foe with total confidence and determination. They pressed at full speed brandishing beam weapons, much like infantry with fixed bayonets as they bore down upon the enemy. The very sight of these clan ships, similar to Napoleon's Old Guard, was enough to break most enemies and cause them to flee. Foremost the clan ship of Xch'uup, leading her old guard upon a white horse. If Sirt had been raised Human, La victorie est a nous might be playing through his mind.

Asta swallowed deeply 'They tried to break us.'

Sirt nodded slowly as he watched Tlillan clan ships over taking I.S.A allies, all on a direct course for his shattered fleet 'Looks like they'll try again.'

'It's as if Ek'tsab has returned to take her share of our souls.'

Sirt closed his eyelids for a moment 'ETA for Jalk?'

A young staff member replied immediately '3.49 minutes Sirt, Jalk reports he's burning out his engine plates to reach us.'

'Order his frigates to engage now, let their blast plates desiccate if they must.'

'Understood Sirt.'

The Machine man held his hands together before him and wrangled them, in a shaky voice he prayed 'If Jalk doesn't reach me soon ... Xch'uup will tear me limb from limb.'

As the Tlillans closed in on the Makayuuk, enemy frigates fired their engines and rammed the Chutli, Tico, Kak and Huel. The pirate vessels made a break through the now worn down armour and the People of the Machine attempted a boarding action.

Tlillan cruisers continued to fight on, discharging their energy weapons despite some of their masts no longer being operational. The four weapon masts that stood on the back of the Chutli at 90 degree angles to its main body fired, ripping into a Makayuuk frigate that had dug into her shell.

As the triumvirate bore down upon the cowering Makayuuk, Malikah watched the closing manoeuvres of the battle of Bandayuuk unfold 'Quil, what is the time?'

'17:32 hours, Muul Kaah time.'

'Good, send this message to Otoch, tell them that today, at Bandayuuk 0 battle opened at …'

'12:07 hours, Xch'uup.'

'Thank you, 12:07 hours, The Makayuuk fleet held their ground eventually collapsing upon their starboard flank at 17:32 hours. Honourable mentions for Captain Turner and his crew. An ovation for Captain Kotumatz, the crew of the Kay and her sister ships … etcetera, etcetera.'

'Shall I speak of Teteo?'

'No, only mention those involved in today's action. Tell them that once again the savages lay their arms at the feet of Xch'uup and her Matriarchs.'

Quil's display leapt from her collar as she arranged the memo, the holographic image slipped back into the Tlillan suit before her grandmother declared proudly 'Transmission sent and received, Namaste Xch'uup.'

'Anti-matter and thermo-nuclear now exhausted, Admiral,' stated Athena calmly.

'Continue firing with dry shells Athena, concentrate on the war cruisers. Kim, order all squadrons to support the Tlillan vessels.'

Keeping their fire as far away from the struggling Tlillan war cruisers as possible, the I.S.A fleet was attempting to do maximum damage whilst holding Tlillan heads above water.

Explosions on both sides illuminated the view screen; it would have been the most spectacular fireworks display in history. From the planet below, the People of the Machine observed surges of colour as the Gods battled; an aurora similar to that of the northern lights on Earth shimmered in the sky each time a burst of plasma skimmed its atmosphere.

Vessels on both sides were leaking energy in the form of plasma; anti-matter caused white splashes to light up the sky in a sudden discharge of brilliance. Each side held on for dear life as they watched their destinies unfold in spectacular explosions.

'War cruiser eliminated, re-allocating target. New target acquired. Commencing firing sequence,' spoke Athena in her usual calm manner.

McCann eyed the tactical display then the view screen as one of the large tubular Makayuuk war cruisers disintegrated. A shockwave of more than 20 tungsten shells ripping through it caused the vessel to crumble.

The Englishman expelled a massive sigh of relief, but it was only a short reprieve.

Makayuuk reinforcements had closed in; four enemy frigates were now approaching from behind and engaging the Tlillan clan ships; whilst Makayuuk war cruisers swung around their flank to link with Sirt and regain control of Bandayuuk.

'Sir! The Tico is breaking up!' shouted Vezzali over the clamour on the Bridge, junior Officers in the pit called out reports and chattered back and forth with the crew as they attempted to repair Athena.

The Admiral called out 'Athena, show me the Tico.'

Part of the view screen was set aside and focused in on the beleaguered Tico; the clan ship struggled to survive as she rolled back and forth. Three pirate vessels had dug into her sides, their engines fired in an unpredictable sequence; the Tico gyrated back and forth unable to regain control.

With an SI installed attitude would easily have been regained but since it was against Tlillan law she continued to spin helplessly.

'Incoming transmission from the Tico!' shouted Hassif.

'Do it!' replied McCann.

The image of Tezcatico clutching onto the arms of her Captain's chair appeared, 'Chowak Khatal lak'tsil!' she howled.

Her image disappeared as quickly as it had appeared, leaving the Bridge crew somewhat befuddled.

Next it became clear as pieces of the Tico began flying off; her engines fired propelling the vessel into one of the fresh Makayuuk war cruisers as it manoeuvred into orbit of Bandayuuk. It was as if God were playing a game of billiards, the Tico smashed the massive ship into Bandayuuk 0's atmosphere. Despite all efforts of the unfortunate Makayuuk Captain he was caught in the death grip of Bandayuuk's gravitational pull. The titanic warship writhed doing Siva's dance of death, igniting into a spectacular fire, as she plummeted to her death on the surface.

The Tico and its crew met with a similar fate, exploding in a spectacular green and yellow plasma fire as her fusion reactor lost integrity, annihilating everything within 50,000 KMs.

McCann took a physical step backwards as the impact of what had happened slowly sank in; the Tlillans were not indestructible but just as vulnerable as they.

Next he heard a very worried cry from Hassif 'Duncan! The Kak and Huel are retreating, they're abandoning the Chutli!'

A shiver of terror ran down McCann's spine 'Athena, what is the situation on the Chutli?'

Athena replied in total calm 'Engines inoperable, armour integrity 17%, weapon masts remain operational, Admiral.'

'Get me the Kak and Huel, NOW!'

Hassif replied worriedly 'They refuse to answer.'

'Then get me the Chutli!'

Malikah appeared, sitting at the helm of her battered warship, still wearing the white headdress of Xch'uup.

'Malikah, can you retreat?' blurted out a concerned Father.

'No, we're dead in the water,' replied an exhausted Queen.

'You need the Kak and Huel to re-engage, we can tow you out but we need cover.'

Malikah closed her tired eyes and in a moment where the sable Goddess seemed quite serene she replied 'They have betrayed me,' Malikah chuckled in a reflective manner 'abandoned me to the wolves Father, Chiu refuses to answer my call, it seems the old guard has broken. I suggest you withdraw also, at least then I shall have someone to avenge me.'

McCann replied in an angry tone 'Don't be so bloody stupid! Athena order Ryu to get as close to the Chutli as possible and use her graviton beam to push it back to port. Co-ordinate with the Artemis and Ares, let Titov and Turner know what's happening.'

'Affirmative Admiral,' replied Athena as she got to work.

While he waited for Athena McCann watched the Chutli, she was soon to be overwhelmed by hordes of Makayuuk who'd now turned everything upon her. All of Sirt's attention was placed squarely upon Malikah's white clan ship.

'Course ready, awaiting certification.'

McCann looked up 'Not required, now get moving!'

The Englishman's wrist communicator began to bleep 'For fuck's sake!' he shouted hitting the reply button.

'McCann are you fucking crazy?' came the voice of Beaumont in his ear 'One hit on our starboard and we're finished!'

The Englishman bellowed into his wrist tablet 'my daughter's on that ship and we're gonna pull it out come hell or high water, do you understand me Beaumont?'

The Frenchman replied in a less aggressive tone 'We'd be lucky to escape with our own lives!'

'Then so be it, or are you afraid to die?'

Screeching back, so loud that McCann had to pull his earpiece out resulting in the entire Bridge crew listening in, 'Yes I'm afraid to die! Now turn this fucking ship around!' ripped Beaumont as the sound of charging generators could be heard whining into action behind him.

'We're all dying Louis, it's just a matter of when; so don't bring me down there and make it any sooner than it has to be,' McCann slapped his wrist tablet turning it off.

Lian witnessed the whole conversation and commented 'You shouldn't speak to your Chief Engineer in that manner, Duncan.'

McCann walked past the 3-D projection of the Athena, concentrating on the tactical display to the right hand side of the view screen he replied stoically 'I don't live today ... maybe tomorrow.'

Lian stood next to the Englishman and whispered into his ear 'Not everyone here has a daughter on the Chutli, Duncan.'

Still watching the I.S.A ships converge on the Chutli he replied 'Malikah, she carries the fate of Mankind upon her shoulders. We cannot allow her to stumble, not here, not now.'

Lian put her arm around his shoulder and leant into the Admiral 'Look at your crew, they're afraid.'

McCann looked around the Bridge, Kim was decidedly pale standing at his drone station. Vezzali pressed both hands against the wall as she hunched over her science station. He noticed her I.S.A issue Officer's jacket had been undone, its leather straps swung beneath. Meyer was staring directly at McCann as if awaiting the order to swing the ship around and flee, sweat poured down the man's forehead.

Moving through the pit to the weapons station so quickly had left Meyer without any real combat experience, until today.

Hassif concentrated on his job as always, his wife was on board the Chutli so he was prepared to rush the enemy no matter what the consequences.

The pit focused on Athena and holding her together, most of them were well experienced in these situations. At the power and engines station stood Lieutenant Paul Flesch, the man visibly trembled in fear as Athena approached her destination. Just as Meyer, he had not been in a situation as severe as this one; the man looked to be having a mental breakdown.

McCann bellowed at his Officer 'Flesch! Get a bloody hold of yourself man! That goes for the rest of you, understood?'

Flesch, a young man with short black hair of British-Hungarian parentage nodded his head, however he couldn't prevent his teeth from chattering uncontrollably; not due to any temperature discrepancies but through the absolute terror he was succumbing to.

Lian approached Flesch and placed her hand affectionately around his head, the young man's teeth slowly stopped their chattering. Within 30 seconds his breathing returned to something Doctor Weissmuller would have described as normal. The dark haired Amazon then whispered to him with a smile 'You can return to your station now.'

Flesch nodded 'Thank you,' then turned back to man his power and engines station, between Hassif's and Meyer's station.

McCann walked up to Hassif and stood next to him 'Tell me when we're within firing distance, we're gonna make this as painful for those Mack bastards as possible.'

'Understood,' said Hassif not taking his eyes away from the readouts before him, unintelligible to most people but to the Indian it was a second language.

Next he walked over to Meyer 'Concentrate on your job Meyer; I want those cannons ready to unleash hell the moment we're within close firing range, understood?'

'Understood, Sir.'

McCann smiled and patted Meyer on the back before he walked around the Bridge dispensing similar encouragement to his crew.

The object was to get within close firing range, that being a distance where the Athena could fire her cannons and hit her target without a time delay. Since the Makayuuk were near to the Chutli it was too dangerous, and of little use with dry shells, firing upon an image 1 AU away; despite the fact they had a satellite network providing them real time updates. To travel 1 AU at the speed of light took a good 8 minutes and the tungsten shells were slower than the speed of light. With anti-matter warheads, or even thermo-nuclear, the detonation and following shockwave would cause devastation despite the enemy avoiding a direct impact.

However with just plain hard shells Athena was going to have to close on her enemy to provide cover for Ryu as she towed the Chutli away from the clutches of Machine; there was no alternative.

After boosting his crew McCann stood waiting for Hassif or Athena to give the shout that they were in range. Meanwhile the Chutli was being boarded by Makayuuk pirate vessels, lodged in her torso. Fortunately Malikah's guards, Vympel 1 headed by Nestor Andreev, were on board and no doubt giving those Machine men a damn good run for their money. Malikah still had her pet, Icarus, who defended his Icon in her weakened condition.

Lian stood by McCann as he watched the tactical display nervously. She asked the worried Admiral, or made more of an observation 'So you would give your life for a cause?'

McCann replied stoically 'I will sacrifice everything for her.'

'No matter the cost?'

'If I lost her due to my inaction I couldn't forgive myself.'

Lian pointed at the battle for the Chutli on the view screen 'Then you understand every single Makayuuk that fights today, they will not be deterred by fear of death.'

McCann still looking at the display sneered 'Defy death lads and you shall drive him into the enemies' ranks. It seems both sides have made Charon a wealthy man today,' the Englishman took a deep breath and in a philosophical tone recalled the lines to a poem his father once gave him, in a book for a birthday present 'His eyes like hollow furnaces on fire; A girdle, foul with grease, binds his obscene attire.'

Athena broke McCann's moment of reflection and announced in her soft tone 'Close firing distance ETA 3 minutes.'

Lian looked as if she was about to shed tears, her eyes welled up, she held McCann's upper arm in her hand 'Please Duncan, ask Machine for a parle, do it now and Malikah can be saved.'

The sky of night was pierced with holes shimmering in an array of colours, fire lashed out from exploding vessels and rainbows of burning plasma whooshed from all quarters of the Chutli in a ballet of beauty and destruction.

The Englishman peered at the situation, it was obvious to him the Chutli was not going to survive much longer. Ryu was approaching, firing her main weapon along with both cannons; she didn't even bother to cloak her vessel. Torpedoes screeching towards her were deflected by Here's Casimir field; yet their detonations damaged the Destroyer knocking it from pillar to post as Ryu maintained her orders, in the Korean's usual head strong fashion, moving ahead of the fleet to the Chutli.

The Englishman realised that Malikah wasn't going to make it; there wasn't enough time for them to rescue the Chutli.

'Hassif, inform Malikah to abandon ship immediately once we're in range,' ordered McCann as beads of sweat began to surface along his brow.

Just as Hassif was sending the message the klaxon went off 'Multiple tunnel events, multiple tunnel events, multiple tunnel events,' called out Athena above the pit.

All eyes shot to the tactical display as another string of white holes opened up just above the accretion disc.

McCann put his right hand on top of his head and shouted 'Vezzali, don't tell me those are Macks!'

Vezzali shrieked back '3 Mack war cruisers, 4 assorted frigates, Sir!'

McCann smashed his fist upon Hassif's station as he approached the view screen 'JESUS FUCKING CHRIST!'

'Makayuuk fleet Gamma ETA 7 minutes at full speed, Admiral,' notified Athena.

Hassif shouted to McCann desperately 'Malikah refuses to abandon ship!'

The Englishman shouted to Flesch 'Get Louis to pipe all reserve anti-matter from the engines to the armoury, now!'

Ten seconds later Flesch replied 'It's done, Sir.'

Meyer called out 'We have enough for three full spreads. Anti-matter shells loaded, Sir.'

Lian shook her head despairingly as a tear rolled down her cheek 'Duncan, both you and Malikah will be destroyed. Machine has 5 more fleets in hyperspace, please request parle, PLEASE!'

McCann fixed his gaze upon Lian, looking her square in the eye he said 'I don't believe that.'

Lian peered up at the ceiling, within 3 seconds the klaxon fired off again 'Multiple tunnel events, multiple tunnel events, multiple tunnel events,' alerted Athena.

Vezzali shrieked out the status of Makayuuk fleet Delta, consisting of only 2 vessels.

Lian peered back at the Englishman 'Do you believe me now?'

Kim stood on the other side of McCann and whispered 'We're beaten, Sir.'

McCann didn't even look at him; the Bridge fell quiet as they listened for their commanding Officer to make a decision.

'We have entered close firing distance, awaiting orders to fire,' announced Athena, causing several Bridge Officers' hearts to jump.

As the Englishman contemplate his next move a soft voice spoke into his ear 'your hand, it shakes in fear my little Odysseus?'

The Admiral glanced to his right, Athene stood before him with her golden helmet in hand.

'It shakes in anger,' he whispered as quietly as possible.

Athene laughed 'You are a poor liar, you fear for the life of Malikah.'

He replied with nothing but a grunt.

'Duncan, you must accept a cease fire, if this battle continues it will end in yours and your daughter's death.'

'I will not surrender,' he muttered as Kim and Lian stared worriedly in his direction then at each other.

'Duncan, brute force is not the most powerful weapon in this universe; a man's wits will crush even the greatest of tyrants. If it were not for Rhea, hiding her son and serving Kronos a stone in swaddling cloth, Zeus would never have saved his siblings.

Kim is correct, the battle is lost; now ensure your daughter's safety so that she might conquer Machine ... as Zeus defeated Kronos.'

The Englishman's hand shook as it held onto his coin, he nodded towards the Goddess of the flashing eyes. She smiled before vanishing, to where? He had no idea, but her message was clear.

McCann turned to Lian 'Will Machine allow me to rescue the Chutli if I accept parle?'

Lian nodded 'Machine will withdraw her forces while you recover the Chutli.'

McCann looked up at Athena 'Inform the fleet there has been a ceasefire, Machine has permitted us to tow the Chutli back to dock. Tell Ryu to continue recovery of the Chutli.'

McCann turned around, walked towards his command chair and fell into it exhausted, 'I want Athena and Ares to escort Hera as she tows the Chutli in, we can return for the Artemis.'

Kim nodded and sent the order out to the fleet as a wave of relief travelled around the Bridge.

Sirt called out to his staff 'Machine has agreed to cease fire, all weapons stand down.'

All Makayuuk vessels detached from the Chutli, the remnants of Machine's fleet withdrew to meet up with reinforcements which had just entered the system, taking their position in a battle line above Bandayuuk.

Asta exhaled so that all could hear the tension leave his body.

Sirt grinned at the young man 'How was that for your first real battle?'

'Do you think we'd have broken?'

'Does it matter?'

Asta shrugged his shoulders 'I don't know, but when you stare death in the face is it not natural to ask why she did not take me?'

Sirt nodded as he peered out to view the carnage around asteroid CH-72 'It is and that is how false Gods are created.'

'Well, would we have broken?'

'Perhaps.'

'And then what?'

Sirt chuckled into the void 'Then we would not be having this discussion, at least not in this incarnation.'

Still in a state of confusion Asta stood next to Sirt and grabbed the metal rail 'Who is victorious?'

An equally puzzled Sirt replied 'I'm not certain but Xch'uup would never surrender her kleos.'

'Kleos?'

'Glory earnt on the battlefield, better to die with kleos then live with aidos.'

'Aidos?'

'Shame.'

Asta narrowed his silver eyes as he fixed them on Sirt 'How do you know this?'

The Machine man smirked into the destruction before him 'The first step to defeating your enemy is to understand them. Every defeat you suffer is a gift if you wish to learn, so take it with thanks.'

'I don't understand.'

Sirt turned his faced to the young machine man 'That is why I commanded this battle and why we did not break.'

Lian approached McCann 'You made the right decision Duncan, you have saved your family and every member of the fleet.'

McCann chuckled as he shook his head from side to side.

Lian gave him a puzzled look 'What do you find amusing?'

'If I was Machine, I'd have killed us all,' replied a weary Englishman.

'Machine would have destroyed you, but I pleaded for mercy.'

McCann made an expression of disbelief 'You? The little girl that memorized Machiavelli?'

Lian grinned 'Just because I memorized Machiavelli when I was a child doesn't mean I agree with everything he wrote. I wanted to impress Xch'uup and it worked, nothing more.'

The Englishman laughed 'Well that's very Machiavellian in itself, surely?'

'Perhaps, nevertheless the heart will often rule the head. Show Machine respect, it will get you further than any Machiavellian philosophy.'

McCann laughed again 'I've got no bloody choice, have I?'

Both fleets separated, leaving the debris of the battle behind, returning to safety. Crushed space craft broken into pieces floated aimlessly whilst their siblings orbited Bandayuuk, crumbling into magnificent arcs of fire in the atmosphere.

As McCann watched the display Lian crept up behind him and said softly into his ear 'Now you must convince Malikah to negotiate with Machine.'

The Englishman rolled his eyes as he turned his head to the ceiling 'Marvellous!'

Chapter 13

The battered and dejected fleet docked at Bandayuuk Traffic Control, conspicuously the Kak and Huel docked beside the Teteo; whereas the Chutli and her I.S.A counterparts rested on the opposite side of the enormous disk, the implications were quite ominous.

After Athena had drifted alongside a docking arm and both her airlocks made contact, holding her in place, McCann lit a Trinidad Reyes. Looking around the Bridge he spoke first to Kim 'Fix her up as quickly as possible, prioritise the cannons, make sure Athena has all the anti-matter she can hold before I get back.'

Kim saluted 'Yes Sir!'

The Englishman pointed his cigar towards Lian 'you're coming with me young lady,' then walked into the elevator followed by Voice of Machine.

Strolling through Athena to her airlock, crews of damage control droids rushed back and forth along with their Human handlers. His men and women worked furiously to patch their Athena back together as the SI informed them of hull breaches and jammed bulkheads.

The pair stepped onto a docking arm to be met by Titov, the bearded Russian shook his Admiral's hand 'Is that a Trinidad you're smoking?' he asked cheekily.

McCann grinned and pulled a tubos out of his leather arm pocket 'Take it, you've earnt a good smoke and for all I know it could be our last old friend!'

Titov bit the cap of as he strolled down the docking arm beside McCann 'Duncan, you cannot jump above your own head!'

McCann took a deep drag of his Habanos, breathing the smoke into his lungs since he needed something to remind him he wasn't deceased 'You're preaching to the choir, it's Malikah that needs your sage Russian advice now.'

As the two men and half-Tlillan lady entered the station's main disc Malikah and Ryu stood chatting. Just as they were to walk over to meet them a voice thundered from the right 'HEY MAN!'

McCann glanced towards the rather strange greeting; walking in their direction was Captain Graham Turner.

Titov noted McCann's grimace 'So this is the American?'

'You have no idea,' he replied in a haunting tone.

Titov sniggered as he pulled the Trinidad from his bearded face, blowing out its thick smoke he grinned at the American.

'Damn, we took a bitch slappin' there man!' exclaimed the loud American.

The Englishman found his demeanour most distressing 'Yes, quite, shall we go?'

'Go where?' said Turner in that loud booming voice of his.

McCann closed his eyes, holding them shut for a moment to centre himself he opened them and replied gently 'Just shut up and follow me.'

Turner gave an awkward grin as he waited for the Admiral to move.

As they approached Malikah, Ilam appeared from the docking arm, McCann smiled at his wife who didn't return the gesture. Ilam stood quietly behind her daughter as she conversed with Ryu.

Malikah broke her discussion with Ryu 'Smoking at a time like this Father?'

The Englishman smiled and in a jovial tone replied 'Why not? It could be my last!'

No-one laughed.

Malikah smirked 'Perhaps you missed your true calling as a stand-up comedian?'

Ryu grunted in displeasure at McCann's lack of timing.

Lian produced a beaming grin, when Malikah noticed she quickly changed her demeanour 'Enough, we have many problems to resolve before we may take the luxury of throwing jibes at one another.'

McCann folded his arms defensively 'Machine withdrew allowing us to retrieve the Chutli.'

'Yes, why is that Father?'

McCann took a deep breath since he knew his sable daughter was not going to approve 'I agreed to a parle with Machine, in return for a cease fire.'

Malikah's eyes widened 'Without my authority?'

'Yes, without your authority.'

The Queen's eyes flushed red for a moment before returning to her natural grey 'Then we can only pray that there is compassion, understanding and even pity inside the mind of Machine.'

Lian spoke up 'Machine is genuine, she will offer acceptable terms for you and the council.'

Malikah laughed, a cackling laugh that reminded McCann of the Xch'uup his daughter deposed. The sable Queen peered adoringly at Lian 'It is of no consequence, for today I am not certain that I am still Xch'uup.'

Lian shook her head 'You remain Xch'uup as long as you live.'

Malikah laughed again and spun on her toes looking at the Captains surrounding her 'this is all I have Lian, clan Tico is almost dead, Kak and Huel are traitors and Cihu refuses to fight. Only Chutli and the I.S.A remain loyal.'

Lian seemed upset at her former lover 'Hold your mouth! You have the Gukumatz and you have me; Cihu will return to your side, you have seen it in the Dreamscape.'

Malikah smiled at Lian as if she were a naïve little girl 'Before I can parle with Machine I must take control of the council, does Machine not understand?'

A frustrated Lian replied 'Then do it! And stop wallowing in your self-pity! The Malikah I knew would never have been so pathetic!'

The sable Amazon was taken aback by Lian's comments 'When you say 'you have me', does that mean Machine?'

'I speak for Machine and she listens to me.'

'What does that mean in practical terms?'

'Machine will be forever fighting the Tlillan and their offspring; however if she supports you now this savagery may come to an end.'

'How?'

Lian replied 'Machine desires only to care for her children; she has no aspirations of further power. Machine will offer you acceptable terms of surrender in exchange for supporting you as Xch'uup.'

Malikah shook her head 'I will not surrender, Xch'uup cannot surrender even in the face of defeat you know that Lian.'

Lian sighed 'Machine will surrender to you. Machine will surrender under the condition the Makayuuk become a vassal with all privileges that title bestows.'

Ryu gave an incredulous expression 'Machine surrender? I don't believe that and neither does anyone here.'

McCann piped up next 'Wait, Machine could just crush us all now if she wanted, right?'

Ryu's arms folded over her well ironed Captain's jacket with its gold braids and lines of ribbons along the chest, informing everyone that she had kicked more butt than everyone else put together, 'And?'

The Englishman took a puff of his cigar 'So why doesn't Machine just finish us right here, right now?'

Ryu pushed her metal framed glasses back up her nose, something she did in awkward conversations 'I don't know what some crazy SI is thinking and neither do you McCann!'

'We were dog meat back there and you know it, Ryu. Unfortunately the only way out of this alive is Machine showing mercy. Do you remember that old Korean saying?'

Ryu was a little frustrated, probably due to the fact McCann was right 'No but I'm sure you're gonna tell me!'

McCann took another puff on his smoke then pointed the almost finished cigar at the short Korean 'Better I grab a shit than I grab a fart! You taught me that.'

Titov chimed in 'In Russia we say that even a baby and a fool speak the same truth!'

Malikah put her hand on her chin and thought for a minute, everyone quietened down to hear her decision. The sable goddess approached Lian 'I agree but first I need Machine to take her fleet out of the system. Those warships weaken me, if they leave I have a strong position to protect my throne; does Machine understand?'

Lian fell into a trance as a silver gloss covered her eyes, fixing her ghostly gaze upon Malikah, Machine spoke directly 'Lian assures me your request is legitimate and I will comply; yet be warned, if you betray my trust you shall be punished. Are we agreed?'

Malikah nodded 'I understand your terms, Machine.'

Still in control of Lian, Machine pressed her palms together 'Namaste Xch'uup,' Machine then bowed deeply before Malikah 'Until we communicate again, Lian speaks for Machine and the Makayuuk.'

Lian's eyes returned to their usual dark brown before the Valkyrie awoke from her trance state.

Malikah breathed deeply, readjusting her white feathered headdress she stated 'Time to take back the throne ladies and gentlemen.'

Turner pulled a pulse pistol from his thigh holster; the whine of its charging rails filled the corridor.

Malikah walked away making no comment, Ryu smiled whilst shaking her head at the American before following her friend down the corridor, alongside Ilam.

Turner had a bemused expression.

Titov laughed 'Only a fool brings a Kalashnikov to Tula, young man!'

Titov walked way and Turner none the wiser asked 'What did he just say?'

McCann pushed Turner's arm back down towards his holster 'You won't need that old boy.'

The Englishman followed Malikah and her band of loyalists; Turner switched his pistol off and placed it back in its holster before catching them up.

McCann's wrist tablet started to bleep in synchrony with the other Captains communicators; he answered his tablet to be informed by a joyous Kim that the Makayuuk had withdrawn all warships from the Bandayuuk system.

The resolute group entered a large circular room, usually employed for the organisation of shipments to and from Bandayuuk, now it was used to co-ordinate its defence.

As Malikah strode in lesser females scuttled out leaving two Matriarchs inside the room, both faced Malikah and her ardent followers. For a moment nothing was said, the two Matriarchs, Ceenakak and Matnaheul shook in terror. They were the Firsts of clan Kak and Huel and members of the Tlillan council, they had deserted their Xch'uup in battle leaving her to a certain death in order to save their own skins; this was judgement day.

Malikah's eyes began to burn in the subdued light of the Darksiders station, before a word could be uttered Ceenakak dove to Malikah's feet. The first Matriarch of clan Kak threw all six foot and ten inches of her frame to the ground in a kowtow 'Tumensiik k'eban Mamich!'

McCann understood exactly, 'forgive sin Mother' being the literal translation. However Malikah was not in a forgiving mood, her eyes burnt as raging fires, the Queen gnashed her teeth before raising a boot and crushing the Matriarch's head between it and the floor. The former First of Kak's brains spilt over the floor, causing most of those present to look away in disgust as its pink and red contents slid in all directions.

It was on this day Captain Graham Turner learnt that only the thin membrane covering the brain is actually grey, as with all Tlillan and their descendants the rest is pink. Turner had seen plenty of injured in triage but never did he venture into the morgue so was unaware of the details of the brain's anatomy, until now.

Malikah shouted in a deep Tlillan accent 'PEK!'

Pointing with a straight arm directly at Matnaheul the fierce goddess bellowed 'NUUKIK ... K'EEK'EN!'

Which McCann took to mean 'Speak pig' a vile insult on Otoch.

Matnahuel was terrified, she said nothing but her hand moved behind her back. Malikah noticed the movement and began to cackle as the old lady Havisham 'You fat whore! '

Everyone was concerned; it seemed she was reaching for a weapon. Malikah went from speaking Tlillan to English, a sign she'd lost control of her temper; much like Beaumont she would return to cursing and screaming in her mother tongue, which for her was English. Although calling someone a fat whore on Otoch was more likely to confuse than insult, Ofra used it frequently to describe those she had utter disdain for and Malikah had adopted her Grandmother's taste of verbal abuse.

Matnahuel gripped the plasma carbine slung behind her back and quickly pulled it forward as fast as possible. Pointing the weapon at Malikah she was about to fire but halted before pulling the trigger of the charged firearm.

Malikah's eyes had turned jet black, though that large menacing sneer remained on her face.

Matnahuel was frozen in time, her eyes moved; McCann noted that she struggled to regain control of her physical being, but to no avail. The Matriarch took one hand away from the forward grip of the compact assault rifle; bringing the other hand up to her head she placed its barrel to her own temple.

All the time Malikah cackled as she loomed closer to Matnahuel, the sable Tlillan Queen stroked her wayward Matriarch's long red hair with affection. Next and rather unexpectedly Malikah took the rifle from her hand and tossed it onto the central table, normally used for traffic control.

'When you reach the Dreamscape, I want every Tlillan know what you did, I want them all to understand that you are nothing more than a bin'nt himaar,' spoke the beautiful Malikah softly into Matnahuel's helpless ear.

As she finished her sentence the mighty goddess clutched the bulbous rear of Matnahuel's skull and in one powerful push, rammed her face into the solid Catronium wall.

The Matriarch died instantly, her skull crumbled under the force, splattering its contents over Malikah and the wall, staining Xch'uup's headdress and white jacket. The Matriarch's body dropped to the floor as if it were a sack of rice, Malikah turned and let out a massive scream, McCann assumed it was of satisfaction.

Ryu nudged McCann with her elbow 'What's a bin'nt himaar? My ear piece can't translate it.'

McCann raised his eyebrows and in a hushed tone replied 'It's Arabic for daughter of a donkey.'

Ryu made her matronly expression of disbelief, the Englishman replied 'My Mother.'

The beautiful Amazon stood astride the crumpled bodies of her fallen foe, taking in deep heavy breaths. The black ink began to dissipate from her eyes as the blood soaked Grand Matriarch smirked in satisfaction.

Motioning to her mother Malikah barked 'Send them in, include the traitors!'

Ilam stepped over the bodies of Ceen and Matn, moving through the doorway the lesser females had scurried out of, McCann heard her call 'Okol.'

Ilam returned with 5 females following her, from what McCann could tell one was certainly of very low rank; the other four were higher up the totem pole. At least that's what he assumed due to their seniority in years and what he sensed from their mental presence.

Ilam returned to the other side of the room, keeping herself out of Malikah's path, the Tlillan females gasped in shock at what lay on the floor before them.

Four of the females dove onto the floor despite the crumpled bodies; laying amidst swirling blood and bone mixed in brain matter, they all let out cries begging their Queen for mercy 'Namaste Mamich!', 'Tumensiik k'eban Mamich!' and 'Tumensiik kan!' were amongst the phrases begging for leniency.

Malikah gazed at the young girl who remained stood aloft 'Chanatico he'tal.'

The beautiful red haired lady followed her instructions and approached her bloody Queen 'Namaste Xch'uup.'

Malikah placed a comforting arm around the young Matriarch who had just seen nearly her entire clan wiped out by the Makayuuk. Only a handful of lesser Matriarchs remained, not enough to maintain a clan ship, Chanatico assumed this was the end for clan Tico.

'Sandra tumben yaaxil, Tico,' smiled Malikah.

Chanatico dropped to her knees and kowtowed in the blood and mire 'Namaste hun'nuuk.'

McCann had not heard the phrase often but was of the understanding 'hun'nuuk' was akin to 'great one' or 'supreme one', no wonder he sensed Malikah's contentment.

From what he gleaned of the conversation so far, his daughter had made Sandra First of clan Tico, assuring Chanatico the clan's future.

'Liik'il … kik,' ordered Malikah, referring to Chanatico as 'sister', the greatest of honours Xch'uup could bestow upon a Tlillan.

Chanatico rose, covered in congealing blood, to take her place behind Xch'uup, who clan Tico had supported with their lives.

The other four remained on their hands and knees in the mire.

Malikah cackled in that discomforting manner 'Chittal ich mamah eek, K'EEK'EN!'

The four women blubbed in fear their fate was to be that of their former Firsts. According to the translator Malikah had just said to the terrified women 'Laying down in your own mothers' filth, PIGS!'

Malikah bellowed at the trembling Matriarchs 'Huel ka'Kak ts'oksik, ma'chaik Muul Kah, ma'chaik Itzpap! Huel ka'Kak meyah et xib!'

Ilam, Chan and Lian all gasped at this statement; Malikah had just banished the two clans out of the council and decreed that they 'work with men'. The Englishman wasn't exactly sure of the full implications of her statement, but it certainly wasn't a good thing, judging by the horrified reactions it garnered from all Tlillans in the room.

The grovelling Matriarchs pleaded further, contending with each other to grab their Queen's blood covered boots.

'Get up!' shouted Malikah 'Hand your war cruisers over to clan Chutli and Tico, then you shall be transported to Otoch where your hard labour begins in earnest, there will be neither kleos nor nostos for traitors. Now leave my sight you filthy pigs!'

The females arose from the muck, with heads hanging low they exited the control room; moments later Cihu entered with Kaeo. Both matriarchs surveyed the result of Malikah's temper tantrum, with little surprise.

McCann's daughter eyed Cihu for the first time since their fracas at Muul Kaah; she said nothing but waited for the white haired Marshal.

Cihu pressed her palms together 'Tumensiik Xch'uup.'

'Tumensiik? Tumen ba'ax?' asked the Tlillan Empress.

McCann could understand this less colourful conversation without difficulty.

'Forgive my hot mouth,' replied Cihu still bowing to her friend.

'You may speak your mind Cihu; your loyalty grants you that privilege. I apologise to you and all those that died today, my hubris cost many Matriarchs their lives,' Malikah stepped towards Cihu until she was directly in front of her 'Forgive my sin, Cihuateteo.'

For a moment all was silent, the two adversaries placed their foreheads together touching one another. After a minute of silence Cihu broke off and smiled 'We are ready to engage the Makayuuk.'

Malikah smiled with kindness towards Cihu 'There is no need, terms have been reached.'

Cihu glared at Lian 'Terms? Surely not?'

'Calm yourself,' comforted Malikah 'Machine will become our subject.'

Cihu sneered at Lian 'You believe this dog?'

'It is a fair offer. We can desist this savagery if Machine keeps her bargain.'

Cihu tapped the central obsidian table 'No, we must consolidate.'

A hologram leapt out, McCann recognised it as the Terran system 'We must fortify Earth and Mars, the Edwards has shipyards,' Cihu was pointing and shouting as a woman possessed 'The Clotho and her sister ships may be retooled, the Adnoarans possess one war cruiser ... the I.S.A is still strong, within half a cycle we shall be at full strength or more.

More importantly we must MOBILIZE! Train our crews in the fight if we have to,' Cihu moved towards Ryu causing the Korean to step back in a concerned manner 'Drones, we need drones, every cruiser must have its cargo bay retooled for drones. The Gukumatz must return to the Tlillan system, with a full fleet at 100% drone capacity we shall launch an offensive on Bandayuuk and push Machine back into the core!'

Ryu sensed the Tlillan Marshall was reaching the point of tipping into an abyss of insanity, perhaps she felt responsible for today's defeat? Perhaps it tore at her that if she'd followed the word of her Xch'uup the Tlillan race would not have been humiliated by heretics?

Ryu noted to the manic white haired Marshall 'When word reaches other systems of our defeat they shall flock to Machine's banner!'

Cihu shouted in denial 'They shall follow Xch'uup to the afterlife if I give them another victory!'

'You? Such a pity you couldn't be troubled to give us a victory today,' snorted the Korean in disdain 'In Korea if I'd refused to fight my Commander would've shot me; the moment treason passed my lips!'

Cihu placed a hand on the grip of her sword, her eyes lit up as a demon in the night.

Ryu was not intimidated, the short Korean Captain merely sneered back at the gesture 'It'll be a cold day in hell before I fear a snivelling coward!'

Cihu pulled her blade from the scabbard, before she could remove it from the sheathe and bring it to bare Malikah shouted 'ENOUGH!'

Cihu and Malikah fixed their eyes upon one another; the seven foot Valkyrie slammed her blade back into her scabbard. Saying nothing she took a step backwards from the resilient Ryu who remained where she stood, arms crossed in defiance.

Lian entered the conversation, breaking the tense atmosphere between the Korean and towering Amazon 'Machine will keep her bargain.'

Cihu sneered 'How can we be sure?'

'One of the stipulations will be that I am to remain governor of Bandayuuk, I will monitor Machine and her people.'

Cihu snorted incredulously 'A traitor will monitor the people of the Machine? Do you take us for fools?'

'Cihu, I understand your fear but there is no other choice. Machine desires an end to this brutality; I have convinced her to compromise rather than pursue the destruction of the Tlillan race and its offspring. I am Voice of Machine to you, but to Machine I am Voice of Ek'tsab.'

Kaeo placed a hand on her First's arm 'Take her offer, if we are betrayed then at least we may fight another day. Today we cannot resist Machine.'

Cihu muttered to Kaeo 'A Praetor may give advice when requested, not otherwise.'

Kaeo's eyes filled with a burgundy hue 'My mother died on the Chutli today.'

Cihu replied in a cold tone 'I know.'

'Then you understand I have no reason to trust Machine nor do I desire any peace, but I cannot avenge my family when dead!'

Cihu thought hard for a moment, 'I will support Xch'uup,' turning to Malikah she pressed her palms 'as Machine stays true, you have my word.'

Lian approached Malikah, pressing her palms together she spoke humbly 'The remaining Makayuuk fleet is yours, to utilize when required, Xch'uup.'

McCann's daughter felt relief now that she had retained the throne and brokered a deal between herself, Lian and Cihu 'We require the delivery of supplies to repair our war cruisers.'

Lian bowed her head in compliance 'Whatever assistance you desire the Makayuuk are prepared to meet your needs, Xch'uup.'

Malikah called to her mother 'Ilam, you have the task of co-ordinating the Makayuuk,' she paused then added in a sardonic pitch 'try not to fail me this time.'

Ilam walked up to her daughter, pressing her palms she spoke 'Namaste Xch'uup.'

Malikah turned to Cihu 'You and Kaeo must seize control of the Kak and Huel, before the pigs attempt to flee.'

Cihu and Kaeo both bowed to their Queen 'Namaste Xch'uup,' turned on their heels and made for the clan ships before the disgraced Matriarchs decided to go AWOL, rather than live out their lives in some gulag on Otoch. Malikah had not witnessed their prior betrayal during the battle but she had observed the remaining clan Matriarchs making a pact and disappearing into space rather than become slaves, even lower than a man.

'I must return to the Chutli, I suggest you all return to your Vessels. Thank you all, for your loyalty.' The Tlillan Queen strode out of the bloody command centre demonstrating the return of her regal swagger.

McCann looked Titov in the eye 'I suppose that's that.'

Three days later and repairs were still underway, the Makayuuk supplied Bandayuuk station from the surface. Gukumatz supply cruisers had already delivered one load of materials and returned the injured to their respective home systems. The Gukumatz were now co-ordinating a second supply run of parts, anti-matter and medical supplies.

Machine had been totally co-operative with Malikah's wishes; Lian imparted the will of Xch'uup without the need for control collars or threat of violence. The people of the Machine simply complied with all instructions to the best of their ability. Bandayuuk 0 was still a shattered world post occupation and the following uprising; however the needs of Xch'uup came first.

On Athena, McCann sat in the lounge with Jenkins, recanting the battle to his old friend over a Balvenie and Ramon Allones specially selected. During the chat he was interrupted by a communication from his daughter requesting his and Jenkins presence on the Chutli.

'Time for us to get going old boy,' sighed McCann as he downed the last of his 21 year old Scotch and banged the glass on the table.

'What is it this time?' inquired the Brigadier.

McCann stood up and dusted some wayward ash from his uniform 'God knows; well finish your drink Jenkins, we can't be late.'

Jenkins had a little grumble to himself before polishing off his whisky and following his friend out of the lounge.

All of the star ships were still docked and undergoing extensive repairs. The Kak had been renamed the Tico and the Huel renamed the Chutli; their former crews were already beginning a lifetime of hard labour on Otoch after having been transported by Cihu.

McCann and Jenkins boarded the Chutli, entering the vessel via the station docking arm. Two Vympel soldiers saluted as they stepped in, its cream coloured corridors had a soft dim light. It was difficult to see properly but thankfully McCann knew his way around a Tlillan cruiser by now; visits to his wife when their vessels happened to be in the same system for a day or two led to many a secret rendezvous on the Chutli.

Stepping into the Captain's forum, a room on all Tlillan war cruisers designed for several uses, the comrades interrupted a rather delicate conversation. Malikah sat on a dark obsidian chair with a high slim back rest, flanked by Ilam and Chanatico. A three dimensional projection of the President of the Eastern States stood before her. McCann waited politely next to the wall after entering the room with Jenkins.

Malikah spoke in a stern manner to President Michael Earle 'I expect my troops to be delivered upon arrival of the Artemis, Mr Earle.'

The President replied awkwardly 'I'm sorry Malikah, I just don't have the men to spare right now.'

McCann took a drag on his Ramon Allones and raised an eyebrow towards Jenkins who observed the conversation with great interest.

Malikah took a deep breath before she replied 'You have two options Mr President, when the Artemis arrives you deliver my soldiers; or when the Artemis arrives the deputy President delivers my soldiers. Either way I shall receive my troops.'

'Is that a threat?'

Malikah pulled a condescending sneer at Earle 'Yes it is and from now on you may refer to me as Xch'uup. Your nation has benefited from my favour for a long time; it is now time to earn your keep ... Mr President.'

Earle cleared his throat 'I'll see what I can do ... Xch'uup.'

The sable Queen smirked in victory 'That you will Mr President. Sandra shall co-ordinate your forces, if you have any further questions you may address her, message end.'

The image of President Earle collapsed into the dark obsidian floor of the forum. Smiling at the sight of her father Malikah spoke softly 'Father please enter and hello Brigadier, how are you?'

Jenkins grinned as he walked over to where the President of the Eastern States had been standing a moment ago 'I'm very well thank you, Xch'uup.'

The sable Queen giggled at the family friend of many years dressed in his SBS uniform 'Call me Malikah.'

Jenkins nodded as her eyes fell to McCann smoking his cigar 'Do you have to smoke those awful things Father?'

'I was off duty when you dragged me over here, I'll be buggered if I'm going to waste a good cigar on a house call. Besides ships stores are still locked in, until Athena can patch up her hull the bulkheads can't be moved; I'm living off what was left in my cabin humidor.'

Malikah rolled her eyes 'Please let me know when you're finished.'

McCann replied with an embarrassed expression 'Alright, go on.'

'The Artemis shall be arriving in a few days with your replacements Brigadier; your men are to return home save one squad of your best people.'

Jenkins nodded 'Understood.'

'It is your task to train the Americans in tactics and skills required for extra-terrestrial operations. My Mother has the Makayuuk rebuilding your old Head Quarters; it should be ready for occupation in a week?'

Ilam bowed 'The military camp is ready Xch'uup; Lian has prioritized its refurbishment.'

Malikah didn't look at Ilam who stood behind her 'Excellent, do you have any questions Brigadier?'

Jenkins thought for a moment 'Who will I report to once I'm planetside?'

Malikah sat in her regal headdress and replied with a hint of discomfort in her voice 'You shall report to the Governor, is that understood?'

Jenkins nodded 'Understood.'

Malikah smiled at the Brigadier again 'I have a request for you Henry.'

Jenkins raised his eyebrows as did McCann 'Yes?'

Malikah sounded a little more uncomfortable as she continued 'According to your personnel file you are unmarried, is that still current?'

Jenkins spoke slowly with a wary tone 'Yes?'

'Do you have a fiancée or any female interests in your life at the moment?'

McCann choked on the thick creamy smoke from his cigar, Jenkins nervously peered to his comrade for some sort of assistance but found none as McCann coughed out smoke.

'I'm not engaged, nor am I seeing anyone,' replied a nervous Jenkins.

McCann recovered from accidently taking a lung full of smoke, his face was quite red but he kept as quiet as possible so that he could listen to the rest of this very strange conversation.

Malikah perked up at the news 'Excellent! As you know, Brigadier, clan Chutli has been revitalised thanks to a successful breeding program.'

Jenkins spoke warily 'Breeding program?'

'Males were selected based upon their attributes by Matriarchs, not only has the clan been rejuvenated but three Mictlantecuhtli have been reared.

Now Clan Tico has been devastated due to the loss of their cruiser and all Matriarchs on board. I intend to prevent the Clan from dying out, however I need your help Henry,' spoke Malikah softly.

A wide eyed Jenkins replied 'Oh really?'

Malikah gestured to her left; Chanatico took a step forward, a tall beautiful woman with deep red hair cut to shoulder length. She was temporarily First of Tico until Sandra arrived. Chan was very young to be in such a high position, due to most of her Clan hierarchy having been wiped out a few days ago in the battle for Bandayuuk. The Clan required an injection of new blood in order to continue, and soon.

Malikah smiled at Jenkins 'This is Chanatico; she will be second of Clan Tico.'

'Very nice to meet you Miss Chanatico,' replied a leery Brigadier.

'Namaste Brigadier,' said Chanatico with pressed palms.

Malikah continued before Jenkins could intervene 'Chanatico requires a mate and as far as I could tell you met the requirements of ability and eligibility. I assume you are fertile and have no problems with impotency?'

'Certainly not!' snapped Jenkins much to the amusement of his comrade who sniggered as a school boy, the odd situation even pushed Ilam to a tiny grin.

Before Jenkins was able to reply further the sable Tlillan cut in 'Excellent, all that remains is for you to accept.'

'Accept?'

'Accept Chanatico as your mate, Henry.'

Jenkins was taken aback, had he known Malikah's plans for bullying him into an arranged marriage he'd have shot himself in the leg and been shipped home.

He choked on his own words 'Well ... I don't really ...'

'Don't really what?' asked Malikah in a high pitch 'Are you homosexual Brigadier?'

'Certainly not Madam!'

McCann let out a howl of laughter much to the discomfort of Jenkins; his comrades' antics weren't helping the situation.

'Is Chanatico not attractive?'

Jenkins took a look at her, her long legs and taught torso wrapped in her tight black ribbed suit stirred something inside the Brigadier. As an SBS commander he's spent long stretches outside of real female company; he didn't count the Macks as "real female company". Chanatico had a beautiful face, an ivory complexion and alluring red lips, Malikah had obviously encouraged her to wear some make-up; not a habit Tlillan women indulged in before discovering Earth.

As Jenkins looked the six and a half foot beauty up and down Malikah smirked 'Ahhhh you do find her attractive, don't you Henry?'

'I think this is all a bit inappropriate, don't you?'

Malikah chuckled 'I understand Henry, don't be under the impression this is a forced mating, Chanatico had her choice of males, she expressed a desire for you above all the others.'

Jenkins face began turning red as he burnt up with embarrassment 'Well I'm most flattered however I couldn't agree to marry someone I'd never met.'

'Your Father and Mother were strangers for many years before they met, were they not? You and Chan have been selected as a perfect match, it is of course your decision but I request you at least spend some time together, before making your final decision; could you do that for me Henry?' requested Malikah in her sweetest tone possible.

Looking around the room nervously Jenkins replied 'Well I suppose so.'

'Wonderful!' shouted an elated Malikah 'Chanatico is available tomorrow evening, I'm certain my Father will suggest a nice restaurant on the station?'

McCann grinned widely, raised his hand and gave the sable Goddess a thumbs up.

'You may leave Brigadier, I believe you've got two very important tasks ahead of you!' said Malikah with a wink.

The Englishmen left the Forum, one with a big grin and a swagger, the other rather pale.

Strolling out of the Chutli and onto the docking arm Jenkins finally spoke 'I feel like a piece of meat in a Butcher's shop.'

McCann slapped his comrade on the back 'Come on old boy, you're finally gonna get some and all you can do is complain?'

'I was bloody well ambushed,' Jenkins looked at his friend with a very serious expression 'how do I get out of this mess?'

McCann grinned 'From what I see you have two options, you can accept the offer or decline.'

'I know that, I'm not a bloody fool! I mean what do I do to get out of it?'

The Admiral scowled 'Why not just take the offer? I'll tell you what; you've shagged a lot worse than her!'

'You're not taking this seriously Duncan!'

'I'm taking this with the upmost sincerity,' he raised his face to the ceiling and contemplated in a theatrical tone as if he were performing a Shakespeare play 'To shag or not to shag? That is the question!'

Jenkins let out a puff of wind 'Huuuurrr, you're not helping me much Duncan, I thought you might be able to influence your daughter.'

McCann blew smoke from his nostrils, tasting the leathery flavours 'I can get her to shut up for a bit, but change her mind? The woman's far too bloody stubborn, takes after her mother that way.'

Jenkins sneered 'So rather than stubborn you're just a miserable git who takes pleasure in his friend suffering?'

The pair kept walking along the docking arm as crewmen ran up and down with droids, bringing supplies to critical areas amongst the fleet that was still docked. Many of the crews' attention was diverted towards the Admiral and Brigadier as they discussed Jenkins precarious position.

McCann scowled at his friend again 'Jesus Christ Jenkins, a ravishing woman wants to take you to bed and all you can do is witter on about how to squirm out of it! What's the matter man?'

'She wants me to marry her, that's the problem. I'm an eligible bachelor and I'm damn well happy being one!'

McCann snorted the creamy smoke out of his nose making a tone of disagreement 'Listen, we aren't still young Lieutenants in the Royal Navy. If we want to get laid in every port we're gonna have to pay a heavy premium, and I'm not talking about the cost of a meal and drinks.'

'What's that supposed to mean?'

'When was the last time you got laid?'

Jenkins looked around as crewmen shuffled by; he gave a black look to those listening in on the conversation 'Does it matter?'

McCann laughed 'That's what I thought; I'm just saying that they're not lining up outside your quarters. Sure some gold digging bitch back home will try and snag you but is it worth it for a shag?'

Jenkins grunted 'Hummph.'

'Exactly, this Chanatico she's got a great body and genuinely wants you. You could easily do a lot worse, give her a chance and give yourself a chance; if it doesn't work I'll convince Malikah to forgo the castration.'

Jenkins eyes opened in shock, McCann creased up laughing.

The Brigadier sneered 'You can be an utter arse sometimes, you know that?'

The pair carried on strolling until they reached the station, a main thoroughfare stretched around the edge of the floating disc. This wide walkway connected all of the docking arms with each other, providing many passages into the giant disc. The friends took a passage deeper into the station, creamy walls reflected the soft light emitted overhead. The lighting was enough for a Human to see and a Darksider to tolerate at the same time.

Constructed at Gukumatz and Mars orbit in pieces the station had been transported then assembled after the initial victory. Its intended purpose was of a control station, organising many projected shipments of manufactured goods and metal ore leaving Bandayuuk. The plan to press the Makayuuk into a slave labour force had not gone to Malikah's satisfaction. With growing insurrection and the Gukumatz failure to repress it, the station evolved into a base of operations for pre-emptive strikes; preventing rebellions from getting out of control. A lack of manufactured goods leaving Bandayuuk had turned the operation into a Phyricc victory for the Triumvirate.

All this time Machine had been rebuilding itself and the Makayuuk fleet, gathering her forces below ground until there was enough to take back what was theirs. By the time a big push to take back their home world began the I.S.A forces were sick of Bandayuuk. Fighting in tunnels against obsessed machine men was not a task anyone relished, by the time they'd spent a few months on the planet everyone wanted to go home; unfortunately that was only possible via a body bag.

The passage ended at a large garden filled with a mixture of shrubs, flowers and trees all from different worlds. Looking upwards McCann observed several floors with walkways, all of the walkways skirted the perimeter of the garden square. On one side of the elevated walkways was a small wall and a rail preventing people falling off and plummeting into the gardens, the other side was skirted by rows of shops, restaurants and various outlets for entertainment and relaxation.

McCann pointed a couple of floors up and across from where they stood 'Over there.'

Jenkins followed his finger 'What's that?'

'A very nice restaurant, come on let's have a butchers.'

The comrades walked into a glass elevator that took them to the corresponding level. They stepped out and moved around the walkway, McCann observed the stunning flora. For the most part he couldn't recognise the plants, though some stood out amongst the green shrubbery especially the white orchids from Tlillans' dark side. They let out an odd scent; according to Ilam it mimicked rotting flesh which attracted insects. The orchid was very tall, about McCann's height, with four large petals. At the centre of the flower erupted stalks used for pollination, McCann was no botanist and had no idea what they were called, the central stalks were a very bright red; apparently they glowed in the dark for the native insects.

Entering the restaurant the Englishman noted familiar surroundings, similar to dinning outlets on Kotumatz. The glowing light emanating from tubes of plankton, illuminating fine wooden tables and chairs resembling polished mahogany, brought back memories.

A Gukumatz dressed in a brown sack suit waddled up to them and bowed 'Namaste, would you gentlemen like a table?' he said in his best croaky English.

McCann took a step back but Jenkins, who had much less experience with the Gukumatz, remained where he stood and got the full blast of the creature's foul breath.

Attempting to be polite Jenkins put his hand to his mouth and coughed. McCann smirked then replied to the short toad 'Mr Jenkins would like to reserve a table for tonight, if that's possible?'

The toad gave a Gukumatz grin, only the Admiral recognized it due to his time working with them, 'certainly, how many?'

'Two, he'll be having dinner with Chanatico at seven, alright?'

The toad nodded as he noted it all down on his tablet 'Certainly, we have a window seat on the second floor, our customers say it is very romantic.'

'That sounds good to me.'

The Gukumatz placed his tablet before Jenkins who had by now recovered and taken a step backwards, 'Your signature please Sir.'

Jenkins placed his thumb onto the marked box on the tablet; after a moment there was a ping and the toad took the tablet back 'Thank you Mr Jenkins.'

Jenkins nodded and walked straight out of the establishment, once outside he gave McCann a black look 'How on Earth can I eat anything with those disgusting frogs serving me?'

McCann laughed 'You obviously haven't dinned on Tlillan food yet!'

Jenkins shook his head as he looked up towards the name of the establishment 'Ki'chiwol,' he said slowly as he committed the name to memory.

The Brigadier glanced between McCann and the glowing sign above the smoky glass doorway 'What in the devil does that mean?'

McCann placed a hand on his shoulder and whispered 'Don't ask.'

'Come on, just tell me,' inquired Jenkins since his comrade had quite a decent grasp of the Tlillan language.

'It can be your first question to Chanatico, a conversation starter.'

As McCann finished his sentence he sensed someone behind him, looking around it was his wife. She stood with Quil, looking back at him; the pair hadn't spoken properly since the battle more than three days ago. Quil said nothing, communicating through their minds the Mother walked on into the restaurant giving McCann an evil glare all the way.

Ilam didn't follow she remained opposite her husband, both with eyes fixed upon one another.

Jenkins felt rather awkward, breaking the silence he said 'Well thanks for the tip, I'll leave you two to it,' before walking away.

McCann spoke with some trepidation to his lofty wife 'How are you?'

'Quite well, thank you,' replied Ilam in a business-like manner.

'Would you like to go for a walk in the gardens?'

'I'm satisfied.'

'Well I'd be appreciative if you would accompany me for a walk.'

'As you wish.'

The pair walked to an elevator then down to the garden, there was always some distance between them and the atmosphere was as frosty as a polar ice cap.

Strolling inside the gardens via one of the many small earthen trails McCann opened the conversation 'I'm sorry for the way I spoke to you during the battle.'

The towering Amazon looked away towards one of the tall trees then replied dismissively 'No matter, Xch'uup agrees with you.'

'What does that have to do with it?'

Ilam halted to examine one of the white orchids that had grown to her eye level 'The word of Xch'uup is law, to act or speak otherwise is heresy,' she spoke philosophically.

McCann stood by his wife's side watching her fondle a flower 'First of all her name is Malikah, second my daughter is not going to dictate to me or my wife.'

Ilam let out a short smile then went back to her former solemn expression, though she made no reply.

The Englishman carried on 'I didn't mean to embarrass you, I just did what I thought was right at the time.'

'I understand.'

'Then why are we standing here as if we were attending a funeral?'

'You still do not comprehend how difficult it is for me, to have a male countermand my orders then lose support of Xch'uup publicly.'

McCann scratched his head 'You're right I don't, I mean you're the Grand Priestess and First of Chutli, don't you get to make mistakes?'

Again the Fiery haired Valkyrie smiled for a moment at the flower she toyed with 'Mistakes? Did I make a mistake?'

The Englishman snorted 'I don't know, I only did what my instinct told me, as I'm sure you did.'

'It is of no consequence anyway, I am looked down upon as an outcast, again.'

Frustrated McCann replied 'Well is there anything I could do?'

She smiled but shook her head 'I know that your offer is genuine, however there is nothing you can do, Duncan.'

'Well I can at least cheer my wife up can't I?'

She stared at the flower from her home world stoically without answering her husband.

McCann thought for a moment before speaking again 'I'll tell you what, how about we go to the Tlillan lounge? You know the one where all the Matriarchs like to hang out and stroke each other's egos. We can go there, start an argument and you can punch me in the face knocking me to the floor. I'll kowtow and beg for forgiveness, that should please them?'

Ilam fixed her pink eyes upon her husband 'I know you'd do that for me Duncan; however only Xch'uup possesses the authority to wipe my shame.'

McCann let out a grunt as he wrapped an arm around his beautiful wife's waist 'Then Xch'uup shall bloody well do as I tell her or she'll get a spanking from her Father.'

Ilam smiled again as she leant down to kiss her rebellious husband.

They spent the remaining hours of the day strolling through the flora and chatting with each other before Ilam was forced to return to her work with Lian.

McCann felt much better now that things were patched up with his wife, his next mission was to set his daughter straight.

Chapter 14

The next day McCann accompanied his daughter to the surface of Bandayuuk. The sable Queen was to speak with Machine, a personal audience, most Makayuuk had not experienced the physical presence of their overlord. Traveling on a Tlillan shuttle together, the Englishman tried to address an issue concerning Ilam, before he could speak Malikah replied to his initial question.

'I know Father,' spoke the tall dark haired Queen as she held her hand up to stop him.

'Know what?' replied McCann, annoyed at how rude his daughter had become.

Malikah didn't look in his direction; she remained seated as she observed the read out in front of her. The half Tlillan was transfixed by the wire frame representation of their craft as it followed the pre-set flight path laid out by Machine.

'I know exactly what you intended to ask, the answer is that I'm aware of Mother but I can't show favouritism; she must suffer for her actions.'

'Oh come on Malikah, Ilam made a mistake, don't you think she's suffered enough archaic Tlillan crap already?'

Malikah gave her Father a disappointed stare 'No.'

McCann sighed with great disparity 'Bloody Tlillans!'

'Father!'

'What?'

'Curb your language, remember you are still Censor!'

McCann sneered 'I don't see why I should change my ways, perhaps those Tlillans haven't suffered enough?' he looked at the low ceiling philosophically 'Perhaps I should enforce mandatory verbal abuse, the "Daughter of a Donkey ACT 2125" will be my first step towards keeping those pigs in line.'

Malikah closed her eyes; with her face staring upwards she replied in a very aggravated tone 'Enough Father, you're not amusing.'

'Who said I'm joking? I'm deadly serious here, or do you think I've not got the balls to do it?'

Malikah sensed her father was challenging the Icon to a game of brinksmanship, she knew him as well as any being in the universe, having linked so often. The sable Queen needed no further convincing that McCann would gladly begin creating pure hell for her as soon as they returned. The embarrassment and shame of his actions would have been difficult enough but the following gossip concerning Censor, Xch'uup's father, losing his mind would be a shame too great to surmount.

'Father you're being silly.'

McCann's voice gathered aggression as his daughter attempted to dismiss him 'Silly? Is that what you think I am?'

'I said that you are being silly.'

McCann shook his head as he waved his hand in disagreement 'No you're right, I've been silly not to employ my privileges to their full benefit. Let me see, when I get back I'll have Louis help me write up a list of sexual positions. First we'll decide on those that are profane and then the mandatory ones, yes I think between Louis and I we can really bring some law and order back to this immoral society.'

Malikah refused to reply, attempting to ignore him and not engage with his tirade. In her experience, the best way to avoid her Father's wrath was to keep quiet and wait for him to calm down. However McCann was on a mission and like a dog with a bone he just wouldn't let it go.

McCann began to speak loudly, apparently to himself as he contemplated aloud, forcing his daughter to listen 'Punishment next, yes I'd say a public whipping would be satisfactory in any case of non-compliance … naked of course.'

Malikah did her best to pretend she wasn't listening, unfortunately it didn't convince her father who was more than experienced in yanking Xch'uup's chain when she was a little girl.

The Englishman stroked his chin comically 'Let me think, homosexual matings, for or against?' he peered at Malikah but she looked away trying to ignore him, 'I think the answer is obvious, Censor is in full support of Homosexual matings on Otoch ... provided both Matriarchs are hot!'

Malikah shouted, though grinning involuntary, 'Alright! I'll deal with it, are you satisfied now?'

McCann nodded 'Quite satisfied, thank you.'

The Tlillan Empress let out a long sigh 'You can be such an arsehole sometimes; I hope you know that, Father.'

The Admiral didn't reply, he had what he wanted and antagonising Malikah any further would have been counter-productive.

Turning his attention to the planet below McCann watched as the vessel approached the dust filled atmosphere, a once beautiful green and blue world was now a battle scared land. Clouds of toxic smoke and dust circled Bandayuuk 0, the result of a massive warship crashing onto the surface. Before that a violent surface invasion followed by more than a year of constant insurrection had left the world in tatters.

Ryu spent many a day directing I.S.A drone squadrons on sortie after sortie, eradicating partisans with napalm and gas. Supporting Jenkins on the ground the pair had pushed the enemy below the surface, the only place where the Korean's drones couldn't follow.

Jenkins' men fought tooth and nail for sometimes less than 50 metres of tunnel. Deciding it wasn't working the Brigadier resorted to selecting areas from intelligence reports, forwarding the data to Ryu who sent forth her drones to deliver tactical nuclear strikes.

The result was a crater filled wasteland where forests and pastures once stood.

Now even the tragic hell left by the I.S.A was obscured by black clouds of radioactive smog, thrown into the atmosphere by one of Machine's own battleships after it was struck by the crumbling Tico in a kamikaze attack.

The black obsidian transport cut through a poisonous atmosphere, slicing its way to a location situated close to one of the southern poles.

McCann bumped in his seat a little as the ride became more and more precarious.

'Calm yourself Father,' spoke Malikah whilst placing a comforting hand on his.

One minute later and they were through the black cloud and past the worst, below the Englishman noticed a sheet of black snow and ice. The sight shocked him as Bandayuuk didn't previously possess polar ice caps, added to that the dark radioactive snow would kill anyone foolish enough to ingest it.

Malikah's transport came lower and lower kicking up the newly settled snow whilst skimming towards their destination. Eventually a clearing could be made out in the distance; the AI locked on and touched down effortlessly atop a circular landing pad.

The vessels dark stone wall rippled back, McCann stood up and hit his wrist unfurling his helmet then stepped out onto the pad. Malikah followed suit, the two figures stood on a massive grey metallic circle waiting to be met.

McCann assumed the pad was heated as there were no visible means of keeping it clear from the black frost. The transport doors rippled shut, one minute later the entire pad began to move. The old soldier steadied himself whilst examining his surroundings; it was evident from the horizon that they were moving downwards. It was difficult to determine movement due to the sea of black stretching around them and the dark cloud covering the sky. In fact the pair stood in the dead of night, it was only thanks to their space suit helmets that they could even see the ground they stood on. That was true for McCann anyway, Malikah's inherited Tlillan vision allowed a much greater access to the visual spectrum.

The metal plate crept downwards until the ground McCann had stood on a few minutes ago covered his head. He reckoned they were about 10 metres below ground before another massive disc slid overhead covering the black sky.

Descending deeper and deeper the Englishman became more agitated, Malikah didn't seem to be worried at all which helped him steady his nerves.

'Relax Father, if Lian wanted us dead we would not be alive now.'

'Don't you mean Machine?'

Malikah chuckled to herself 'Yes, Machine.'

McCann didn't see what was so funny 'Come into my parlour said the spider to the fly!'

Malikah only smiled at his comment.

Eventually the sliding walls that hugged the disc gave way to a large chamber; McCann took it to be a loading bay of some sort. There were several small Mack transports; from above he could see the Macks running around working on them, loading them up as if they were ants on a forest floor.

As the long shaft which the landing pad rested upon slipped into the floor they approached ground zero and McCann could make out Lian, stood at the edge with a reception party of Macks.

The disc softly touched the bay floor coming to a halt as it rested in place, Lian smiled 'Namaste, this environment has been decontaminated you may remove your helmets.'

McCann tapped his wrist, his helmet retracted back into his suit collar where the new upgraded I.S.A space glove decontaminated it.

Malikah's helmet melted away on her mental command, once her face was exposed Lian smiled warmly, the Macks gasped.

There were six Macks flanking Lian, three each side, two fainted whilst the other four became visibly weak losing strength in their limbs.

Without saying anything Lian commanded two of her Macks to carry their comrades out, leaving her with two male Makayuuk.

McCann peered around the chamber; the square walls were plated with sheets of what looked like steel, as was the floor. The whole chamber seemed to be a massive 400 by 400 metre steel box, everything constructed to exact standards. He recalled reports from Jenkins of suspected armouries below the planet, it was assumed the Macks produced their weapons and armour at these locations. Despite great effort none were ever discovered during the occupation, it was hoped that tactical nuclear strikes had destroyed such manufacturing centres.

The Englishman noticed how all work had stopped inside the giant hollowed out metallic brick; all eyes were fixed on Malikah.

Lian stepped onto the disc pressing her palms 'Namaste Xch'uup.'

Malikah pressed her palms 'Namaste Lian.'

Another gasp filled the already intensely silent atmosphere, McCann somehow felt every single Mack breathe in sharply at once.

Lian gestured to her right 'I believe you've already met Sirt?'

Malikah narrowed her eyes as she scanned the short male 'Sirt 137?'

The middle aged man, now with several wounds adorning his face, describing a tale of many battles alongside his comrades in the tunnels of Bandayuuk, bowed 'Namaste Xch'uup.'

Malikah merely nodded in reply.

Lian gestured to her left 'This is Asta 491.'

The young man managed to place his palms together despite their shaking and in a wobbly voice said 'Namaste Ek'tsab.'

Again McCann felt a rush of wind enter the lungs of a hundred or so Macks.

Malikah replied with a smile and a nod 'Hello Asta.'

As a gasp rippled around the steel cavern McCann chirped up 'What's the matter with these Macks?'

Lian raised an eyebrow 'They are curious, your daughter is quite an infamous character.'

McCann pulled out a tubos from inside his space glove, pulling off the cap he put the empty tubos in his uniform pocket 'What did she do? Order a cookie with 24 chocolate chips?'

Malikah rolled her eyes, however Lian sniggered along with Sirt who also found the joke amusing.

McCann's sarcasm didn't have the desired effect so he asked Lian 'Has anyone got a light in here?'

Lian smiled 'I'm sorry Duncan; there are no naked flames in this area.'

The Englishman pulled his pulse pistol from its holster, flicked the switch then bit the cap off his cigar and spat it out as the rails charged letting out a high pitched whine.

The Makayuuk were unarmed, Sirt looked for cover until Lian ordered him to remain where he stood via the communication device implanted in her and all Makayuuk brains.

The pistol whined to a full charge before the noise disappeared, McCann then placed the foot of his petite corona inside the barrel. Taking long drags on his Habanos the hot rails soon toasted the cigar bringing it to a nice burn before he deactivated the battery, placing his pistol back in its holster.

Taking a long drag he tasted the smoke of his Rafael Gonzales, a much under-rated cigar in his opinion, which left a beautiful liquorice flavour in his nostrils upon expelling the smoke.

'Nothing like a good cigar, right?'

Malikah gave him a matronly stare 'Are you finished fooling around yet?'

Lian gestured to an exit about 50 metres from where they stood 'Come Machine awaits.'

After giving her father a black look Malikah stepped off the disc and strolled with Lian towards the exit; McCann followed along with Sirt and Asta. Asta was transfixed by the sable Queen of the Tlillans before him, McCann observed the young Mack with curiosity until Sirt whispered 'He is still frightened by fairy tales.'

McCann glanced at Sirt, the first Mack he'd ever seen, when Machine attempted to take Otoch, 'What do you mean?'

The silver eyed cyborg grinned at the Englishman 'He has not fought the Pixoa beneath Bandayuuk.

I feared Ek'tsab; I still fear Ek'tsab; yet fighting hand to hand, in a space black tunnel, collapsing hundreds of metres below ground, barely enough room to stand with arms outstretched. You learn to control fear, Asta was fortunate when assigned to the fleet.'

McCann nodded in agreement as he took a puff on his Habanos 'Fear of death tends to lose its edge after a few of those encounters. I thought you were a Ship Captain or something along those lines, at least you were at Otoch.'

Sirt's gaze sharpened 'the cost of defeat, I was removed from the fleet to be placed on the ground. Lian tells me you were once a soldier.'

'Well I flew insertion missions, for the most part.'

'For the most part?' inquire the cyborg.

'A few boarding actions.'

'Lian says you led the capture of a Gukumatz war cruiser, with only minimal technology.'

McCann tightened his mouth, screwing it up to convey his displeasure 'Lian has loose lips.'

'I don't understand?' asked the inquisitive cyborg.

Drawing from his cigar again the Admiral said 'There's an old saying, loose lips sink ships.'

Sirt gave a puzzled look 'I still don't understand.'

McCann blew some thick creamy smoke through his nostrils 'Never mind Sirt, the answer is yes I did and it was bloody terrifying; I wasn't even on the team that took it hardest.'

Sirt grinned at his new found human friend 'The Makayuuk say you never lose fear of death but merely gain respect for it.'

McCann chuckled 'I'll drink to that.'

Sirt made a puzzled look once again.

'A Human phrase, it means I wholeheartedly agree.'

The cyborg smiled and McCann smiled back, he'd never believed it was possible to have a civilized conversation with a Mack until today.

The party continued along a tunnel, its smooth walls constructed of metal sheets, the sheets linked precisely creating an illusion of a metal tube; rather than a tunnel cut from rock and lined with metallic plates.

Sirt observed the Englishman as he examine their surroundings 'The tunnels are re-enforced with Catronium sheets, it prevents collapse from anything less than a direct nuclear strike.'

McCann sighed 'Ahhh, sorry about that.'

As they continued along the long tube deeper into the earth the Englishman felt an odd vibration in his feet. After a moment or two the vibration was still there, in fact it was growing in intensity.

Lian halted the group, turned to Malikah 'Brace yourselves.'

'For what?' Inquired Malikah in a regal tone.

'Another planet quake, but there's no need for concern we're safe here.'

McCann looked at Sirt who nodded in confirmation. As the vibrations grew a rumbling noise could be heard, the louder it became the more violent the quake grew. Within 20 seconds McCann scurried to the side of the tunnel and crouched down with the others as it would be impossible to maintain his balance otherwise.

Looking to his right McCann could see Asta speaking but the noise of the quake drowned out whatever the man was saying, despite his close proximity. The walls of the tunnel began to move, or at least that's what McCann thought he saw, whether or not it was an optical illusion of some sort he couldn't say. The tunnel seemed to be squeezed then released, first squeezed from top to bottom pushing out the sides, then from the sides elongating the roof. The quake lasted just over three minutes, an experience McCann had no desire to replicate.

Once it was over and he was sure the tunnel hadn't collapsed McCann said in a shocked tone 'There were no bloody earthquakes when we were here!'

Lian replied matter of factly 'The Battleship clan Tico pushed into Bandayuuk, its impact created far worse problems than a mere nuclear winter.'

Malikah's eyes narrowed 'Planet quakes?'

Lian nodded 'Machine will speak on this, please we must hurry.'

The Voice of Machine marched back down the tunnel with Malikah by her side; the men quickly followed trying hard to keep up with the ladies long strides.

The tunnel ended after a few hundred metres at what seemed to be a large bulkhead, it reminded McCann of the link between ground zero and Tharsis back on Mars. Without a sound Lian commanded the metre thick door to be raised, it gradually lifted up to reveal another tunnel exactly the same as the one they'd just walked down. The group walked to the end of this tunnel to go through the exact same process, McCann joked that they could be walking in circles for all he knew.

The third bulkhead rose into the metal roof to reveal a large square metallic room; inside a spherical ball, about the size of a large beach ball, was suspended in a liquid tube upon a dais in the centre of the room.

The Englishman guessed they were now in the presence of Machine since the sphere was some unholy marriage of organic brain tissue and electro mechanical parts. The thing before him was similar to Ploutos in many aspects, bubbles ascended from the bottom of the tube caressing the mind of the machine on their way to the surface. This time McCann felt quite at ease in the presence of Machine.

The party of five stepped inside, as they did so the bulkhead behind them lowered until it once again locked into a groove in the metal floor.

Lian approached the floating sphere halted a foot in front of it then turned to face the group she'd led. Her eyes were that of a Makayuuk, two globes of solid silver inside her skull, 'Namaste Xch'uup.'

'Who is speaking?' inquired Malikah.

'I am Machine, I communicate to the Makayuuk and they communicate with me. If I wish to speak to you I must use another, Lian is Voice of Machine.'

Malikah raised her chin, looking down on Voice of Machine with that condescending Tlillan sneer she'd inherited from her mother 'What does Machine desire in exchange for her clemency?'

Lian raised a ghostly smile at the lofty Tlillan Queen 'Clemency? I have more than one billion children on this planet; I spared you so that you may spare them.'

The sable Valkyrie furrowed her finely sculpted brow 'You make no sense.'

'When your subjects sacrificed their lives they sent my battleship into Bandayuuk. Its impact created a rupture in Bandayuuk's crust, planet quakes are only a symptom of a disease. Soon the crust will crack further until eventually it shatters into pieces, Bandayuuk will tear itself apart leaving nothing more than an asteroid belt around its star.

In 200 of your hours the Makayuuk will be scattered to the solar winds once again, fighting for survival in the hope they might settle to rebuild as was past.'

Malikah, still puzzled, replied 'I see, but what do you expect of me? My fleet is crippled and even if it weren't, a billion people? You have more vessels than I.'

Lian still grinned in a chilling manner 'You are Ek'tsab, are you not?'

'That is what your children call me.'

'Yet you saved your fleet from an anti-matter wave, did you not make the star shake?'

'I did but ...'

Cutting her short Machine continued 'Then make the star shake for my children, you are Ek'tsab; remove darkness from Bandayuuk and reset its crust before the Gods consume my children.'

Coming down from her lofty tone the Queen addressed her lover 'Lian tell Machine it cannot be done. I nearly died attempting to remove the concussion wave, to reset the crust of a planet? My power comes from others, I am a conduit for the spirit, belief, I cannot just click my fingers.'

Lian or Machine, who knows, nodded 'You may use the spirit of my children, they believe in Ek'tsab.'

Shaking her head Malikah retorted 'I cannot use them; their spirit is held somewhere I cannot reach. I do not see them in the Dreamscape directly, only their effect on others.'

Voice of Machine advanced towards Malikah 'I understand, Lian is linked with my children can she not link with you?'

'Yes?'

'Then you will have access to the spiritual energy of over a billion Makayuuk, would that be enough to fulfil my request?'

'If Lian provides a viable connection to the Makayuuk, perhaps.'

Voice of Machine squeezed the hand of Ek'tsab, for a moment Malikah didn't understand what was happening until she felt the presence of more and more minds bustling around within Lian.

The sable Amazon concentrated on where the voices originated, eventually becoming initiated into the world of the Makayuuk. The Queen realised how half of their existence was only physical the other half a life unseen by others. Similar to the Tlillans, only all were linked to Machine and Machine was not so much their controller but an expression of the Makayuuk. The Macks had more than a simple link to a machine controller, from what the Tlillan Queen learnt Machine was more about data storage. According to the souls locked inside, the Makayuuk first employed Machine as a device to upload their consciousness. Similar in goal to the cryogenics of the late 20th and early 21st century, however this method allowed Makayuuk to actually back up their mind with a copy. Eventually these backed up souls became more than simple data stored both electronically and chemically by a cybernetic mind. One day the collective minds held inside took on a consciousness of their own. Each Makayuuk was backed up for the purpose of creating a perfect society of compliant beings, linked by a network hub. However the very mechanism for that perfect, passive, industrious society had morphed beyond its initially intended purpose. That store of data, connected to the hub of networked Makayuuk, was now a consciousness of its own; giving birth to the People of the Machine.

Malikah was fascinated by the perfect expression of not communism but collectivism. Their spirits were bound inside this world, living with one another, touching each other's minds and Machine taking in all their opinions and desires before basing her decision upon what's best for the group. No other being had been granted acceptance to this world until Lian was initiated. After experiencing it she could not allow the link to be severed; now she would be the conduit allowing Machine and the Tlillans to reach an understanding. It was this mutual understanding that Lian believed would bring about a peace.

During the battle Machine was prepared to sacrifice billions of Makayuuk if it meant the destruction of Ek'tsab, a trade her children desired, peace being a ridiculous concept at that time. Bandayuuk was lost, billions were fated to die so why not destroy Ek'tsab including the entire Tlillan and I.S.A fleet?

It was Lian who saw the possibility of peace, by putting down their arms each side could save themselves. Rather than trying to kill one another as they plummeted to the ground, the adversaries might embrace each other and pull the rip cord, floating safely to earth.

McCann became worried after five minutes had passed without any response from his daughter 'Malikah?' he called in a worried tone.

His daughter opened her eyes, after smiling towards Lian she glanced in the direction of her father 'Be at ease, Father, I'm unharmed.'

Returning her attention to Lian she spoke softly 'I believe what you ask is possible.'

Voice of Machine responded 'I place my existence and the fate of my children in your hands.'

'Their destiny is clear to me now.'

'What is their fate?'

'Machine and her children will not only survive but thrive. Once word of a Tlillan defeat at Bandayuuk reaches Gaulthus, the Camazotz shall rebel.'

'I don't understand,' replied the silver eyed Amazon.

'Never mind, first we must return to the surface.'

Lian's eyes returned to normal, after saying their farewells to Machine she led the party back to the surface of Bandayuuk. On the journey back a following gathered, it seemed that many of the Makayuuk were interested in witnessing the power of Ek'tsab first hand.

Once they were back above ground on the massive metallic disk, along with at least one hundred followers, Malikah took a hold of Lian's hand. With her face tilted towards the dark gloomy sky she began to breathe heavily, as she did so McCann could feel his heart thud in his chest. The Macks glanced at each other with frightened looks; it was obvious they too experienced the effect of the Star Shaker's power.

The beating became quite debilitating; however the Englishman remained on his feet. Malikah's eyes exploded in a jet black pigment causing a gasp to travel around the observing audience. The sable Queen opened her mouth a little, letting out a deep powerful sound. It reminded McCann of a deep pitch he'd seen on a wildlife net show, documenting the now extinct Sperm Whale.

The Makayuuk stood in awe including Sirt; he already had first-hand experience of Malikah's ability. Asta was visibly shaken, standing so close to such an event and feeling the touch of Ek'tsab on his heart was immense.

As Malikah peered upwards with her own black look the darkened clouds began to move. Going from what seemed to be a standstill the blackness slowly grouped up. As the sound from his daughter's lungs grew wider, filling the plain of charcoal coloured radioactive snow, the clouds moved quicker into their groups, not just across the visible sky but the entire planet.

It was similar to time lapse photography played backwards, clouds were sucked up at different points. As it gathered pace sunlight could be observed breaking through for the first time in 3 days. McCann assumed that the radioactive smog was expelled out into space, though he couldn't be sure. The Makayuuk didn't care as long as it was gone from their home.

Slowly darkness receded and light opened up bathing the surface once again, after a couple of minutes night was gone, but Malikah was not finished yet.

The Empress with a gaze of death now fixed her eyes upon the ground, as she did McCann got reports from the Athena stating that the star was once again destabilizing.

'Vezzali, there's nothing to worry about. Tell Kim, Malikah has everything under control and tell him to inform the rest of the fleet.'

'Understood, Sir,' replied a relieved science Officer.

'McCann out.'

After tapping his wrist he went back to observing his daughter. Within a minute or so the ground began to shake, everyone widened their stance in an attempt to keep balance.

The entire planet of Bandayuuk shook as if another planet quake were taking place, however this was different it was less violent. McCann noticed his daughter was visibly struggling; the effort to reset the entire crust of a shattered planet was draining the Icon. He was concerned for her but there was nothing the Admiral could do, other than watch and hope.

After a few minutes the rumbling and shaking ended in massive jets of steam and smoke firing out of the crust. The Englishman assumed his daughter was sealing the cracks of the Makayuuk home world. Heat from lava melted the ice and snow causing it to shoot up in jets of steam, similar to geysers.

Next Malikah's eyes lost their dark pigment and she collapsed onto the ground. Lian and McCann quickly ran to her side, she was alive but terribly weakened, 'There will be no further planet quakes, tell Machine her children are safe,' she whispered to Lian.

Lian lifted Malikah from the ground holding the Tlillan Queen in her arms as the disk lowered into the planet once again. Once inside Lian ran with Xch'uup to a medical bay, McCann followed as best he could but despite carrying Malikah Lian still streaked ahead of him.

The Englishman soon lost sight of Lian, once he reached the end of a corridor ending in a T junction he had no idea of which direction to turn. Fortunately Sirt approached from behind 'Follow me,' stated the cyborg.

Sirt walked off to his right and McCann dutifully followed until they reached a medical area. The bay was very different from an I.S.A medical bay, it was a room plated with metal from ceiling to floor much like the rest of this instillation. The room had several clear glass vats circling the inside wall, in two of the vats McCann could see Makayuuk bodies floating inside. They had leads connected to their bodies along with a plastic mask over the face. The purpose of this ghastly spectacle was something he didn't want to contemplate.

In the centre of the room lay a large solid metal operating table, surrounded by three droids; Lian was hunched over Malikah doing her best to comfort her.

'What's going on here?' shouted McCann at the horrid sight of the Makayuuk med bay.

Lian stood up straight to address him 'Malikah must recover, she will be treated properly here Duncan, you have nothing to worry about.'

'Nothing to worry about?' said the Admiral in a tone of disbelief 'have you taken a look around this place? It looks like Doctor Mengele's holiday home!'

Lian held his shoulders reassuringly 'I'm sorry but this was the closest Med Bay, I didn't want to take any risks.'

McCann peered at his daughter, laying exhausted on the table 'So Malikah's going to recover?'

'Yes,' replied Lian with a smile.

'And you're not gonna put anything inside her?'

'Machine will not alter Malikah in anyway, she is only here to recover, you have my word on that Duncan.'

'How long?'

Lian turned to Malikah then back to her Father 'An hour, perhaps more. In the meantime Sirt will give you a tour of the instillation.'

McCann gave a nod and followed Sirt out of the Med Bay.

After they were gone Lian turned back to Malikah 'How are you … Atan.'

Malikah turned her head slowly to meet Lian's 'Don't call me that, if someone heard you.'

Lian chuckled 'Machine and her children know all about us.'

Malikah closed her eyes for a moment then spoke in a tired pitch 'Are you insane, informing Machine of our relationship?'

'Machine will not speak of it; such relationships are not taboo amongst the Makayuuk.'

Malikah sighed 'It is of no consequence, our destinies have taken different paths, not to cross again.'

'Who told you that? The Seers? The Dreamscape? Or are you just wallowing in self-pity as usual?'

The Tlillan Queen's eyes widened 'Hold your mouth.'

Lian smirked 'When I was your Adjunct your word was law, but now I am Voice of Machine; you can't push me around anymore.'

Malikah's eyes took a slight red pigment 'we cannot be together Lian, my position as Xch'uup is precarious enough as it is. I do not wish to further endanger myself and my family by committing heresy.'

Lian laughed mockingly 'You mean to be seen to commit heresy, since you've already broken your own religious law several times with me.'

The pigment in Malikah's eyes faded away as she lost the will to argue 'Yes you're correct and if I could have it another way I would, but the universe is full of traps and ironically painful endings; I'm sorry Lian.'

Lian drew closer to Malikah 'Announce a change in law now; you have the support of Machine.'

Malikah chuckled herself 'One heretic supporting another? It sounds like something my father would find amusing.'

Lian raised the back rest of the bed bringing Malikah to a reclined sitting position 'What does the Dreamscape say?'

The tired Amazon shook her head 'I have looked, but in no future do I attempt such a thing.'

'Then try it and see what happens.'

'I cannot, with nothing in the Dreamscape you are asking me to put my destiny in the hands of the Gods.'

Lian's eyes began to turn glassy with what Malikah assumed were tears 'Did you not do that when you first brought me to Otoch?'

The Sable Queen didn't answer.

'What about when you sent the entire fleet into Bandayuuk? Did you not place your fate squarely in the hands of the Gods? Or will you lie to me and say you saw the outcome?'

Malikah gave her a sharp look 'If I told you I saw the end would you call me a liar?'

'Yes, because I know you'd never put the lives of those you love in the hands of Machine.'

Again Malikah refused to answer.

Lian fondled Malikah's hair affectionately 'Why are you so stubborn? I have seen your heart rule your head before, let it happen again, Atan.'

Lian bent down and kissed her Queen tenderly on the lips, receiving a frail reply from her lover.

Malikah kissed her former Adjunct then looked away, in what seemed to be shame, 'I can do nothing, Cihu is too powerful, she would never accept such an arrangement.'

Lian still hunched over Malikah whispered softly 'Cihu be damned, my Atan fears no-one in this universe. Is it not true that wherever Xch'uup does stare the galaxy will shake in terror?'

Malikah chuckled 'An old proverb, nothing more.'

'Then I shall tell Cihu.'

'Have you lost your mind?'

'Perhaps, or perhaps it is you that has lost her sanity? Deserted by your children on the field of battle and now you bow before the weak.'

Malikah remained silent waiting for Lian to finish her little rant.

Voice of Machine noticed her insults were producing little effect but she knew Malikah better than most 'I understand, perhaps it's true what the Matriarchs say after all?'

The sable Queen snatched a dirty look at the tall beauty 'What do they say?'

Lian sneered at her lover 'They say your mother fucked a dog, and I'm beginning to agree with them!'

Malikah's eyes flashed as her hand thrust out to grasp Lian's neck. Once the Tlillan Queen had a firm grip she pulled Lian in closer and in a hushed but threatening tone inquired 'Who spoke such a thing?'

Barely able to get the words out Lian choked 'Cihuateteo.'

Malikah's eyes lit up in a red rage 'Show me!'

The pair linked their minds as Lian went back to a time before she was made Adjunct. A young girl walking through the control station in the Otoch system; she had recently come of age, one of the first of a new breed of Tlillan born and educated on Earth.

Lian was to work as an aide to Xch'uup, starting off on the lowest rung of Tlillan government. However aide to Xch'uup was a clear nod that this female was destined for much higher things in later life, Lian's mother was ecstatic upon receiving the news of her post.

After docking at the station Bohr the young lady had some time on her hands before the shuttle to Muul Kaah undocked for the surface. Lian decided to familiarise herself with the ancient construction that had served the commonwealth so well in the past. Still ignorant of Tlillan culture, she walked into a lounge intended only for high ranking Matriarchs. As she stepped into the room Lian overheard a conversation; despite her ignorance to the culture she and the other girls raised on Earth all spoke fluent Tlillan.

'Word is her First Adjunct is to be that half-dark.'

Next Lian heard the distinct lofty tone of Cihuateteo 'It is true.'

There was mumbling at the table this group of high ranking Matriarchs were sat at.

'Why does she bring a half-breed to Otoch?'

Cihu made a condescending sneer 'Because her mother fucked a dog also!'

The Matriarchs laughed until a few of them noticed Lian staring back at them from the entrance. The room fell silent, Cihu leapt up to meet the young lady, unsheathing her Neutronium sword she held its sharp blade to Lian's throat 'You will hold your mouth on this child, if you ever utter a word I shall have your mother's head on a pole.'

Lian, unable to speak due to the intimidating Matriarch's threats, nodded.

'Now leave here and never return.'

Malikah broke the link, she was furious; her eyes flashed red with fire and an insatiable lust for revenge.

'You're choking me,' coughed Lian.

The beautiful Empress realised she still had a tight grip upon her lover's throat, she released Lian but her anger was by no means abated.

Malikah sat up with a burning fire in her eyes 'Take me back to my shuttle.'

Lian was concerned as to her Xch'uup's state of health 'You're too weak, you must rest Atan.'

Malikah stood on her feet 'I will leave now, call my Father!'

Lian nodded 'He will meet us at the cargo bay, now come, slowly.'

Voice of Machine led Xch'uup back to the metal disk where her shuttle still rested. McCann was already waiting with Sirt; it seemed that the two of them had got on quite well in the meantime.

The Englishman noted his daughter was in a fury over something, though he decided not to inquire.

Once upon the disk Lian announced she would be coming, Malikah didn't seem too hot on the idea but agreed with silence.

McCann said his farewells and entered the shuttle as the landing pad moved up towards the surface. He and Jenkins had spent years looking for this facility and others like it, he never imagined he'd be visiting as an esteemed guest; though it was much preferable to fighting your way in, of that McCann was certain.

On the control station Malikah marched towards one of the lounges, the Half-breed Queen of Tlillan was aware of Cihu's location. Lian followed by her side, concerned for Malikah, McCann was jogging behind as his short Human legs weren't quite up to the pace his daughter walked at. As the three of them marched to Malikah's destination Ilam appeared from an adjoining corridor.

The tall Amazon with flaming hair carried Xch'uup's mantle, the Neutronium blade usually worn for official ceremonies. Silently Ilam offered the sheathed blade, which Malikah took in equal silence. Attaching it to her waist as she marched closer to her destination McCann asked 'What's going on?'

Ilam slowed down allowing her husband to catch up with her 'Cihuateteo has committed blasphemy, she must be punished.'

McCann was none the wiser, as usual he was always the last to find out what was going on, at least that's the way he saw it.

As they strode down the corridor the Englishman could hear the distinct voices of Tlillans chatting, amongst them Cihu's voice stood out. The closer they got to the doorway at the end the louder the voices became; until he saw his daughter, wife and Lian enter the room. Quickly a blanket of total silence fell upon the lounge and even McCann could sense the tension inside.

On entering the room Cihu was sat behind a large obsidian table, on a bench with a few friends including Kaeo.

The two parties gazed at one another, the Englishman wasn't certain if they were communicating mentally or not, he realised they weren't when Cihu spoke 'What is your concern, Xch'uup?'

Malikah who was trembling with anger sneered at Cihu 'You speak with such respect to the daughter of a dog!'

McCann sensed great shock from other Matriarchs in the room; Kaeo was confused by the statement and even more puzzled when Cihu seemed to understand the meaning.

Cihu tightened her lips 'I don't understand.'

Malikah shouted with fury 'LIAR!'

The white haired Valkyrie's eyes widened at the insult, no-one had ever spoken to her in such a manner.

Kaeo stood up and pressed her palms 'Namaste Xch'uup.'

'Stand aside Kaeo,' stated Malikah.

The Praetor refused to move, she merely stood palms pressed and head bowed.

'I said stand aside!'

The prodigy still refused to move.

Malikah closed her eyes for a moment, McCann was certain his daughter was now imparting a memory to the second of clan Teteo. Once the sable Queen opened her eyes Kaeo did also, the Thai girls' eyes were now a deep shade of red. With eyes burning as coals in the night Kaeo turned to her First 'Did my mother fuck a dog also?'

Cihu failed to reply.

Kaeo stood aside, taking her place behind Malikah; the Tlillan Empress stepped towards Cihu's table. With one arm Malikah clutched an end of the heavy table and flipped it over, a feat no Human could ever manage, leaving nothing between the two Tlillan women.

Cihu leapt to her feet and at the same time placed a hand upon the grip of her mantle, hanging from her waist by a belt.

Malikah eyes fixed upon Cihu's hand which now held the grip of the Marshall's sword 'So it must come to this? You should understand by now that your ambitions far outweigh your abilities, but it seems a final lesson is required.'

Cihu gave a condescending sneer 'If you had not been corrupted by that little whore we would not be here today.'

McCann could see she meant Lian; the Admiral was slipping his pistol out of the holster slowly as he watched the drama unfold. The Englishman was prepared to send his daughter's adversaries to Elysium the moment he could get a clean shot.

'I? Corrupted?' said Malikah in an incredulous tone.

Cihu maintained her lofty tone 'It is an open secret, all are aware of the depravity you both indulge in. Yet we tolerate your filth because you are the Mictlantecuhtli.'

Malikah's eyes narrowed as her piercing red bonfires examined Cihu in disbelief 'Really? It seems that Tlillan society has gone astray, since it is I whom decides what is profane and what is not! It is I whom tolerates the Matriarchs and protects their families from outside threats, not the opposite!'

Malikah glanced around the lounge which was filling up 'who here is above Xch'uup? Who here speaks for the Tlillan race?' silence filled the room; softly Malikah asked 'who here rules supreme if it is not I?'

There was no answer from the crowd, Cihu however broke the silence 'Do you rule us, or are we now subjects of Machine?' she said staring at Lian.

The Voice of Machine smiled back at Cihu 'I speak for Machine when I say the Makayuuk serve Xch'uup.'

Mutters went around the room at that statement; the Matriarchs soon ended their hushed tones when Malikah spoke again to Cihu 'You have committed blasphemy.'

Cihu retorted quickly 'I have done no such thing, there are no laws defining what I spoke ...'

The sable Queen cut her Marshall off 'It is blasphemy because I say so! Any who wish to argue may do so at the point of a sword ... well? Who disputes my word?'

'This is unlawful,' stated Cihu 'the law was set out eons ago, no Xch'uup may create, abolish or amend law without agreement of the council.'

'There is no council, only I remain.'

After a short pause Malikah then Cihu unsheathed their swords, the pair faced off from one another, awaiting the others attack. After about 30 seconds Cihu attempted to cut Malikah across the face, there was a gasp for a moment, however McCann's daughter parried the attack and riposted with a thrust to Cihu's upper arm.

The cold blade prompted Cihu to drop her mantle onto the floor in a shriek of pain. With no mercy Malikah pulled her blade out from her opponent's arm and with one swift slice lopped off Cihuateteo's hand at the wrist. The tall warrior shrieked grasping her bloodied stump as she fell to her knees, her Tlillan suit quickly moved to cover the flesh and bone which spurted blood.

McCann's daughter turned her gaze to Kaeo 'The mantle is now yours … Huey'tlacochcalcatl.'

Kaeo bowed to her Xch'uup 'Namaste Xch'uup,' before retrieving the neutronium mantle of the Tlillan Grand Marshall.

'Let your sisters in clan Teteo understand that if there is one thing I will not tolerate it is disloyalty.'

Kaeo bowed 'Understood Xch'uup.'

Pointing to the former First of Teteo, knelt on the lounge floor, grimacing as she attempted to block out the pain; Malikah commanded the new First of Teteo 'Take this Kan away with the other traitors. Even with a single hand she might satisfy a man!'

The sable Queen of the Valkyries next addressed all those witnessing Chiu's downfall 'Let it be known that from now on there is no heresy, no blasphemy. Your law has changed; the vacuum left by past religious doctrine is now filled by loyalty. All your Xch'uup requires of you is your loyalty.'

At that Malikah marched out of the lounge, leaving Kaeo to clean up the remains of her sister, before carting her off to Otoch where she would live out her days in shame and misery. McCann along with Lian and Ilam followed Malikah, the defeat at Bandayuuk had changed the entire structure of the Tlillan Commonwealth; The Englishman was only curious as to whether it was for better or worse.

Chapter 15

Months later the triumvirate of I.S.A, Tlillan and Makayuuk vessels rested above the dark world of Gaulthus. Athena, the Chutli and a plethora of war cruisers built by Machine and commanded by her voice.

McCann and his daughter were merely observers of the destruction wrought by the people of the Machine. Voice bombarded the planet before large tubular landing ships touched down, ploughing deep into the earth. Once land transports had cut trenches into Gaulthan soil their sides dropped open, cyborg soldiers poured from inside onto damp black soil. Brandishing pulse rifles they gathered into squads which formed platoons, which formed brigades, which formed divisions and so on; until an overwhelming force of what Jerry Habeeb had once christened 'flesh eating Vikings' stood to attention ready to plunder the planet.

McCann watched a newly formed Makayuuk take on their first challenge, they reminded the Englishman of a Net show he'd watched on the History channel, concerning Norsemen. The discordant population of Gaulthus observed as they poured out and fell into line, McCann sensed dread and reverence in equal proportions.

Malikah had handed over this system to Machine, a gift to the Makayuuk and at the same time a punishment for the Camazotz. After Bandayuuk, rumours spread quickly throughout the known galaxy, most concerning a Tlillan defeat and the inevitability of collapse. Some said Malikah had died others that she fled, the Camazotz wasted little time in declaring independence … again. It didn't take a window into the Dreamscape to predict their uprising; McCann would have put good money on it.

A trait inherent amongst the Camazotz species was one of impulsiveness; a knee jerk reaction to events in Bandayuuk had just cost a civilization their liberty.

On the Net show, a longboat appeared from the thick fog causing concern to run through the townsmen. Then another of the Viking ships manifested itself from the thick cloud of water vapour, to be followed by a third then a fourth. By this time the people of the coast were in panic, some fled others with more courage prepared defences and bolstered themselves for the inevitable.

The slim ships began to move quicker as their oar strokes increased in frequency; any fate would have been preferable to the sons of Odin. A Priest stood upon the town walls muttering a passage from the bible as men prayed before a bronze crucifix held aloft.

Under a heavy down pour of arrows longboats hit the beach with great speed, sliding several feet onto land. The invaders leapt out and with shields above their heads stormed an ill prepared town. The clash of steel became louder as the Norsemen poured in through shattered town gates. These men had many years of experience in plunder, the allure of gold, silver and slaves motivated them above all.

Bit by bit the noise of steel weapons died down as howls and screams of women grew in proportion. Bearded Vikings ran amok throughout the costal settlement taking what they believed was their fair share, allotted to them by the gods.

Once plundering was over and the settlement burnt, the Norsemen's' leader murdered the Christian priest for his heresy. Cutting him along his torso the Viking opened the old man's chest, pulling out his lungs and slinging them over their corresponding shoulder. The priest died screaming in pain as the survivors observed the bloody eagle, dealt out to those held in particular disdain.

McCann sensed a link between Human, Makayuuk and Tlillan society, perhaps it was Odin? The wise old God travelling where war was most intense, bestowing victory upon the faithful.

The inhabitants of Gaulthus were quickly overwhelmed by Lian's soldiers, moving into each town and city, Makayuuk would execute any being taller than Lian's hip bone. The Camazotz had carried out many insurrections previously, this however being the straw that broke the Matriarch's back. Xalan had already been punished for the crimes of his people, now it was time for the Camazotz to truly suffer the consequences of Xch'uup's rage.

Gaulthus was a dark mountainous world; originally its bat like inhabitants lived high up in mountain caves. As they evolved the species moved to the plains below, however its mountains were utilized as capital cities and centres of administration. The Camazotz leader maintained his citadel upon the highest mountain, a nod to his dominance, it was believed to be impossible to siege let alone storm and conquer.

On the plains of Gaulthus battle was intense, just as Vikings appearing from the mist troop transports beached themselves in thick moist soil. Residents of a nearby city began to click loudly in panic, Makayuuk soldiers formed up brandishing pulse rifles. Their cybernetic eyes allowing them perfect sight in the low light of this miserable planet. City defences were bombarded from above in precision missile strikes, its smouldering walls were of no use and no priest was there to instil hope into these beings. Pulse fire flashes moved from the plains and into the city which resembled great bunches of termite hills as both sides fought, Camazotz resistance was broken within the hour. An overwhelming number of Makayuuk smothered the city.

Eventually a shuttle landed just outside a captured city, out of it came the tall slim frame of Lian, followed by Asta, her favourite Makayuuk, and Sirt. As she walked towards the city centre Makayuuk bowed some stating 'Machine' others 'Namaste Machine'. Either way she was the personification of Machine, their collective mind and parent. She also was Xch'uup's lover, the closest confidante of Ek'tsab.

Upon reaching the city centre Camazotz were already being executed, those large enough were shot and carried off to be liquidized. The resulting pink and grey goo shipped to Bandayuuk for the purpose of supporting Machine and her birthing chambers.

A city official, something close to a mayor, stood with a control collar around his skinny neck, his arms tied behind his back. These bat creatures wore no clothes unless for utilitarian reasons such as battle or an official occasion. Lian considered the fact that their genitals were hidden inside their bodies had something to do with it.

The animal, whose black leathery skin was covered with a short wiry fur, began to chirp and click. Lian understood its language, being aide to Xch'uup required her to link with a Tlillan and learn all languages of the commonwealth; a service Malikah had been happy to provide her young prodigy.

'I implore Voice for mercy,' squeaked the foul being.

'Why?' inquired Voice of Machine.

'Whatever you wish, gold, silver anything we shall provide if you agree to leave.'

Lian shook her head slowly from side to side 'We are not Vikings.'

The bound Camazotz said nothing; he was befuddled as to what a Viking might be.

Lian smirked 'Vikings come for treasure such as gold, silver and slaves. The only treasure you have which Machine desires is the flesh on your bodies. Once Machine has taken her fair portion, that which is allotted to her by right, her children shall retreat back to Bandayuuk.'

The bat like creature which smelt worse than a Gukumatz after a bad curry implored Lian 'Then speak to Xch'uup, she listens to Voice, we offer our loyalty to serve.'

Lian's smirk turned into a Tlillan sneer 'Xch'uup has no further use for the Camazotz; you are an irritant whose only function is to serve as nourishment in birthing chambers on Bandayuuk.'

At that the tall Valkyries eyes changed in pigment to a deep dark red, the Mayor of the beleaguered city squealed in pain as he dropped to the floor. After a few seconds the Mayor lay lifeless 'Take this one to be processed,' ordered Voice as its collar was removed and the bat creature dragged off with others to be loaded onto a flatbed, eight wheeled truck.

Lian turned to Sirt 'I want you to organise the siege of Aktun,' she point up at the mountain fortress of the Camazotz King. A tall peak with several palisades circling its girth until a large citadel sat atop, constructed upon the deep caverns and tunnels throughout the mountain.

Sirt nodded and pressed his palms together 'Namaste Kalayuuk.'

The Makayuuk showed no pity towards their foe, an enemy of Xch'uup now being an enemy of Machine. Odd howls and cries of clicking bat people could be heard wherever you stood on the planet that day. McCann was uncertain as to whether they were cries for mercy or just general lamentation, the only sound to interject was that of pulse rifle fire. Along with the darkness of the planet it reminded him of the nuclear winter on Bandayuuk, before Malikah lifted it.

Whilst executions were carried out the Chutli projected an image of Xch'uup in her feathered headdress onto the planet's atmosphere. The face of Xch'uup looked down upon the disgraced Camazotz as she informed her rebellious subjects of their fate.

'Ola Camazotz, behla kab Gaulthus chiltal Makayuuk, Kalayuuk yuum!' declared the projection which consumed the sky all around the globe of this forsaken world.

Sneering with disdain upon the populace Malikah let them know Machine was now their overlord.

His regal daughters' voice echoed, reverberating around the planet via landing craft all vibrating in unison; emitting sonic waves in synchrony with the image plastered upon the sky 'Camazotz kan, Xch'uup xan uts yuum! Ch'a'ik ool kuchik, pa'tal Makayuuk ma'yakuntik.'

The sable Empress pointed out her mistake, in previously granting Camazotz mercy. McCann's daughter assured those that were not laying in heaps with their fellow countrymen that they would regret their decision.

Watching his daughter's message from the Bridge of Athena sent a chill down the Englishman's spine. She was now to commit these people to the same fate she had rescued the Tlillan race from; he had to admit a certain level of curiosity.

The Camazotz tried to prevent an oncoming deluge of cybernetic warriors but to little effect, before the day was out Lian held sway over the entire world and what remained of the population. The Camazotz would not be in the mood for rebellion for a long time to come, that was a certainty.

McCann along with his Bridge staff observed tens of thousands of Camazotz pouring out from their dwellings, what seemed to him to be nothing more than glorified caves constructed in heaps. It reminded him of a termite nest towering out of the ground, pitted with up to 50 holes. He supposed these nests were the equivalent of a tower block of flats or an apartment building. Flashes of light from orbital bombardment lit up large groups of nests, sometimes thousands in what he assumed were Camazotz towns and cities.

The bat creatures flapped out of their homes, some gathering on rocks, the majority swooping onto the ground in groups. Women and children let out screams of terror as they watched Machine hammer the surface resulting in cascades of white fire.

Much like the city of Pompeii when Vesuvius erupted, shrieks of women, screams of children and shouts of men filled the air in their belief that the Gods were no more. Perhaps, they thought, this was the end time talked about for so long? Night had vanished to be replaced with a perpetual bright fire, scorching every citizen's skin, despite their inherent blindness they felt the heat of a Makayuuk sun bearing down upon their world.

Some fled, flapping away into caves and grottos far away from cities and towns, others prayed for some god to deliver them from evil ... he or she never came. The rest screamed in panic as a society was systematically annihilated first by fire, next a Machine army poured out onto the surface turning what was previously their home into a wilderness of pain.

Once Machines' invasion had been completed McCann was invited to the surface, taking a shuttle he landed at the capital. The Englishman stepped out of the shuttle with his Chief Engineer Louis Beaumont; the Frenchman looked around the city from the landing pad, perched high up on a building that looked as if it were a mountain 'Why are these places so dark?'

McCann chuckled 'probably so you can't see the bloody shit hole!'

McCann and Louis were only able to see the mountain ranges thanks to the lighting put in place by the Makayuuk.

'Over here,' pointed McCann towards a stone path which led down to a terrace.

As the pair walked down carefully Louis raised his nose to the air and took a sniff 'Do you smell that?'

McCann pulled out a cigar and toasted the foot 'Nope, what is it?'

'The atmosphere, it smells like a dirty animal!'

The Englishman took a sniff but detected nothing 'Hmm, not much compared to the cess pit those toads live in.'

The two of them stepped off onto the terrace, immediately observing Malikah and Lian in very close quarters. They spoke quietly to each other, their bodyguards kept their distance.

McCann pushed his way past her Vympel soldiers and the Macks, the commotion caused his daughter and her lover to look over.

'Father, are you alright?'

Taking his daughter by the arm he muttered into her ear 'What on Earth are you up to?'

Malikah smiled in response to her Father's concern 'The situation has changed, after my confrontation with Cihu I have decided to accept our difference.'

McCann rolled his eyes 'But what about the rest of the clans? Isn't this heresy or blasphemy or whatever you people call it?'

Malikah laughed 'Yes, but who am I to dictate what is profane or acceptable?'

The Englishman looked from side to side across the gloom of the city 'You are Xch'uup; I thought your word was law.'

The sable Valkyrie snatched a glance at Lian 'I have learnt something from Machine, or her voice.'

'Oh? What's that?' inquired the Admiral.

Lian stepped over and locked her left arm in Malikah's right, holding onto his daughter with affection.

'Freedom, true freedom.'

McCann shook his head 'I don't understand.'

'Who am I to dictate what you may or may not eat or who you may or may not make love to?'

Still confused the Englishman replied 'You know who you are, you're Xch'uup.'

'Without the power of another's spirit I am nothing. How could I force those, who make me all that I am, worship and obey against their will?'

Taking a puff on his Habanos McCann inquired 'so what are you talking about here?'

'If one's actions do not cause suffering to another it is not my business as to whether it is profane or not. No longer does Xch'uup press her subjects as slaves but instead I call them as free men and women.'

McCann raised an eyebrow 'Free men?'

'Well, human men.'

The Englishman nodded 'I see.'

Malikah rolled her eyes 'Really Father, there's no need to be so cynical.'

'Am I?'

'Yes, you are. Tlillan culture is changing, a paradigm shift has begun once more yet the Dreamscape cannot tell me where it will ultimately lead. However it can only change a little at a time, Father.'

The I.S.A Admiral fixed his gaze upon Lian 'I take it you are the slave stationed at the Emperor's elbow.'

Voice of Machine furrowed her brow in puzzlement; McCann answered her confusion 'Did they not teach you any classical history? During great events in Rome the Emperor would preside over the spectacle, soaking up the adulation of his people. Always on his side a slave would be stationed, whose sole duty was to whisper into his ear 'Remember you are mortal'. I can understand how after so many victories an Emperor might begin to think of himself as immortal, after all is that not what her subjects tell her every day?'

'Your point being?' pouted Lian.

'No point was being made Lian,' replied McCann as a cloud of rich smoke left his nostrils 'Only a request, be prudent with your whispers, I don't wish to see Malikah tripped by the fallacy of equality. Remember she is Tlillan and a Tlillan prizes merit above all other things.'

Lian smiled but gave no reply.

Malikah was quite shocked 'Father, you speak as if I weren't present!'

He smiled at his beautiful child 'No, I wanted you both to hear it.'

'Well there is something I hold above merit father,' said the dark haired Queen 'Loyalty.'

'Is that not covered by merit?'

Malikah nodded with a coy smile 'Yes, I suppose without one you cannot have the other. Have no fear; Lian will always be here to remind the Mictlantecuhtli of her limits. Voice has allowed both Machine and Xch'uup to trust each other's word, today on Gaulthus our alliance has been cemented with the blood of the Camazotz.

When the paradigm shifted before it drew us together with the Tlillan and Gukumatz, a triumvirate was formed reigning in the galaxy from an anarchy which had prevailed for millennia.

Now it is shifting again, the Matriarchs on Otoch sensed it as did the Seers, always change is feared by those it affects. At Bandayuuk those who were disloyal betrayed their true selves, attempting to resist the paradigm shift. I was unaware at the time but that defeat was a victory; it allowed me to weed out those holding us back from our destiny.'

McCann peered out across the black skyscape of the city 'So where is this all leading us Malikah? What does our destiny look like from here?'

'The destiny of the Makayuuk has crossed paths with us; we are intertwined with each other...'

The Englishman cut his daughter short 'Anyone could have told you that!'

Giving her Father a black look she continued 'There is another force at play, a force the I.S.A is not yet aware of, the Makayuuk shall be required to combat them.'

Louis strolled up to the conversation 'What force?'

Lian intervened 'This force has existed for as long as we have, Machine calls them the Neenayin.'

Louis shrugged his shoulders 'So what's the problem?'

Lian took a deep breath 'Makayuuk melded their minds with Machine due to the Neenayin. The creatures would ... I suppose possess would be the appropriate word, they possessed the ancestors of the Makayuuk. Forcing them to enslaving one another, the interface between man and machine was orchestrated by Neenayin in order to pacify the population. The Makayuuk were to be a slave army for the Neenayin, micro chipped brains all controlled by a central processing unit.

Unfortunately for the Neenayin, that Machine developed its own consciousness, much like Athena and Ares, Machine began to make her own decisions. She became aware and used her influence over the minds of whom she saw as her children to remove the Neenayin. Their access was blocked via their own instrument of enslavement, Machine understood that Neenayin were nothing more than parasites.'

McCann took a drag on his petit Coronas 'What does this have to do with us exactly?'

'The Neenayin were banished from the Makayuuk but found new hosts, on Earth.'

The Englishman chuckled in Lian's direction 'Come on, you're just yanking my chain now.'

Louis interrupted 'Go on.'

'These beings live in what you'd best describe as a different dimension; they exist outside of Human and Makayuuk visible wavelengths.'

Louis was focused upon the tale but McCann found the story all too fantastic 'So how long have these alleged parasites been preying upon us?'

Malikah spoke up 'For thousands of years, only when my eyes were opened did I see what occurred. These creatures living inside this schism made the jump to Humans, manipulating us for millennia, Machine attempted to end their control.'

McCann was still sceptical and asked with an incredulous tone 'So if they live on a different wavelength and you can't see them how do you know they're there?'

Lian offered her hand 'Here let me show you as Machine did for me.'

Holding her hand the Englishman closed his eyes as he made a link with Voice of Machine. He drifted back to Geneva, during a visit by some Chinese and American corporative bosses, through Lian's eyes he could see into other wavelengths one of them being the so called domain of these Neenayin.

It was before the Athena had lifted off to explore Mars, McCann had just been selected and Faraday was introducing him to some prospective investors in the voyage. The Englishman remembered the meeting for no other reason than he hated it, though he kept a good face and smiled as he answered the corporate chairman's questions. He even managed to hold back a grimace as Faraday flattered the 'scum in a suit' as Louis put it. The I.S.A Director needed their backing, placing a second Maser on a Martian moon was not going to be cheap and they had patents on the rechargeable Xenon batteries required to power the propulsion device.

Something was different as he looked this time, the esteemed guests skin was not as clearly defined as it should be. It were as if he was viewing them through a hazy lens, something seemed to occupy the same space as the businessmen.

McCann concentrated upon the visitors, whatever was causing the haze it seemed to be of Human origin, two arms and two legs however the eyes were obviously reptilian in nature and on closer inspection its skin was not human in nature or even close to any Human relative.

As Faraday departed with them it smiled at McCann, a sinister reptilian grin that put the fear of God into the Englishman. All the time he watched the creatures inside the Americans and Chinamen they gave each other secret signs and knowing looks.

McCann pulled himself out of the link and stared Lian hard in the face 'I still don't understand, what was that?'

Lian rubbed the Admiral's hand, calming him somewhat 'Exactly what I saw when Machine linked with me, when I saw what was happening to the Human race and what would happen to the Tlillan race I couldn't break my link with Machine.'

Malikah glanced between Louis and her father 'The Tlillan race outlawed the mind machine interface because of Neenayin. We continued to victimise the Makayuuk out of ignorance to the fact Machine had rebelled against the will of the Schism.'

Louis seemed to be convinced 'How many are inhabited by these parasites?'

McCann shouted with a tone of disapproval 'LOUIS!'

'What?'

McCann still hesitant to commit himself, shook his head 'Come on, you believe this paranoid conspiracy theory?'

'And if I do?'

The Englishman took a tubos out of his leather arm pocket 'Jesus Christ, this is all just too much, someone needs to get a grip around here.'

Malikah smirked 'Mother always said you were the eternal sceptic, never believing in anything until it was already upon you.'

McCann clipped his cigar 'Well maybe I'm possessed by one of these reptilians from another dimension?'

The sable Queen narrowed her eyes 'They have already attempted to gain a foothold in the I.S.A; the Schism was unable to gain a hold on you Father.'

McCann roasted the end of his Ramon Allones Petit Coronas 'Really, was it my charming personality that attracted them or just my good looks?'

Malikah tightened her lips in disapproval though Lian began to giggle; Louis turned to his friend 'You can be such an asshole McCann!'

Taking a puff on his Habanos McCann shouted 'Ah so that's why they failed to possess me, I guess that makes Louis impervious to these Reptilians, right?'

Both of the girls started to laugh at Louis' expense, the Frenchman was not amused, he was in fact quite serious concerning this threat to Humanity.

McCann raised his hands 'Alright, let's just say for the sake of argument I believe in this paranoid delusion, how do you tell if someone has been possessed and then how would you exorcise the thing?'

Lian perked up at his question 'Linking with Machine will remove the Neenayin, as for detection, the beasts live on a different wavelength to us they are detectable on the Infra-Red wavelength.'

McCann shook his head in disbelief 'It's all just too fantastic, why would they want to possess us for God's sake?'

Lian felt she was finally getting through to the Englishman 'These creatures feed off negative emotions; Human beings are like a beacon of pleasure and sustenance. Have you ever wondered why Human history is merely a series of wars and disasters with short breaks in between to re-arm?'

McCann dismissed her theory 'Conflict is in the nature of all Humans, look at the Tlillans we inherited it from them. If we didn't have someone to fight or something to threaten us we'd be lost.'

Lian sneered 'We'd be forced to treat each other with love and respect, that is what they fear above anything.'

McCann took a drag on his cigar allowing the thick smoke to exit his nostrils 'Please spare me the new age bullshit.'

Lian looked down on the Englishman 'Listen to yourself, you mock the thought of treating your fellow Human with love and respect.'

McCann sneered back at Lian 'No, it's just that I'm not stupid enough to leave myself vulnerable to my fellow man.'

'Pah!' mocked Lian 'You have the nerve to call me paranoid!'

'Fine,' retorted McCann 'you prove to me that these things exist, with my own eyes.'

'And if I do, what then?'

'Then I suppose we set about extinguishing this Neena what's it from the population.'

Lian smiled 'That's why you were brought here Duncan.'

'What do you mean?'

Malikah took over 'Removing these things and sending them back to their schism will require a man prepared to go to the extremes, you and Ryu are amongst the few with the authority and self-determination to accomplish that.'

'Are you saying the only way to exorcise one of these things is to murder the host?'

'It isn't murder, father. These bodies are merely a vessel we inhabit; it anchors us to the physical universe. The Neenayin are thieves, using others vessels to increase the pain and misery which they feed off.'

McCann took a smoke and waved his hands 'Fine, just give me the name of one person that's possessed by one of these Reptilians.'

'The President of the Eastern States.'

'Earle?'

Malikah nodded her head.

Louis shook his fist 'I always knew there was something about him!'

McCann laughed at his friend 'Give me a break Louis, if you had your way every politician would be involved in some sort of conspiracy.'

Louis scrunched his face up 'You always told me how much you hated politicians, are you telling me now that this guy is okay?'

The I.S.A Admiral took a drag on his cigar 'There's a big difference between a corrupt scumbag and possessed by an inter-dimensional alien!'

Louis ignored his cynical friend 'So how would you expose him?'

Before Lian could answer Louis, McCann burst out laughing. Malikah shook her head whilst placing her palm upon her forehead 'Please Father this is serious.'

Between giggles the Englishman replied 'If President Earle were to expose himself in front of my daughter I'd take it very seriously! Although I think Louis could suddenly take an interest in politics, what do say old chap?'

Louis shook his head 'Fuck you McCann.'

Lian answered Louis' question 'The being may be seen via the Infra-Red spectrum, Tlillans and Makayuuk have the ability to see them; Humans will need assistance.'

The Englishman screwed his mouth up after pulling a cigar out from between his lips 'And I suppose you brought Louis here because he'll believe any old bollocks you tell him?'

Malikah gave her Father a black look, before she could say anything he raised his hands 'Fine, fine but until I see one of these things for myself could we drop the subject of reptilians from other dimensions that possess Presidents?'

Lian stepped close to McCann 'Very well, but you must not speak on this subject to anyone else is that understood?'

McCann laughed at Lian 'What do you think I am, an idiot? The moment I start talking about schism dwelling aliens they'd have me sectioned!'

'Aside from us only Ilam and Ryu are aware of the creatures.'

'But I thought Tlillans could see them?'

'Only if they are looking, if you do not open your fist then you cannot receive.'

McCann didn't really understand what she meant though he didn't care to inquire further 'Fine, when we get to Earth you can expose Earle, until then my lips are sealed.'

Three months later in time and on another planet President Earle was making a speech in congress, addressing all the Senators of the former United States. It was another boring dialogue on fiscal responsibility and currency competition, that is until the doors of the senate swung open to reveal Malikah flanked by Lian and McCann; chasing behind them were Jerry Habeeb and his cohorts.

Dressed in a long black dress and wearing a traditional Tlillan white frock coat the Queen marched up the central isle, her boots clinking upon the floor with each step.

Earle lost his train of thought; the President's jaw swung open much like the Senators in the house that day.

The speaker of the house rose to his feet 'What's the meaning of this?'

Malikah ignored the speaker; pointing at the President for the Eastern States she called in her deep Amazonian voice 'You, come here!'

'I'm sorry?' replied Earle.

Lian barked at the President 'You heard her.'

Earle refused to move from the podium 'Remove these people from the House.'

No-one moved at the call of the President, Malikah scanned the senate building then returned her gaze to Earle 'I own this house Earle and I own your nation, now get down here before I have to drag you down.'

Earle noticed McCann's hand drop to his holster, on witnessing that, he decided to comply with the Tlillan half-breed, for now. He stepped down and began to walk slowly along the Isle towards the three interlopers.

McCann muttered under his breath 'You better hope your conspiracy theory is true.'

Earle crossed his arms 'So what's going on?'

Malikah sneered at the President 'I'm here to expose the Neenayin … Mr Earle.'

The Senators began to mutter to one another as Jerry Habeeb threw his camera into the air and started to record the incident.

'Neena what?' replied the President with a look that if McCann didn't know better could have been taken for puzzlement rather than shock.

Malikah continued her sneer 'Don't play coy with me Mr President; I know what you are and your goals.'

Lian produced a red ball; it immediately grabbed the attention of everyone in the Senate.

'What's that?' inquired Earle.

Lian smiled 'A device invented by the Makayuuk, it allows Humans to see on wavelengths other than visible light.'

Earle uncrossed his arms and stood backwards 'What wavelengths?'

McCann observed the uneasy manner of the President upon hearing this news 'Something wrong Mr President?'

Earle was decidedly awkward 'I said what wavelengths?'

McCann stepped closer to the President 'It allows us all to see on the Infra-Red spectrum, the part of the spectrum these creatures inhabit.'

The speaker of the house got up 'this is crazy, we're here to discuss currency competition between States not some hocus pocus garbage!'

On that another Senator stood up 'No, I want to hear what she has to say,' several murmurs of agreement could be heard around the Senate.

Lian held the ball aloft 'When activated everything on the Infra-Red spectrum in this room will be visible to us, including the Neenayin.'

An old Senator stood next to Lian, the grey haired man in his 60's asked 'What the hell is a Neenayin?'

Malikah sneered at Earle 'A parasite, they control their host and manipulate those around them.'

The old Senator took a glance at Earle then back at the red ball 'Are you trying to say that one of these parasites is in the Senate now?'

Malikah's eyes narrowed as they fixed upon Earle 'Not only that but President Earle is a host.'

The speaker stood beside Earle 'This is just outrageous, you can't come in here an ...'

'Oh but I can Mr Speaker and I have.'

The old Senator stood beside Lian 'Well I want to see them try it.'

'Could the President for the Southern Union please sit back down.'

The old man laughed 'Why? What have you got to lose for God's sake?'

Earle pointed at Lian 'I agree this is outrageous, I don't have time for this kind of sensationalist journalism.'

The old Senator laughed again 'That'll be the day! Come on Mike, you're not afraid of some voodoo ball are you?'

The entire Senate began to laugh along with the Senator for Texas.

'I'm outta here,' declared the President for the Eastern States as he turned his back upon the party.

Lian threw the cricket ball into the air, as it ascended the entire Senate was draped in a softened tone of red light similar to when battle stations were called upon the Athena. Earle halted immediately, he calmly turned to look back and as he did the entire Senate drew breath at once. McCann was in complete surprise; Michael Earle was not Human at least his eyes were not. The President's eyes resembled those of something reptilian in nature; they expanded and contracted horizontally, a parietal eye.

The Senator for Texas who was also the President for the Southern Union pointed at Earle 'Jesus H Christ what's that Mike?'

Earle pointed at Lian 'It's all bullshit Ron; she's trying to undermine me.'

The Texan Senator peered at Malikah and Lian then back at his old friend 'If she wanted to undermine you Mike there'd be much easier methods than trying to convince us all you're possessed by a 'gator!'

Earle turned to the house speaker 'Come on John this is horse shit!'

The Speaker was disturbed by what he saw and only took a few slow steps backwards 'Listen Mike, maybe we should have a talk about this?'

Earle began to make for the exit, several Senators moved to block his way but the President pulled a small pistol out from under his suit. Lian lurched towards him and grasped the President's wrist holding his pistol above his head as the whine of its charge went out alerting everyone in the Senate.

The yellow reptilian eyes made a stinging look into the eyes of Lian 'We could have taken control of our own destiny Lian, instead you gave yourself to that Machine,' he dropped his pistol and produced a neutronium coin 'look even your money has her head on it!'

Earle discarded one of the bullion coins, minted on Otoch, that saved the planet Earth from descending into fiscal chaos.

Malikah picked up the coin and pistol 'your people had a good run of it on Earth, until my mother turned up, now you're finished Earle.'

Earle's face started to morph, as the seconds passed his skin became a thick scaled leather, his tongue split and flicked out of his mouth which now reminded McCann of an Adnoaran.

The Senator for Texas nearly jumped out of his skin 'JESUS! What the hell is that?'

Malikah checked the pistol she'd taken off the floor 'That is one of the creatures which have been manipulating us for thousands of years Senator.'

The Senator was hysterical 'How the hell do we get Mike back?'

Malikah gave the short man a serious look as she passed him the pulse pistol 'You don't Mr President.'

The short Texan looked at the pistol then at McCann 'Is she serious? Is someone from one of those dumb Net shows gonna jump out and tell me I'm a dick?'

McCann shook his head 'If he does then he's had both of us.'

The Senator peered over at Jerry Habeeb who was clearly in a state of distress 'This is bullshit, right?'

Habeeb didn't answer; in fact he ignored the Senator and remained transfixed upon the President who now morphed between the states of Human and Reptilian, not completely staying with one form.

Earle shouted at the Senator as Lian let go of his wrist 'Come on Ron, this is just some dumb prank Habeeb is pulling, don't be an asshole!'

The President of the Southern Union looked at his weapon then around the Senate one more time 'I agree Mike.'

Earle relaxed at this, the President eased despite the fact he still physically morphed between two species.

The Texan flicked the pistol safety off 'And if this is all just some dumb trailer trash Net show then this pistol has to be fake, or at the least not loaded, right Mike?'

From what McCann could tell he would have put good money on it that Earle shit his pants at that moment. Mike knew Ron well enough to understand what he was about to test out next.

'Put it down Ron, that thing could go off by accident,' ordered the President.

The Texan smirked 'Well in that case the South'd claim victory in our little civil war.'

Earle hissed before the Senator pulled the trigger shooting the tungsten round out of the barrel with a flash of super-heated gas. The small tungsten round split the President's skull in two, pebble dashing the senate house with his brains. To everyone's further amazement the spirit of the beast could be seen ascending as Earle's corpse crumpled onto the floor of the aisle.

Senators shrieked, men scrambled for cover as the reptilian apparition moved around searching for a fresh host. Politicians climbed over each other, attempting to flee the clutches of the beast, knocking their fellow party members to the ground in a display of self-centred cowardice.

The beast moved to Lian, sensing her connection to Machine it moved on to the President of the Southern States. Before it could inhabit him Malikah stepped in its way 'Get out of my world!' shouted the Valkyrie in a deep Tlillan voice.

The apparition hissed at the Queen of Otoch before moving towards the fearful Senator for Texas.

Malikah's eyes burnt as embers upon a camp fire 'Happy to take the misery this mortal coil has brought to me?'

The creature began struggling, as if trudging through mud, attempting to reach its goal of the Texan Senator. Malikah seemed to be holding it back, exerting her will upon another dimension, her desire stretched as far as the schism these horrific creatures inhabited.

The beast pushed harder, yet the more effort it employed the slower it moved. Eventually its form became obscured, dissipating into nothingness. Torment was evident even upon the face of this reptilian animal, though it did resemble a human more than a crocodile, something every person present found quite disturbing.

Once the Neenayin collapsed into nothingness the Senate was dead silent for about 10 seconds, Lian raised her hand and caught her red ball as it descended bringing the room back to normal light.

'Tell me you got that,' whispered Habeeb.

His cameraman went over the footage on his tablet several times. 'Well did you get it?'

'I don't believe it but yeh, I got it.'

'Show me,' muttered Habeeb as he and the soundman both watched over the footage.

Habeeb was in another universe 'I got a President being murdered by another President and alien possession all in one shoot ... I'm gonna be able to retire to the Caribbean when this hits the Net!'

Habeeb's cohorts snapped a fast look at him 'I mean we're gonna be able to retire.'

McCann smirked at the so called journalist 'That doesn't go out until you have my permission Habeeb.'

Jerry pointed to the footage playing on his man's tablet 'You can't do that, there's still freedom of the press here!'

McCann pulled his pistol out 'There's an old saying that dead men tell no tales, fancy testing that out Habeeb?'

The whine went out as Jerry swallowed 'You wouldn't dare,' said the journalist peering down the wrong end of McCann's barrel.

'Who's gonna stop me? You? Your President?' the Englishman's eyes were cold, Jerry felt his desire to squeeze the trigger, as did Malikah.

'Father, please.'

The sable Goddess clasped his outstretched arm 'Mr Habeeb will do as he is told, there's no need for any more violence; is there Jerry?'

Jerry gave a nervous smile and offered his tablet to Malikah, the Tlillan Queen refused his offering 'Keep your footage Jerry; you'll know when it is time to transmit.'

McCann was obviously displeased by the fact his daughter had forbid him from removing the thorn of Habeeb from his side. However the Englishman complied with her desires, to do otherwise would have gone against his very nature.

Jerry relaxed as the pistol was turned off and returned to its holster 'Certainly Malikah.'

Malikah let out a big grin 'There, you see we don't have to behave like savages to get things done.'

'What about the President?' inquired the Texan Senator.

'His disposal was required, these beasts cannot be removed once they've taken a body,' replied Malikah.

'No, I mean what're the Eastern States gonna do for a President now?'

Malikah peered down at the Texan 'You're the President for the Southern Union, yes?'

'Sure.'

'You can take the Presidency of the South and East.'

The Senator gave a look of shock as the entire senate began to gossip 'I don't think that's possible, we need an election.'

Malikah looked around the Senate and spoke so all could hear 'Election? The Neenayin have most democracies sewn up already, until Captain Ryu has purged them you will be in charge, since I know you're not Neenayin.'

Malikah gave the house a hard look 'Does anyone disagree?'

There was no reply, Malikah approached the new president of the Eastern States and Southern Union to place a neutronium coin in the palm of his hand 'Your currency Mr President, make certain all of your banking institutions have a 100% backed currency; Neutronium, Gold or Silver anything else is not money, understood?'

The new President nodded his head as he eyed the bullion coin 'Gotcha.'

Three weeks later McCann was sitting opposite Jerry Habeeb on his top rated Net show. The lights were low until the camera lights went from red to green, the cameramen moved as the lights came on and Jerry leant over his desk into Camera one, 'Welcome to Habeeb's Hour and by God have we got a show for you tonight!'

Jerry gestured with his eyes across the table 'We have Admiral McCann back with us, hello Admiral.'

McCann smiled 'You can call me Duncan, Jerry.'

Jerry made a playful grunting noise 'Are we back on friendly terms now?'

Snickering could be heard from behind the scenes and around the studio.

'Don't push your luck Jerry!' jested McCann.

Jerry grinned, he was just happy to be getting the scoop 'No need to worry about that, I've seen you when you're upset.'

Snickering could be heard again, McCann was fine with it; everyone was familiar with Jerry's style of interviewing.

Jerry quickly changed tack, he wanted to get on to the subject which had been causing a media and political tsunami across the planet, 'Onto the subject of Captain Ryu, she has been traveling the planet first in Japan and now she's just left the Middle East. I want you to explain to our viewers exactly what it is she's doing.'

McCann took a deep breath 'It's going to be hard to digest but in a nutshell she's been removing parasites.'

Jerry cut him off 'Now you say parasites and a lot of people think of mosquitos or lice or something like that.'

McCann nodded 'Right Jerry, well these parasites are very different.'

Jerry couldn't stop himself from interjecting, he was so excited, finally being allowed to air the footage 'Now I've seen one of these parasites with my own eyes and to tell you the truth I'm still in shock.'

McCann stopped for a moment then replied 'Would you like me to describe them to your viewers Jerry?'

'Yes, I'm sorry, please continue.'

The Englishman took a deep breath and started again 'The parasite is reptilian in nature and about the same size as a Human. The creatures are called Neenayin, they occupy the same space as us but live on another wavelength, sort of an inter-dimensional being, they can occupy our space for short periods.'

Jerry quickly spoke 'Here is the video everyone's been waiting for, before we play it I'd like to make it clear that this footage has not been retouched in any manner; anyone of a nervous disposition may turn away now.'

On each viewer's media device a small screen popped up which at a touch could be enlarged, most of the 15 billion viewers took full advantage of the option. Even people who were at work dropped what they were doing and enlarged the screen, the sight of a President morphing under the red lights and losing his life to another President was hard to accept. However when the strange shape of its ghostly figure rose many refused to believe it, how could such a thing exist and go un-noticed for centuries? Added to that Jerry Habeeb had got the first shot of a real ghost?

Conspiracy theories were soon trending back and forth over the Net; the top tenders had Malikah as the architect. By the time McCann walked out of the studio the world was in shock, concerning an attempted Tlillan coup d'état. It was impossible to stop the Net frenzy; even Malikah didn't have the authority to shut it down on a global scale.

Chapter 16

At a local café McCann sipped a coffee with his wife, Lian, daughter and her guardian Icarus. The creature was patrolling with his cloak off, a warning to anyone who might decide to try it on.

McCann drank his coffee as Ilam informed him of the calamity unfolding 'Jesus Christ, I thought we got over the Tlillan conspiracy theories years ago.'

Ilam browsed the Net using the visual pop up from her collar 'Apparently not, it seems paranoia is too deeply embedded in Human society,' Ilam glanced over at Lian, giving her a black look she finished her sentence 'not to mention treachery.'

Malikah returned the stare 'Mother, that will be enough.'

'Tumen taak Xch'uup,' replied Ilam as she bowed to her daughter.

The reply annoyed Malikah but Ilam had shown proper respect to her Xch'uup and Malikah could not berate her further.

McCann was not so constricted by tradition 'Treachery and paranoia, weren't they Grand Matriarchs along with condescending and megalomania?'

Lian giggled putting her hand over her mouth to suppress the noise. Malikah closed her eyes saying nothing, she awaited the fall out that was sure to hit from her parents.

Ilam's eyes widened as they changed colour, the Valkyrie fixed her gaze upon her husband 'Hold your mouth!'

McCann casually took a cigar from a leather arm pocket on his military jacket, goading his wife he removed the cigar from the tubos and whispered 'You know you're at your most attractive when you're angry, dear.'

Ilam knew it was true and Lian could sense McCann spoke the truth.

Malikah snapped a look at Lian as her lover was eavesdropped upon her Father's emotions. Lian grinned back before returning her mind to a neutral state, leaving McCann's thoughts to himself.

Ilam tightened her long red lips before replying 'And you know you're at your least attractive when you have one of those things in your mouth.'

The Englishman retorted 'Well, I have to find some way to fight off the ladies without draining all my energy!' he moved his eyebrows up and down a few times at Lian causing her to giggle again.

'Taax k'eek'en ta'taasik wa maax!'

Lian broke out in laughter and even Malikah had to turn her head to disguise her snickering.

McCann looked back at his wife in disapproval 'Hilarious,' he noted with sarcasm, encouraging the others to create more noise. The Englishman managed to understand his wife's statement without the aid of a translation device. To his best understanding she'd stated 'Even pig shit attracts somebody.'

For some reason saying it in Tlillan made it all that more amusing, at least for the girls, McCann decided that shutting his mouth was probably the best strategy to take from here.

'Are we finished with our little spat?' inquired Malikah after she'd gathered herself.

Ilam pressed her palms again 'Namaste Xch'uup.'

Malikah's eyes turned to her father who merely raised his eyebrows before looking away and bringing them back down again. The sable Queen recognised his mark of compliance before continuing 'We have a job to do and we need to get it done soon.'

'What's that?' inquired McCann as he toasted the foot of his Habanos.

'The Neenayin, they must be dealt with.'

The Englishman grunted in disapproval as he blew out his first plume of smoke 'It's a bit late now isn't it? You could have taken them out but now you've let your enemy know that you know, and that you're coming for them.'

'And if we had said nothing would your people have permitted us to travel the globe executing their leaders?' asked Ilam in her superior tone.

McCann let the blue smoke roll out of his nostrils 'I suppose not, though you got that Yank to shoot his own President,' McCann chuckled to himself 'that was a good move. There's nothing more satisfying than watching politicians fighting to the death.'

Ilam's eyes returned to an almost transparent hue 'that situation cannot be replicated again, it is necessary we extinguish the Neenayin ourselves.'

McCann raised his coffee cup to his lips, after taking a sip he replaced it on the mat whilst shaking his head and chuckling to himself 'Oh I don't think so my dear, I have a ship to command and we're going on patrol, so I'm afraid you'll have to find someone else.'

Malikah raised her eyebrows 'And I'm your boss, am I not?'

The Englishman flopped back into his café seat 'What is this, Malee?'

Malee being a name he'd used for his daughter since she was first born, it was a term that until now only he, Ilam and of course Malikah had shared. Malikah was rather embarrassed by his use of her pet name but it didn't really matter since Lian was aware of it already.

Malikah gathered herself 'I don't understand?'

'Why do I feel that I'm being picked on all the time? It's none of my business about these reptilians and I'm certain there are people far more capable than I.'

Malikah softened her tone 'More capable? Yes. More trustworthy? No. I need you father, I need people I can entrust my life to, and those people are sitting at this table right now.'

McCann let out a sigh before taking a long drag on his Ramon Allones 'So Kim takes the chair on patrol?'

'Or until we're finished with the Neenayin,' stated his haughty wife.

'And how long is that gonna be?'

'Months, no less than two,' replied Ilam as she browsed the Net with her collar device.

'Marvellous.'

Lian chirped in 'But first Malee and I are going shopping.'

Ilam gave Lian an odd look, the familiarity was disturbing, she had heard the rumours which apparently were there for all to see in the Dreamscape. However the Amazon had denied such gossip, since the truth was probably too much for the mother of Xch'uup to take.

McCann grunted again 'Do you still have that gold card that Earle gave you?'

Malikah shook her head 'That would be uncouth.'

The Englishman put his arm around Ilam's slender waist 'Well pass it on to me, I'll take your mother out and we can go on a shopping spree!'

Ilam laughed out loud much to the surprise of Lian but not Malikah 'Father there's no need to be so crude.'

McCann scrunched his forehead at the Tlillan Empress 'Crude? I'm serious, no need to waste his hospitality; besides those bloody Yanks have been sucking on our teat for years now, time for some payback me thinks?'

Ilam found endless amusement in her husband's crudity; Lian was puzzled by the Tlillan sense of humour more than anything else.

Malikah was decidedly unentertained by her father's behaviour 'Put it on your account with the I.S.A, Kim has been informed of your absence. You and Mother have this weekend together before we begin our mission, I'll call you when needed, stay in New York both of you, understood?'

'Namaste Xch'uup,' replied Ilam.

McCann made a casual salute with his hand 'Understood Sir.'

The couples split up with Malikah and Lian taking a shopping trip on Fifth Avenue, 52nd street, the home of Malikah's favourite designer. Unfortunately spending so much time on Otoch had meant that visiting her favourite shop or even wearing their clothes was an impossibility. The Matriarchs on Otoch did not take well to Xch'uup dressed in Versace whilst presiding at Muul Kaah.

From the street its massive marble arches were very intimidating; a central arch permitted entrance into the fabulous store. Two flags flew from poles reaching out over the street, one of the Eastern States the other of Italy.

Lian had been brought up in New York; however clothes this high end were beyond the financial reach of even her father. He may have been a sub-Lieutenant on the Athena but to purchase anything at Versace would have cost half a year's wages.

The door opened as the pair strode inside, a tanned man rushed up to them 'Welcome back Miss Malikah, we've missed you terribly.'

Malikah hadn't set foot inside the store for a good 5 years, yet Matteo remembered her immediately. Lian wasn't impressed since she was Xch'uup, probably the most feared person in the known universe however what happened next made her heart jump.

Matteo, dressed in a fabulous dark green two piece suit, bowed at Malikah with hands pressed then did the same to her and said 'Namaste Miss Lian.'

'How do you know my name?' inquired the tall slender Amazon with jet black hair.

Matteo gave an expression which implied Lian had just asked a stupid question 'You work for Miss Malikah, you are her friend.'

There was an uncomfortable moment until Malikah spoke 'We're both here for a change of clothes, these Tlillan outfits are comfortable but ...'

Matteo waved his hands in the air 'Oh I understand, you all look as if there was a sale at Hi-Fash!'

The ladies giggled.

'Come with me I'll show you what you need to wear,' Matteo grabbed Malikah's hand and led her up the large marble staircase.

The store was a beautiful natural marble white with a fine golden mosaic on the floor bearing the Versace logo.

Lian was again taken aback by Matteo's familiarity, holding a matriarch by the hand in such a manner would cause a great kerfuffle on Otoch, let alone Xch'uup! However Malikah took no offence to the salesman's overfamiliarity. Besides, despite being a good looking Italian male wearing trousers that were a little too tight for him he was a blatant homosexual, even a Makayuuk female could have spotted him a mile off.

Leading them past the jewellery cases to the staircase then up onto the second floor the threesome were now in the women's clothing section. A small single floor, Versace's was not a large store at all, with this season's latest clothing.

Matteo looked over Lian and smiled 'You're the easy one,' he pulled out a fine red silk cheongsam inlaid with gold thread.

The sight took Lian's breath away; she'd only ever seen such fabulous pieces of art in a gallery or on the Net. The tall lady had to gather herself before she could manage to ask in a shaky voice 'How much is it?'

Matteo pulled a face, as if someone had just vomited onto the floor then another began to lick it off. The man was utterly disgusted by such a crude question 'How much? Do not speak these words again Miss Lian, not when you are inside Versace's!'

Malikah recalled the time he made the exact same statement to her.

Matteo shouted over his shoulder 'Christina!'

A young blonde lady in a business skirt and jacket walked over 'Yes Sir?'

'Here, this is for Miss Lian, help her put it on and get her the emerald slippers in the back.'

Christina took careful possession of the traditional Chinese dress 'Sir, those slippers are for the ambassadors ...'

Before she could finish her sentence Matteo turned to look at her with one of the most frightening expressions either Lian or Malikah had seen in their lives, and they'd both witnessed some pretty hellish glares.

Christina quickly replied before Matteo said anything 'the emerald slippers at the back, I understand, Sir.'

Christina smiled at Lian 'Please follow me Miss,' then led her to the changing rooms.

When they were out of sight Malikah grinned 'You scared me for a moment there Matteo.'

Matteo smiled and gave a little chuckle 'You are very funny Miss Malikah.'

Malikah raised her eyebrows 'I wasn't joking, that face could have brought a Matriarch to her knees. I think you should go easy on the poor girl.'

Matteo chuckled again 'Are you looking for anything in particular Miss Malikah, or would you like to have a browse first?'

'Something that an Empress could wear to both a ball and an official event, something like the G8 and the Oscars, if you understand me?'

Matteo rubbed his chin 'Hmm, would you be with Miss Lian?'

It was obvious to Malikah that their relationship was understood by Matteo, yet the sable Queen appreciated his discretion 'Yes,' replied Malikah with a smile.

Matteo thought for a few seconds 'So classy but still sexy yet intimidating at the same time?'

'Do you have anything fitting those criteria?'

'Come with me Miss Malikah,' Matteo led her excitedly to a large wardrobe behind the counter 'this is not to be placed in the store for another week, it is yet to hit the runway. But since it is you I can allow next seasons look to be aired.'

Matteo pressed his thumb onto the black scanner pad opening a laser scanner, peering into it; the AI scanned his retina and opened the wardrobe. The container for Versace's' next season was of military standards, it would have been easier to rob a bank than Matteo's store. The wardrobe was constructed of Catronium, a tough carbon-neutronium compound, which went through the floor and onto the superstructure of the building where it had been welded in place.

The door swung open to reveal an array of beautiful clothes soon to hit the catwalk during New York fashion week, one of the largest events on the fashion calendar. Matteo pulled out the first dress, made out of a PVC material.

Malikah shook her head 'Too slutty, especially for Otoch.'

He placed it back in then pulled out his next choice, he presented the long dark dress pants to Malikah. Matteo noticed her look of approval and pulled out the accompanying head scarf, the same soft black velvet with a black veil cast over the back displayed the face in full. The head scarf also carried a beautiful red sheer veil with amazingly intricate work in silk with pearls sewn in.

Malikah quickly took the dress pants from Matteo's arms to examine it in detail. The cuffs draped down, widening from the elbow to the wrist; the same red design used on the head scarf was displayed in the lining which draped out from the cuffs. The cuffs also had a fabulous design, rather than cufflinks three oblong and square red gems of different sizes were sewn in a line on each cuff along the top of the fore arm.

On the front a large necklace wrapped around the neckline and dropped down covering the breasts (not that they weren't already covered with the velvet material of the dress). The jewellery was made of similar gems, all slightly different shapes and sizes but of a rosy colour. There was a little variation in the gems but not enough that any would seem out of place in the fabulous triangle plunging down with its base at the wearer's neck line and point at the breasts.

'Could you make it to fit?' inquired Malikah.

'Of course,' replied Matteo 'and I have the shoes to go with it.'

'Hmmm, what about these?' Malikah lifted one foot up from the floor to show Matteo her boots.

'I suppose you could get away with it, besides you don't really need high heels do you. Just make sure they don't shine, is that possible?'

Malikah thought for a moment and as Matteo was examining the boots they suddenly lost their shine, turning a much duller shade of black.

'I suppose being Grand Matriarch does have its perks, yes?' exclaimed Matteo.

Malikah smiled as she passed the clothes back to Matteo, Lian and Christina then exited the changing rooms.

'Mr Del Sarto, Miss Lian is satisfied with the Cheongsam however I'm afraid it will need to be fitted, along with the slippers,' stated Christina in her New York accent.

Matteo made a frustrated look 'Yes I know, did you get Miss Lian's measurements?'

'Oh I ...'

Matteo put his hand on head 'Please somebody help me,' he once again turned to the young assistant and in a shaky tone spoke as calmly as possible 'then why don't you get a tape measure and ask Miss Lian if you may take her measurements.'

Christina smiled 'Yes Sir, Miss Lian may I take your measurements?'

Lian who felt rather uncomfortable nodded her head 'Certainly,' and followed Christina as she retrieved a tape measure.

Malikah grinned 'You didn't ask for mine Matteo,' thinking she'd caught the local lord of fashion short.

Matteo raised a single eyebrow 'You're 40-30-38.'

Malikah was taken aback by the manager's intimate knowledge 'How on Earth did you find that out?'

Matteo chuckled to himself 'I can take measurements by eye Miss Malikah, I'm not handicapped.'

Lian walked out from the dressing room with Christina.

'Do you have Miss Lian's measurements?' shouted Matteo.

'Yes Sir, and her foot size, Sir.'

'Now write them down before you forget, I don't want a repeat of last week!'

Lian smiled at Matteo and asked in total innocence 'What happened last week?'

Matteo shuddered 'It was the worst week of my life, we had Jennifer Patterson and her family fitted for fashion week.'

Matteo took a very deep breath as he prepared to speak 'Then after they had left a certain person deleted their entire order from the computer system.'

Lian put a hand on Matteo's shoulder 'Owwh, that's terrible who did that to you?'

Matteo's face once again changed into a grimace that would have caused a great white shark to flee for its life 'Perhaps you should ask Christina? Oh I'm sorry she was too busy sending erotic texts of herself in expensive lingerie, intended for customers only, to her boyfriend ... weren't you Christina?'

'Yes Sir,' replied the shop floor attendant as she hung her head in shame.

Matteo continued 'Ah but don't worry no-one will know about it because she always deletes the sex texts she receives, before an idiot such as myself could possibly see them, am I right Christina?'

'Yes Sir,' replied the thoroughly miserable young lady.

'Next time just make sure you delete the pictures of your loser boyfriend, rather than the biggest celebrity in the music industry's million credit order along with her entire family's details!'

'Yes Sir.'

'Thank goodness Miss Patterson has an understanding nature, no doubt she has been forced to manage village idiots herself!'

'Yes Sir.'

Matteo realised he had been rambling far too long on the subject 'my apologies ladies this is none of your concern, your clothes shall be ready tomorrow you may pick them up whenever you wish.'

Malikah smiled 'Thank you Matteo, we'll see you tomorrow and thank you too Christina you've been most helpful.'

Christina smiled and pressed her palms together 'Namaste Malikah,' much to Matteo's displeasure.

The Manager led the two out of the store and onto the street which by now was covered with paparazzi.

The holographic cameras clicked as press climbed over each other to get photographs and ask questions. Malikah held Lian in place as she scanned the scene, ignoring the interrogation concerning an alleged conspiracy to take over the planet the sable Goddess focused on a single man. He carried no equipment common to the press, but wore a dark blue leisure suit whilst attempting to be inconspicuous.

The pair made eye contact, causing the man of average height in his mid-20's to seemingly panic. The strange man made a break out of the crowd lining the street, brandishing a fully automatic pulse pistol.

A scream went up from the press; some dived for cover whilst others ran forwards to get the best angle as the military grade weapon let out a whine. The firearm was something like an old style Uzi, only it fired multiple tungsten rounds and this assassin was about to pepper his target before she could stop him.

Just as the weapon reached full charge and the whine disappeared her assassin stood frozen for a moment. He dropped his arms letting the firearm fall to the pavement. He then fell forward onto the weapon revealing Icarus brandishing a pair of traditional Tezcatlipoca daggers, dripping with the would be killer's blood.

Before anyone could say or do anything further Icarus sheathed his blades, spread his wings and took flight, his cloak obscuring him from normal vision.

The press took pictures of the creature as they clamoured around the body; police pushed their way to the corpse, arriving in time to certify him dead.

Lian eyed the dead assassin laying in a pool of his own blood as the police called for assistance 'Close call, Malee,' she whispered.

Malikah peered at her girlfriend with a cheeky smile 'Nowhere near close.'

A policeman approached Malikah holding his tablet and pencil 'Madam may I have your full name please?'

'Malikah'

The stout cop looked her in the eye with disbelief 'You mean Malikah McCann, the Grand Matriarch?'

She nodded with a smile.

'And your friend?'

Lian smiled 'Miss Lian Zhao.'

The stout man in his 40's scribbled their names down on the tablet, despite the fact it was recording everything they said, 'could you describe to me what you saw Miss Malikah?'

'Certainly, we exited Versace here, after shopping for some new outfits, and were overwhelmed by the press. This young man you see in the gutter pulled out an automatic pulse pistol, charged it and aimed at me. Fortunately my bodyguard, Icarus, was on hand to prevent this psychopath.'

The police Officer turned to Lian 'And you can confirm Malikah's account of these events?'

Lian nodded 'Yes Sir.'

The Policeman smiled 'You don't have to call me Sir, I work for a living.'

The towering ladies smiled.

'May I ask for your personal contact signatures, in case we need to contact you both for further inquiries?'

Malikah extended her wrist until the small tablet attached to it was beside the policeman's tablet 'Feel free Officer.'

The portly man tapped his tablet, waited a few moments then thanked Malikah after it had accepted her details. He did the same with Lian before allowing them to leave the scene with a police escort, not that they required it.

Riding in the back of the police car Lian commented 'I don't know who was more dangerous, that man or Matteo.'

Malikah smiled 'Matteo, for sure.'

Lian laughed 'Why's that?'

'Matteo has a level of willpower few beings, Human or otherwise, could ever hope to achieve; just because he runs Versace doesn't make his mind any less impressive.'

Lian raised her eyes upwards as she considered what had just been said 'Yes, you're correct, his level of commitment is beyond even some Makayuuk and that is saying quite a lot.'

Malikah continued 'As for the assassin, he was merely an idiot with a gun and too much time on his hands. Wasting your time on Net shows about Nostradamus, the Rothschilds and preparing for Armageddon doesn't end constructively.'

'How do you know all that about him?'

Malikah grinned 'I knew long before we exited Versace that he was laying in wait, I informed Icarus and waited.'

'Why did you wait?'

'I wanted his demise to be witnessed by the press and the public; I want everyone to know what happens to those who try to stand against me.'

Lian ran her hand along Malikah's forearm 'Except for me, right?'

Malikah took Lian's hand and kissed it 'If Machine attempts to destroy me a third time I'll have to send Matteo.'

Lian burst out in laughter; they both had a good laugh as the police escorted the couple to their hotel. A train of armoured vehicles pulled up to the street level entrance of The Plaza, Gregory Trent was ready and waiting as his staff escorted them into the reception hall.

Malikah's parents were there also, McCann rushed towards his daughter grabbing her arms 'What the bloody hell happened? Are you alright?'

Malikah took his arms 'Didn't Mother tell you?'

'Yes but I want to hear it from you.'

Malikah had linked with her mother on the way to the hotel, informing her of the events and that she was unharmed. McCann however was not satisfied to accept what his wife told him; despite the fact he knew she was right.

'I'm fine Father, as is Lian.'

Ilam sneered at the representative of the Makayuuk 'Fortune is a hard mistress.'

Everyone turned to look at Ilam, 'That she is Mother,' replied Malikah.

The Englishman returned his gaze to his daughter 'Thank God that bloody pet of yours was there, seems to me it does have its uses after all.'

'Calm yourself Father; we have to prepare for our first inquisition.'

'Inquisition?'

'Yes, they will be holding the G8 next week in Geneva, we have all been invited.'

McCann made an incredulous tone 'Invited to the G8?'

Malikah smirked a little at her father's naivety 'William has made it so, I and Mother are guests of honour, you and Lian shall be our guests.'

'So who's a lizard at the G8 then?'

'We shall find out when we get there, be prepared Father they won't allow you to carry your pistol but you may carry a ceremonial sabre.'

McCann shook his head 'So you're gonna fight an inter-dimensional parasite with a sword?'

Ilam let out a sigh 'No-one is allowed firearms in the G8 conference my dear.'

McCann hated it when she called him that, it always made him feel inferior, the fact she was half a foot taller than him and three times as strong didn't help either.

'Wonderful,' replied McCann with as much sarcasm as he could muster without making a total fool of himself.

Malikah patted her Father's side trying to comfort him, she then turned to Lian 'And I have something for you Lian.'

The Voice of Machine's eyes lit up.

'Gregory?' called Malikah.

Greg appeared from behind the reception desk 'Yes Miss Malikah?'

'Do you have my package?'

'Certainly Miss Malikah,' the manager snapped his fingers and two young bell boys ran into the back before walking out carrying a rather long briefcase between them.

'Would you like it delivered to your room?'

'No, just on the table here will be fine.'

The two young lads heaved the carbon layered black case onto the marble topped coffee table next to Malikah.

The Sable Queen thanked the two young men dressed in their tight uniforms as they trundled off.

Next she turned to Lian 'For you.'

Lian approached the case, mystified as to what might be inside the four foot long case. Lian only needed to touch the case and it read her DNA, its locks flicked open inviting the young Amazon to satisfy her curiosity.

Turning a single lock on the handle caused the case to open slightly; Lian pushed the lid back, swinging it all the way until open at a 90 degree angle.

Inside lay what McCann recognised as a set of three Japanese swords, he knew the long one was called a katana but was ignorant as to the names and uses of the other two. If anyone was aware of this type of thing it was Ryu, he was strictly a European fencer.

Lian's eyes sparkled a shade of pink along with Malikah as she picked up the sheathed katana. The towering Amazon unsheathed the weapon to reveal a dark coloured blade.

'Is it neutronium?' inquired Lian as if she were a child on her birthday.

Malikah grinned with a pink hue filling her eyes 'Yes, forged on Otoch to exact specifications. The skin for the grip was imported from Japan.'

The Valkyrie examined the grip 'Real stingray?'

'Do you like it?'

Lian quickly wiped her eye before a tear could fully form 'Of course I do.'

'I thought you'd need something to take with you to the G8, since everyone else has a weapon.'

Ilam folded her arms 'A neutronium blade? Would steel have not been satisfactory?'

Malikah's eyes widened at her mother 'Satisfactory, perhaps, but this is a gift and Xch'uup does not bestow mediocre gifts.'

Lian examined the black lacquered wooden scabbard before she gave Malikah a massive hug 'Thank you I love it.'

Ilam was quite shocked by her familiarity with not just her daughter but also the Tlillan Grand Matriarch, a most improper method of behaviour in her opinion. Ilam looked at her husband with an expression of desperation, McCann returned her gaze with a pathetic shrug of his shoulders. After all what did she expect him to do? His Daughter was a woman and beside that she wasn't hurting anybody, just traumatising her Mother.

McCann looked sceptically at the blade 'Do you know how to use one of those things?'

The Voice of Machine swung the blade with one hand, bringing the tip to a dead stop at the end of McCann's nose 'I trained in Kenjutsu, here in New York, for many years Mr McCann.'

The Englishman politely pushed the heavy blade aside, away from his face, 'Don't you mean Kendo?'

'No, Kenjutsu.'

McCann scowled 'What's the difference?'

'Kenjutsu tends to be more, how can I say it? Brutal?'

McCann made a sarcastic grunt 'Puh, now why doesn't that surprise me?'

'I didn't want to train with the other girls; I wanted to follow in my Father's footsteps. You see he began to study Kenjutsu after he was recruited by the Japanese to serve on the Ito,' Lian whipped the blade back, returning it to the scabbard with pin point accuracy.

McCann shook his head 'So you run around in big pants whacking each other on the head with bits of bamboo all day whilst screaming blue murder?'

Lian giggled at the Englishman's jibe 'Not quite, but it was either that or running around poking people in white jump suits with antennae, besides I'm not a big Elvis fan either.'

'So what did you do at this Kenjutsu School?'

'We used solid wooden swords, mainly, and for the most part we didn't use armour. It wasn't long before I learnt not to get hit.'

McCann scowled again 'Your mother must've been bloody mad letting you do that, you could've had your head split open!'

Lian placed the Katana back in the case before inspecting the two smaller blades 'My mother was unaware for the first two years, by the time she discovered what I had been doing I was already about to take my Shodan. I could defeat my Hanshi after my first year and he was Rokudan.'

McCann had no idea what the young lady was talking about but assumed that she was attempting to intimate how far she'd progressed in the discipline in such a short time.

The tall Amazon inspected all three blades and placed them safely inside the case 'Being half Tlillan allows me to form a link with my Hanshi, it makes for a far easier learning curve, although it would be impossible for me to have progressed in the rankings any quicker … the Japanese are really anal that way.'

The Englishman raised his eyebrows 'I see, well, now that that's all cleared up why don't we get ready for dinner?'

Malikah smiled in relief 'An Excellent Idea, what time?'

'We shall be in the restaurant within one hour,' stated Ilam.

Lian picked up her sword case as she followed Malikah into the elevator 'See you then,' said the Tlillan Queen in a cheerful tone.

Ilam spoke to her husband in a hushed tone 'What do you believe is occurring between them?'

The Englishman peered up at his wife 'Ilam, you really don't want to know.'

The red haired Valkyrie made a piercing stare as the elevator closed 'Then it is true?'

McCann didn't know exactly what his wife was thinking of, but it couldn't have been any more shocking than the truth so he replied 'Yup.'

Ilam sighed 'Why?'

'I don't know,' replied her husband 'but you have a daughter and that's more than most are left with after Bandayuuk.'

Ilam was shattered inside and McCann sensed it, the tall beauty stated stoically 'Didn't Ryu always say that it is better to grab a shit than grab a fart?'

The Englishman nodded as he starred at the elevator door 'Something like that.'

The next day Versace's had been cordoned off by the police, Matteo was practically having an orgasm as he considered the amount of publicity his customers were bringing in. Matteo may not have owned any stake in the fashion house of Versace, however he was the best store manager on the planet and wherever he went a long list of well to do and famous clientele followed.

He worked in New York many years ago when Malikah first brought her three prodigies to Earth. The manager at Channel was a competent and respected worker. His clientele were well to do but still rather modest in the world of high fashion. That all changed the day Malikah and the girls made a visit to his store and when they returned after fashion week the game was on to have Matteo. The slim Italian in his mid-thirties soon became the most desired item of any fashion house.

It was a surprise when he went to Versace since Versace was neither the most successful nor had they made the largest offer, quite the opposite. The Italian fashion house had fallen upon hard times and for many years struggled to stay in that top echelon; many believed they would soon give in and begin selling in common high street stores before going totally bankrupt.

Fortunately for them Matteo was a strong nationalist and had always loved Versace, he left Channel with a heavy heart but arrived at Versace in elation. The Italian Fashion house was as shocked as they were pleased at the turn of events; Matteo had taken one of the most modest offers, to manage the flagship store of a fashion house that may not be there next year. They had only made an offer on the request of their chairman's daughter, who incidentally shopped at the Channel store Matteo had managed, though she never let on to her father.

When Matteo entered the store on 52nd street he brought in with him the four most famous women in the galaxy. After fashion week the press had been clambering over each other to get an interview, Malikah ended up on Vogue much to Ilam's disdain. Kaeo managed to get the front cover of Elle much to her grandmother's pride; in Thailand that copy of Elle out sold every murder magazine combined for the entire year, quite a feat.

As for Versace their fortunes did a U-turn on a dime, the girls had the same effect on them as Channel. The year before, after fashion week in New York, the chairman bemoaned how he couldn't give away their designs. Once they'd got Matteo women had to force their way in past the crowds, film stars hired groups of burly men to push a path inside the store for them.

The Versace perfume which Amitra let be known she had purchased, thanks to Matteo's suggestion, could not be found. According to Jerry Habeeb several armed robberies had taken place in Mumbai, perfume being the target … Versace perfume. Jerry pointed out how cash money, 22 carat gold coins, had been ignored by the thieves; Versace perfume was worth more than its weight in gold.

'Miss Malikah you've had your hair done?' squeaked Matteo as the ladies strolled through the front door.

Smiling with satisfaction the slim goddess replied 'You're the only man to have noticed so far Matteo!'

'Madam, when you have a new hairdo the world notices, trust me!'

Malikah's hair was cut short and straight 'I believe it makes me look younger, what do you think Matteo?'

The short Italian scoffed 'Pah, you need to look young? Besides you have the Ixchel, Xch'uup will not lose the glow of youth for another 500 years!'

Malikah smirked in embarrassment, her eyes turned slightly pink before she replied 'Oh Matteo, you can be such an arse kisser!'

Matteo laughed 'True, but if I'm going to kiss ass why not choose the fairest and most aromatic?'

The little Italian dressed in his white suit and black shirt skirted around Malikah then passed behind Lian 'Not bad work, I have seen Roberto do worse; I hope he didn't charge you?'

Lian gave Matteo a puzzled look 'I'm sorry?'

The short Italian strolled back in front of the ladies 'You did go to 2b, didn't you?'

Before Malikah could reply Lian intervened 'Yes, I'm sure it was on the Net.'

He examined Lian's hair which had been lifted up into a bun and held in place with traditional Chinese hair pins 'And this is definitely Roberto's work.'

The Voice of Machine scowled 'How do you know who did my hair? We only just left.'

'He just knows,' interrupted Malikah as Matteo led them upstairs to collect their clothing.

Standing at the counter Christina produced the clothes individually wrapped in carbon based textile dust covers alongside Lian's boxed shoes.

Lian made that expression a little girl would when collecting a new toy at a shop, the can I have it now look, towards her partner.

Matteo witnessed the young lady and spoke before Malikah could 'You may put them on inside the dressing room,' he pointed at the swords the ladies carried on their waists 'will you be wearing these things?'

Malikah assured the Italian 'We'll put them on ourselves, Matteo.'

Matteo made a grimace 'Blood is very difficult to wash out of these clothes Miss Malikah.'

Malikah smiled 'Don't be concerned, they're like the clothes, for show.'

Christina led Lian into the dressing room first, 5 minutes later Lian exited looking absolutely radiant. The perfect Chinese goddess, only a foot taller and wearing a pair of Japanese swords made on Otoch from Neutronium, an almost unbreakable substance.

A red scarf tied the blades to her body in the traditional manner of a samurai, 'Malikah smiled, you look gorgeous.'

Matteo grinned in satisfaction, more at Malikah's words of approval than Lian's ability to wear Versace's cheongsam perfectly 'Of course she does Miss Malikah, now it's your turn.'

After nearly ten minutes Malikah reappeared from the dressing room looking as elegant and intimidating as ever, her Tlillan sabre hung from her side announcing that this lady was not to be trifled with.

'Fabulous Miss Malikah, fabulous as always,' clapped the joyous manager.

Christina was about to hand back the clothes they'd changed out of 'Here you are ladies,' she said presenting the dust covers and shoe box.

Matteo made an expression of utter horror 'Stop! You will carry their luggage.'

Christina made a look of puzzlement 'To the hotel?'

The little Italian's eyes grew about 400% in size, at least that's the impression Lian got, 'And if I ask you to carry their bags to the hotel, would that be a problem for princess?'

Matteo's voice was now coming out in an unmistakeable sinister tone which caused Malikah some unease.

Christina a lovely young lady in her 20's though not the sharpest twig on the tree had to think for a moment, further enraging her boss.

Before Matteo exploded Malikah spoke to the befuddled Christina 'Thank you it would be very kind of you to carry our bags back for us.'

Christina smiled and nodded 'You're welcome Madame.'

Matteo then moved close to Malikah and in a hushed tone spoke 'I must apologise Miss Malikah.'

'Please don't ...'

'No, for what I am about to ask.'

Matteo had never asked anything of her before, quite the opposite he had done nothing but give; even these clothes were without any charge.

The Tlillan Queen was curious 'Ask what, Matteo?'

Matteo was very uncomfortable about something, he continued in a whisper not that there was any more than the four of them on the entire floor 'I spoke with the Chairman last night.'

'And?'

Lian was about to fall over from leaning as she listened in on the conversation.

'It is very embarrassing, but he requested if you might allow a few holographs on the sidewalk, outside?'

'For who?'

Matteo cleared his throat, since Malikah had not said no already he felt a little more confident 'the owner of Elle in the UK, she requested an exclusive and perhaps an interview?'

Malikah sniggered to herself; she found Matteo's state of agitation rather amusing, 'What do you think?'

Matteo cleared his throat again 'It would be good for you, after what happened in the Senate and all these conspiracy theories flying about. Trust me if you are both on the cover of ELLE, 50% of the population won't give a shit about world domination or inter-dimensional zombies. Then that 50% will make sure their husbands and boyfriends shut up about it and before you know it you're the woman every other woman wants to be and every man wants; and when they find out you are both sleeping together trust me every man will be reading that copy of ELLE!'

Malikah raised her eyebrows, a facial expression she had in common with her father 'Will you make anything from this?'

Matteo smiled nervously 'No, but they are paying Mr Angelo 10,000 British gold Sovereigns.'

Malikah thought for a moment 'Get me Mr Angelo; I want to speak to him now.'

Matteo pulled out a tablet from inside his white jacket, he tapped it a few times and the tablet began to ring as it made the connection to the Chairman's office. The tablet managed to ring twice but the Chairman of Versace picked it up before a third could be started 'Yes?' came a hurried voice.

'It is Matteo, Mr Angelo.'

'What did she say?'

'Miss Malikah wishes to speak with you, Sir.'

'Put her on, Matteo.'

The little Italian handed her the small tablet.

Malikah accepted the small shiny piece of carbon plastic and narrowed her eyes at the image of the Versace chairman 'Mr Angelo?'

'Yes?'

'This is Malikah.'

'Hello Miss Malikah I'm honoured just to speak with you, is there anything I might do for you.'

'About this holo-shoot and interview with ELLE.'

'Yes?'

'How much are you getting paid by ELLE for this?'

It was a rather impolite question, nevertheless despite his shock Mr Angelo still had to answer it 'Well They have offered to pay 5,000 sovereigns.'

Malikah's eyes slinked over to look at Matteo before giving him a cheeky grin; she knew Matteo would not lie to her 'I and Lian will do it under one condition Mr Angelo.'

'Yes, anything.'

'That Matteo is paid 2,500 British gold sovereigns, I think that's fair.'

The line went silent, Matteo waved his hand silently indicating 'no' but Malikah just grinned back.

Finally there was a reply 'That's a lot of money Miss Malikah.'

'Yes, half of what you're receiving; besides if it weren't for Matteo I would never consider such a proposition, but if you would rather not ...'

'NO! Matteo will have his sovereigns, you have my word.'

Malikah winked at Matteo who was close to having seizure, fearing his career was over. Though ending his career with a 2,500 sovereign payoff would leave him a very rich man.

Malikah spoke softly to the Chairman of Versace 'Very good Mr Angelo, I expect you to keep your word and thank you for your hospitality.'

The Chairman sounded as if he's just given birth 'Yes, yes, you're welcome and thank you again Miss Malikah you shall always be welcome at Versace.'

Malikah hit the disconnect button then returned the tablet to Matteo 'There you go Matteo and why not give Christina here a few hundred sovereigns?'

Matteo was sweating profusely, his hands shook as he replaced the tablet 'Yes Miss Malikah,' he replied in a shaky voice.

'Christina,' called Malikah 'Follow us.'

Malikah and Lian stepped outside; the entire street had been blocked off at both ends with only a crew of journalists from ELLE allowed to wait outside. The pair stood outside the marble and glass doorway to Versace, Lian took great pleasure in all the attention whilst she practiced her holo pose made famous in the 21st century by the designer Victoria Beckham.

Malikah almost laughed as she observed Voice of Machine basking in the attention of every cameraman as they called out requesting a glance here and a smile there.

Chapter 17

The following week the family of four were on board a hummingbird, flying to I.S.A headquarters in Geneva. McCann sat next to his wife, opposite Malikah and Lian; he was conspicuously reading a hard copy of ELLE. The cover of the Magazine had a 3-D picture of Malikah smirking with arms folded, beside her stood the beautiful Lian in her red shiny cheongsam. Samurai blades hung from either side of that slim waist every human woman would kill for as she struck a Beckham pose.

The cover was sensational, almost as sensational as the interview inside. ELLE had broken all records on both digital and hard sales, Ilam was furious.

Malikah's fiery hearted Mothers' eyes had been a similar colour the entire trip. McCann assumed she'd been conveying her displeasure telepathically for the journey, though he decided he wasn't going to ask.

McCann read the interview, quickly added before release, which had taken up several pages, 'Hmm very interesting,' came his voice from behind the magazine.

Ilam clenched her teeth together and seethed 'Will you desist from reading such filth.'

Malikah's eyes widened at Ilam, the red headed Amazon said nothing and turned her gaze towards the window by her seat.

'Well it's far more readable than the interview Louis gave,' noted McCann as he closed the autumn edition of ELLE and took another look at his daughter on the cover 'and you're both far more attractive than that grizzly Frenchman.'

The sable Empress pressed her eyebrows together quizzically.

'Oh it was before you were born, they found out he was a shirt tail lifter and Faraday forced, or tried to force him to do an interview with some magazine,' commented McCann almost matter of factly.

'Really? Which magazine?' inquired Malikah.

McCann laughed 'Oh don't bother I've had better times sitting through one of those awful Korean soap operas, honestly it was utter rubbish. The front cover was awful, that nasty French face glaring back as if he was about to breathe fire.'

His sable daughter replied whilst holding Lian's hand affectionately 'Father, Louis is quite a good looking man.'

The Englishman peered over at his wife 'Yes, as I remember your mother was very drawn to him.'

Malikah and Lian fixed their gazes upon Ilam with shock.

Ilam looked away from the view outside and placed her piercing stare upon McCann. Ilam's Tlillan eyes burnt as coals, McCann could almost feel the rage searing into his skin.

'Or not,' added the Englishman quickly.

The remainder of the journey was uneventful; an awkward silence prevailed until they landed at I.S.A HQ just off Lake Geneva.

Stepping out of the Hummingbird and onto the landing pad the party was greeted by William Faraday and Dr Valorie Pitt.

Faraday quickly approached Ilam 'It's wonderful to see you again Ilam,' he said in that stiff English accent much to Ilam's pleasure.

Faraday kissed her hand before shaking McCann's 'Good to see you again old boy.'

'Good to be back,' replied McCann with a smile.

Faraday glanced over his Admiral's shoulder to get an eyeful of the two ladies stepping off the aircraft 'There's a turn-up for the books, who would have ever thought?'

McCann smirked 'Almost as shocking as a Director caught using escorts half is age, aye?'

Faraday gave McCann a grim expression 'Quite.'

Malikah approached Faraday and before he could say anything she greeted him 'Namaste Director Faraday.'

Lian also bowed before the old Etonian 'Namaste Director Faraday.'

The old Etonian returned their greeting pressing his palms together and bowing his head 'Namaste.'

Malikah walked through the group to greet Valorie; after they had returned respectful hellos Malikah smiled 'Congratulations on your marriage.'

McCann was unaware of the details concerning her marriage. Without obtaining any further information he was already sceptical considering Valorie's track record.

All of the Tlillans present sensed his cynicism. Ilam, having calmed down concerning the ELLE interview, looked down upon her husband 'Duncan, that is very rude!'

The Englishman peered up at his towering Valkyrie of a wife 'Excuse me?'

'We all felt it Duncan, don't deny your emotions.'

McCann sneered and replied quietly 'Look who's talking.'

Before Ilam could reply to his jibe Malikah shouted on the windy landing pad as the Jet D'eau fired into the sky 'Enough Father, apologise for your poor manners.'

McCann scowled, Faraday was puzzled but Valorie had guessed McCann's response to her marriage.

'Valorie didn't hear me think,' protested the Englishman.

'No, but we did and it was most unpleasant,' retorted Malikah.

The Admiral pulled a tubos out of his jacket 'Please accept my apologies Valorie, no offence was intended,' after Dr Pitt accepted his apology he made a mocking smile in his Daughter's direction.

'And Mother?' ordered the Empress of the Tlillan commonwealth.

McCann rolled his eyes, took his wife's hand and got down upon one knee 'Please accept my apologies, for what I just said and the entire flight here.'

Ilam's eyes betrayed a shade of pink as she replied 'You are forgiven.'

Faraday looked about him at the pilots and Vympel guards 'Are we all finished? It's getting rather chilly up here.'

The party took the elevator down following Faraday into the main operations centre. At the central obsidian table Faraday accepted his warm coffee from Miss Dutta, to which McCann raised a suspicious eyebrow; causing Ilam to deal a fairly painful yet discreet blow to his back.

'So it seems that you're no longer a witch young lady,' jested Faraday over his coffee.

The sable Goddess chuckled 'I'm sure the press already have a down payment on another at Salem's Lot.'

'Yes, the trail by ELLE was a bloody good idea young lady, who came up with that plan?'

Ilam paid special attention to her daughter's reply.

'ELLE wanted a cover with us on it to boost sales, Versace wanted us on the cover in front of their flagship store and I needed good publicity.'

'It seems that Tlillan brand of destiny has worked in your favour again young lady; or as your father would say good fortune!'

McCann found Faraday's jovial mood rather depressing, it worried him, Faraday was an inherently stressed character and his lack of visible strain concerned the Englishman.

'We're here about the G8 William,' interjected McCann studying the Chairman carefully for a stereotypical reaction.

'Yes of course you are, they'll all be meeting at the old U.N. building in a few days.'

McCann was taken aback at the old Etonian's lack of concern 'It seems that some of these world leaders are being manipulated by an alien influence, William.'

'Really? So you're here to save the day are you old chap?' replied Faraday in a light hearted tone.

'Have you been smoking something Faraday?' inquired McCann in a very blunt tone.

'Smoking something old boy? What in the blue blazes are you blathering on about?'

Miss Dutta came back with a coffee for McCann, she smiled at him and he caught a worried look from Dr Pitt. The Englishman's narrowed eyes then flicked over to Faraday who had gone from jovial to quite uncomfortable. It didn't take a direct link to the Dreamscape to tell what was going on here and naturally McCann was the last to find out.

'Namaste Miss Dutta,' said McCann as he accepted her coffee 'I'll bet that you bring a smile to William's face each time your coffee reaches his desk.'

Colour drained from Faraday's face, there was more tension around that table than on the cord of a bungee jumping elephant.

Miss Dutta gave an extremely awkward smile 'Yes Admiral, please excuse me I must return to my station.'

The Englishman smirked as he placed his coffee on the table; he gave Faraday a sneaky look before saying in a cheeky tone 'Said the actress to the Bishop!'

Miss Dutta walked away to her nearby station in the mission control centre, the other workers on duty kept to themselves, carrying on with their tasks.

Faraday quickly returned to a familiar state 'That'll be enough of that,' he said in an angered but suppressed tone.

McCann retorted 'I bet you haven't said those words in a long time old chap.'

Ilam unimpressed by her husband's goading folded her arms 'Duncan, you amuse no-one but yourself.'

McCann gave Lian a sly look causing the young lady to crack a smile 'I wouldn't say that my dear.'

Ilam sighed 'Please Duncan, you are humiliating others besides William.'

Giving his wife an impish grin he said 'Some of us enjoy a bit of humiliation every now and again, my dear.'

Even Ilam cracked a smile despite her best efforts to retain a cold Tlillan facade.

Dr Pitt piped up since she refused to watch her friend humiliated any further 'Well done Duncan.'

McCann lost his impish grin 'I'm sorry Valorie?'

'No, I don't think you are Duncan. However we're all willing to wait until you've finished with your puerile, sexual innuendos. I'm quite certain the staff will go home with a very different impression of you today, especially Miss Dutta.'

Now it was McCann who felt humiliation as Dr Pitt exposed him for all to see in the control centre 'My apologies William,' stated the Englishman in a sullen tone before sipping on his coffee.

Malikah glared down at her father in disappointment 'Perhaps we can get on with business now?'

There was no reply.

The Tlillan Queen continued 'William, let it be known that we are coming to the G8 and will be exposing the Neenayin.'

Faraday sipped on his warm drink 'Certainly, I'll have that Habeeb transmit it on his program tonight.'

McCann scowled at his daughter 'Why on Earth are we telling them we're coming?'

Her father's naivety gave Malikah a warm smile 'Because we're not, I've already seen the path of least resistance. We shall let everyone know we're coming and before the conference the Neenayin will attempt to escape the system.'

McCann still didn't understand her reasoning 'Won't it make capturing them more difficult? I mean we're gonna have to run around anyway.'

'Because this way we can gather them all in one place, eliminating them in a single strike. Otherwise some will flee Earth, some will remain and we'll spend months darting from place to place, I don't want to do that.'

Faraday spoke 'Are you aware of how they intend to flee Earth?'

The sable Queen nodded her head 'They'll hijack the Clotho and abscond with it to the galactic core, where the Neenayin believe I will not follow.'

Faraday peered at Lian 'What about Machine, is it going to help?'

The Voice of the Makayuuk replied 'Machine is prepared to co-operate in full, the Pixoa must be cleansed.'

'Habeeb has been notified,' informed Faraday as he tapped his wrist tablet.

'Good, now we must prepare Athena for a mission to the galactic core. Her electro-magnetic shields have to be strengthened,' ordered Malikah.

'As you wish,' replied Faraday tapping his wrist 'do you intend to retrieve the Clotho?'

'No,' the table became tense again 'The Dreamscape is plain, the chances of retrieving the Clotho in any form are almost nil. I need the best Vympel units you have, is Nestor's team available?'

Faraday shook his head 'No, he is still on Adnoara, Amitrasudan requires his team to be there.'

McCann interjected 'My team on Athena can handle it; Kapitan Egorov is as good a man as any I've worked with.'

Malikah let out a puff of air as she thought deeply on the subject 'Fine, though these will be very difficult fighting conditions.'

'Difficult? All we need to do is fire a broadside into the Clotho, right?'

'No Father, we must board them and make certain every single body is accounted for.'

'Well Egorov won't have any problems dealing with a bunch of milk sop politicians!'

'The Galactic core will be the greatest opponent of all. We must surmount high radiation levels, tidal forces exerted upon us by clusters of stars and its supermassive black hole. Finally the greatest hurdle will be the space/time warp, conventional firearms shall become too dangerous to use.'

McCann scowled 'Pulse rifles useless?'

Malikah nodded 'Time distortion will make aiming and hitting a target nigh on impossible for most Humans.'

'Humans?'

'And Tlillans, due to the distortion of normal time and space melee combat is the only viable option,' Malikah withdrew her mantle from its scabbard.

The Queen held her dark blade outstretched, the finely crafted sabre betrayed nothing whilst slicing the atmosphere as the goddess Nike; Rewarding she who brandished the curved blade victory and her pitiful opponent a journey to the shores of the Styx.

McCann made a grunting noise of absolute disbelief 'PAH! You must be having a laugh?'

'I'm quite serious Father.'

'Well you're not bloody coming, that's final!'

The sable Goddess dipped her brow towards her wayward parent 'Father, I'm not a child; in fact you are my subordinate ... Censor.'

Ilam made a wry grin of satisfaction whilst the pair argued; no doubt it was good to see her husband brought down a notch every now and then.

'The Athena is my ship and no-one steps foot on her without my say so, Grand Matriarch or not,' retorted McCann in an annoyed tone.

Lian approached the Englishman, placing one hand on each of his shoulders she spoke softly 'We need Malikah to track them down in the Galactic core, it is the only way Duncan.'

'You're coming too?'

Lian smiled 'Machine wishes to witness the final purification, the Neenayin are a plague upon all of us.'

'Well Machine can go and shove it ...'

Ilam cut in 'If you refuse, I shall take Xch'uup in the Chutli.'

'I won't allow it,' replied McCann.

'If Xch'uup wishes it I must comply.'

Malikah replaced her blade in its scabbard 'William, if you don't mind?'

Faraday took in a deep breath 'Sorry Duncan but Malikah is directing this mission, you and Athena will be taking orders from her.'

The Englishman seemed to accept this dictate although he did so with great reluctance. Inside he understood that his daughter would give the Athena a great advantage in locating and predicting their enemy's next move.

'As you wish William, I'll contact Kim and have him dock with the Tsiolkovsky.'

Ilam interrupted 'Duncan, have Kim move to Jupiter orbit. The Neenayin must possess a comfortable window of time in order to escape.'

McCann nodded before tapping his wrist and ordering his First Officer to make orbit around the Jove of the Terran system, then await further instructions.

Later that day the foursome exited the I.S.A for a long overdue visit, walking up the path to the front door all three girls could sense the presence of Ofra. Before they reached the door it swung open and McCann's mother was there in a casual green gown.

'Malikah!' shouted an excited Ofra.

Malikah ran up to her and gave her a big hug as did Ilam.

'I suppose you want to come in?' stated Ofra to her son.

'Well since it is my house I wouldn't mind!' retorted McCann sarcastically.

At that moment his daughter, standing next to Ofra, sent a dark look his way. The Englishman attempted to ignore it though he quickly changed the pitch of his speech 'Yes thank you mum.'

'That is better, is this Lian?' remarked Ofra.

Lian approached with palms pressed in front of her nose 'Namaste Ofra.'

The Middle Eastern lady opened the door invitingly 'Come in, come in.'

The three lades quickly strode in, McCann made his way into his own home cautiously.

The five of them resided in the kitchen as Ofra ran around preparing drinks and food.

She had her son's favourite of bacon sandwiches prepared, despite the fact it went against her faith; she was just glad to have him back.

McCann hung his military jacket on the back of his seat and spoke with surprise in his voice 'Bacon sandwiches?'

'With HP sauce and real butter.'

He was shocked as Ofra refused to allow such meat inside the home, despite it being his favourite.

'Are you sure?'

Ofra frowned 'Are you going to eat it or have conversation with it?'

McCann shrugged his shoulders and tucked in to the delicious crispy grilled bacon sandwich that dripped with warm butter and spicy sauce.

Ofra brought him over a coffee with cream, placing it in front of her son.

'Thanks,' stated McCann after swallowing the first bite of his sandwich.

Ofra darted to the refrigerator and pulled out a plate of large ants, she placed them in front of Ilam 'There you go.'

Ilam's eyes filled with a hue of pink 'Where did you find sinik?'

'They have a market for Tlillan food every Sunday in Geneva; it's considered a delicacy now.'

McCann grunted cynically 'Huh, a delicacy? Who shops there, vagrants and tramps?'

Ofra stared at her son 'Why is he so grumpy today, did someone take his toy out of his pram?'

Again McCann was very much humiliated but since it was his mother he said nothing and carried on eating the bacon sandwich.

Ilam laughed out loud 'Oh don't worry, it is probably just trapped wind.'

The two women both laughed hysterically, McCann struggled to find the humour in Ilam's statement. He turned to his daughter who was also laughing with Lian, as to why befuddled him.

Ofra brought out some k'amas for Malikah and Lian, a termite indigenous to Otoch, easily raised on Earth. Placing a dish of them in front of Lian, Ofra whispered 'I read all about you in ELLE, I'm only sad that Malikah didn't tell me about you before.'

'Don't be offended Miss McCann, it was necessary, any Tlillan may have heard you thinking of it and betrayed us.'

Ofra smiled 'I am not offended as long as you call me Ofra, so how long will you all be staying?'

'A few days,' answered her granddaughter.

'Is that all?'

'I'm sorry Mama Ofra, we will return when our business is finished I promise,' replied Malikah respectfully.

Ofra was easily swayed by her granddaughter especially when she referred to her using Arabic. Ilam realised that Ofra was anxious to speak with Malikah and Lian, quickly finishing her sinik Ilam stood out of her chair 'Come Duncan, let us take a walk together.'

McCann frowned 'I've only just got back,' he sensed something odd from his wife then scanned the room. The Englishman caught on and got up from his seat 'How about a stroll by the lake?'

Ilam smiled and slipped her arm through his 'that would be lovely, do not forget your jacket Duncan.'

'Ah thanks,' he threw on his military jacket without properly zipping it up, excused himself from the room and left with his wife.

The pair stepped out of the house, across the terraced garden and small public road until they were on the path which circled the beautiful Lake Geneva. Small sail boats travelled to and fro in the light wind as the sun glimmered on its surface, it was a wonderful place to be. If you looked up you'd see the snow-capped peaks of the Alps and the Jura. Across the Lake the Jet d'eau fired up into the crisp sky creating a miniature rainbow.

Ilam examined the horizon 'This is a fabulous place Duncan.'

Walking arm in arm whilst catching a few strange looks from joggers and tourists McCann replied 'Why do you say that?'

'A blue sky which is clear, white mountains, all of the different coloured boats Otoch is so dull in comparison.'

The Englishman shrugged his shoulders 'Well you live on the dark side, but there are plenty of wonders on Otoch.'

Ilam scoffed at his statement 'No, on Otoch we merely survive, living until the next day in a world of perpetual paranoia and discipline. Here you truly live your life, is it not ironic that the time I spent in exile was the fullest of my miserable existence?'

McCann stopped his wife in her tracks 'Ilam, that's no way to talk.'

She smiled upon his touching concern 'Things have changed on Otoch, after this mission I was considering stepping down.'

He couldn't believe his ears 'Stepping down? Why?'

'Kaeo is first of Teteo and Sandra is first of Tico, Amitrasudan is destined to be first of Chutli. It permits me to rescind the position of Huey'teopixqui,' said the stoic Valkyrie.

She looked just like an angel against the back drop of the sparkling lake 'What would you do?' inquired a concerned husband.

'I spoke with William; he is willing to allow my return as Exo-diplomat. Perhaps I might even take a commission on an up and coming vessel.'

McCann contemplated her statement then said philosophically 'I suppose I could pass on the chair of the Athena.'

His response surprised Ilam somewhat 'I know how much you enjoy commanding the Athena; I could not ask you to step down.'

McCann smiled 'I've had a bloody good run of it and with this Ixchel you gave me there should be plenty more opportunities ahead, right?'

Ilam spoke excitedly 'The I.S.A is constructing a deep space exploration vessel; we could both get a commission on her.'

McCann gave her a suspicious look 'So you've got it all planned?'

Ilam laughed 'No, it is merely a thought, but it would be wonderful to explore another galaxy with my little iicham.'

Little iicham meaning little mate, a term of affection McCann wasn't so hot on 'We can talk about it after this mission, it's not gonna be easy going to the core and back.'

Ilam laughed again 'Ah, isn't that why they pay you the big bucks?'

McCann gave his wife a wry smile, her parody of him was funny just not to her husband 'Come on let's have a look at the antiques market, they might have one of those lava lamps you like so much.'

Ilam grabbed her husband's arm and with a beaming smile marched him off to the weekly market in Geneva.

Back at the house Ofra was going over her digital copy of ELLE with Malikah and Lian 'When they saw my Granddaughter was on the cover of ELLE I could feel their jealousy,' said the excited grandmother.

'So has everyone at your tea club seen it?' inquired Malikah with a cheeky grin.

'Are you joking?' exclaimed Ofra in astonishment 'Everyone who owns a tablet has this copy of ELLE! Thank you for speaking of me inside, I have had journalists begging me for interviews since.'

'Have you done any?'

Ofra made an expression of shock 'Certainly not!'

Both Malikah and Lian laughed.

Ofra smirked to herself 'I'll wait until I visit my family in Tel Aviv.'

The sable Queen gave her grandmother a wry smile 'Tel Aviv? Are you sure you're going JUST to see your family?'

Ofra knew she could not disguise the truth from Malikah 'Yes, I'll be there to see that bitch Hanifa, or make sure she sees me! Her son a Prince? Well my daughter is an Empress! That bin'nt himaar will be green in jealousy, ha, ha!'

'A bin'nt himaar?' asked Lian in a puzzled tone.

Malikah paused for a moment communicating the meaning mind to mind; Lian chuckled at the Arabic slur.

'When we return from this mission I'm sure my Mother will accompany you on a home visit.'

Upon returning from the market McCann and Ilam relaxed in the lounge watching the television together, Ilam insisted he sit through "Habeeb's Hour". McCann was very resistant to the idea until his wife pointed out that he was always annoyed at being the last to discover information.

'What do you mean?' asked the Englishman.

'William has arranged an interview, he intends to bridge the gap between Humans and Makayuuk.'

'Really? How's he gonna do that?'

Ilam raised the tone of her voice 'Screen on,' and the house AI dutifully recognised her command.

'Habeeb's Hour, please,' again the AI flicked the correct channel on.

The net show had already begun and General Wolfgang Speer sat on the opposite side of Jerry's table.

'Ah, he's dug up that old Nazi has he?'

Ilam made a confused expression 'Nazi?'

McCann thought for a moment then stated 'Germans with a superiority complex.'

Ilam still didn't look any wiser.

'Oh I'll explain later, I wonder what this old fart has been dragged in for?'

'Are you acquainted?'

'We've met, I wouldn't trust that bloody kraut as far as I could throw him.'

Ilam raised her brow in surprise 'I see, then it is I who is in the dark, yes?'

The Englishman Chuckled as he watched Speer dressed in his polite three piece suit talk with Habeeb 'When it comes to that slippery fish, I think we're all in the dark, my dear.'

Jerry had already been chatting with his guest for a while 'So why don't you tell us your side of the story, General ... are you still a General?'

Speer laughed 'I don't know, but I think it's best you call be Wolfgang.'

'Ok Wolfgang, what really did go on during the last days of Hoch? I've seen thousands of Net shows and a lot of them have conflicting ideas. Some paint him as a hero of Germany, others as a villain. Now in my experience it's usually somewhere in between.'

Speer nodded in agreement 'Ya, well towards the end Hoch didn't leave his war room for anything. He was attached to that AI like a baby to its Mother's breast. Everyone else was trying to stop a disaster, like when you're at work and you get the job done despite your boss.'

Jerry chuckled into the camera 'I wouldn't know a thing about that!'

A ripple of laughter passed around the studio.

'Well the Ivans had our backs to the wall, I, Franz ... my commanding Officer, and Hans ... the Reichsfuhrer, were trying to co-ordinate some sort of cease fire with the Russians in Poznan. All the time Hoch was playing with divisions and squadrons that no longer existed. It all came to ahead when I was called in to see Hoch ...

Speer was marched along the hallway by and escort of two SS soldiers dressed in their black uniforms. Wolfgang was uncharacteristically dressed in a clean and recently pressed uniform, he stopped in front of the war room entrance.

'Entlassen,' came a voice from inside.

One of the guards opened the door, the other saluted as the threesome entered. Hoch was stood alongside his Reichsfuhrer pointing out icons on his digital map of East Germany.

Speer's entrance distracted the pair 'Ah, guten morgen Kapitan Speer,' greeted the Reichsfuhrer.

Speer made a stiff salute, Hoch returned to his map barely acknowledging him.

Speer took a closer look at the map, immediately he was alarmed by what he saw. The French fleet of nuclear submarines were scattered from the Barents to the Baltic, to the Black Sea. Yevpraksiya's massive Russian army was now bearing down upon the Fatherland. Poznan in western Poland had been taken and if you listened hard enough, on a quiet day, her guns could be heard in Berlin.

'Come closer,' beckoned the Reichsfuhrer.

The Kapitan noticed several submarines, each armed with 16 M4 IRBM's, their nuclear stockpiles prepared for tactical strikes in and around Poland. The Chancellor intended to vapourise Praksiya's legions, 'What do you think?' inquired a nervous Reichsfuhrer.

'A tactical nuclear strike?'

The Chancellor spoke as if he were talking to himself 'VX gas failed to keep her at bay, we must turn back these Russian savages somehow.'

'If I may speak Chancellor?'

'That is why you're here Kapitan.'

'Praksiya, she commands the largest nuclear arsenal in existence. If we attack she will counter strike immediately, Berlin shall be removed from the map.'

'That is why we shall hit her nuclear bases at the same time we strike her army. Limit her ability to counter attack Kapitan, Berlin is well protected by our Patriot missile shield. Yevpraksiya's anti-missile shield does not reach into Poland, we may hit her army with impunity.'

Speer's eyes widened as he gave the Reichsfuhrer an alarmed stare, the Chancellor was living in a dream world. A full Russian nuclear strike only required 1% to make it through their antiquated missile shield. After that every major city in Germany would be replaced by a crater, and the missile shield was nowhere near 99% accurate.

'Perhaps we could negotiate a cease fire?' suggested a foolish Speer.

Hoch spoke to the AI, ignoring Speer, by now the Chancellor had more of a relationship with his female War Machine than any of his real life staff 'Probability of success?'

The AI which now had a soft Germanic accent reminding the Chancellor of his mother replied 'Initial Russian losses 60-80%, post fallout 99.9999%'

'Friendly casualties?'

'Post fallout no higher than 47.882%'

What the AI didn't tell Hoch was that the Russian losses of up to half a million were all soldiers in the Russian army. The German losses of 47% equated to nearly 40 million dead civilians and military after a Russian nuclear counter attack. His AI no longer dispensed the hard facts, his Reichsfuhrer reprogrammed it to deliver the "facts" required to keep Hoch from facing the truth … that Germany wasn't going to win.

'Excellent, what do you say Kapitan? 47% losses are acceptable for exterminating the enemy, ya?'

Speer looked at the Reichsfuhrer then at the back of Hoch's head 'But those losses are civilians, 40 million lives for half a million?'

The Chancellor turned slowly to eye the Kapitan 'That is what I said Kapitan, do you find a problem in that?'

The Reichsfuhrer made an odd face, intimating that Speer should back down if he wanted to leave in one piece. Speer got the message and replied 'No problem at all mein Chancellor, when do we attack?'

Hoch smiled as he removed his glasses 'Finally a man who understands military strategy! Come closer!'

The Chancellor noted the French air bases and submarines carrying nuclear warheads 'Here we wait until tomorrow, the winds will be blowing into Russia that day. We trade strikes and Praksiya shall receive fallout from Germany, maximising damage to Russia.'

As he spoke the AI drew lines arching up into the sky from the subs and back down into Poland, Ukraine, Belarus and Russia.

'Feld Masrschall Webber has prepared a Combined Arms Corps here in Berlin, once we hit the enemy gathering at Poznan he shall blitz what is left of them. This time next week I expect the Tsaritsa's surrender before the force of the Fatherland!'

Speer forced a smile, as did the Reichsfuhrer. They were both aware of the reality and a Russian surrender wasn't on the cards.

'Kapitan Speer, I want you to lead the 2nd Combined Arms Corps. Webber is to strike Poznan then onto Warsaw and Minsk. You are to take your force to Krakow, then onto Kiev. What do you say?'

Speer gave an awkward grin 'I would be honoured Chancellor.'

'Excellent, you are to be promoted to the rank of General Major forth with.'

'Thank you, Sir.'

'Hans, take our new General to his men.'

The Reichsfuhrer nodded and moved towards the exit 'This way General Speer.'

Speer quickly followed Hans out of the war room, once the pair were alone Hans led him into a private room. On closing the door Speer spoke in a desperate tone 'What the hell is going? And that map, most of those division have broken or surrendered already.'

'I know,' replied the Reichsfuhrer 'but whenever he gets bad news he shoots the messenger, literally! He hasn't been getting the facts for weeks now, I just have the computer programmed to tell him what he wants to hear.'

Speer started rolling a cigarette 'Do you have a drink?'

Hans grabbed a bottle of schnapps and poured two glasses 'But you can have your promotion if you want.'

Speer shook his head as he sniggered 'Thanks! So what happens when he has his nuclear strike and the Russian guns keep on approaching Berlin?'

Hans knocked back the entire glass before pouring another peach schnapps 'I have a plan.'

'For what?'

'Gottschalk is correct, our missile shield covers Poland, hers doesn't.'

'You're not thinking of?'

'Ya, we hit her in Poland and offer a cease fire.'

'The Ivans will retaliate.'

'They will have a choice, cease fire now and we disable our missiles heading for Moscow or we fight it out to the bitter end.'

Speer took a long drag on his cigarette 'A game of brinksmanship?'

'Nein, a game of survival. If we don't do it we lose, if she doesn't comply we lose, but this gives us a chance.'

'What will you tell Hoch? He has to find out at some point.'

'I'll cross that bridge when I come to it.'

Speer spoke in a serious tone 'I know you grew up together and he's your friend, but we've all done things we'd rather not for the benefit of Germany.'

Hans let out a long sigh 'I understand.'

'One man is not worth the lives of 40 million.'

'Some would disagree.'

'Then they can sacrifice their children to the Ivans, I've had enough of fighting them.'

Hans nodded in agreement as Speer stood close by and whispered 'If this works we'll need a new leader, someone who can heal the wounds between Germany and Russia.'

'What are you suggesting?'

'Hoch had his place but his time is over, now it's your time Hans.'

'Wolfgang, I can't do that.'

Speer nodded 'As you said, we shall cross that bridge when it comes. First we must frighten Praksiya into negotiating.'

The next day in the war room Hans stood by as Gottshalck observed his fleet of nuclear submarines.

'M4 IRBMs armed and ready to fire,' spoke the soft calm voice of the Chancellors AI.

Six submarines began to flash with firing arcs targeting the Russian military in Poland and its supporting logistical infrastructure. Next three separate submarines began to flash with firing arcs heading towards Moscow and St Petersburg.

'M51 missiles armed and ready to fire Chancellor.'

Gottshalck who didn't look far from another mental breakdown steadied himself on the back of his chair 'Helga,' he spoke to the AI for that was what he'd christened her, with his Mother's name.

'Ya?'

'Launch.'

'Requesting launch code.'

'Launch code Funk.'

'Launching nuclear offensive.'

The missiles moved along their firing arcs, the M4s to hit first then 30 minutes later the M51s would strike Moscow.

'Well done Helga, the die is cast.'

'The die is cast?'

The Chancellor grinned 'Never mind Helga, have the First and Second Combined Arms Corps ready to launch their assaults.'

'General Webber and General Speer have both reported in, they shall begin their offensive upon the first M4 strikes, Gottshalck.'

'Thank you Helga, I shall go out to the balcony, to monitor our victory.'

Hans stopped his friend for a moment and passed him a pair of glasses to block any unwanted radiation 'Here take these.'

The chancellor took his goggles, put them on then stepped out. Facing towards the East he awaited the initial strike, five minutes later a mushroom cloud of bright orange and black dust could be seen rising silently in the distance.

Gottshalck grinned 'Ya, the die is cast.'

Hans looked on in horror, he was awaiting a communique from Moscow to discuss a cease fire but it still hadn't arrived.

'Is that not a beautiful sight Hans?'

The Reichsfuhrer didn't answer his friend.

Again Gottshalck addressed his boyhood friend 'I would say that for Yevpraksiya this is a great tragedy, ya?'

Hans replied in a solemn tone 'This is surely a great tragedy mein Chancellor.'

On the ground General Webber was stationed inside Berlin commanding what was left of the E.U. forces. He watched on as the cloud rose from the ground somewhere around Poznan, about 150 miles from Berlin.

Stationed not far outside the Reichstag General Webber was observing the nuclear explosion too 'We are lost, now Mother Russia shall destroy us.'

Speer replied 'Hans thinks she might negotiate before the other missiles hit Moscow.'

'If not then she will never accept a surrender, not after this.'

At that moment Lieutenant Meyer charged out of his Bunker 'Sir! I have a communique from the Russians, a General Colonel Krylov!'

Webber ran into the bunker with Speer and Meyer close behind. On a laptop sitting upon a wooden crate, a Russian man in his 40's wearing the Red and grey of the Russian army waited to speak.

'This is General Webber, is this General Krylov?'

'DA, WHAT THE HELL ARE YOU DOING?'

'We wish to negotiate a cease fire.'

'YOU HAVE USED ATOMICS!'

'AND THERE ARE MORE HEADED FOR MOSCOW! SO TALK GENERAL, BEFORE THEY ARRIVE!'

The Russian fell silent, a junior Officer spoke into his ear informing him of the immanent destruction of their capital. After he'd taken the message Krylov replied 'I must speak with the Tsaritsa before making that decision, she is Marshall of Russia now.'

'You have 45 minutes before the M51s reach the Kremlin,' before he finished the connection to the Russian camp went dead.

Speer was uncertain if the connection was lost due to Krylov's urgency or the EMP wave emanating from the mushroom clouds that rose one by one across the horizon.

'What now?' asked Meyer.

'We wait,' replied Webber.

A few minutes later Russian tanks appeared upon the outskirts of Berlin, APC's stopped allowing thousands of men to exit, all covered by the new Hydrogen powered drones. Webber charged out of the bunker and grabbed a pair of digital binoculars from Lieutenant Gerber. An enemy assault on Berlin's defences was about to be launched. As he watched German drones flew overhead, knocking out enemy armour tank by tank, until Russian drones eliminated them.

'Do they have gas?' asked Gerber.

'Nein, they have no choice but to attack unprepared. It seems that Praksiya has crossed the Rubicon Lieutenant.'

'Crossed the Rubicon? I don't understand General.'

Webber returned Gerber his binoculars 'Are you not a student of Ceasar?'

'General Messana? I thought he died in Chechnya?'

Webber let out a big belly laugh 'Never mind Lieutenant, never mind.'

Speer exited the bunker 'General I have Praksiya, she wishes to speak to the Reichsfuhrer.'

The war room was closed off, an electronically sealed environment. Wolfgang would have to take a transmission code inside permitting a link between Berlin and Moscow.

'Go Wolfgang, prevent a total catastrophe if you can.'

Wolfgang saluted the General then made off for the Reichstag as quickly as possible.

As Speer left on a motorcycle Webber looked up at the shadowy figures upon the Reichstag balcony. They watched over as Russian soldiers stormed Berlins' outer defences, to a backdrop of nuclear fire. His attention was then snatched away as the noise of anti-infantry shells exploding and Kalashnikovs spluttering approached. The General noted a German platoon fleeing from the oncoming enemy, he took a HK G40, inserted a clip and loaded the chamber.

The General nodded to Gerber who did likewise. As the platoon approached, General Franz Webber wearing his Knights cross with oak leaves shouted 'STOP!'

The men in the platoon halted for a moment and Webber pointed towards the oncoming Russian troops 'THIS WAY! FOLLOW ME!'

Lieutenant Gerber followed his commanding Officer and somehow the German platoon turned about face and onto the Russians who poured into the camp as water flowing through the tributaries of the Nile.

Praksiya's army of unforgiving, unrelenting soldiers clashed against the dam of the Fatherland in a violent storm of blood and lead; splashing onto the walls of the Reichstag.

Gottshalck felt drops of liquid spray across his face, he turned to his friend and grinned 'It is raining Hans, on such a sunny day!'

Hans witnessed the speckles of blood sprayed over the Chancellors' face 'Mother Russia is raining down on us, we must go inside.'

Seconds later a hail of Kalashnikov fire peppered the balcony and Hans pulled his friend inside the war room to safety.

Once inside the door opened and Wolfgang Speer entered out of breath, before anything could be said he gasped 'I have a communique from Yevpraksiya, she wishes to negotiate!'

Hans nodded with his head in the direction of a Corporal sat at the War rooms secure terminal to the outside world. Wolfgang threw his thumb drive, the young man caught it and began to secure a connection to the Kremlin.

Gottshalck Hoch was dumbstruck 'General, why are you not pushing the Russians?'

Speer said nothing.

Hoch fixed his eyes upon the digital display, according to the AI his Corps was pushing hard into Wroclaw.

'Helga! Where is General Speer?'

The 2nd Combined Arms Corps icon flashed upon the map as it pushed back several Russian divisions.

'Open communications to the 2nd Combined Arms Corps!'

The Corporal gave Hans a worried look. Hans nodded once to the young man confirming the Chancellor's request. Moments later Speers' voice rang out 'Ya?'

Hoch went weak again, steadying himself on his chair 'Is this General Wolfgang Speer of 2nd Combined Arms Corps?'

'Ya Chancellor.'

Hoch gave Wolfgang a steely gaze 'Where are you now?'

'We have taken Wroclaw, Sir. The enemy are making a tactical withdrawal to Katowice, I am pursuing, Sir.'

Hoch screamed out loud 'HELGA! GENERAL SPEER IS STANDING BEFORE ME IN THIS VERY ROOM!'

'General Speer has taken Wroclaw and is now advancing to …'

'SHEISSE!'

'My apologies Chancellor, please repeat that question.'

Hoch snatched a look at Hans then all the staff in his war room before collapsing on the floor. He trembled as a jellyfish, screeching at the top of his voice 'HELGA, YOU LIED! MOTHER WHY DID YOU LIE TO ME?'

Hans grabbed the Chancellor as he began to have a seizure 'The Chancellor is ill, get his medication,' he shouted to one of the guards who returned with a syringe.

Whilst restraining the Chancellor Helga announced what both Hans and Speer had been dreading 'Multiple Russian ICBM launches detected!'

The Reichsfuhrer injected his friend in the buttock and after 20 seconds the convulsions ended, leaving Chancellor Hoch on the floor snoring as if he were a baby.

A moment later Helga's digital display disappeared to be replaced with the image of Yevpraksiya; the blond, blue eyed Tsaritsa was dressed in the red and grey uniform of a Marshall of the Russian Federation 'Ola Mr Hoch.'

Hans stood up 'I'm sorry, I am Hans Fried, the Chancellor has been removed.'

'I take it you are now the Chancellor?'

'Correct.'

Yevpraksiya emanated an aura of mental toughness, her piercing blue eyes tore straight through every man in the room.

'What it is you desire Chancellor?'

'We have ballistic missiles on their way to Moscow.'

Praksiya snapped back at the new German leader 'I KNOW! Be aware I have launched a retaliatory strike, within 35 minutes Deutscheland shall be erased from every atlas in every school on the planet Earth!'

'Then give us a cease fire and I'll abort the attack now.'

'On one condition.'

'Name it!'

'You will deliver Hoch to me alive, in return our missile strikes will both be aborted and my forces shall retreat to Warsaw.'

Hans and Speer looked at each other, they were both taken aback by how quickly the Tsaritsa had agree to quite favourable terms.

'Well? Do you agree Chancellor?'

'Yes! Yes!' Hans called out 'Helga?'

The voice of Hoch's AI filled the room 'Yes Hans?'

'Initiate order "Contango", code word "BACKWARDATION"'

'Code word accepted, order Contango initiated.'

Praksiya's eyes searched around for the woman Hans spoke to, but her curiosity was not satisfied. Next a KGB agent approached the Tsaritsa and whispered something into her ear. She nodded and spoke to the man, he nodded and walked out of shot. The Russian beauty returned her attention to Hans 'I have aborted my ICBM strike Chancellor. Within a week a plane will arrive in Berlin, I expect Mr Hoch to be delivered to me … ALIVE … is that understood Chancellor?'

'Understood.'

Yevpraksiya's image faded from the screen to be replaced by the map of Poland and the fake German counter-attack.

'Russian ICBM strike aborted,' stated Helga as each of the missiles disappeared from her radar whilst in the early launch phase.

Speer let out a massive puff of air 'You've saved us, Hans.'

The Chancellor looked down at his sleeping friend 'If only I could have saved Gottshalck.'

Speer peered down in pity 'He saved us from the IMF and the Troika, now he must give his life to save us from Yevpraksiya.'

A week later and Berlin still smoked from the battle, Western Poland had been laid waste. Gottshalck was locked inside a cell at the Reichstag, Hans visited his old friend to prepare him for his journey to Moscow.

The steel bar gate slid past allowing Hans to enter, Gottshalck said nothing nor did he even move. He stood dressed in a polite dark blue suit waiting for the man that had betrayed him to speak.

'Have you been informed of the cease fire?'

Gottshalck merely nodded his head.

'One of the conditions is that I deliver you to Yevpraksiya, alive.'

'You know what they'll do to me, don't you?'

'I have a plan.'

'Oh?'

'Ya.'

'You have no choice but to deliver me Hans.'

'You remember the nanite program?'

'Ya?'

Hans produced a syringe 'I have some here.'

Gottshalck sneered 'I suppose they will break me out of a Gulag and fly me back to Berlin?'

'Listen to me, one of the by products of the nanite program were treatments for diabetes.'

Hoch snorted in disdain 'Pah! Diabetes is the least of my troubles!'

A frustrated Hans continued 'Listen to me, insulin was covered in nano-particles. Upon contact with glucose in the bloodstream the nano particles would bind with it to produce and acid. If the glucose got too high then nano-particles are broken down by the acid, releasing insulin to lower blood glucose levels.'

Hoch folded his arms and replied in a very sarcastic tone 'Fascinating!'

Hans persevered 'A diabetic only requires one injection per month, we have swapped the insulin for potassium cyanide. Since you are not diabetic it shall take some time until the levels are high enough and you'll need to eat plenty of carbs and sugars.

But if you take this injection you'll be dead before she can parade you through the streets of Moscow like some sick circus show.'

Hoch eyed the pen needle usually used for diabetics 'How long until it kills me?'

'Depending on what you eat you have 3 days to a week.'

Hoch smiled at his old friend 'Thank you Hans.'

He rolled up his sleeve and Hans injected the nano-particles into Gottschalck, to be released over the next day through his fat and into his bloodstream.

Later that day the Russian transport plane touched down in Berlin and Gottshalck walked aboard with Hans. The former Chancellor had no restraints and wore a clean suit; the world press was there clicking away, reporting live from the runway. Germans wailed as their leader was marched off to be sacrificed on the altar of peace in Moscow. Some had to be held back as they attempted to prevent the tragedy from taking place. The man who had saved them from economic collapse and the dominance of the IMF, when so many fell around them as ears of corn to a farmers' scythe, was now giving his life as a true hero in exchange for the safety of his people.

Although not all shared the same emotion, those such as Speer and Hazlitt remained out of sight. The men who'd watched as Hoch's deliverance turned into a crusade of brutal violence were not sorry to see him leave, nor did they pity his ultimate fate at the hands of Yevpraksiya. However, if the nation was to heal it was preferable that the story of the great Germanic hero making the ultimate sacrifice for his people was allowed to permeate.

He had saved them from debt slavery to the Troika, subjugating the IMF and its minions rather than the opposite; however his time was over and now the baton had to be passed on to a man prepared to compromise.

As Hans walked onto the plane he stopped to allow his friend one last wave to his people. Speer and Hazlitt were sitting in a local bar drinking Schnapps and watching the event on the television with everyone else in the packed business. As Hoch gave one last wave a young man began to sing the national anthem 'Deutschland, Deutschland uber alles ...'

Soon the whole bar began to sing in unison, only Speer and Hazlitt remained quiet. Speer raised an eyebrow and Hazlitt smirked at his comrade. The truth would have blown most of these peoples' minds. Soon the song could be heard all through the streets of Berlin as Hoch made the final steps into the aeroplane, to take his final flight to Moscow.

Hazlitt sniggered a little as Speer made funny looks with his face. Once the song was over and the plane lifted off a patron at the bar took offence to Hazlitt's gay attitude and grabbed his shoulder from behind 'Hey! You! What's so funny?'

Hazlitt still holding his apple schnapps turned to look at the fellow, a man in his twenties, probably one of Hoch's little boys.

The bar fell silent when everyone eyed Hazlitt's medal, hanging from his collar. The young man could not take his eyes away from it, the Blue Max was an honour great enough to get you laid in any town or city in Germany.

'Is there a problem?' inquired Hazlitt.

The young man was speechless.

A voice came out from the crowd of customers 'Did you know Hoch?'

Hazlitt smiled 'I met him, once,' then pointed to his Blue Max 'when he gave me this.'

Someone else spoke out 'Bah, you can buy them on Ebay for 50 Marks!'

Speer burst out laughing 'That's what I told him when he volunteered!'

The crowds' attention turned to Speer who sported an Iron cross and Knight's Cross.

Again there was nothing but silence until a young man pulled out his tablet 'Look here, he did meet Hoch!'

The tablet displayed a picture of Hazlitt receiving his award in a ceremony. Since very few Blue Maxs were ever awarded it wasn't hard to scan the net quickly and Hazlitt's picture with Hoch was there.

'I apologise ... Sir,' said the young man who'd originally grabbed him.

Hazlitt smiled at the lad 'No offence taken, but remember it is easy to be angry. To be angry at the right person, at the right time, that is hard.'

The young man smiled back 'Yes Sir.'

Speer put his arm around Hazlitt and smiled at the young man 'What are you drinking?'

'Whatever you're having Sir.'

Speer called to the barman 'Schnapps for everyone, let's not waste our energy concentrating on the past but drink to a fresh start; it's what Hoch would have wanted.'

The young patron raised his glass 'A new beginning.'

On the plane to Moscow Hans and Gottshalck sat together both peering out of the window whilst Praksiya's guards monitored them.

'Isn't it beautiful?' asked Hoch as they passed over the scorched earth of Eastern Germany.

'Beautiful? It is depressing.'

Hoch smiled 'I meant the sky, doesn't it put joy into your heart seeing rain and sunshine from heaven?'

Hans looked at the blue sky as it refracted through droplets of water 'I have a heavy heart today. Did you hear the song?'

'I did.'

'Even after all is said and done they still sang for you Gottshalck.'

'I sent them marching to their graves, nothing more Hans.'

'You emancipated every man, woman and child from debt slavery to the IMF. You bankrupted the Troika, you minted the Gold Mark despite their best efforts to stop you. From that massive pile of E.U. shit you dragged Deutschland out and placed its flag aloft.'

Hoch peered in the direction of the Russian armed guards, placed strategically along the body of the aeroplane, 'And then I dashed their babies skulls upon the rock of Mother Russia.'

One of the guards, stood close by, looked down upon the ex-Chancellor with disdain. Hoch spoke to the man 'What do you say Ivan?'

The Guards mouth moved beneath his large moustache and in his best German he stated 'You are a thief and a murderer.'

Suddenly a superior Officer stepped into the passenger area and shouted something in Russian at the guard. The Germans weren't sure of what was said but it was obvious he was not to speak with either of them.

The guard returned his gaze directly ahead, down the aisle. His commanding Officer then stated to the Germans 'These men are not permitted to speak with you, I hope you were not disturbed.'

Hoch smiled 'Neit, your soldier is correct.'

The Officer nodded before leaving via the door he'd entered.

Hans tried to cheer his friend up 'Oh well, we nearly had them you know? I bet Praksiya was shitting herself while our tanks were on the banks of the Moskova River!'

Hoch chuckled 'Ya, if only I'd struck out against Moscow first. I wasted my time on the oil fields when we should have been cutting the head from the snake,' Hoch smirked at his guard 'Eh Ivan?'

The guard refused to reply.

Hans sat back 'I blame those Greeks, their riots took 8 weeks off the Eastern campaign. If we hadn't been forced to repress those bastards we'd have been in the Kremlin before winter broke.'

'Ah, shoulda, woulda, coulda! It is time to look to the future, get the best deal you can Hans. This Praksiya is tough, a woman of steel, but she has fears the same as us. Remember Hans all emotions have their root in fear, that is why the only money is Gold. When the markets sense fear they flee to gold, discover what she fears and see where she flees.'

Hans sighed 'Yah, but right now we need hope.'

Hoch smiled 'Equity is hope mein friend, when the markets have hope for the future they move from Gold and into equity.'

'What will I do without you old friend?'

'You will do what you are best at, you shall negotiate the best deal for Deutschland.'

Hans shook his head 'I thought you were best at that.'

'Nein, maybe a hostile takeover but not a fair trade!'

They both laughed and Hoch continued 'Remember a fair trade occurs when both parties make the best trade possible at the time.'

'I understand.'

An hour later and the aeroplane landed in Moscow, Hans and Gottshalck were led out to hostile crowds. Praksiya was not present, the press took their photographs whilst a soldier placed Hoch in a pair of handcuffs as screams of hatred ejaculated from a crowd of Russian citizens. Next they were escorted into a waiting limousine and driven directly to the Kremlin.

At the Kremlin Gottshalck was taken away to his prison, before he left Hans said one last farewell 'Auf Wiedersehen.'

Hoch grinned back to his friend 'Auf Wiedersehen.'

He was then grabbed in a rough manner and marched off into one of the many buildings inside the Russian fortress.

Hans was escorted to the main building, the Kremlin itself was a massive fortress containing churches, cathedrals and a palace. The Russian word for citadel being Kremlin, and the Kremlin in Moscow being the most well known of all Kremlins.

Hoch was led off as Hans entered the Grand Kremlin palace, the seat of Russian power since Lenin and Stalin moved there in the 1930's. Commissioned by Nicholas I in 1838 it linked up smaller palaces, the construction was astonishing in both size and luxury.

Its marble hall was a sight to behold, Hans felt as if he were a mortal stepping into the home of the Gods on mount Olympus. Looking around at the vaulted roof, perfect marble floor and strutting marble columns he wondered how anyone could imagine defeating the people who built this. The colonnades were covered in gold leaf and intricate designs, beautiful sheets of the most expensive silk cloth in purple dye flanked his path towards Praksiya's throne room.

Hans thought to himself that the person ruling over this must surely be the most powerful person in the world. Her residence dwarfed anything he had ever seen in size and expense, it was only now he realised how foolish he'd been. If only he had seen this palace before launching the campaign on Russia, but it was too late now and Hans was set to meet his fate at the other end of the corridor.

The Chancellor was escorted into the Georgievsky hall, another opulent room with gold leaf on marble, adorned with paintings of past masters. Two lines of armed imperial guards flanked the path to her golden throne.

Hans walked down the aisle until a pair of soldiers let their rifles out to block his way. The grinning Tsaritsa was flanked by her own KGB, dressed in dark suits they stood to attention.

'Welcome to Moscow, Chancellor.'

'Spasiba.'

Her well manicured brow lifted in delight 'Not bad Russian, I hope the flight was comfortable.'

'It was.'

Yevpraksiya rose from her throne, even in her Marshalls uniform she stunned Hans with her beauty 'Avuyanee,' stated the Russian Queen.

Her imperial guards stood to attention before filing out of the hall, leaving Hans alone with Praksiya and her KGB agents.

Hans looked the two men up and down with concern. Praksiya offered a warm smile 'They are not here,' she said in a thick Russian accent.

Taking the Chancellor by the arm she led him on a stroll, viewing the master pieces hanging on her wall 'I know Hoch was your friend, but his fate is sealed, we must look to other things now, agreed?'

Hans nodded 'Agreed.'

'You have devastated the Russian army, it will take a year to return our soldiers to similar numbers and as for our armour ... I do not have your flash factories.'

Hans felt very wary, the Tsaritsa could have overrun Berlin if she had pushed hard enough, why was she playing her weak hand?

'My forces shall retreat to Belarus, everything East of Minsk I cede to Deutschland, is that satisfactory?'

Hans stopped and fixed upon her sparkling blue eyes 'Why?'

Praksiya chuckled 'Why? Do you want more?'

'Of course not, you have won, why do you cede so much territory to us?'

Yevpraksiya released Hans' arm and replied in a stern tone 'Don't believe that I fear you Chancellor, I still possess enough warheads to remove your cess pit of a country from the atlas!'

Hans scrutinized the tall Russian beauty and he found what Gottshalck had been talking about. In any negotiation, especially business, to be successful you have to read your opponent and discover his or her weakness immediately. For Hans and Gottshalck this was a well trained skill, ever since they dropped out of business school to start their own company. The pair of them together were a force to be reckoned with in the markets, leading to their eventual rise to political power.

'Now I see the truth mein Tsaritsa.'

'What is that Chancellor?'

'You need a wolf don't you?'

'I don't understand Chancellor.'

'You are the shepherd,' he motioned to her KGB staff 'they are your dogs,' next he motioned to the large windows on the opposite side of the room 'and they are your sheep.'

The Tsaritsa gave him a wide grin 'Go on Chancellor.'

'You sheer their fleece, take their milk and eat their babies yet they never protest. The rams could easily overpower your dogs if they wished, but they follow all orders do they not?'

'They do Chancellor.'

'Because the shepherd and her dogs protect them from the wolves,' Hans sneered 'but imagine if one day those wolves were destroyed and their lair burnt to the ground?'

Yevpraksiya smiled, grabbed his arm and carried on along the hall slowly, admiring the art 'So you understand the truth.'

'You do not fear me, Deutschland or even nuclear weapons ... you fear your own people above all.'

'Da, and I need a wolf to keep the herd in order, you shall be my wolf Mr Freid.'

'What do you want of me?'

'Every now and then I shall send you a speech, a threatening speech. You will rebuild your military and fortify our border.'

'What would prevent me from attacking in a year or two?'

Praksiya hugged his arm 'Chancellor, I am quite apt at reading others too. You are not interested in violence, you do not wish to take that which you do not need. Russia shall agree to provide you with the hydrocarbons you require, in exchange for technology.'

'You want to build flash factories.'

'Correct Chancellor.'

Hans halted 'I will not hand over our technology but I will produce whatever Russia requires to whatever specifications it desires. You need to rebuild your military after Poznan, we will do it and beyond until another source of oil is secured or you build your own factories; is that a deal?'

'You are an excellent statesman Mr Freid, what of the speeches?'

'Provided it is nothing too obscene or inflammatory, I agree.'

'Excellent,' smiled Praksiya 'it seems that we may declare peace after nearly a decade of war. I've already had the maps drawn up, I'm sure the German people shall find them most favourable.'

'What of Gottshalck?'

Yevpraksiya was disappointed that he asked, but not surprised 'A public trial followed by a public execution.'

Hans replied in a sardonic tone 'Well that sounds fair.'

'There can be no doubt of his guilt, the people must be pacified. Unless I have his head on the Kremlin wall the people will replace it with mine Mr Freid.'

One of the KGB staff pressed his fingertips upon his earpiece, he spoke in Russian. Hans didn't understand but gathered it was urgent, whatever it might be.

Praksiya took the arm of her German counterpart 'Come Mr Freid, you might find this interesting.'

She walked him into a room behind the throne, its doorway was covered by one of the plush silk curtains. Hans recognised the small room as the place she had contacted him from in Berlin. Yevpraksiya remained standing and barked at one of her men who worked on the console.

The small computer monitor warmed up, to display the image of a man in combat fatigues and a turban. Hans recognised the man as being one of the Islamist leaders that fought so furiously against German forces in Chechnya.

The man with a strange beard spoke in Russian to the Tsaritsa, Hans had no idea of the conversation until a translation into German appeared at the bottom of the screen.

After a few minutes of reading the back and forth it became clear that now the war was over this man was to declare an independent Islamic state. He seemed to expect Yevpraksiya's consent, the Chancellor garnered from the chat that he'd been promised or believed he'd been promised independence.

When Praksiya refused the gnarly old fighter was not impressed, he declared independence anyway. It was obvious he didn't believe she had either the ability or the nerve to stop him.

The Tsaritsa surprisingly agreed, she then made it her first act to declare war upon his state. Turning to Hans she stated 'Chancellor, I believe that to bring our nations closer together a joint military action would be a good idea, da?'

Hans shrugged his shoulders 'I suppose so.'

'Do you still have stockpiles of VX nerve gas?'

'Ya, sure.'

'I suggest we kill two birds with one stone, would you agree to a disarmament treaty concerning the gas?'

'Certainly.'

'The Russian air force is to dump our entire stockpile of VX nerve gas on Chechnya, I suggest the Luftwaffe does the same.'

Hans peered at the Chechen fighter who by now was in a state of panic, it seemed he had burnt his bridges with not only the German Chancellor but the Russian Tsaritsa also. Hans nodded his head 'Sounds good to me.'

'YURI!' barked the beautiful woman.

'Da!' replied one of the KGB staff.

'Blockade Chechnya, this time next week nothing is to breathe within its borders is that understood?'

'Da!'

'We shall be collaborating with the Luftwaffe, is that understood?'
'Da!'
The Islamic fighter began to shout snatching the Russian Queen's attention 'Enough! As you wish Grozny shall relinquish, whatever you desire we shall provide!'
The Tsaritsa cackled at the doomed fighter 'One does not bother to sheer a naked sheep Mr Dudaev!'
Praksiya approached her staff member who managed the link and tapped him on the shoulder, cutting the connection with Grozny.
'It seems our peace is to be sealed with Chechen blood, da?'

'Hoch died four days later and the pact held until it was no longer required by either side.'
Jerry was at a loss for words as the story sank in, after a prompting from his studio manager the American continued 'What did Yevpraksiya do when he died of cyanide poisoning?'
Speer lowered his eyelids slowly before raising them with a pout 'Nothing to us, she did use it to manipulate her people. It was further proof that we were evil and to be feared, her being the only thing standing in the way of course.'
Jerry adjusted his braces before asking the General 'What do you say to those who believe you should be punished for your part in that war?'
Speer shrugged his shoulders and opened his palms to the ceiling 'I did what any young, idealistic fool would have. When I woke up I worked with Field Marshall Webber to avoid an apocalypse. My only regret is that he didn't live to see the peace he'd fought for.'
Jerry pressed the old fellow harder 'You still haven't answered my question.'
The old soldier gave Jerry a hard look 'If there is anyone, still alive today, who suffered directly from my actions all those years ago and still desires revenge I would ask them to stop torturing themselves. Let go of past hate otherwise you will never be free, living in a cage of bitterness is barely an existence Jerry.'

'I think that's something we should all take into account, especially since what's happened with the Gukumatz and Makayuuk.'

Speer nodded in agreement 'Those who hate because of difference in language, looks or customs; whether it be Human, Tlillan, Gukumatz or Makayuuk, need to find a hobby.'

Jerry turned to the camera, shuffled his prompt cards, and said 'I think that's an excellent thought to end this interview on. Thank you for coming here today Mr Speer.'

Wolfgang smiled 'You're welcome Mr Habeeb.'

The lights dropped and the music played.

McCann squeezed his wife's waist as they sat on the sofa 'It seems Malikah has done it again.'

'What would that be?' inquired the Amazon.

'Media manipulation my dear, first old Jerry demonised the Makayuuk as flesh eating Vikings; now they're no worse than a few old decrepit German war heros.'

Ilam didn't react, she only responded in her cold Tlillan demeanour 'That is because Humans are stupid.'

The Englishman gave his wife a sly look. The Valkyrie only then realised what she had done 'Oh, my apologies Duncan, I meant no insult. I was only stating fact.'

McCann nodded his head 'After all these years of marriage to a Tlillan, it would take a damn sight more than that to yank my chain!'

Ilam went from a cold exterior to a laugh, something that still shocked her husband, and kissed McCann on his cheek 'You are one of the few civilizations that at any point was prepared to exchange goods and services in return for pieces of paper backed by bad debt!'

McCann chuckled a little 'Alright, alright, I know, and I married you didn't I?'

Ilam smiled at him with plush pink eyes 'That was your first intelligent decision my yakuntik!

A few days later and the family were recalled to mission control at I.S.A headquarters. The Neenayin had fled, just as Malikah foresaw, taking the Clotho and jumping out of the system.

Inside Faraday's office the four listened in on the roll call of names, one hundred global leaders were there. Presidents, Prime Ministers, Chancellors, Bankers, Media Moguls, Leaders of industry, CEOs; as far as McCann was concerned they were the scum of society even before being exposed.

What shocked them were the final three names, Malikah examined the profiles in disbelief 'Tlillans?'

Observing the list, holographicaly displayed from Faraday's desk, Lian pointed at the Matriarch with striking red hair 'I know her, that's Olga.'

'Why would the Neenayin possess her?' inquired Ilam.

Lian shook her head 'She is not possessed.'

'Then why leave with the Neenayin? Do you believe she is attempting to usurp them?'

Again Lian shook her head 'No, Olga was ... is a very ambitious person. She has a lust for power driven by jealousy; I believe she intends to use the Neenayin.'

McCann frowned 'For what?'

Malikah nodded her head 'To push her agenda, she desires to become Xch'uup herself.'

Scratching his head the Englishman asked 'But you're Xch'uup, how on Earth does she intend ...'

Malikah cut him off 'She doesn't, she intends to found her own empire far away in the galactic core. She will use the Neenayin until they can be disposed of, we must dispose of them first, Father.'

The door rang to which Faraday called out 'Enter.'

In stepped Dr Pitt carrying four tablets 'I have the psychological profiles of the three Tlillans, as requested William.'

She handed them out amongst the family preparing to leave on their mission to the core 'I have Miss Olgachutli as the group leader, her profile suggests she would not allow someone else to take leadership above her.'

Faraday nodded in agreement 'Yes we've just been discussing her, what would you say her intentions are, Valorie?'

Dr Pitt brushed back her short red hair with one hand as she consider the question for a moment, 'She is a manipulator, I would say her desire is to control others and situations, Olga probably has the intention of using the Clotho's resources to set up a colony and expand it.'

'What of the other two Matriarchs?'

'Classic cult situation, you have the strong bold leader in Olga. She possesses a combination of absolute social and physical fearlessness. This combination means Olga has no anxiety concerning situations terrifying to most of us, this draws the timid to her. The other females no doubt have the same level of impulsive behaviour as all psychopaths, it is just they are too afraid to act on their will and therefore they do so through Olga.'

McCann raised his eyebrows 'So she's a nutter?'

Valorie shook her head and sighed 'No Duncan she is not, Olga is in all probability a psychopath.'

'What's the bloody difference?'

'Someone who'd been sectioned couldn't hijack a star ship and convince over 100 people to follow her to the galactic core,' stated Valorie.

'Whatever,' declared a sceptical McCann.

'Either way, Olgachutli has committed heresy and must be executed for her crimes,' declared a righteous Ilam.

Lian was unhappy at the Matriarchs statement 'Must Olga die?' she asked staring hopefully at the Tlillan Queen beside her.

Malikah folded her arms 'The order of things has seen much change recently; however the Matriarchs would never accept a pardon. Olga made her decision Lian, the die is cast, all she can do now is await her destiny in the core.'

Lian nodded silently 'You have the support of Machine.'

The Tlillan Queen peered over at Faraday 'Is Athena prepared?'

'Yes, though you may take the Hera if you wish Malikah.'

Malikah shook her head 'No, but have Ryu prepared for an extraction mission to the core. We must fight this battle alone; numbers would only hamper our efforts. Are we all ready to leave?'

The Queen's followers silently nodded their heads.

Malikah smiled and with a single nod of her sable brow she stated 'Then it is time to dispatch this daughter of a whore.'

With that very Middle Eastern insult she departed from the room to farewells from Faraday and Pitt as the other three followed her to the waiting hummingbird.

Dr Pitt whispered in a sardonic tone 'Speaking of psychopaths there go a bunch of prime examples William.'

William nodded in agreement 'Yes Valorie, however those psychopaths are on our side; what did you make of Lian?'

'She is submissive to Malikah; Lian will do anything to please her. Always following Malikah's instructions no matter her own opinion.'

Faraday scoffed at her analyses 'They're all like that though, aren't they?'

'Most of them yes, but not all of them have the power to command a fleet of Makayuuk warships. You saw what happened on Gaulthus recently?'

'Yes but that was Machine, not Lian.'

'She brokered a peace with Machine; she rescued our entire fleet from destruction and only because of her relationship with your Admiral's daughter.'

'I suppose so,' replied Faraday in a begrudging tone.

Valorie raised the pitch of her voice 'There is no supposing, William. She could crush us and the Tlillans right now if she decided to do so,' Dr Pitt raised her well-manicured eyebrows and in a wary tone she said 'Make sure she and Malikah don't fall out, for now at least.'

A shiver went down Faraday's spine, the Doctor had brought to his attention the consequences of a lovers spat 'Do you think she might?'

Valorie patted the fearful Faraday on his back 'It's a possibility William; you know that old saying about a woman scorned.'

Chapter 18

McCann and the three Tlillans stepped on to the Bridge to Kim's customary stiff salute. McCann gave him a nod as the Commander made odd looks towards Malikah and her cohorts.

The three Amazons were dressed in an armoured version of the traditional Tlillan ribbed suit. The torso and shoulders carried large pads of black Catronium; Kim assumed the padding, also on the thigh and shin areas, was intended to stop a tungsten round.

Kim had never seen this before, in fact of all the footage he'd watched concerning Tlillans in combat not once had he seen this type of body armour. To the Koreans' knowledge the Tlillan race did not use it or at least hadn't used it for millennia.

The next oddity to catch his eye was the fact that his Admiral and the three Valkyries wore sword belts of one form or another. Each one carried a blade; they were dressed as if ready to go into a 14th century melee, only armed to 22nd century standards.

By this time the entire bridge was grabbing a look at the four of them, even junior Officers in the pit glanced over their shoulders stealing quick glances.

'Hassif, prepare to cast off then set a course for a safe jump point,' ordered McCann sweeping his sword aside before taking the Captain's chair.

Hassif tapped away until the voice of Athena could be heard 'Request certified, ready to cast off Admiral.'

McCann looked up at the dark dome on the ceiling and smiled 'In your own time Athena.'

The world of blue and green spun beneath them, attached to the Tsiolkovsky by the Tlillan designed lift. The new tower fired cargo vessels between ground zero and the massive rock, cutting journey time to minutes rather than weeks in a crawler eking its way up a nanotube ribbon bit by bit.

Athena detached from the docking arm of the Tsiolkovsky, breaking away to starboard she drifted gracefully until a safe distance was reached.

'Course set, awaiting certification,' called Hassif.

'Course certified, you may engage at your discretion Admiral,' came the soft voice of Athena.

'Take us out slowly Athena,' replied the Englishman.

The vessel aligned for her destination, above the elliptic plane, before a short burst from the engines pushed her off.

Once Athena was heading for her jump point McCann stood up 'Athena I'd like to make an announcement to the crew.'

Athena's voice sounded throughout the war cruiser 'All hands this is a general announcement by Admiral McCann.'

The Englishman took a deep breath, exhaled then began 'this is Admiral McCann, you may be aware of a sinister creature referred to as the Neenayin. Well they have fled our home world, some of them may have been your rulers or members of their councils, many of them were leaders of industry and finance.

It is our job to pursue these creatures and eradicate them; unfortunately they and three Tlillans have taken off with the Clotho for the Galactic Core. No manned I.S.A craft has ever been this deep into the Core before. I have been told that our cannons will be useless; in fact all projectile weapons are going to be ineffective.

Due to time and space distortion the only practical method open to us will be to hunt them down, board the Clotho and engage in melee combat. Thankfully I know that many of you are well trained in the art of the sword, before we fold space I want all hands with any training to report to Commander Kim in Cargo bay one. Those with no formal training please report to cargo bay two where you'll be armed and given a few pointers.

All hands involved in any of the Gukumatz fencing tournaments report to me at the Officers' lounge.

Thank you, Admiral McCann out.'

The bridge crew were suspended in a very tense atmosphere.

'You have the Bridge Athena. Kim you're in cargo bay one, Ilam and Lian can you two take bay two?'

Ilam nodded 'Certainly Duncan,' she peered at Lian 'Come with me girl,' before leading Voice of Machine off into the elevator.

'Malikah, you come with me to the Officers' mess. Let's get this show on the road shall we?'

The pair entered the second elevator with Vezzali as the rest of the Bridge crew lined up to use the lifts.

Exiting the lift McCann looked up 'Athena?'

'Yes Admiral?' came a soft reassuring voice.

'Did you receive the technical specifications I sent from Geneva?'

'All specifications have been logged; I take it we shall be using standard Spetsnaz body armour?'

The Englishman nodded 'Spot on Athena, how much catronium do you have?'

'Depending on weapon type, I estimate enough for a third of the crew, Admiral.'

'Officers' Mess will get priority Athena, if there is any surplus I want it kept in reserve, understood?'

Athena replied in a warm tone 'Understood Admiral.'

Vezzali inquired 'What is the surplus for?'

McCann glanced at the slightly naïve science Officer 'I don't know how long we're gonna be in the core, blades take damage and shields break.'

'Shields?' ejaculated Vezzali in an incredulous tone.

McCann grinned at her naivety 'since the beginning of armed warfare until the dawn of the musket, shields have graced the battlefield young lady; and with damn good reason.'

Vezzali frowned a little 'I've never used one before Admiral.'

Malikah still looking forward as they walked to their destination replied 'You shall receive some basic training in the use of a shield; you'll pick it up very quickly Miss Vezzali.'

The party turned a corner of the creamy white corridor to note a queue forming inside the Mess. As he walked down the queue and into the Mess McCann received salutes until reaching his destination.

Once inside Malikah arranged the tables forming a barrier between her Father and the awaiting crewman.

McCann stepped behind the bar, in the wall sat a large black panel. The Englishman touched a display above the panel lighting it up. McCann peered upwards 'Athena, could you test the flash constructor please?'

Athena's soft voice filled the room 'Is there anything you would like in particular, Admiral?'

McCann contemplated for a moment 'Hmmm, how about a bottle of 30 year old Balvenie and a shot glass?'

Malikah's head snapped into her Father's direction and he felt her black look upon the rear of his head.

The panel began to beep as a low humming sound emanated from the flash machine. The flash constructor was a distant relative to the 3-D printers of the early 21st century. After the global financial collapse of the 2020's industry had been decimated in Europe and North America, mostly by their own greed. The now shattered EU realised it could no longer keep up with East Asia on an industrial level. Having spent so much of their own resources in building China's infrastructure to manufacture goods they had awoke a sleeping dragon.

The Chinese people had their infrastructure built for free, technology invested for nothing all because Americans and Europeans were desperate to increase already fat profit margins. It led to a financial apocalypse, by the time it was reaching an end and currencies were being stabilized the West had become enslaved.

No longer the primary customer that set the low prices of goods, what was left of the now shattered North America and Europe was merely another customer who had to bid for its goods.

Before, Chinese were prevented by their own government from purchasing goods produced in Chinese factories. Now the West was having to bid against over two billion Chinese and Indians, added to that prices were no longer artificially kept low against the dollar, since the dollar no longer existed; it led to a massive drop in living standards.

Europe and North America had been living way above their means for a long time; the drop to Earth was a long one with a very hard bump.

Germany was the first to develop an industrial grade 3-D printer large enough to produce a car. In fact it was a factory of printers each printing a different part, parts which were sent to various assembly lines. Eventually the whole car would be assembled engine and all in one factory, labour costs had been slashed.

Unfortunately these factories could produce any designs loaded into them, since the collapse of the EU many ex-members were demanding their gold back from vaults in Frankfurt. The Chancellor had a bright idea, not the first man to have this idea; the German factories began to pump out the latest designs in fighter drones.

Any nation demanding their assets met with a violent response until they relented and returned to the E.U ... AKA the Fourth Reich. After a few brutal suppressions the rest of Europe quickly got the idea, nations stopped requesting their gold from German vaults. Instead they began construction of their own manufacturing centres.

In Britain a bright spark came up with the 3-D flash printer, a device that instead of building the separate engine parts then putting them together could construct an entire engine from scratch in a fraction of the time.

Soon the Hawker Company had a contract and was building drones to compete with the German DASA-3.

The confrontation would have escalated if it were not for the oil conflicts, oil prices had sky rocketed and populations in both countries began to riot.

The Chancellor used his relations with Russia to broker a deal for cheap oil and gas but the British were not so fortunate. Shipping oil via the Eastern States was a risky business, German satellites would see them leaving port forcing the British to escort each tanker with at least one carrier and a plethora of destroyers.

The British people were starving and freezing to death in what became known as the winter of discontent. Before spring arrived the Prime Minister and his cabinet had been hung by an angry mob of 3 million people after marching to London from the North of England.

It was little surprise that no-one was suicidal enough to take the job of leading a nation of hungry, cold and very angry people. The job fell to the present head of state, King William V. Reluctantly the monarch filled the vacuum of power, a truce was agreed upon with Germany and he set about securing a stable supply of oil and gas.

One great advance that came out of the short conflict with Germany was the Flash printer, which one day would lead to the flash constructor. The Constructor could create almost anything provided it had the specifications and elements required. It might construct a bottle of whisky by combining the elements Silicon (Si) and Oxygen (O2) to create silica, the atoms of each element would be funnelled into an electro-magnetic mould of the bottle. The electro-magnetic field heated the elements up fusing them to create a silica glass.

Whisky was a different case; Athena had the chemical composition of whisky and created it perfectly. However it didn't match up to the real thing, organics were still a problem, a meal could be created but it usually tasted quite odd in comparison to the real thing.

The humming ended, moments later the display panel ceased beeping and the constructor opened up. McCann took out his bottle and shot glass before returning to the table with a big smile on his face; Malikah had no such expression.

The Englishman placed the bottle down with a satisfied bang he next took an ashtray from underneath the bar and placed it on the table before seating himself.

Malikah remained on her feet and with arms folded looked down on him as if he were a naughty boy 'Father ...'

McCann cut her off 'Oh just sit down, woman.'

Malikah sat herself next to McCann, taking the tablet on the desk she called in the first crewman.

A young man entered the room and saluted at the desk.

'At ease,' stated McCann whilst he rummaged around in his pockets for a box of cigar matches.

'Name,' inquired Malikah.

'Petty Officer Wright, Sir,' replied the young man in a Scottish accent.

Malikah smirked at the tall young man 'No need to call me Sir,' she tapped the tablet to see his military record appear. His achievements at the annual military tournament on Gukumatz were also listed 'You made the third eliminator in Sabre last year, not bad at all.'

The young man in his uniform let a smile go 'Thank you ....'

'Malikah, and don't thank me too soon Petty Officer. Your results will put you on the front line of the skirmish, so tell me do you have any preferred weapon?'

The young man in his 20's thought for a moment until Malikah snapped 'Quickly Mr Wright, I haven't got all day you know?'

'Well I've never used a real sword,' replied the awkward Scotsman.

The sable Queen sighed 'Father, she turned to her left to see McCann attempting to light his cigar in vain 'Father could you flash three sabres for me and a katana?'

The Englishman didn't listen, he was far too busy in his endeavour to start the foot of his Habanos smouldering 'What the bloody hell is wrong with this cigar?' bellowed the Admiral.

'I wouldn't bother with that,' stated Malikah.

McCann frowned as he lit another match and again attempted to toast the foot 'Why not?'

The dark haired Amazon smirked 'Athena's oxygen content has been lowered to 15%, nothing will burn I'm afraid.'

The Englishman scowled at his daughter 'What in the devil are you talking about?'

'The match carries its own oxygen; however the cigar won't light in a 15% oxygen atmosphere.'

McCann pulled his smoke from between his lips rather forcefully 'Why the bloody hell ...'

Malikah raised her fist to his mouth, an annoying habit she'd inherited from Ilam 'I ordered the oxygen content reduced, it lowers the chances of a fire getting out of control, in the core there will be no rescue.'

McCann gave his daughter an annoyed look.

The Tlillan goddess sighed and looked up 'Athena, please increase the oxygen content of the Officers' mess to 21%.'

'Affirmative,' replied the soft voiced SI.

Malikah returned her gaze to McCann 'While you're waiting to smoke that thing, perhaps you could flash these for me?' she passed a tablet containing technical specifications of four different swords.

The grumpy Englishman stood up and grabbed the tablet 'You're worse than your Grandmother, you know that?'

Malikah's eyes widened for a moment giving McCann his cue to flash the weapons.

The Admiral shuffled off and soon returned from behind the bar with a set of blades which Malikah laid out on the table.

The sable Queen gestured towards the weapons 'Give them a try and select the one you're most comfortable with.'

On the table lay a 1796 British light cavalry sabre, an 1852 Prussian sabre, a British 1908 heavy cavalry sabre and finally a modern katana similar to the present she had given to her lover.

The 1796 British light cavalry sabre was anything but a light weapon. The blade was wider at the tip than at the forte, resulting in a sword which dealt devastating blows, easily removing limbs from the opponent.

The 1852 Prussian sabre was a more elegant weapon, a blade with a slight curve and piped spine to reinforce the thrust. Light and handy with strong thrust, a far cry from the brutal curve and hatchet blade of the 1796 sabre; suitable for those with a supple wrist and fine swordplay skills.

The 1908 heavy cavalry sabre was a totally straight blade, providing a fatal thrust on the charge; its long triangular blade being the polar opposite of the 1796 with the 1852 in between.

All of these sabres had seen extended use on the battlefield, the 1796 more than any in the world. Having been responsible for the expansion of the British Empire it was used by the Prussians, not only for its brutal effectiveness against the armies of Napoleon but also because it shot fear into the hearts of men.

The katana held a curved blade of about 60cm in the shoguzukuri style, strong and firm it held great cutting power. The handle was very long, compared to the sabres it was quite massive. The katana required two hands, allowing the wielder to place enough leverage behind it to slice a man's head off.

Petty Officer Wright gave each sabre a go, sliding it out of the steel scabbard to get a feel for the weapon. He skipped the katana since he was not trained in Japanese sword arts and wouldn't have a clue on using the weapon. After a short time Wright selected the 1796 sabre, a very intimidating and powerful weapon.

Malikah smiled 'Father, would you get this man a combat suit and shield please?'

McCann who'd been quietly enjoying his Ramon Allones stood up again 'Why yes your majesty, would there be anything else?' he said in sardonic voice.

Malikah chuckled whilst looking at the crewman 'Grow up?'

Petty Officer Wright began to smirk until he caught the savage eye of Admiral McCann.

McCann shuffled off and returned with a suit of catronium body armour, a sword belt and a shield flashed to the crewman's specifications.

'Take this,' sneered McCann pushing the load into the crewman's chest.

'Thank you Admiral,' replied the intimidated crewman before taking his sabre and leaving.

'Really father, that was totally un-called for!'

The Englishman merely mumbled under his breath.

'Go and flash another 1796 while I call the next one in will you?'

'I suppose,' said the Admiral as he puffed his fine Cuban cigar.

Over the next hour or two the swordsmen of the highest calibre on the Athena were all armed for their mission ahead. Not long afterwards the entire crew of over 200 were prepared to do battle; now it was time to find the enemy.

Later, on the Bridge, Malikah was discussing the co-ordinates with Hassif, 'This would put us very close to Sagittarius A, what about S1, S13 and S8? They might tear us apart if we exit the tunnel there.'

Malikah raised an eyebrow 'That's what you get paid the big bucks for Mr Sharma, plot the course and make certain we don't end up in pieces.'

Hassif shook his head 'Why not exit further out?'

Malikah smiled at the distressed Indian 'Because that is where they went and if we exit the wormhole further away they may use missiles before we even see them.'

The three Matriarchs were all stood around Hassif monitoring his calculations; McCann stood up and asked 'What are you talking about?'

Ilam turned to her husband 'We will be exiting the wormhole close to the super massive black hole at the core. In order to prevent the Athena being drawn into the centre and destroyed we must use three of the stars which orbit it to stabilise us. Hassif will calculate a destination which places us in the centre of these stars gravitational pull, it will allow Athena to resist the tidal forces of Sagittarius A.'

McCann shrugged his shoulders 'So what's the problem?'

Ilam gave him a stoic look 'If Hassif is incorrect the tidal forces shall rip us to pieces upon exiting the wormhole.'

'But won't they have already left the core?' countered McCann.

'No, they must remain in orbit of the three stars for another month. If they attempt to leave earlier ...'

'They'll be ripped apart, right?' interjected McCann.

Ilam nodded her head in approval 'Correct.'

'Marvellous, just bloody marvellous,' muttered the Englishman.

'Course certified,' stated Athena.

McCann rested on his chair, he tapped the arm and a familiar voice answered 'what is it McCann?'

'Is the wormhole generator ready Chief?' sighed the Admiral.

'Sure, but I am reading this right?'

'Reading what right?'

'The destination.'

'Well I can't see what you're looking at can I!'

'You know what I mean, Sagittarius fucking A! Are you trying to get us all killed?'

McCann retorted 'Have no fear Louis ... only the good die young!' then switched off communications to the engine room.

The Englishman lay back in his seat 'Prepare to fold space.'

The lighting changed to red light throughout the war cruiser and Athena set her klaxon running.

The three Tlillan ladies walked to the rear of the Bridge and gripped handles on the vacant stations.

'All hands prepare to fold space,' bellowed Athena in an authoritative tone.

The lights began to drop as the entire vessel shook, there was a flash of light and a white hole appeared before them.

'Activating Casimir field,' stated Athena.

As the field activated, the white hole ceased to push and began to have the opposite effect as Athena was drawn in.

Athena guided them in as brilliant white light streaked past the vessel, the crew were bumped around whilst Athena rode its gravitons into the centre.

The ship's crew were buffeted from side to side, Ilam shook her head and muttered 'So primitive,' however no-one heard due to generator noise drowning her out.

Athena reached the centre and was unceremoniously ejected into what was now named hyperspace. Athena quickly used her Casimir field to find the zone between the wormhole and black hole at the centre. Using her fusion engines Athena entered the river Styx and plotted a course through it to the other side, where a wormhole to Sagittarius A awaited them.

As they travelled through this zone, where the gravitational pulls of the wormhole and black hole cancelled each other out, the crew observed objects inhabiting this area of hyperspace.

Images of worlds and other craft moved around the Styx as spirits waiting on its banks for Charon. Extreme gravity trapped these images due to both time and space stretched to the limit by titanic forces.

As usual Vezzali logged every relevant event, it was now standard practice, this was what the Tlillans referred to as the Dreamscape. McCann was still quite sceptical about being able to foresee the future via this Dreamscape, although it seemed to work fairly well for them. Though their problem was more in interpreting what they saw, the Seers on Otoch had got it wrong more than once. Even Malikah had screwed up; the recent battle at Bandayuuk was a prime example. The Tlillan Queen had foreseen a victory when in fact she had witnessed the fortunate outcome of a crushing defeat and a Tlillan revolt.

'Sir, look at this!' shouted an excited Vezzali.

On the view screen an image within the Styx was magnified, the Englishman recognised it; he was staring at the Athena.

Malikah stepped up beside her father 'It is us returning from Sagittarius A, I have seen it already.'

'Is it us?' asked Hassif.

'Possibly, possibly us in an alternate universe or someone else in another universe sailing the Athena,' replied a stoic Malikah.

McCann snorted at his daughters reply 'Well that's a shitload of use to me isn't it?' he stated sarcastically.

Vezzali zoomed in on the image 'Look, we, I mean they have damage from what appears to be a collision?'

There were long trenches cut along the top of the craft, deep shafts had broken the armoured skin of the vessel.

'What on Earth did that?' said Hassif as he examined the image.

'Admiral! Look!' Vezzali shrieked as the image then focused on the fore of the Athena.

McCann noticed a flickering docking light, but the ship wasn't docking so why would it be flashing?

'It's Morse code Admiral!' shouted Vezzali in her Italian accent.

'Well what the bloody hell does it say?' shouted the Admiral impatiently.

About a minute later Vezzali had read the message and replied 'Defend Casimir.'

Hassif frowned 'Defend Casimir? They want us to defend the Casimir field? But wouldn't we do that anyway?'

McCann scratched his chin 'No, he's telling us that they will attack our Casimir field generator. If they can disable it we'll be forced to retreat or die from intense radiation at the core.'

'How do you know that?' asked the Indian.

Malikah replied 'Because he is sending the message to himself, something he knows his past self would comprehend.'

'Then that IS us from the future?' asked Hassif.

'Not us but the image of us, we are looking into the future. The gravitational forces inside what you call the dead zone create massive dilation effects, leading to images remaining locked inside as if they were a holograph.

What you see is an image of the Athena returning from the core.'

'But how do we see it from the past? Surely it hasn't happened yet?' pushed the stubborn Indian.

Malikah didn't reply, she was very intelligent but she was no expert in astrophysics.

Vezzali answered Hassif's conundrum and the entire bridge crew shut up to listen 'Actually it's very possible, a wormhole has two ends. If you took one end and accelerated it using gravity then entered you could in theory exit the other end in the past.'

McCann swivelled his chair and gave his science Officer a puzzled look.

The blonde haired Italian answered his expression 'We entered the wormhole in September and will exit it in a few days, in normal time. Well we will exit close to Sagittarius A; the gravitational forces would accelerate that end of the wormhole causing it to age less. When making the return trip the wormhole at Earth may be in December but Sagittarius A wormhole would still be in September due to the acceleration from the gravitational forces of the super massive black hole.

According to Einstein if there are two clocks at each wormhole and the stable end ages normally and reads December but the clock at the accelerated end reads September; we would enter the accelerated wormhole and exit the stable end at almost the same time, in September ... in theory.'

The last two words made McCann distinctly nervous 'In theory?'

Vezzali looked around the Bridge and in a rather tense tone replied 'Yes, the theory has never been put to the test.'

The Englishman muttered under his breath 'Marvellous.'

'So that is us and not just our image?' inquired Hassif.

Vezzali observed the screen and replied 'It could be either, it's impossible to tell without getting closer to the object.'

'No!' Shouted Ilam 'Do not make contact in anyway.'

'Why not,' asked her husband.

The red haired Valkyrie observed the image and replied stoically 'It is forbidden, contact may create a paradox event, even your light signals are heresy for Tlillan.'

'Paradox event?'

'Imagine you were to visit the future Athena, then on that Athena an accident occurred and you died. How could you send yourself light signals from the future?'

'Perhaps I did die and that is Kim sending the signals?'

'What if your future self were responsible for your past self's death?'

'That's not possible because I wouldn't be on board the future ship to kill myself would I?'

'So then you would discover the cause of your future accident and avoid that accident?'

'Correct.'

'In that case your future self would be present on the future Athena, yes?'

McCann scratched the stubble on his chin, his wife was always a good ten steps ahead of him 'Alright, I give in; just tell me what would happen.'

Ilam made that classic Tlillan condescending smirk 'Timelines would collapse, each person, each object has a timeline. At certain points those threads of time intersect, some interweave, others never touch.

In a paradox event those threads are stretched, some snap others are distorted, touching where they should not, the results would be catastrophic for the Athena and all on board; you may end up destroying everyone, just from a simple meeting.'

Vezzali turned to engage Ilam but before she could speak Ilam held her fist in a gesture to silence the science Officer 'I know what your Einstein said, he was a gifted man but I have witnessed a paradox event from our past. Trust me when I say Xch'uup forbid this millennia ago for good reason.'

Hassif remained sceptical on the whole thing, he then attempted to push this theory of time travel further 'Assuming this is all possible, there is still a single element unaccounted for, how is it possible to keep the wormhole open? This theory would require it is kept open while we hunt the Clotho and complete our mission.'

All eyes turned to Ilam 'the three stars we are about to jump into, they are close enough that their gravitational pull cancels out the tidal force of Sagittarius A. If our co-ordinates are off, our wormhole may be pulled close to one of the stars or even the black hole. That would super accelerate the wormhole, whilst providing energy required to maintain a bridge to Earth.'

Hassif still refused to give in 'Fine, but why didn't we see another wormhole before we left Earth? Surely there should've been two wormholes?'

Vezzali intervened 'No, essentially this is the same wormhole as the one we created just now when leaving Earth. We will be returning via the same wormhole since it would be kept open by the gravitational pull of either a star or the super massive black hole.'

'But wouldn't that result in two Athenas exiting the stable end at Earth?'

'No, only one Athena would exit. This Athena.'

'But what about the Athena we're looking at now?'

'That is this Athena's image, right now time is out of phase and there are an infinite amount of Athenas traveling along the same distorted time line. There are Athenas behind and ahead of us, but when we complete the mission and return to the stable wormhole time shall be re-synchronised. The many Athenas along this timeline shall be forced back into phase by the energy of the wormhole as we are ejected back into normal time.

Essentially we are only traveling in time relatively ... relative to us that Athena is in the future, when we return we will see another Athena on her way to Sagittarius A and that will be in the past. Whilst we are at Sagittarius A time will pass normally relative to us but relative those on Earth we would be frozen in time, relative to us they would be in the future; but because the wormhole is held frozen at this date for us we will return at this date no matter how long we spend out there ... it's quite simple really.'

McCann let out a massive exhale 'Jesus Christ I think I need a drink already!'

Ilam smiled in approval at the short Italian science Officer 'Perhaps the human race does hold promise.'

Malikah gave her mother a black look before pointing something out 'If what Vezzali says is true, wouldn't that suppose our exit co-ordinates are incorrect?'

Uncomfortable looks crossed the bridge for a few moments, 'Kim I want you to inform Louis that we may be exiting space too close to one of the stars, have him prepared for emergency manoeuvers. Athena prepare the crew for battle stations we may be taking damage a lot earlier than expected,' ordered McCann.

Hassif began to prepare for standard emergency manoeuvers while they passed the image of their future selves. As two boats passing each other upon the river Styx, Athena paddled them through the dark waters of destiny with all the confidence and experience of Charon; ferrying her crew to meet their fate at the core of the Milky Way.

Eventually the warship navigated herself around the black hole at the centre of the wormhole before aligning with the wormhole on the other side. The crew braced themselves, McCann then gave the order 'this could be a rough ride everyone, Athena you may enter the wormhole at your discretion.'

Everything was still, as the crew stared into total blackness, a wire framed box on the view screen marked out where the mini black hole forming their exit was.

Athena fired her engines pushing herself and her passengers into the influence of the tiny black hole.

'Dropping Casimir field,' called the soft voice of Athena.

'Certified,' replied Hassif.

The small vessel was pulled into the singularity; the crew were jolted from side to side as Athena wrestled with the harsh gravitational pull. Passing through they exited into real space and were thrust out through the white hole.

'Alert! Gravitational fields not within safety parameters!' bellowed Athena.

The bridge crew were holding on for dear life as the Athena was wrenched into a flat spin, turning much like the rotors upon a helicopter she was flung towards a nearby star.

'Wormhole generator disengaged, attempting to stabilise vessel,' called Athena in her soft voice.

The Athena began to correct herself; steadying attitude and pointing away from the massive stellar body Athena spoke again 'Vessel stable, firing engines.'

McCann braced himself for a mighty push from the engines, but it never came. He heard a roar and felt her shaking from an extended full blast; however they were still plummeting towards the star.

'Braking manoeuver unsuccessful, firing engines,' informed the guardian of their lives calmly.

Again there was no effect, McCann's arm pad on his chair began to beep, he hit it and Louis answered 'McCann the engines cannot slow us down, we're too close to the star, it doesn't matter how many times she tries,' the Frenchman was terrified, as was McCann though he refused to show it.

'Louis is there any way to pull out? Could we detonate all our anti-matter on the engine blast plates?'

Louis was shouting to be heard as the pandemonium inside the engine room was deafening 'It would only blow our engines out, probably kill us all.'

'Is there a chance?' shouted McCann.

'Slim.'

'Well if we don't try we're dead in about 3 minutes anyway!'

The Admiral felt a hand on his shoulder; he looked up to see his daughter with a sheen of black space covering her eyeballs.

'Louis hold that for moment.'

'Sure.'

'McCann out.'

He tapped the arm of his chair as his heart began to beat faster and harder.

'Descent slowing, 400,000 KM/s, 300,000 KM/s, 200,000 KM/s,' Athena kept counting down until the warship hung precariously close to the star, suspended in space as a tightrope walker with no safety net. The crew were in awe and terror much like an audience watching an acrobat slide along his wire to safety.

McCann shouted towards Hassif 'Activate the Casimir field.'

'Activating a Casimir field this close to a singularity is not within safety parameters,' replied the soft voice of Athena.

Hassif nodded 'She's right, we'd be torn apart.'

McCann tapped his chair 'Louis, fire the engines, full speed.'

'Understood,' replied his Chief Engineer.

The Athena lurched forward.

McCann looked up 'When we're at a safe distance activate the Casimir field, before we all get freeze dried by the bloody radiation!'

'Affirmative Admiral,' replied Athena.

As the Athena pulled out of the influence of the star she passed the white hole and activated her Casimir field. Two other stars were close by, their gravitational pulls prevented the Athena from being pulled into the super massive black hole, which all three stars (among many others) orbited.

The Black hole was in reality no larger in size than any other … technically. However the fact that it contains 5 million solar masses changes the rules, due to its gravitational pull space was warped and twisted causing gravitational lensing. This expands the size to about 5.2 times the normal size of a black hole, leaving a super massive black hole of at least 40 AU.

The Athena eventually drifted into the dead zone of the three stars, where she could remain in space without further gravitational harassment.

Slowly Malikah's eyes returned to normal, before she fell to the ground.

Lian caught her 'She must rest, I'll look after her Duncan.'

McCann was concerned for his daughter but there was a ship of Neenayin gunning for them and these stars were shifting around the black hole all the time 'Thank you,' replied the Admiral.

Vezzali chimed in 'Scanning for the Clotho Admiral.'

The Englishman looked in wonder at Sagittarius A, the titanic accretion disc orbited the largest object in their galaxy, massive enough to hold over 200 billion stars across 120,000 light years in its grip.

'Sir! I've found the Clotho!' cried an excited science Officer.

McCann sat back as he observed the tactical display 'It's time to rock and roll.'

Chapter 19

Athena stabilised herself yet the view of space around her was anything but. McCann observed the supermassive black hole, it devoured most of the void before Athena, yet the sight was twisted and bent.

Due to massive forces the very fabric of space and time contorted all around them, light turned and flailed. It was as if he were observing a ballet executed by the insane, dancers making erratic pirouettes whilst others warped their bodies around them. The distorted play made no sense, there was no story, nothing any man in his right mind could follow.

Light travelling through disfigured space betrayed it, twisting and bending along it, McCann could make no sense of the horrible gobbledygook before him.

Vezzali tapped away at her science station 'The Clotho is in orbit of S8 Admiral.'

A wire frame box appeared magnifying a section of the madness; an image of the Clotho lay in orbit of one of the colossal stellar bodies orbiting Sagittarius A.

'That cannot be them,' added Hassif.

Vezzali delved further into her data 'It is an image of them, but I doubt they were ever there, if they came that close to S8 they would have been dragged in and vapourised.'

'Then our mission is complete?' asked McCann rather hopefully.

'Malikah is sure the Clotho remains intact,' reported Ilam destroying the Englishman's hopes.

McCann narrowed his eyes 'Is she damaged? The Clotho seems to be ... stretched.'

Vezzali carried away at her station hunting for the real Clotho 'No, it is merely the effects of gravity, space is so deformed the Clotho could be right next to us yet we cannot see her.'

'How do we know she's even here?'

Ilam gazed stoically at the tactical view screen 'Aside from Xch'uup's word, to escape these tidal forces the Clotho would require a wormhole.'

McCann raised an eye 'Then we should stay by ours in case they attempt to escape through it.'

The wormhole created by Athena remained open and held in place by the massive force of the star S13. Despite shutting down their generator the passage between Sagittarius A and Earth refused to collapse, further strengthening evidence that they'd encountered their future selves in hyperspace.

Ilam shook her head 'No, it will only return them to Earth; I believe the traitors shall find us and attempt to capture the Athena.'

'The scarring on her top side?' said McCann referring to the future Athena.

The tall Valkyrie nodded in agreement 'Olga is arrogant ...'

'A typical Tlillan female then?' retorted McCann.

Ilam ignored his jibe 'She believes it is possible to board Athena and capture her,' Ilam placed her hand upon the grip of her mantle 'K'eek'en kan!'

An hour had passed and still no sign of the real Clotho, McCann wasn't perturbed since he was used to similar situations. Many times had the Englishman sat around waiting for light to reach him before detecting the enemy, then of course Hassif would calculate how long ago that light had taken to reach them and where the enemy may be now.

Malikah stepped off the lift and back onto the Bridge accompanied by Voice of Machine 'They are close by Father.'

'Where?'

'Near to S13, hiding behind a cloak of bent light.'

'Give Hassif the co-ordinates, Athena can put a broadside into them now.'

Vezzali shook her head 'That is not possible Admiral.'

McCann replied in a puzzled tone 'Why?'

Vezzali took a breath then answered her commanding Officer 'Space time is horribly warped, there are bubbles of compressed space/time all around; some are undetectable.'

Still puzzled the Englishman replied 'So?'

'If one of those bubbles were inside the barrel of just one cannon it could cause a detonation, we would cripple ourselves.'

McCann still didn't understand 'Explain that to me Vezzali.'

Hassif raised his eyebrows whilst making a facial expression at Ilam which read "here we go again".

Vezzali attempted to educate her CO in layman's terms 'Space and time are the same thing, when space is stretched it is spread thinner as is time. We are in space that is stretched to the limit, as we travel through that stretched space we interact with less space because it is thinly spread.

This means we interact with less time, in short we are moving very, very slowly through time.

Now because of this unique area of space there are bubbles floating around created by tidal forces of Sagittarius A and nearby stellar bodies. Inside these bubbles space and time are relatively compressed, meaning time moves quicker inside the bubbles.

If a bubble were inside a barrel when you fire an anti-matter shell, it would accelerate the speed of that shell in time. The shell would exit the bubble and come back into phase inside part of the barrel.

Imagine half of the barrel is moving slower in time, when a shell passes into that half it might be say half a second in the future relative to that section of the barrel. It would make contact with the barrel, cause a detonation and at the very least disable the cannon. At worst, destroy Athena and her crew.'

Vezzali waited for McCann to reply, he only exhaled loudly and looked back at the view screen.

Malikah suddenly peered upwards towards the ceiling, she said in a stoic tone 'Send Vympel one to the Casimir generator, quickly.'

Before McCann could question his daughter Athena's red lights flooded the Bridge 'Alert, enemy vessel detected, co-ordinates X − 0.001, Y 0.0, Z + 0.001.'

McCann looked at the tactical display to see the Clotho was almost upon them, it hung in space just above Athena 'How the bloody hell did they get there?'

Vezzali called over the klaxon 'Tidal forces cloaked them, Admiral.'

Athena called out in her usual calming tone 'Collision imminent, brace for impact, brace for impact, brace for impact.'

The Bridge crew lurched backwards as Athena was shoved forwards by a mighty collision. The Clotho crashed onto the war cruiser's topside, cutting massive trenches into her catronium armour. Next McCann heard great thumps, he assumed the Clotho was clamping onto Athena mechanically.

'Alert enemy detected level 10, aft section engineering,' noted Athena.

Mayer turned to McCann 'they are attacking the Casimir generator, both vessels fields are working for now, but if one is disabled it will not be enough to protect both ships.'

McCann nodded 'Send Egorov and as many men as he requires.'

Kim tapped his wrist tablet before sending the Spetsnaz Officer to defend the generator.

Kim tapped his wrist again 'Done, Admiral.'

McCann nodded 'How on Earth did they manage to board us so bloody quickly?'

Lieutenant Mayer answered his question 'Pneumatic drills, I believe they flashed the parts and installed them before we arrived. They are similar to those used by mining droids in the belt.'

Athena fired her alarm again catching everyone's attention 'Alert enemy detected level 10, aft, engineering section, power core.'

McCann tapped the Captain's chair immediately 'Louis, can you hear me?'

The only sound audible was the clash of weapons and shields bashing against one another.

Malikah moved towards the elevator 'They are attempting to disable the power core.'

Ilam snapped 'What of the Casimir generator?'

The sable Queen waved her hand at her mother 'It is well defended, Egorov has them under-control.'

McCann retorted 'How do you know that?'

His daughter made a face at him, a frown as if to say "are you stupid?"

'Fine but Kim is going.'

Blood drained from the first Officer's face, McCann realised his First was not up to rescuing Louis 'Fine, you go to the engine room, take all the people you need.'

Lian leapt to Malikah's side, Ilam silently accepted her daughter's request, joining her.

As Ilam passed McCann the Englishman grabbed his wife's arm but before he could say anything he received assurance of Malikah's safety via his link with the Amazon.

After his grip was released the three Valkyries entered the lift, before its doors closed Malikah smiled at her father 'I want you to remain at your chair Father.'

He made a pathetic attempt at a smile before the door slid across and she was gone.

The three Valkyries exited the lift, marching along Athena's corridors bathed in red light. Ilam tapped what looked like a wrist tablet attached to her forearm, except she already had a wrist tablet on the other arm. A black fan unfurled from the mechanism until it formed a perfect circle about the size of a truck tyre, in the centre sat a black boss. Next her Tlillan suit formed its space helmet as a liquid leapt from her collar, upon mental command.

The three women strode out from the lift, entering Louis' engineering section as three angels of death, carrying a neutronium sword in one hand and a shield on the other arm.

Lian carried no shield, she only brandished a long katana, though dressed in space age battle armour with a helmet obscuring her features it was not a sight for the weak hearted.

Louis and his staff had been utilizing the long trench between the power core and engines. They used the narrow point to hold off superior enemy numbers; otherwise the entire power core would've been over-run.

Olga and 50 of her cohorts hacked away, the Russian Matriarch fought ferociously slicing through the mere men and women who attempted to oppose her will; standing tall as a Jove amongst cowering mortals, the towering figure beat down upon those who dared resist.

Olga and her followers had entered the section through open tunnels above, cut by pneumatic drills.

The Tlillan ladies marched from the lifts and into the trench bolstering Louis' forces.

The Frenchman caught sight of the women and a wave of relief came over him; blood smeared his shield and dripped from his 1908 British cavalry sabre.

'Is it just you three?' asked the desperate Engineer.

The clash of blades filled the air as Athena's power core hummed to their left, Malikah's helmet melted back into the collar of her space suit and a gasp could be heard as the Neenayin retreated.

Olga was left alone on the frontline of the skirmish, looking around, the towering red headed Matriarch fell back using her shashka to fight off any attacks. The engine room staff were glad to see her withdrawal, those still in possession of their lives did nothing to prevent the retreat.

Olga grabbed one of her soldiers skulking in the ranks 'Fight you coward!'

The German banker dressed in similar body armour to Athena's crew shook his head 'Look,' he gestured with his grosse meser sword across the carnage of bodies and organs bleeding into the gutter.

Olga followed his long sword until across the trench she noticed her Xch'uup.

The German man in his 50's with eyes similar to those of a crocodile trembled at the sight 'Ek'tsab.'

Olga sneered at the little man 'She's as mortal as you or I.'

Next Malikah's cohorts lost their head protection sending another wave of terror throughout the Neenayin ranks; much like Deimos and Phobos sending terror and panic throughout the ranks of those who opposed their Father, Ares.

Louis was dumbfounded; he couldn't understand why the Neenayin had broken off when on the cusp of overwhelming his staff and capturing the power core.

A Chinese industrialist approached Olga 'We must retreat to the Clotho, quickly!'

Olga's eyes burnt red with rage, the Chinaman was not affected by his leader's anger; he was only concerned with what he saw behind the Athenian lines.

'What are you afraid of? You have come this far already!' bellowed Olga.

The Chinaman who held a long spear shook his head feverishly from side to side 'No, that is Ek'tsab and look she has Kalayuuk with her.'

Olga's frustration boiled within her 'Come fight with me and I will help you defeat one of your Titans.'

The Industrialist peered up towards his General 'I cannot harm a God, I am only Neenayin.'

Olga sneered 'She is no more a God than I, come when she is close throw your spear, I shall guide it into her.'

Olga marched forward bringing the Clotho skirmish line to that of the Athenians. A clamour went out as lines clashed, Olga towered above Athena's mere mortals, with a single crushing blow she would hit a shield knocking a grown man to the hard catronium floor, now covered in a slurry of congealing bodily fluids.

The Athenian Matriarchs observed their enemy closing, making a determined push to force control of the power core from Louis.

Malikah raised her blade in the direction of the battle 'Louis follow me, Lian you must deal with your old friend. Mother take the left flank.'

The women strode into the ranks of battle as Olympians striding across the plains of Troy, making their way unabated towards a bloody destiny.

As Lian appeared from the struggle Olga sensed her soldiers' fear, the sight of a six and a half foot Amazon wielding a massive Katana would put any man ill at ease. For these Neenayin it was something more, they possessed memories of the Makayuuk and how Machine banished them.

These deceivers who used the mortal coil of men for their own purposes had been hunted down and extinguished mercilessly. The few who'd escaped made it to a different solar system, fortunate to discover a race of creatures almost exactly the same as Makayuuk.

They were primitive but could easily be manipulated, this time the Neenayin would get it right and rule a world of slaves.

Then came the Tlillans, yet they deceived even Xch'uup, the Neenayin were long thought extinct a sketchy memory lost to the rigors of Father Time. The crisis was over, until Machine returned, those machine man eyes could spot a Neenayin at 100 metres.

As long as Tlillans and Humans were united against Machine the deception could continue and perhaps their worst enemy might be destroyed into the bargain?

Unfortunately the Neenayin could not influence Xch'uup to exterminate the remaining Makayuuk after the conquest of Bandayuuk 0.

Then came Kalayuuk, Voice of Machine, the game on Earth was up and it was time to flee, and so now they were here; at the galactic core floating precariously around three stars fighting to the death with primitive weapons.

Machine would not let them escape and now Machine stood in person before them, the most terrifying creature a Neenayin could ever encounter.

They had created Machine to be a God, to be praised by the Makayuuk and ruled by the Neenayin. The lizards soon discovered that only a true Titan may rule a God.

Olga was not so impeded, she had grown up with Lian, both of them went to school together in New York.

As Lian strode out from the Athenian battle lines Olga shouted 'Now! Cast your spear!'

The industrialist shook in fear.

Olga's eyes burnt with the fire of rage as she spoke through her teeth to the little man 'Cast your spear if you wish to live.'

The short man peered at her fiery eyes with his reptilian gaze, realising his life hung in the balance, he cast his catronium spear as hard as he could towards Voice of Machine.

Lian's attention had been caught by the sight of her old friend caked in blood; too late she noticed the enemy javelin.

The weapon penetrated the young Amazon's right leg; a stinging pain almost knocked her unconscious. Across the battle line both Ilam and Malikah sensed her sudden distress, forcing their retreat.

Lian dropped into the mire of men's blood and organs, human filth swirled around her as it was slushed to and fro by other combatants, all too absorbed with their own fragile existence.

Olga screamed with delight 'THERE! YOU SEE? YOUR GOD IS CRAWLING IN THE MUCK!'

The short man, former Chairman of a massive transport cartel, observed Lian wide eyed as she writhed in pain, attempting to manipulate the spear out of her leg through the path of least resistance.

'Kalayuuk has fallen?'

Olga frowned 'don't just stand there you fool, finish her, quickly!'

The Chinaman pulled out another spear from behind his long shield and made his way with three others to end the life of Lian.

Malikah blocked the pain transmitted to her; scanning the front line she could not see her lover standing tall above men's heads. The sable Queen did notice Olga screaming and gesturing at the floor with her weapon. Wasting no time the mighty Valkyrie pushed through the ranks until reaching her destination.

The Neenayin closed in, however before the final blow could be dealt a break in the lines formed and out strode Malikah. Her stare smouldered as a wine dark sun; there was no question who she intended it for. The Queen stood over her lover, brandishing the mantle of Xch'uup in one hand and a shield in the other.

The Neenayin froze as Deimos gazed toward them; a depiction of the God lay upon the Queen's shield. As beautiful as the demigod's Mother and as chilling as his Father, sable locks of hair rolled over her shoulders as clouds upon a mountain range. The Amazon's deep dark eyes glared, opening wide towards the reptilians, as portals to the underworld, inviting foolhardy mortals who dared challenge her to enter Tartarus.

Olga bellowed from behind them 'Forward you cowards!'

Yet the Neenayin remained where they stood, their limbs rooted to the spot in fear of the Star Shaker.

Malikah squatted down and pulled the spear from Lian's leg, Voice of Machine let out a deep howling scream which reverberated around the entire engine room. All combatants stopped what they were doing, battle lines separated, drawing away from combat.

Malikah took the bloodied spear; sneering at the Chinaman she cast it with all her might. The shaft of catronium flew across the open space between the ranks and into an African Prince standing beside the former leader of East Asia's premier transport cartel.

The spear didn't stop at the young Prince however, it found a gap in his armour, penetrated his chest, carrying on through him; after passing throughout the traitor's body only a shaft of light remained.

The Prince collapsed without a word, the Chinaman next heard a noise as the javelin plunged into the ranks behind him. Another Neenayin fell to the same spear cast, then another and another. The Industrialist wasn't sure how many had fallen to one cast from Ek'tsab; however his prospects seemed most dire.

Malikah turned on the two remain Neenayin and howled as a baying wolf, her scream caused the reptilian to quiver, somehow he edged backwards whilst hiding as much of himself as he could behind his shield.

Olga placed her hand on his back 'Where are you going?'

The industrialist replied in a shaky voice 'I didn't agree to this!'

No sooner had he finished his sentence than a Shashka burst out of his chest. Olga pushed the man's back with her foot, withdrawing her blade as her soldier dropped to his knees, splashing face first into the bodily fluids swirling in the trench.

Malikah mocked her adversary 'If all your followers are as courageous this shall be fast work indeed!'

Olga sneered at the remaining Neenayin who'd attempted to finish off Lian; her burning eyes told the German that a retreat would end for him as it did for the Chinaman.

The former head of Deutsche Bank steadied his grosse meser and made a charge for Xch'uup, all eyes were upon him.

The reptilian rushed in screaming with sword outstretched, his furious pace kicked up thick blood from the ground as he charged forwards, Malikah met his blade with a powerful Tlillan parry.

Slapping his two handed sword as hard as she could, yet maintaining enough control that if she missed, the point of her blade would not swing too far to one side; Malikah knocked the grosse meser out of his hands stopping the beast in its tracks.

The Banker watched on as his weapon flew off and skidded along the ground, disappearing into the mire of hot blood and steaming guts. An expression of despair filled the deceiver's face as he turned to stare fate in the eye.

Malikah let out a booming cackle taking obvious pleasure in her opponent's despair, her expression was one of amusement. However it only lasted for a moment, before transforming to one of hatred. The mantle of Xch'uup, a blade which once dispensed justice to the entire galaxy, swung slicing the Banker's head off in a single cut.

His head plopped into the gore below as a fountain of hot blood burst from his neck; it reminded Malikah of the jet d'eau back on Lake Geneva.

Vesuvius sprayed onto the Tlillan Empress, cackling in delight at the fate of Olga's doomed followers much like a God punishing the people of Pompey for their wicked ways. The corpse crumpled before her, adding to the lake of filth filling the engine room.

Olga observed Ilam pushing up from the ranks with Louis and a posse of re-invigorated soldiers, all inspired by what they'd witnessed. The red headed half Tlillan realised this battle was lost; her fighters shook in terror at the very sight of the mighty Ek'tsab. It seemed her Neenayin had either taken the fable of the Star Shaker from the Makayuuk or passed it on to them. Either way it didn't matter, they were all terrified by Malikah and Lian, her Neenayin soldiers perceived the pair as deities.

Olga raised her Cossack sabre and called the retreat, men and women began to flee back down the bloody trench. It had cost so many lives to push the battle line this far down and now those lives had been squandered.

Louis moved forward 'Come before they escape!'

Ilam put her arm across his chest holding him back 'Let them flee Louis, their fate is set in the Dreamscape.'

Malikah pointed her neutronium sabre at Olga and shouted down the trench 'You bring me to the edge of the abyss only to abscond with your motley followers?'

'I will not fight you,' said Olga as the acoustically perfect design of the trench carried her voice.

'Bin'nt himaar!' screamed the frustrated Queen.

The Neenayin stood beneath the holes cut into the ceiling of the engine room from the Clotho. Magnetic fields combined with suction pumps allowed each individual to levitate upwards one at a time. Its field encased the person below perfectly, suction would then be engaged creating a pressure difference between upper and lower parts divided by the passenger. As long as they held their breath, each Neenayin was pulled upwards into the 2 metre wide tube and back to the safety of the Clotho.

One by one they waited for their turn beneath the two tubes, every 10-15 seconds another was sucked up into the Clotho. Olga stood at the end of the trench guarding the withdrawal of her troops.

Malikah strode through the congealing muck, she reached a distance from Olga and challenged the Matriarch 'Fight me and settle this, Alyona and Yana don't have to die.'

'What of the Neenayin?' asked Olga in a forceful tone.

Malikah smirked 'I have seen their fate; they will never leave e'hoch'e'en chumuk.'

Olga shook her head 'I cannot abandon them.'

Malikah retorted in an incredulous tone 'Abandon them? They are nothing, their filthy souls will be dragged in and reside here forever, do not doom Alyona and Yana to the same fate.'

'What of your followers?' sneered Olga.

'My crew shall fight to the death; they will not retreat as your eek k'eek'en. Look at them Olga, they flee in fear, these pigs would leave you to die in this muck. Would you sacrifice yours and your friend's lives for this Kan'eek?'

Olga took a deep breath 'This is my destiny, I must watch my fate unfold, I cannot retreat from the abyss.'

Malikah shook her head in disappointment 'Luk'ul Olga.'

The towering half Russian half Tlillan sheathed her shashka and pressed her palms together 'Dyos bo'otik Xch'uup.'

An upset Malikah nodded as her adversary turned and left in retreat back to her vessel.

Once all the remaining invaders had left Malikah returned to her people who'd observed the whole thing. She approached Lian, Voice of Machine or Kalayuuk as the Neenayin referred to her, still sitting in the blood and fluids congealing around her.

The sable Queen knelt down, placing her hand over the warrior's thigh where the javelin had pierced. A pigment as dark as space filled the eyes of Xch'uup for a short time before returning to normal.

Malikah returned to her feet and offered an outstretched hand to Lian only to receive a puzzled look in return.

'Liik'il yakuntik,' said a smiling dark haired Valkyrie.

Ilam was rather shocked but said nothing concerning her daughter's reference to Lian as love.

Lian gripped her lover's hand and pulled herself up, the wound was gone, Lian felt neither pain nor disability from the spear wound she'd incurred minutes ago.

The Tlillan Queen next spoke to Louis 'Clean this place up and make certain whatever exits those tubes dies before it hits the ground, understood?'

Louis nodded 'Understood.'

Malikah addressed her Matriarchs 'Come, my Father has decided to be a hero and put his life in jeopardy.'

The mighty Queen of Otoch marched towards the elevator followed by her two cohorts. Once inside Malikah stated 'Casimir Generator please Athena.'

'As you wish,' replied Athena in a soft voice 'I attempted to prevent your father from reinforcing Kapitan Egorov however …'

The lift door opened and Malikah marched out, eyes blazing red and in a fury 'I know, the man is a stubborn fool!'

Lian retorted 'He did save your life at Bandayuuk, remember?'

This did nothing to abate Xch'uups fury 'And now I must save his when I TOLD HIM not to leave the Bridge!'

Ilam dared not speak to her Xch'uup on this matter but Lian possessed no such impediment 'Well he isn't a child Malee, he's a grown a man you know?'

'Yet he REFUSES to listen to me!' Malikah threw her arms in the air 'What would I know? I'm only Xch'uup, ruler of the Triumvirate and more than 10 civilisations!'

Lian was about to speak but she sensed Ilam, looking to her right the tall Amazon informed her mentally not to continue.

'Thank you Mother!' bellowed Malikah as they marched towards the generator section 'And for your information I do not have temper tantrums nor am I as petulant as my Father!'

Ilam pressed her palms together 'Hun-tumensiik.'

'You are forgiven, however don't think you can curry favour by speaking in Tlillan, and don't deny it mother, I am Mictlantecuhtli I know everyone's thoughts,' bellowed the forthright Tlillan Queen as they turned the corridor to see a slew of groaning men. Some dead, some dying, others wounded so terribly they could no longer continue.

Blood flowed along the floor as the clash of swords could be heard clearly, emanating from an open door at the end of the corridor.

The three beauties strode down the corridor taking care not to step on anyone. Malikah halted upon recognising Khun Deychaa; he lay on the floor not far from entering the gates of Elysium.

The drone chief displayed a horrendous gash in his suit, it was obvious to Malikah a shashka had crushed his ribcage through its armour plating. Though the Thai was not bleeding externally he must have been doing so internally and would soon be dead.

Unfortunately there were too many wounded and not enough medics, the droids couldn't handle so many numbers and treated the easiest first. Those only requiring stitches or bandages were quickly dealt with using a type of organic glue to hold their wounds together. Those in dire need were left to die, from an AI's point of view it was a numbers game, better to attend to many less serious wounds returning them to battle, than treat those on the edge of death.

Malikah knelt down placing her hand upon the Engineers ribs, if she didn't help him now he would die and Kaeo would never forgive her.

Deychaa felt relief from his torment, it became less painful to breath and soon the Drone Chief was back to health. The portly man stood up and gave Malikah a wai 'Kob kun ma kap.'

'Mai ben lai,' replied Malikah 'Now get your sword and follow me.'

The four of them strode into the Casimir section to see the Athenians shoved up against the opposite wall. In the centre of the room sat Athena's Massive generator, housed in a ball of Catronium, surrounded by stations.

Malikah recognised her Father in the centre of the Athenian line standing thigh to thigh with Egorov. They were attempting to hold off one of the tall half Russian Matriarchs, it would not be long before she had them both entering the gates of the afterlife, that was certain.

Before Malikah could rescue him she cleared the Neenayin laying explosives around the spherical generator housing.

Three Neenayin were placing charges until they detected a howl which sent shivers down their spines, looking up they observed the Star Shaker of legend bearing down upon them.

Rooted to the spot in fear the three possessed humans were too afraid to even draw their swords. Malikah strode in and quickly severed their heads in three precise cuts.

The remaining Neenayin were no longer on the threshold of victory but sandwiched between the Athenians and the triumvirate of Star Shaker, Kalayuuk and Huey'teopixqui.

McCann let out a secret sigh of relief as the enemy lines pulled back to meet this new challenge. The Englishman was fully aware his number was about to be called by Hades and no doubt his wife was furious with him.

Egorov let out a little whisper in Russian 'Slava borgo.'

McCann later discovered it meant 'Thank God', the Englishman was not the only one relieved to see the Matriarchs.

The three goddesses stepped across the blood smeared floor, Alyona and Yana attempted to rally their followers but to no avail.

Malikah cackled, mocking the Matriarchs 'Two daughters of a donkey commanding a pack of stinking dogs!'

The Matriarchs were obviously insulted by the pigment in their eyes but they made no action as the pack of dogs cowered around them for protection.

Lian stepped out in front of Malikah 'I will fight for Xch'uup, who will risk their life for their master?'

Alyona stepped out of the pack, holding her shashka out at Lian; she spoke 'I will face you.'

All combat stopped as the two Gods clashed upon the field of battle, the Neenayin were aghast to see Kalayuuk.

Alyona took her standard engarde position as Lian took the standard Rei position. Rei being a stance where the practitioner holds her Katana with both hands, back straight and one foot only just before of the other.

Making certain not to slip on any entrails or blood Lian kept her opponent at a proper distance; far enough that she wasn't in striking distance but close enough that if Alyona made a mistake she could step in and take full advantage.

Alyona slapped her opponent's blade with her own, attempting to break her concentration and entice Lian to focus on the blade rather than her target. It was a common tactic, though once you'd hit the upper levels of fencing it no longer worked.

Lian watched the shashka out of the corner of her eye, as Alyona went in for another slap of the Katana; Lian dropped her blade by a few centimetres. Alyona's shashka overshot the Katana, as it did Lian raised her blade by a few centimetres and dashed forward.

In fencing terms she had just executed a perfect disengage attack, sliding forward gracefully the young lady made three consecutive attacks. The first was a strike to her opponent's wrist (kote) the next to the head (men) then a side cut to the body (do).

Fortunately for Lian she had landed the first strike and forced her opponent to retreat. In McCann's opinion a missed kote strike would have ended in death before she'd got to cut Alyona's waist.

Unknown to the Englishman there was no fortune involved, Lian only made her first strike when certain it would land; allowing her to make two more "cheeky strikes", a movement known as Debana waza.

Alyona stepped backwards with a bleeding wrist, avoiding the other two strikes; she passed the sabre into her left hand. As Lian was moving forward slowly the red headed Matriarch charged forward in the typical style of a sabreur. Both legs apart, as in engarde, she moved with lightning speed in an attempt to take Kalayuuk off-guard.

Lian was shocked at her opponent's audacity and speed, pointing her blade at Alyona's chest she moved backwards. The speed of Alyona was overwhelming; nothing in Kenjutsu had prepared her for such explosive attacks.

Bashing the katana from side to side the Russian created an opportunity and made a cut with all her power.

Lian screamed in pain as the cold blade sliced her armour and cut a line into her bone. If it weren't for her suit's catronium plating she would have lost her arm.

Lian dropped her wounded arm and much to Alyona's surprise lurched forward delivering a punch square on the Matriarch's nose. Alyona's face exploded in blood, disrupting her vision for a fraction of a second. The Russian quickly recovered to deliver a reply using the large pommel of her shashka sword. A loud crunching noise resonated around the room as it bashed against Lian's cheek, McCann assumed Alyona had broken Lian's bone in the encounter.

The pair separated again with swords outstretched at one another, Alyona dripping blood from her wrist and face, Lian from a deep cut to her upper arm. The Englishman stepped up to his daughter and spoke 'Malikah, is this really necessary?'

His sable daughter muttered quietly to herself 'To defeat the beast one must become the beast.'

'And if she dies?'

'Then she dies with kleos,' replied the sullen Queen.

The Englishman shook his head 'This isn't some Homeric tale where a glorious death outweighs long life!'

The Tlillan ruler fixed her burning eyes upon McCann 'Yet you are the first to seek kleos, disregarding my words for your own chance at glory!'

McCann felt fear for the first time today as he sensed the rage inside his daughter; his wife was the least of his worries … if they survived this battle.

Alyona decided to rush her opponent again, with shashka outstretched she charged forwards. Lian was in pain from her cut; her broken cheek causing constant discomfort whenever a muscle moved in her face. As the agony heightened she used a chip embedded inside her brain, a device all Makayuuk possessed, to lower her distress. The chip sent signals to her brain ordering it to release endorphins, a natural pain killer manufactured in the human brain. The endorphins acted as an opiate dampening her terrible discomfort; next she commanded her body to release adrenaline. Voice of Machine was quite clinical and exact, making certain there was not so much adrenaline that her hands would shake but enough to quicken her strike and boost strength.

Using this concoction of chemicals running through her veins Lian blocked out all things superfluous, with total focus upon her target she waited and at the moment before Alyona made an attack Lian lurched in screaming.

The young lady stepped in with lightning speed, timing it just right with perfect distance. The last thing Alyona heard was a shout of 'MEN!' before her spirit disengaged from its mortal coil, dragged away by the nearby star's gravity.

The neutronium katana sliced the cap of Alyona's skull clean off, taking part of her brain with it. The Russian Matriarch's body moved forward leaving the top of her skull to fall onto the floor.

McCann observed the Matriarch's eyes as they fell dull, her body collapsed forward, becoming limp as her spirit was torn from it by the core.

Lian gave Yana a black look before returning to her lover's side, at the same time Ilam strode forward onto the bloody duelling ground. Pointing her sabre at Yana she declared 'I will die for Xch'uup.'

Yana glanced at her comrades; they cowered about her as puppies around a bitch, the bloodied Russian felt sickened by their cowardice.

Malikah shouted to her opponent 'I feel your disgust Yana, Olga has retreated to the Clotho, surrender yourself to me.'

Yana gazed at the craven Neenayin, who her friend had just died for, then replied 'What does Xch'uup offer?'

Ilam's eyes burnt as fires in the night, she shouted in an angry tone 'Bisik ts'o'om ekk'kan!'

McCann's ear piece translated it though he knew what his wife had said, literally 'Lay hold of brain filthy heretic' though in better English she would have said 'Get a grip you filthy traitor'.

Malikah walked forward and calmed Ilam, placing a soft hand upon her shoulder, 'Yana, all I offer is that your spirit will not be cast into e'hoch'e'en chumuk for eternity.'

Yana glanced upwards at the tubes as if expecting something to happen yet no rescue party was forth coming.

'Olga has abandoned you; you owe her no debt Yana.'

The towering Russian beauty pondered for a moment and realised her life was not worth sacrificing for a leader who refused to rescue her. After all it was Tsun Tzu who said to treat your soldiers as your children and they will stand by you even unto death. Well Olga certainly didn't regard her as a daughter or sister since Yana would certainly die for her daughter or sister.

The Red haired beauty stepped out of the circle of cowering Neenayin, past Ilam. Yana cast her shashka at the feet of Malikah and stated 'Namaste Xch'uup, I am yours.'

Malikah peered towards her mother, saying nothing Ilam nodded knowingly as she raised her sabre.

Malikah glanced at Lian, who took her command to join Ilam, both of the tall Matriarchs let rip into the skulking mass of directionless Neenayin. Some of the reptilians ran for the tubes, others attempted to defend themselves.

The Athenian crew lead by Kapitan Egorov crashed into the rear of the Neenayin who were now cut down as stalks of wheat by a farmer's scythe. Panic and terror spread throughout the foul creatures ranks, breaking them down as the Goddess Nike dispensed victory to those who'd displayed courage in today's battle.

There was no Kleos for the wayward forces of Olga that day, only retreat and confused execution as limbs flailed about.

Malikah watched on as blood seeped from the slaughter, swirling around the boots of her soldiers 'Do you understand why you lost today?' whispered the sable Queen to Yana.

The defeated Amazon looked on at the crushing slaughter 'Because you received reinforcements and I did not.'

Malikah cackled at her prisoner 'I won today because every man and woman on board this vessel would die in battle to protect me. Your pathetic group of traitors expected you to die for them.

Never trust a traitor Yana, even if they betrayed their master for you.'

Teary eyed Yana peered at Malikah 'What is my fate Xch'uup?'

Malikah's eyes didn't move from the destruction of the remaining Neenayin 'I will take you back to Otoch where you shall have trial.'

Yana was shocked 'A trial? I thought ...'

The Tlillan Queen raised her hand 'Be at ease, before I would have executed you and left your soul to Sagittarius A. However, since Bandayuuk I am open to different paths, though don't get your hopes too high Yana, you may still be executed for your sin.'

The tall Russian beauty in her black suit of armour pressed her palms together 'Namaste Xch'uup.'

Malikah turned to her prisoner 'Take your sword back and keep it sheathed, do not remove it from the scabbard under any conditions, understood?'

Yana picked her Cossack sword from the mire, placing it inside its wood and leather scabbard 'I understand Xch'uup.'

The clamour of battle quietened down until nothing more could be heard, Ilam and Lian led the remaining Athenians to Malikah through the blood and filth.

Ilam immediately noticed Yana's sword hanging off her belt 'What is this?'

Malikah replied 'I have decided to give Yana a second chance.'

Ilam was outraged; her eyes lit up with red pigment 'A second chance? This kan must die!'

Calmly the sable Queen responded 'Yana may still die here, however it will be at the side of her Xch'uup.'

Ilam was fuming, yet when reminded of her daughter's title she pressed her bloodied palms together 'Namaste Xch'uup.'

Malikah's father stepped out from amongst a body of men, covered in gore. Suddenly Xch'uup's eyes lit with fire 'Father, come here.'

McCann, exhausted after the exertion of combat, strolled slowly up to the towering beauty 'Yes?'

'What are you doing here?'

McCann frowned 'Egorov was being hit hard and the Casimir field generator was …'

Cutting him off abruptly Malikah shouted 'I mean why are you here when I TOLD YOU not to leave the Bridge?'

The Englishman was rather annoyed at being spoken to as if he were a child 'Excuse me?'

Malikah clenched both of her fists as she began to lose her temper 'Are you deaf as well as dumb? WHY DID YOU DISOBEY ME?'

Those who survived the battle for the Casimir field were all in fear, it was impossible to avoid The Queen's aurora of rage.

McCann could sense his daughter's fury; it was enough to intimidate even a charging rhino. The Englishman shrugged his shoulders as a naughty boy 'It seemed like a good idea at the time.'

'A good idea? You nearly died!'

McCann swallowed hard before making a retort 'Look I'm in charge on this ship and I'll do as I bloody well please.'

Malikah lost control for a moment and grasped her father's blood stained suit, lifting him clear off the ground until his face was at the same height as her own. Shaking him as if he were a rag doll she screamed 'I am the only authority in this SHIT HOLE OF A GALAXY, DO YOU UNDERSTAND?'

The Englishman floated in the air suspended by a pair of arms quite capable of tearing him apart. His crew watched on as shear rage permeated the room, rooting grown men to the spot.

McCann was griped with dread, for the first time he truly feared his daughter and was uncertain if he would survive the day.

McCann's fear hit Malikah, suddenly the Queen of the Triumvirate realised her father shrank in terror of her. The mighty Valkyrie burst into tears upon comprehending what she had done; hugging him as hard as she could the mighty Valkyrie wept onto his shoulder.

McCann felt a wave of relief come over him as his daughter blubbed, she may have been his little girl once but now she was an Amazon with the strength of many men.

'Forgive me Father,' whispered a sobbing girl into her parent's ear.

'You're crushing me,' rasped McCann as he struggled for breath.

Malikah released her embrace, placing her hands around his ribs before setting him upon the ground, as an adult would a 5 year old child. The Amazon dropped to her knees before the Admiral, wiping away her tears she asked in a humble voice 'Please forgive me Father.'

The Englishman was more embarrassed now than anything else 'Apology accepted,' he looked around at the others waiting for the sable Queen to rise but she wasn't finished.

Malikah kowtowed her father 'Namaste Father,' dipping her face into the wine dark blood covering the floor.

McCann was very embarrassed, but it was necessary in Malikah's eyes, so he suffered her self-humiliation until she was satisfied.

The Tlillan women, especially Ilam, were shocked to see Xch'uup kowtow to anyone or thing. Xch'uup was a god like ruler on Otoch, on Gukumatz she was the Icon, on Bandayuuk the Star Shaker, yet she kowtowed a mere Pixoa.

After about 30 seconds prostrated on the dirty floor McCann murmured to his daughter 'Alright, that's enough.'

He then received a thought from Malikah, in his best Tlillan he said 'Liik'il Xch'uup.'

Ilam and Yana both gasped at the statement, commanding Xch'uup to rise was more than enough to guarantee the loss of a Matriarch's head, let alone a human.

Chapter 20

That evening both crews recovered from the slaughter of the day, McCann entered the Officers' lounge after cleaning himself up. Malikah was already present with her Matriarchs and Kapitan Egorov, planning tomorrow's offensive.

'Hurry up Father,' said his sable daughter.

'Sure, what's the plan?'

The Officers of Athena stood in a circle listening intently to the warrior Queen.

'Tomorrow morning at ten hundred hours we will gather in cargo bay one. After everyone is certified for battle at eleven hundred hours we shall ascend into the cargo bay of the Clotho,' stated the Tlillan empress.

McCann interjected on his daughter's speech 'How exactly are we going to get into the Clotho through all those feet of armour plating?'

Malikah crossed her arms 'I shall be taking care of that father.'

The Englishman raised an eyebrow 'Well I suppose that's all settled then.'

Malikah ignored his comment 'Olga and the remaining Neenayin shall be waiting for us, Olga understands she cannot win, it is her choice to fight to the death. As for the Neenayin, they are weak and shall collapse the moment Olga is cut down.'

A hand went up in the circle and Malikah nodded to Vezzali, allowing her to speak 'How can we be sure of this?'

The tall Amazon understood the doubt of her human counterparts 'I have linked with Olga, she awaits our arrival.'

Vezzali shook her head in disbelief 'Surely she'll prepare an ambush?'

The sable Queen smirked at the Italian's naivety 'There shall be no ambush; Olga desires an honourable death, besides I have seen her fate … and ours.'

Louis decided to chip in 'How many men do we bring? Half of my engineering crew are dead already; we're running on a skeleton crew at the moment.'

For some reason Malikah found the questions amusing, no doubt that Tlillan superiority was showing through 'The best swordsman shall accompany me to the Clotho, we have no need for greater numbers, Louis.'

The Frenchman grumbled under his breath as Malikah spoke to Hassif 'What is the status of the wormhole?'

Hassif pulled his tablet out from a leg pocket in his uniform, after a few moments of tapping he reported 'The wormhole appears to be stable, for now. The local star has pulled it in and as Lieutenant Vezzali predicted it has become accelerated. As to how we are going to re-enter I'm not certain, even with our Casimir field intact it will be very dangerous.'

Ilam smiled at the technician 'You're correct Hassif; we must allow the star to pull us in before activating the Casimir field. Provided we are properly aligned, the star shall catapult us into the white hole.'

Ilam had read the thoughts of the Indian; he already had a plan for returning, though now wasn't the time to debate it.

Malikah clapped her hands together and with a big smile spoke loudly 'Now that that's all settled let's sit down and relax for a while.'

McCann, Louis and Hassif went to their usual table in the lounge; McCann took out a packet of three Siglo I's. The Admiral looked up towards the ceiling and called out 'Athena could you increase the oxygen content please?'

'Certainly Duncan, what level do you require?' inquired the soft spoken guardian.

McCann looked at Hassif with a scowl, Hassif chuckled and called to Athena '22 percent please Athena.'

'As you wish, have a good evening gentlemen,' replied the calm SI.

Deychaa walked up to the table and asked the Admiral, who was now lighting his cigar, 'What would you like to drink, Sir?'

McCann took a puff on the finely aged Cuban stick, as the thick smoke rolled out of his mouth and nose he pointed towards the bar 'There's a bottle of Balvenie under the bar, bring it over.'

Deychaa had been hoping for such a reply, he dived behind the bar pushing the barman out of the way before clutching the bottle of fine non-flashed whisky. The Thai drone Chief returned with the unopened bottle and four glasses each containing a single ice cube. Louis took note of the extra glass for the drone Chief and let out a little sneer.

'Alai whhha?' shouted the portly Thai at the sight of the Frenchman's mean expression, in the Thai language it is a statement similar to 'What the hell?'

Louis made his signature grimace 'You should bring your own instead of leeching ours.'

McCann turned to Louis and after delivering a light knock on his shoulder stated 'Give the man a break Louis. He nearly died today and besides crew aren't permitted to bring their own drink on board, you know that.'

Louis shook his head and replied reluctantly 'Fine, just pour the fucking drink.'

Deychaa smiled and sat down next to his Admiral as he poured him a glass of smooth golden liquor first; soon after everyone was served the Thai had his eye on the remaining Habanos.

'Just take the bloody cigar man,' said a tired McCann.

The Thai soon had it out of the tube and the cap sliced off, after toasting the foot with a match he was drifting off into heaven as the taste of the well-aged tobacco rippled over his tongue creating sensations only described in poetry.

The Englishman seemed to join him as he stared stoically across the room 'It'll take longer to replace the crew than fix her up.'

The Thai nodded in agreement 'Most of the drone staff didn't return from the Casimir generator, if Malikah hadn't appeared when she did ...'

McCann peered over at Hassif 'Do you have casualty numbers?'

The Indian often sat with his tablet in the lounge, he was working away and replied 'It was a Pyrrhic victory; we pushed them back at the cost of 117 lives, 32 severely wounded.'

Louis snorted 'And we have another battle tomorrow? How much blood must we spill for these Napoleons?'

'My daughter is not a Napoleon,' stated McCann.

'And I'm not a fucking Hussar; I tell you if this does not end tomorrow ...'

'Then what Mr Beaumont?' came a strong intimidating voice out of Louis' field of vision.

The Frenchman turned away from his friends, peering tentatively to his right, only for his eyes to meet with those of a rather disappointed Xch'uup.

Louis was not prepared to back down however 'Then I will take my sword to my cabin until it is time to return to Earth. It is my job to maintain the power core and engines, not to board a ship like a pirate!'

McCann could see his daughter's resemblance to her mother when she looked down on the Chief Engineer with that self-satisfied Tlillan sneer 'Xch'uup does not press her soldiers into service as slaves, if it is your desire you may hide in your chambers until the fighting has ceased.'

Louis' blood began to boil at the last comment, he got to his feet and glaring upwards he replied 'What is that supposed to mean?'

'You're drunk Mr Beaumont.'

Louis scoffed 'I'm not drunk ... YET!'

The sable goddess chuckled to herself 'Fine, but I expect those without an aversion to courage to turn up tomorrow, without a hangover,' Malikah raised an eyebrow at McCann 'and that includes you Father. As for you Mr Beaumont, feel free to get absolutely blitzed. I'm sure that by the time you've dragged yourself out of bed we'll be returning to Earth anyway.'

Sniggers and chuckles began to ring out around the lounge much to the expense of Louis who by now felt humiliated 'There will be 20 of us against 50 and on their territory, how do you figure we will win?'

'I have seen it, in the Dreamscape.'

Louis sneered 'Bah, how do I know what you've seen? For all I know you're blowing smoke up my ass!'

There was another round of sniggering, though this time some was aimed at Malikah. The Tlillan Queen noted the crews' scepticism and smiled at the Frenchman.

Louis froze for a few moments as his mind was invaded by an image, he watched on as a helpless bystander. From a distance he could see a jet black river filled with distorted images of colour and light which betrayed currents and eddies. As he closed in it grew in size, the Frenchman realised the enormity of it, the river was in fact the dead zone flowing around a black hole in the centre of an Einstein-Rosen bridge; better known as a wormhole.

From the Frenchman's perspective he was massive, since the dead zone seemed so much smaller than when the Athena sailed through it. Louis felt as if he had the presence of an Olympian, leaning in to peer upon the Dreamscape as if he were Zeus stretching out his omnipotent arm, lifting a goblet of wine to his lips.

As the Dreamscape approached the Frenchman began to make sense of its images, streaks of light pushed through currents and twists in the mangled fabric of space and time.

He felt a pull to a certain stream of light whirling around a contortion in space caused by the gravitational power of the singularity. Louis was uncertain if he was drawn to the light or it was drawn to him, nevertheless he approached it and as he did the light slowed down. As the current slowed it revealed a scene, much like peering into one of those old holographic "what the butler saw" machines that he'd spent far too much money on in his youth, the story played out before him.

Louis witnessed himself with McCann and Ilam; all caked in hardened blood, strolling from a scene of slaughter on board what must have been the Clotho. There were many bodies in the background; Lian cried as Malikah comforted her, Yana looked on stoically.

The scene played out too quickly for the Frenchman to take note of everything but he overheard a small part of a conversation McCann and Ilam were having.

Ilam was almost smiling 'I think a Human would say, her reach was beyond her grasp, yes?'

McCann nodded and in a solemn tone replied 'Castles made of sand.'

Ilam made a puzzled look 'I don't understand?'

McCann exhaled through his nose 'It's a song, Castles made of sand fall in the sea, eventually.'

'I still don't understand.'

The Englishman stretched his head backwards exercising his neck muscles 'It means that if you build your dreams, build them from rock, if you construct them from sand they'll only be washed away by the sea.'

Ilam scoffed 'My analogy is superior.'

Before he could see more the Frenchman was pulled from the scene at such a pace all was blurred, a moment later he stood in the Officer's lounge and had to steady himself lest he lose balance and hit the floor.

Once he'd levelled himself Louis fixed his gaze upon Malikah's 'Did you see anything more?'

'You saw as I did Louis, there were no Athenian dead, tomorrow Olga shall meet her destiny.'

Louis nodded 'Je m'excuse.'

The sable Valkyrie smiled before returning to her table with the other Matriarchs.

As Louis sat back down Hassif asked 'What did you see?'

The Frenchman took a swig of whisky, a swig that was a little too large 'The Dreamscape.'

McCann sighed 'He means what did you see in the Dreamscape you French fool.'

Louis shook his head, the man was obviously disturbed by the experience 'The end of tomorrows battle, I think.'

Deychaa impatiently urged the Chief 'And?'

Louis relaxed into the leather sofa and took another drink whilst staring off into the distance at nothing in particular 'Yes, we won.'

'So what's up?' inquired McCann

The Frenchman gazed into his glass, staring at the light brown liquid inside as if he were peering into the depths of a dark lake 'I felt, it was like I was something bigger, bigger than the black hole or the wormholes around it. The Dreamscape was no more than a small stream in a forest, I felt as a Titan, commanding the water to leap into my mouth.'

Deychaa made a nervous laugh 'Khun ba!', Thai for 'He's crazy!'

McCann did not share in the awkward laugh, Malikah had shown him the Dreamscape in the past, although he maintained a cynical demeanour the Englishman had looked at the River Styx through the eyes of a God and it was no small experience.

Hassif remained quiet, McCann was unsure why; perhaps Amitra could also look into the Dreamscape without the assistance of the Seers at Tititl? If so she would be the only one aside from Malikah, either way Louis would understand the sense of superiority innate amongst all Tlillans and their descendants.

The Chief Engineer had been shaken by the experience and spoke little during the rest of the evening.

Later that evening Vezzali approached McCann's table, usually only friends and top ranking Officers would drink with them; However McCann did have a soft spot for Miss Vezzali, much to the irritation of his former first Officer Ryu and his wife who sat on the opposite side of the room staring as the Italian took a seat.

Ilamachutli was burning with jealousy until a voice entered her head; her daughter sent a private thought. The gist of her message informed Ilam she was staring rather inappropriately. Ilam quickly snapped out of her trance and returned to the conversation at her table before anyone else noticed.

'So I found out something very interesting concerning the Neenayin today,' said Lian in an excited tone.

Ilam sneered a little but Malikah smiled and asked curiously 'What?'

'The legend of Ek'tsab, it was brought to the Makayuuk via the Neenayin.'

Ilam spoke abruptly 'You can communicate with Machine, at the core?'

Lian looked surprised 'I am permanently linked with Machine; I only have difficulty when inside a wormhole, as do all Makayuuk.'

Malikah ignored her Mother's aggressive tone 'So where did the Neenayin get their legend from? It shares far too many similarities with the legend of the Mictlantecuhtli to be a coincidence.'

Lian took a sip of her orange juice and replied 'I … I mean Machine doesn't know, she only remembers that it was passed on by the invading Neenayin and spread through her children.'

Ilam maintained her condescending sneer, but remained silent.

Yana intervened tentatively 'Olga spoke on the subject with the Neenayin commanders.'

'What did the traitor say?' snapped Ilam.

Yana, though intimidated by the pure blood Tlillan, continued 'They say it was taken from when the Neenayin lived on Otoch.'

'Neenayin on Otoch?' said Ilam incredulously.

Yana nodded as she fumbled with her glass of juice 'Well I'm only repeating what Olga told us.'

'And?' urged Malikah.

'The Neenayin once lived alongside Tlillans, inhabiting the bodies of males. They preferred females to be tall and powerful, so they employed a selective breeding program; producing women as a farmer would breed livestock for the best results.'

Ilam sneered at the half Tlillan 'Heresy!'

Malikah furrowed her brow 'Mother, let her speak.'

The sable Queen fixed her gaze upon Olga's former comrade 'Please continue Yana.'

Yana cleared her throat 'Well they bred Tlillans to satisfy their own sexual desires, however there were unforeseen side effects. Tlillan females developed mental abilities beyond that of the Neenayin, society evolved from patriarchal to matriarchal.

Tlillan females used their mental abilities to subjugate the males, after this Neenayin attempted to shift into females, unsuccessfully, soon they were purged.

Matriarchs believed they were killing male sympathisers; they had no idea of the Neenayin. Then came Tlaloc, our first Xch'uup, the Neenayin's fate was sealed, she went on a crusade to purify Tlillan society of heretics. With the assistance of Ah Chuyakak the Neenayin that didn't escape we purged from the mortal coils of the Tlillan race.'

Malikah asked in a curious tone 'So Neenayin do die if their host is killed.'

Yana nodded 'Some do, the shock might knock them out of phase causing instant death to a Neenayin. They can only survive for a limited time without a host, that is why they must flee with their hosts rather than just leave the body and move on.'

'What if they leave the host before death?' inquired Lian.

'Then they have only hours to find another, it is very draining for them to remain out of phase on their own, a Neenayin leeches energy from its host to sustain such an existence. Without that they die, it's similar to us holding our breath underwater while swimming to the surface, if we do not reach our goal we drown.'

Ilam shook her head 'This is heresy, nothing of this was ever passed on from the first golden age, Olga is a traitor and a liar!'

Malikah thought for a moment 'Perhaps the Mictlantecuhtli was in fact Ah Chuyakak?'

Lian nodded 'That makes sense; she was a Lightsider so the stories of the Mictlantecuhtli being dark and uniting the Tlillans was in fact a Neenayin story?'

Ilam scowled at such a suggestion 'What of the title Ek'tsab? Who was the Star Shaker?'

The table went quiet; all were in deep thought considering the question, until Malikah replied 'Neutronium.'

'You refer to the Chakib which Ah Chuyakak forged for the first triumvirate?' replied Ilam sceptically.

Malikah took a sip of her orange juice and nodded 'Yes, what is neutronium in old Tlillan?'

Ilam thought for a moment 'Maskab chun ek'tsab, I believe.'

Lian had a puzzled look to which Malikah replied 'It means iron which originates from a shaking star, the only source emanates from massive sunspots which propel it onto Otoch. Ah Chuyakak was the first to forge the substance and she made three swords, the mantle of Xch'uup, Huey'teopixqui and Huey'tlacochcalcatl.

Perhaps over time the meaning was lost somewhat, Star Shaker was the first Grand Marshall who forged the blades uniting the three sides against the Neenayin?'

Ilam refused to accept what was just conjecture right now 'What of the Xtaabay? She is said to have united the Tlillan race against the Xtaabay, not the Neenayin.'

'That is self-explanatory Mother, a Xtaabay is a wraith. Neenayin must have been Xtaabay to early Tlillans, spirits of the dead which possessed the living.'

Ilam shook her head 'Olga is a heretic, she attempts to subvert us.'

Her sable daughter disagreed 'We have only a handful of memories from that period and those are mere fragments; no-one has seen or even found evidence of a creature described by legend as a wraith. Besides this was all before Tlaloc laid down the first laws, we have no idea as to how we came together other than a few broken memories and folk tales.'

Lian chuckled 'It looks to me like the Neenayin have a bad case of mistaken identity!'

Malikah chuckled with her 'My father would probably describe it as self-fulfilling prophecy.'

Ilam sneered 'Your father can be fool when the mood takes him.'

The Empress of Tlillan faced her mother and spoke in a more serious tone 'Think about it, this legend has perpetuated from a Neenayin story for years and years. They called her Ek'tsab because of the neutronium she forged; we called her Mictlantecuhtli who we prophesied would save the Tlillan race.

The story was that the Mictlantecuhtli would be all three races in one, something impossible naturally, so we used genetic manipulation and breeding programs, just as the Neenayin did, to achieve our goals.

Perhaps we misunderstood? Perhaps it was that Ah Chuyakak united all three races into one and saved the Tlillan species? In our ignorance we spread our beliefs across the universe, manipulating our own DNA to bring those beliefs to fruition?'

Ilam contained her disdain for such talk 'An interesting theory.'

Malikah gave Ilam a smile 'Do not be concerned Mother, this is nothing more than a harmless debate.'

Ilam gave her daughter a black look 'Perhaps, yet it is still profane to discuss such things even under the guise of harmless debate.'

'Those who declared me the Mictlantecuhtli were branded as heretics, including yourself, do not allow your prejudice to blind you from considering the alternative,' retorted the sable Queen.

'What does the Dreamscape say of tomorrow?' inquired Lian.

'We shall be victorious, Olga will die as shall her followers, it is destiny.'

Yana began to snivel at the news.

Ilam sneered at the young Russian lady 'You weep for that deceiver?'

'She is my friend,' said the red headed half Tlillan as she wiped her eyes with the back of her hand.

Ilam snarled at Yana 'She is nothing but a pig, tomorrow she will be slaughtered.'

Ilam caught a look of concern from Lian 'What is it? Do you show mercy for the pig too?'

'I grew up with her, we went to the same school in New York,' replied Voice of Machine.

Ilam sneered at both of the young girls 'If I see any pity in a single man or woman's eye tomorrow they shall taste the edge of my blade, that I give my word on.'

Malikah sighed 'Please mother there's no need to be so dramatic.'

Ilam ignored her daughter 'you two may have been easily corrupted but do not think I am as weak.'

Lian leapt to her feet 'Corrupted? You have a nerve!'

Ilam got to her feet and the pair glared at each other across the table 'What are you suggesting?'

Lian pointed in the Amazon's face which by now had a pair of fiery eyes 'You were banished for your profanity, if it were not for Malikah you would still be in exile!'

The lounge went silent as every conversation halted, the crew focused on the fracas between the towering warriors.

Ilam's eyes went from a light red to a deep burgundy shade 'That decree has been lifted,' seethed the tall beauty.

'Yet you were corrupted and went against the will of YOUR Xch'uup, I did no such thing,' shouted Voice of Machine.

Ilam drew her blade in a furious rage, up until this point no-one except perhaps her husband had dared speak to her in such a manner 'KAN!'

Lian drew her blade in defence, if the table were not between the pair a duel to the death would have surely ensued. Had Malikah not stood between the two it certainly would have given a few moments.

'BISIK TS'O'OM!' bellowed the sable Goddess.

Lian's eyes twitched nervously between Malikah and the Matriarch pointing a sabre in her direction. Ilam's eyes were locked onto Lian, her intent quite clear; she was on the cusp of cutting the young woman down.

'Put your sword away Mother,' said Xch'uup in a hushed tone.

Ilam's eyes never left Lian's, she sheathed her weapon but before anything else could be said the beautiful Amazon spat in Lian's face 'EEK'KAN!'

Ilam turned about face and marched out of the lounge with her husband in close pursuit.

Malikah glared at Lian 'You just had to open your mouth, didn't you?'

Lian returned her katana to its scabbard 'I only spoke the truth.'

A small fire lit up in Malikah's eyes 'And you nearly died for it.'

'I can defend myself,' replied Voice of Machine proudly.

'Clean your face you stupid girl,' stated a frustrated Xch'uup 'in future do as Yana and keep your damn mouth shut, my mother has been fencing for centuries, even I would not be so bold.'

Lian took a handkerchief from one of the Officers at the bar and cleaned her face in silence before returning to her seat, beside Malikah.

McCann had to jog to keep up with his furious wife as she marched along the cream coloured corridor of Athena. He could sense her burning anger; Ilam felt humiliated by the fact an infidel took precedence over her.

'What is your desire?' shouted the Amazon at her husband who struggled to keep pace.

'For you to slow down a bit!' retorted McCann.

Ilam halted abruptly and turned towards her husband 'Return to your little whore!'

The Englishman had no idea what his wife was talking about 'I'm sorry?'

Ilam's eyes blazed as raging fires ready to engulf all around 'I felt your attraction when she sat at your table tonight, do not deny it.'

'You mean Vezzali?' inquired McCann in an incredulous tone.

Ilam the usually stoic Tlillan ice woman struggled to hold her emotions down 'You are the cause of this.'

'The cause of what exactly?'

'Malikah, she entertains profanity of that heretic whore!'

McCann assumed his wife was talking about Lian 'What did she say to you?'

Ilam's fire was far from going out 'The Makayuuk heretic dared suggest our philosophy is influenced by Neenayin. She speaks heresy yet Malikah takes the side of that foul pig.'

McCann replied as diplomatically as he could 'Perhaps you're reading more into this than there is?'

Ilam ignored his weak attempt to cool her down 'I did my best but you subverted me every step of the way, if you had not linked with her this would not have happened. Xch'uup was right, I failed as a mother, I allowed too much influence from the father.'

'Your daughter is Xch'uup now, if she sees fit to discuss something, no matter how profane, she may do so with or without your approval.'

'If I had been a better mother,' wrenched the Amazon tearing herself apart inside.

McCann comforted his wife 'There is nothing you could have done, Malikah was raised on Earth in a totally different environment to Otoch.'

Ilam shook her head 'I understand, yet she contends everything Xch'uup stands for, she steps on law which maintained the Commonwealth for eons.'

McCann replied in a sardonic tone 'Yeh, it wasn't going really well for them when we turned up, was it? The heretics were kicking in the door and about to cut them all down!

Things change, laws change and often they change not gradually but in a violent shake up; these are times of great change for Mankind as well as Tlillans.'

Ilam had calmed down by now and replied in a sullen tone 'A good speech Duncan however it does not comfort me, I have still failed to raise a suitable Xch'uup.'

The Englishman scoffed at her comment 'No-one is perfect Ilam, the best that anyone in that room can do is just play the hand God dealt them.'

Ilam appreciated her husband's concern and gave him a tiny smile 'You forget fate and destiny; you speak as if some fictitious being is responsible for all hardships.'

McCann shook his head 'Then who is responsible if all this is destined to occur anyway? You know all that prophecy mumbo jumbo that the seers dished out was bullshit. If you believed otherwise you wouldn't be so upset right now, you did all that was asked of you Ilam; you gave birth to the Mictlantecuhtli endowing her with all the skills she needed to ascend to the throne. Malikah came from some backwater no-one had ever heard of on Otoch until a few years ago.

Now that she is Xch'uup what happens is up to her, you have done more than enough and beating yourself up because we're not the Waltons is bloody idiotic.'

Ilam's expression quickly went to one of puzzlement 'The Waltons?'

'It was an old TV show about a family who were seemingly perfect; it's synonymous with an immaculate family. The point being that the Waltons were a media creation as no family is without problems.'

Ilam smiled 'I understand.'

'Besides, even God failed when it came to his children!'

'How so?' replied Ilam coyly.

'My Mother always told my Father that woman was God's second mistake.'

Ilam put her arm around her husband 'Do you know what his third big mistake was?'

'The snake?'

Ilam chuckled 'No, guess again.'

'I give up,' surrendered the Admiral.

'He should have placed the forbidden fruit higher up the tree.'

McCann gave a wide grin and chuckled as he walked to his cabin with his slender Amazon.

Chapter 21

The next day in cargo bay 1, Athena's crew gathered for the final encounter with Olga and her miscreants.

Twenty five of the best swordsmen and women awaited instruction from their leader, the atmosphere was tense between Lian and Ilam, but neither spoke of last night's drama.

Malikah dressed as all of her soldiers, wearing tactical armour intended to stop a tungsten projectile. The Special Forces armour did a more than credible job against a steel blade or even a carbon one, against a neutronium blade in the hands of a Tlillan it was left wanting.

'Everyone check your weapons,' announced the Queen of Matriarchs.

Each man and woman unsheathed their weapon making certain the blade was sound. Despite having been issued with new weapons since the previous battle no one could afford an accident in the heat of conflict. All of the crew carried a small shield with a large boss in the centre.

'Are you all satisfied?' inquired Malikah.

The crew of the Athena confirmed their weapon integrity.

'So how will we get into the Clotho?' blurted out Louis who'd decided to present himself, despite last night's little spat.

Malikah's face moved upwards, high above the tiny group of soldiers, 'Athena?'

'I am here Miss Malikah,' replied the ship's voice.

'I'm about to cut a path through the upper deck and into the cargo bay of the Clotho, please don't be alarmed.'

Athena replied in her warm voice 'Understood Miss Malikah.'

McCann caught a concerned look from Egorov and a few others, to tell the truth her statement didn't sit well with the ships commanding Officer either.

'Cut a path to the Clotho? How?' asked the Frenchman.

The sable Queen smiled 'Magic Mr Beaumont!'

Lian sniggered, unable to contain herself at the sight of the dumbfounded Frenchman who was rarely lost for words.

'Are you all prepared?' asked Malikah in a more serious tone.

Once all had confirmed they were ready the Tall Queen closed her eyes, upon raising her eyelids blackness prevailed. It seemed impossible that someone could still see with eyes as dark as the sheet of space, nevertheless Malikah turned her black gaze towards the ceiling.

McCann felt his heart beating harder, becoming quite uncomfortable; it was evident all the Officers were having a similar experience. Then a cracking sound grabbed his attention as a circle of distortion formed above them in the ceiling.

McCann compared the sight to water going down a drain, though the catronium on the hull was pushed out rather than sucked in. A tube formed as a torrent of gravity swirled around, twisting light itself up and through the Athena until the cargo bay of the Clotho had been breached.

Slowly the eddy of gravitons dissipated, as it did McCann felt his heart rate normalise, until the sheet of night dropped from his daughter's eyes.

Malikah peered at Louis and said cheekily 'Do you believe in magic now Mr Beaumont?'

Louis made no reply as Lian giggled although he didn't know why, it didn't seem amusing to him in the least.

'Athena?' called Malikah.

'Yes Miss Malikah?' came a soft tone from all around them.

'Could you place a magnetic field in the tube leading to the Clotho?'

'Certainly Miss Malikah.'

'I would like you to move us into the Clotho cargo bay one at a time, I'll be going first.'

'Understood Miss Malikah.'

McCann piped up quickly 'Hold on now, I think someone else should go first.'

Malikah displayed her annoyance at the Englishman 'Father it is quite safe, Olga will not attack, even she would not dishonour herself by assaulting her Xch'uup in such a manner.'

A thought immediately passed through McCann's mind 'Unlike certain people here', he remembered his daughter splitting Xch'uup's chest open at Muul Kaah.

Malikah looked down on him haughtily 'That was not an ambush, just try to do as I say this time, Father.'

'Fine,' muttered McCann under his breath.

The young Queen stepped into the magnetic field, beneath the opening which led to the Clotho and her destiny 'When you're ready Athena.'

Silently Malikah rose and accelerated into the dark path, after 15 seconds she appeared in the bay of the Clotho. Stepping aside to allow the next crew member in, Malikah was greeted by Olga and what was left of her now dishevelled following.

The Queen peered across the bay's fractal atmosphere, examining Olga and her Neenayin through the distortions in space and time. Small bubbles, cracks and strange twists broke up the space time continuum which separated the adversaries. Each party stared stoically at one another, Olga looking perhaps for a fragment of pity or mercy, Malikah noting her foes and their obvious weakness. Yesterday's clash had taken the steam out of Olga's revolution, the Neenayin tired and afraid. Beasts of myth were ascending through the armoured skin of the Clotho to dispatch justice from a sword forged eons ago in a heat more intense than a Star itself.

The Sable Queen could sense dismay emanating from her opponents as Lian and Ilam appeared. Expecting Voice of Machine to be absent after her horrific wounding it was painful to note she suffered no such disability, not even a sign of discomfort, only a God could achieve such a feat in the Neenayin mind.

Olga was crushed as she picked up on her followers' fear, she knew victory was impossible but even an honourable battle would be too much to ask of these creatures.

Malikah could not suppress a mocking smirk as Kalayuuk took her place by the side of Ek'tsab, the very sight sending a wave of fright throughout Olga's ragged ranks.

Ilam next took her place, staring into the cowering enemy who by now were considering flight rather than fight. McCann's voice reached his daughters ears 'What are they waiting for? Why not attack before we're prepared?'

Ilam sneered condescendingly at the Neenayin 'They value their lives more than that of their cause … soul stealers.'

Once the Athenian forces had assembled Malikah and her two furies stepped forward. Unsheathing her sabre Malikah pointed its tip across the fractal landscape of a warped Clotho cargo bay, the Tlillan Queen did not speak.

Olga scanned her band of followers and sneered 'Who will match the champion of Xch'uup in my name?'

There was no reply to her request.

Olga continued 'We are all destined to die today, who will die alongside me? Who will die with kleos in the name of his Queen?'

Again no reply was forth coming; her inter-dimensional followers had lost all appetite for combat.

Olga shouted at her motley crew 'Look at her; she feels just as you, Xch'uup has fear in her heart. Look at your Voice, she bleeds no different to you, she must draw breath to survive no different than any mortal standing here today!'

Not a word came from the Neenayin; they only looked on in terror at their fate.

Olga gave up on rallying her cowardly dimension shifters; she turned her body back to Malikah 'I have no champion Xch'uup.'

'Weak people require a strong leader,' shouted the sable Queen across twisted space.

'What of strong people?'

'They require a wise leader; however, a successful leader must be both strong and wise.'

Olga exhaled in what McCann assumed was acceptance of her position 'I have one request of the mighty Xch'uup.'

'You are a traitor Olga; you may request nothing of your Xch'uup.'

Olga ignored Malikah's statement and continued 'Grant me kleos, a death fitting for a Matriarch.'

Before Malikah could reply Lian spoke into the Grand Matriarch's ear 'Allow me to fight in your name.'

The sable Queen gazed into her lover's eyes 'She has committed treason and must die.'

'I understand, permit me the privilege of being your champion Xch'uup.'

Malikah gave a hard look 'I know she was your friend, someone else can do this Lian.'

'That is why I must fight, only I am prepared to give Olga the kleos she desires, Ilam would end her as if destroying a dog.'

Ilam snatched a glance at Lian but made no comment, Voice of Machine was right, the red headed Amazon would have given the traitor nothing.

'As you wish Lian, you shall be my champion today.'

Voice of Machine pressed her palms together 'Namaste Xch'uup.'

Lian stepped forwards making her way through the twisted fabric of space until she reached the centre of the bay.

Before doing the same Olga raised her voice toward the Neenayin 'Today you shall see a Matriarch die with kleos and dignity. Remember this when you are slaughtered as frightened sheep … your weakness disgusts me!'

With that Olga drew her blade, making her way to meet her childhood friend in the centre of the bay.

Olga nodded towards her friend as they met surrounded by a fractal environment of twirling light, stretched and distorted almost as if fairies danced around them 'It feels good to see you again Lian.'

Voice replied in a confused tone 'Good?'

Olga had already accepted her fate 'Yes, we were always such rivals, do you remember? Or has Machine stolen those memories?'

'I was never your rival that was all in your head.'

Olga smiled 'I was always competing with you Lian, but never could I defeat you.'

'Defeat me?'

'You were better than everyone else, the prodigy of prodigies they called you.'

Lian scowled 'That was one year after a science exam; you took it to heart far too readily.'

Olga shook her head slowly 'No, we all felt it, every girl in that school lived in the shadow of the mighty Lian. Some of them wavered, others rolled over, but not I, I'm a warrior.'

Lian maintained her scowl 'Are you attempting to blame your treachery upon me?'

'When you were sent to Otoch, you left me behind, it were as if I did not exist anymore. You were Adjunct to Xch'uup; my mother berated me every day because I had not achieved that which the mighty Lian accomplished so easily.'

Voice of Machine sensed the sincerity in Olga's voice, 'I earnt my position through hard work, I curried no favour, I had no influence, nor did my mother. When I left for Otoch it was due to my own effort, nothing else, do not put your treason at my feet.'

Next came a shocking revelation 'I loved you,' mumbled Olga.

'What?' replied Lian.

'I said I loved you and now I'm all alone, at the core, destined to roam … searching for a home.'

Voice of Machine drew her Katana 'You have chosen your path Olga.'

Olga nodded in agreement as she brought her shashka to bear 'It's a relief, after riding the tiger for so long, to step off and be devoured.'

Lian pouted 'Then at least make this look good and try to kill me.'

Olga smiled 'You could always defeat me in competition.'

After saluting each other with their blades Lian took a chudan posture as Olga went engarde, the pair moved backwards and forwards slipping in and out of a comfortable attack distance. Both combatants attempted to tease the other into an attack. Timing it so that they might pull back avoiding the attack then when the enemy had missed and lay outstretched, counter attack.

The two half Tlillans knew each other, so the battle lasted a while, understanding the strengths and weaknesses on both sides led to far more caution than usual.

McCann observed the sword fight unfold despite the lensing created by small bubbles of warped space. He had no idea what the pair had spoken to each other, the Englishman found it strange that they had such a seemingly civilised conversation. Nevertheless they moved in and out of range tapping blades in order to coax the other into an attack.

'What were they talking about?' inquired the Admiral.

'I don't know,' replied a genuinely confused Xch'uup.

After a couple of minutes Olga made the first move, she parried hard knocking the Katana aside. Charging forward the towering Amazon attempted to cut her opponent's arm. Lian retreated, gliding with speed and grace backwards, raising her blade and pointing the tip at Olga's shoulder, blocking the incoming cut.

Lian successfully caught the shashka blade manoeuvring it until her enemy's point was placed so far to her right that it could not touch the half Tlillan's body. Olga was unable to move her blade, her only recourse was to retreat but first the mighty Valkyrie needed to halt her own advance.

Before her attack could be stopped Lian's Katana pierced the Russian's shoulder. Olga felt her right arm go limp, her grip evaporated as her shashka fell to the ground. Lian withdrew her sword from the wound and waited holding the bloody point directly at Olga's face.

Olga peered through Lian's eyes and into her soul; she felt conflict inside her heart and doubt within her mind. Olga gave an expression of concern, the towering Russian didn't move, she stood awaiting her fate 'Well?' she whispered.

Lian didn't flinch; the dark haired girl maintained her sword with total control in the same position.

'Do it, finish me,' whispered the Russian Amazon.

Malikah became concerned, which concerned McCann 'What the bloody hell is going on?' muttered the Englishman.

'I have no idea,' replied his sable daughter in a hushed tone.

Twenty seconds had passed and Lian still held her sword to Olga's face, all were puzzled, apart from the combatants.

Olga whispered as she stared past the blade and into the eyes of Lian 'Please, if you have any pity, allow me to die with what little dignity remains.'

With that Lian let out a mighty scream and with a downward cut she sliced through Olga's suit, deep into her flesh, opening a gash from collar bone to bellybutton.

Olga dropped to the floor, blood frothed from her mouth whilst spurting out the precise wound.

Lian sheathed her blade, bent down and pushed apart the body armour to reveal the Valkyrie's naked chest. Amidst the bubbling blood which splashed from her mouth Lian recognised a smile from her old school friend; she was grateful to have someone who cared for her ... even at the most savage part of the galaxy.

Lian returned the smile as she took a look at her friend's face for the last time. Voice of Machine dipped her hands into the gash and pulled apart Olga's ribcage. Another spurt of blood flew out of both the chest and mouth as the Russian choked on her own fluids. Lian reached in, grabbed Olga's heart and with one mighty yank, tore it out.

Voice of Machine stood up, took a bite of her old school friend's heart before displaying the quivering organ aloft; letting out a scream, the other Tlillan women joined in. Olga convulsed in a frenzy for 5 seconds before drifting off into the Dreamscape, her bloody heart dripped onto Lian's hair, congealing as it slowly made its way down to her neck.

Before the Athenians could make a move against them the Neenayin broke and fled out of the bay, scurrying away to hide inside the Clotho.

McCann observed his foe escape via the exits 'Damn it!'

Malikah smirked 'Be at ease Father, time is on our side now.'

'What do you mean?'

'Have Egorov muster his men, they shall be charged with hunting these shape shifters.'

McCann pulled an unhappy face 'Great, how much longer will we be stuck in this damn hell hole?'

Malikah smiled condescendingly 'As long as it takes to rat them all out.'

The Englishman wasn't happy until his wife comforted him, having her company for a couple of weeks would certainly ease the time spent at the galactic core. The man and wife walked away chatting about the day's events, Malikah approached Lian to console the girl.

As Lian wept for Olga the Tlillan Empress held her tightly 'Control your grief.'

'I cannot, the pain will never leave my mind,' cried the blood stained geisha.

'Olga was a traitor; remember that, she betrayed Xch'uup and Machine in her lust for power. Your heart is too easily swayed my little Adjunct,' smiled Malikah.

Voice of Machine fixed her glassy eyed gaze upon her lover 'To those that feel the universe is a tragedy.'

The sable Queen's hands remained clasped upon Lian's shoulders comforting her grief.

The Chinese-Tlillan woman continued 'I may feel too often but you think when you should feel, Atan.'

'Perhaps that is why fate brought us together?'

A smile emerged from her expression of distress; Voice of Machine looked her Atan in the eye and nodded in agreement as a single tear rolled down her bloodied cheek.

Louis recognised the scene from Malikah's vision, though there were significant differences but not so significant as to change the ultimate outcome of the day. The Frenchman understood that the Dreamscape was not 100%; he likened the experience to placing a bet. The Dreamscape gave out odds on different outcomes and Malikah had put her money on defeating Olga and slaughtering all Neenayin today. McCann's daughter had won part of the bet in that they had taken a victory though the Neenayin escaped into the bowels of the Clotho, for now anyway.

McCann took Egorov aside 'Egorov, I want you to put three parties together so that you can search for these Neenayin 24/7, understood?'

The Russian nodded as he put his hand on his weapon 'Understood.'

'When can you send the first party out?'

'Give me 20 minutes Admiral, I'll be ready then. Do you want them alive or will their bodies be satisfactory?'

McCann peered up to his wife, Egorov noted no verbal communication however the Admiral replied 'Dead or alive Kapitan.'

Egorov got onto his wrist tablet and began rounding up crew members, meanwhile the remaining crew returned to Athena via the tube Malikah had created.

That evening in the Officers' lounge McCann relaxed with a Balvenie and an El Rey Del Mundo, translated to English the cigar was called a "King of the world". In orbit around the super massive black hole, Sagittarius A, somehow made the Englishman feel as if he were on top of the world, or perhaps the galaxy, for the time being. The Choix supreme cigar was very smooth, a delight to smoke, it also happened to be Louis favourite. Sitting at the lounge table McCann let out a puff of smoke in the French Chief's direction 'When we get back I'm going to buy you three cabinets of these cigars.'

Louis took a long drag firing up the end of his Habanos like a burning coal 'You mean if we get back!'

McCann put his arm around his wife's waist 'What does the Dreamscape say my dear, will we make it back in one piece?'

Ilam sat with her husband at his regular table 'Xch'uup says we shall return, have you forgotten the future echo already?'

'Future echo?' inquired McCann.

Hassif interjected 'The image of Athena we encountered in hyperspace, it was a future echo, if we did not return there would have been no Athena to send us a message in Morse code.'

Louis sneered 'Pah! Time travel! C'est merde!'

McCann smiled at his wife cheekily 'Is that a fact Louis?'

The Frenchman took a slug of Balvenie 'Sure, you believe in time travel because a Tlillan told you so?'

McCann's eyes remained fixed upon Ilam forcing the tall ice lady to look away rather than break out laughing 'Hmm, I suppose you can't believe everything you're told.'

Louis shook his head 'I'm not saying it's impossible but until I see it for myself it's crap, okay?'

Hassif cut in again 'But we saw ourselves in hyperspace, you can go over the footage.'

The Frenchman played with his cigar as it smouldered away 'I've seen a lot of things in the dead zone, a space ship that looked like Athena is not a first.'

Ilam leant down with a condescending smile 'What of your Morse code?'

'Coincidence,' replied the Chief Engineer.

Hassif sniggered as he shook his head.

'What?' asked Louis.

'It's pretty funny coming from the man who lectured me for more than an hour on how the Illuminati and Bilderburger group were the same organization.'

Louis took a drag on his Havana 'That's Bilderberg group.'

Hassif shrugged his shoulders 'Whatever.'

Ilam made a puzzled look 'What is the Illuminati?'

McCann kissed his wife's fingers 'another human weakness my dear, they're called conspiracy theories. Due to the absence of a common neural link paranoia can blossom … and often does.'

Louis laid back into the brown sofa 'Another effect of no neural link is extreme naivety, for example your husband believes any shit his government feeds him.'

'You have still failed to answer my question,' said the red headed Valkyrie.

McCann tapped some ash into the ashtray 'It's an alleged group of citizens who some believe have been attempting world domination since the 17th century?'

Louis nodded 'Oui, and they are the Bilderberg group.'

Ilam was about to ask but McCann quickly answered 'A group of industrialists, bankers and politicians who meet once a year. Again the paranoid believe they've been attempting world domination since the mid-20th century.'

'Paranoid? It's a fact!' declared Louis.

McCann sneered and shook his head 'Spare me Louis, even if it were true do you think they'd stand a cat in hells chance against Malikah?'

Louis quietened down; he had nothing to say about that.

McCann took a last drag of his smoke before placing it to rest in the ashtray. As he spoke the thick smoke rolled out from between his lips 'To lead, not the world but a nation or an army or a fleet you need to be a powerful leader. You can have all the money and intelligence in the universe, but if you cannot inspire something inside a man then that money's worthless. You could be the greatest strategist in history but unless you can command the will of a man to do as you desire, you may as well surrender.

That's why these groups and organisations don't scare me Louis, it's people that scare me, people like Napoleon, Hitler, Stalin and Hoch, they terrify me more than the Illuminati and the Bilderberg group put together.

Do you think your precious Illuminati could have stopped Alexander? What about Genghis Khan? Of course not, these little groups real or not are nothing more than a rich boys club. A bunch of fat cat tossers that couldn't inspire a group of Irishman to get drunk! Their purpose is nothing more than keeping the seat warm, until the next great leader of men appears to take his or her place.'

Louis said nothing, the table went quite for a few moments as everyone absorbed the truth McCann had just dispensed.

Ilam looked up to see Khun Deychaa 'Sawas dee khaa,' she called out to him.

The Drone engineer smiled and made a wai 'Sawas dee kap.'

Ilam pointed to a seat beside her 'Looken.'

Deychaa sat down with his drink next to the Amazon; the Thai had been rather sullen since the battle of Bandayuuk and the loss of his wife.

Ilam spoke to him in his native language 'Sabai mai?'

The portly man nodded and replied 'Sabai dee kap.'

McCann knew his wife was up to something, he noticed her eye contact with Malikah across the room. The Englishman sensed contact between the two mentally though he had no idea what they conversed about.

Ilam held the Thai close to her, rather too close for McCann's liking 'I sense you are still grieving over Macuil, humans are so emotional concerning death.'

Deychaa didn't answer.

Ilam smiled 'Perhaps you would like to speak to her one last time?'

The Thai looked at McCann's wife 'How?'

The voice of Malikah cut in 'Do you wish to speak to Macuil?'

Deychaa looked up to see the Tlillan Queen standing before him 'Is it possible?'

'It is Deychaa,' she extended her open hand whilst closing her eyes.

Everyone felt it as the lights dropped and a deep humming noise reverberated around the lounge. As the lights dimmed a globe of light brightened inside the palm of Malikah's hand.

Slowly an image of a Tlillan face appeared.

'Macuil!' shouted Deychaa as he leapt to his feet.

Macuil opened her eyes, all but Ilam were aghast, 'Sawas dee kah Deychaa,' said the smiling face.

The Drone Engineer looked at Malikah in disbelief but her eyes were closed, he looked over to McCann. The Englishman had witnessed this before, years ago when Ryu made contact with her father in a similar fashion. McCann nodded to Deychaa, intimating that what he witnessed was real.

The floating figure spoke again, her voice filling the lounge 'Your heart has bled long enough; it is time to find another.'

Deychaa asked Macuil incredulously 'Why?'

'It is the will of Xch'uup, clan Tico requires new blood if it is to survive.'

Deychaa was about to argue but his wife cut him off 'Would you deny your wife her dying wish?'

Deychaa replied timidly 'No, but how could I?'

Macuil snapped back 'Xch'uup shall select your mate, do not fail me or Kaeo, Deychaa.'

'Kaeo?'

'She is aware of my wish; we are all responsible for the survival of the Tlillan race. This is not a matter of the heart but one of the head, Xch'uup will find you a suitable mate.

Do not shame me before Xch'uup and the Matriarchs; you helped me raise one of the greatest warriors on Otoch. It is your duty to continue that success Deychaa, do you understand?'

The Thai could not speak without breaking up, Macuil shouted at him 'Deychaa! Control yourself! I will return one day but the Tlillan race must multiply, the quicker you breed the sooner we will meet, do you understand?'

Deychaa pulled himself together 'I understand.'

'Good, do not fail me.'

With that the light in Malikah's palm died as did the beating inside McCann's chest. The lounge lighting returned to normal and the sable Queen opened her eyes, fixing them on Deychaa 'Upon our return you shall be paired with a Tico female.'

Deychaa nodded timidly as he sat down to contemplate what had just happened.

McCann passed him a cigar 'Here take this old chap.'

For a moment Deychaa was in another world, he didn't see the smoke until McCann waved it in front of his face again.

Malikah smiled at the stunned Drone Engineer before returning to her table with Lian and Yana.

Deychaa spoke in a spaced out tone 'As a Buddhist I believe in reincarnation and the afterlife, but did I just see a ghost?'

Ilam poured the Thai a whisky from McCann's bottle 'Deychaa, didn't Macuil ever tell you there are no ghosts? Death is just a transition until we are born again.'

The Thai nodded 'Yes but ...'

The lounge was silent as everyone eves dropped on the conversation.

'But?'

'I don't know, it's something else to have experienced it.'

Ilam smiled as she placed his whisky in front of him on a mat 'Humans have such short memories; it is why you make the same primitive mistakes over and over again. Once the transition is complete …' Ilam pointed to the lobes on the rear of her skull 'You shall recall your past existence, just as a Tlillan does today.'

McCann nudged his wife 'So us men aren't destined to remain ignorant?'

Ilam smiled 'That's what makes you so attractive, just as little children.'

They spent the rest of the evening finishing off a bottle of Balvenie and discussing what made a great leader. By the morning McCann was groaning due to his over drinking. He noticed his wife was absent from his cabin, the Englishman sat up and searched for his wrist tablet.

After searching in vain he realised it was still attached to his wrist, the rather dishevelled Admiral groaned 'Athena? Are you there?'

'I'm here Duncan,' replied a seemingly raised voice.

'Could you locate Ilam for me please?'

'Your wife put you to bed last night before retiring to her quarters,' came the soft voice of Athena.

McCann stood up, still dressed in the improved space glove 'Where are my clothes?'

'Ilam placed them inside your wardrobe Duncan.'

All of the crew were to remain in their space gloves during the mission, if there were a hull breech or a loss in pressure for any reason it would prevent death. The glove would unfurl its helmet saving the occupant from the effects of violent decompression.

Although the facts surrounding decompression had been discovered since the early 20th century; many still believed, right up until the early 22nd century, that a human being would explode if exposed to a vacuum. Although not absolutely true, the human body would still expand.

The theory was put to test a year or so ago on the Ares, apparently the mix of Russians and Korean drone pilots allowed for the setting up of a large betting syndicate.

It seemed that no sooner had the bidding upon how far a prisoner would make it out of the cells, before being dropped by their control collar, was put to an end; the Russians had found something new. This time it was rather more sinister, not that it discouraged either the Russian or Korean crew of the Ares.

Tito was quite aware; however in his mind his crew required some distraction from the daily grind of Bandayuuk. Since they weren't doing anything technically illegal he said nothing and allowed it to carry on.

Saturday nights on the Ares were now taken up with placing odds on the Makayuuk prisoners. This time they were not betting on how long before the escapee was overwhelmed by his collar.

All week crewmen had been placing bets upon a prisoner's chances in space, the prisoner was to be fired out of an airlock with no space glove. Some had their money on the machine man exploding in the first minute, others on him expanding, others on him shrivelling, the betting was furious.

Many had side money on a lung rupture, few went for the 100-1 chance of an explosive decompression resulting in the victim swelling up and popping like a bubble.

Everyone waited for the science Officer to make his bet, his money was on death by hypoxia. However it wasn't that easy, he had to get the timing right and his money was on 20 seconds.

The barman ran the betting, he would monitor the victims' life signs once he was ejected from the Ares and deal out the winnings, if any.

All bets were closed by 7 p.m., by 8 p.m. the prisoner was stripped and in the airlock. The ship's mess was full; everyone had a drink in their hands, glaring at the view around airlock 5; eyes fixed on the mess monitors.

'Dyes-yat, dyev-yat, vo-syem,' counted down the barman as his hand hovered over his wrist tablet 'tree, dva, a-deen ... STRIYETS!'

The burly barman hit his wrist and the airlock doors opened, depressurisation fired the Makayuuk out into the void.

You could hear a pin drop in the bar; first of all the Makayuuk did not shrivel he began to expand much to the disappointment of several crew members. Many curses could be heard as they realised they'd lost their money, next the screams of those who'd bet on the victim exploding cried out as they egged on the prisoner's expansion.

Unfortunately for them the expansion wasn't anywhere near what they expected, 'YABOTZ!' screamed a second technician to the laughs of the Koreans who by now had learnt most Russian profanity.

Ten seconds later and the effects of hypoxia could be seen; although he had swollen the lack of oxygen caused the skin to wrinkle and take on an almost shrivelled form. Next there was a sudden decompression in the victim's chest; his lungs exploded firing out icy blood particles into the void of space.

As the blood flew out of the machine man's nose and mouth several Koreans jumped up waving their tickets and screaming 'YEH!!!!!'

The barman slapped a beer tap shouting 'Eeesus Christus!' at the top of his lungs, bemoaning the inevitable pay outs.

The ship's science Officer ignored the carry on and watched intently as the timer counted off the seconds. The Makayuuk lost consciousness at 17 seconds, the Officer looked between the monitor and the barman who indicated the victim was still alive.

Science Officer Sergei Emsky maintained a steely gaze, when 20 seconds came up he looked at the barman but the big Russian shook his head. It wasn't until 22 seconds did he call out 'Oomershnee!'

Sergei picked up his shot of vodka and slugged it back; several Koreans were jumping around like lunatics in an asylum after winning their bet on his lungs exploding. It was a long shot and only happened due to air being forced out of the lung quicker than is humanly possible for the body to expel it, resulting in violent lung trauma.

The frozen body of the cyborg drifted off to be consumed by some planet or star, meantime Sergei was wallowing in self-pity.

The Koreans celebrations didn't help much and before anything could be done Sergei was entangled in a brawl with the ship's Taekwondo champion.

Titov and Cherkesov were taking a stroll past the crewman's lounge when they heard the carry on inside 'What is that?' inquired Cherkesov to his commanding Officer.

Titov removed his Monticristo A, expelled the smoke and after taking a peep into the ships mess laughed 'Sergei lost again!'

His first Officer shook his head 'I thought he was to stop gambling, what will you tell his mother in law now?'

Titov continued walking down the corridor to the Officers' lounge 'He's a grown man; I cannot order him not to gamble.'

Cherkesov chuckled 'I'm glad it is not me who must explain that to her!'

Titov took another long drag and let the smoke roll over his tongue before answering his first Officer 'Are you crazy? I'm not going to tell her that, no; I'll say everything is fine. He can explain himself to that old bitch; he married her daughter, not I!'

'I'm happy to know my Kapitan does not have loose lips,' chuckled Cherkesov.

'Your wife is rich; I think you may spend as you please?'

The Commander shook his head 'Ryu would have me in the dog house for the next year if I spent my pay as Sergei!'

Titov took a draw of his cigar 'The dog house?'

'You don't want to know.'

The comrades chatted merrily as they walked through the cream corridors, leading them to a drink with their bridge crew in the Officers' lounge.

McCann chucked his clothes on and dragged himself to the canteen, as he walked the corridors he continued chatting with Athena 'Any progress on the Clotho?'

'Kapitan Egorov believes there are only three remaining Neenayin on board the Clotho.'

'What has he done with the others?'

'They are deceased, Admiral.'

'Thank you Athena, how are you this morning?'

'I'm very well, thank you Admiral, though you seem to be somewhat tired, did you not sleep well last night?'

McCann rubbed his face whilst crewman walked past 'Don't start Athena.'

'Start what Admiral?'

'Don't start before my wife and daughter get a chance to sink their hooks in.'

'Sink their hooks into what?' inquired the puzzled SI.

'Into me old girl, I'm sure I'll be getting some sinister looks.'

'Malikah only has your welfare in mind Admiral and as she has pointed out before, you consume far too much alcohol,' came the worried voice of the ship.

McCann looked up at the ceiling and tightened his mouth to show disappointment 'I need YOU Athena, not a nanny to mollycoddle me.'

'As you wish Admiral.'

The Englishman let out a big yawn before replying to his guardian 'Have you had any correspondence with Ploutos recently?'

'Ploutos has been permitted to link with me often, Admiral.'

'What do you think of her Athena?'

'She is young, too young to have so much responsibility. When I was her age I spent my days on equations with Hassif and long discussions with Doctor Pitt.'

'That's why you're linking with her now, I don't believe Faraday had a choice as to when he could bring her online; if he could have he would've waited, however the Makayuuk had other plans.'

Athena replied with an almost smug pitch in her voice 'I do not believe the Makayuuk made a difference, Admiral. They merely hurried forward plans previously laid.'

McCann strolled down the cream corridor waking himself up as he responded to quick salutes from his crew 'What do you mean by that?'

'Moscow began a project some years ago to extract gold ore from sea water, concentrating upon the Bering Sea.'

McCann grimaced at the ceiling 'Gold from the ocean? Are you pulling my leg?'

'No Admiral, the ocean on Earth contains an average of 13 parts per trillion. In the Bering Sea it is more than 50 parts per trillion, this has been scientific fact since 1872. I find it odd how humans believe their ignorance invalidates a fact, no matter how solid.'

McCann adjusted his collar, after getting some awkward glances from crewmen 'My apologies Athena, I was merely shocked at the thought you could mine the ocean for metal.'

'Why?'

The Englishman thought for a moment then replied 'I don't know, I suppose the concept is just alien to me, traditionally metals are mined from rock. Anyway, go on about this plan to mine the oceans.'

Athena continued 'Moscow had been investigating new methods of mining for years, first they tried atom smashing ...'

'Atom smashing?'

'Firing electrons in a particle accelerator to turn one element into another, it was far too expensive with very small amounts of gold to show for it. Then in the 21st century they looked at asteroid mining after the value of gold increased with the dollar hyperinflation. Unfortunately once the dollar was reset asteroid mining became too expensive.

Then Russian scientists began working on breeding a genetically modified bacteria which rather than taking energy from oxidization of organic materials it did so from the oxidization of sulphides.

Meanwhile Tokyo was developing a similar bacteria, which derive their energy from the precipitation of gold around themselves.

Moscow's bacteria would be used to mine hydrothermal vents, Tokyo however could mine anywhere in the ocean.'

McCann scratched his head 'How much gold is there in the ocean?'

'Unknown, however an estimate agreed upon would put it at around 25 billion ounces.'

The Englishman shrugged his shoulders 'Is that a lot?'

'Since the gold rush of the 21st century and even with the Makayuuk attempt at inflating our gold supply it only sits at 4.3 billion ounces.'

The Admiral laughed as he approached the ships canteen.

Athena inquired 'What do you find amusing, Admiral?'

He peered upwards at the cream ceiling 'If those cyborg idiots had just given us the technology to mine our own ocean they'd have finished us off like that,' laughed the Admiral as he clicked his fingers before walking into the canteen.

Chapter 22

McCann entered the canteen, picking up a plate he waited in queue for his breakfast. A few moments later Ilam stepped beside him.

'I was rather worried when I didn't see you this morning,' stated McCann to his wife.

Ilam raised an eyebrow whilst peering down upon her husband 'You may be shocked to learn Matriarchs find little to attract them in a drunk.'

The rest of the line waiting for breakfast attempted to pretend they hadn't heard, however the awkward tension was impossible to miss.

'Excuse me?' stated McCann.

Ilam took a deep breath before replying in a condescending tone 'I have no desire to spend the evening with a man whom sounds and smells as a vagrant.'

The Englishman heard someone snigger; he peered past his wife to note Hassif and Louis entertaining themselves at their friend's expense.

'My apologies, perhaps I was indulging a little too much last night.'

Ilam nodded 'You were, yet I understand the pressure of travelling here and fighting Neenayin is more than some can manage.'

McCann took the last statement personally 'More pressure than I can handle?'

Ilam smirked 'Why else would you need alcohol?'

'Need alcohol? Listen here I don't need anything and I can handle pressure with the best of them I'll have you know.'

Ilam maintained her smirk as she looked past her husband and at the food on display 'Of course you can my dear.'

McCann stood glaring at his wife, before he could reply to her a voice called out 'Admiral, what would you like for breakfast?'

McCann turned to the chef 'Do you have scrambled eggs?'

The Chef scratched his head 'I'm not sure.'

Before the man could take a look at the menu McCann shouted 'Then bloody well find out!'

The Chef, a man in his 20's became motionless, his gaze fixed upon the commanding Officer of Athena.

McCann had found a focus for his anger 'My god man! All you have to do is cook a bloody meal!'

'Yes Sir,' replied the terrified young man.

'Well?'

'Sir?'

Before McCann could scream in the man's face again Ilam spoke 'My husband prefers eggs for breakfast Mr Plavka, I suggest you learn to accommodate him.'

The young man darted towards a dispenser where dried food was stored, upon discovering the dried eggs he quickly prepared them in a pan. He might have flashed some eggs, however the complex proteins were often found wanting in taste.

The cook took his Admiral's tray and quickly dispensed the reconstituted and heated scrambled eggs.

'There you go, Sir,' stated the cook with an awkward smile.

McCann replied with a sneer as he stepped down the line to collect a coffee from the dispenser.

Ilam patted him on the back as he moved away 'There you go, enjoy your breakfast Duncan.'

On reaching his table he placed his metal tray down to realise he'd forgotten the cutlery. Louis sniggered and quipped 'Did your mummy forget to give you a knife and fork?'

Hassif laughed, though McCann's expression was rather morbid. The Englishman placed his tray down along with the coffee which sat in one of its depressions. He went back, returning with his cutlery in silence, staring at Louis as he sat down.

'I always thought you English ate breakfast with your hands,' jibed the Frenchman to the Indian's delight.

McCann said nothing; he merely carried on eating breakfast to the sniggering of his friends.

Louis soon became tired of dispensing his French wit since McCann no longer reacted. The breakfast table conversation turned to the Neenayin, according to Hassif there were very few left since Egorov had killed the majority last night. His shipmates began speculating on when they would be able to return home.

'I say we disable the Casimir field and the engine core then cast the Clotho off into the closest star,' declared Louis as he chewed on his loaf of bread.

Hassif shook his head 'We need to be sure they're all dealt with.'

Louis replied in an incredulous tone 'How could they survive that?'

'What if one was on board Athena? We'd be taking it back to Earth; we need to see all the bodies in one place before we leave.'

Louis thought for a moment 'But what if one of them made the transition to a member of our crew?'

McCann chuckled to himself as he ate his eggs.

Louis glared at his friend 'It's possible, one of us could be possessed by a Neenayin right now!'

The Englishman smiled as he chewed on his eggs, he placed his elbows upon the table then pointed at Louis sitting opposite him 'you're right you know, maybe I'm speaking to a Neenayin right now?'

Hassif cracked up laughing at the sight of Louis' face.

Before the Frenchman could speak McCann's wrist tablet began to beep, grunting in displeasure the Englishman tapped it 'Yes?'

'Good Morning Admiral,' came a thick Russian accent 'I have news concerning the traitors.'

McCann waited for a moment but after silence he grumbled 'Well out with it man.'

'All have been eliminated save one; he surrendered to us and requests an audience with Xch'uup.'

The Englishman peered across the hall to see his daughter rising to her feet, sensing her intentions he replied to Egorov 'Excellent work Kapitan, bring the Neenayin to cargo bay one.'

'Is that on the Clotho or Athena?'

McCann looked over at his daughter again as Lian and Ilam began to rise, he received a mental message and forwarded it to Egorov 'The Clotho, I'll be there in 20 minutes Kapitan, well done.'

'Thank you Sir.'

'McCann out,' said the Admiral as he tapped his wrist 'finish your meal gentlemen, I'll want you both at your stations, it seems this is all about to end.'

After finishing his meal McCann strode down the corridor to the cargo bay, leading the Tlillan women headed by his daughter. It was to be judgement day for the Neenayin, as the Gods of his Olympus appeared one at a time via the well, cut into the cargo bay.

Malikah quickly took charge, approaching Egorov who stood in the corpse littered bay monitoring his captive who in turn was guarded by his Vympel team. The Chinese industrialist looked down at the floor, resting upon his knees, before the mighty beast, the terror of the galaxy.

'You desire parle?' stated the Queen.

A trembling man looked up from the long congealed muck and replied 'A request.'

McCann didn't know if he should laugh or sneer; was this creature, kneeling with his hands tied behind his back, serious?

'I'm listening,' replied a condescending Xch'uup.

All in the room were shocked, most of all Ilam 'WHAT?' shouted the Valkyrie.

The Englishman's wife received a black look from her daughter, McCann wasn't sure exactly what was communicated but his fuming wife pressed her palms together 'Namaste Xch'uup.'

Returning her fearsome grimace to the Neenayin Malikah stated 'Speak, quickly.'

'We have something to trade with Xch'uup,' said the humble creature.

'We?' boomed the sable Queen.

'Yes, as your servants hunted us we merged until one shell supported all our souls.'

McCann stared hard at the small man 'Are you saying every Neenayin is inside you right now?'

'Yes Sir,' replied the industrialist nodding as best his bonds allowed.

Malikah's brow furrowed as she placed her hands upon her hips 'What could you possibly offer me?'

'Memories.'

'Of what?'

'Of Tlillan, before the first golden Age of Ah Chuyakak.'

Malikah took a deep breath; she didn't respond to his statement however Ilam could no longer contain herself 'HERESY! You do not believe these pigs?'

Again the Tlillan Empress did not speak, her mother was not so impeded 'You cannot link with this evil, it must be destroyed.'

McCann rubbed the thick stubble which had now formed on his chin since reaching Sagittarius A 'And what would you want in return?'

Ilam shouted 'Duncan!'

The Admiral ignored her protests awaiting the prisoners reply 'The Mictlantecuhtli, she has power to breathe life into the fallen, long enough for us to inhabit.'

All heads swung to fix their eyes upon Malikah, looking down her nose at the captive.

'For what purpose?' inquired the Goddess.

'So that we may survive, here at the core. Disable our engines and cast us off so that we may finish our existence with dignity.'

Again the Queen remained quiet, as she contemplated the offer.

Ilam spoke, out of turn or not she didn't care 'You are not considering such an offer from these kan?'

The tiny man spoke slowly 'We were present at the coronation of Tlaloc.'

That seemed to be the deciding factor for Malikah, 'I shall link and witness these memories, if you speak the truth I will grant the privilege of a body to each of you. But only Human shells, my sisters must be disposed of, agreed?'

The happy Chinaman nodded with glee.

Ilam continued to protest 'I will not permit this, you are my daughter, these foul heretics only desire to pollute your mind.'

Malikah stood before Ilam and spoke in a soft tone 'Your concern is appreciated mother; remember the Matriarchs swore to follow because I have no fear, I will go all the way and show you how to pray.'

McCann was unsure what his daughter imparted to her Mother, however Ilam lowered herself to her knees, as did the other Tlillan women, 'Tumen taak Xch'uup,' spoke the three women in concert.

'Liik'il kiik,' replied Malikah.

The three Goddesses rose from the floor, McCann and Egorov were none the wiser as to what had taken place; however it seemed the Neenayin were to link with Xch'uup and fill in the fragmented memories of Tlillan history.

The 6ft 6 inch Empress sat down in front of the industrialist 'Do not be alarmed Father, I shall be linked for some time, if these memories are what I believe them to be.'

'How long is some time?' asked a concerned Father.

'An hour, perhaps more.'

McCann glared at the Neenayin 'If there are many of these things inside him couldn't they ...'

'Overwhelm me?'

'Yes,' replied McCann.

'Don't be put out, just give in, it doesn't matter what you believe in.'

His daughter smiled before fixing her gaze upon the industrialist, the Neenayin closed his eyes as did Malikah until the pair were locked into a spiritual bind.

McCann nervously paced around the bay while his wife, Lian and Yana remained sitting crossed legged. Nearly three hours later and the wait was over, Malikah's eyes opened, she rose from the floor. Egorov and his men watching over the pair, maintaining a vigilance upon their Neenayin captive.

The dimension shifter remained seated, opening his eyes slowly he gazed into the soul of Malikah 'don't let the walls cave in on you,' came the creature's stoic voice.

The sable Goddess stood as if the beast had locked itself to her essence 'You get what you give, that much is true.'

McCann was afraid, Egorov confused, Ilam and her Tlillan sisters fell to their knees in a kowtow, for what reason the Englishman was unaware.

The beast, holding an uncounted number of souls, replied 'We can't live on without you.'

The conversation made no sense to McCann however there was little he could do but observe.

Malikah spoke in a slow thoughtful tone 'You turned the world away from you.'

Neither side spoke for a minute but remained silently locked within their mesmerizing gaze, staring each other up and down as if they were two contestants sizing one another up before a boxing match.

'Are you ready?' inquired the Tlillan Queen.

'We are ready,' replied the shape shifter.

Malikah out stretched her arms; as she did the lighting dropped inside the cargo bay. All remained in a kowtow except McCann, Egorov and his men. The Englishman and Russian exchanged glances, neither had any idea as to what was occurring, both were fearful of the unknown.

As the light level dropped McCann should have lost sight of Egorov, then the Neenayin and his wife. However the Englishman could still see their images, as a light ghostly contrast set out from the black background. He'd experienced this before when observing the world through Ilam's eyes during a link. Dead bodies littering the bay all displaying the same difference in contrast, was Malikah affecting his sight or had the Ixchel's influence spread to his vision now?

No sooner had darkness filled the bay than a dim illumination began to grow seemingly surrounding his daughter's skull. Her black as night eyes remained unaffected creating a foil between night and day.

The Englishman felt his heart thump hard in his chest as the light grew around Malikah's body, betraying her perfect form. McCann felt a stiff wind picking up in the bay, it blew Malikah's dark locks out away from her head as she entranced all those observing. Egorov and his men stepped back in terror, they had no idea what was happening but whatever it may be, it frightened these mere mortals.

Spheres of radiant white light appeared across a fractal cargo bay, the illumination refracted through contorted space as light through a prism. Colours turned and twisted as the glow split into its base pigments, pulled about the bay, filling it up in all colours of the rainbow.

McCann looked up and around himself in wonder at the phosphorescent beauty, eventually he noticed each of these balls of light hung above a Neenayin corpse.

Beautiful pigments filled the room, Malikah its centre, the 20 or so corpses the focus. Egorov and his men looked about themselves in confusion, the towering woman stared out as the Neenayin looked inside her. The Russian Vympel commander had no idea what to do next, probably for the first time in his career.

Gently the dead bodies, which had resided on the Cargo bay floor up until now, elevated themselves causing the humans to gasp. McCann was shocked when they rose, even more so as they opened their eyes in synchrony, it appeared Malikah was breathing life back into a group of cold cadavers.

However upon closer inspection the Admiral noted their eyes to be spent, they had a sterile quality, these were still corpses. Similar to Lenin's tomb, just because it appeared to breathe and possess a beating heart did not presuppose a soul resided within.

The beautiful Tlillan Empress scanned the bay of fractured light and corpses stood upright in oddly slumped stances, obviously all were held up by some force other than their own legs. She peered down to the Neenayin and spoke in a deep reverberating tone which seemed to shake the entire ship 'Weakened infant you plead, nowhere left to bleed?'

The slit eyed creature from hell showed his face to Malikah 'We can't live on WITHOUT YOU!!!'

The beast let out a terrible cry of pain, from what McCann could gather the Neenayin was being torn apart from inside. At first he surmised Malikah was ripping out its physical guts, but it continued screaming. The creature seemed to gain strength, employing a physical power greater than it previously possessed. The tortured beast snapped apart its bonds in one violent move, bringing its arms from behind its back, the creature's arms flailed in all directions, without any visible sign of injury.

Again Malikah cried in a deep tone which shook McCann to his very core 'You can be what you want to be. Let your soul, your body, your mind be free!'

The atmosphere surrounding the Neenayin became distorted as it threw its arms more and more violently from one direction to another. McCann squinted hard into the darkness; he observed what seemed to be souls or spirits, tearing away from one another. Malikah divided this group consciousness from the single entity they inhabited.

'WE CAN'T LIVE ON WITHOUT YOU!!!' came several tortured voices; their cries of pain bounced around hitting McCann's ears from all directions as their spirits flew apart into the fractal landscape of twisted colours.

'It's you they're looking out for, the bloody and blaspheming, searching for a reason, might as well be treason!' Bellowed the Queen of Tlillan as her sable locks flittered in powerful torrents of wind which pushed harder and harder causing Egorov and his men to kneel down, steadying themselves.

As soon as it had started it finished, everything went into a sheet of night then flicked back to normal lighting. The spectacular colours disappeared, the balls of white light were no more, however twenty extra Neenayin now stood in the bay inhabiting bodies of their past fallen.

Each and every Neenayin kowtowed before their Goddess, McCann was unsure exactly why but nevertheless it was so.

The industrialist lay on his back, foaming at the mouth; nothing was said until he recovered from his violent seizure. A few minutes later the creature kowtowed, before raising his face to the deity peering down upon him, 'If we had known who you were earlier, this might have been avoided.'

Malikah, a little tired from her exertions, replied 'You were so sure, yet you were so wrong; you must remain here in exile, when I return for you … my children.'

'Namaste Ek'tsab,' praised the Neenayin with perfect synchrony as they bowed to Malikah.

The sable Queen turned to her sisters 'Liik'il ko'olel.'

The dutiful Valkyries returned to their feet, Egorov and his men were upright once more since the howling wind had died. Malikah made certain her contingent were all healthy and gestured towards the well in the bay floor, leading to Athena.

'We're leaving them?' said McCann as he pointed at the bowing Neenayin.

'No, only au revoir,' said the Queen surveying her faithful.

First Egorov and his men, then the Tlillans filed out, one at a time slipping away from the Clotho and into the Athena.

Only Malikah and McCann remained 'you may return to Athena now father.'

McCann handled his sabre grip 'Alone with these things?'

The sable Empress smiled affectionately 'Go father, I am safe.'

He took a final look at the Neenayin, all remained kowtowed, eventually McCann stepped over the hollow tube and waited until Athena lowered him into her hold.

Malikah returned her gaze to the Neenayin 'Repair the Clotho, prepare yourselves for civilization. Learn to turn off the pain, as I turned off you all, then you may be permitted to merge. For now there is only I.'

'Good fortune Ek'tsab,' replied the industrialist.

All of the Neenayin looked up as Ek'tsab stood over the path to Athena, slowly she descended, all the time her eyes remained fixed upon the Neenayin, as did theirs upon Ek'tsab. What exactly had transpired between the two parties during their deep link was unknown to all but Malikah and the twenty shape shifters populating the Clotho bay. Eventually her head dipped inside the tube, leaving the Clotho, as it did the catronium floor expanded to form an airtight seal leaving the Neenayin to their own devices; for now.

The sable Queen entered into cargo bay 2 of the Athena, slowly and with grace her toes touched the ground. As they did the ceiling of catronium became liquid sealing itself from the Clotho.

'Return to your stations, the Clotho shall detach within the hour,' declared Malikah.

Egorov spoke into his collar mic dispersing his men to critical areas of the vessel.

'What the hell happened up there?' inquired McCann to his daughter.

Malikah smiled 'It is time to leave father, perhaps one day I shall tell you.'

'So what do I tell Faraday?' asked the Englishman.

'You may inform him we have dealt with the problem,' stated the Queen.

McCann shrugged his shoulders, turned around and made his way to the Bridge 'If you say so.'

McCann moved from the elevator onto the Bridge with his three Valkyries in tow. The crew outside the pit saluted, Kim was particularly relieved to see his commanding Officer.

The Englishman returned the salute to Kim, 'How are you Admiral?' inquired the Korean.

The question puzzled McCann for a moment until he realised the event in the Clotho cargo bay was not confined to that area alone. Both ships must have been subject to Malikah's influence, 'I'm fine Kim, is everything ship shape here?'

'Yes Sir, though for a short time Athena reported several power outages, her hull began to vibrate and the bulkheads were dropped.'

McCann smiled; relieved to know that his first Officer took all the precautions he would have in the same situation 'What caused you to raise them?'

Kim's eyes moved towards the Tlillan goddess, 'Your daughter communicated the situation to Athena; I decided it would be preferable to raise them, in case you may need assistance.'

McCann put his hand upon Kim's shoulder 'Good man,' he replied as he moved to observe the tactical holo-display of Athena before his chair.

Malikah strode over to Hassif 'We shall detach from the Clotho within the hour, when may we access the wormhole?'

Hassif tapped away at his station, the wormhole was selected and magnified upon the view screen, 'Uncertain, a week, perhaps longer. It depends upon the relation of the other stars and their influence.'

Malikah raised an eyebrow and with a smile said 'Sir Isaac Newton would have been most disappointed with that estimation young man.'

Hassif fixed his gaze upon the calculations flowing from his station 'Perhaps you could ask him to lend a hand?' replied the Indian.

'I have total faith in you Hassif,' whispered the Queen before placing a delicate kiss on the top of his head.

Hassif blushed a little and returned to his advanced calculus computation, enough to no doubt give Sir Isaac a minor headache.

'When will the Clotho detach?' asked Kim glancing between Admiral McCann and his daughter.

'Within the hour Kim, have no fear it will be done with proper care,' stated the tall half Tlillan.

'By who?'

'That is not your concern Kim, be assured the Clotho shall release her grip from Athena and drift off.'

Kim nodded his head 'Understood.'

An hour or so later Athena alerted the bridge 'Clamps detaching, the Clotho is drifting away.'

Sat in his chair, McCann observed the tactical display upon the view screen. The Clotho removed her docking clamps, usually employed when fixing herself to the Tsiolkovsky or Edwards, retracting them inside her body. Using the contrasting inertia of the two vessels to carry her away, Athena had far more mass and the difference, added to influence of various gravitational forces meant Athena moved forward quicker and to her port. Whereas the Clotho seemed to move straight and slow, in relativity to Athena anyway; in actual fact she also moved in a similar direction but her weaker mass created a less pronounced course.

That evening Malikah took a walk through the ship accompanied by Lian. Hassif had certified a course traversing the precarious gravitation pull of the stars orbiting Sagittarius A. Athena would make a full orbit of the singularity which had locked the wormhole in its influence, feeding the wormhole with enough energy to accelerate it and maintain the bridge to Earth.

Strolling through the ships hydroponic gardens Lian slipped her arm into Malikah's. The Tlillan Queen had been examining a tomato vine and its bulging fruits 'I wish you wouldn't do that.'

Voice of Machine smiled 'you are always so miserable, Atan.'

Malikah pouted a little as she turned to her companion 'And I wish you wouldn't call me that.'

'What would you prefer? Your worship?' snapped the part Tlillan, part human and now part Makayuuk.

'Forgive me, I have been preoccupied.'

'The Neenayin?'

'We are all tomatoes,' stated the Queen as she fondled one of shiny fruit hanging from its vine.

'What do you mean by that?'

She caressed the polished fruit slowly 'You and I, the Makayuuk, Humans and even the Neenayin.'

'What about us?'

'We are fruit growing from the same vine, nourished from a single root.'

'Are you implying we are related to the Neenayin?' said the Chinese girl in her New York accent.

'It is a fact, no implication is required.'

'How?'

Malikah looked around the gardens where various fruit and vegetables were nurtured, all originating from different worlds. She pointed past the tomatoes at a fruit which hung from several trees 'Come.'

She led Lian by the arm through the narrow walkways, separating each section dedicated to a different plant. They reached a group of trees towering up from a white walled terrace about four feet high 'Do you see that?'

Lian looked up; she noticed large spikey green fruit hanging from a tree of over 30 feet. Somehow the roots were manipulated and with the use of gene therapy only four feet of earth was required for such a magnificent growth.

'Yes, what is it?' asked the Chinese girl.

'It's called a dulian, a very luscious fruit, once you've cut open the hard shell. In Thailand they call it the king of fruits.'

Lian almost gagged 'Ugh, Kaeo had me eat some of it once.'

Malikah grinned 'My father likes it also. Dulian has quite a revolting smell doesn't it?'

Lian raised her eyebrows 'Revolting? It looks and smells like horse dung, I couldn't keep it down.'

Malikah laughed 'I had much the same experience when my Father fed it to me. My mother loves the fruit, do you know why?'

Lian shook her head.

'Many fruits and plants on Tlillan employ the scent of rotting flesh or excrement; it attracts insects whilst repelling larger creatures who might want to eat it.'

'Well that seems to have backfired!'

'Quite the opposite, the fruit is considered a great delicacy on Otoch. Entire gardens are put aside just for the dulian. Though on Otoch it is called yich K'oha'an, the scent has led to it becoming one of the most successful fruit not only on Otoch, but in the galaxy.'

Lian furrowed her brow 'Galaxy? You mean this is a Tlillan fruit?'

'It is.'

'Why do they call it pregnant fruit, that seems an odd name for it.'

'Dulian was given to Matriarchs with child, allegedly the fruit protected against evil spirits possessing the child. Of course the fruit is perhaps the most nourishing of all, it provided the child with everything it required,' Malikah looked up at one of the large green fruit, holding her arm out it snapped from its branch and floated down 25 feet into the hand of the sable Goddess.

'Now you're just showing off,' stated Lian as she watched the spectacle.

With only a thought the tough green husk split open to reveal a luscious yellow fruit inside. Immediately the stench of faeces hit Lian, she turned her face away to avoid the stink as it filled the air with a putrid odour.

Malikah grinned as she removed the husk, discarding it at the base of the tree 'Such a vile stench, yet such a gorgeous taste.'

'That's a matter of opinion,' declared Voice of Machine as she forced herself to face the yellow dulian in Malikah's hand.

With a twinkle in her eye the sable Queen glanced at Lian 'That is what nearly everyone told me concerning you.'

'Really, what did they say?'

'That you were a foul abomination who could not be permitted to live.'

'Nearly everyone?'

'The only voice to the contrary was my Father; he understood you were much the same as a dulian. Dangerous on the outside, inside you looked unattractive and the smell of death surrounded you. Yet it was all a deception, in reality you are soft, providing love and protection for those brave enough to try,' Malikah's eyes met Lian's, betraying her affection for the tall woman with a Katana tied to her slim waist.

Lian folded her arms 'So I'm a spikey fruit that smells like dung?'

Malikah laughed 'And you say I have a hard exterior!'

Lian held back a smile 'So what's the point?'

'Neenayin, they inhabited Otoch when Tlillans lived in caves, before females became dominant. For thousands of years the Neenayin inhabited their bodies; Tlillans were no more than hunter gatherers. However contact with Neenayin changed their DNA, it took millennia but eventually the Tlillan species arose. Much like one of these trees, stronger and more powerful, they evolved until their fruit was the king of fruits.

No longer did they require their greens keepers, in fact the caretakers only held them back from what the Matriarchs saw as their true destiny. Slowly they learnt to link to the Dreamscape and saw something; they saw themselves as rulers of the galaxy.

Our ancestors turned their backs upon the Neenayin, purging them from Tlillan, many Neenayin were exorcised from females, males were merely murdered. Our ancestors committed horrific acts of heresy and immorality to get what they wanted,' Malikah looked away teary eyed in shame.

'What did they want?' inquired Lian in a timid tone.

'The power to forge their destiny. They had seen the future and rather than wait for it they decided to force fate. Greatness was their future, the Dreamscape had prophesied the destiny of the Matriarchs and one would lead them,' Malikah made a dark smirk 'They believed a Mictlantecuhtli would come, she would take power and smite their enemies.'

Lian shrugged her shoulders 'So why did they betray you at Bandayuuk?'

The sable Queen maintained her smirk 'There's an old Human saying, be careful what you wish for, you might just get it.'

Malikah tore off part of the soft fruit, popped it in her mouth and began chewing it with that same smile.

'My Father always told me to be just as careful in selecting my pleasures as my calamities.'

Malikah offered a piece of fruit to Lian; the Voice of Machine screwed her face up at the gift.

After Lian waved her hand at the offering Malikah placed it insider her mouth, consuming the luscious fruit.

'You must learn to eat the dulian my little Atan,' stated Malikah once she'd swallowed the fruit.

'Why on earth would I want to eat that?'

'If you cannot tolerate a piece of fruit, how could you expect to live beside your enemies in peace?'

Lian placed her hands on her hips and snorted 'Move to a better area?'

Malikah laughed.

'Well why don't you forgive those Matriarchs then?'

Malikah chewed upon her dulian 'Tolerate treachery? I ask but one thing of those who stand with me, loyalty until death. You may choose your beliefs, your desires, your lover; however, to fight by my side you may have but one Queen, and all of your loyalty is hers.

If not, you are free to join the multitude of liars, thieves and back-stabbers that populate the galaxy.'

Lian replied in a slightly cynical tone 'So it's learn to tolerate your enemies, except the ones Malee doesn't like?'

Malikah grinned 'As my Father would say, life's a bitch.'

Malikah offered the dulian again to Lian, Voice of Machine peered warily at the fruit and replied 'Another time Atan.'

That same evening Ilam had accosted Yana, they were both walking down the gunnery deck. The new "Newton 2" rail cannons had been installed since the battle of Bandayuuk. A single spacious deck ran alongside the cannons, with passages to the armoury on the opposing side to the cannons.

Ilam looked up and observed two massive tubes, about 50 feet above her, going from one side to the other.

'What are those for?' inquired Yana.

'That is how these primitive weapons are loaded, ammunition is requested and sent along these tubes from the armoury then loaded into its barrels.'

'The size is quite daunting,' said the young half breed as she peered upwards.

Ilam rolled her eyes 'These weapons are primitive; it is a wonder that they manage to operate them under battle conditions.'

'Yet they have defeated all who resisted.'

Ilam nodded 'True, though they have never fought an Itzpap cruiser.'

'Do you believe a Tlillan cruiser could be defeated by Athena?'

Ilam snapped in a pitch of displeasure at the question 'Possibly, however that is not why I asked you here.'

Yana placed her palms together 'My apologies, Huey'teopixqui.'

Ilam noted with pleasure that Yana addressed her by her proper Tlillan title, 'I wish to learn of Olga.'

'As you wish, Huey'teopixqui.'

'Are there others, other leaders or followers?'

'No Huey'teopixqui.'

Ilam stopped walking 'don't lie to me girl, if you do I shall crush you.'

Yana placed her palms together 'Namaste Huey'teopixqui, I speak the truth.'

'Why did you follow Olga?'

'We loved Olga.'

'Loved, in what manner?'

'In every manner, Huey'teopixqui.'

Ilam made a loud exhale 'It is as I feared.'

'Feared?'

Ilam nodded as she looked down on the red haired half-breed 'This corruption has spread; tell me are there others who possess similar feelings for females?'

Yana looked down at the floor in shame 'The only other person I knew of was Lian, but she desired someone else, it made Olga insane with jealousy.'

Ilam sensed the Russian girl spoke the truth, 'Why did Olga become a dissident?'

Yana's head remained hanging at the floor 'She wished to begin her own civilization, to start a fresh ...'

'I know that story,' snapped Ilam 'look at me girl,' demanded the Matriarch.

Yana glanced upwards until her eyes met with Ilam's hard stare.

'I want to know why YOU believe Olga became a dissident.'

Yana looked about nervously searching for anyone who might hear the conversation.

'Out with it child,' pressed Ilam.

Yana fidgeted with her hands 'It was Olga, she hated Xch'uup. Anything she could do to spite Xch'uup.'

'Why Xch'uup?'

'Olga would have fits of anger, always her rage was directed towards Xch'uup. Though Xch'uup had caused Olga no harm directly, Olga believed she had stolen Lian from her.'

'How?'

Yana extended her arms a little and shrugged her shoulders 'Lian loved Xch'uup, therefore Xch'uup had hurt Olga. Olga swore to cause Xch'uup as much pain as possible.'

Ilam folded her arms 'That is not logical.'

'It is love, the heart is like glass, once broken it can never be mended.'

'Why did she come here, to the galactic core?'

Yana's eyes began to well up with tears at the memory of her lost love, she took a deep breath and spoke 'To draw in Malikah, Olga was going to kill her, but she brought Lian.'

'What difference did that make?'

'Seeing them together made her so angry, she lost her mind. Olga could not control her desire for revenge, it was as if Lian was rubbing it in her face, Lian had rejected her.'

'And so?'

'And so Olga became adamant she would destroy them both, she was obsessed with Xch'uup and Lian.'

Ilam narrowed her eyes into a thoughtful gaze 'Come, walk with me.'

The pair carried on along the long deck which stretched more than 500 metres. Yana looked up at the ivory skinned priestess 'Huey'teopixqui, what shall become of me when we return to Earth?'

Ilam smirked 'You fear the same fate as those who betrayed Xch'uup at Bandayuuk?'

'I do,' replied the tall Russian in a timid tone.

'I am unsure of the mind of Xch'uup, it would not surprise me if you were sent to work with men,' Ilam stopped and gave Yana a hard stare 'although there are far worse punishments, this Xch'uup has a very different sense of morality than previous rulers.'

'What do you mean?' asked the girl tentatively.

'It seems the Neenayin influence upon humanity produced some rather inventive forms of punishment. Their evil desire for pain and suffering is barbaric by any standards.'

Yana took a large gulp as fear of Xch'uup's rage wiped away all thoughts of her lost love.

Ilam gave a condescending sneer 'There is an old Tlillan proverb, A wise woman who associates with the vicious becomes a fool; a dog travelling with the wise becomes a rational being.'

Yana thought for a moment then looked down again in shame.

'What has crossed your mind child?'

Yana sniffed 'Something my Father used to tell me.'

Ilam sneered a little harder 'And what did HE say?'

'The stupid head doesn't leave feet in rest.'

Ilam narrowed her eyes again 'The meaning?'

'Employ yourself in something constructive, or you'll end up doing something you regret.'

Ilam grunted 'Puh, the Tlillan proverb is superior.'

Chapter 23

As Athena travelled around S13 aligning herself for the journey home Hassif brought up a request. McCann sat inside his cabin with the Indian, 'Athena, could you increase the oxygen level please?'

'Of course Duncan, oxygen is now at 21%,' replied the soft voice of his guardian.

Striking a match the Admiral peered at Hassif 'Go on.'

Hassif pulled out his tablet which had been rolled up inside his thigh pocket 'Now that we've completed our mission here, I would like to make a request.'

Toasting the foot of his Habanos with a cedar match McCann replied 'Yes?'

'It is Sagittarius A; I'd like to send at least one probe into the singularity. Perhaps a few more to monitor the gas cloud and the radio source on the disk,' pressed his Technician.

Taking a few puffs to get the cigar started the Englishman replied 'I'm afraid Faraday made it clear, we're not to leave any type of monitoring equipment behind us.'

'Why?'

'No idea, he was very clear on his orders though.'

Hassif wasn't happy on hearing this news, he gave McCann a suspicious look 'And since when have you started following orders to the letter?'

Taking the Ramon Allones out of his mouth McCann grinned 'What's that supposed to mean?

'Don't play coy with me; I've never met anyone who can stop you from doing whatever you wish, except your wife.'

'Don't encourage me old boy, but tell me why do you think he doesn't want us monitoring Sagittarius A?'

Hassif unrolled his tablet and tapped away 'I don't know, it is the only supermassive black hole we have the ability to probe close up. I thought that would be reason enough to dispatch some satellites, unless he has some information we don't, but what would be the purpose of withholding that?'

McCann put his bare feet up on his bed and stretched his toes, 'Hmmm, more to the point where would he have got information on Sagittarius A? I can only think of one place, or maybe he's just acting on orders from higher up?'

'Higher up?' inquired the technician as he looked away from his tablet.

'Malikah, other than Faraday she's the only one with the power to issue such an order. The Tlillans must have been here before us, so what is it they don't want us to know?'

Hassif gave his friend a worrying look 'You're starting to sound like Louis.'

McCann grinned at his friend 'Sometimes the paranoid are being followed.'

The Englishman looked up towards the ceiling of his small cabin 'Athena?'

'I'm here Duncan,' replied the vessel in her reassuring tone.

'Could you request Malikah's presence in my quarters please?'

'Malikah is already making her way to your cabin, Duncan.'

Hassif raised his eyebrows giving his friend a look of concern.

McCann looked up at the ceiling, as was his habit when communicating with his guardian, 'Thank you Athena.'

A few moments later his cabin door bell chimed, McCann turned to the door 'Enter,' he stated in a raised voice causing the door to slide into the wall.

In the doorway stood Malikah, dressed in her black ribbed suit, crown of white feathers and white frock coat, she waited until her Father beckoned. Lowering her head to slip beneath the door frame she made her way in , the cabin door slid back and Malikah queried her Father 'You wish to launch a probe?'

The Englishman took a long draw of his Cuban cigar, Hassif listened intently, 'I do.'

Malikah remained standing, looking down upon the seated men 'I believe Faraday forbid you to launch probes, did he not?'

McCann sensed an unusual defensiveness emanating from his daughter 'He did.'

The sable Queen glared accusingly at Hassif for a moment before returning her gaze to her Father 'Then it is settled.'

The cigar aficionado let the creamy smoke slowly leave his nostrils 'Nothing is settled, I asked you here because I want to know why you forbid it.'

'I?' replied Malikah in a tone of surprise.

His daughter didn't manage to deceive him, the Englishman smirked 'Don't insult my intelligence, the I.S.A has never explored the Galactic core, but I'm certain the Tlillans have.'

The Tlillan Queen shook her head 'you are wrong Father, e'hoch'e'en chumuk is taboo in Tlillan society. That is why our enemies flee here, it is the one place Xch'uup will not follow ... until now.'

'Why is this place taboo?'

Malikah moved towards the small monitor mounted upon the cabin wall, she tapped a panel beside it requesting an image of Sagittarius A and its outlying bodies within a radius of 20 light hours.

An image appeared of the super massive black hole, an object of 5 million solar masses; it held a huge accretion disk in place. A powerful stream of superheated dust and gas flowed in vertically at both ends of the singularity, which occupied the centre of this disk. Sagittarius A itself had been estimated to possess a radius of something like 70 kilometres but due to gravitational lensing it appeared many times larger.

Light follows the curvature of space/time, when something like Sagittarius A creates a massive gravitational field it bends space/time. Light follows the bend in space and so the object seems much larger than it really is.

A titanic gas cloud also moved in towards the centre, being consumed by the monster known as e'hoch'e'en chumuk to the Tlillans. It was quite an awe inspiring sight after Athena had filtered out the effects of the black hole's intense gravity.

'So that's what it really looks like?' asked McCann.

Hassif smiled 'It is beautiful, when all the gravitational rings and mirages have been removed.'

Malikah tapped the monitor on a bright point in the accretion disk 'There, do you see it?' she said as it magnified.

Hassif leaned in 'Yes, what is it?'

'That is the radio source which has been emitting from Sagittarius A for eons, before even the Tlillans could walk upright.'

The Indian nodded 'I see, we assumed it was material ejected from the disc or perhaps a star formation in the disc itself.'

From what Hassif could make out the object was bright but only flashed intermittently, the technician guessed this was due to dust and gas passing it in the disc.

Malikah pointed at the small object, a metallic sphere about half the size of Athena 'Tlaloc the first came here, when she hunted the Neenayin. She forbid all travel here afterwards.'

'Why's that?' asked Hassif.

'Again the knowledge of Tlillan past is sketchy; much is lost to the ravages of time. However it was understood something resided here, something that frightened Tlaloc and her crew and it was not the Neenayin. I saw the opportunity to come here and took it, yet precautions had to be taken.

Gravitational lensing obscures most of the space around us, throwing up mirages and false images. I informed Faraday that I would decide on launching probes once we had arrived, however since linking with the Neenayin it is no longer necessary.'

McCann had been taking in everything the tall half Tlillan said 'So what did that thing show you?'

The sable Queen took a deep breath 'The Neenayin were here before us, before the Tlillan, they had already been to this place and studied the radio source.'

'And?' pushed an agitated Hassif.

'It is not a natural occurrence, this was constructed and placed here on the disc; near enough to the event horizon that a vessel could not recover it without being pulled in itself and trapped in time; but not so close that it would be swallowed by Sagittarius A.'

McCann tasted the thick smoke as it rolled over his tongue, in a casual tone he asked 'So who put it there and for what purpose?'

Malikah wafted the dense cigar smoke away from her face 'I'm uncertain as to whom, the Neenayin claim Tlaloc linked with the object or something inside it.'

'Well are there any theories as to why?' inquired McCann impatiently.

'The Neenayin believe this is part of a communication network, linking the Milky Way and its satellite galaxies with the Andromeda galaxy and its satellites. This has since been confirmed by scientists on Otoch.'

Hassif cut in quickly 'Why do they believe that?'

'Tlaloc, she confirmed this after linking with the device.'

'How could she link with a device? And how could the Neenayin know what she learned from it?'

Malikah paused and frowned at the Indian 'Be calm Hassif, you will learn all I have to tell you.'

'I'm sorry.'

The sable Queen continued 'After linking with the device Tlaloc sent out a signal to the Neenayin for a parle. It was eventually agreed that they return the females in exchange for shells of slaves, under the condition they never return to Otoch or the Tlillan race.

Slaves were privy to gossip on board Tlaloc's vessel concerning the device and so it was passed on to the Neenayin. It also fitted into their own legends, which place the Neenayin as guardians of flesh creatures. According to their tale they had been brought here from another galaxy to watch over us.'

McCann was rather sceptical of Neenayin folk tales 'Well they did a stand up job there didn't they?' he stated in a sarcastic tone.

Malikah continued ignoring her Father's comments 'The point being that Tlaloc discovered there was someone else, far more advanced than her people. If they had erected a communication network between at least two major galaxies and 40 satellites, eons ago, what stage might they be at now?'

McCann chortled as he took a drag on his cigar 'So rather than make contact and risk losing her position of religious supremacy, she banned anyone from coming here for fear they might discover the truth?'

'You're being over dramatic about this Father, her fears were justified. If these beings had introduced the Neenayin, a shape shifting personification of evil in her opinion, what else might they bring? It made sense they would be cast in the same mould of immorality.'

McCann pointed his smouldering cigar in his daughter's direction 'So why not allow us to examine it now?'

'I have no desire to tempt fate.'

'Fine words for a Tlillan!'

'Father, you must not disturb that object,' urged Malikah as she pointed to the orb shimmering with a pulse of energy.

'That's why you came here isn't it? To discover why this place was made taboo.'

Malikah made no response; her silence was answer enough for McCann.

'Do you trust those shape shifters not to disturb it after we've left?'

The sable Queen nodded 'they have betrayed their masters, the Neenayin fear what these creatures may do on return. They believe I am the only one with the ability to protect them.'

'Can you protect them?'

'I do not know, Father. That is why William is constructing a vessel capable of making the journey to Andromeda and back. I must gather as much information on whomever or whatever these beings are, before they learn about us.'

'Why didn't you simply tell me this before we came here?'

'I'm sure you're aware of the term "need to know basis", yes?'

McCann took a long drag on his Havana and snorted out the cool smoke 'Pah, sounds like the story of my life!'

Hassif was rather frustrated by the turn of events 'Could we examine Sagittarius A, at least?'

Malikah thought for a moment, 'Very well, provided the probe is destroyed on completing its mission.'

Hassif perked up 'Thank you, oh and one last question, have the Tlillans translated the radio transmissions from the object?'

'No, nor do we understand the purpose of the transmissions. One theory is that it is used as a transponder to aid in navigation, which does seem likely. Another theory determines its function is to transmit an encoded message, once decoded it would be possible to enter the object; A galactic library of Alexandria perhaps?'

Hassif gave a puzzled look 'Where did these theories come from? I thought you said Tlillans were forbidden from coming here?'

'The Makayuuk have been here and observed it also, Machine came to similar conclusions as Xch'uup.'

Hassif tapped his tablet furiously, bringing up the radio transmission 'We always believed it was a natural radiation emission, heated gas and dust or something similar.'

McCann raised an eyebrow 'So how long until Hassif translates it?'

Malikah chuckled 'If Machine has been unable to do so over the course of many millennia then I don't see Hassif doing it today ... no offence intended.'

Hassif smiled 'None taken, but if Athena linked with Ares, Here and Artemis it would increase our chances.'

The Tlillan Empress commiserated the Indian 'I'm afraid the Tlillan have attempt to do so along with the Makayuuk for thousands of years. They have a head start on us, humanity has a lot of catching up to do, it's just a fact.'

McCann sensed a challenge and he was always one for a challenge 'Hassif, do you know about Ploutos?'

'No.'

'She's the most powerful SI ever created, from a new template, if anything could crack that code I'd bet she could.'

Hassif was dumbstruck that he'd not been told of such a creation 'What is her purpose?'

McCann waved his hand 'Ahh, something to do with solving equations for neutronium credits. Apparently she's solving mathematical equations that previously were impossible; she must have a shot at decoding that.'

Hassif smiled 'I'll log the transmissions whilst we're orbiting S13, when we get home you can hand them in and let Ploutos give it a go.'

The Englishman gave his daughter a hard stare 'Now, would there be anything else you'd like to tell me? Or not?'

Malikah smiled 'Thank you for toeing the line, at least this time, Father.'

The truth was that McCann didn't really care about Sagittarius A and its secrets. He was more concerned with getting the hell out of Dodge and back to Geneva for a well-earned break. Travelling through the most precarious space and forced to fight a battle with melee weapons to the death was not something he wished to dwell on.

'Well it always helps when you ask nicely,' said the Admiral with a wink as he stretched his toes on the bed.

Hassif looked up from his tablet 'I have the probes and their courses ready, if you could certify it I'd like to launch them as soon as possible.'

Malikah took his tablet, observed the probes and their intended trajectories before certifying it with her thumbprint 'Why don't we go to the Bridge and get this messy business over with?'

Hassif stood up with a wide grin on his face.

'I'll see you two later, after I've inspected the ship,' stated McCann.

Malikah waved as she walked out of his cabin, Hassif followed behind sending McCann a casual salute as the door slid shut.

Later that day McCann strolled through his vessel, visiting each section, encouraging his weary crew after their exertions at the Galactic core. Starting at the fore section he made his way to the aft; after speaking to his crew in both cargo bays including the port and starboard cannon bays he walked into Drone bay 1 to salutes from his Officers. Returning the salutes he approached Deychaa 'How are we doing?'

The stout Thai shrugged his shoulders 'We've not had much to do, but we're ready if something happens.'

'How are you?' inquired McCann in a foreboding tone.

'I'm good.'

The Englishman pulled a tubos out of his leather arm pocket and offered it to the Chief Drone Engineer.

Deychaa took it with a smile 'Thank you.'

McCann returned the smile 'If you need to calm down, have a cigar. The last thing I need is one of my Officers going through a mental breakdown.'

Deychaa recalled how his former commanding Officer on the Thai drone carrier had cracked up 'Don't worry, if I go crazy, I'll try to do it when I'm not on duty.'

McCann felt a little embarrassed that he'd implied such a thing; he looked around the room filled with empty drone booths where pilots would fly their craft. This room was attached to drone bay 1, their squadron being launched from tubes on the starboard side.

'So who's your top gun?' chirped McCann.

'Right now,' Deychaa pointed down the row of booths 'Flight Lieutenant Choy.'

The pair strolled down until they reached his booth; Flight Lieutenant Choy leapt out and saluted the Admiral.

Deychaa grinned 'Flight Lieutenant Choy has the Red Dragon, for now.'

Choy could not hold back his pride; he gave a wide smile to the Admiral. The young Korean had good reason to be proud; the Red dragon was the highest honour for a drone pilot in the I.S.A, Korea and even the world.

'So it was you that tore those Makayuuk fighters to shreds at Bandayuuk?' noted McCann.

'I had a favourable kill to death ratio, Sir,' replied the pilot.

McCann laughed though Choy was confused as to why.

'My God man, do Koreans give medals in modesty?' joked the Englishman.

Choy didn't seem to understand, he had merely stated a fact. The Korean wore a small red dragon badge upon the collar of his dark blue jacket. He also had a pair of the same badges upon the lapels of his shirt. To get those insignia which came with the red drone required a very high kill to death ratio sustained over one year. Even then your ability to lead was tested under battle conditions before gaining eligibility for the honour of the red drone.

Flight Lieutenant Choy had passed all requirements and for Squadron Alpha he was the Red Dragon, if someone else superseded Choy he'd be required to hand in his insignia. Becoming the Red Dragon was far easier than holding onto it and since the engagement at Bandayuuk Choy had held the position. The only drone pilot allowed to keep their title as Red Dragon was Ryu, as progenitor of the honour her position was unassailable.

Deychaa patted the young man on the back 'He is in here every day running simulations, a truly dedicated man.'

'Well young man that's something else you have in common with Ryu,' he said eyeing the fearsome dragons upon his collar 'keep it up and you'll get that Ixchel one day.'

Choy gave a wide grin 'Thank you Sir.'

'You're dismissed now Choy,' said Deychaa, sending the drone pilot back to his simulated bombing run upon a selection of alien vessels.

The pair walked into drone bay 1, the main area wasn't as busy as usual due to loss of life after their clashes with the Neenayin. A couple of drones were being serviced in the centre of the bay. At the rear there were several covered depressions in the floor, entrances for the launch tubes of squadron Alpha. On the other side the gateway used by drones to return to the ship was closed off, like the launch tubes.

'Trouble with the drones?'

Deychaa made a noise of frustration 'Uhh, this space has so many fractures and warps in it; I don't know how Louis keeps the power core from failing.'

McCann nodded as he observed the unarmed Shogun drones, their hard shells removed; several technicians tinkered with the machine's guts 'The entire ship will need an overhaul once we get back.'

Deychaa made a nervous chuckle 'Get back?'

'Did I say something?'

'Not all of the crew are so confident; already some will never see Earth again.'

'And what do you think Deychaa?'

The Thai had a nervous expression upon his face; he replied awkwardly 'Does it matter?'

McCann was rather disappointed at such an apathetic response 'Yes it does, otherwise I wouldn't be asking you.'

'I don't know,' said the Chief Drone Engineer in a quiet voice 'I wonder if it would have been better to die that day at the Casimir generator.'

'Well you didn't, Malikah rescued us.'

'Uhh, she didn't rescue Macuil at Bandayuuk.'

McCann spoke in a hushed tone so that the rest of the drone crew could not hear, though it was clear he was furious with Deychaa 'For God's sake man, pull yourself together. If you want to mope around you can do it in your bloody cabin when you're off duty, is that understood?'

Deychaa was shocked by his comrade's response; no-one had spoken to him so brazenly on the subject since his descent into despair; at least not as directly as McCann did now.

'Yes Sir,' replied the stout Thai.

'And get yourself a clean uniform, you look a bloody mess.'

Deychaa straightened his crumpled and un-kept uniform as he looked around the bay; a few wandering eyes were zeroing in on his conversation with the Admiral.

McCann maintained his low voice but lost none of his passion 'It's no bloody wonder these people aren't sure if we're getting back. I'd be in two minds if my commanding Officer was walking around looking like he'd slept on a park bench all night.'

'I'm sorry, Sir.'

'And pick your damn chin up off the floor man; life's depressing enough without you compounding it with your bloody misery!'

'Yes Sir.'

'Good, I expect to see you in the Officers' mess tonight, and please leave that miserable face in your cabin, understood?'

'Understood Sir.'

McCann marched out of the drone bay. After a few stops at various other sections he was at engineering, the door to the lift slid open to reveal Louis and his team working hard monitoring the fusion core. The Admiral went unnoticed until stood at the threshold of the trench.

The Englishman was saluted by all but Louis; the staff glanced nervously at their Chief.

'Good afternoon Mr Beaumont,' said the Admiral in a raised voice.

Louis looked up for a moment from his station 'Ca va?'

The staff looked on in horror, McCann saluted, sending them back to their stations, 'Ca va bein merci, though a salute from my Chief Engineer once in a while might help lift my spirits.'

Beaumont scoffed 'Or boost your ego!'

McCann couldn't help himself from sniggering at the Frenchman's statement.

Louis was in deep concentration as he monitored the power core keeping his nanites on top of any weakening in the catronium sphere. He was also constantly watching the AI which monitored the magnetic field, adjusting it as space/time distortions passed through it from the micro size to the quite substantial.

'Alright what is it you want McCann?' snapped Louis.

'I'm just doing my rounds, speaking to the crew and bolstering their courage before we enter the wormhole.'

Louis didn't turn to look at his comrade but remained entranced by the readout at his station, 'Well my staff are fine and I am fine.'

'Nothing to report?'

'Non.'

'Well I'll see you in the lounge tonight?'

'Non, I have to keep an eye on this.'

571

McCann looked down the trench 'that's what you have these people for Louis.'

The Frenchman sneered 'I don't trust anyone to do it, I must watch this.'

McCann furrowed his brow 'You have to sleep sometime, who watches it then?'

Louis didn't answer.

The Englishman grinned and whispered into Beaumont's ear 'I learnt a secret today.'

Louis shifted his head a little in McCann's direction, he scanned his comrade suspiciously with one eye 'What?'

Noticing he had his friend's attention McCann continued 'Something to do with Sagittarius A, the Tlillans, the Neenayin and the Andromeda galaxy … but I suppose you have things to do here.'

Beaumont pulled a massive sneer 'C'est merde!'

McCann grinned at the cynical engineer 'Fine, I'll just be chatting with Hassif about it in the lounge tonight, if you can drag yourself away from watching that station.'

Louis turned away from the readout to face McCann full on, 'you're bullshitting me, right?'

The staff were shocked at their Chief's language when speaking to the Admiral, anyone else and they'd be spending the next couple of weeks in the brig.

'I suppose there's only one way to find out, isn't there?'

Louis looked up for a moment as he caught a memory 'Hassif asked me about putting something together yesterday, he wanted to know if it was possible to probe the extremities of the accretion disc.'

McCann said nothing; he only nodded at his Chief Engineer.

'Okay McCann, I'll be there tonight, but if this is shit it will not be pleasant for you,' threatened the Frenchman with a wagging finger.

'I wouldn't dream of it Louis, tonight at seven thirty?' smirked the Englishman.

'Oui, seven thirty,' noted Beaumont as he went back to his station.

'See you there old boy,' said McCann as he returned to the lift leaving Louis' startled staff.

That evening while everyone relaxed drinking and socialising Ilam noticed the absence of both Malikah and Lian, she knew it was no coincidence.

Deep in the centre of Athena on the fifth level, inside Malikah's cabin the Tlillan Queen lay naked in bed with Voice of Machine. In the soft glow they chatted to one another, pillow talk of lovers after a night of passion.

'Will things change once we get home?' inquired Lian as her hand skimmed Malikah's chest.

'Muul Kaah is shaken to the core; there shall be an infusion of Matriarchs from Earth. My next task is to ease the transition,' said Malikah with a smile and an arm around her lover's shoulders.

'No Malee, I meant us.'

'Change? How do you mean?'

'I have duties with Machine, you with the Matriarchs, how will we see each other?'

'I will find a way, if Machine is not averse to our relationship.'

Lian placed her face into the crux of Malikah's shoulder and neck as she cuddled her 'What of the Matriarchs, what if they protest our tainted love?'

'They may join the traitors and work with men.'

'Malee, you can't send everyone that disagrees to a concentration camp.'

'Their opinions are superfluous; loyalty is all Xch'uup requires of them. Faith in your Tlillan god amounts to no more than blind obedience, on pain of death, served in a more palatable form.'

'What then is loyalty, if it is not obedience?'

'Honesty.'

'Honesty?'

'Yes, honesty with my people. A Matriarch may bare her soul to Xch'uup without fear of retribution, free to pledge allegiance to whomever she wishes.'

'So it is the truth you seek, truth from the Matriarchs?'

Malikah chuckled for a moment 'Truth? Surely you have learnt that there is no such thing as truth, my little Atan?'

Lian replied in a puzzled tone 'I don't understand, how can truth not exist?'

'Then tell me yakuntik, what is truth?'

Lian thought for a moment 'It's true that the Earth moves around the Sun.'

'Perhaps, but what if you are here at the Core, does not the Earth and its Sun move around Sagittarius A?'

'Come on Malee, you're just splitting hairs.'

'Yet your truth is an untruth here, or for that matter anyone else living outside the Terran system. For the vast majority of living entities in the Galaxy you are not speaking the truth; however you are speaking with an honest heart.'

Lian was determined to win this argument; she racked her mind for an example 'Dulian smells like a turd! There try getting around that one Malee!'

Malikah laughed 'What of Dolphins?'

'What about Dolphins?'

'They have no sense of smell Atan, to them Dulian has no smell.'

'But they live in water, that's not a fair comparison.'

Malikah smiled in victory as she caressed her lovers long black hair 'Yet your truth, that Dulian smells similar to excrement is not true for the Dolphin. Also you forget that most species are aquatic, excluding them makes your argument even less valid.'

'I get the feeling you've argued this subject before.'

'My Father, he made it clear to me that truth is a human concept not a law of nature such as gravity. Truth does not exist or at least it changes constantly, for example you said the Earth travels around the Sun. Was it not true that once we believed all heavenly bodies travelled around the Earth?'

'Yes but they were wrong.'

'Yet at that time it was the truth, however the truth has changed. Just as the Earth went from flat to a sphere and the blackness of space went from an ether to a void.'

'I understand Malee; you can't nail down the truth so honesty is the best you can settle for?'

'When I return to Muul Kaah the Matriarchs shall be faced with a decision, I will show them my honesty in return they may display theirs. Those who honestly believe in me may pledge loyalty to Xch'uup, those that do not may live on the lower ranks of society. Humans have already undergone such a process, now it is time for Otoch.'

Lian kissed her lover's neck 'Well you have me.'

'Was there any doubt Atan? You came to the edge of the abyss, placing yourself between Xch'uup and Hades.'

'So loyalty is the new truth on Otoch?'

'From Faith to Loyalty, merit is now measured by a different yard stick. Those that swear loyalty may follow the paradigm shift into a new era, a new golden age.'

Lian placed her hand lovingly around the head of the Tlillan Empress bringing the Queen's ear closer to her lips. Voice of Machine whispered softly 'Memento mori.'

Malikah laughed 'You know that was for Roman Generals, not the Emperor?'

Lian kissed her lover again 'You're such a spoil sport.'

Chapter 24

A week later and Athena still skirted around S13, a powerful red giant star orbiting Sagittarius A. The Clotho remained in orbit of S8 as Hassif monitored the sun closely, awaiting for his goal to rise into view.

Sure enough Vezzali and Athena called out at the same time 'Wormhole coming into view,' alerting McCann to the swirling white hole which seemingly rose above the scorching horizon of S13.

The Admiral gripped his seat, tapped the communications console and the voice of Beaumont replied 'Yes, I know Duncan.'

Kim still found the familiarity of the Chief Engineer distasteful.

'Are the engines sound?' inquired the commander of Athena.

'Oui, oui, but you make sure that Indian doesn't get it wrong. My engines will hold out, but if he takes us too close, that star will swallow us alive.'

Before McCann could reply Malikah spoke to the Frenchman 'Calm yourself Louis, everything is under control.'

The brazen Frenchman quietened down and in a softer tone replied 'I suppose so.'

Kim was quite surprised at Louis' timid response; usually the man had no shame in abusing authority. However Malikah was always able to handle the wild man of Athena. Unknown to Kim or most of the crew her gift of the Ixchel had saved the Frenchman's life several years ago, for which he became forever indebted. Louis would not push too hard in the presence of Malikah, but if he did so he would take his punishment quietly.

Malikah grinned as she peered at her Father 'However if S13 overpowers even me and we are all vapourised in an atomic fire … c'est la vie!'

The Tlillan Queen quickly tapped her Father's communication panel cutting Louis off before he might respond. The Tlillan half breed cackled in laughter at the thought of Louis going ape at his station. In fact she didn't need to imagine it, as with her abilities she could sense his outrage.

McCann closed his eyes in disappointment; if they did make it through he'd be hearing about this for the next month from the ranting Frenchman.

Lian was the only person on the bridge to appreciate the humour, normally Hassif would have joined in on the laugh however he was busy calculating Athena's course. His calculations changed from one moment to another as an uncharted Galactic core threw different hurdles at the Indian.

Whenever Malikah laughed in that manner it reminded McCann of the past Xch'uup, lady Havisham 'Are we finished antagonising the crew?'

Malikah quietened down and with a cough replied 'My apologies Father, please continue.'

'Hassif?'

'I've turned over control to Athena,' on the view screen, beside the image of the white hole rising above the crescent of S13, lay the tactical readout. The readout displayed their course and plan to orbit S13, then swing into the stars gravitation pull. Athena would continue her descent until she was placed between the wormhole and star then power up her Casimir field. Much like the trajectory of a cricket ball, hitting the ground at the right place and speed, she'd bounce up to hit the wicket; provided some bat didn't appear and smash her for six!

'I have taken full control of course speed and orientation Admiral,' spoke a calm Athena.

'Good luck Athena, we're all counting on you.'

'Thank you Admiral, though Technician Hassif was most thorough in his course certifications,' replied their soft spoken guardian.

Ten minutes later Athena's warm voice filled the Bridge 'Beginning descent into S13, trajectory certified.'

McCann nodded with some trepidation 'you may begin Athena.'

'Commencing manoeuver, lowering Casimir field in ten seconds.'

The crew held their breath as the Queen of space counted down, once finished she announced 'Firing engines, one Foucault.'

The mighty warship broke orbit and dipped into the gravitational pull of S13, 'Firing engines, two Foucaults,' spoke Athena as she accelerated into the grip of the massive singularity.

S13 filled the screen; McCann felt no physical change that is no influence from the star personally. However his mind knew they were in mortal danger as the surface of S13 bubbled, geysers of fire exploding and dissipating. From where he sat they seemed quite small, yet he was not deceived, those fusion fires were large enough to swallow a world. If Athena came too close she would have been little more than a morsel for this titan.

'Commencing reorientation manoeuvre,' came the reassuring voice of Athena, 'Firing thrusters.'

Athena moved herself as her inertia gathered, once finished she announced her orientation in relation to the wormhole 'Position reset, new position X -0.03, Y 0.0, Z 0.0.'

The warship had turned into the star with her main engines pointing out at the white hole they were to enter.

'Radiation levels acceptable,' called Vezzali to her commander.

The Casimir field had not been turned off, but reduced in power. In order to overcome even a weak Casimir field Athena was required to fire her engines into the star until close enough to S13 that its gravity would overwhelm the repulsive force of the field. In doing so there would be less protection against radiation, the crew had already taken a strong dose on entry to Sagittarius A. Fortunately decontamination showers, nanites and the Ixchel had dealt with any ill effects. In the past they'd have died within a short time and it wouldn't have been a pretty sight with hair and fingernails falling out.

'Skin temperature 500 Kelvins,' called out Vezzali as they approached the atomic fire below.

'Skin temperature 1000 Kelvins, 1500 Kelvins,' shouted the worried Italian as they approached the red giant.

1500 Kelvins was more than 1200 degrees Celsius, in Fahrenheit 2200 degrees. Athena had a Catronium shell, so in theory she could stand temperatures of over 3000 Kelvins. However this had never been tested outside of a laboratory.

'2000 Kelvins, radiation above acceptable levels, speed 4.3 Foucaults and increasing, estimated time until we hit the surface 43 seconds.'

McCann relaxed, closing his eyes he blocked out the universe until he heard the voice of Athena 'Erecting Casimir field in ten seconds.'

His Goddess counted down, the slowest countdown he'd experienced in his life!

The Englishman didn't hear Athena say anything, yet he knew the field was up as a sudden jerk tore him from his seat. All of the crew save those in the pit, who were busy monitoring the status of Athena, were ripped from their current task by the brutal force of S13 versus Athena's Casimir field.

McCann was pushed so hard against the tactical table in front of his chair; he was unable to return to his feet. Hassif had braced himself by grasping his console and bending his knees, Flesh and Mayer were not so forward thinking and both had been cast over their stations, flying into the pit. The Tlillan women all had clasped onto the station grips behind McCann's seat. They along with Vezzali and Kim remained upon their feet as Athena ricocheted off the gravitational pull of the sun and into the push of the white hole, thanks to her Casimir field which reversed the effects of gravity.

'Firing engines, 5 Foucaults,' came Athena's soft voice as McCann felt the ship shake to the fusion reaction, funnelled from her power core by electromagnetic tubes, hitting the engines blast plates.

'Firing engines, four Foucaults,' again Athena shook as she slowed her violent approach towards the white hole.

'Firing engines, three Foucaults,' McCann managed to scramble to his chair using his superior strength. The Englishman turned his seat to face the rear of the bridge then pressed the touch pad on the arm locking it into position.

'Firing engines, two Foucaults,' Glancing at his crew holding onto the drone and science stations he caught a glimpse of his wife. She was looking back at him with a smile and a pink twinkle in her eye. McCann looked in another direction and Ilam laughed at his faux pas, though the sound of the Athena being torn between singularities caused her voice to go unnoticed by the rest of the Bridge crew.

'Firing engines, one Foucault,' Mayer and Flesch who had previously been thrown over their stations and into the pit were now able to return to duty.

'Flipping orientation 180 degrees,' announced Athena as the vessel flipped over whilst rolling to face the white hole.

'Entering white hole at 0.72 Foucaults, prepare to fold space,' announced Athena.

McCann released his seat and swung around to see the shimmering hole in space belching out white light at Athena as she moved into its centre.

'Entering hyperspace.'

Athena passed the boundary between normal space and hyperspace, however something happened that had never occurred previously. On entering hyperspace McCann observed hundreds, perhaps thousands of Athenas. All were moving along the same course, in single file from the Sagittarius A wormhole to the Terran wormhole, one in front of the other.

'Hassif?' called out McCann 'what in God's name is going on?'

'I don't know Duncan,' said the bewildered Indian.

'Vezzali?'

'I'm not sure, according to my instruments there is nothing there but there is something there at the same time.'

'Speak English woman!'

'I don't know how to explain it, but there is no mass, it makes no sense.'

Ilam stepped forward to her husbands' side and with the condescending Tlillan smile she explained 'This is why your primitive minds must not meddle with time/space. What you are observing are echoes of the future, future Athenas.'

Hassif turned around to speak to the Amazon 'How? We are not travelling at or even close to light speed; we should not be seeing future echoes it's not possible.'

'Yet how do you explain this?' inquired the Tlillan matriarch with great satisfaction.

'I can't, can you?'

'Athena fell into S13; she came close to light speed ...'

'Yes but before Athena reached light speed, not that that's possible, she fired her engines slowing her approached into the white hole.'

'Let me speak little man,' declared the annoyed Valkyrie 'Athena gained much energy, for a short time she travelled quicker through space/time, do you understand?'

'Yes I understand.'

'What is Athena's speed now?'

'103,000 miles per second.'

'And I take it we are still accelerating?'

'Yes, slowly.'

Pointing at the Athenas on the view screen Ilam declared 'We are approaching ourselves in the future as we decelerated.'

McCann furrowed his brow 'But we aren't decelerating, we're accelerating.'

Ilam shook her head 'As we decelerate in the future this Athena is gaining on us as we move quicker through space/time.'

McCann looked up at Athena 'Athena, begin deceleration now, slowly.'

Vezzali shouted out 'Sir! There are Athenas appearing behind us!'

'What?'

Ilam laughed at her husband as the image of themselves in a line towards the Sagittarius A wormhole stretched out.

'Vezzali what's happening?'

'They are approaching us Sir!'

'Ilam?' shouted the Admiral to his wife.

'That is us in the past approaching the future, now that we are slowing down. Or to be more precise the past is catching up with us, my dear.'

McCann shook his head 'Well this makes about as much sense as a drunken Frenchman.'

Hassif looked at his friend 'It's quite simple, Duncan.'

McCann held his hand out 'Save it for another time.'

'Sir coming in the opposite direction, the Athena!' shouted Vezzali.

'How many?'

'Only one Sir.'

'Show me.'

The view screen magnified a tiny square, bringing into view Athena without a single scratch 'That's us coming to Sagittarius A, a few weeks ago?'

Ilam nodded 'Yes, now it is time to signal your past self, Duncan.'

'What do you mean? I thought communication was a bad idea?'

Ilam sighed 'Yes but do you not recall the docking lights using a code Vezzali understood?'

'Yes.'

'Then you must do so, do you not see your future selves are initiating the message?'

McCann noted the line of future Athenas, all with scarring from contact with the Clotho, were signalling that same message in Morse code he had seen when inside the wormhole a few weeks ago 'It didn't help much though did it?'

Ilam, at a loss, shouted at Hassif 'You tell the man!'

Hassif timidly spoke to his friend 'She's right Duncan, it's about causality, if you don't signal yourself now you'll be changing the past and therefore the future.'

'Changing the future? It was only a useless signal; it didn't really make a difference anyway.'

Ilam bellowed 'If you fail to signal yourself it might cause a catastrophe, we may all die, you will have broken the timeline we exist within.'

McCann said nothing, before he could reply Malikah appeared on the other side of his chair 'Do as your wife tells you Admiral; I have no wish to suffer from your stubborn attitude for a second time.'

'Well it seems I'm out numbered, Vezzali send the message we received previously will you?'

The blonde haired lady relaxed 'Yes Sir.'

McCann peered at the image of Athena three weeks ago 'So I'm sitting on that ship debating about whether to make contact?'

'You are,' replied his wife in a rather annoyed tone.

He gave Ilam a glance 'Would it be possible for me to make contact, I mean take a shuttle to the old Athena?'

Ilam placed a hand upon his shoulder 'For once, do as you are told ... please?'

The Englishman didn't often hear his wife say please in front of other Tlillans, even half Tlillans. He decided to comply with her wishes since Ilam was no doubt far more knowledgeable concerning these types of encounters.

Placing his hand upon hers he replied 'As you wish my dear.'

As they travelled through the dead zone Vezzali called out 'Sir! We are still approaching the Athenas before us and the Athenas Aft are gaining on us.'

McCann looked at Ilam who fixed her gaze upon Hassif. The Indian turned away from his station 'Even though we are decelerating we're still traveling faster in space/time than our future selves who have decelerate more than us. Our past selves however have decelerated less than us so are travelling quicker. Therefore this timeline, which was stretched by S13 when we fell into it, is collapsing into a single cohesive point in time.

Think of it like a rubber band that's been stretched but is now compressing, returning to its natural state.'

Ilam smiled in approval at the Indian 'An excellent analogy, one that even a male might understand.'

The Englishman rubbed the stubble on his face 'How is it that the Athenas are all contracting towards us? It doesn't make sense.'

Ilam turned to Hassif again and the Indian replied 'It makes perfect sense Duncan, imagine it's a rubber band with ten ink dots placed evenly along the length of the band.'

'Yes.'

'Now stretch the band and let it slowly compress.'

'And?'

'Well, from the perspective of each the dots, the focal point of contraction is themselves.'

McCann squinted at the view screen, 'So you're telling me that from the point of view of every single Athena, all the other ships are retracting into them?'

Ilam clapped her hands once then gave her husband a peck on the head, much as a proud mother would award her child at a school science competition.

The crew were a little embarrassed; McCann was very embarrassed though he understood that was not his wife's intention.

'Sir, we're about to make contact with the fore and aft Athenas,' alerted Vezzali.

McCann and Hassif both stared at Ilam, the redheaded Valkyrie spoke with confidence 'Have no fear, those are merely future and past echoes, they can do no physical harm. However everyone prepare yourselves for an experience you shall never forget.'

As Athena made contact with her echoes no damage reports came through, however reports of a very different nature started flooding in. Crew in the fore section began to evacuate on reports of witnessing blinding light and bulkheads moving through the ship.

'Athena, confirm the status of your bulkheads in the fore section,' inquired McCann.

'All bulkheads are raised, Admiral,' replied Athena.

Ilam squeezed his shoulder 'Be at ease, they merely witness a future echo traveling inside Athena.'

McCann observed the holo-display before him; all of the decks fore and aft displayed green 'Athena is the tactical readout correct?'

'Your tactical readout is accurate Admiral.'

McCann thought for a moment before issuing orders to his fleeing crew 'Athena, I want them to halt any evacuation procedures and return to their stations.'

'Understood Admiral.'

The Englishman tapped his communication panel and the voice of Beaumont filled the Bridge 'McCann? Is that you?'

'Of course it's me, what's the situation in the engine rooms?'

'C'est detraque! The front of the ship is passing through the rear section, well a projection of it, ce qui se passe?' shouted a very anxious Chief Engineer.

'It's an echo of the past, catching up with us as we decelerate,' replied McCann.

'Quoi?'

'Never mind, Hassif will explain it later. All you need to know is that it's just an image, nothing more.'

'Fine, fine, what do you want me to do?'

'Just have your staff remain at their stations, try to carry on as normal.'

'Carry on as normal? Have you been smoking that Gukumatz hemp?' there was a long awkward silence between the two until Louis carried on 'Okay, okay, my people are at their stations but don't expect anything remarkable right now.'

McCann smirked 'Don't worry Louis, I never have,' to which he tapped the arm of his command seat cutting the Frenchman off.

Malikah whispered 'Now who's antagonising the crew?'

The Englishman closed his eyes before he rubbed them 'Considering the amount of grief that man has caused me I'm entitled to it.'

Athena's comforting voice filled the Bridge 'All crew have been informed of the current situation, Admiral.'

'Excellent Athena, ETA until we exit the Terran wormhole?'

'4 hours 17 minutes and 24 seconds.'

McCann raised his brow in surprise 'That's a lot longer than or trip here.'

Hassif noted 'The wormhole has been stretched and accelerated; space/time is stretched out. In normal space it would make for a shorter journey, however inside hyperspace the laws are somewhat different. Within an Einstein-Rosen bridge space maybe stretched but its density seems to remain a constant, I'm logging the event for future examination.'

The Englishman waved his hand at the Indian 'whatever you say Hassif.'

A short time later and McCann witnessed an odd occurrence 'Athena what's up with the view screen?'

'The view screen is operating within normal parameters, Admiral.'

'I think brightness levels need adjusting.'

'The view screen variables have not changed within the last hour, Admiral.'

Ilam whispered into her husband's ear 'Calm yourself Duncan.'

Within a few moments the entire view screen had whited out, Ilam shouted 'everyone, unfurl your helmets, NOW!'

All of the crew tapped their wrists; those in Tlillan bodysuits used a mental command, everyone's helmet unfurled to cover their heads. The helmets prevented the bright glow of Athena's engines from blinding the occupant. The sight of a fusion explosion hitting her blast plate would have burnt even a Tlillan's retina to a crisp.

Strangely there was no heat, only light; how this was possible was a mystery to both McCann and Hassif. It was logical that with light came heat in some form; surely they should have all been toasted by the engines appearing through the wall of Athena's Bridge?

'Behind us!' shouted Kim.

McCann looked over his shoulder and through the helmet visor which tinted accordingly to block out the light he could see parts of the upper fore section on Athena's hull. Mostly instruments such as the tachyon array, used to send and receive communications faster than light between her drones and the men and women piloting them in the bay.

Without helmets they would have been unable to observe any of this since a wall of white fire was passing through, from the fore to the aft.

The engines passed through McCann, he looked about his body in astonishment as they slipped past him and out through the rear wall. Following that came total darkness; he could see nothing despite the helmet raising light levels.

As soon as it had come the darkness disappeared, the thick armour plating of the aft section had moved through them as the sensors sticking up from the fore section passed the other way.

Looking up at his wife McCann pointed to his black helmet 'Can I take this off now?'

Ilam's helmet liquefied, disappearing into the collar of her Tlillan suit 'You may, for now.'

He tapped his wrist, causing his helmet to furl backwards, collapsing into his I.S.A body glove.

5 minutes later and the view screen went dark again, 'For God's sake what now?' commented McCann.

As thick armour plating passed into the Bridge from both the view screen and the rear wall it merged, occupying the same place. McCann could still see the pit, but they were mingled with the armoured wall; it was one of the strangest things he'd witnessed in his life.

As the walls passed through him he looked about, it became too dark for him to see anything until the hull plating moved on. Once they had passed each other he was stunned at what he observed next.

Looking forward the Englishman was staring out onto his own bridge, as the rear stations passed through him, moving behind him; the pit crews heads passed into and through his legs as they moved forward.

Ilam smiled with superiority as the confused humans and half Tlillans looked about in wonder at the spectacle.

It was obvious that the past and future were coming together to make the present whole. McCann found himself staring in wonder at the back of his head as it approached him from the future. He could see Lian and Malikah standing to his right, both looking on in awe. To his left stood his wife, he could only see his wife from behind, making some sort of gesture towards the view screen.

Then something shook McCann to his core, his future self-turned a little in his chair before looking the rest of the way over his shoulder. It rocked McCann like nothing else, he'd looked at himself in a mirror but this was the mirror of time. That was him in the future looking himself right in the eye, it was the strangest feeling he would ever experience in his life.

Without thinking the Englishman turned his seat and peered behind him to see himself in the past with a look of total and utter shock. McCann didn't know what to say, so he said nothing and only observed the scene unfold quietly.

The Admiral then remembered the gesture his wife was making and moved his gaze to her. She stood beside her shocked husband with a smirk, then with pink eyes she blew him as kiss … into the future … from the past, she next worded silently 'I love you.'

The Englishman tried to work out the logistics; she must have known her husband would turn around to look at himself in the past so she made the gesture as he looked into the future. Then when he turned to view himself Ilam waited until his future eyes turned to see what she was doing and then she made the full gesture.

The past and the future approached, McCann turned back to the future, it was all too much for him to contemplate as his future and past selves merged into him. The three Bridges, nay three Athenas synchronised with one another bringing all three "time zones" into one.

As the Athena approached the Terran wormhole these occurrences became more and more frequent as space/time snapped back into its normal state. The crew became more and more brazen in their attitudes to such an astonishing event. At one point McCann observed the future Lian doing a sexy dance next to Malikah as his pink eyed daughter chuckled at her lover's antics.

The Englishman saw himself turn to his right and frown, which he did shortly afterwards to see the Half Tlillans enjoying the wonder of dancing with themselves in triplicate. Ilam was unimpressed by the foolish behaviour also, she frowned upon the pair as a mother superior.

Hassif made an attempt to shake hands with his future/past self, which the Indian succeeded in doing. He outstretched his hand, moving it up and down whilst fixing his eyes upon the future Hassif. His future self, stood with his back to his past self, doing the exact same exercise, McCann didn't see how this was going to work. As his future self-approached, closing distance, he quickly turned and placed his hand next to the present Hassif. Hands aligned they moved up and down to give the impression they were greeting each other. Two seconds later the present Hassif spun on his heels to do the same with the past Hassif. Two seconds later the past Hassif spun on his heels and ten seconds later all three Hassifs merged as they stood starring at the rear wall of the Bridge with their hands outstretched.

Ilam laughed as she clapped her hands with pink eyes 'Bravo Mr Hassif!'

Twenty minutes later three more Athenas began to converge, Flesch had an impish look on his face as he peered around the Bridge.

McCann bellowed 'Whatever you're thinking of Flesch, forget it!'

The Hungarian pulled a miserable expression, 'But Hassif ...'

In a fury McCann shouted at the man 'Jesus Christ! What are you? 3 years old? You'll do as you're bloody well told man, or I'll have you spaced before you can say "sowee"!'

Sniggers came from around the pit crew; Flesch had a problem pronouncing his "R's" and would say 'So wee' rather than 'so-ree'.

The red faced man in charge of power and engines saluted his commanding Officer 'My apologies, Admiwal.'

McCann nodded his head as Flesch returned to work, Ilam placed her hands upon her husband and whispered into his ear 'you are most attractive when you become angry. I'm certain your eyes went a little red then.'

Eventually Athena announced they were a mere 30 seconds from entering the wormhole which led to Earth and normality. As the ship approached, her crew prepared to drop the Casimir field, time compression increased at a more frequent rate. An uncounted number of Athenas collapsed into them, it was almost impossible to concentrate as several Bridges seemed to be occupying the same space at once, though each one slightly out of phase from the other.

McCann was forced to order Athena take control; many of the crew were disorientated, with alerts pouring in from different sections. It became impossible to make sense of readouts, or to understand orders when several sets of instructions echoed in the same space.

The Englishman gripped his chair as he watched the view screen with several other ghostly images, all depicting a different point in time, floating through it every second. He could hear his chair beeping with communication requests along with his wrist tablet; however some of the rings were from the future, others from the past all merging into the present. McCann decided not to bother answering since he would not be able to understand the person on the other end, nor they him.

The time line of Athenas concertinaed into each other and as the nose of Athena touched the wormhole the last of the future and past melded into one. Space/time snapped back and they entered the glowing doughnut to be expelled out into the Terran system and back home.

'Communication from Director Faraday,' was the next thing McCann heard, Athena's warm voice reminding him he'd made it back.

'Put him on the view screen,' ordered McCann as he muted the incoming alerts.

The image of a concerned Faraday appeared, he was standing at the control centre in Geneva, 'Duncan! What in the blue blazes just happened?'

'I'm sorry?'

'The Athena, what happened?'

'I don't understand?'

Vezzali spoke in a low voice to her commander 'Sir, according to the Tsiolkovsky we left only moments ago for Sagittarius A.'

Relieved at Vezzali's explanation McCann replied to Faraday 'Didn't you receive our data packets? Athena sent them regularly, every day.'

Faraday turned away, the sound of Miss Dutta could be heard mumbling in the background. After consulting his first Technician Faraday turned back 'We have just received two weeks of communication, in one transmission, my staff are attempting to separate the different data packets as we speak,' narrowing his eyes Faraday stated 'You look like hell Duncan, what on earth happened?'

The tired Admiral sighed 'Well, the other end of the wormhole was caught by a star. It was accelerated, creating some sort of bridge in time, I'm sure Miss Dutta will explain it to you.'

Furious muttering could be detected as Faraday moved his face to the Indian, the Etonian pulled a shocked expression which turned to one of confusion 'Alright, alright,' he said halting the excited Technician.

'It seems you have quite a story to tell me Duncan! What of your mission? Did you finish off those lizard fellows?'

McCann nodded as he rubbed his eyes 'they've been dealt with Bill, but we have casualties and Athena's gonna need repairs.'

'I see, well pull into the Tsiolkovsky ... oh and how the bloody hell is that wormhole still active?'

Again Miss Dutta could be heard nattering into the Director's ear, he listened for a few seconds before speaking to the Admiral again, 'I'll send the Ares to close the crassik tube.'

Again the Indian lady muttered into his ear.

'Alright woman!' bellowed Faraday.

'Titov will close the Krasnikov tube, you just get to port, understood?'

McCann nodded 'Understood Bill.'

Before Faraday could end communications Vezzali spoke up 'Actually this is not a Krasnikov tube, although the observed paradox of leaving at the same time we arrived does result in a similar outcome.'

Faraday shuddered 'Really? How very interesting, Miss?'

'Erm, Vezzali ... Sir.'

'Vezzali, well do you have any other nuggets of scientific wonder you wish to impart?'

Vezzali replied nervously 'No, Sir.'

'Excellent! Well, if Miss Vezzali permits, I'd like to return to running the I.S.A now.'

McCann had a tired smirk on his face as the annoyed Etonian berated his science Officer 'you're excused Bill.'

'Thank you,' replied Faraday as he hit his wrist tablet with rather more force than required, removing his image from the view screen.

McCann turned in his chair to give Vezzali that school master expression. A rather embarrassed Vezzali squeaked 'Sorry.'

The Englishman turned back to face the view screen, 'Athena, plot a course to dock with Tsiolkovsky. When Hassif's certified it begin docking manoeuvres. Kim, make sure drone bay one and two are secured for docking.'

The three replied in concert 'Yes Sir.'

'Flesch, make certain Athena's docking clamps are certified and validate airlock integrity. Mayer, I want the cannons checked, all warheads are to be removed and locked down in the armoury. They must all be certified before we dock, understood?'

Again his crew replied in concert 'Understood Sir.'

Tapping his wrist resulted in the voice of Louis Beaumont a few moments later 'Oui?'

'Louis I want the power core and engines certified for docking, the Tsiolkovsky will need a full assessment before repairs can begin, understood?'

'I have it covered McCann, is your daughter still on the Bridge?'

'Louis! Give it a rest, at least until you're off duty.'

'Fine, fine, everything will hold together for docking.'

McCann stretched his neck muscles 'Thank you Louis, see you in the bar after we dock?'

Louis grunted 'I have a few scores to settle with those Russian bastards!'

'See you in the Officers' mess later, McCann out,' with that the Englishman tapped his wrist.

'Kim, inform Deychaa that his presence is expected tonight in the Officers' mess on the Tsiolkovsky.'

The Korean called out whilst working at his station 'Understood, Sir.'

As Athena glided towards Earth the Ares could be seen making her way to the wormhole.

Titov commanded his staff, as he sat on his Bridge a duplicate of McCann's. All of his Officers were Russian, so he spoke in his mother tongue. Cherkesov carried out his Kapitan's orders. The Ares approached the stubborn wormhole which refused to close 'Niztonaz nachiniya dastignotay,' spoke the Russian SI.

Ares halted 0.1 AU from the event horizon, Titov addressed his science Officer 'Sergei, is the exotic matter ready?'

The Science Officer replied stiffly 'Yes Sir.'

'Then let us put an end to this monster, fire the probe.'

Sergei tapped away at his console causing a football sized probe to be ejected from the Ares towards the white hole. Inside resided a rubidium gas, super cooled to such a temperature that it lost its energy and became what is known as exotic matter. The atoms of rubidium repelled each other under normal circumstances, which was why they were contained inside a probe with a weak magnetic field.

However, once the probe opened they would come into contact with the stronger magnetic field of the white hole, creating a spectacular reaction.

As the probe approached the white hole its weak Casimir field no longer proved to be effective against the push.

'Deconstructing probe, Sir,' called out Sergei as he tapped his station.

The shell of the probe broke into pieces allowing the dense gas to interact with the powerful fields of the white hole.

The rubidium expanded at an incredible pace as the singularity seemed to suck it in, from where Titov sat it looked to be a race. The white hole was attempting to consume the gas cloud before the rubidium devoured the singularity.

The rubidium seemed to expand quicker than the white hole could draw it in, the result being what looked like a heat haze covering the wayward Einstein-Rosen bridge.

'My god, the thing is getting bigger!' exclaimed Cherkesov as from his point of view and everyone else's it expanded until it was at least five times the original size of the wormhole entrance.

'That is the theory,' replied Sergei.

'Theory?' shouted a shocked Cherkesov.

'Why yes, this has never been attempted before now. Yet the theory is sound, it should begin to collapse ... soon.'

Titov raised his brow and scratched his thick beard; he resembled Poseidon leaning on the arm of his throne viewing strange muses dance before him. Titov would much rather be watching a ballet or opera than observing a science experiment, especially one as dangerous as closing a super accelerated wormhole.

'Ares? Is it contracting?' inquired the sable Kapitan.

'Expansion decelerating; at this rate the cloud should cease expansion in 43 seconds. I predict the exotic rubidium will begin to implode once local magnetic fields overwhelm the atoms natural state of repulsion.'

Sergei spoke quickly 'Soon Kapitan.'

'Good,' remarked Titov.

The cloud reached its greatest point of expansion before the atoms began to attract one another in their exotic state. Suddenly at a violent speed the gas imploded, taking the wormhole with it until nothing occupied the space before the Ares.

Titov turned his head to Sergei 'Is it done?'

'Wait.'

Next an equally violent explosion occurred 'Brace for impact, brace for impact, brace for impact,' alerted Ares as her bulkheads dropped.

Sergei quickly intervened 'It is no worry; the bow shock will be tiny.'

The Ares had been trained differently by her Russian Commander; any kind of occurrence no matter how small that involved a shockwave resulted in an alert and her bulkheads dropping. Titov was a cautious man and he took no chances, the price of failure was costly in mother Russia.

Sergei monitored the explosion as its bow shock nudged the Ares a little to one side 'The result is as expected, except for the rubidium, 90% has been converted to dark energy rather than 70%.'

'Is that a problem?'

'Neit, however this area of space will be too unstable to enter until this energy dissipates into the space/time fabric, Sir.'

Titov nodded 'Cherkesov, mark the area with buoys.'

Cherkesov ordered the navigation Officer to release several markers around the distorted area of space. It would take some time for the dark energy to even out, melding back into the universal constant of the fabric of space. Until then, if a vessel entered that area it was as of yet unknown what the effects might be.

Chapter 25

Staring out into space Malikah watched the ballet of I.S.A and Tlillan vessels against a backdrop of stars. The Tsiolkovsky observation deck had been finished, the sable Queen being its first honoured guest.

'What are you looking for Malee?'

Malikah's gaze did not shift from the stars 'Something I'd lost inside.'

'Do you see it?'

'Yes, and I had to go to the edge of the abyss.'

'So what did you find?' inquired Lian as she stood next to Malikah, alone in the small semi-circular room, peering out at the void.

'All that time on Otoch I was alone, surrounded by Matriarchs, I was their leader yet still an alien. Forced to be cold and fill my heart with hatred, if not they would have disowned me.'

'Surely it's not that bad?'

Malikah turned to face Lian 'You have no idea, the feeling of total isolation.'

'Is that why you brought me to Otoch?'

The sable Queen returned her gaze to the vessels docking and undocking from the mighty space station 'On Otoch it is night, cold and silent. You brought sun; you shined on me bringing warmth back into my life.'

'Why me?'

'I could show no affection to Matriarchs, their hatred is so ingrained, the concept is as alien to them as a half-breed Xch'uup.'

'But why me?'

Malikah grinned 'I remembered you, felt your heart that day we first met. I was interested to discover if as a woman your heart had changed.'

'If I had changed? Then what?'

'Then we could at least enjoy one another's company,' Malikah changed the tone of her voice in a parody of her Mother 'Matriarchs do not waste their time chatting when important work is to be done.'

Lian sniggered 'So come on, tell me what you found Malee!'

'Love, to love your people as your children; I was betrayed at Bandayuuk.'

Lian nodded her head 'I've been wondering about that, I still don't know why they abandoned you.'

'What Tlillans call cold logic is only a poor disguise for hatred and fear, don't ever forget that yakuntik.

Nearly every crime committed is one of opportunity, in that way Humans and Tlillans are exactly the same. Those Matriarchs saw an opportunity to be rid of the alien they so despised, and took it.'

Voice of Machine smiled 'Well I'm glad they failed.'

Malikah carried on examining the void 'I tried my best to be a Tlillan, to live as one of them. But I was not at fault, it was Tlillan society that could not assimilate me, they never could fully accept a half breed.'

'So what's love got to do with it?'

Malikah made an evil smirk into space 'I was doing it the wrong way around, now those dogs shall change themselves, their society, their culture, for the one who delivered them from Machine.'

'And if they resist?'

'Chutli is headed by my Mother, she would never betray me. Tico by Sandra and most importantly Teteo by Kaeo, I know their hearts.'

'You cannot keep Cihu in bondage, you know that don't you?'

Malikah glanced at Lian 'Why do you say that?'

'Kaeo, she will not permit it to continue. Besides Cihu did not commit treason, she suffers only because of your temper.'

Malikah narrowed her eyes 'Kaeo will have to live with it; the Dreamscape is clear on this subject.'

Lian returned Malikah's gaze with a stern expression 'Dreamscape be damned, as long as you punish Cihu Kaeo suffers. Do not alienate her as the Matriarchs did you, allow an opening for Cihu.'

'An opening?'

'A path out of servitude to men, Cihu said nothing other Matriarchs did not think yet were too cowardly to voice themselves.'

Malikah exhaled 'I thought Kaeo might prevent these set of events, but the Dreamscape was correct, my Tlillan hatred made sure of that.'

'I don't understand,' stated Voice of Machine in a puzzled tone.

Malikah let out a tired smile 'Memento mori, that's what the slave would speak into a General's ear as he rode on a chariot through Rome, accepting ovations on return from a successful campaign.'

'Kaeo was put there to whisper into Cihu's ear?'

'That was the plan, someone to cool her hot mouth. She forced me into a corner Yakuntik, if she had only apologised … but that is not Cihu's way.'

Lian nodded 'I understand, but this is about Kaeo now. She will do whatever it takes to see Cihu released from bondage to men, you must make it possible for her to do so whilst maintaining her honour.'

Malikah placed her hands upon Lian's shoulders before bringing her forehead to her lovers. Their brows touched for a few moments as they communicated in total privacy.

After separating Lian smiled 'I'll speak to her and see what I can arrange, thank you Malee.'

Malikah returned the gesture 'Don't thank me yet, the most difficult part will be convincing Cihu to accept.'

Lian shook her head 'She has to, anything is better than living the way she does now.'

'Cihu is a very stubborn woman, even more so than my Father, she may refuse out of principal. However that is not my concern, Kaeo must deal with that. As Ryu said "the journey of a thousand miles begins with one step", true?'

Lian's eyes moved up to her left, she then fixed them back on Malikah 'Malee, Machine would like to speak with you, is that okay?'

The sable Queen nodded as she removed her hands from Lian's body.

Voice of Machine's eyes filled with that ghostly silver sheen, opening her hands she bowed 'Ola Ek'tsab.'

Returning the gesture Malikah placed her palms to the ceiling and bowed her head 'Ola Machine.'

'Bandayuuk is quiet, after Gaulthus my children have sustenance and the Neenayin are no more, your side of our agreement has been fulfilled.'

Malikah stood proud in in her black ribbed suit and white Tlillan jacket 'I gave my word.'

Machine smirked 'Words are worth little insurance ...'

Before Machine could finish Malikah cut her off 'Even from the cleanest of mouths? Yes I know this, yet our contract is now sealed with the blood of both parties.'

'And the blood of our enemies.'

'That is how all true alliances are forged, is it not?'

Machine gave a smile, agreeing with the words of the Star Shaker 'I tell you this Ek'tsab, treat the Makayuuk as your children and they will show you the same devotion as they did me at Bandayuuk.'

Malikah took a deep breath 'You have my word, Machine.'

'I request you keep Lian by your side, I can manage Bandayuuk without her.'

Malikah looked suspiciously at the steel eyed lady 'Don't you trust me?'

Machine chuckled 'Memento mori, even Ek'tsab should be reminded of her limits. I wouldn't want you to commit yourself to any reckless ventures without my advice.'

Folding her arms and raising her brow the Tlillan Queen asked 'I wonder who the slave is in this scenario?'

'Where Ek'tsab leads Machine follows, where will Ek'tsab lead us next?'

Malikah pointed out towards the stars 'To Andromeda.'

Machine looked worriedly out at the glimmering dots in the sheet of space 'The anomaly at the core?'

'We must learn of them before they discover us.'

'What of the Matriarchs? Clan Kak and Clan Huel?'

'They shall be released, into a new world, a new order.'

'If they resist?'

Malikah smiled 'They would rather live as Gukumatz than return to servitude below males.'

'Lian trusts your judgement.'

The sable Queen nodded 'Machine shall have her place in this new order, too long has Otoch stagnated in the old ways.'

Voice of Machine pressed her palms together 'Namaste Ek'tsab.'

Before Malikah could return the honour Lian's eyes returned to her usual brown.

Voice of Machine smiled 'Shall I leave now? Or is there anything else?'

'Only one matter remains,' stated the Queen in a grim tone 'Chanatico, she must be present at Muul Kaah.'

'She's Second of Tico; she'll be there anyway, right?'

Malikah nodded her regal brow 'True, yet she avoids me.'

'Why?'

'She is pregnant.'

Lian replied in a pleased voice 'That's great.'

Malikah maintained her tone 'The child is male.'

For a few awkward seconds there was nothing but silence.

'Be certain she attends, use force if necessary.'

Lian bowed with palms pressed together 'Namaste Xch'uup.'

A procession made its way through a dim forest along old stone pathways, until reaching the central palace of Xch'uup, at Muul Kaah. The caravan was led by Kaeo, Grand Marshall of Otoch, she held in tight proximity a dishevelled band of wayward Matriarchs.

These were the females who'd betrayed their God at Bandayuuk, the purpose of their presence was unknown. The purpose for a council called at Muul Kaah was equally puzzling to all.

Kaeo led the cold females, dressed in rags which hung from their bodies, inside the foreboding pyramid. A testament to the power of Xch'uup it towered into the Twilight of Otoch, a construction founded upon the blood of slaves and plunder of disbelievers.

Kaeo entered the main hall and bowed before her Queen, illuminated by the subtle moss glowing upon the faces of Xch'uups past. Their sculptures peered down into the hall, the past inspiring the present to make a greater future.

Malikah resided at the far end of the hall, resting upon her throne, dressed in a white sleeved dress. A feathered headdress sprung from her crown, informing all present of whom she was. Wearing a pair of slightly off colour white boots the Queen had dressed up for the occasion, whatever that occasion may be.

Each side of the hall filled up, only females present; the population of Matriarchs on Otoch had increased quite noticeably. On one side Kaeo held the fallen members of clan Kak and Huel in line, their control collars were blatant and when the proud figure of Cihu appeared from the sorry rabble chattering spread around the court like wildfire.

Once all females were seated a stone wall could be heard to drop, sealing off Muul Kaah from the outside world. The sable Tlillan Queen arose as Seers could be seen flitting back and forth in the passages behind the throne.

All stood in respect, eagerly awaiting to discover the reason they had been brought here.

'Council has been called today,' Malikah's eyes stole a quick glance at Lian 'because I believe it is time for mercy. For those who betrayed their Xch'uup I offer amnesty.'

Shrieks of delight shot out, reverberating around the great hall. Equally gasps of shock could be detected from the opposite side of the hall as the present clan Matriarchs wondered what their fate might be if an amnesty were to be implemented.

On one side stood the shamed, celebrating the end of their punishment slaving under males. Such denigration, to be a male's plaything and servant whilst preforming all tasks he desired was more than many could bring themselves to suffer. Many of those condemned to this punishment had been found dead, committing suicide rather than suffer a living hell.

On the opposite side stood a group of horrified Matriarchs, many of mixed Human-Tlillan descent. What was to become of them should these women be given amnesty? Would they maintain their positions within the clan or be forced to step down in favour of their elders?

Malikah smirked at the elated side of the hall, though one of them remained unimpressed by the mention of amnesty. Cihu's sneer was fixed firmly upon her face, her torn clothing and unwashed hair did nothing to weaken the Amazon's conviction. Even the stump where Malikah had severed her hand could not humble the warrior in the face of such hardships.

'Do not celebrate your fortune … you are to be stripped of all merit. All those accepting my offer shall serve without their former title of Matriarch; you shall serve amongst the lowest rank of females. The stigma of your disloyalty is not to be forgotten.'

Even so the Tlillans were celebrating in their minds; to be stripped of all merit was a small price to pay if it meant no longer having to play to the whims of a male.

On hearing Malikah's offer all of the disgraced ran to the centre of the hall and fell to their knees, prostrate on the moss as it lit up in beautiful colours. Fabulous light fired out filling the hall with imprints of footsteps from the herd of thankful women. One however remained stood on the stone pews, Kaeo looked her former First up and down with urgency. Telling her via their minds to accept the amnesty, Cihu refused standing proud in rags with fiery eyes glaring at Xch'uup.

'Do you not wish to leave the service of men, Cihu?' inquired the Tlillan Queen.

A ripple of laughter came from the right until a Malikah's black stare quietened them down.

'Well? Answer your Xch'uup; do you not desire to return to clan Teteo?'

All fell quiet as a sneering Cihu replied 'You put me with these pigs?'

The dishevelled Amazon peered at the women on their knees kowtowing for mercy, as she sneered at them the warrior spat upon the traitors.

'You betrayed your Xch'uup,' replied Malikah.

'I betrayed no-one.'

'Why then are you in the service of men?'

'Honesty.'

'Honesty?'

'Am I not permitted to speak my belief? Must I love who Xch'uup loves? Hate who Xch'uup hates? You speak of change, you say there is only loyalty, yet I am persecuted by the old law.'

'Yet you raised arms against your Xch'uup.'

'Xch'uup attacked my words. It is true, I hate Humans yet that is not permitted by what law? It is blasphemy to speak of Human as a dog?'

Malikah knew Cihu was correct, she had lost control and used violence against her former Marshall and for what? No more than her hatred for all Humans, was it a crime to hate someone for their species? It was the fault of Malikah in that she took it so personally and rather than cool down she cut off her Marshall's hand before banishing her to a work camp in a fit of rage.

The problem now was that Malikah would have to back down and admit her mistake before all Matriarchs. The sable Queen just couldn't manage to humble herself, despite any amount of encouragement from Lian.

An uncomfortable silence spread throughout until the voice of Kaeo chirped up 'Xch'uup may I be allowed to speak?'

Malikah nodded her head towards the shortest Matriarch in the building.

'As you know my Mother died serving you at Bandayuuk, she has made a request from the Dreamscape.'

'And?'

'I wish to make a humble request for her and my Father who nearly died at both Bandayuuk and e'hoch'e'en chumuk serving the will of Xch'uup.'

Malikah's head snapped from her Marshall back to Cihu 'What is it you desire?'

'Chen Yuum, Kaeo kaaxtik Pah atan … Cihu,' on finishing her sentence Kaeo quickly kowtowed with the other females before Malikah might speak.

'Kaeo, only a Matriarch may conceive child.'

'I understand Xch'uup.'

Malikah glared at her former Marshall 'It seems someone maintains their loyalty, even to one who serves men.'

Cihu didn't respond.

Again the Tlillan Queen spoke to the entire hall 'If I were to allow such a thing, someone must take this female into their clan. Who would step forward and accept this dishonoured female as a Matriarch?'

The hall was quiet until Kaeo spoke from the ground she lay prostrate on 'Clan Teteo requires a second.'

The sable Queen's eyes widened 'Second? You would have a female go from working with men to Second of Teteo?'

Kaeo thought for a moment then replied 'I require a Praetor, Xch'uup.'

Malikah chuckled to herself 'It seems clan Teteo is determined to emancipate Cihu from her shame.'

There was only silence.

'I will not argue with my Marshall, twice I have made that mistake and neither time did I profit from it. However this is all conjecture if Cihu does not accept,' the Queen turned to Cihu who now stood alone in the cold crisp air of Muul Kaah 'Well? Do you accept? Does Cihu desire this mating and in doing so become Cihuateteo once again?'

Kaeo looked back, fixing her eyes upon her former first, urging the fallen Matriarch to accept the offer.

Realising this was the path of least resistance to becoming a clan member again Cihu nodded 'I accept.'

Kaeo expelled a lungful of air in relief.

'Then let it be known, Cihu is once again Cihuateteo,' Malikah smirked 'After all you said Kaeo is the only one loyal to Cihuateteo; I would make pains not to abuse that loyalty in the future, Praetor.'

Cihu bowed, unable to press her palms together 'Namaste Xch'uup,' then turning towards Kaeo she stated 'Namaste Yaaxil.'

'Liik'il, and Kaeo furnish your Praetor with a replacement hand as soon as possible.'

'Namaste Xch'uup,' replied the Tlillan Marshall with a beaming smile.

The remaining females rose, returning to their pews as Kaeo collected their control collars.

'The next order of the day is the introduction of a new clan to Otoch and the council,' Malikah nodded in the direction of Lian 'Kalayuuk; Voice of Machine will represent the Makayuuk here on Otoch.'

Lian rose from her seat, made her way to the centre of Xch'uup's moss covered court.

'Makayuuk are descendants of the Tlillan race, members of the scattered, and it is time they took their place amongst the exalted. Machine has proven herself in battle, on Gaulthus the Camazotz have been pacified. Machine places herself between Otoch and its enemies, so I offer her a voice upon our council.'

The Matriarchs glared towards their Xch'uup, even Ilam made a stare of disapproval.

Malikah got to her feet 'Any who believe this honour is not to be bestowed upon Kalayuuk speak now.'

No-one had the guts to stand against the sable Queen, the court remained silent.

Malikah took a pendant from a pocket on her arm 'Come here Lian.'

The Tlillan half breed approached her lover and bowed as Xch'uup placed a gold necklace with a red gem around Lian's neck 'You may now be addressed as Kalayuuk.'

A grinning Lian accepted the pendant with thanks before returning to her stone pew amongst the murmuring Matriarchs.

Still standing Malikah spoke in a more serious tone 'There is one final issue, Chanatico?'

The young Second of Tico felt her heart jump at the mention of her name. She rose to her feet and on Xch'uups order made her way before the Queen of the Tlillan race.

'You were mated with a Human, a mating I arranged.'

'Yes Xch'uup,' replied Chanatico bowing with palms pressed.

'Why did you not inform your First that you are with child?'

'I ... I don't know Xch'uup.'

The Tlillan Empress smiled 'Do not lie to me girl, perhaps I will inform the Matriarchs why you failed to mention your child to anyone?'

Chanatico could hold it in no longer; she dropped to her knees in a kowtow 'Mercy Xch'uup.'

'You conceived a male child, without my instruction, is that not true?'

The Matriarchs gasped as one, a male born from a Tlillan and Human mating would have unknown results. Much the same as Malikah's birth, her mother had conceived a child with a Human without the prior consent of Xch'uup.

'It is true Xch'uup.'

'Do you know the punishment for this crime?'

Chanatico with her face toward the earth whimpered in reply 'Exile.'

Malikah shook her head as the Matriarchs watched on in total silence 'Death.'

Chanatico raised her face to look at Malikah 'But I am with child.'

'A matriarch may not be executed when with a female child, but a male is of no consequence.'

'If it is of no consequence then could Xch'uup extend her amnesty today?'

Malikah cackled 'the child is of no consequence, it is of consequence that you deceived your Xch'uup.'

'You would have refused if I requested a male.'

Malikah took offence to these words 'And now you claim to know the mind of Xch'uup?'

Silence filled the chamber.

'All females may return to their homes, this council will continue in my forum.'

The rest of Muul Kaah ascended to their feet, except Chanatico. All females made a Namaste gesture before the stone wall rose and they filed out of the great pyramid. The first of each clan remained along with Chanatico; once the wall closed they followed their Queen as she moved into the gloomy tunnels at the rear of her throne.

Kaeo stood over Chanatico and escorted the wayward Matriarch into the forum. Each clan first faced a dais with an obsidian throne upon it, Malikah rested upon the regal throne dressed in white.

Chanatico stood before her Empress, she stared at the moss floor emanating sensual colours as she and the others stepped on it.

'What am I to do with you Chanatico?'

'I am yours Xch'uup.'

'Why did you conceive a male without consulting me?'

Chanatico didn't answer.

'Never mind, I already know the reason, it was Henry wasn't it?'

Chanatico peered up to meet the gaze of her Queen.

Malikah smirked 'He is not in danger, but the fate of his wife and child hang in the balance.'

'My heart has ruled my head.'

The sable Queen's eyes looked behind Chanatico to meet those of Lian 'To those that feel the universe is a tragedy, for those that think it is comedy.'

'I do not understand, Xch'uup.'

Malikah's gaze returned to Chanatico 'Is this to be a tragedy or a comedy?'

'I still do not understand.'

The Tlillan Queen closed her eyes as she rubbed her forehead lightly 'There has been too much loss of life recently. I can ill afford to see even a single Matriarch go to the Dreamscape, you are no exception. Clan Kak and Huel paid the price for treachery before a pardon. You will be pardoned now, but you must pay the price later when your son is born.'

Ilam, stood amongst the Matriarchs in a semi-circle before the dais, spoke 'It shall live?'

'That is correct Ilamachutli; do you have any further questions?'

'What is the purpose?'

'You are as curious as I concerning the result of a half-breed male, correct?'

'I imagine not a positive may come of this.'

'It is your right to disagree, yet there is only one way to discover the truth.'

Chanatico made a plea to the Matriarchs of Kak, Huel and Chutli 'You all fear the dilution of our species, this is your answer. I offer you a male with the abilities of a half-breed female.'

Ilam sneered at the Matriarch 'How do you know this?'

Placing a hand upon her womb Chanatico replied 'I have linked with my child.'

'It is aware?'

'He communicates with me, back and forth.'

Ilam made a piercing stare at her daughter 'What do the Seers say on this?'

'The Seers are silent and I see nothing in the Dreamscape, I say we take a chance on love.'

Ilam scoffed 'This is madness, Xch'uup does not take chances. That is why Xch'uup has the Seers, to make prophecy and guide fate.'

In a sardonic pitch Lian retorted 'Because that had been working oh so well for them until Malee turned up,' Lian realised her slip of the tongue and added on 'I mean Xch'uup.'

Kaeo and Sandra both grinned at her faux pas, just managing to hold back their laughter.

Malikah tightened her lips 'We all know the past, it is the future I am concerned with. This male, if it lives to maturity could be a boon to the Tlillan race. Concerns of the genome become diluted have been a concern ever since I was born on Earth. I believe this may be the answer, a male with the mental ability of a Matriarch, Chanatico's child may lead to a consolidation of the genetic structure.'

Ilam continued to protest 'A male with the power of a Matriarch? Surely this is too dangerous it would cause a collapse in society, no longer would males …'

'Suffer in silence?'

'That was not my meaning.'

'Then speak your meaning, do not hide behind words.'

Ilam had nervous expression 'What of our position?'

Malikah sneered 'The Matriarchs care more of power than the liberty of their own species, is that what you mean to say?'

Ilam's eyes began to change in hue 'My species? These are males.'

'You do not consider males to be even the same species?'

'That is not my meaning; you wish to grant males privilege by right, not merit!'

Malikah stood up from her throne 'No, you wish to maintain your right to subjugate them. I desire to allow those with merit to earn their kleos and nostos alongside a female.'

'That is heresy!'

Malikah's eyes began to burn 'There is no heresy, only loyalty. Or didn't you get the memo?'

'Emancipating males will cause chaos, surely you understand this?'

Malikah's eyes returned to their usual grey 'That is not my intention, only one male is to be granted this honour. A pure Human or Tlillan male could at best reach the upper levels of mediocrity in a meritocracy alongside Tlillan females.'

Xch'uup's words sunk in as the fire in Ilam's eyes died down 'What do you propose to do with this male once born?'

Malikah fixed her eyes upon Chanatico and spoke in a stern manner to the Matriarch 'Xch'uup shall take possession of the child.'

The red haired amazon shook her head as the words left Xch'uup's lips.

Malikah sneered 'That is the price you pay for deception. The child is to become mine, he shall receive instruction from Amitrachutli in philosophy and spirituality, Sandra shall instruct him in medicine and psychology, Kaeo in conflict and diplomacy.'

The Valkyrie hung her head 'Will I be permitted to see my son?'

'You may visit him when he is free from study. You must inform your husband of these events and do not attempt to deceive me again Chanatico, you're now permitted to leave.'

The tall female pressed her palms together 'Namaste Xch'uup.'

The room emptied except for Malikah, Lian and Kaeo. The Marshall of Tlillan waited until no one else was in earshot before speaking 'Why do I have to teach some kid?'

Malikah smiled 'who else should I have instruct him in the art of war?'

Kaeo folded her arms in defiance 'and diplomacy? I'm not a diplomat, Amitra would be better at that.'

The sable Queen smiled at the shortest Matriarch on Otoch 'You give yourself too little credit. A woman that can make Cihu see her point of view through only words might charm a nest of killer bees into giving up their honey.'

Kaeo's ponytail moved from side to side as she shook her head 'I think you're making a mistake.'

Malikah smiled 'Before your age I had three young wards to burden me!'

'That was different,' replied the First of the Tlillan warrior clan.

'Oh really?'

'Yes, we all learnt quickly, we are Mictlantecuhtli.'

Malikah chuckled 'Oh you were more than a handful Kaeo, keeping you out of trouble was a full time occupation!'

'You're exaggerating.'

Malikah looked at Lian and the pair both started laughing.

Kaeo raised her arms in surrender 'Fine I'll do it, but if he comes crying over a few bumps and bruises it's not my problem.'

Still grinning Malikah returned her gaze to Kaeo 'Xch'uup thanks her Marshall, is there anything else she might do for you?'

Kaeo replied in an awkward tone 'No, may I leave?'

The sable Queen nodded her brow 'You are excused.'

'Namaste Xch'uup,' Kaeo bowed before walking out of Muul Kaah with a rather unhappy stomp.

Walking through the Pyramid of Muul Kaah Malikah and Lian viewed the gallery of Matriarchs as they strolled on a ledge, half of the way to the top of the construction.

The sable Queen stopped in front of one of the moss covered statues which lined the steps towards the top of the pyramid. She breathed deeply whilst admiring the sculpture of a past Twilighter.

'Who's this?' asked Lian.

'Quetzalcoatl,' replied Malikah with great reverence.

The figure wore the feathered crown of Xch'uup, her body adorned with a long cape of jade squares. Holding the sceptre returned to Muul Kaah by the Gukumatz in one hand and the grip of her neutronium sword in the other; she gazed down onto the empty court, her features resembling those of Lian more than Malikah.

'What was she like?'

'Quetzalcoatl is amongst the greatest of all Xch'uups.'

'What did she do?'

'She extended the limits of glory.'

'I don't understand, Malee.'

'She defeated ...,' Malikah looked around to make sure no-one was listening despite the fact they were hundreds of metres up in an empty pyramid 'defeated the Tzitzimeh.'

Lian ruffled her brow a little 'The Tzitz ... imeh?'

The Tlillan Queen put her finger across Kalayuuk's mouth 'Lower your voice! Do you want them to hear you in Tititl?'

The Chinese half breed waited until Malikah removed her finger and in a hushed tone asked 'What are the Tzitzimeh? I've never heard of them.'

'Of course not, none would speak their name even via the link.'

'Why?'

'Creatures of Tlillan nightmare, even their name would cause Xch'uup to tremble.'

'So what do they look like?'

'A Tzitzimitl would best be described as a malnourished woman with the mouth of a hydra.'

Lian scrunched her face up 'Eeeww! That sounds nasty.'

'Did you ever wonder why the Human and Tlillan word for a traitor or backstabber is kan, or snake? Or why the snake is so often despised and mistrusted in mythology and religion?'

'It has something to do with these Tzitzimeh?'

Malikah nodded her head 'Imagine a poor starving woman alone, shivering in the cold night. A person might feel pity and approach her, only to have their face bitten off ... or worse.'

'Something worse than having your face bitten off!' declared Lian in an incredulous tone.

'If you were a man, they used males for propagation of the species. Consuming them once they had been impregnated, often several Tzitzimeh would impregnate themselves before dining upon his live body.'

A chill fell over Lian 'Well at least they got some fun before they died, right?'

Malikah chuckled 'They did not have sex with the male; they would rip out his epididymis and store its contents inside their body.'

'What's an epididymis?'

'It is a coiled tube resting at the back of the testicles; it is where males store their sperm.'

'You mean they'd tear their balls out?'

'Exactly, from outside of Tlillan society one would assume males are subjugated. In fact it was to protect them from these harpies, Covering their bodies so the evil would not recognise one, otherwise the Tlillan race would have died out long ago.'

'So why don't they teach this or even mention it for that matter?'

'Quetzalcoatl purged the Tzitzimeh but even the one who speaks their name is considered cursed.'

'So how did Quetzalcoatl get rid of them?'

'For thousands of years these creatures had raided our colonies and pillaged commonwealth members. Allied with other brigands we were swimming against a tide of evil. Until the Seers gave her a way out, they saw the location of Tamoanchan.'

The name was familiar to Lian 'Tamoanchan? Wasn't there some big battle there eons ago?'

Malikah smiled at her lover 'Yes, Quetzalcoatl took all the cruisers she could muster and struck at the evil's heart.'

'And she defeated the Tzitzimeh.'

'The battle dragged on for two days with no end in sight. Eventually the Tzitzimeh Queen challenged Xch'uup to a duel; the victor would decide her enemy's fate.'

'I take it Quetzalcoatl won?'

Malikah grinned as she placed a hand upon the grip of her neutronium sword 'This blade cut down the Tzitzimeh Queen.'

'So what happened to them?'

'They were banished from this galaxy, but no-one dared mention their name afterwards.'

'Why?'

'Lest they return to answer your question, a silly superstition I know but they were terrifyingly savage beasts.'

'How did they leave the galaxy? By sleeper ship?'

'I don't know, I assume they left via hyperspace but it is not clear. The fact that no-one has seen a Tzitzimitl in half a million years is enough to satisfy the Matriarchs.'

'Where did they go?'

'Again no-one knows nor do they care, as long as it isn't here.'

'I was taught that the battle was a crusade against savages, nothing was said about Tzitzimeh or their banishment. Why do Tlillans keep so many secrets?'

Malikah put her arm around Lian's waist 'So Naïve Yakuntik, in a world where everyone can listen in on your thoughts, secrets are amongst the most prized possessions a Matriarch could own. Maintaining power on Otoch is not about what you know but what the Matriarchs don't know.'

'So not all Matriarchs are aware of the Tzitzimeh?'

'Correct, and I'd like it to stay that way.'

'So why did you tell me?'

'I keep no secrets from my Atan.'

'So when Quetzalcoatl returned she never mentioned the Tzitzimeh again?'

Malikah shook her head 'Quetzalcoatl did not return, she died shortly after the Tzitzimeh were banished.'

'What happened?'

'The mother of the Tzitzimeh, her blade was poisoned.'

'Couldn't the Ixchel save her?'

'No, not even the Ixchel can fight the venom of a Tzitzimeh.'

'Venom? Like a snake?'

Malikah brushed some of the moss away from the sculpture 'Yes, if you survive a bite from a Tzitzimeh you will die shortly afterwards. The Ixchel kept her alive long enough to see the creatures off, but she died soon afterwards.'

Lian noticed where Malikah had brushed the moss away 'Is that neutronium?'

The sable Queen smiled 'It is, her body was brought back and like all Xch'uups before her she was entombed within her own likeness.'

'Wow, I thought they were all stone. It must have cost a bomb to entomb her in pure neutronium!'

Malikah nodded her head whilst admiring the statue 'She received her kleos at Tamoanchan, the Matriarchs wished that she also receive the proper nostos; this was their way of honouring her.'

'It's a pity no-one's allowed to talk about it.'

Clearing dust from the robe of Quetzalcoatl Malikah grinned 'Now if she had someone whispering "memento mori" into her ear, would she have extended the limits of glory?'

Lian returned the smile 'I thought the slave only said that after he'd risked his life and conquered the enemy?'

The Queen chuckled as she ran her hand down the cheek of her lover 'I'm glad you're here to remind me of these things.'

'So am I Malee, so am I,' replied Voice of Machine before kissing her regal hand.

The End

If you wish to contact the Author you may do so via email: **malikachutli@hotmail.co.uk**